Petticoat Ranch © 2007 by Mary Connealy
Calico Canyon © 2008 by Mary Connealy
Gingham Mountain © 2009 by Mary Connealy

ISBN 978-1-61626-216-7

All scripture quotations are taken from the King James Version of the Bible.

Published by Barbour Publishing, Inc., P.O. Box 719, Uhrichsville, Ohio 44683, www.barbourbooks.com

Our mission is to publish and distribute inspirational products offering exceptional value and biblical encouragement to the masses.

Member of the
Evangelical Christian
Publishers Association

Printed in the United States of America.

MARY CONNEALY

BARBOUR
PUBLISHING

ONE

Mosqueros, Texas, 1867

Sophie heard God in every explosion of thunder as she listened to the awesome power of the approaching storm. But there was more. There was something coming—something more than rain.

Over the distant rumble, Sophie Edwards heard pounding hoofbeats. Her heart sped up, matching the pace. The horse came fast. Something about the way it ran echoed the desperation in the pulsing of Sophie's heart.

Sophie whirled to race inside the cabin. Exhausted after another day of grinding work, she prayed for strength and courage. God would have to provide it; she had none left. She scrambled into her disguise and waited until the last minute to wake the children, hoping the rider would pass on. She stood near the can that held the vile-smelling Hector scarf, hoping she wouldn't need it.

Was this the night someone would come for her and the girls? The night she couldn't talk fast enough or hide well enough to survive this rugged, lonely life?

The back of Sophie's neck prickled in horror as the horse veered from the main trail and came toward her cabin. For a second, she thought the rider meant to come to her place, but there was no letup of the running hooves. Sophie's fear changed. No one could safely ride the narrow, rocky trail down the slopes of the creek bank behind her cabin at that speed.

The horse charged on. Sophie could hear it blowing hard, its wind broken, the saddle leather creaking. She hated the rider for abusing his mount, but inside Sophie knew it wasn't the rider's fault. This pace—this reckless, dark ride—could only mean one thing.

Pursuit!

And pursuit might mean a fleeing criminal with a posse on his trail. But not all pursued men were justly accused. No one knew that better than Sophie.

She almost ran out to wave the rider down. She let fear freeze her for a second. Then, ashamed, she grabbed at the door latch on her ramshackle cabin, praying, "Help me, Lord. Help me, help me, help me." Her prayers, like her life, had been stripped to bare bones.

The horse stormed past the heavy brush that concealed the house.

"No! Stop!" Sophie dashed out the door and down the stoop. "Stop! The cliff!"

She was too late. The rider was past. Within seconds she heard the dreadful screams of the falling animal, the coarse shouts of terror ripped from the throat of the rider.

Rocks dislodged along the top of the bank as Sophie ran in the direction of the accident. There was the rumble of falling rocks and the softer sound of the horse's big body striking stone as it plunged thirty feet to the creek below, neighing its fear and pain into the night. She heard the splash as the avalanche, and its unwilling cause, hit the moving water below.

She skidded to a halt and her long, white nightgown billowed around her. A gust whipped her blond hair across her eyes. Blinded for a moment, a cold, logical part of her mind told her that the best way to handle this was simply to ignore it and go back to bed.

But God asked more of her than cold logic. He even asked more of her than her own survival. It was a relief to admit it, because her strongest survival instincts couldn't stop her from going to someone

in need, and she was glad to have God's support in the matter. She whirled away from the embankment and ran back to the house.

"Girls!" Her voice lashed like a whip in the darkness. The girls would be so frightened to be awakened this way, but there was no choice. If ever a family had learned to do what needed to be done, it was the Edwardses. "Girls, someone's fallen on the creek path."

Sophie tore at her disguise, putting everything in its place with lightning speed. She couldn't ever afford to be unprepared. "I need help. I'm going down. Mandy, bring the rope and the lantern and follow me. Beth, catch Hector and bring him. Don't take time to get dressed: just pull on your shoes. Sally, stay with Laura. Get blankets out and heat water. If he's alive he'll need doctoring."

Sophie heard the girls jump out of bed as she headed outside in her nightgown with untied boots on her feet.

She saw where he'd gone over and her stomach lurched. He couldn't have picked a worse drop. She stumbled and skidded toward the bottom of the creek, risking her own neck on the treacherous path.

Hearing Amanda call out from overhead, Sophie yelled, "Down here, Mandy. Quickly." Sophie picked her way over the jumble of dirt and stones edging the swollen waters of the creek. In the starless night, she couldn't make out anything. She glanced behind her and saw, with relief, ten-year-old Mandy coming with a brightly lit kerosene lantern.

Sophie continued to scramble over the debris. She stepped in mud and sank until water overflowed her boot. The thunder came more steadily now, until it was a constant collision of sound. The approaching lightning gained enough strength to light up even the depths of the creek.

Feeling her way, on her hands and knees now, she tried to pierce the utter darkness with her vision. *Where is he, Lord?*

A wailing wind cried at them that it was bringing disaster in its wake. Suddenly, the thunder and lightning held a worse threat than savage rain. The storm was coming from the north. It was probably already raining upstream. The creek might flood without a single drop of water falling here. And she now stood in the path of that flash flood. Worse still, she'd just ordered her children to come after her.

Sophie listened intently for the roar of oncoming water. She heard nothing. They still had time.

Mandy caught up with her. "Here's the lantern and rope."

Sophie took the lantern. "A rider and horse went over that drop-off. Help me find him, and hurry! It's raining up north!"

Her girls had lived in their little thicket hideaway long enough to know what it meant when rain came in from the north. Sophie saw Mandy glance fearfully over her shoulder into the darkness of the creek. Then, practical girl that Mandy was, she started searching for the rider.

"Oh, Ma. Can he have lived?" Mandy went ahead of Sophie to the very edge of the dimly illuminated area.

"I don't know, honey," Sophie said grimly as she surveyed the area, looking for a glimpse of fabric or a bit of horsehide. "I don't hear him. He might be buried under these rocks. He might have been swept away by the creek. We only have a few minutes to search."

"Here, Ma. I think I found him!" Mandy's voice was sharp with excitement. A bolt of lightning lit up Mandy's frightened face. Sophie saw Mandy's blue eyes, so like her own, glow in the jagged glare. Her blond hair, identical to Sophie's and the other girls', hung bedraggled and muddy to her waist.

Sophie rushed to her daughter's side and saw a single hand, coated with dirt, extending from a pile of mud and rocks. The two of them fell to the ground and began digging away the soil. They ignored the tear of jagged stones on their hands and the damage to their nightgowns, the only ones they owned. Sophie heard soft trudging steps as Hector came down the creek path. She dug faster, knowing that with the mule's help they could move the man as soon as they freed him.

Another rumble of thunder sounded closer. The lightning lanced the sky just as Sophie uncovered the stranger's face and pushed away the mud. The man was utterly still. As limp as in death. She didn't stop

to check his condition. If there was life left in him after the fall, the suffocating dirt would snatch it away. She and Mandy uncovered his shoulders as eight-year-old Elizabeth came up.

"Get this rope around his shoulders, Mandy. Beth, hitch it around Hector's neck. We've got to get out of this creek before the water comes!" Even as she said it, Sophie heard the first distant crash of waves against the sides of the creek. Once the sound was audible, there were only minutes before the wall of water would sweep by their cabin.

She kept digging as she shouted commands. She reached deep into the muck to make sure there were no heavy rocks pinning him. Her girls worked silently beside her, following her orders. Sophie felt a surge of pride in them so great, she knew it to be almost sinful.

"Ready, Ma." Mandy turned her attention from fastening the rope under the man's arms and went back to digging.

"Hector's ready anytime, Ma," Beth shouted over the raging wind. A bolt of lightning flashed brightly enough for Sophie to see the man. His legs were still well buried, but there were no rocks on him.

He was so coated in mud that Sophie couldn't have told anyone what he looked like. She remembered the desperate speed at which he'd ridden and thought again the word: *pursuit.* Yet no onc had come along behind him.

The thunder sounded again. The water roared ever nearer. Sophie shouted to be heard over the sound, "Once you start pulling, just take him all the way up! The floodwater is coming!"

Sophie knew Elizabeth, her second born, would handle the stubborn, rawboned old mule better than she could. Hector was a cantankerous beast on the best of days, but he had a soft spot for Beth, as did most animals.

Beth's gentle cajoling urged Hector forward to take up the slack in the rope. Mandy knelt at the man's head, and in the few remaining seconds, pushed more dirt off his arms and chest. Sophie braced herself to support his head and neck as he began to inch free. A bolt of lightning lit up their strange little group, this time with blinding brightness. The thunder sounded almost at the same instant. Sophie prayed for the man and asked God if the floodwater could just hold off another few minutes.

In answer, God sent the first icy drip of rain down the back of her neck. Sophie took it as a heavenly warning to hurry.

The man emerged slowly from the slide. As soon as he was free, with another lightning bolt to assist the lantern, Sophie yelled, "Keep going. All the way to the top of the bank. Mandy, you run ahead with the lantern." Anything to get her girls to safety, even if she didn't make it herself.

She looked at the man, now being battered even further by his ride up the hill. His body was coated in mud. The slime helped him slide along the rough ground. One particularly nasty jolt over the rutted path almost woke him. He took a deep breath and turned his head sideways. He vomited up filthy, muddy water and gasped deeply for breath as he was dragged along. It was the first sign he was alive. Sophie kept to his side to make sure his head didn't encounter a rock.

The rugged upward trail twisted and turned. Just as it faced the north along one of its steeper sections, a bolt of lightning split the sky. Sophie saw a wall of water raging toward her like the wrath of God. "Faster, Beth! The floodwater's coming! Get to the top!"

Elizabeth kicked Hector and yelled. Sophie knew her mule well, and whatever unfortunate qualities Hector had, stupidity wasn't one of them. She knew he headed for the top of that creek to save his own mangy mule hide, and if he saved the lot of them along with himself, well, that had nothing to do with him.

The path snaked back to the south. A few more feet. Twenty at the most. Sophie knew the water would come along right to the top of the bank. It had been cut to its current depth by these raging torrents over thousands of years. Sophie glanced over her shoulder and saw it coming. They weren't going to make it. Lightning lit up the sky just as Hector crested the top of the path. The roaring water changed to a scream. The thunder had become a constant jarring drumroll that only added to the fierce growl of the approaching flood. The rope dragged

against the ground, and knowing she was out of time, Sophie reached down and twisted her arms through the rope that bound the man to the only anchor there was for them in the world.

The water hit like a crashing fist. Sophie heard her own cry of fear as she was swept sideways. Her arms wrenched nearly from their sockets as the rope tightened. Her body, literally tied to the man, lifted with the angry waters. The flood caught them as if it were a greedy child not wanting to let go of its toy. Sophie had a second to despair of Hector's strength and prayed Beth wouldn't be swept away with the mule. Flood water filled her mouth. The life her precious babies had to face without her was the image she'd die with.

Then they were up. They landed on the top of the creek bank like a couple of battle-weary trout. Sophie was too battered to move. She lay there, choking on muddy water as the world began to right itself. She tried to catch her breath and was having precious little luck, when Mandy got to her side, followed by Beth. Only when they rolled her off the man did she realize she'd been stretched out fully on top of him.

"Ma! Are you all right?" Mandy's anxious voice reached into her sluggish mind.

Her girls. She felt the scrambling fingers on the ropes that bound her to this stranger, and she heard their fear. She had to be strong for them. She forced the panic from her water-logged head. "Yes, I'm fine. Just got a good soaking. Let's see if our friend here survived it."

Sophie almost staggered when she got to her knees, but she didn't. The girls were watching. She turned her attention to the man and pressed her hand firmly against his chest. Beneath her palm was a strong heartbeat, even though, after his one spell of coughing, the man hadn't stirred again. She felt his chest rise and fall with a steady breath.

Sophie heaved a heartfelt sigh of relief. "He's still alive."

The spitting rain grew steadier, and Sophie wondered what a chest full of dirty water did to a man. A deep chill now might well be the last straw. With a renewed surge of strength, Sophie decided that, after all she'd been through, this man could just think twice before he up and died on her. Thinking aloud, she said, "There's no way we can carry him to the house, and we're not strong enough to get him up on Hector's back."

"If Hector goes slow, maybe we can just drag him," Mandy suggested. "Reckon it'll kill him, though."

Elizabeth said lightly from where she knelt beside her mother, "I don't know how he could get much worse. He appears to be mostly kilt already."

Sophie prayed in her heart, as she had been nonstop since she'd heard the first hoofbeats. But no better suggestions were forthcoming from the Almighty.

"Okay, we drag him. Take it real slow, Beth. Stay by his side, Mandy and. . .and. . ." Sophie was out of ideas. A sudden gust of wind and a prolonged glare of lightning, with thunder rumbling constantly now, prodded her. "Let's get on with it then."

They hauled him the same way they hauled logs to split for their fire. Hector pulled the unconscious man right up to the front door. When Elizabeth stopped Hector, Mandy asked, with the practicality her life had forced onto her, "Reckon Hector can drag him into the house?"

The house was small—one room, with a loft, no back door, and two front steps that passed for a stoop. Sophie tried to envision the big mule climbing the stairs, ducking through the narrow door, and then turning around in the cramped space. Hector was large and not given to cooperation at the best of times, even with Beth's gentle urging.

"How about we put him in the barn," Mandy suggested.

Barn was a highfalutin word for the Edwards's one and only outbuilding. The building remained standing more out of pure ornery stubbornness than sturdy construction. It was a three-sided shed that stood upright, thanks to the bramble that had wound itself around every inch of the building and practically reclaimed it as part of the vast thicket that hid the Edwards's home. Hector seemed inclined to head for it, though he usually disdained to go under the rickety roof.

The wind began driving the steadily increasing sprinkles straight

sideways. The lightning and thunder continued, and the icy drops of rain grew fatter, soaking into their thin, mud-soaked nightclothes. This was all the man needed to finish the work of his fall. Sophie finally said, "The barn it is. Let's go."

They hauled the injured man down a nearly invisible trail that wound away from the cabin. Another small clearing, one of hundreds that appeared inside the twisting maze of the thicket, opened up at the decrepit *barn*. Mercifully, the rain was coming from the north and the shed opened to the east. The inside was dry except for the multiple leaks in the roof. A stack of the first spring prairie grass Sophie and the girls had cut took up the driest corner. With some quick pitch-forking, they got the man situated on a soft bed of fresh-scented hay. It was a better bed than the one Sophie had.

Hector was released. As if in a huff at the uninvited company, he went to the far corner of the tiny shed. That put about ten feet between him and the intruders in his domain.

Sophie knelt in the hay beside the still-unconscious man. "Bring the lantern up close, Mandy. Be mindful of fire."

"I'll fetch blankets and check on the little 'uns, Ma." Beth darted out into the storm.

As the lantern light fell on the man, and with a sudden extended flash of lightning, Sophie saw bright red soaked through the coating of dirt on his face and across the front of his shirt. The stranger was drenched in his own blood.

With a dart of aggravation, Sophie thought the man was determined to die one way or another. She felt stubbornness well up inside of her that would have humbled Hector. After all she'd been through, he'd live if she had to grab his worthless life and hold him on this side of the pearly gates with her bare hands!

TWO

"Where'd he get to, Harley?" Judd Mason roared into the storm.
Judd wheeled his horse around in a circle and looked along both sides of the forked path ahead of them. The rain slashed and their quarry's trail washed away like dirt in a Chinese laundry.

Judd pulled back hard on his mustang. The horse reared and fought the brutal hand on the bit. Judd whipped his mount hard with the long reins and swore at the unruly horse he'd caught wild and never really mastered.

He'd seen the horse that thieving trash rode. If Judd could have gotten his hands on that magnificent thoroughbred, he'd have put a bullet in the brain of this ornery cuss and kept the beautiful bay for himself. After all, a man catching horse thieves deserved some payment.

That was why Judd had sent the bulk of the gang after the rest of those no-account varmints when they'd split up, while he, Harley, and Eli had kept after this one.

He'd have made a deal with Harley and Eli somehow. Let them keep whatever was in the man's pockets or given them a bigger cut of the next windfall. He wanted that horse! It would have made a sound start for breeding on the ranch he'd be buying on Monday.

He thought of the Mead ranch and the twisting, turning path he'd followed so the Mead brothers' disappearance wouldn't be noticed. Now, the Meads' ranch would be his. But it wasn't enough. He wanted that thoroughbred bay!

"I'm sick of this weather, Judd. We're not going to track him in this." Eli wiped an arm across his face, but it did no good. Even with foul-weather gear, they were all soaked to the skin.

It was all Judd could do to not knock Eli out of his saddle. The day would come when he quit putting up with the constant carping. But for now, Eli had his uses.

Instead of knocking Eli down, he turned his temper on Harley. "Where'd ya lose him, Harley?"

"We ain't a-gonna catch 'im tonight, Mason." Harley, calm as usual, hunched his shoulders against the driving rain and tugged his hat low over his brow.

Judd jammed his spurs into his horse's scarred sides. The horse reared up, fighting the heavy hand. "He can't have gone much farther in this rain. I want that horse! No two-bit horse thief is gonna ride a horse like that while I'm stuck on this nag!"

Judd hated the black mustang. He'd done his best, but he couldn't beat the fighting spirit out of him. The animal was so vicious, he couldn't turn his back on it.

Harley didn't argue. "I might have seen a trail into the thicket back a piece."

"You think he left the trail?" Judd hollered. "Well, why didn'cha say so earlier?"

Harley said coolly, "Let's go back and see if he went down that way. He might have ducked into that thicket and found a hidey-hole we can flush him out of. If he's ahead of us, he's gone. We won't catch him tonight."

Judd turned back, determined to sniff out their prey like a wolf would sniff out a three-legged elk.

"Elizabeth, wait," Sophie shouted after her rapidly disappearing daughter. "He's bleeding."

Beth skidded to a stop and looked back.

"Bring rags and the water Sally was warming."

"Got it, Ma!" Beth ran on.

Sophie had lived on the frontier for a long while. She'd given birth to Mandy beside a jumbled shelter of fallen logs on her way west with her husband, Cliff. She'd fed two babies at her breast at the same time, because there was no other milk for growing girls. She'd buried a tiny boy, born too soon after she'd fallen from a horse while bull-dogging cattle, and watched Cliff withdraw from her. He'd wanted a son so badly. She'd run the ranch herself, with two old men her only help, while Cliff went off to war. Then she'd cut her husband down from a tree and dug his grave with her own hands.

All of this she had endured. In truth, she'd flourished under the hard life. The West did that to people. It changed them. They either grew bigger, stronger, reveling in the freedom that could be wrested from the wilderness with two strong hands. Or it broke them and revealed them as small, unfit for the bounty that could be wrested from the land. Cliff had been such a man.

And now, in the rickety barn, with no tools but warm water and rags, she set out to save a man's life. She began unbuttoning his tattered shirt. "We have to see if he's injured anywhere, Mandy. Now this is doctoring, so it's not improper to remove his clothes, like it'd be otherwise."

Mandy nodded easily and started coaxing the shirt off one broad shoulder.

It was hard to tell where the mud ended and the bruises began. His chest and arms were bleeding from a dozen cuts and scrapes. Sophie pressed against his ribs, checking to see if any bones gave where they shouldn't. The man groaned softly once, when she pressed high on his right side. The bone held firm, and Sophie was encouraged by the sign of life.

Something stirred in Sophie as she worked over his bared chest. It was almost—for want of a better word—recognition. She hadn't given much thought to the man's identity, assuming him to be a stranger. But

now, she looked closer. His face was so filthy she couldn't make out features, even in the occasional burst of lightning. But his chest, the light covering of coarse hair across the top and the long, ever narrower line of hair down his stomach, struck a familiar chord. Sophie knew she couldn't identify a man from his chest, unless maybe she'd doctored him before, and she had only used her skills on Cliff and the girls.

She shook off the feeling. It didn't matter. Whoever he was, she'd help him. And if he turned out to be one of the town storekeepers, who were so cruel to her, she'd still get him on his feet and send him on his way—she just wouldn't be polite while she was about it.

She hesitated about his pants. It really was too bold to remove them. She looked up at Mandy, who seemed to feel the same way, and shrugged her misgivings at her mother. After a long struggle with her own sense of propriety, Sophie said, "We'll have to get them off later or he'll catch a chill, but let's leave him dressed for now."

She settled for running her hands down the man's muddy pant legs, firmly enough to satisfy herself that he had no broken bones. She came away with her hands caked with mud but satisfied that his lower half was intact.

The black sky opened up while she examined him, and the rain, whipped with the fury of the thunder and lightning, poured down. Sophie wiped her hands clean as best she could on the hay, just as Beth returned to the shed with a sloshing bucket of water and a bundle of rags.

"Thanks, honey. How were the little 'uns?"

"Good. Laura's asleep. Sally had everything ready for me. Is he dead yet?"

Sophie took a rag from her pessimistic daughter, wet it, wrung it out, and dabbed at the blood on the man's forehead.

"Nope," Mandy said placidly. "Pretty soon I s'pect, but not yet."

"Get that lantern closer, Mandy."

Beth began spreading the blanket over the man's filthy, inert body.

Sophie searched for the source of the bleeding on his head and found a nasty gash just under his hairline. The bleeding had already slowed to an ooze. "He should have stitches." Sophie cleaned the cut carefully.

"He should have a doctor," Beth said quietly.

Sophie didn't answer. It was one thing to do all she could; it was another to bring in someone from town. Once the townspeople knew she was here, the menfolk, with their dishonorable propositions and their anger at her refusal, would be back. Those men had driven them into this thicket.

A doctor to save this man's life might cost her daughters theirs. Of course, when this man woke up, their secret would be out anyway. Still, Sophie could do no less than her best to save him.

After she was satisfied his head wound was clean, Sophie explored his skull further and found another lump on the back. Between the two blows, it was no wonder the man was unconscious. Sophie was just ready to turn her attention to wiping the grime from his face when she heard, in the far distance, the sound of more hoofbeats. The pursuers? After all this time?

She knew she didn't have a moment to spare. "Riders coming. Elizabeth, stay with him. Put the lantern out. If he starts to wake up, do whatever you must to keep him quiet, including gagging him. Mandy, get to the house and cover things, then get up in the loft with Sally and Laura. Don't let them see you!"

They ran to get ready for intruders as if their lives depended on it. They had done it before many times.

The hoofbeats turned onto her path just as she darted into the door a step behind Mandy. Mandy tossed several large cloths over Laura's crib and high chair to disguise the presence of others in the cabin. Then she flew up the ladder behind Sally, who had heard the sound of someone coming and had gone into action without being told. Sally had the sleeping Laura in her arms and Sophie's disguise laid out.

Sophie grabbed her bulky housecoat for the second time that night. She pulled it on over her slender form. She dove for the fire and scraped a bit of ash out from the glowing coals with a knife.

She took the little bits of carved wood down from the shelf over the front door and slipped them between her front teeth and lips. A pillow came hurtling down from overhead, and she stuffed it up under her housecoat, into the special pouch sewn just for it. She tucked two pieces of clean, white cotton between her bottom teeth and her cheeks.

She twisted her rain-bedraggled blond hair into a bun, then grabbed for the nightcap, to which she had attached a heavy tress of Hector's tail, liberally greased, and pulled it on, so it looked like her hair was dark brown and stringy with oil. She checked the ash and found it cool enough. With a light, experienced hand, she dabbed it under her eyes just enough to look naturally hollow-eyed.

As her last act of self-preservation, she did something she hated above all—she popped the top off the tin milk can and pulled out the scarf. It was her masterstroke. It was what happened when you let a mule wear a wool scarf for a month. She heard Sally gag.

Mandy hissed, "Just hold your nose and keep quiet!"

Laura slept through it all.

The horses thundered to a stop outside. Sophie heard the creak of saddle leather and the treading of heavy footsteps. She rolled the long sapling from the side of the room so it would wedge against the door once it was open about three inches. Just as the pole was in place, a fist pounded on the front door.

Sophie took her time, letting them think they'd woken her, but judging by the battering force of the fist, she didn't dare wait long or the door might be knocked in.

She cracked open the door and looked into the red-veined eyes of the man who had killed her husband.

She couldn't go into her routine as the slovenly, crazy woman who lived in the thicket. She was too shocked to do more than stare. She'd never seen the man before that terrible night when he'd killed Cliff, but his face was burned into her memory.

In the seconds she stood frozen, the man tried to force the door, but it wouldn't give. Then, after a bit, he reeled back with a sickened grunt and pulled the kerchief, tied around his neck, over his mouth and nose.

Seeing him—this brute, this murderer, reacting with revulsion because she smelled bad—jerked Sophie out of her shocked silence. He wouldn't recognize her from that night. He wouldn't see through her disguise even if he did notice her the night he hanged Cliff.

"Whadaya want?" She spoke over the wooden mouthpiece that made her appear grossly buck-toothed. The teeth and the wadded cotton altered her speech, slurring it and giving it the thickness of someone who wasn't mentally quite right.

"A man!" The vicious, bloodshot eyes of the beast on her porch began to water from the acrid stench. Sophie's eyes watered, too, but that just gave her a rheumy look that was all the more repellent. He took another step away, which took him down the two steps.

From a safe distance he snarled, "We're chasing a horse thief! We lost him on the main trail and think he may have come this way."

"Hain't no one be comin' this way, this foul night." Her voice cracked, and she cackled with laughter. "No one stupid 'nough ta do it cept'n y'all. The path goes across the crick, and it's flooded right up to the rim. Has been for a while now."

The man, away from the meager shelter of her stoop, was battered by the wind and rain. Sophie could see the battle going on inside him. He was torn between the desire to run roughshod over anyone who turned him aside from his plans and his aversion to the squalid, stinking woman in front of him.

A voice from the darkness behind him said, "He's gone, Judd. Give it up, and let's go have a drink. This rain'll wreck his trail. So what if this one gets away? What say we just hang the next one twice." A burst of crude laughter followed that suggestion.

Judd.

Now, for the first time, she had a name. She had no way to use it—had no way to gain justice for her husband. But it was more than she'd had before.

The man whirled around at his grumbling companion. "I want that horse, Eli! He must have come this way!"

The other man, the one who hadn't spoken before, spoke up. "There are a dozen trails into this thicket. We can't explore 'em all."

The rain hit Judd full in the face and sent a visible chill through him. Then, with a dismissive grunt, as if his killing rage had only been some fun he'd missed out on, he gave a rough laugh. "All right. Let's go. Let's get out of this weather."

He turned again and stared at Sophie, who let her mouth sag and her eyes cross just a bit. With a shudder of obvious disgust, he turned away.

Hatred ate like acid at Sophie's soul. For that moment, when he stood with his back to her, it was as if there was a target painted on the man. She had a loaded shotgun hung over the door. She could kill him.

She'd die for it. The man's friends would see to it. Her girls would die, too. And maybe, before they died, they might face horrors so great it would destroy them, all the way to their souls.

But she was tempted. God forgive her, she was tempted to kill him where he stood. She knew she harbored hatred. She had carried the burden of that hate for two years. But she had never been so nearly overwhelmed by it—to the point that she was almost beyond control of herself. She shuddered under the weight of that temptation—to sacrifice everything for revenge.

The two men behind Judd rode off into the storm, their identities cloaked by darkness. Judd, just a few steps behind, swung himself up onto his horse's back. The animal fought against its rider and danced toward Sophie enough that she saw a brand.

J Bar M.

Judd and Eli. J Bar M. She had two names, a brand, and a face burned forever in her mind. At last, she had somewhere solid to pin her hate.

Sophie now called up another of her standard prayers. *It's evil to hate the way I do, Lord.* She gathered the shreds of her self-control and let the men ride away. It was the only thing she *could* do. She shoved her hatred down deep inside her, and if she couldn't bring herself to forget it, she would lock it away and ignore it, which was almost the same thing.

She closed the door and whipped the foul-smelling scarf off her neck. She shoved it into the covered pail and slammed the lid shut tight. It seemed to ripen in that pail, getting more hideous with every passing day.

"Ma, it takes a week to air the house out after you've done that," Sally groused from overhead.

Mandy started down the ladder.

"Sorry," Sophie answered. There was no point discussing it because it had to be done. Her disguise had evolved over the course of time. She had come to fear the attention of the men around Mosqueros, so she'd decided to play down her appearance. The trouble was, her main appeal was her ranch, and no disguise could conceal that.

Then the ranch loan had come due, and Sophie had been forced into choosing between the banker, Royce Badje, and eviction. It hadn't taken her a second to decide on the latter.

"I want to see the hurt man before he dies, Ma." The ladder creaked under Sally's feet as she brought the sleeping baby down to her crib. "I don't want to stay with Laura."

Sophie sighed at her insistent daughter. Her children's safety had been the reason she'd ended up here. She had no family anywhere, and nowhere to go. She had discovered this cabin during one of a hundred picnics with her girls. It had been like a little playhouse to them, deep in the thicket. When it became apparent that she was losing the ranch, she'd shifted what possessions would fit into it before the ranch was sold.

"You'll see him in the morning, Sally. I know you're curious, but someone has to stay with Laura, and I need Mandy. We might have to lift him, and she's stronger." Sophie removed her costume quickly, while Mandy threw open the two little windows so the smell would get

out. Sophie removed the rest of her disguise and ran a quick hand to tidy her bun before giving it up as a hopeless cause.

"Can't I just take a peek?" Sally persisted. "If I have to wait till morning, he'll most likely be dead. I want to see him afore he croaks." It occurred to Sophie that her children were remarkably calm in an emergency, and just the littlest bit bloodthirsty. Part of being Texans, she supposed. They'd adopted Texas ways along with the drawl.

Sophie had to smile at Sally's wheedling. Really, the child didn't ask for much, and this was the most excitement they'd had in a long time. It had long ago become clear to Sophie that excitement was usually a bad thing, and she never quit being thankful to God for a boring life. "Is Laura fast asleep?"

Sally laid her little sister down and gently patted the baby's back to keep her asleep, but there was really no need. Once the toddler dropped off for the night, she could take a ride on a cyclone without waking.

"Just like always, Ma. I'll only stay out a minute. I promise." Sally acted like it was Christmas. Then Sophie remembered their scanty Christmas and knew this was easily bigger.

"All right, just for a minute. You girls can run on out while I get changed out of my nightgown."

The girls dashed off, and Sophie quickly discarded her cold, muddy flannel and pulled on a dry calico. She rushed after the girls, not wanting them alone for a second longer than necessary, even with an unconscious stranger. Beth knelt beside him, holding a damp cloth on the cut on his forehead. Her second born, who had an unusual love for all living creatures, was caring for the injured man as well as anyone could.

"Has he shown any signs of waking?" Sophie asked.

"Nope. He's been knocked witless. Out cold as a carp."

Sophie knelt on the other side of him and let Sally get in close to have her look. It took Sally about ten seconds to figure out nothing was going on.

"We may as well clean him up a bit." Sophie took a clean cloth from the stack Beth had brought and soaked it in the now-cool water. "It's chilly out here, but there's nothing for it but to bundle him up. We can't risk a fire in the shed with this dry prairie grass, and until he can walk, we can't get him in the house."

She wished she'd thought to put more water on to heat. She began bathing his face, the mud now almost dry and beginning to cake and fall off. It only took her a few seconds to clean away the grime. While she turned to rinse out the cloth, first one, then another, then the third of her girls gasped out loud.

Sophie became instantly more alert. Had the night riders doubled back on foot? She looked into the darkness for trouble, but the trouble wasn't out there. It was right here under the dirt.

Mandy said incredulously, "It. . .it can't be."

"What can't be?" Sophie turned her attention sharply to Mandy, still trying to find the danger.

"But it is!" Beth cried out. "It is, isn't it, Ma?"

Sophie realized both girls were staring in stunned fascination at the wounded man. Sophie turned to follow their gaze, but before she could look, Sally started to cry.

Sophie put her arm around her daughter but saw where she was staring. She turned to see what her girls were seeing.

"It can't be." Beth's voice broke. "But it is."

It was.

"It's Pa," Sally spoke through shuddering tears.

The husband Sophie had personally cut down out of a tree. Had personally released from the noose around his broken neck. Had personally buried on a rise overlooking the ranch they'd worked on so hard.

The husband whose death had etched her heart with hate and made her long, only moments ago, to commit cold-blooded murder. He was lying here unconscious, as men sought him to kill him all over again.

After what seemed like hours of stunned silence, Sophie leaned closer to the man.

Cliff.

"It isn't possible." She scrubbed more quickly at his face as if, when enough dirt was removed, the truth would be revealed.

"But it is, Ma. This is Pa," Sally said firmly.

Sophie considered herself to be broad-shouldered and levelheaded. She took what life handed to her, and with fervent prayers to her Maker for help, she made do with what she had. She wasn't a woman given to fancy. She stared at the man in front of her and knew it was Cliff. She thought back to that awful night two years ago and knew she'd buried Cliff. Those two absolutes clashed inside her brain and nothing that made any sense emerged. She stared and she washed and she tried to make the impossible fit into her sensible head.

Beth started crying next. She lifted the hand of the man who lay before her. "Pa?" She spoke so softly, it had the reverence of a prayer.

Mandy added her tears in next. "I c—can see it's him, but I saw you bury him. We all helped wr—wrap him"—Mandy's face crumpled—"in the quilt. How can this be, Ma?"

Sophie noticed several things about the man. He was more muscular than Cliff. He had an ugly round scar high up on one shoulder that could be nothing else but an old bullet wound. He had three slashing cuts on his right arm that were scarred but looked pink and fairly new. Cliff had none of these things. But that proved nothing. A man could build a lot of muscle in two years. And he could get himself shot and stabbed. Sophie remembered that sense of familiarity when she'd been bathing and doctoring his chest. The reason it had seemed familiar was, despite the bigger muscles, the man had hair on his chest the exact color, texture, and thickness of Cliff Edwards's.

With a sudden start, she thought of Cliff's birthmark on his right shoulder blade. "Help me roll him over. Your pa had a mole." All three girls added their strength, and they lifted the heavily muscled man a bit.

What they saw was an exit wound from the bullet. In the exact spot where Cliff had a large black mole, nearly an inch across. Or was it the exact spot? The wound was close enough that she couldn't be sure.

"Let him lie back, girls." Sophie sank from her knees to sit fully on the shed floor. Feeling boneless from the shock, she almost sank all the way down. The girls were all crying softly, and with a start, she realized she was, too.

She shook her head to clear away the fog, and then she gathered her senses. "I know one thing." The girls tore their eyes away from where they drank in the sight of their father and looked at her. "Your father is dead."

Sally shook her head. Sally had always been Daddy's girl, more than the rest of them. He'd left when Sally was too young to remember him, but in his absence, he'd grown into a heroic figure in her mind. And he'd only been back a few short months when he'd died—just long enough to get that longed-for son to growing in Sophie's belly, the one that turned out to be another girl.

Sophie had tried to help Sally see Cliff as he was, without harming her little girl's love for her father. But Sally had never been able to protect her heart from Cliff's small cruelties. She'd believed her pa's criticisms were just and tried harder than ever to win his love. She had been the one to be the tomboy. To be the son they'd never had. She'd carved out a special place in her pa's heart by tagging along with him everywhere for the little time they'd had together after the war. And it was no small trick to carve out a place in Cliff's heart. He wasn't a demonstrative man. He was a decent, honest man, but he was given to dark moods and sarcasm. Now, Sally had her pa back. She wasn't giving him up easily.

"It's him, Ma. We know our own pa!"

"It's. . .it's. . ." Sophie struggled to let go of the wild surge of hope that was building in her. Although their marriage hadn't been perfect, she'd loved her husband, at least to the extent he would allow it. But she couldn't build her life on a fantasy. "I've heard it said that for each of us, somewhere in the world, there is a double. Now, I've never put much stock in that myself, just because I've never seen any evidence of it. I've never seen two people who looked exactly like each other, except sometimes brothers or sisters come close, or a parent and child. But

maybe it's true. Maybe—no, definitely—your pa has a double. Because here he is."

"Did Pa have a brother?" Mandy, the analyzer, asked.

"No. He was an only child and his pa died when he was little. His ma had passed on several months before I met him. He told me there was no one. Not even cousins. No, this man can't be a relative. At least not a close one. That's one of the reasons we ended up here after Pa died. With my folks gone, we have no family on either side to help us."

"So you think this man looks like Pa, even down to that birthmark?" Sally began chewing on her bottom lip.

"Now, Sally, honey, we don't know if there's a birthmark under that scar."

"It was right there, Ma, I remember," Sally insisted.

"Do you really think it's possible two men could look this much alike?" Beth asked skeptically.

Sophie was skeptical herself. But she also knew who she'd cut down out of that tree. "There can be no other explanation, girls." Sophie said quietly to her weeping daughters, "Look at me."

One by one they tore their hungry eyes away from a dream that all children who have lost a parent carry with them. They looked at her and waited.

"I don't know who this man is," Sophie said. "But I know who he is not. He's not your pa. Your pa is dead."

Mandy and Beth nodded. They knew it, too. They'd seen it with their own eyes. Only Sally wouldn't give up the dream.

They all turned back to look at him again. As they did, his eyes fluttered open.

Sally began sobbing and leaned over him. "He's alive!"

THREE

He was dead.

That was the only possibility. He was dead, and he must have been good, because he was in heaven being ministered to by angels. They floated around his head. They cried for him as if his death were a sad thing, which made him feel like his life must have been one worth living. They touched him, held his hand, leaned against his legs, and knelt and bowed over him. And every one of them had her blue eyes riveted on his face, as if he held the answers to all the world's problems.

He'd never known there could be such love for him. He'd never seen so many blue, blue eyes. The closest one caressed his head with a gentleness that almost broke his heart, it was so sweet. He sighed under the loveliness of heaven.

The angel who touched him spoke, but he was having trouble making sense of what she said. His mind seemed to be groggy, not working much at all. He thought a man should listen carefully when an angel spoke, so he tried his best to pay strict attention. Finally, after she'd repeated it several times and stroked his cheek as if to coax an answer out of him, it made sense.

She said, "Who are you?"

Shouldn't an angel know the answer to that?

The nearest angel was also the biggest. He looked from one angel to the others. They seemed to come in all sizes. One of them was crying

hard, broken sobs that stabbed into his heart, as he wondered if he was the cause of her unhappiness. He couldn't remember the angel's question, and instead of answering her, he said to the one who wept so, the littlest one, "Don't cry, little angel."

He reached a hand up to comfort her. A spasm of pain cut across his chest. He cringed, as his head spun and his stomach lurched with nausea. He thought he might be sick all over his glorious angels.

Funny, he wouldn't have expected there to be pain in heaven.

Even with the agony, he reached for that one brokenhearted angel, to try and make amends with her. Then he saw his muddy hands and knew he didn't dare touch her.

Funny, he wouldn't have expected there to be dirt in heaven.

He dropped his hand, but the little one grabbed it. "Pa? It's you, isn't it? Tell them it's you. No one believes it, but I know it's you."

Pa? He didn't understand. He knew she was talking to him. She was clasping his filthy hand to her chest, as if it were the greatest of treasures. He looked at that one little blond angel and wished he could be her pa.

Maybe that was it. Maybe this was his lot for eternity. That sounded very good to him. Tears of gratitude for God's goodness cut across his eyes. He held that little hand firmly, until darkness caught hold of his mind and pulled him under.

Sally almost flung herself down on top of him. Sophie grabbed her.

"It's him! Did you see the way he recognized me? Oh, Ma! Ma, he called me a little angel!" Sally looked up at Sophie. Sally's joy was so precious, Sophie wanted to say whatever Sally wanted to hear.

Suddenly, Sally gasped aloud. "If there *is* a double, then why not the other one, Ma? Why couldn't we have cut the double down out of the tree?"

Sophie ran her hand gently down Sally's uncombed white curls.

"They took him from right in front of me, Sally sweetheart. I was there. He was in the yard, just walking away from the house after supper. You remember how it was. You were there. I was standing in the door, watching him go."

They'd come charging in and surrounded Cliff. One of them, Judd she now knew, shouted that they'd tracked a horse thief to this property—right to this yard. Then they dragged him away before Sophie could so much as speak a word in his defense and tell them Cliff had been with her all day.

They'd galloped off, and Sophie had run after them, screaming. They hadn't even acknowledged her existence. When they'd left her hopelessly behind, she'd dashed back to the corral and caught a horse. She was good at it, having done largely for herself during the war years. She'd been riding after them within minutes. And she'd caught them just as they rode away laughing and sharing a whiskey bottle—leaving Cliff swaying in the wind.

She'd raced to the tree, thinking she might be in time to save him. But Cliff's face was a horrible, lifeless gray. His blue eyes gaped open, staring straight ahead at nothing. His neck was bent at an unnatural angle. All that had been left to do was cut him down and carry him home.

Sophie had gone for the sheriff, but he'd begun questioning her about the horses on the Edwards's property, as if he suspected the vigilantes might have been within their rights to hang Cliff. The sheriff had gone back to town without offering to so much as chase after Cliff's killers.

Sophie, beyond grief, with the fight battered out of her body, simply dug a hole next to the grave they'd dug for their baby boy. Late in the evening Parson Roscoe showed up with several townsfolk. The parson tried to comfort her, but Sophie couldn't even respond to his Christian faith. She was afraid if she accepted even a moment of comfort, she'd begin crying and never stop.

Others came out to pay their respects, but except for the parson,

none of them were really friends. On top of Mosqueros's aversion to the Edwards's Yankee affiliation, Cliff had a knack for alienating people. There'd been a short ceremony, and Sophie had bitterly refused all help filling in the hole.

She'd also turned down four marriage proposals. Sophie was mortified her girls had witnessed the crude men trying to convince her to marry them over the fresh-turned earth of her husband's grave. The parson had ordered them off her land. The next day, Royce Badje, the banker, had ridden out to the ranch to notify her that when the next loan payment came due, he'd expect the full amount left on the loan.

Sophie had cattle to sell and a large part of the principal of the loan paid down. Mr. Badje said once the man of the household was dead, the woman was a poor risk. She'd either have to pay her loan in full or sell.

Sophie countered by pointing out she'd kept things going while Cliff was away fighting the war.

"Cliff was at Gettysburg, wasn't he?" Mr. Badje asked coldly. The banker's sons had died at Gettysburg, fighting for the Confederacy.

Sophie didn't answer. They both knew. Mr. Badje had given her thirty days to pay up or vacate the property.

While she was still shaking with anger, the banker proposed marriage. He offered to let her keep the ranch for their home, if she said yes. She'd said no. Then Mr. Badje asked how many years until Mandy was of marrying age.

Sophie's skin was crawling by the time he left.

The man stirred beside her and brought her thoughts back to the present, but he remained unconscious.

All three of the girls leaned forward, as if they were hanging on every breath that passed through his lips. Sophie studied his relaxed features, willing his eyes to open again, so he could answer some questions. A sudden fierce gust of wind rattled the shed, reminding Sophie of where they were and how late it was. She needed to get the girls away from him anyway, before they could fall more completely into the dream of getting their father back.

She studied her daughters, grim and mourning in a dark night split by lightning and shaken by thunder. She saw them as she hadn't seen them in a long while. They were tough as shoe leather, she knew that, but tonight, for the first time, she saw they were gaunt. She had waged a battle to survive on wild game and sparse greens.

Tonight, for the first time, she saw that she was losing that battle. Her girls were being hurt by this lean, hard life. She had to do something. She couldn't go on hiding, afraid of the hostile, hungry-eyed townspeople. Something had to change. But change took thought and planning. She didn't have time for either right now. She never had time for either.

"Girls, we have to get some sleep. And we can't leave Laura alone any longer."

Her girls each had a look of Hectorish stubbornness. Sophie understood, but they still had to put one foot in front of the other. And that started with sleep. She judged the situation and decided now wasn't the time for patience and kindness. She started issuing orders. "Amanda and Elizabeth, you go back to the house for now."

"No, Ma, we want to stay," Mandy protested.

Beth stormed, "It's not fair that Sally gets to help first."

Sophie hardened her heart to their pleading. They had to get through the next day without being exhausted. "Sally didn't go down into the creek. She's not soaking wet and shivering." That was true, but it wasn't the real reason. Sophie knew she would never pry Sally from this man's side.

She didn't waste her time trying to be reasonable. "Do as you're told. Get some sleep. Sally and I will sit up with him and keep him warm as best we can. You'll have to spell us later, so try and rest. Laura will wake up just as usual at dawn, and someone's going to need to have the gumption to take care of her. I'll send Sally in later to wake you, Mandy. Then Beth will have a turn."

In the intermittent lightning, Mandy and Beth looked stubborn-still, but the chance at keeping vigil later placated them somewhat. Sophie saw the dark circles under their eyes from the strain of this night, and she knew they'd sleep if they'd only lay their heads down. She didn't think Sally would. She'd just lie in the house and spin pipe dreams and hope.

In a slightly more gentle voice, Sophie said, "Go on now, girls. If he wakes up and can walk, we'll bring him in the house where it's warmer."

They grumbled, but Sophie had been in charge of this family for a long time. At last they moved away from their patient's side, and after hesitating in the opening of the little barn, they dashed out into the slashing rain and disappeared into the narrow pathway of the thicket.

Sophie exchanged a long look with Sally, who could barely tear her eyes away from the man. "It's not your pa, Sally. I'm sorry, and I know you don't believe me. We all want it to be him so badly. But it's not."

"But Ma, he's. . ."

"Don't you think I want it to be him?" Sophie interrupted. "Don't you think I've been fishing around inside my head for some way I'm wrong about who I buried that night? It was two years ago. You were only five. It's possible for you to convince yourself that things were different than they were. But I can't fool myself."

"But, Ma," Sally wailed. "All you have to do is look at. . ."

"I don't know what's going on," Sophie cut her off. "Maybe we'll find out your pa had a. . .a distant cousin or something. I think, with the way he looks, there has to be some connection between this man and your pa, but it's not him." Sophie softened her voice. "I'm sorry, sweetie, but it's just not him."

Sally's eyes wavered between the man and her ma. She finally whispered, "Okay."

And while Sophie knew her daughter believed her, she also knew the hope wouldn't die. The man stirred. The heavy woolen blanket that covered him slipped down, and goose bumps covered his arms and bare chest.

Moving slowly, as if in a trance, Sally stretched out beside the man and rested her little body along side of him. Just above a whisper, she said, "I'll keep you warm."

It was as if Sophie saw her daughter falling in love with this stranger right before her eyes. She didn't know what to do or say to stop it. In the end, when the man shivered again more violently, Sophie decided to leave it until morning. She rubbed the man's arms and pulled the blanket a bit higher. When that didn't make the goose bumps go down, she decided Sally had the right idea. She stretched out beside the man and huddled up close to him to share her warmth. She reached her hand across him to touch Sally's pale, worried face.

"Would it be so bad to pretend—just for tonight?" Sally asked.

Sophie smoothed her little girl's bedraggled hair back off her forehead. Then she felt a sudden easing of her heart. Sophie knew it came from a loving God who had proclaimed worry a waste of time.

"You're going to pretend anyway, aren't you, sweetie?"

Sally looked a little sheepish. With a shrug of her tiny shoulders that had already borne a lifetime of sadness, she said, "I reckon."

"So just enjoy it. It wouldn't be so bad to pretend we've got Pa back—just for tonight."

Sophie saw Sally unbend inside. Sophie knew Sally was pretending and feeling guilty over it, and that had lent strength to the fantasy of her father returning from the dead. But talking about it turned it into something less weighty. Almost a game.

He shivered again. Sally hugged him a little tighter. "Just for tonight."

The man's chills lessened as they held him. Sophie looked across that broad chest and noticed that Sally had fallen asleep with her head cradled on the man's shoulder.

Sophie lay awake and felt him begin to make more natural movements, as a person might do in his sleep. The tension that had been riding her since she'd heard his horse's pounding footsteps so long ago eased.

And that's when she remembered her children's hollow cheekbones and Judd's cruel, bloodshot eyes. Judd's viciousness had driven them to this life. The taste of hate burned her tongue.

It grew in her, like mold in that damp, musty shed, until it filled her and threatened to explode. She shook as she lay there beside the man Judd now wanted to kill. Her eyes stared into the black, drizzling night and saw nothing but hate. Satan gripped her heart, and she gave full sway to her thirst for vengeance. Hate roiled in her heart, guilt ate at her soul, and tears burned in her eyes. Then she forced her burning eyes to close. It was evil to feel like this about one of God's children.

With typical brutal honesty, Sophie admitted to God that she didn't want to let go of her fury. It was a betrayal of Cliff to forgive. It was ludicrous to love enemies such as these. She forced herself to pray, "Dear Lord, remove this sin from me. Soften my heart. Help me not to hate the way I do."

For Sophie it was a flowery prayer. Usually, she had neither the time nor the strength to be eloquent. She was too busy living through whatever life crushed down on her next. So exhausted, cold, and afraid, much the same as any other day, she spoke to God in words that summed up everything, "Help me, Lord. Help me, help me, help me."

That plea to God, that futile cry for something she didn't even want, was on her lips as she fell asleep. "Help me."

Help me.

Adam looked away from the horror before his eyes and glanced into the darkness behind him. He heard someone calling to him.

"Help me, help me, help me."

But there was no one here who needed him. The only ones left were beyond help.

His friends dangled from a tree. A noose around each neck. All dead. All but him.

Adam had crawled into the underbrush when the drunk, who was lashing his back with the bullwhip, had stumbled and fallen to his knees and passed out. Adam had tried to regain his feet, but the loss of blood from the gunshot low on his side and the ripped up skin on his back were too much. He got as far as one knee, thinking to go back and save Dinky and the other men he'd been ranching with, when he lost consciousness.

He awakened to the sound of fading hoofbeats and the triumphant laughter of cowards.

And his friends, lined up three in a row, each swinging slightly from a tree branch. In the chaos, they must have lost count and thought they had everybody. All black men looked alike to them, Adam thought bitterly. They hadn't noticed one was missing.

Adam watched his friends and tried to swallow his terror and his hate. And then he heard the voice.

Adam looked in the opposite direction of the hanging men. A woman. Adam gained his feet and took a few staggering steps toward the voice. Then he heard it again.

"Help me, help me, help me." So familiar. So precious to him. When he'd worked for her daddy, she'd tagged along after him, begging for a turn riding the horses or feeding the cattle, until he'd begun to love her like the child it seemed certain he'd never have. He'd know Sophie's voice anywhere.

It wasn't in any direction he could walk. It was inside his head. A message from her to him sent on the wings of the wind, blown to him by the breath of God. She called to him from Mosqueros, Adam knew that—somehow. Mosqueros, where he'd left her with that fool she'd married. Cliff had made it impossible for him to stay.

With one last heartrending look at his friends, Adam started out. He didn't take time to bury them. He couldn't save the dead, but maybe he could help the living.

The horses. The herd. Ten years' work. Gone. All of it gone. Right now that didn't matter, and it was a good thing it didn't. If he'd let it

matter, he'd have hunted down those men and torn them apart with his bare hands. Sophie's call, "*Help me, help me, help me,*" turned him aside from that path—but only for now.

He took the handkerchief from around his neck, pressed it solidly against the bullet wound in his side, and walked. It was three hundred miles, but what difference did distance make? Sophie needed him. He'd go.

"Ma, you said you'd wake me!" Mandy's quiet, scolding voice hissed her awake.

Sophie moved, then groaned from aching muscles. She tried again to sit up and found she was anchored to a man by one strong arm.

In the full light of dawn, Sophie tried to take stock of where she was and why she was sleeping with a man.

Sleeping with a man! With a sudden squeak of surprise, she pulled against the man's grip—the man she'd just noticed lying beside her. He grunted when she pushed against him, and she remembered everything. Including that he might have some broken ribs. The ribs she was right now being rough with. She subsided immediately and looked sideways at Mandy, standing over her in a snit, with almost two-year-old Laura kicking and wriggling in her arms.

Sophie tried to get control of herself. She firmly reached for the arm that had found its way around her in the night. Just when she would have unwound it from around her neck, she saw him looking at her.

He said, "You're no angel."

Sophie opened her mouth to tell him he wasn't so great himself, but because of his condition, she controlled herself.

Then Beth came into the shed to announce that breakfast would be ready in five minutes. She looked down at the man. "You're not our pa."

Sally, barely awake and very content to be held close against the man's side, said, "Yes, he is."

"He is?" Beth asked in wonder.

"I am?" The man pulled his arm out from under Sophie, and her head dropped with a *thud* on the hard, packed hay.

Sally spoke securely from her little nest of warmth and comfort. "He's our pa. I've thought it over and decided God sent him back to us. Why not? He rosed Lazarus from the dead. Jesus can do anything, and God knows we need a pa."

Sophie sat up and looked from Sally to the man to see what he'd have to say about being declared resurrected and gifted with four children and a wife.

He was no help at all.

"I've been raised from the dead?" He spoke as if he had trouble accepting it but was willing to take Sally at her word.

"He's not raised from the dead, Sally."

"Why not?"

"It just doesn't happen, honey. Pa's gone, and that's that."

"It does too happen." Sally's voice rose. "What about Lazarus? God can do anything!"

"Yes," Sophie said. "God can do anything. But He just—He just— doesn't. . .do things like this. . .very often."

Mandy said smugly to Sally, "Why do you think it was a big deal to raise Lazarus up? It's 'cuz it doesn't get done very much."

"So that means I'm dead?" He rubbed his forehead. "Or I was at one time?"

Sophie felt kind of sorry for the poor, injured man. "No, you've never been dead." Then she thought of a way to solve the whole problem. "Who are you?"

All of them froze.

Sophie waited patiently.

Sally held her breath, hoped etched on her face.

Beth and Mandy exchanged wondering glances.

Laura. . .well, Laura tried to put her foot in her mouth and look at Hector at the same time.

"Didn't you just say my name was Lazarus?"

Sally patted his chest. "No, that's someone else who was raised from the dead, like you."

The man said uncertainly, "I—I don't know. I can't seem to remember anything. Except. . .except last night I woke up in heaven."

The minute he said that, he knew it was the wrong thing to say, because these females were who he'd seen there. So he must not have been in heaven at all. He must have been right here.

Another reason it was the wrong thing to say was it made the lady mad.

"You're not helping a bit." She crossed her arms and glared.

He shifted his weight and groaned from the pain, and the lady looked satisfied. No, she was definitely *not* an angel.

The girl who'd announced breakfast said, "Let's go eat. We'll talk this out in the house where it's warm."

The lady stood slowly. He heard her knees cracking. The little girl in his arms seemed content to stay where she was. The lady rounded him, reached down, snagged the little girl, and pulled her gently but firmly to her feet. Then she bent over him and put her arm under his shoulders. "You took quite a fall last night. Let's see if we can get you up."

He leaned on her as he tried to get to his feet. His chest was in agony. His head felt like it was full of angry gold miners, trying to chisel their way out. His knees seemed to have the consistency of apple jelly. He wobbled once, and the lady put her arm around his waist and helped him balance. All three of the girls reached for him. He was surrounded by swirling skirts and gentle hands and the sweet sounds of someone worrying about him. He reveled in it, until he thought his heart might break from the pleasure. Maybe he *was* in heaven. Or maybe the angels had been allowed to come back to earth with him.

The oldest girl, the one with the baby in her arms, caught him around the waist on the side the lady wasn't on. The little one—he remembered she'd wept over him in the night, and he wanted to hug her close and thank her for caring so much—she wrapped her arms around his middle and clung to him, as if she'd bear every ounce of his weight if he needed her to. Her head hit him right at his belly. She turned her worried face up and looked at him with pure love in her eyes.

The other one, the cook, rested her hands on his shoulders from behind and said with a voice that instilled confidence, "Steady there, mister. You'll be all right in a minute. Let us help you."

They all smelled wonderful. Sweet and pretty, except—he hated to find a sour note in what was one of the sweetest moments of his life—the lady was really rank. He tuned out that unpleasant discovery when she started fussing at the girls to be gentle with his ribs and the cuts and bruises. He looked down at his body and was stunned at the wreckage. He looked like he'd. . .he'd. . .

The lady said, "You fell over a creek bank."

He looked at his battered chest. "That sounds about right."

"You don't remember?" the lady asked.

The wiggling little worm of worry in his brain was growing into a coiled, sixteen-foot prairie rattler of panic in his gut. The truth was, he couldn't remember anything. Not how he came to be in this place. Not where he'd come from or where he was going to. Not even his name!

He looked between all these pretty women, in their gingham and calico, with their soft kindness, and said, "I don't remember anything, ma'am."

"Sophie," she supplied.

"Sophie." Suddenly, that name was the only solid thing that existed in a wildly out-of-control world, and he was determined to hold on to it. "I—I don't know why. . ." He faltered from admitting anything more. It seemed like a weakness to admit he had no memory, and it went against some instinct within him to admit to any weakness.

"So you're not Clifton Edwards?" the lady—Sophie—asked. There was a strange tone to her voice when she asked it, and he looked hard

at her. He could tell from her tone that "no" was the right answer. But Clifton Edwards? Something about the name touched a chord inside of him.

"Clifton Edwards." He whispered the name aloud and tried to focus on what exactly bothered him about the name. The image of a face, a little boy's face, flashed in his mind. He didn't know who the boy was. He saw an older man, stooped with age. He saw a naked man—or nearly naked—leap up from the grass and raise a tomahawk in the air. An Indian. Blackfoot. He knew that. Then the parade of pictures faded. He absently reached his hand up to rub his aching head. He flinched from the stabbing agony of his ribs when he moved his arm. His stomach twisted and surged, and then the fact that he seemed to have no memories made the world spin.

"You fell a long way," Sophie said. "You took two hard blows to the head. Hard enough to leave big bumps and knock you senseless for hours. I reckon you'll be okay when you've had some rest."

"Don't any of you know who I am?" His voice sounded like it came from outside of himself. He saw a dead man lying on the ground in front of him. The vision widened. Ten dead men. A hundred. Blood everywhere. Bodies dressed in blue and gray. Severed limbs and the screams of the wounded. The smell. War. Sickening. Brutal. He wished he could forget it all. Forever.

From a great distance the lady answered his question, "No."

The littlest one said, "You're our pa."

The cook said, "You're not our pa."

The baby-sitter said, "You just look like our pa."

The toddler kicked her feet and landed one on his ribs and said, "Papa."

His knees went from apple jelly to apple cider, and all the girls' strength didn't keep him from sagging back to the ground. Through a roaring in his ears, he thought he heard someone, the cook maybe, say matter-of-factly, "We shoulda got him to the house whilst we had the chance."

He also thought the lady, who smelled so bad, grew a second head that looked like a mule's head. Now that he thought of it, a mule was what she smelled like. A really filthy, old mule. Maybe one that'd been dead for a while. His last impression was that the mule kicked him in the ribs as he hit the ground, and maybe, just maybe, the mule said vehemently, "You are too our pa! You've been raised from the dead and that's that!"

Then everything went black.

FOUR

Mandy knelt beside the unconscious man. "Drat, he's out cold again. He really took hisself a whack."

Sophie shoved Hector's head off her shoulder. "Beth, can you get this ornery beast out of here?"

Elizabeth came around and soothed Hector, who had wandered outside after the storm but now wanted to see what the fuss was about in his house.

Sally fell to her knees beside the man. "He said he doesn't remember nothin'. Does that mean when you come back to life you don't bring your memories with you? Your whole life starts over at that moment? Does that mean he don't remember he's our pa?"

Sophie sighed at Sally and her resurrection theory. When you came right down to it, it made about as much sense as anything else. "It's much warmer this morning. The only danger he's in out here is from Hector stepping on him."

Beth came back without Hector. "I wouldn't put it past him, Ma. Unless you want to keep Hector tied up all day, someone's gonna hafta stay out here."

"I'm staying," Sally shouted.

Sophie took charge. "We'll eat in shifts. You girls go and eat now."

"I'm not leaving him, Ma!" Sally said adamantly, clearly planning to hold her ground until she died.

"You'll do as you're told, young lady!" Sophie gave Sally a stern look and continued, "I'll sit out here and nurse Laura while you girls eat. Then I'll eat while Beth watches him. Sally, it's your turn to wash the dishes, and there'll be no shirking. Whoever is with him gets Laura, too, so your hands won't be idle. We'll take turns sitting and doing the chores. If he wakes up, come running."

With a raised eyebrow at her third daughter, she added, "We're all just as curious as you are Sally, so don't ask for special treatment."

"The only trouble with that, Ma," Mandy said sensibly, "is that you smell so bad, I don't think Laura will eat. Plus, you'll stink her up."

"Yeah, and I already gave her a bath this morning," Beth added. "I've got water hot on the stove for you, Ma, and the washtub set up. Let Mandy and Sally stay here with Laura. I'll finish breakfast while you bathe. It's just biscuits. I can bring Mandy and Sally some out here."

"I promise I'll do my chores, Ma," Sally pleaded, "I'll go as soon as you're done washing up. I know we all want to spend time with Pa. I won't hog him."

When the girls ganged up on her, especially armed with common sense like this, she marveled at them. It was only then, as she thought of the logic of their reasoning, that she realized how much *she* didn't want to leave. Was it possible that she was harboring resurrection theories of her own? She looked at the unconscious form of her husband who wasn't her husband, and a sudden twist of longing made her breathing falter. That's when she knew she had to be the one who went to the house. She needed to get away from him and clear her head. And she took pity on Laura, who was already clean and sweet smelling.

"All right. Sally and Mandy take first shift watching out for him. Holler if he wakes up." Before she left, she took one last hard look at the man who kept falling back to sleep in her shed. As she turned away from him, she thought of all that lay ahead of her today. There was enough flour left for one more baking of biscuits. They needed food, and she would have to go into the thicket and search for it. She'd hope for a nest of pheasant eggs. If there weren't any, she'd have to set her

snares and hunt for early-spring greens.

The girls could do a lot, but in the end it all fell on her shoulders, shoulders made strong by hard work and faith. There was Laura to tend and laundry to do after last night's muddy soaking. That meant hauling water and heating it. And on top of the regular struggle to survive, she now had an injured man to look after. All this came on top of a poor night's sleep. Her shoulders sagged as she made her way to the house.

Her morning prayers were the same as her night prayers and most of the prayers in between. Tears she would never let fall burned her eyes as she prayed, "Lord, give me the strength to get through another day. I can't do it on my own. Help me, Lord. Help me, help me, help me."

Luther awoke with a start and slid into the brush, away from the glowing embers of the fire. He glanced behind him and saw Buff roll out of sight into the woods. The two of them lay silently for a long time. They knew how it worked in the West. Get stupid, get dead. Simple.

What had made him move? The more Luther thought about it, the more he was sure it wasn't a sound that had awakened him. It was a—a nightmare. But that didn't quite cover it. Finally, into the darkness, Luther said quietly, "Buff, I've a hankerin' to see the kid."

There was an extended silence. "That what sent you runnin' for cover? Ya missed the boy?"

Buff didn't sound sarcastic, which Luther appreciated. Sheepishly he admitted into the night, "As I lay here, I reckon that's exactly what woke me."

Buff came to the fire matter-of-factly. "Movin' first an' askin' questions later keeps body and soul together."

Buff looked to be settling back in, but Luther knew he could not ignore that call for help. " 'Twas one o' them consarned dreams where a fella is fallin' and lands afore he wakes up."

"Had 'em," Buff said.

"Only 'tweren't me fallin'. It was Clay. An' it was almighty real. And a call for help. I think the boy's in trouble."

"Best check it out."

Buff put on the coffee while Luther led the horses to the creek for water. Without more than ten words between them, they ate breakfast and broke camp.

As the sun rose to the middle of the sky, Luther spoke for the first time since they'd set out. "Texas is a big state."

"Clay's a big man," Buff said. "He'll leave tracks."

Luther nodded. "Blackfeet're feisty in the spring anyhow. Might'uz well find a differ'nt spot."

"Yup," Buff said grimly as he swung his horse into a ground-eating lope aimed at Texas, most likely a thousand miles away or more. "Let's see if Apaches're friendlier."

Sophie bathed the Hector stink off herself and ate her biscuits and jelly, while Beth stood behind her and braided her still-wet hair. She was just getting up from the table when Mandy came tearing into the house.

"He's awake again!" Mandy dashed away.

Sophie and Beth were hard on her heels.

Sally was kneeling beside the man, talking earnestly to him, when Sophie got to the shed. Sophie heard her say, "And I'm your third daughter, Sally."

Sophie skidded to a stop and tried to walk sedately into the shed. Her patient turned his eyes toward her and tried to sit up. Sophie forgot to be sedate and dropped to the ground beside him. "Don't try yet. We shouldn't have let you get up earlier. It was too soon."

As if he appreciated being given permission to lie still, he sank flat on the ground.

"Now," Sophie said calmly, "can you tell us who you are?"

He rubbed his head and didn't answer for a long moment. Sophie

saw her daughters lean ever closer. Even the practical Mandy seemed to be hoping this man would be their father.

When he didn't respond, Sophie added, "You rode your horse over a creek bank last night. We heard you fall and got you back up here. This is going to sound strange to you, but once we got you to where we could see you. . ."

Sophie really didn't know how to say it. "The thing is. . .you look exactly like my husband. And he's been. . .he's been. . ." She thought it best to break it to him gently. "The thing is. . .my husband—the girls' father—is. . . He's. . ." Sophie could find no gentle way. "He's dead."

The man was watching her like a hawk, hanging on every word. What little color he had faded from his poorly washed face. Sophie hated to go on, but there was no solution to this in silence. "I buried him myself two years ago. There can be no mistake. So you can see why the girls and I are. . ." Sophie faltered then went for a Texas-sized understatement, ". . .interested in who you are."

The man quit rubbing his head. He was staring at her and listening so intently, it was as if every word she spoke was coming straight from the mouth of God. "Earlier you asked me about a name?"

"Clifton Edwards."

His eyes narrowed, and Sophie leaned closer along with the girls.

"Clifton Edwards. Cliff," he muttered. "It means something to me."

He felt himself withdraw from the women as he searched inside himself. Visions flashed one after the other. A towering mountain. A battlefield. A half-naked Blackfoot charging him with blood in his eyes. A star. A silver star pinned on his shirt. When he saw the star, the floodgates opened. He sat upright so quickly Sally almost landed in his lap. "Clifton Edwards. I remember. No, I'm not Clifton Edwards. I'm Clayton McClellen. I'm Cliff's brother. His twin brother."

Sophie gasped at the same time she reached her hand out to support the man's unsteady shoulders. "Cliff didn't have a brother. He didn't have any family."

"Yes, he did. We'd been separated for years. My ma couldn't stand life in the West and went back to her family in Boston. We were young, three or four, but even then I knew I wanted the life we were living in Montana. Pa said Cliff hated it, so Ma took him and left me."

Sophie shook her head. "But. . .Cliff never said a word about you. Or about a father."

"Pa died while I was away fighting the war." Clay tried to make sense of what she said. Could Cliff have been so indifferent to Clay that he wouldn't even mention his twin brother's existence? "I guess when he picked my mother over Pa and me, he decided we were dead to him."

Sophie's blue eyes were kind and warm. Even though Cliff was long dead, Clay envied his brother. Sophie said, "No, I don't think that's true. Cliff used to talk about having a son. He wanted one so much. He said often enough that he was the last of his family line, and he wanted someone to carry on the name."

"The child would have been carrying on my mother's family name if Cliff called himself Edwards," Clay said bitterly.

"Yes, but his name wouldn't be his doing if he didn't know you and your pa existed. Three's awfully young. Maybe. . . Did you ever see your mother and brother again? Is it possible he forgot he had a brother?"

"Forgot? How could he? I never forgot him. Never!"

"But did your pa talk about him? Did he keep the memories alive for you?"

Clay nodded as he thought of the stories his pa had always told about the mischief he and Cliff had gotten into as toddlers. He thought of the sympathetic way his pa had talked about how unhappy Clay's mother had been during the brutal Montana winters. Clay had seen the sadness in Pa and he knew, even then, that Thomas McClellen had missed his wife and had loved her until the day he died. His pa had kept the memories alive, and he'd made those memories good ones. So

he was never angry at his mother and brother. Only lonely for them—terribly, endlessly lonely—especially for the twin brother that he knew was out there somewhere. And then he'd heard that Cliff had died.

"Maybe your ma didn't do that for Cliff," Sophie said gently. "I know he would have wanted to have a brother. There was a loneliness in Cliff. I think in some way he knew you existed and he missed you."

Clay suspected Sophie said it mainly to offer comfort to an unhappy man, but even as she said it, he knew it was true. Cliff had been his best friend. Cliff would have wanted to know his twin brother.

Sophie added, "*Loneliness* isn't the right word exactly. It was more like he had a way of being alone even when he was surrounded by people. He kept everyone at arm's length."

From the sad way she said it, Clay wondered if "everyone" included her.

"So you're not our pa?" Sally asked with a downward droop to her mouth.

Clay looked away from Sophie to the little girl who'd offered him unconditional love from the first moment he'd opened his eyes. He squeezed her hand. "I'm sorry, no, I'm not."

A sudden burst of clarity in his befuddled brain made him think of something else. "I'll tell you what I am, though. I'm your uncle." He felt a wide smile spread across his face, and even as a single tear ran down the little girl's face, a shy smile bloomed on her lips.

"My uncle?" she said with wonder in her voice.

"Yeah! I'm your uncle Clay. I didn't even know I had a niece, and here I have four of them. I like the idea!"

"I do, too." Sally nodded and swiped an arm across her cheeks to dry her tears. "Are you going to stay around then?"

Clay sat up and looked from one girl to the other. His eyes paused on Laura, and he couldn't stop himself from smiling at the cheerful little girl. Then with a shake of his head that made his stomach lurch from the pain, he remembered why he'd come here to begin with. A hundred more details washed aside the joy of finding a family, when he thought he was the last. He'd known Cliff was dead. He'd heard about the lynching. He reached for his breast pocket, searching for the star the Texas Rangers had pinned on his chest when he'd accepted this one and only assignment he'd ever do for them. Not only was there no star, there was no shirt.

Vigilantes were terrorizing this corner of Texas. When Clay had heard about Cliff, he'd gone looking for justice, and he'd gotten a star. But where was it? He remembered taking it off and tucking it in his saddlebag before he'd ridden up to that campfire last night. Then he remembered how the campfire had been attacked and they'd all scattered. And he'd been pursued.

He said firmly to Sally, "You bet I'm gonna stay around. I heard about Cliff, and I came to see what happened." For now Clay didn't mention the Rangers. "I didn't even know he'd gotten married and had a family."

Clay's eyes traveled to Sophie. She was a pretty little thing. And she was even sweet-smelling now. "Is there a mule around here somewhere?"

Before anyone could answer him, Sally announced, "We're your family now, Uncle Clay. Our pa used to do all kinds of things with us girls and with Ma. Now you can do all those things."

All the things Cliff had done with Sophie. Clay looked at her. Their eyes caught and lingered for a second too long. Sophie looked away first. Clay forced himself to forget about the charged moment and turned back to Sally. "You are, for sure, my family now."

It sounded like he was staking a claim. Or making a vow. And that suited him right down to the ground.

"Let's see if we can get you up and into the house," Sophie said, rising to her feet. "We have breakfast ready."

The girls all grabbed hold, but he was steady on his feet this time. They'd delivered all the shocks while he was still sitting. He walked slowly to the house with Sally on one side, Sophie on the other, Mandy following, and with Laura and Beth running ahead.

Clay marveled again at being surrounded by so much femininity.

The gentle touches and worried looks. The soft cooing sounds of concern. He'd grown up with only his pa around. Luther and Buff most times, and a dozen others who had come and gone. He'd rarely seen a woman, and until the war, he'd never seen a child, except for a few Indian children who lived in Fort Benton when he and Pa made the long trek every spring to trade their furs for supplies. Those children had fascinated him, but the Indian women wouldn't let a curious, half-grown mountain man near their babies.

The Edwards women escorted him to the house and seated him at their table as formally as if he were visiting royalty. He was appalled. "This is where you live?" The minute the words burst out of him, he wished them back.

Sophie bristled, and all the girls frowned at him—even Laura.

"What's wrong with where we live?" Sophie asked defensively.

Clay decided to forge ahead. "It's the most pathetic house I've ever seen. It's so small." Clay rose from the table and stepped to the door to stare out. "Are we in the middle of some kind of. . .weed patch?"

Sophie appeared at his side, her hands on her hips. "This is our home. There's nothing wrong with it."

"But you can't live in this—this shack in the middle of a thicket."

Sophie crossed her arms and glared at him. "Define *can't*, Mr. McClellen. Because my girls and I have proven you can."

"And it's just one room? How do the five of you fit in here? What are you thinking, to be raising my nieces like this?" Clay looked into the fire in Sophie's eyes and wondered what was the matter with her. He'd been bending over backward to say it as nicely as he could. Of course, he'd grown up with men. They talked straight, and the closest they came to watching their mouths was when they'd refrain from saying something that might get them shot. Sophie didn't seem to appreciate his efforts at all.

"Raising *your* nieces? I've been making do pretty well raising *my* daughters for two years with no help from you or any man! What do you suggest I should have done? The banker threatened to foreclose on

53

the ranch unless I married him. The town marshal offered to marry me, in between accusing Cliff of horse thieving. I had fifty proposals, not all of them decent, I assure you. Life in a thicket was a better idea than any of them."

"You should have taken one of them up on his offer!" The thought of Sophie with another man made his gut twist. But common sense should have made her pick the best of the lot and accept his proposal. "A woman can't live alone in the West, and you're the proof of it with this leaky house and that rickety shed!" Clay was shouting by the time he finished talking.

"If you need better accommodations, there's a path leading straight out of the thicket and into Mosqueros, about ten miles down the road. If you think you can make it in your condition, feel free to go."

He looked at the path that disappeared into the thicket. It looked like she'd settled herself into the middle of a wasteland. Then he turned and stared down into Sophie's defiant eyes. He told her the simple truth. "No, I don't want to go."

Their eyes locked again.

After a long, tense moment, Sally came and tugged on his arm. He tore his gaze away from Sophie's beautiful blue eyes.

"Well, that's settled then," Sally said. "Come and eat."

Clay looked past the sweet little girl and saw the table set with a single plate, with only biscuits and jelly for breakfast. His heart clenched as he realized this might well be all they had. Clay looked back at Sally's adoring little face, and then he turned and looked at his brother's wife. Wasn't there a Bible verse about marrying your brother's wife if your brother died? Clay looked into Sophie's pretty face and thought he had God on his side. It was his God-given duty to take care of them all.

Then he thought of a second verse about a brother dying without leaving sons. It was the job of the second brother to give sons to the wife, to carry on his brother's name. His eyes lost focus when he thought about it. He was barely aware that Sophie grabbed his arm and, with all the girls helping, eased him into a chair. His head cleared, and he was

fairly certain that he'd almost passed out because of his injuries—not because he'd thought about how it was really his Christian duty to see that Sophie had another baby. Cliff still needed that son.

Clay didn't look at Sophie again. He wasn't sure he'd survive it. But he decided in that moment that, if they wanted to carry on Cliff's name, it was going to be the name Cliff was born with. McClellen. Everyone in this house was changing her name to McClellen and like it!

He pulled the plate of biscuits toward him and started spreading on jelly as he continued making plans in his head. And while he was making changes, he'd get them out of this thicket and make sure they had meat on the table. And her next child was definitely going to be a son.

With grim satisfaction, Clay decided they'd name the boy Cliff.

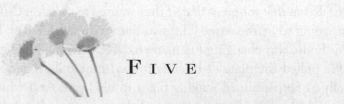

FIVE

Sophie paced around the outside of the cabin and fumed. She stopped and glared at the closed-up house and thought dark thoughts about the occupant. He didn't emerge. She started pacing again. After a long time she started to think he might have died in there. That softened her anger somewhat. True, he'd insulted her years of backbreaking effort to keep a roof over her girls' heads. True, he'd told her she should have married one of the rabble who proposed to her—and she included the banker and sheriff in that lot. True, he'd looked at her with Cliff's eyes, and she'd seen straight into his soul.

She stopped pacing and admitted that the way he made her feel when he looked at her was the real reason she was so mad at him.

Once Sophie stopped being angry, she started to worry in earnest. She was a mother, after all. Worrying was her job! He'd been in there too long. How long could it take a man to bathe? She'd left some of Cliff's clothing—rescued from the rag bag—for him to wear. How long could it take a man to dress? He was still unsteady on his feet. What if he'd fallen? He might have hit his head again. What if he'd passed out in the tub and sunk under the water? Sophie gave up her pacing and charged toward the door. She might already be too late to save him.

She was on the step when he opened the door.

"Coming to scrub my back, Sophie?" he drawled.

Sophie felt her cheeks heat up. "I was afraid you'd fallen. . .or something. You've been in there a long time."

"Trying to soak out some aches and pains." He tilted his chin slightly and gave a little one-shoulder shrug. It was a gesture so like Cliff's Sophie almost gasped out loud. He was watching her intently, but he didn't outwardly react to what must have been blatant fascination on her part.

"First things first. Where's my horse?" he asked.

Sophie and the girls, who had been waiting impatiently with her, all looked at each other.

Mandy said bluntly, "I reckon he's dead, Uncle Clay."

"Dead!" Considering all the shocks the man had endured so far today, Sophie was surprised how upset he seemed about the horse.

"You went over the creek bank," Beth reminded him. "And your horse went with you."

"We never saw any sign of a horse, Clay," Sophie said sympathetically. "It was pitch black. You were half buried in mud. I suppose your horse was down there, too. But there was no time to look. A flash flood came through the creek, and we were lucky to get out alive."

"I 'spect the fall kilt him, but iffen it didn't, I reckon the flood got him," Sally said, patting Clay on the arm.

"You girls went down into that creek, in front of a flash flood, to pull me out?" Clay asked incredulously.

Sophie hadn't been called a girl in a long time. She hadn't felt like a girl for even longer. She kind of liked it. She said in exasperation, "Well, we didn't know there was a flash flood coming when we went down!"

"You could have been killed!" Clay growled.

Sophie replied sarcastically, "I promise, if we'd have known there was the least danger, even of a stubbed toe or a broken fingernail, we'd have left you to die without a second thought."

Clay glared at her. "You need a keeper."

Sophie saw Mandy roll her eyes, and the two shared a grin.

Clay returned to the subject of his horse. "Has anyone gone down and looked? What about my saddlebags? And I had. . ." Clay stopped talking, and Sophie could see he was holding back something about what he had in those saddlebags.

Clay shook his head as if to accept the fact that he'd been wiped out by the flood. Accepting what couldn't be helped was very Western of him. It was something Cliff had never learned.

"I've got to get to a telegraph. How far is it to the nearest town?"

"Mosqueros is ten miles straight west." Mandy pointed toward the narrow trail.

Clay nodded. "I'll have to take the mule, but I'll only be gone—"

"Oh, you can't take Hector," Sally interrupted him.

"I'll bring him back." Clay's eyes slid from one to the other of them. "Don't you trust me? Do you really think I'd steal your mule?"

He sounded so hurt Sophie almost smiled. "It's not that. People would recognize Hector. He is so ornery he's almost a legend around these parts."

"So what if people recognize him?"

"Well, they'd know he was ours, and then they'd know we were here abouts," Beth explained.

Clay tilted his head again, and Sophie had that same wrenching reaction to him. She clenched her fist and held it close to her side when she realized she wanted to reach up and touch Clay's chin as he reminded her so much of her husband.

"Are you saying no one knows you live here?"

Clay spoke quietly, but Sophie heard an intensity in his voice that made her wary when she answered. "No. We were getting. . .bothered by a few of the townfolk."

"The men," Mandy said flatly.

Sophie didn't like the way Clay's eyes narrowed. She continued quickly, "So I led them to believe we'd gone to live with family."

" 'Cept we don't have any family," Beth said sadly.

"Till we got you." Sally grinned.

Clay rubbed his mouth with his hand, and Sophie thought he was trying to not say something. She forged ahead. "And if you show up with Hector they'll think we're here somewhere."

"And they might start coming around chasin' after Ma again." Sally, bouncing with energy, clung to Clay's hand.

"No one's going to bother your ma now that I'm around." Clay sounded like he was making a threat and a promise in the same breath.

"Then they'll just pester Mandy," Beth said philosophically.

"Mandy is only ten!" Clay exclaimed.

"Men!" Mandy snorted as if she'd noticed the same thing.

"There's a shortage of women 'round here," Sally said matter-of-factly. "They're thinkin' to the future."

"They won't be bothering Mandy either." Clay patted Sally on the shoulder.

"And besides," Sophie said, "and this is the important part: They might think you're Cliff, and he was supposed to be a horse thief. So you might not be safe in town."

"But everyone knows Cliff is dead!" Clay protested.

"Lots of them came and watched him be buried," Elizabeth remembered.

"Still, *we* wondered about you," Sophie reminded him. "They might, too. It was quite well known Cliff didn't have any family, especially after he died. And for a while I had nowhere to go until I remembered a 'cousin' who'd take me and the girls in."

"You better not go into Mosqueros." A furrow formed in Sally's brow. "We don't want to lose you like we lost Pa. They might just round you up and hang you to be on the safe side."

Sophie wondered if Sally could bear losing Clay. The little girl had never really gotten over Cliff's death. Sophie turned to Clay, more determined then ever to convince him to stay out of Mosqueros.

Clay snapped, "Let 'em try!"

He headed toward the back of the house without another word. Sophie exchanged anxious looks with her daughters then she hurried after him. They found him dropping a halter over Hector's head. Sophie waited for Clay to get bucked off into a thornbush. She was still waiting when he rode the disagreeable mule around the house. He headed for the gap in the thicket, and just as he rode out of sight, he stopped and turned Hector around without any effort, steering mostly with pressure from his knees.

He looked straight at Sophie for a long minute. "You know what needs to be done here, Sophie?"

Sophie most certainly did know what needed to be done. She'd been managing her life and seeing to her girls single-handedly for. . . well, honestly forever. She felt herself puff up with indignation. What did he think? Was he planning to give her instructions on what chores to do while he was gone?

She said waspishly, "Of course I know!"

"And you're willing?" Clay asked.

"Of course I'm willing. You didn't even need to ask."

Clay nodded silently for too long. "Then so be it. I'll see to it."

Sophie wondered what he'd "see" to. She opened her mouth to ask when Clay said, "Are you a God-fearing woman?"

Anything she'd been going to ask fled her mind when she pondered the question that seemed to come out of the blue. "I am, Clay. God is who has helped me through these last hard years."

Clay nodded again as he sat on Hector's back and seemed to consider all the great questions of the universe. Finally he quit nodding as if he'd worked it all out. "I'm a believer myself. I reckon it wouldn't have mattered. Taking care of you and the girls. . .well, I have it to do. But it's for the best, as far as raising the girls, that we agree on doing right by God." He nudged Hector, and the old mule obeyed Clay like the gentlest of lambs. Hector turned and Clay rode into the thicket.

He was gone before Sophie thought to call out, "What is it you have to do?"

There was no answer, but she assumed he meant something about helping with the chores later on. Sophie sniffed. She wasn't about to wait around for him.

She dusted her hands together. "Girls, let's get on with our day's work."

Sally set up a clamor about Clay leaving. Laura picked that moment to start crying her lungs out.

Beth's shoulders drooped as she headed for the house. "I'll get some dinner cooking."

Mandy bounced Laura and rubbed Sally's back and exchanged a very adult look with her mother. "Whatever he's up to, I'm planning to go along with it if it means we don't have to keep that mule scarf in the cabin no more."

Sophie shrugged and nodded. "Stay with the girls until they cheer up, Mandy. I'll go see to tidying the house."

She and the girls spent the next few hours pretending things were normal. They did their chores and ate a noon meal none of them wanted. Sophie scrubbed Clay's torn-up, muddy clothes and draped them over a bush to dry. Mandy and Beth explored downstream of the now-receded creek for over a mile, looking for any lost possessions that could be Clay's. They found nothing of his, but they did bring back a decrepit wooden pail with no handle and a tin coffee cup. Treasure.

The day wore on and Sophie was preparing their biscuits for supper when she heard a wagon come creaking into the yard. Branches from the bramble slapped back as the wagon squeezed though the thicket trail. The wagon had two horses tied on the back.

She pulled her biscuits out of the fire and ran out to see who'd come by. It was Clay with Parson Roscoe and his wife. Clay rode Hector like the old firebrand was a house pet.

She walked out to meet the parson, with the girls scrambling past her sedate walk. As she passed the unusually obedient Hector, she whispered, "Traitor!"

Speaking normally she said, "Howdy, Mrs. Roscoe. Parson."

"Get the house packed up," Clay said brusquely. "We're getting out of here."

Sophie opened her mouth and looked from Clay to the parson to Hector. None of them were any help.

"Where are we going?" Mandy, always calm and sensible, asked.

"I went to town looking for a better place for us to live. It turns out Cliff's ranch was for sale, so I bought it back. We're moving. I want to be over there before sunset."

Sally squealed and ran into the cabin. "I'll have my stuff packed in ten minutes, Uncle Clay."

Sophie was abstractly aware that she kept opening and closing her mouth, not unlike a landed catfish. She just didn't know what to say. Sally ran past her with her arms full of clothing, and Sophie realized they could indeed leave this place in about ten minutes.

"Y—you bought the ranch back?" Sophie finally managed.

Sally dumped her things in the wagon and ran back in the house. The other girls were hard on her heels.

Clay was wearing new clothes. There was no sign of Cliff's old clothing anywhere. He swung down off Hector's back and yanked the front of his new Stetson in an abbreviated tip-of-the-hat to her. "The owners had taken off a few weeks back, owing on the mortgage. No one else has shown any interest in it. I bought it."

"With what money?" Sophie asked. "You left here in borrowed clothes with no horse or saddle."

"I had my bank in Denver telegraph the one in Mosqueros confirming my draft was good." Clay headed into the cabin. Sophie followed after him. She was slowed by her girls passing her with the kitchen pots and Laura's crib. By the time she got inside, Clay was carrying the kitchen table outside. She almost got knocked back down the stairs. She stepped inside, and the girls dashed past her to grab bedding and the kitchen chairs and anything else that wasn't nailed down. Beth even thought to grab the cooling biscuits. Sophie noticed Mandy pull up the loose floorboard and take out the meager family purse.

Beth disappeared into the thicket for a minute, and when she came back, she said, "I tore down the snares so's we won't catch a rabbit and leave it to starve to death."

Clay came back in to the nearly empty little house and grabbed the milk pail with Sophie's Hector scarf in it. He pulled open the lid and

dropped the pail with a gasp of shock.

He looked wildly around the room. The girls were stripping the last of their things out and running past him.

"Leave it and get out while you can," Beth yelled as she dashed past him.

Clay grabbed Sophie's arm and dragged her out of the empty cabin.

Sophie found herself plunked into the back of the wagon. The parson and his wife sat on the bench. Sally sat in front of Clay on Hector, chattering away. Clay had untied the horses from the back of the wagon and put Mandy and Elizabeth each on horseback so they could ride along beside him. Sophie held Laura.

Sophie heard Clay say to Sally, "What do you mean 'disguise'?" as they disappeared down the trail.

The steady rocking of the wagon lulled Laura to sleep almost immediately. Sophie sat quietly so the baby could sleep, even though she was fuming at being moved without being consulted.

Of course, she'd have gladly moved. She wanted to move! She couldn't wait to get out of that shack they were living in. But couldn't Clay have said something? Talked to her like she was a competent, thinking adult instead of just issuing orders?

They were thirty minutes down the trail when Sophie's jaw finally unclenched enough that she could say to Parson Roscoe, "Where did you meet up with Clay?"

The parson chuckled. "Word travels fast around a town the size of Mosqueros. I came out to see Cliff Edwards come back to life, and by then he'd been to the telegraph office, the general store, and the bank to buy his ranch back. I approached him and asked him who he was. He laughed and asked me, 'Don't you think I'm Cliff? Everyone else seems to believe he's back.'"

"I was right beside him," Mrs. Roscoe said in her peaceful voice. "I said, 'We saw Cliff Edwards buried, and although we are believers in Jesus Christ and as open to miracles as the next person, we aren't

63

about to believe God resurrected a man after he was two years dead and buried.' "

"Clay said," Parson Roscoe continued, " 'It does seem like if God's going to resurrect someone, He'd do it right away when it'd done some good. By two years later everyone's gotten used to the idea of him being dead.' "

Mrs. Roscoe reclaimed the story, "So Irving said to him, 'Are you family?' He said, 'Twin brother. I've come to see about his death and care for his family.' "

"Then I said," the parson interjected, " 'We heard Cliff didn't have any family.' "

Mrs. Roscoe added, "Clay said, 'You heard wrong.' And since there he stood, big as life and as surely a twin brother as any man could be, we welcomed him to Mosqueros. Then he said you were all moving, which is a good thing and high time. We've worried about you something fierce out here, Sophie," Mrs. Roscoe said severely. "So we offered to help, and he said you'd be moving immediately. He said he'd bought a wagon to haul you and could use a driver."

"I see," Sophie said weakly. It wasn't that she minded moving. The thought of getting back the lovely home that she'd been forced out of made butterflies soar around in her stomach. But it was a little overwhelming to just be whisked away. Why, it bordered on kidnapping!

Then Parson Roscoe distracted her from the house. "Now you know I'm a Christian man, and if my time is up and the Lord calls me home, I expect to go praising God's name. But that doesn't mean I need to be a reckless fool. Time was, a parson's collar would protect a man of God from most everybody, but those days are gone. You and Clay will have to say your 'I do's' quick. I don't want to be on the trail after dark. Those vigilantes were out riding again last night."

"*I do's?*" Sophie stopped listening or caring about anything, except getting her hands around Clay McClellen's arrogant neck! There was a roaring in her ears by the time they reached the ranch house.

Clay was already dismounted and coming out of the barn. Sally

skipped along beside him, holding his hand, and Beth stood in the front door of the house wielding a broom. Mandy ran from the corral to take a groggy Laura into her arms. For just a second Sophie forgot her need to beat some sense into her brother-in-law and admired the ranch she and Cliff had built.

She'd had some money when she left Philadelphia. Her father owned a large farm. He felt the need to be generous to his only child and her new husband. It had been her father's money that had made the down payment on the ranch and built the house.

Adam, one of her father's farmhands who suddenly confessed he'd always wanted to move west, was persuaded to drive the second team and stay with the Edwardses until they were established. Adam, a black man with emancipation papers, did more than help. He did everything. Cliff and Sophie wouldn't have survived without him.

Cliff had come to resent Adam. That was Cliff's way. Out of loyalty to Sophie, Adam stayed as long as he could stand Cliff's rudeness. Before he moved on, shortly after Elizabeth was born, the Edwards ranch had seen itself off to a good start.

She looked at the large one-story ranch house and remembered the adventure, excitement, and occasional disappointment of coming west as a new bride. Then she remembered her high-handed brother-in-law.

"Let's get this marriage over and done, Sophie," Clay said as he removed his Stetson to whack some trail dust off his pants. "Parson, if you don't want to climb down, you can just do the pronouncing from where you're at."

Sally giggled and whirled in a little circle without letting go of Clay's hand. The mention of marriage didn't seem to come as a surprise to her, so maybe Clay had gone so far as to mention there was going to be a wedding while he'd been riding with the girls.

"Clay!" Sophie hadn't really meant to yell, but her ears hurt just a little from the single word, so she supposed she had. The girls all froze and looked at her.

Sally's happy smile turned down at the corners. Beth quit sweeping.

Laura woke up. Mandy said, "Marriage?"

"I need to talk to you." Sophie started marching toward the house, but she didn't go in. She went around the side of the house and was almost out of sight when Clay grabbed her arm.

"We can talk later, Sophie. The parson needs to get home. Let's get this out of the way."

Sophie wrenched her arm loose and whirled to face him. "We will talk now, Clay McClellen." Sophie glanced over Clay's shoulder and saw all four of her girls watching in fascination. The parson and his wife were mighty interested, too.

"Sophie, there's nothing—"

"Not here," Sophie snapped. "In private!"

Clay narrowed his eyes. They were cold, blue, gunslinger eyes, and if she hadn't been so furious, she might have backed down and married him just to get him to quit looking at her so angrily. But she was furious, and it gave her the courage of a west Texas cougar.

"Back of the house. Now!" she roared. She jerked her arm, and he must have been agreeable to letting her talk, because she got loose, and she knew she never would have if he wasn't willing.

She marched on around the house. He was right behind her. When she thought she was out of earshot of the girls, unless she started ranting of course, she turned. "Where did you get the outlandish notion that we were getting married?"

"Outlandish notion?" Clay's brows shot up. "We talked about it. You said yes. What do you think I went to town for?"

"The parson?" Sophie screeched.

"Yes," Clay answered in a sarcastic drawl. "The parson!"

"We have not talked about getting married." Sophie jabbed Clay in the chest with her index finger. "I think I would have remembered a proposal!"

Clay grabbed her hand. He must not like being poked. Good. She'd remember that if she ever needed his attention again.

Clay got a very thoughtful look on his face. "I asked you if you

66

knew what we had to do."

"Yes, but I can't imagine how you got, 'Yes, I'll marry you' out of that brief exchange."

Clay released her hand, lifted his Stetson, and ran his fingers through his hair, tousling it before setting his hat back on. "I asked you if you were a God-fearing woman," Clay added.

"And I am one." Sophie crossed her arms, stiffened her jaw, and waited for the man to make some sense.

"Well, we have to get married!" Clay said tersely. "So that's what I meant when I asked you if you knew what we had to do. What did you think I meant?"

"I had no idea!" Sophie could hardly remember him making the comment.

"Then why did you say you knew what we had to do?" Clay asked indignantly.

Sophie tried to think what in the world he was talking about. Clay waited as he stared at her with growing belligerence.

At last she fetched around what she could of the memory. "I guess I thought you were telling me we had the usual chores to do around the place." She snapped her fingers suddenly and said, "That's right. I said, 'Of course I know!' "

"And you said you were willing."

" 'Of course I'm willing,' " Sophie said with vicious sarcasm, "*to do the chores.* I thought you had a lot of nerve telling me that since I've been doing all the chores for two years now!"

"Why would I try and tell you to do the chores you'd been doing alone for so long? That would be stupid!" Clay bellowed. "Do I strike you as a stupid man?"

Sophie arched an eyebrow and didn't respond.

Clay's gunslinger eyes got even narrower. "We talked about having the same faith."

Sophie mulled that over. He'd asked if she was a God-fearing woman. She remembered thinking that was a question best left for a time when they could talk more. "Okay, I guess you asked me that," Sophie conceded.

"And we talked about raising the girls. I know I said something about it being best if we raise the girls in a church-going household."

"Yes, you said all of that. But I never imagined you were talking about. . ."

"It doesn't matter anyway, whether you've been asked proper or not. I guess I've heard of women who want fancy sweet talk and even rings and such, but I didn't take you for a woman who'd need that nonsense."

Sophie felt a little twinge of regret that she seemed like that kind of woman. She liked sweet talk real fine. But she wasn't the kind of woman who would ever dare ask that of one of these rough-hewn Western men. Cliff had given her those words at first, but they'd dried up almost as fast as the roses Sophie's ma had picked for a wedding bouquet. She'd missed them.

Sophie's throat closed just a little, and she tried to go back to being mad. She felt a lot more able to control Clay McClellen when she was mad than when she was near tears. "Why doesn't it matter?"

Clay shrugged. " 'Cuz we're getting married right now, whether you understood what I wanted or not."

Sophie opened her mouth to tell Clay to go try and talk a Texas sidewinder into marrying him, but her throat seemed to swell shut, and she thought for a humiliating moment that she might break down and cry. With a sudden rush of weakness, she wondered what difference it made. Why not marry him? At least she wouldn't have to live in a thicket like a mama jackrabbit anymore.

He seemed to have some misplaced desire to take the worries of the Edwards family on his own shoulders. And he was standing there with a Hectorish look of stubbornness on his face, as if it were a forgone conclusion she'd marry him. And all she was really doing was holding up the parson, who needed to get back to town before dark.

She shrugged. "All right. Let's get it over and done."

Clay curled up the corner of his mouth in a way that wasn't a smile. It almost looked like he was hurt in some way, but she couldn't imagine how. He was getting what he wanted.

He took her arm and led her back around the house. They met everybody, Parson and Mrs. Roscoe included, rushing out of the house. Sophie knew the layout of the house, and she'd bet next spring's calf crop that they'd all been standing at the kitchen window, listening to every word Clay and she had uttered. The embarrassed guilt on their faces was evidence enough.

"So what's the verdict?" the parson asked.

Sophie thought "verdict" was right. This was a life sentence. Clay looked to be a man who wouldn't die easily, unlike Cliff, so she was probably stuck with him.

Clay led her up onto the porch and said to the group waiting there, "We're getting married."

In her mind, Sophie heard a prison door slamming shut.

S I X

He was free! Free from the burden that had been riding him from his earliest memory. He'd wanted his brother back as badly as he'd have wanted back one of his arms if it had been cut off. He'd spent his whole childhood bumping hard against the longing for Cliff. He'd felt the aching pain of the loss every time he laughed out loud. He'd tasted guilt every time he realized he hadn't thought about his brother for a while.

Clay held Sophie's hand, and with a feeling of triumph so strong he could almost hear angels singing, he gave up the years of loneliness. In a heartbeat the heavy weight he'd carried all his life lifted from his shoulders, replaced with a fierce desire to take care of his brother's family.

He gripped Sophie's hand. When she turned her head toward him, he smiled at her.

She scowled back.

Clay wanted to laugh out loud. He might be free, but he had his work cut out for him.

He looked around at the pretty little girls he was getting for a family and almost threw his arms around Sophie to hug her and thank her. He was a little *too afraid* of her to actually do it. Women were foreign creatures to him. He wondered why she wasn't happy. After all, she now had a man to take care of her. Wasn't that all a woman wanted? She'd actually hurt his feelings just a little bit when she'd agreed so gruffly to

his proposal. The little woman should be at least as happy as he was.

The parson said, "Do you. . ." Clay didn't listen. He figured he knew what he was getting into without hearing the exact words the parson said. He just waited for a pause and said, "I do."

Then he heard Sophie say it, too. The parson pronounced some blessing Clay heard part of. He shook Clay's hand and congratulated him. He tipped his hat to Sophie, and he and Mrs. Roscoe got back in the wagon to head for town.

"I'll be in to pick up the wagon and the supplies I ordered from the general store tomorrow," Clay called out.

Parson and Mrs. Roscoe waved as they made for town to beat the sunset and the dangers inherent in the dark.

Clay turned to look at his wife. She was his. The burden of Cliff was gone. He was free!

He wanted to toss his Stetson into the air and give one of those victory yells he'd learned from all the Blackfeet who'd tried to kill him over the years. Then he had a momentary vision of Sophie fat with his child and he had another thought. He'd never in his life been to a wedding, but he'd heard of "You may kiss the bride." Was it time for that now?

Sophie looked like she might punch him if he tried. Still, he considered it.

Sally distracted him when she threw her arms around him. He ignored his tender ribs and hoisted her high in the air. He forgot about trying to coax a kiss out of his cranky new wife. Sally squealed with delight and accidentally kicked him in the stomach. Clay set her down. The other girls came up and hugged him. Even Laura in Elizabeth's arms seemed pleased.

Clay hugged them all. "I've got a family."

The girls giggled and held on tight.

"I always wanted my ma back so bad." He ruffled Sally's pretty blond hair. "And I wanted my brother back until it was an itch under my skin that I couldn't scratch. I reckon I've got something just as good as that now. Maybe better!" He mussed Beth's hair and gave Sally a kiss on top of her head. He slung his arm around Mandy and tickled Laura under her soggy chin.

The only one not having a good time was his wife. She said over the din, "I'll start getting us settled in," and headed for the ranch house.

Clay saw her go and wondered what in tarnation was the matter with her. He thought about it as he watched her walk away from him. She was a fetching little thing, with a trim waist and a beguiling smile, what little he'd seen of it. He enjoyed the view for a second, and then he dismissed her from his mind. Whatever bee was in her bonnet, she'd have to get rid of it herself. He had a ranch to run!

He headed for the barn. Sally caught up with him and clung to his hand. Clay grinned down at the little girl who wanted to be his shadow, and she smiled her heartfelt total adoration back up at him. "I'll show you around, Uncle Clay," she offered.

His niece. Clay shook his head. No, his daughter.

Never had he thought his search would come to this. He remembered when he'd started searching for Cliff in earnest. He'd fought in the war and heard rumors of another soldier that looked like him back East. Clay's time was spent along the western edge of the madness. He'd wondered if it could be his brother, and he'd tried to track down the rumors, closely questioning anyone who came to him with the tales.

Clay didn't like the East. He missed the wilderness and felt hemmed in by the crowds of people and the old hatreds and the artificial loyalties to Yankee or Confederate, just because of where a man was born. Clay had fought for freedom for the slaves. His conscience wouldn't let him stay out of it, but he couldn't believe being born south of the Mason-Dixon line made a man think it was all right to own another human being.

So he'd fought until the fighting was done, and after the war, he'd ignored his instinct to return home and headed east to search for his brother. He'd received a telegraph somewhere along on his quest that told him Pa had been killed. Luther had given him all the details he

needed in a four-line telegraph, including that the killers, four of them, were dead and Pa had found a good strike and left it to Clay. Having money didn't make up for losing his pa. If anything, it made it worse, as if he'd profited from his father's death.

It had hit Clay hard to realize he was alone in the world, and finding Cliff became twice as important. He'd gone all the way to Boston. Once there it took over a month to find his mother, because it didn't occur to him that she would have gone back to her maiden name. When at last he found that out and visited her grave, he'd started searching for his brother under the name of Edwards and found out he'd gone to Texas over a decade ago.

Clay had taken the time to track down evidence of Cliff's war service, because once he headed for Texas, he didn't want to have to backtrack to the East if his brother had abandoned Texas as he'd abandoned the mountains. The men who had served with Cliff at Gettysburg knew little about him. They described him as stiff-necked and moody but smart and dedicated to the war effort. A few of them heard him speak of a west Texas ranch.

Clay had, by now, become stubborn to the point of obsession. He had gone to Texas, started in the farthest west corner of the panhandle, and worked his way east. He'd been doggedly at his search for two years when he met up with a Texas Ranger who was all heated up about a gang of vigilantes who had been terrorizing people all along the Pecos River, especially in the area north of Fort Davis.

That's when Clay had mentioned Cliff Edwards, and the ranger had told him his brother was dead. There was nothing about a wife and four children in the story.

From the obsession with finding Cliff, a new obsession grew: finding his killers. Clay, who had spent time scouting for the army in Wyoming and later in New Mexico before going to fight the war, had volunteered to work with the Texas Rangers this one time to track down Cliff's killers.

And that had led him here. Clay studied the barn and corral, proud of the sturdy construction that spoke so well of his brother. Sally skipped along beside him. The other girls were lingering around the yard, maybe a bit shyer than Sally but just as sweet.

He said to the gaggle of girls around his ankles, "The banker said there's a passle of cattle run wild in the hill country around the ranch, most of 'em ours but some of 'em maverick, so they go to whoever can catch 'em an' slap on a brand. I'm gonna ride out and see what the property looks like and find the best place to start. I'll be back at dark. Have your ma get supper." He settled his Stetson firmly on his head and went to catch up his horse.

"Can I come with you, Uncle Clay?" Sally asked, her hands clutched together as if she were begging.

Clay hadn't thought of that. He shrugged his shoulders. "I reckon there's no harm in it. You'll have to stay out a long time," he warned. "And you'll have to ride double with me. I 'spect you're a mite young to handle your own horse."

Sally grinned and promised, "I'll stay out till you're ready to come home. No matter how late that is, Uncle Clay."

Clay said, "Okay, you can come on one condition. . ."

"Anything," Sally said, clapping her hands together joyfully.

"If you come, you gotta call me 'Pa.'" Clay tried to sound stern, but a grin broke out on his face as he said it.

Sally's eyes got as bright and round as double eagle coins. For a second she looked so awestruck Clay was afraid she was going to swoon or something. Then she said fervently, "I'd be right proud to call you 'Pa,' Pa."

"Can we call you 'Pa,' too?" Beth asked.

Clay drawled, "Well, I reckon that's what I am now, your pa, so I'd say you'd better get to calling me that."

The girls all giggled and squirmed. Clay lifted Sally up off the ground and plunked her in front of him. He had a fight on his hands to wrestle her skirt and petticoat down around his Appaloosa mare's sides, and the horse didn't like it none too well. Clay knew how to handle a

horse though, so after a bit of a battle of wills, Sally was settled in, and they headed out.

"You other girls want to come along on Hector? You older girls can probably make him mind."

"We'd better help Ma with the moving in," Mandy said practically.

"But I'd like to come some other time," Beth said.

"Fine." Clay wrapped his arm around Sally's stomach when she twisted around to smile at him.

"We'll have a good supper waiting for you, Pa." Mandy giggled when she called him "Pa."

Clay nodded. "Obliged, darlin'."

He turned his Appaloosa to the north, toward the rugged foothills where the high plateau country climbed into a spur of the Rockies. Plenty of places for a longhorn to hide in this terrain, but Clay had seen worse growing up in the northern Rockies. This just looked like some rolling hills to him. He rode eagerly out to explore the land that was now his home.

Sally started talking before they were out of the yard. Shocked at first, after years of riding with taciturn soldiers and trappers and cowpokes, Clay got to liking the sound of her little voice. He found he didn't have to say much to keep her talking. Whatever she said, it all boiled down to one thing: Her pa was a giant of a man who could do no wrong and whom she loved with every ounce of her heart. And now she loved her new pa just as much.

Clay was humbled and proud, and when he found evidence of a large herd of cattle coming to water at several springs, he realized he'd bought himself a fine ranch. All in all, a perfect day. Just maybe the best day of his life.

There never was a worse day landed on the shoulders of a single woman who had walked on the face of this earth!

Sophie tried to tell herself Eve had a worse day when she got herself kicked out of the Garden. And Lot's wife had to have been unhappy about being turned to salt. That was a long time ago, though. What was happening to Sophie was happening right now—and to her! She would put it up against the worst that had been handed out to anyone.

And the day showed no signs of ending. She'd been insulted for breaking her back keeping her children alive, in a country that chewed hard on regular folks and swallowed weaklings whole.

She'd been married, without really being consulted about it, to a man she didn't even know. Or so far—like!

She'd been dumped in a house with next to no food and been ordered to make supper.

Well, she'd show that man what she was made of! She made supper by taking Hector out and shooting a whitetail deer. She'd had snares set in the thicket that kept her supplied with pheasant, grouse, and rabbit. But this animal was a lot more to deal with. She knew how to skin and gut a deer, but she had no desire to do it the first night in her new home.

The deer had been the first game she found, and she'd been looking for a long while before she found it. Clay would have been her first choice of shooting targets, but he wasn't available, so she settled for the deer. Her hunting had proved difficult because, remembering the vigilantes, she had no choice but to take the girls along with her when she went. And that brought her to the worst of it. She was missing a daughter. That ornery man had kidnapped Sally!

What in the world had Clay been thinking, taking Sally with him without asking permission or at least telling Sophie.

And all the girls were calling him "Pa" now. She wanted to scold them and tell them Clay McClellen wasn't their pa and he never would be. She wanted to say they were showing disrespect to the memory of their real pa by tossing him aside so quickly. But she held back the angry words. It was Clay she wanted to punish, not her girls.

After shooting the deer, she hung it from a handy tree to bleed it

and gutted it where it hung. She then slung it over Hector's shoulders, got the girls settled on Hector, and walked back to the ranch house, leading the whole bunch of them.

Then she had to find firewood. She didn't have so much as an ax, so she had to find sticks that were small enough to fit in the fireplace or were thin enough to break. That wasn't too hard; there was a nice stand of trees near the house. But it took time to get it done.

It was full dark by the time she had venison steaks roasting on a spit in the fireplace. She also was up to her elbows in a bloody deer carcass, cutting it up for jerking.

"Pa's home," Beth shrieked with pleasure.

All the girls dashed off to greet him. Sophie saw Clay set a very bedraggled but cheerful Sally on the ground and then ride to the stable, with the girls dancing in his wake.

Sophie ground her teeth together and turned back to her butchering with a vengeance.

Clay came around back with Sally on one hip and Laura on the other. Beth and Mandy were close behind. He studied her and her blood-soaked apron for a long minute. Then he said, "When's supper gonna be ready?"

Sophie didn't throw the knife at him by sheer willpower. She said through clenched teeth, "Mandy, check the steaks broiling in the fireplace. Beth, get out those biscuits we brought along."

"Good. I'm hungry." Then Clay added with a smile, "You're sure a pretty sight."

Sophie looked up, and her grip tightened menacingly on the knife. Clay didn't seem to notice. "You're sure making a mess of that buck. Leave it and I'll finish it later."

Sophie spoke through gritted teeth. "No thanks!"

Clay shrugged, as if he hadn't even noticed her outrageously sarcastic tone of voice. "Okay, if you want to do it. Come on in to supper when you're ready."

He turned and left her with two more hours of work to do on the deer! And the sun already fully set! She almost cried, which would have been ridiculous. She never cried. She was so tired and so hungry. She settled for her usual pastime when she was trying to live through the next backbreaking minute. Prayer. The usual prayer. "Give me strength, Lord. Help me, help me, help me."

Luther kicked at the fire all of a sudden and stood up in a huff. "Best be movin'," he muttered in disgust. He'd almost let himself relax before the pestering voice started in again.

"You're sure in an all-fired hurry," Buff grumbled, bolting the rest of his meal.

"Reckon," Luther said. It was the first time they'd stopped to eat all day.

Buff sighed until Luther thought the hair on his beard would part. But he didn't complain.

Luther had never intended to sleep this early anyhow. There was starlight aplenty, and the boy needed 'em.

They'd put a hundred miles behind them today, which was no small trick with a game horse and flat land. But in the mountains it was brutal, and their horses had taken the brunt. They needed the breather.

"Need horses," Buff said.

Luther just shook his head and wondered why Buff was so consarned chatty. Luther knew what was needed as well as the next man. He clucked his horse into a trot.

SEVEN

Clay tried to wait up for her. She finally came in so late, though, that he'd fallen asleep in his chair. She deliberately slammed the door. He started awake then studied her wet hair for a second before he asked drowsily, "Did you wash up in the creek?"

Sophie said tightly, "Yes."

"Don't go down there again without me standing watch. I saw cougar tracks today and a few wolves. And there could be bear in this country. It's not safe."

"Anything else?" she asked through clenched teeth.

Clay shook his head. He stood up and brought out the remaining steak. He set it on the table. "The girls said you didn't eat. That was stupid."

Sophie almost picked up the plate and threw it at him. She would have if she hadn't been starving. The smell of the meat she'd started smoking had been taunting her for the last hour until she'd almost chewed on it raw. If she'd have met a cougar at the creek, he might have been in more danger of being eaten than she was.

Instead of attacking Clay, Sophie focused on the incongruity between Clay holding supper for her and then calling her stupid. It was a good thing she was too tired to think, because it didn't bear thinking about. She started eating the tough, succulent venison, and she could tell Clay had been careful not to let it dry out. He silently brought her coffee and set what was left of the biscuits in front of her.

Sophie's stomach started to fill enough that she could think about something besides eating. She realized the house had been put in order. There were no more cobwebs in the ceiling corners. The windows shined brightly against the lantern light. The girls—she glanced around sharply—the girls must have all gone to bed. How had Clay managed all this? And why? Why hadn't he come out and taken over the butchering, surely a man's job, and left the house to her?

"The girls are asleep?" Sophie asked.

"Yep. I put all three of the older girls in there." He pointed to the bedroom on the northeast corner of the house.

"And I put Laura in there." He pointed to the northwest corner of the house.

"Why didn't you split them up two and two so the one room isn't so crowded?"

"Mandy and Beth said that room was always the nursery. When I tried to put Sally in there, she thought that meant I was calling her a baby, and that didn't set well," Clay said with a faint air of panic.

Sophie bit back a smile, afraid he'd take offense since he was obviously upset. She knew exactly how it had gone. The tears and the whining and the begging. "No, I don't suppose it would have."

"Are they supposed to cry so much and giggle every second when they're not crying? They never quit finding something so funny that I thought it'd break my eardrums a few times. And Laura pitched a daisy of a fit when Beth tried to give her a bath. Then Beth asked me to help, but Laura was stark naked, and I didn't think that was proper, so I said no. Then, well, maybe I said no a little. . .loud. Beth started crying." Clay ran his hands into his hair and made it stand up on end.

"Anyway, they're finally asleep, so please. . .please don't move them. If you can convince Sally to stop wailing about it, we can move them around tomorrow."

At least he'd been doing something. She'd pictured him sitting in here warming his feet by the fire while she butchered the deer.

Her belly filled as her plate emptied. She rose from the table to wash up.

"You look real tuckered. Go on to bed. The girls said you always slept in there." Clay pointed to the bedroom on the south side of the house. She had always loved the view from the window in there. She would rise each morning and look out on a sweeping green valley descending away from her and know she had a place where she belonged in the world. A place that was truly hers. Then she'd learned the hard way that nothing was ever truly hers.

She almost staggered when she took her first step. Clay steadied her. It occurred to her that he might not be so strong if he'd been working as hard as she had been today. Even so, she appreciated the strength of his grip. Without looking at him, she gathered herself and went to bed, thinking kindly of her new husband for the first time.

That wasn't strictly true. She'd thought kindly of him when she'd first found out he was Cliff's brother. She'd had several very kindly thoughts of him in fact. Then he'd married her without even really asking her permission. He'd left her to move into the house and hunt supper. He'd kidnapped Sally. And he'd left her to butcher and smoke the deer. Of course she'd told him she would, but if the man hadn't registered her sarcasm, then he wasn't making the full use of his ears.

But before all that, she'd thought kindly of him. And now she was again, just a bit. Cliff had certainly never washed a dish in his life or helped give a baby a bath. Sophie couldn't imagine a husband doing such things.

As she went into the room he called after her, "Sophie?"

She turned back. She tried to wade through her exhaustion and respond pleasantly. "Yes, Clay?" That was the first time she'd said her husband's name. She thought it fit comfortably on her tongue.

She'd married a very nice man.

Very politely he said, "Don't forget what I told you about the creek. The girls would be mighty upset if their ma got herself eaten by a cougar. You've lived on the frontier long enough to not be acting so stupid."

She'd married a troll.

She closed the door to her bedroom with a sharp *click*. She slipped her nightgown on. She was so tired she barely had the covers pulled up before she was sound asleep. As she nodded off, she wondered where the troll was going to sleep. Then he came in and set about proving identical twins could be very different.

"We'll be goin' in to services in Mosqueros this morning." Clay announced. "Parson Roscoe said the preachin' starts around nine so the country folks can have a long morning at their chores and still get there on time."

"We never go to services, Clay," Sophie said quietly.

Clay looked at his brand-spanking-new wife. He didn't give much thought to what she said. Instead he gave some thought to last night. He pulled her into his arms and planted a hearty kiss on her lips.

When he came up for air, he said, "We'll need to be on the trail in an hour." Then he kissed Sophie again, just 'cuz he wanted to. She sighed kind of sweetlike, and he enjoyed the sound while he helped her let go of his neck. When she was steady, he went out to see to the horses and Hector, with Sally tagging after him.

"Why do we have to go to church, Pa?" Sally asked.

Clay had never lived in a settled area, and although he'd stumbled on to a preacher here and there and sat through a Sunday service when he had the chance, he'd never been in any one spot long enough to have the habit of church attendance.

"I'm a believer. I've lived in the northern Rockies all my life, with my pa and the mountain men who were our friends. To my way of thinking, no one can live in the grandest cathedral on earth, the Rocky Mountains, and not know there's someone bigger than man in charge of the world."

"I'm not asking about believing in God." Sally tugged on his hand as she half walked, half skipped along beside him. "Everyone does that. I just don't know why we have to go to church."

"Well, you're wrong about everyone believing in God, Sally. When I was younger, I went through a spell when I was too big for my britches. I wrangled with my pa something fierce." Clay wondered at how comfortable he was talking to the cheerful little girl. He'd never done much talking when it was just him and pa sitting around a campfire.

Sally's eyes opened wide with fear. "You fought with your pa?"

Clay wondered why that scared her. He shrugged and went on jabbering. "There were lots of little fights when I got to thinking I was too much of a man to take orders from anybody. After my first real big blow-up with pa, I struck out on my own. That's when I learned there were folks who didn't believe in God."

"Those poor people."

Clay almost grinned. "The truth is I felt kinda sorry for them myself. Anyway, I was fourteen when I took off that first time. I was nearly six feet tall, and I'd been working a man's job since I was eight, so I didn't see anything wrong with making my own way."

"When you were fourteen?" Sally gasped.

"Yep."

"Mandy is ten; that's only four years from now."

Clay almost stumbled when he thought about his little girl going off and leaving him so soon. Then he shook his head to clear it. "Girls are different. Mandy isn't going anywhere for a long time."

"So what did you do after you left your pa?" Sally stood aside as Clay began slapping leather on his Appaloosa.

"I hunted grub and worked for a meal time to time. By the time I reached Cheyenne, I'd calmed down and went home." The truth was he'd been so homesick for Pa and the mountains, he'd signed on with a cattle drive heading into Montana and meandered home.

"I lived in unsettled places where there wasn't any church, and now that I have a chance to go worship with people, I'm looking forward to it." Clay talked with Sally as he saw to the meager chores and made note of some sagging fence posts and a couple of barn doors hanging from one hinge.

"We don't like Mosqueros much," Sally said.

"Why not?" Clay barely listened to her as he looked at the neglected ranch. It would have to wait until he got a handle on the cattle and ranch land. There were several spots he wanted to dam up on the creek before the spring rains quit, and then he had to get to the fence. He stretched his battered muscles and felt the strength of his back. He loved the life he'd gotten himself into.

Sally said, "I reckon it's 'cuz we're Yankees."

Clay suppressed a smile. He knew of the lingering hatred some people were capable of, and it sobered him to think of some of the cruelty his wife and daughters had no doubt been subjected to while Cliff was gone fighting. But everyone in town had been very friendly to him yesterday. His new family just hadn't been to town in a while.

He couldn't think of what to say to reassure her. Then he thought of those girls alternately crying and giggling at him at the same time, he already loved them. They scared him to death! So he thought he ought to head off another bout of tears. All he could think of to say was, "Don't you worry yourself about it. I'll take care of you."

Sally smiled uncertainly, and they both turned back to the chores. She was eager to do any little task for him, and although she actually slowed him down, he enjoyed being with her. When he was nearly done he said, "You better run on back to the house and get on your Sunday dress."

With wide, solemn eyes, Sally said, "But this is the only dress I have."

Clay looked at the bedraggled little dress, neatly patched but worn as thin as parchment paper. His family needed to do some shopping. "Well, go on and clean up anyway. Your ma will want to find the pretty face under all that dirt."

Sally giggled and gave him a big hug. Her soft, little arms were a wonder to him as he hoisted her up in the air to hug her tight. She ran off to the house, giggling some more. As he headed back in to gather his women, he slowed a bit as he thought of the house full of their giggling

and the sudden way they had of bursting into tears. He wondered ruefully if he'd ever get used to them. Then he remembered their beautiful blue eyes and all that long, golden hair and Sally's soft, generous hugs and how they all seemed to adore him. And he remembered Sophie's warmth and hurried his step.

He was looking forward to going to town.

The thought of going to town made her sick.

Sophie thought of the evil eyes of the man who had come to her house in the thicket last night and wondered if she would run into him in Mosqueros. She thought of that arrogant sheriff and the greasy banker, and she dreaded town so much, she felt goose bumps break out on her body.

Clay hadn't even asked her if she wanted to go. The Edwards family had never attended church! Cliff hadn't cared for Parson Roscoe when they'd first moved here, Cliff being a staunch Episcopalian and Parson Roscoe coming from a Methodist persuasion. The small town she'd lived near in Pennsylvania had one church building and a circuit rider, like so many other small towns. Sophie's family had worshiped with everyone else in town, paying little heed to the denomination of the parson.

She'd tried to go to church in Mosqueros for a while, after Cliff had left for the war. But by then there'd been such hostility toward her and the girls, Sophie couldn't bear it. She'd found a firm champion in Parson Roscoe though.

They didn't announce it around town, but he and his wife had made their parsonage in South Carolina available as a stopover for the Underground Railroad, before they felt God call them to a frontier ministry. They'd been here five years before the Edwardses. But Sophie firmly believed that God had put the Roscoes in Mosqueros as a direct answer to prayers she wouldn't begin praying until many years later.

She wiped dry the last of the breakfast dishes, then with apprehension churning in her belly, she turned her attention toward preparing for church. Getting ready herself was easy. She owned one decent dress. She had it on. There were two others, but they were out of the question. She'd butchered a deer in one last night. Even though she covered it with an apron, that one was so awful she wouldn't think of wearing it out in public. And her other dress was the huge one she wore for her disguise. There was enough fabric in it to make dresses for all three older girls, providing she could get the Hector stink out of it.

She let her hair out of the braid she'd slept in, combed it smooth, then rebraided it and coiled it into a neat bun at the base of her neck. She went from one girl to the other, fixing the hair of each, although Laura didn't need much fixing with her little cap of white blond curls. Mandy had tried to braid Sally's hair. The braid was a little lopsided, and too many hairs had escaped for it to be suitable for church, so Sophie quickly tidied it, complimenting Mandy on her efforts and giving pointers at the same time. Mandy was learning. With a sigh of contentment, Sophie knew Mandy would be doing more of these little chores every day.

Sophie had put each girl's hair into a braid with nimble fingers and began tying a pink ribbon into Beth's hair.

Mandy shouted, "It's *my* turn to wear the pink ribbon!"

Beth gasped so loud it was almost a screech. She whirled around so fast she whipped Sally in the eye with her braid. "It is not your turn! It's mine!"

"My eye!" Sally squealed. She grabbed for her eye and wailed at the top of her lungs, "You hurt my eye!"

Beth ignored Sally and kept at Mandy, "You got to wear it for Christmas! That's the last time we got dressed up, and you wore the pink ribbon!"

Laura, up until now sitting on the floor contentedly watching her sisters, started crying in sympathy with Sally.

Mandy balled up her fists at her sides. "It was not Christmas! It was

that night Parson Roscoe came out to visit. We got all dressed up, and Sally wore that ribbon. She's the youngest. We go oldest to youngest, so your turn must have been before that. It's my turn!"

Mandy reached for Beth's hair, and Beth slapped her hand.

"Sally, let me see your eye." Sophie added sharply, "Girls, don't fight! Mandy, it's Eliz. . ." Sally backed up, sobbing and wiping at her eye. Mandy and Beth were wrestling with each other and screaming to raise the dead. Sally knocked into Sophie, and Sophie staggered backward and would have fallen, except strong hands were there to catch her. She looked behind her as she was set back on her feet. Clay.

Mandy got her hands on the pink ribbon and, not purely coincidentally, one of Beth's braids. The screaming reached the point where it could make ears bleed.

Clay roared into the chaos, "Quiet! Every one of you girls, be—quiet—right—now!"

Dead silence fell on the room. The girls all looked at Clay, and after a few seconds of shock, Sally started crying. "Don't you love us anymore, Pa?"

Elizabeth started crying next. "I didn't mean to be so naughty!" She buried her face in her hands and wept. After a few seconds she reached back and dragged the pink ribbon out of her hair and tossed it at Mandy. "Here—" she said brokenly, "take the stupid—ugly ribbon—if you want it—so bad!"

The ribbon hit Mandy in the chest, but she didn't even try and catch it. Instead tears welled in her eyes. "I'm sorry, Pa. I didn't mean to make you stop loving us. Don't leave us. Please!" Mandy's voice cracked. With a sudden burst of grief that almost sounded like a scream, she whirled away from all of them and dashed out the door, crying.

Laura tottered toward Sophie, who was studying the drama calmly. Sophie curled up one corner of her mouth, shook her head, then she picked Laura up.

"Enough, girls," she snapped. "We're going to be late for church!"

"Don't yell at them!" Clay grabbed her arm and spun her around.

She wanted to snarl at him for grabbing at her like that, but she held her tongue when she saw the stricken look on his face, as he looked from her to each of the sobbing girls and, with complete panic, looked to the door.

"I'd better go after her! She could get hurt running around so upset." Clay hurried out the door, looking backward fearfully.

Once he got out, Sophie turned back to the girls. Beth was still sniffing a bit, but she was already tying the pink ribbon in her hair with a faintly satisfied air.

Sophie said, "Next time is Mandy's turn, and don't any of you forget it! Now Sally, it's your turn for the blue ribbon. Come over here."

Sophie had them all ready in just a few minutes. She found Clay in a near panic, searching for Mandy. Sophie told him to ready the horses. He seemed eager to obey her. Sophie rousted Mandy out of the barn hayloft, a favorite hidey-hole since she was little. She tied the yellow ribbon in Mandy's hair and plunked her on the horse. The six of them rode double on the two horses and Hector and headed for town.

Clay carried Sally in front of him. Mandy rode double with Beth in complete harmony. Sophie carried Laura like a papoose on her back.

Sophie rode beside Clay. Companionably she nodded at Beth and Mandy, riding slightly ahead on Hector's broad back. "It's certainly easier to get the girls ready for church since they got older. Going to town used to be a real struggle."

"It used to be harder than this?" Clay asked in a horrified whisper.

Sophie arched an eyebrow at him. "Well, of course. I had three girls under five years of age at one time. My goodness, it was a battle getting them all dressed and keeping them clean until we'd get to town."

Clay gave Sophie a wild-eyed look. She had no idea what he was so upset about. He shuddered slightly and spurred his horse into a trot. Sophie shrugged and increased her own speed to keep up with him. Clay treated them all like they were part sidewinder and part crystal, afraid they'd bite or break if he made a single wrong move.

Go figure men.

EIGHT

The trail to Mosqueros passed the thicket where they'd lived. Sophie looked at the familiar little path. A shiver of fear ran up her spine. She jerked back on the reins so suddenly her horse reared. So much had happened since the night she'd seen Judd, Eli, and the other man, she'd forgotten to tell Clay that the men who had killed Cliff had been chasing him. They'd called him a horse thief. They'd spoken of hangings. She wheeled her horse around to where Clay lagged behind them. He was immediately alert.

Mandy and Beth were ahead of them, but there sat Sally, enjoying the ride she was getting from her new pa. Sophie hesitated.

Clay said, "What?"

She shook her head sharply at him, just as Sally looked up from petting the horse. Sophie couldn't baldly announce, in front of her little girl, that men were looking for Clay to kill him.

Sophie immediately wiped the concern from her expression. "I was just thinking about the old place."

Clay caught her hint that what she wanted to say was best said away from the children. His eyes had that narrow, dangerous look about them, and his already cautious way of watching a trail became even more careful.

Sophie dropped back beside him. "I should tell you about life in that place sometime, Clay."

Sally piped up, "We ate roots and greens and jackrabbits. There

89

were fish in the creek, but they were almighty hard to catch, and Ma could fetch us a deer when she had a mind to."

"Like last night?" Clay asked. "We went out riding herd, and here your ma finds food for a week."

Rather tartly Sophie replied, "Hunting with three children is quite a trick, Clay. Remind me to let you try it sometime."

Clay gave her a long, slightly horrified look, as if it hadn't occurred to him that she'd had to take the girls. Or maybe he was imagining hunting with them. "I may remind you, and I may not."

"There are other things I have to tell you. But later." Sophie held his gaze.

He tightened his grip on Sally as if to protect her. "Right after church soon enough?"

Sophie said with a brisk nod, "Just barely soon enough."

"Let's catch up to the girls a mite." Clay clucked to his horse.

Sophie stayed right beside him the rest of the trip. She tried to let go of her fear for her new husband, as well as her thirst for revenge for her old one. Every time she turned her mind away from vengeance, she thought of the enmity that was sure to face them in Mosqueros, and she tried to control her resentment.

In her opinion, her neighbors had chosen the wrong side in the war. They'd held it against her and her family when they lost, and they'd turned their backs on the Edwards family when Cliff died—when she'd needed help so badly.

None of these were emotions fit for a church service. She wasn't having much luck, but still she struggled against her anger. All over the United States, people had hard feelings against their neighbors and life needed to go on. Sophie was determined to put it behind her. While she rode along she prayed, *Help me, help me, help me.*

Adam jerked awake. He lifted his head and peered around him. There

was nothing. He seemed to be lying flat out on grassland. He'd passed out after staggering along for what seemed like hours.

He fumbled for the wound on his side. The bullet had entered from the back and passed clean through. Adam wasn't surprised he'd been back-shot by that pack of cowards. He felt the dried blood, and just that little movement cut razor sharp through his side and back.

His girl needed help. "Give me the strength to take one more step, Lord. One step at a time, let me get to her."

He had nothing necessary for survival. Not food nor a weapon. Not even a fit set of clothes. But Adam figured God wouldn't give him the powerful message that Sophie needed him then not give the strength to go and help. Adam was a man of the West now. He'd learned to live with the land and let it provide for him. He pulled himself to his feet and staggered on toward Mosqueros.

"They're here, Irving. Oh, I so hoped they'd come!" Sophie heard Mrs. Roscoe's joyful pleasure when they rode up to the sagging picket fence that surrounded the little wooden church.

The small group of people milling around outside the church were staring. Sophie dismounted with grave misgivings. She tied her roan to the hitching post, alongside a dozen others, swung Laura around to her front, and pulled her out of her little leather carrier.

Clay helped Sally down, then swiftly went to lift first Mandy, then Beth off of Hector. He took Laura and had a steadying hand to spare to help Sophie alight.

Sophie took a minute to fuss over the tendrils of hair that had escaped from the girls' braids. The girls looked fine, but Sophie was delaying the moment she'd have to walk into that crowd. Clay came to stand beside her, with Laura in his strong arms.

Sophie smiled up at him. "Thank you."

Clay nodded and grinned. With his hand resting on Sally's back, he went to say hello to the parson.

"Good morning, Parson Roscoe." When Clay spoke, several people approached him.

"Clay McClellen!" the banker's voice boomed.

Sophie braced herself for trouble.

The banker extended his hand and said jovially, "Glad you could make it in to worship with us."

"Wouldn't have missed it, Royce," Clay said easily, reaching out to shake hands with the short, stocky man.

"Let me introduce the missus." Mr. Badje swept his arm sideways with a flourish.

The missus! Sophie almost choked, she was so surprised. A pretty young woman approached shyly, and Royce Badje took her hand. She clutched his hand in both of hers and hung on as if she'd caught a lifeline. Badje looked at her bowed head with adoration. Sophie knew the banker hadn't given her a thought in a long time.

"Clay McClellen, I'd like you to meet my wife, Isabelle. Isabelle, say hello to Clay." The banker gave the order and little Isabelle performed on command.

"Hello, Mr. McClellen." Isabelle nodded her head and held on to her husband even tighter.

Clay lifted his hat clean off his head and held it against his chest. "Howdy, Mrs. Badje. Have you met Sophie and my girls?"

It was as if a dam broke. Everyone flooded toward them and welcomed them genially to church. Sophie spoke to everyone, and all her girls were fussed over, especially Laura. Before long the girls were off chattering with other children, and Sophie and Clay were visiting pleasantly with the congregation.

A lady Sophie had never seen before approached her. "How do you do? I am Grace Calhoun, the new school teacher." Each word was clipped and perfectly pronounced—no Texas drawl for this young woman.

Sophie nodded her head at the extremely proper teacher. Grace

Calhoun's demeanor reminded Sophie of her more formal upbringing in Pennsylvania, and she dusted off some of her more genteel manners. "I am pleased to meet you, Grace."

"Excuse me, Mrs. McClellen, but I prefer Miss Calhoun. I feel my students must hear me referred to with respect in their homes if I am to keep order in school."

"Um. . ." Sophie felt herself blush a bit. "Of course, Miss Calhoun. As I said, I'm pleased to meet you. This will be the first school in Mosqueros, won't it?"

"No, Mrs. Badje was the teacher before she married. I mean to see things are well run. Are you intending to send the girls to school, Mrs. McClellen?"

The woman had a chilly manner. Her hands were folded primly. Her bonnet was carefully tied with a bow precisely angled under one ear. Her lips were pursed, not unlike someone who had just had a drink of vinegar. But Sophie thought behind the prissy behavior she saw truly kind eyes.

School. She'd never given it much thought. Survival had been too much work. She'd taught the girls to read with books she owned, mainly the Bible. And she'd taught them their numbers and simple arithmetic. There was so much more, though. Sophie looked sideways at Clay.

Before she could ask, Clay said, "We'll be there for sure, ma'am." Clay reached out his hand to shake Miss Calhoun's.

She flinched just a bit. "It is a lady's decision if she will shake hands with a man. It is improper of you to offer me your hand first."

Clay's hand stayed where it was for an awkward second or two, then he lowered it and rubbed it against his pant leg. "Uh, sorry, I didn't mean nothing by it."

"No, I don't imagine you did." Miss Calhoun nodded her head. "I'd best be getting inside." She turned stiffly and headed into the church. Sophie noticed Miss Calhoun went in alone and felt a stab of pity for her. She wondered if the young woman had any friends.

A flurry of friendly faces came up and greeted them. Parson Roscoe broke up the fellowship time by waving the congregation inside. Mrs. Roscoe took Sophie's arm firmly and escorted her to the front pew. Clay and the girls filed in beside her.

Sophie's head was spinning. She'd never been treated so kindly by the people of Mosqueros. It could only be due to Clay and whatever passed between him and the townsfolk when he'd done his shopping yesterday. Buoyed by the happiness of it, she faced the parson, ready to listen to the first preaching she'd heard in years.

Parson Roscoe held his big, black Bible open in one hand, lifted it to eye level, and roared, "Avenge not yourselves!"

Sophie almost jumped up out of her seat. She reached sideways without thinking what she was doing and clutched Clay's hand. She wanted to shake her head and deny the verse the parson had selected, but she held herself still. She didn't want to hear that it was wrong of her to want vengeance for Cliff. And now vengeance for Clay. She didn't want to let go of her hate for Judd and Eli and the men who rode with the J BAR M.

"Leave room for God's wrath," the parson thundered.

Sophie realized her own hand was hurting she was holding Clay's so tightly. She tried to relax her grip, only to realize she wasn't the only one holding on. Clay's hand was crushing hers.

Relentlessly the parson said what Sophie didn't want to hear, "For it is written, 'Vengeance is mine.' "

Mindful that she was sitting front and center in a very small church, she dared a quick glance at Clay.

Parson Roscoe said vehemently, " 'I will repay, saith the Lord'! "

The parson's voice faded from her hearing as she looked at her new husband. His face was flushed, and his eyes were locked on the parson. His jaw was rigid. Sophie sensed a terrible battle going on within him for self-control. She knew the words were striking home just as hard with Clay as they were with her. Clay wanted vengeance, too. Every bit as badly as she did.

But vengeance against whom? Sophie saw the anger on Clay's face,

and even though she'd already had a few arguments with him, she sensed Clay was capable of anger far deeper than she'd suspected.

She'd had the impression he was a very Western man in his philosophical acceptance of bad luck—like his horse dying. And she'd noted a certain glint in his eyes when he was challenged that told her Clay could be dangerous. But this rage frightened her. Clay hated someone. Hated him or her deeply and wanted revenge. Just like Sophie did. She tightened her grip on his hand and turned back to face the parson, with stubborn dislike of the chosen topic.

Parson Roscoe had been talking for some minutes while Sophie paid attention to her new husband. Now the parson asked, "How many of you are afraid to ride the roads around Mosqueros at night?"

Sophie knew the parson himself was afraid. The self-appointed lawmen were dangerous.

"We have vigilantes working around here. Men bent on vengeance. Men who have gone too far, taking the law into their own hands."

Sophie got it. The parson wasn't talking about her and her thirst for vengeance. It was her own knowledge of the wrongness of her hatred that had made her take the parson's words personally. Yes, she knew it was wrong to hate so passionately, and she'd keep working on it. But no one, not even a loving God, would ask her to forgive the men who killed her husband. The parson was talking about the renegade lynch mob and the need to stop them. Sophie agreed completely.

"They have hurt too many people. Killed honest men. Killed guilty men who, in this country, are promised a fair trial before a judge and jury."

Sophie relaxed and her heart rose. The parson agreed with her. The parson knew that crowd of murderers needed to be hunted down and. . .

Parson Roscoe jabbed his finger straight at Sophie, then swept his hand across the entire congregation and roared, "You have to let go of your hate!" Then his voiced dropped nearly to a whisper. He said with a voice so kind it was heartbreaking, "You have to let go of your hate."

All in the church visibly leaned forward, so enthralled were they by the challenging sermon. " 'Thou shalt love the Lord thy God with all thy heart, and with all thy soul, and with all thy mind. This is the first and great commandment. And the second is like unto it: Thou shalt love thy neighbour as thyself.' To harbor hate, even against men as fearful as those who ride these hills in the night, is a sin. Do you think you harm them by sitting in your home and raging in your heart against their evil? Do you think you make the world a better place or bring a single person to believe in the Lord Jesus by gossiping about how deserving the vigilantes are of death? No! The anger only harms you!"

He pointed right at her again. "The hatred only keeps you away from God. There are only two commandments according to the scripture. Not ten. Two! If we obey those two we obey all the others. Love God. Love your neighbor. We have to find it in ourselves to love everyone."

No! Sophie didn't cry out, but everything in her rebelled against the parson's words. God could not ask her to love the men who killed her husband. He didn't ask His followers to look the other way while people were being killed.

"That doesn't mean you should be foolish. It doesn't mean that these men don't deserve prison. It doesn't mean we should let ourselves be killed while evil walks the face of the earth."

Sophie breathed a sigh of relief. He was giving his blessing, after all, to her desire for—she knew better than to call it *vengeance* now—justice. She'd call it *justice*. That was better.

"But He does call us to love. Yes, even love those who persecute us. Don't fool yourself that you can walk through life harboring hatred and still call yourself a believer in Jesus Christ. Love is what Jesus demands of us. First! Last! Always!" He looked right at her and finished his sermon in a voice full of tenderness and kindness. "First, love. Last, love. Always, always, love!"

It wasn't the ferocious demand that had begun his sermon. It was a prayer. His words washed over Sophie's restless soul and offered her, for the first time in a long time, peace.

"Dearly beloved," the parson said quietly, "avenge not yourselves.

Leave room for God's wrath. For it is written, 'Vengeance is mine; I will repay, saith the Lord.'"

The parson then led the congregation into a rousing chorus of "Rock of Ages."

"Rock of Ages cleft for me. Let me hide myself in Thee."

Her whole body trembled as she stood to sing along. Sophie heard the words of the faithful old hymn. She had spent the last two years hiding herself, literally. But had she hidden herself in God? Had she depended on Him?

The song ended, and only then did Clay release her hand. And only when he released it did Sophie realize they'd held hands tightly through the whole service. The parson swept up the aisle. Mrs. Roscoe followed.

Clay and Sophie had a second as they stood alone in the front pew of the church. "I don't think it was right," Clay said curtly, "for the parson to pick out a scripture and use it to scold me the first day I attend his church."

Sophie stumbled. Clay caught her. She looked sideways and couldn't quite stop a smile from flickering across her face.

"You think that's funny?" Clay growled.

Sophie glanced forward. In just a few steps they'd have to shake the parson's hand, so she didn't have time to say much. She tucked her hand through Clay's elbow. "I thought he was preaching it at me, not you."

Clay's eyebrows rose in astonishment. "You? What do you need revenge for?"

The girls surrounded them: Mandy with Laura, Sally holding Clay's hand, and Beth just a step behind. Sophie didn't want to get into her hatred in front of them. She said quietly, "Cliff."

Clay stopped so abruptly, Beth bumped into his back. "You reckon everyone in that church figured the parson was aiming his words at them personally?"

"If God blesses his words, I imagine they do."

Clay let a small, humorless grunt of agreement escape his lips, then he stepped forward and shook the parson's hand. "Excellent message today, Parson."

Sophie didn't think Parson Roscoe gave her a look more stern than usual. So his sermon hadn't been for her—or Clay. It was God who'd made her think that. The peace she'd felt earlier deepened and settled on Sophie's heart as she considered that. It was God who chastised her, not the parson.

She could say honestly, "I enjoyed the service, Parson."

He shook her hand and moved on to Sophie's girls. Sophie and Clay walked toward the horses.

"You wanted to tell me something on the trail?" Clay asked.

Sophie glanced over her shoulder. The girls were coming right behind. She said quickly, "I didn't tell you about the men who came to the cabin in the thicket after we pulled you out of the creek. They were hunting you. They were the same men who killed Cliff. Or at least one of them was."

"Did you. . ." Clay cut off his question when Sally came around front of them.

Sally asked, "Can I ride double with you again, Pa?"

Sophie murmured to Clay, "We'll talk later."

Clay nodded at Sophie, then turned to Sally and said, "I reckon it's Beth's turn, darlin'."

Sally pouted something fierce. But after a nice long visit with their fellow believers and a stop at the general store, whose owner was kind enough to fill their order on Sunday, the McClellen family headed home, with Beth taking her turn.

NINE

Sophie was so excited about all the food they had in the house, she almost forgot men were trying to kill her husband.

It had been so long since she'd had choices. She didn't have to try and contrive bread; she had the ingredients to allow her to choose between making rising bread, biscuits, or corn bread. She didn't have to hunt for whatever greens were growing; she had canned vegetables and fruits of every kind. Clay bought a ham and a side of bacon. He had also purchased flour, sugar, baking powder, yeast, potatoes, carrots, and onions. They'd hitched up their horses to the wagon the Roscoes had driven home and filled it with wonderful, delicious, precious food!

It took some doing for Sophie to remember how to cook with it all, but it came back to her, and they had a feast for their Sunday dinner.

Sophie told Clay she'd like to go for a short ride with him after lunch. They went alone, despite the wailing of the three older girls. It was good luck that Laura was taking a nap, or no doubt she'd have joined in with the other banshees. Sophie had to bite back a smile when she thought of the terrified look on Clay's face every time one of the girls started crying.

Before they'd ridden a hundred feet, Clay said, "We don't dare go out of sight of the ranch. We're far enough they can't hear us. Now tell me about those men who were hunting me."

Sophie told him everything. The parson's words rang in her ears, and she wondered if it wasn't a sin to pile her own list of enemies onto Clay's shoulders. She was inviting him to hate along with her.

"Judd was his name?" Clay asked. "That's all you heard? No last name?"

"Just Judd and Eli."

Clay's eyes flashed with anger.

Sophie tried not to join with him.

"And J BAR M," he said with grim satisfaction. "That should be registered. It should be a simple matter to track down the owner of that brand."

"Unless the horse was stolen, Clay," Sophie reminded him, afraid he'd act rashly.

Clay nodded. "It might have been stolen by Judd from someone from the J BAR M. Or maybe someone else stole it and the vigilantes caught up with the thieves."

"So even if we find who owns that brand, we still might not know anything," Sophie said forlornly.

Clay sighed. "It might lead to a dozen dead ends."

They rode around a small stand of trees, thin enough they didn't block the view of the house. Sophie pulled her mount to a halt and leaned forward, resting her crossed arms on the saddle horn. "Clay, what did you think about Parson Roscoe's sermon this morning?"

Clay looked at the skyline, and Sophie realized that he had been sharply alert the entire time they'd been riding, much as he had been on the ride to town this morning. It made her feel safe. Sophie tried to remember the last time she'd felt safe. They were sandwiched between the thin clump of oak trees that had sprung up by a little spring, and a vast woodland that stretched up into the rugged hills which surrounded the ranch house on two sides.

"I thought he was aiming it right at me." He gave her a sheepish grin.

Sophie smiled back. "Me, too."

"So do you think he wrote the whole sermon with the two of us in mind?" Clay teased her.

Sophie shrugged. "He could have."

Clay moved his horse. Sophie knew he was checking all around them, watching for danger.

Without ever letting his eyes rest, he said, "I guess everyone in the place might have felt like we did. It's not just the vigilantes either. I reckon every man and woman alive carries anger around and wishes for revenge for something or other."

"I have hated that man who lynched Cliff for so long my hatred is almost like an old friend." Sophie realized she was looking around, too. And it wasn't just Clay's heightened awareness that was making her do it. She had learned all the hard lessons the West had to teach.

"I don't want to give it up."

Clay nodded. "I heard that my brother was dead and all I could think of was revenge. I rode down here hunting his killers with no thought except to even the score. To pay them back for what they did to Cliff."

"I've prayed every day to stop the anger in my heart," Sophie confessed. "I've always known hatred was a sin. But to give it up seemed like a betrayal of Cliff. And those men are dangerous. How do we love them when there's a very good chance that, one of these days, they're going to come riding onto this ranch and kill you, just like they did Cliff?"

"I don't want to wait for that day either. I have been fully intending to hunt them down."

"And kill them?" Sophie asked.

Clay lapsed into silence for such a long time that Sophie had her answer. Finally he focused on her and said quietly, "I'll turn them over to the sheriff instead. That would be justice, not revenge."

Sophie raised her eyebrows, and a quirk lifted the corners of her mouth. "That might be okay. But what do we do about the hate?"

"I've been using the hate to keep me inspired," Clay said grimly. "It pushes me to never give up."

"But it's wrong," Sophie reminded him.

"It's not that I don't agree that vengeance belongs to God. I just don't see why we can't both have a turn."

"Both?" Sophie asked.

"Yeah, God and me—both." With a little grin, Clay said, "First I can have a crack at 'em, then God can punish 'em eternally in the fire."

"Clay!" Sophie interrupted. "I don't think that's quite what Parson Roscoe had in mind."

"I reckon not." Clay shook his head and looked away from Sophie to scan the woodlands and flatlands. "What the parson has in mind is to give it up to God, I s'pose. So far I'm not having any luck. I don't even want to let it go. I've never prayed, like you have, to quit hating. I've never prayed to catch up to 'em either. I figured when I got my hands on 'em, I'd kill 'em. And I guess, even without the parson's words, I knew God wouldn't want to hear a prayer like that. I think, sweetheart, that you're one step farther along the way to doing it right than I am."

He'd called her *sweetheart*. It actually made her heart feel kind of sweet. "Well, then maybe we can pray for both. We'll pray for me to quit hating and for you to want to quit hating."

"Okay. I won't go after 'em." Then Clay added playfully, "Anyway, I don't have time. I got me a wife and four daughters and a ranch to watch out for. I only got time to hate 'em part-time these days."

Sophie smiled at him, then her smile faded and she said hesitantly, "Clay."

"Huh?"

"I want us to do what God wants, but I don't want you to be hurt. Those men might not have seen you enough to know who they were chasing that night, but we can't know that for sure. They might still be looking for you."

Clay leveled his blue eyes at her. "I've lived a long time in a hard land, Sophie. I'd take a lot of killing."

He had eyes exactly like Cliff's and yet so different. They were identical, and yet she knew them apart. His eyes were the reason she'd

never really believed he was Cliff, even when he was just regaining consciousness, even when he couldn't remember his name. She could take one look at the confidence in Clay's eyes and never get the two of them mixed up.

"We'd better get back to the house," Sophie said with some regret. She'd enjoyed this time with Clay. He'd actually done a little talking. In fact, this might be the first time he'd strung two sentences together. She'd like to stay and ask him questions about his life growing up in the mountains and his pa—her girls' grandfather.

Clay turned his Appaloosa toward the ranch. Just as Sophie wheeled, a wild boar burst out of the dense undergrowth in the small grove of trees about a hundred yards away from them. Sophie jerked her Winchester off her saddle and shot the boar before it could run ten feet. She dropped her rifle back into its sling, clucked to her horse, and turned back for the boar. Clay reached out and grabbed her arm.

She held up on the reins before he pulled her out of the saddle. She tugged on her arm. "I've got to bleed him."

He didn't let up his hold. If anything, it tightened. "Where did you learn to shoot like that?" he asked faintly.

Sophie took her eyes off the hog she'd brought down. "I taught myself, mostly. Adam showed me the basics." She looked at Clay, pleased with her shooting, although the boar was certainly a large target. She was surprised to see the incredulous look on Clay's face.

He kept looking from Sophie, to the boar, to her rifle.

Finally she said defensively, "What? It's a good shot. I caught him just ahead of his front leg. A clean shot through the heart. I didn't damage the hams, and there won't be powder or bone fragments in the headcheese."

Clay's grip slipped a little. "You mean you even took the time to pick a spot to hit him?"

Sophie was flustered by the question. "Well, sure."

"No woman knows how to handle a gun like that," he said flatly.

Then Sophie saw what was bothering him. She couldn't believe it. "You mean you're all ruffled because I'm good? That doesn't make sense."

"I'm not ruffled!" Clay growled. "Men don't get ruffled!"

Sophie bit back a grin. Then she remembered the deer from last night. "If it ruffles your manhood to see a woman whose aim is fast and true, then why don't you prove how tough you are by butchering that boar? You do know how to do it, don't you?"

"Of course I know how to do it." Clay narrowed those eyes at her, like he'd done time to time, and her heart sped up just a bit. He ignored the jab at his masculinity and got right to the heart of her insult.

"If you wanted me to clean that deer for you last night, you shoulda said yes when I offered to do it."

Sophie met his gaze with the coolest one she could muster. She had the feeling that many a man would back down under that look in Clay's eyes, but she had no fear of him. "I won't make that mistake again."

A flicker of surprise passed over Clay's face. Sophie wondered when the last time was that he'd been sassed.

Then he did something that took her completely by surprise. He closed the few inches between them and kissed her. He pulled back. "See that you don't."

The kiss had been over almost before it began, but it had still left Sophie's lips tingling. She had to hold herself from leaning toward him again. Then he let her arm go and turned his horse toward Sophie's catch.

Clay stopped his horse to turn and look at her. After a few seconds he said gruffly, "Get back to the house and take care of the children, woman."

Sophie laughed again. "Yes, sir!" She gave him a sharp two-fingered salute. She was afraid she'd irritated him, but not very afraid. And when she heard his deep-throated chuckle, she wasn't afraid at all.

Sophie tasted him on her lips and wondered how foolish it was to be falling in love with a man she'd only known two days. Somehow it

seemed more foolish than marrying him.

Still, he was her husband. Who better to fall in love with? Then she caught herself. She thought of how much she'd loved Cliff and how much his rejection had hurt.

Of course she'd respect Clay and work hard at his side and honor him whenever possible. But love? No. She rode away, determined not to ever be such a fool again.

"What ya mean it's been sold?" Judd smashed both fists on the banker's desk so hard he shoved it back against Royce Badje's paunchy belly.

Badje stood and pulled his handkerchief out of his breast pocket to dab at his forehead.

Judd smelled the fear in the man and enjoyed it. "Who bought it?"

"R–Really, sir," Mr. Badje stammered, "b–bank transactions are c–confidential. It isn't my place to say who—"

"I want to know *who* now!" Judd reached for the massive oak desk to wrench it aside so he could get his hands on this pasty-faced city slicker. He wanted to make this man afraid of him. He wanted to crush him under his heel like the bug he was.

But Judd prided himself on his wiles. He had held back after Cliff died, so as not to draw attention to himself. He had kept his cool, played the game out his own way. Now, he had to do that again. He fought for control of his rage. Finally, he felt capable of straightening away from the desk and lowering himself into the chair, where he'd been sitting so comfortably a moment ago.

He'd been savoring the moment when he'd impress this overbearing banker with the show of cash he could produce. Instead, the banker had said dismissively that the land Judd had been working two years for belonged to someone else.

"Just give me a name," Judd said through clenched jaws. "I heard the owners had abandoned it. So I scouted it. It looked like a right nice piece of property. I might go out and see if the new owner would dicker with me."

The stout, little man puffed up, dabbed his forehead again, and with a huff of indignation, returned to his seat. "I can't give you any details. A banker has a certain position to maintain in a community. . . ."

Judd leaned forward in his seat and reached for the desk, outwardly just to balance himself while he stood, but he knew the effect he had on milquetoasts like this. He let the full weight of his fury blaze in his eyes.

Without Judd saying a word, the banker caved. "There is really no reason I shouldn't say. After all, it is common knowledge who the new owner is."

Judd settled back and smiled coldly at the banker. Judd could feel the money burning in his pocket. Thousands of dollars. The full price of the ranch. Two years' work.

"Clay McClellen. Twin brother of Cliff Edwards, the former owner. Clay bought the ranch when the Mead brothers missed their payment. He married Edwards's widow and moved out there just last Saturday." As if to make up for his unethical telling of the new owner's name, the banker added with a sniff, "It's very doubtful, with his ties to the property, Mr. McClellen will want to sell."

"Edwards's widow?" Judd's fists curled. "I heard she was long gone, living with relatives."

"How did you hear that?" Mr. Badje asked. "You're not from around here."

A killing fury made Judd want to put his hands around the banker's fat neck. After a bitter struggle, he found the self-control to say sharply, "Never mind. If it's sold, there's no point in discussing it."

He got up from his chair and left the room. He stalked out of the building, already making new plans. He'd played it too safe before. The law had been watching because the sheriff was sweet on Mrs. Edwards. But in the unsettled West, the only real law was strength. Once he owned the Edwards's place, buying the sheriff, or getting rid of him and

handpicking a successor, would be his first order of business.

He strode down the street of the town he was planning to control. He was tired of waiting around. He'd worked too long and hard to get his hands on that ranch. A twin brother? Where had a twin brother come from? Judd had learned for a fact that Cliff Edwards had no family, except for his wife and a pack of worthless girl children. That had been part of what made the ranch easy pickings for him. Judd didn't ponder the twin brother's existence for long. It didn't matter where he came from; it only mattered that he was here.

Judd shrugged it off. The last brother had proved to be an easy mark, and he'd had no friends to stand up for him after his death. A twin brother would be cut from the same cloth. Judd planned to make short work of him. He stormed down the street and jumped on his mustang. He spurred the mangy critter into a gallop. The night riders weren't going to get to retire quite as soon as they'd planned.

Royce Badje straightened his string tie with all the dignity of a very big fish in a small, small pond. "Humph!" He strode out of his office and said to his teller, "I'll be out for a few minutes." He lifted his black, flat-brimmed hat off the rack by the front door and, after carefully checking that Mr. Mason wasn't about, he stormed down to Sheriff Everett's office. He found the office empty, and at the diner, he learned the sheriff was transporting a prisoner and would be gone for a day or two.

Royce Badje returned to the bank a very nervous man.

"Eeeiiyy!"

The high-pitched scream made the horse Clay was riding crow-hop to the side and rear up until Clay thought he might go over backward.

Clay hadn't been unseated by a horse since he was 15, except when he was busting broncs. He didn't wait to find out if the horse would throw itself on over. He'd known some to do it.

Clay slipped from the saddle and jumped back from the Appaloosa. The horse snorted and wheeled away from the barn. It charged toward the open field where Clay had just spent the day branding strays.

Just as Clay dropped from his horse, Laura came charging around the corner of the barn stark naked. Clay flinched when he saw the little cyclone fleeing from her mother. Sophie was hot on Laura's heels, and she scooped her up before she could get any farther. Clay whirled around and faced away from the bare-bottomed toddler. He felt his cheeks heat up, and he pulled his hat low over his face for fear he might be blushing.

Sophie had a firm grip on Laura now, and she rested the little fire-brand on her hip. "She got away from me, Clay. I'm sorry. Hope you didn't get hurt when you fell off your horse." Sophie turned and went back to the house.

Clay heard her footsteps recede, along with the screaming load of wriggling girl child she was toting. Clay looked up. Four of his men were smirking in his direction.

Clay knew he needed help to run a ranch this size, and he'd needed it quickly. He had put out the word that he was hiring hands, and cowpokes started to straggle in. He hired several of them immediately. Others, who didn't measure up, he told to move along.

One of them, Eustace, a good hand but young, said, "Fell off, did'ja, boss? Them babies can be almighty scary, I reckon."

Clay amended his ideas regarding Eustace. Not just young. Young and stupid.

Two of the men turned their backs and started heading for the bunkhouse. Clay could see their shoulders quivering. It was a wise man who could laugh silently at his boss.

Eustace wasn't wise. He cracked up and started chortling until he had to hang on to the fence to keep from falling over. The other man, an oldster named Whitey, who reminded Clay somewhat of his pa,

wasn't having any part of any laughter. He was trying to settle his own horse down. Whitey had ridden up Monday morning hunting work. Clay had liked what he'd seen and hired him on the spot. Whitey had worked tirelessly at Clay's side ever since.

Clay snapped, "Eustace!"

Then Clay told the young pup to pick up his pay and clear out. Eustace was laughing too hard to hear himself getting fired.

Clay planned to do it all over again, but he calmed down before Eustace stopped laughing.

"Naked babies. On a ranch!" Clay shook his head and muttered as he hunted up more work for himself to do so he could stay outside until maybe that house full of women would be asleep. He didn't do much more than round up his horse before Sally came out to lend a hand. So he wasn't going to get to escape them anyway. He was dog tired, saddle sore, and he'd had dirt for his noon meal.

Sally said something about apple pie, and after she said it, he could smell it, even if it was just his imagination. And Sally kept holding his hand with her soft fingers and looking at him with those adoring blue eyes until he wanted to see the other girls' eyes. Especially Sophie's. He gave up and went to the house.

Clay's life was better than it had ever been.

Clay's life was worse than it had ever been.

He couldn't figure out to have the better without taking the worse along with it, 'cuz they were all mixed together. And better and worse came flocking toward him all the time. He felt like he'd fallen through a hole into another world. A girlish one.

He spent the night after his fall with Sally sitting on his lap, talking about her hero of a pa. Cliff. He got a chance to referee when Mandy and Beth quarreled about whose turn it was to do the dishes. He was unfortunately handy when Laura twirled around in a circle for too long and threw up on his boots. He got drafted to hold on to slippery Laura while she was given a bath, and he thought his ears would break from the high-pitched toddler giggles. Those giggles were nothing compared to the steady stream of whining when Sophie told them to go to bed. It was a normal night.

He could have stood all of that, if it hadn't been for the crying.

It terrified him and left him feeling helpless and brutish, even if he had nothing to do with their tears. He'd tried everything he could think of to get them to stop. Yelling was the way he related to his pa if there was ever an upset. That didn't work with the girls. It only made it worse. He'd bought a little cheerfulness one night with a handful of coins, and another night he'd come up with a sack of candy that he'd picked up in town and saved for just this occasion.

Sophie was horrified when she found out about it and put a stop to the bribery.

Too bad. It had worked pretty well.

If he ran, which he did from time to time, they all thought he was going to quit loving them and leave. And there were more tears.

Once Sally had asked him between broken sobs, "Do you want us to go back to the thicket and leave you alone, Pa?"

It would have made him crazy except he also got to eat Sophie's good cooking. And he got hugged by every soft, sweet one of them when they headed off to bed. He liked the smell of Sally's hair after Sophie had washed it. He sat in the cleanest, prettiest house he'd ever lived in, full of shining surfaces and Texas wildflowers picked fresh every day. He wore clean clothes that had nary a button missing nor the littlest tear left unmended. And he was told, "I love you," ten times a day.

His pa had spoken those words to him two or three times in his life, and Clay had said them back as often, or maybe grunted an agreement. Pa loved him, and Clay figured if that ever changed, Pa would have mentioned it. He'd always figured that was enough said. Clay was surprised to know he liked hearing it more often. And he said it back

to all of them. If he didn't, they'd get all teary eyed and scared.

He said it back to all of them except Sophie, who also never said it to him. He'd caught himself lately wishing she would say it.

After all, the girls loved him.

What was she waiting for?

TEN

Clay had claimed the brand C BAR for his own, by right of marriage to Cliff's widow. He'd claimed the cattle along with the brand. When he'd bought Cliff's old place, Clay had also used the healthy account in Denver, where Pa had banked gold, to buy up some surrounding property. So he'd expanded his holding considerably.

Clay rounded up over two hundred head of cattle that first week. Most of them were old, branded to the C BAR, the brand registered to Cliff.

Anything younger was branded M SLASH M. No one seemed to know what had happened to the Mead brothers, who had registered that brand. Clay knew the code of the West, as it pertained to an abandoned herd: If you caught 'em, you could keep 'em. But Clay was a careful man. He knew local peace officers could be almighty prickly, and Clay didn't want to antagonize Mosqueros's sheriff.

He headed for town Saturday morning to consult with the law. Sheriff Everett was just entering his office, covered with trail dust, and looking like he'd been ridden hard and put up wet.

Clay tipped his hat to the burly man. "You look like you've been over the trail, Josiah. I'll buy you a cup of coffee, if you've got the time."

With a heavy sigh, the sheriff said, "A cup of coffee would go down mighty good right now, McClellen. I've been delivering a bandit to the territorial prison, and I haven't had a good night's sleep in a week. I'd thought to ride out and say howdy one day soon."

112

The sheriff went inside the jailhouse as he talked and locked his Winchester into a gun rack behind his desk. "Esther has the best coffee in town, because she has the only coffee in town. She starts out in the morning making it black as coal dust, and she keeps it boiling all the day long. We're lucky it's still fairly early. By the end of the day it gets mean enough to fight back when you try an' drink it."

"Just the way I like it." Clay's boots rang hollow, his spurs adding a sharp metallic ring, as the two men walked down the creaking board sidewalks of Mosqueros.

The sheriff pushed the diner's door open, and the smell of burnt coffee nearly took the skin off the inside of Clay's nose.

"Just coffee, Esther." A small puff of dirt rose up around the sheriff as he lowered himself onto a bench.

The dirt had a better scent than the food, to Clay's way of thinking.

Esther brought them both a cup of coffee. "I've got huckleberry pie."

"That sounds—"

"Not today, Esther," the sheriff cut Clay off. "We're in a hurry."

Esther harrumphed at them, as if it were a personal insult, and stalked away from the table.

The sheriff chuckled softly. "You'll be wanting to thank me later for saving you from Esther's huckleberry pie."

"I've never had a bad piece of pie," Clay protested.

"The woman doesn't believe in a heavy hand with the sugar."

"I'll eat a tart pie over none, any day." Clay wrapped his hands around the lightweight tin coffee cup, enjoying the warmth, even though the day was already heating up.

"And whatever berries she's using are none too ripe, undercooked, and I'll be surprised if they're even huckleberries." The sheriff shuddered. "I've yet to see a huckleberry bush out here."

"Still, now she's offended." Clay regretted that.

"I've never been able to figure out how she can leave the berries raw and burn the piecrust at the same time." The sheriff looked up from his coffee with an obviously mystified expression. "It just don't stand to reason. I once broke a tooth on her piecrust."

"It was probably a pit. A pit can get in any pie. These things happen to even the most careful cook. . . ."

"It wasn't a pit. It was a button."

"A button?"

"Off her shoe," the sheriff added darkly. "When I complained, she came and acted as close to happy as Esther ever gets, thanked me, took the button, then sat down. She pulled off an almighty bad-smellin' boot and sat beside me whilst she sewed it back on."

Clay lapsed into silence. He finally said quietly, "I'll just go ahead and thank you now."

The sheriff nodded. "Now, what did you want to see me about?"

"I've been finding strays from the Mead brothers' herd mixed in with Cliff's brand. I wondered if you have any idea how to reach them."

The sheriff took a long drink of coffee, and Clay saw him shudder all the way to his toes. "No one seems to know why they took off. I'm suspicious for a living, and the only thing that makes sense is that something happened to them."

"A lot of ways to get yourself lost in the West," Clay observed.

"I know that. And the Meads weren't neither one of 'em a ball of fire, if ya know what I mean. They weren't the hardest workers, and they weren't the smartest managers I've come across."

Clay thought of the deterioration he saw in the buildings and knew the truth of what the sheriff said.

"Still, they were getting by. Keeping their land payments up, if only by the skin of their teeth."

"You think they ran into outlaws or renegade Indians?" Clay speculated.

"I reckon it's something like that. Truth to tell, I've been assuming they're both dead almost from the first. But no bodies have turned up. They were a two-man outfit, so no cowhands were out there with them to come and report them missing. We only decided they'd taken off when Royce Badje reported their payment didn't come into the bank.

They could've been gone a month before we noticed 'em missing."

"Do they have any family?" Clay sipped at the vile excuse for coffee in front of him. "Those cattle I'm rounding up should go to their heirs."

Sheriff Everett swallowed the last of his coffee and chewed on the dregs thoughtfully before he said, "How many head?"

Clay fished something solid out of his cup and wiped it on his pants. He didn't look close. He didn't want to know what it was. "Forty-five last count. We're not done shagging 'em out of the hills."

Clay watched Sheriff Everett swish his cup around to liquefy the solid black goo separating at the bottom, then take a healthy swig while holding his breath. "They had a sight more'n that. Maybe a couple hundred head. They were so scattered when I went out to look around, I couldn't be sure if any had been stolen or not, but it sounds like they have been."

"To some people one hundred and fifty head of cattle are worth killing for." Clay strained the coffee grounds out with his teeth.

The sheriff nodded. "I talked to the Meads time and again since they bought the place two years ago. Neither of 'em mentioned any family. Just keep track of how many you find."

"I'll fatten 'em up a bit and cut out the older stuff. When I market the herd, I'll be mindful of what should be the Meads'."

Clay watched the sheriff signal to Esther for more coffee.

"I'm impressed, Josiah. I didn't know if you were man enough for another cup."

The sheriff narrowed his eyes at Clay. "Watch it, McClellen, or I'll order you a piece of pie."

Clay started laughing, and he and the sheriff were still chuckling when Esther poured their coffee. Then Sheriff Everett introduced Clay to Esther and proceeded to sweet-talk her out of her mad.

The three of them talked awhile longer, as other citizens of Mosqueros came in and met Clay. With everything settled, Clay invited the sheriff to drop in after church for Sunday dinner. Then he headed home.

"Where is that man?" Sophie muttered as she combed the few snarls out of Laura's white curls.

Sally stood at the window, staring out. Suddenly she whirled around. "He's coming. He's got the wagon hitched up."

"Oh, good. We can all go to church together then." Sophie smiled at her tidy little family.

"Is Parson Roscoe gonna yell at us again?" Beth's eyes got as wide as saucers.

"That's his job, honey." Sophie brushed the wisps of hair off Beth's forehead. "He's trying to point out the error of our ways."

Beth stared at the floor for a long second. "I reckon he can't do a fearful thing like that if he's speaking softly."

Mandy buttoned up the back of Sally's dress. "Still, we get in trouble when we yell too much. Why is it okay for him?"

Sophie didn't have an answer for that, so she was glad Clay chose that moment to come inside. He glanced at them all standing, ready and waiting. Sophie saw him heave a sigh of relief. She couldn't imagine what he was relieved about, unless he thought they wouldn't be ready on time.

"Let's hit the trail."

The girls ran past him for the wagon, in a swirl of calico and braids. Sally called out, "I get the front seat between Ma and Pa!"

"You don't get to sit up there! We need to take turns, and since I'm the oldest. . ." Mandy's voice faded as the girls raced away.

Sophie heard Clay sigh again, so deeply she thought it stirred a breeze in the room.

"What's the matter?"

"They're fighting again."

Sophie cocked her head a bit to listen to the squabbling that distance had nearly erased. "You call that little spat fighting?"

"What do you call it?" he asked impatiently.

Sophie shrugged. "There isn't room for any of the girls on that seat, and they all know it, so they're just making noise. I didn't pay it any mind." She walked up to him and patted him on the arm. "That's just how little girls are. You'll get used to it soon enough."

Clay nodded silently for a while, then turned to go to the wagon. As he walked out Sophie heard him mutter, "I'll get used to it or go deaf. In the end, I reckon that's the same thing."

Sophie smiled all the way to town.

This Sunday wasn't such a shock for Sophie. She was prepared to be greeted politely, and she wasn't disappointed. She leaned over to Clay as he guided the wagon toward the church. "How did you get all these people to like us so quickly? They've never been anything but awful to me."

"The war is fading from people's minds." Clay pushed his hat back on his head with one gloved thumb and looked at her. "The country is healing. It's time for them to forgive and forget. They'd've been kind, even if I hadn't come, if you'd've given 'em a chance."

"Except for them all trying to marry me, of course."

"Well, that was another lil' thing that got in the way of you living peaceably around here." Clay smiled down at her.

She couldn't quite help smiling back. "I guess marrying you solved that."

Clay pulled back on the reins to halt the horses. "Indeed it did, Sophie darlin'. Indeed it did."

They mingled with the other worshiping citizens of Mosqueros.

Miss Calhoun came up and said a prim, "Good morning."

Sophie smiled and returned the greeting, careful not to forget to call her "Miss Calhoun." She studied the young woman. Miss Calhoun was a first-year teacher, most likely still in her teens, but she carried herself as if she had a steel rod in place of a spine—a steel rod so long it tilted her neck up. Either that or Miss Calhoun kept her nose in the air on purpose.

Sophie put aside her misgivings about the young woman's acutely

117

"proper" behavior. There was kindness in Miss Calhoun's eyes, and Sophie had heard good things about how the school was run.

"I have my appointment book with me today, Mrs. McClellen. I'd like to schedule a time when I can come out and see you."

Sophie, mindful of all her manners, said, "We would love to have you join us for Sunday dinner."

Miss Calhoun industriously consulted the small, black book in her hand. "Today isn't convenient, but next Sunday would work nicely."

Sophie noticed a fine trembling in Miss Calhoun's hand as she poised her pencil over the blank spot in her carefully kept book. It struck Sophie that a lot of Miss Calhoun's fussiness could really be a cover for shyness. It warmed her toward the teacher.

Sophie rested her hand on Miss Calhoun's arm. "Are you from around here, Miss Calhoun?"

Miss Calhoun seemed startled by the question. Sophie noticed a faint tint of pink darken Miss Calhoun's cheeks. She immediately regretted asking such a personal question.

Sophie didn't wait for Miss Calhoun to answer. "Next Sunday will be fine. You can ride out to the ranch with us after church, and we'll see you have an escort back to town. It's no time for a young lady to ride the trails alone."

Miss Calhoun seemed to gather her composure during Sophie's little speech. "That sounds excellent. It's very thoughtful of you to provide me with an escort. Not everyone around here thinks of things like that."

Sophie had a moment to wonder if Miss Calhoun had ever put herself in danger to visit her young charges. She seemed like the type of woman who would do what she saw as her duty, regardless of how difficult that might be.

Sophie wanted to warn Miss Calhoun to be careful, but the parson chose that moment to shoo them inside. They settled in the same pew as last week, alongside Mrs. Roscoe. Only this week Mandy was on Clay's left, Beth was on Sophie's right, Laura was on Sophie's lap, and

Sally insisted on squishing in between them. They were all scared to death.

When the parson stepped up to the pulpit, Beth grasped Sophie's hand until Sophie thought she heard her knuckles creak. Sophie had to be very careful not to smile.

The parson opened his mouth. Sophie saw her big girls lean forward as if bracing themselves against the force of the words. Parson Roscoe spoke so softly, the whole congregation, as one, leaned forward to catch what he said. "An expert in the law said to Jesus. . ."

Beth fell forward off the pew and banged her head on the wooden panel in front of them.

Sophie reached and pulled her back up.

Beth rubbed her head. "He snuck that soft voice in when I was ready for him to go to yellin'."

Without a pause, the parson went on preaching in a near whisper. "Which is the greatest commandment? Jesus replied: 'Love the Lord thy God with all thy heart, and with all thy soul, and with all thy mind, and with all thy strength: this is the first commandment. And the second is like, namely this, Thou shalt love thy neighbour as thyself. There is none other commandment greater than these.'"

The parson solemnly closed the big, black Bible in front of him and lifted it up into the air. "This whole book of God's Word is full of the call to love. And the darkest parts of the Bible deal with the failure of people to love. You don't need anything else, brothers and sisters. You don't need a parson preaching fire and brimstone at you. You don't need a parson at all, or this church, or. . ." The parson's voice dropped to a rasping whisper, "Or forgiveness."

After another extended silence, broken only by the sound of the breathing of his mesmerized followers, he said, "If only we would love God and love each other completely."

The parson spoke a bit louder, but Sophie noticed Beth's hand was no longer gripping hers, and all the children were listening closely to the words.

Sophie thought of how violently she had hated the men who had come for Cliff and chased after Clay. She was guilty. She needed God's forgiveness. Even as she listened and prayed, she could feel the rebellion in her heart. The anger wouldn't go away easily. She knew it was Satan battling for control of her life. She turned from the anger with all the meager strength a human can muster and begged for forgiveness. Begged for an end to her need for vengeance. Begged, *Help me, help me, help me.*

She left the church feeling more at peace than she had in years. They milled around for a bit outside, saying good-bye to the other church members. Sophie barely registered that all her girls but the baby had run off to play with a group of very noisy little boys Sophie had never seen before.

Clay stood at her side, holding Laura, and introduced her to Daniel Reeves. "Daniel just bought the mountain valley to the north of us, Sophie. He's got himself a houseful of boys to match our girls."

"Hello, Mr. Reeves," Sophie said.

Daniel reached out with more enthusiasm than Sophie was prepared for. Hesitantly she offered her own hand, and Daniel's huge mitt swallowed her hand whole. He pumped her arm up and down.

"It's Daniel, ma'am." He almost shouted his greeting. "Don't 'spect I'll be thinkin' to answer to any other name. I'm one up on y'all, ma'am. Got me five strappin' boys, I do. Every one of 'em a chip off the old block!"

Sophie had to control a desire to recoil from the man's loud voice as she tried to remember her manners. "Is your wife here, Mr. Reeves?"

"Daniel. Daniel it is, ma'am. Nope, no wife. Died birthin' the last of my boys, she did. Five sons in five years."

Sophie didn't want to imagine what the poor woman had gone through bearing that many children so fast. Everyone in the West knew childbirth was dangerous, and most men were thoughtful enough to spare their wives.

Daniel mentioned his wife's death with such negligence that Sophie

felt a surge of anger. Then, annoyed, she looked closer at the callous brute and saw a shadow settle in his eyes.

"Sad when it happened. Almighty sad. The kind of thing that makes a man believe in God or wash his hands of Him altogether. Well, I'm here, so I guess that tells the story."

Sophie watched Daniel Reeves slap Clay on the back and turn to shout a greeting at someone else.

She said faintly to Clay, "Do we have to have a baby every year until we have a boy?"

Clay's laughter pulled Sophie out of her strange mixture of sympathy and annoyance with Daniel Reeves.

"Daniel's story isn't as bad as it sounds."

Sophie said emphatically, "I suppose that's true since *nothing* could be as bad as that sounds."

"He had one set of twins, and then five years later the poor woman gave birth to a set of triplets."

Sophie gasped. "You're right. It's not as bad as it sounds; it's worse!"

Clay grinned. "You can't blame the twins and triplets on Daniel though."

"Triplets! I've heard of such a thing, but I've never known any."

"Well, take notice when they come by. They're as alike as two peas—or I guess I should say three peas—in a pod. They're five now, and the older boys are ten. They look like older versions of the triplets. They're all full of mischief, from what I've seen."

Sophie stared across the expanse of stubbly weeds that grew around the church. She watched a crowd of children, her own included, run and scream and laugh. There was no problem picking out the Reeves boys. They all had shocks of snow white hair that hung shaggy, well past their shirt collars. Then, after the startling resemblance, was the fact that they were the loudest, the most reckless, and by far the dirtiest and most ragged children in the group.

Clay laughed again. "I bet they'll keep Miss Calhoun's hands full if he sends them to school."

Sophie only shook her head. "Thankfully, I'm not their teacher."

As Sophie had that unkind thought, she remembered the sermon and immediately felt guilty. She wasn't going to think unloving thoughts. She was a new woman. From now on she was going to let all the happiness of her heart flow over everyone.

"Clay McClellen, I can't believe you invited that man over to our home for Sunday dinner!"

Sophie was looking at him like she was a wolf ready to fight the pack for fresh meat.

Clay froze, just in the house from waving Josiah off. He purely hated being scolded. It wasn't like when a man started taking after him. He'd just slug the guy till he shut up, and that would solve everything.

Clay didn't know much about women, but his gut told him that wouldn't work worth spit with Sophie. Sophie was a soft little thing, and he liked holding her close at night, so he didn't want her mad.

But mad she was, and he took it to heart, especially when the three older girls, Beth carrying Laura, gave their ma a fearful look and dashed into their bedroom.

"What's the matter with the sheriff? He's a good man."

"Good man?" She turned back to her dishes. Clay hoped the plates survived her temper. He hoped he did.

"He's a low-down scoundrel! He accused Cliff of being a horse thief, refused to chase after the posse that hung him, and asked me to marry him, all in the same breath!"

A woman could sure get upset over the least little thing.

"Now, darlin', don't get all fussed about that."

"Fussed! About a man calling Cliff a horse thief," Sophie stormed. "I will never stand by and listen to talk like that!"

Clay carefully reached for his hat, hoping Sophie wouldn't notice he was planning to run for it. She was fuming at him with her back

mostly turned, only peering over her shoulder once in a while to scorch him with a furious look.

Clay tried to placate her. "After all, the man had a job to do, Sophie darlin', and what man wouldn't want you to marry him?" There, a little flattery. Wasn't that what women wanted?

In case it wasn't, because more often than not he guessed wrong, he slid the hat off the peg and hid it a mite behind his back. He got a firm grip on the doorknob. "And he's been right nice about the herd. He told me I could round the cattle up and sell them. And if the Meads show up, I have to turn the money over, but I can take out cash to pay for feed and time and the like."

He inched the door open, lifting, mindful of the squeaky hinges if he didn't. "And since the Meads seemed to have quit the country, it figures the animals are mine until someone tells me different."

Sophie whirled around, but Clay was too fast for her. He swung the door shut and was all the way across the yard at a fast walk—only a coward would actually run from a woman—before he heard the cabin door open. He ducked around the corner of the barn.

He caught up a horse and rode out to check a few more cattle, careful to keep the barn between him and the cabin until he'd covered a lot of ground.

Sophie went back to wiping the dishes with a fine fury riding her, when suddenly she remembered the parson's words. She almost dropped the plate. "Oh, Lord, help me."

"What's the matter, Ma?" Beth came in from outside and settled in the rocking chair to soothe Laura into a nap.

"I made a promise to myself this morning. And I've already broken it." Sophie frowned down at the churned-up dishwater.

"Ma, you've told us never to break a promise. And you promised you'd never break one," Sally said fearfully from the doorway.

Sophie was almost sorry she'd spoken out loud. But she was also determined to be honest. "My promise was to try and be loving to everyone, just like the parson said. I don't think I was very nice to the sheriff, and I'm sure I wasn't nice to Pa."

"I couldn't tell you were mean to Sheriff Everett." Mandy brought up the rear. The most practical of the bunch, the girl usually let time pass when tempers flared. "I didn't even think of such a thing until you started hollering at Pa."

"In my heart, I wasn't a bit nice to the sheriff. And I'm pretty sure God counts what's in your heart just as much as how you act."

"That don't seem fair." Sally took the washcloth from Sophie's idle hand and wiped the cleared but still messy table off. "You oughta get some credit for controlling yourself."

Sophie fervently hoped she did.

Beth, half asleep herself from the rocking with Laura, murmured, "Well, I reckon that's what Jesus died for. So you could be forgiven for things like this."

Sophie looked at her very wise daughter and thought of what Jesus had said about having a childlike faith. She immediately felt better. "You're right, Beth. I need to ask God to forgive me, and then I'm going to tell Clay I'm sorry and I'm going to start over. Even if I have to start over ten times a day, for the rest of my life, I'm going to keep at it. If Jesus died for us, we'd better be smart enough to accept the sacrifice He made."

Sally went to the window. Absently she said, "Might as well."

Sophie imagined she was looking for Clay to tag along after him. Sally loved him so much. All the girls did. And he'd done so much for them in the brief time since he'd come hunting Cliff. Sophie definitely didn't want Clay to be upset with her.

Mandy took the towel out of Sophie's idle hands. "I'll finish the dishes. You'd best get on with it."

Sophie smiled at her girls and left the room. She knelt humbly by her bed and prayed for a new attitude toward life. A new ability to love. She began, "Oh, dear Lord, help me. . . ."

Luther groaned and tossed out the last swallows of his coffee. His muscles ached, and his backside was saddle sore, and he hadn't had a good night's sleep since that woman had started hounding him.

Buff didn't say a word. He got up and started saddling the horses. He didn't need to ask; he knew what was eating Luther.

"The boy has got himself tied up with a naggin' woman."

"Is there any other kind?" Buff asked.

Luther shrugged. "Don't rightly know nothin' about the strange little critters."

They made tracks down the trail for Texas.

Adam pulled at the last of the disgusting, unripened juniper berries as quickly as he could and swallowed them. He'd gotten through the day without opening up his bullet wound. If he could drink a lot of water, maybe get lucky with a rabbit snare or find a creek with some fish, and get a good night's sleep, then he could regain enough strength to start pushing hard for Mosqueros tomorrow. But all of that was driven out of his mind the instant he heard her. His Sophie. Calling to God for help, and God giving the great honor of sending that message on to Adam.

Adam knelt by the spring that gushed out around the roots of the evergreen shrub and drank his fill. Then he got to his feet, careful not to put any stress on the skin around his wound. He started toward Sophie. He didn't need a good meal and a long sleep. He only had to find the strength for each step. God would have to provide that.

ELEVEN

I love owning a ranch." Clay leaned forward to rest his forearms on the saddle horn.

Whitey sat his horse alongside Clay's as they watched the newest batch of a dozen mavericks gambol down the hill to join the herd. "I've been with enough operations to know which ones are well run. You've picked up most of the ways of ranching along the trail, and it's already starting to show."

Clay sighed with pure contentment. Having Whitey's respect meant a lot to him. There was nothing about cattle and ranch land the old codger didn't know. "I've been wondering though, this ranch—there's a kind of weird quality to it. Maybe it's just the Mead brothers' working over what my brother did and nothing matches, but it seems like more than that."

"I know what you mean." Whitey studied the ranch laid out below them. "This ranch was selected by a knowin' man. This has to be one of the few really good stretches of lush grazing on this plateau. Your brother really had an eye for land when he picked it."

Clay pointed to the house, barn, and corral so far below. "And they're laid out so the northern winter wind is blocked but the summer breeze comes through. And the buildings are well built, sturdy, and nice to the eye. And the springs have been dammed in exactly the best spots and spread out to water more acres. Still, there's something. . ."

Clay's respect for his brother grew daily. But under that respect was

126

a tinge of jealousy. All the girls spoke of their father as if he was the nicest, strongest, smartest man who ever lived. It was demonstrated to him almost daily that he would never take his brother's place. That might be why he noticed every little flaw he found around the place.

"I don't think it's the Meads who did the shoddy patchwork or who added the lean-to on the barn," Whitey said as he stared down at the ranch yard. "They only came here two years ago, and the poor work looks older than that. And I see a different hand in some of the newer repairs."

Clay had had the same thought himself. "Did someone live here between Cliff and the Meads?"

Whitey shrugged. "I'm new around these parts. I didn't even know the Mead brothers."

"It doesn't matter." Clay smiled. "It's just that it's mine, and I want to know everything about it. I'll need to fix the place up."

Whitey grunted his agreement. "First things first, though. Gotta get those cattle rounded up and branded."

Clay sat a few minutes longer and stared at his home. He saw Sally dash out of the house so far below and run to the barn. Clay couldn't hold back a smile. Yes, he loved everything about owning a ranch.

By the end of two weeks of ranching, he had some steady cowpokes on the place. He knew these men. He didn't know them personally, but he knew their type. They were men of few words. Men who worked from sunrise to sundown. Men who knew the job and didn't need to be given orders but who knew how to take orders.

He'd grown up around men just like this, and he felt comfortable with them. He had to fight the inclination to stay out on the range with the men till all hours, so he wouldn't have to go into the house and get giggled at, or worse yet *cried on*.

Then he'd get lonely for his girls and the sweet kisses he'd sometimes steal from Sophie, and he'd find himself practically running for the house. He loved his nieces—daughters, he corrected himself. He'd sort of expected to do that. But he hadn't expected Sophie.

A quiet woman most of the time, she worked hard, was a stern disciplinarian with the girls, but quick with a laugh and ready with a comforting word. She was always turning her hand to something he would have thought was man's work.

He shook his head. "Time to quit thinking and start working."

He and Whitey rode out to hunt strays. He stayed out until the sun was setting.

As he unsaddled his horse, he looked between the uncomplicated friendship of the men in the bunkhouse and the "nuthouse" he couldn't resist. He couldn't decide where to go. While he considered what kind of coward that made him, Clay loitered around the corral, trying to work up the gumption to go into the house. Pounding came from the back of the barn, and he walked around to see what was going on.

Sophie knelt, holding a sagging board in place on the shabby little lean-to tacked on to the otherwise tightly constructed barn. Clay intended to tear the little room off and start from scratch. Now here Sophie was patching it, and it sparked his temper. She treated him like he didn't take care of her.

"What are you doing?"

Sophie jumped at his harsh tone and whacked her thumb. "Ow!" She grabbed her finger and looked at it for a minute, then stuffed the tip into her mouth and glared at him.

Clay forgot his temper and chuckled at the sight.

"There is nothing funny about me smashing myself with a hammer!" she growled around her thumb.

"You look like Laura sucking her thumb. It's cute." Clay smiled at his wife. Her hair was bedraggled. She had on her stained work dress. She was wearing boots five sizes too big for her, and she was wildly irritated. He thought about how pretty she was and wondered if he could tease a kiss out of her.

Cute? Sophie withdrew her thumb, scowled, and bent over to go back to work on the board.

Clay remembered why he'd hollered at her to begin with. His

amusement faded. "I'll do that. You wouldn't have hurt your thumb if you'd been doing the work God intends for a woman to do. Get back in the house!"

He strode over to where she crouched beside the board and jerked it out of her hands. At the same time he noticed that she was half finished, and the job was well done. It reminded him of. . .

Sophie yanked the board back. Distracted, he lost his balance and fell over on top of her. They tumbled to the ground.

A bullet ripped a hole in the barn just over their heads.

Clay grabbed Sophie, kicked the new boards—and a couple of old ones—out of the lean-to, and literally threw her through the hole. Gunfire exploded all around them, and Clay rolled well into the barn. Keeping low, he dragged Sophie toward a stall. Splinters of wood shredded the barn under the hail of bullets.

Sophie got her feet under her.

"Stay down," Clay roared.

Sophie cried out and fell flat on her back. Clay looked at her, and from the way she was squirming around to get behind the stall, he figured she was all right. The pounding gunfire eased up. Return fire erupted from the bunkhouse. That turned his attention from surviving to finding out what was going on. He edged himself around the corner of the stall and scrambled to the back wall of the barn.

He heard the barn door slam and turned to face an assault. All he saw was Sophie gone. Outside! Maybe right into the teeth of more rifles! Running scared, the fool woman. She should have trusted him to do repairs around the ranch, and she should have trusted him to protect her.

The girls trusted her to protect them.

They might come outside when they heard the commotion. They knew right where Sophie was working, and they might come running straight for her. But no, her girls wouldn't come. They'd know just what to do. Just as they'd know she'd come.

She dashed for the house, grateful that the barn was in a direct line between where she was heading and where the bullets were flying. She did the little quickstep that avoided the traps on the porch and slammed her way into the house. Mandy tossed her a loaded rifle. Then Mandy pulled the shotgun off the rack and commenced loading it.

"Where are the others?" Sophie dropped to her belly, double-checked the load, and skittered along on her elbows to the front window. Mandy didn't need to answer. Sophie knew where they were. Her girls were Texans after all.

Still, Mandy responded, "The crawl space under the house. Beth and I went down with 'em right off. I watched from the crack under the porch, and when I saw you coming, I came up and started loading."

"Good girl. Did you pull out the support boards on both sides?"

"Yep." Mandy crawled close and laid another rifle next to Sophie. "First thing after the little 'uns were safe. The front and back porches will collapse if anyone tries to step on 'em. I haven't closed the front window shutters yet."

Sophie listened and heard that the gunfire was still focused on the barn. She hoped Clay was all right. Cautiously, she inched up to the glass windows and pulled the heavy, wooden shutters closed.

"I got the ones in the back and on the sides. There was no gunfire from that direction." Mandy jacked a shell into the shotgun and then loaded the second barrel. Matter-of-factly she added, "I knew you wouldn't want me going close to the front. Although the gunfire seems to be aimed at the far side'a the barn."

Sophie took the shotgun when Mandy was finished with it and added it to their arsenal. She looked out the narrow slit in the shutters, just wide enough for a gun barrel, ready now to pinpoint the exact location of the assault. She heard shots from the little grove of trees that the boar had come charging out of and studied the situation in her mind. She was listening to at least five different guns booming from up

there. She heard return fire from the barn, which meant Clay was faring well, and there was plenty of noise from the bunkhouse.

Sophie waited with bated breath, never taking her eyes off the landscape. She glanced over her shoulder and saw Mandy looking out the gun portal of one side window. Then Mandy crossed the room in a crouching run and looked out the other side.

As Mandy lowered herself to the floor, she looked sideways at Sophie, and a furrow appeared on her very young brow. "You're bleeding, Ma."

Sophie saw that the left sleeve of her dress was soaked in blood. She reached for the little hole that marked the highest point of the bleeding—about halfway between her elbow and her shoulder—and tore the hole a bit wider. She studied it for a long second. "It's just a scratch. He must have clipped me in the barn. Humph. This dress had another year left in it. Now it's ruined."

She went ahead and tore the sleeve all the way off and fashioned a bandage around her freely bleeding arm. Mandy came over and helped her tie it tight, then went back to checking both windows.

Beth popped her head up through the trap door Mandy had covered with a rug. "Need any help, Ma? Sally's got Laura safe. I could go out through the tunnel to the cave and scout around."

Sophie knew Elizabeth could move as quick and quiet as an Indian, when she chose. It made Sophie's stomach lurch to think of Beth out in those dangerous woods, but if it had come to life and death, Sophie would have sent her.

Help me, Lord. Help me, help me, help me.

The gunfire from the grove fell silent. Sporadic shooting continued a few more minutes from the bunkhouse and barn, then quit. Beth wouldn't have to go. *Thank You, Lord.*

"It seems to be over," Sophie said. "Replace those braces in the porch so we don't catch one of our own menfolk in our trap."

Beth grinned and ducked out of sight. Her head reappeared a second later. "Your arm's bleedin', Ma. Are you okay?"

Sophie waved the concern away. "Just nicked me. I didn't even notice it till I had things secure in here."

"Good. I'll have a look at it later." Beth vanished back into the floor, and the rug dropped neatly in place.

Sophie heard the sound of running horses from a distance and knew that whoever was shooting at them was riding off. Men came pouring out of the bunkhouse and fired a few shots at the retreating gunmen, but the riders never showed themselves, leaving the grove and riding into the heavy woods.

Clay came charging out of the barn. "Whitey, get some men and make sure they keep moving! Don't try and run 'em down, though. They're pure coyote to shoot from cover thatta way, and they might do it again. Just lag back, and see what you can learn from readin' their tracks."

Sophie opened the front door. She heard the posts that supported the crosscut boards in the front porch being wedged back into place and noticed that Whitey, as well as the rest of the cowhands, had headed for the corral before Clay had begun giving orders.

Clay looked at the house furiously, and his eyes zeroed in on her arm. Sophie sighed. She knew what was coming. It was going to be just like repairing the barn. Apparently staying alive wasn't woman's work either.

Judd sat his horse and worked the action of his carbine. The sound eased his fury a bit.

So they'd missed today. There was always tomorrow. He'd ridden up to scout the McClellen place, thinkin' to go charging in and drop a necktie on McClellen, like he had Edwards. This time Judd would step right in and buy the land.

He'd have to deal with Clay's wife, too. Judd hadn't thought of it at first, but now he remembered that Sophie Edwards had seen the men that took her first husband. Judd had worried about it at the time,

because she'd raised such a ruckus. But then he heard she'd quit the country, and he'd forgotten all about her. There were others who had seen him, in the early days of his night riding, before he'd gotten smart and started seeing to it that there weren't any witnesses.

It didn't sit well with him to kill a beautiful woman, but Judd knew it had to be done. McClellen first, then the woman. It needed to look like an accident when he did her in. Or maybe he could stage something that looked like an Indian attack. There hadn't been any in these parts for a while, but there could always be just one more.

One way or another, Sophie Edwards McClellen had to die.

He'd come today thinking to take care of McClellen. He'd figured the hands wouldn't be much trouble. They'd all be drifters who wouldn't measure up any better than Cliff Edwards had. Since Edwards had been a weakling, it followed that his twin brother was one, too. And the next step in reasoning told him a man wouldn't want cowpokes around him that showed him up. But McClellen had hired himself a salty bunch. And plenty of 'em, all armed.

Studying the layout, Judd had seen a chance to take McClellen out from cover.

With a quirk of humor, Judd thought of the look on Harley's face when he'd been ordered to back-shoot McClellen. Harley hadn't like it one bit. Judd had enjoyed making his saddle partner do as he was told.

And then that no-account Harley had missed! McClellen must be a lucky one to have stumbled forward at the exact moment Harley had fired. The missed shot gave McClellen the warning he needed. He'd taken cover until Judd had called off the attack.

Judd rode off in a fine fury, but his calculating mind told him anything he wanted this bad wouldn't come easy. He'd regroup and pick his time more carefully.

He pulled Harley aside as they strung out over the rugged trail that led over the bluff behind the McClellen ranch. "Harley, I need someone watching this place."

"I'll do it." Harley studied his back trail.

"No, I need you with me. Pick whoever's best at ghostin' around. I want to know McClellen's routine. I want to catch him when he doesn't have his guard dogs so close to hand."

Harley nodded. "Percy is the best, and Jesse's good. There are a couple of others who'll do."

"Get 'em started," Judd ordered.

The two of them moved out. Judd couldn't remember the last time they'd had to hightail it. It was a bad omen. Harley fell in behind him, and they picked up the pace to leave the C BAR far behind.

"Sophie," Clay growled as he strode toward her. "You are the most ridiculous. . ."

Her husband was a man of few words. This wouldn't last long. But he surprised her. He kept up his lecturing the whole time he bandaged her arm.

Beth edged up next to him. "Let me do it, Pa. I've done a sight of doctorin' alongside Ma."

"I'll do it," Clay grumped at the little girl.

Beth's eyes got round and filled with tears.

Clay hunched his shoulders like he was taking a beating. "Now don't start in crying. I have some experience with this from the war, and I want to see to it."

The tears spilled onto Beth's face. "I'm sorry, Pa."

Clay sighed deeply, but Sophie noticed he didn't run, which was his usual approach to the girls' tears. He turned back to the wound on Sophie's arm and started fooling with it. Sophie wished for Beth's gentle touch, but she didn't tell him that.

"Get some rags and tear them up for a bandage, Beth honey," Sophie said quietly, wanting to include her daughter.

Clay was still fuming over the wound and scolding her to beat all.

Sophie interrupted his tirade as soon as Beth was out of earshot.

"So who wants you dead, Clay McClellen?"

Clay stopped fumbling. They stared at each other for a long moment. Sophie found herself caught in the worry she saw in his eyes. Kind eyes. True, he was being as grouchy as a grizzly bear with a sore tooth, but she could see it was because he cared about her. Something warm inside of Sophie heated up past warm, and she rested her hand on his where he touched her arm.

With a swift glance at the girls, he whispered, "I don't think he was after me, Sophie. It would take them awhile to get set up in that grove. Why did they pick that spot? It's mostly blocked off from the rest of the yard by the barn. I think they were after you."

Clay's hand came up and caressed her cheek. Suddenly he looked dismayed. "I'm sorry." He pulled his hand away and looked around for the wet cloth Beth had brought when she was preparing to clean the wound.

"Sorry about what?" Sophie asked, not wanting him to look away.

"I got blood on your face." He touched her cheek with the cool cloth, so gently that Sophie forgot the sting in her arm and the bullets that might have caught one of her girls.

"I'm so sorry, Sophie. I should have been more watchful. They should never have gotten so close to the place." Clay looked from her cheek where he caressed her with the cloth to her eyes. His eyes flickered to her lips and then to her arm, and he seemed to gather himself. Suddenly brisk, he washed her face, then went back to his ham-handed doctoring. Sophie didn't mind his rough skill anymore.

"Who do you. . ." Sophie's voice was husky—not her normal voice at all. It seemed to sharpen Clay's attention on her. She cleared her throat. "Who do you think it was?"

"I don't know." Clay tied off the rough bandage. "But it appears someone. . ."

"I counted five different guns."

"There were at least five of them. And it appears they want one, or both of us, dead."

Clay and Sophie exchanged long, solemn looks. Their silence was broken by the giggling and chattering of the girls in the background.

"Well." Sophie's jaw tightened. "I'd say that *someone* is going to be disappointed."

Clay nodded in firm agreement.

Sophie hoped he'd say something complimentary right then. Something along the lines of, "It takes quite a woman to pick out five different gunmen in all that excitement." Or maybe, "I'm right proud of you for running in to protect the girls and having the house all closed up and safe." Or maybe even, "That was quite a carpentry job you did on the barn, before I kicked it in."

As usual, he failed her.

"What kind of blamed fool notion got into your head, to go running out of the barn while there were bullets flying. There I had you all tucked away safe, and instead of staying put, like anyone would who had half a brain, you had to go haring off. . ."

It went on the rest of the day. He even woke up a few times in the night. At first he'd hold her tight and close and long and touch her as if he were desperate to make sure she was alive and well.

Then he'd start in on his scolding again.

Adam chafed at the slow pace. He had no money, and no one would be inclined to trust a black man enough to loan him a horse, so he didn't ask.

The world was full of food to anyone who would just open his eyes. He unraveled enough thread from his tattered shirt to rig a snare. He caught grouse or rabbit most nights. He fished. There wasn't much growing yet in the early spring, but he found a few wild strawberries and a steady supply of greens.

He wouldn't have minded living like this forever, if it hadn't been for the voice. He refused to think about his murdered friends. He was

afraid the hate would overcome his need to get to Sophie. He kept his mind always on her.

His back still hurt like fire. The gunshot dragged on his strength, but he didn't let up on himself. One night, he made himself a soft bed of pine needles under a loblolly and had the best night's sleep he'd had since he'd been heading for Sophie.

He awoke with a jerk. He froze, trying to think what had disturbed him. Maybe he'd heard Sophie again. He stared straight up, and looking through the limbs brought memories. Branches. Nooses. Swinging bodies. His friends had been lynched. Adam had been presumed among the dead, and he'd walked away. Guilt wracked him. He should have gone after the killers! He should have hunted them and killed every man jack of them!

Adam swallowed the hatred and remembered why he'd walked away. Sophie. He reached for his side and felt the tender bullet hole. He swore that when he had done whatever Sophie needed doing, he'd find those men and make them pay.

He lay flat on his back and stared up at the sky through the pine boughs. He had to get to her. He didn't know why, and he didn't care. He wasn't a superstitious man, and he wasn't given to notions. Sophie needed help. God had placed it in his heart.

He hoisted himself to his hands and knees and started to crawl out from under branches that sagged so low to the ground he had to lift them to get past. Just as he reached for one, he heard in the distance the sound that had awakened him. Hoofbeats.

He held himself as still as a wild hare and listened to silent men, riding fast in the direction he was headed. He slowly, carefully, moved his head, aware that any motion on his part could attract their attention. He saw stirruped feet, he heard creaking saddle leather, but faces were blocked from his line of sight. He didn't see anything that he could recognize. Then the last few riders went by.

One of them wore Dinky's boots.

They were ridiculous black boots, overloaded with glittering silver trim. Dinky had them special made with money from his first cattle sale. He'd laughed and talked about how he hadn't owned a single pair of shoes until he'd joined up with the Union army. He'd picked cotton and tended horses barefoot until he was twenty-five years old. The man who owned him thought shoes were above the station of a slave.

Dinky loved those boots. Adam had scoffed at him and told him his boots would spook the herd, but Dinky, always happy, always finding joy in life, only took those boots off when he slept. Adam looked closely at the last few riders. He saw William's rifle. It was a .50 caliber Sharps. William, handy with a knife, had carved scroll work in the wooden butt.

He saw a rawhide rope that had old Moses's fine braiding about it, and a single pearl-handled pistol that also belonged to the elderly man, who had been the steady one of the foursome.

Then Adam saw his own blanket rolled up behind another saddle. It could have been another blanket, nothing special about it. But the bloodstains settled it in Adam's mind. Couldn't this lynching party even count? They'd stolen the outfits from four men, but they'd only hanged three.

Adam's fury built until it was all he could do to stop himself from leaping from cover and begin killing. He'd grab the last one, take his rifle, and empty it into the lot of them, grabbing another rifle from a fallen man when his was empty.

But he held himself frozen. He'd die with a plan like that. But it would feel good every last second of his life.

Then he thought of dying that way, in a killing rage, and finally that gave him the strength to hold his hiding place. God had blinded their eyes to the obvious. Maybe he'd survived for some reason of God's. Maybe he'd done something right to earn him a few more years here on this earth. More likely, he was alive because Sophie needed him.

Adam let the men go. What other choice did he have? But he counted twenty of them, and he risked his life to see a few faces. Then he noticed the brand. . . .

J Bar M.

TWELVE

Luther rode steadily into the night, with Buff galloping relentlessly by his side. They could make Texas before they slept, if they kept up their pace. But the closer Texas got, the bigger it loomed.

A distant pinpoint of light had them both pulling up.

"Coffee'd taste almighty good 'bout now, Buff. Whataya say?"

Buff grunted, and they headed slowly for the light. The fire was miles away. They knew from reading signs, they were riding into the camp of a herd being pushed up the trail rather than into a bunch of outlaws.

They weren't afraid of being shot by no-accounts now. They were afraid of being shot by law-abiding men.

Before they got within shooting range, Luther hollered out, "Hello, the camp!"

A voice out of the darkness called, "Ride in easy."

They heard the clicks of a dozen rifles being cocked.

Buff and Luther knew how to approach a cow camp, and the drovers knew how to hold their fire until it was needed. Within minutes, the two were settled in with coffee, biscuits, and beans. The fire crackled, and the scent of boiled coffee and mesquite wood soothed Luther's edgy nerves. He hoped it was working on everyone here. The *clink* of the coffeepot on the tin cups melded with the soft lowing of a cow out on the range and made Luther feel right at home.

Every cowhand in the group had left his bedroll and joined the new-comers at the fire. A cowboy was always hungry for news and a different

139

voice than the few he heard all day every day for weeks and months on end. And cowboys were a friendly lot. But Luther knew, the cowpokes came to the fire mostly to help with the shooting if there was trouble.

"Huntin' work?" the trail boss asked. "We can always use a few more men."

"Headin' to Texas," Buff replied.

"Looking for a friend of ours," Luther added. "Anyone know of a young feller by the name of Clay McClellen?"

One of the drovers said, "I served with a Clay McClellen during the war. We were with Grant up to Shiloh. Then I got stuck in the siege of Vicksburg and lost track of the major. I remember he was always huntin' news of his brother."

"Cliff," Buff said.

Luther nodded. "His twin brother. He hadn't seen him since they were kids."

"That's right," the young cowboy said. "There was talk of some soldier in the East that looked just like Major McClellen. He was tryin' to track him down."

"My last job was scouting for the Texas Rangers. I heard of a Clay McClellen workin' with the Rangers over some trouble with vigilantes in west Texas," an old-timer said. "There's been real bad doin's along the Pecos. Lotta men hung. Good men along with the bad. Heard McClellen hired on to help out."

"Why would Clay quit searchin' for his brother to take a job with the law?" Luther knew Clay wasn't the type of man to get sidetracked. So if the trail boss had it right, and there weren't two Clay McClellens, working for the Rangers must have something to do with Cliff.

"Maybe he just needed to make some money along the trail," one cowboy said reasonably.

Luther exchanged a quick glance with Buff. Clay didn't need money, not with all the gold his pa had left him.

"Whereabouts in west Texas?" Luther asked.

The old-timer said, "Vigilante trouble is all over the panhandle and

up north almost to Indian territory. The place I heard the name Clay McClellen mentioned was in connection with a little cow town name of Mosqueros."

Luther drank the last of his boiling hot, inkblack coffee in a single swallow and wiped his hand across his mouth. "Mosqueros," he said with some satisfaction. He stood up and headed for his horse.

"You oughta stay in camp for the night," one man offered. "You'd be safer in a crowd, and it's already mighty late."

Luther changed his saddle from one of his horses to another they'd picked up along the trail, while Buff did the same. *We might as well ride,* Luther thought. *We're getting too close to bother with sleep.*

"Whereabouts is Mosqueros?" Luther wasn't a man who had traveled much in his life. He'd come from the East, like everyone else who was in the West, except the Indians. But he'd headed straight up into the peaks of the Rockies like he was kin to the mountain goats. And he'd stayed.

Still, he was a man who'd sat at a lot of campfires, and like all Western men, he listened to talk of the world away from his mountain home. He tucked away information about trails he never figured to trek and rivers he had no notion of ever crossing. He knew a sight about Texas, even though he'd never laid a foot in it.

"If you're pushing hard," the trail boss said, "you can be there in four or five days. This herd is out of Lubbock, three days' ride straight south of here. Mosqueros is another day south."

Luther said, "We'll find it."

"Obliged," Buff called over his shoulder.

"Five days," Luther muttered to himself.

"You got something powerful ridin' you, Luther."

As powerful as the voice of God. "Let's make it in three," Luther said as he kicked his horse into a ground-eating lope.

Clay was on razor's edge, trying to track down the men who had taken a shot at him and Sophie. All the men were working double time, scouting the hills and standing the night watch. Clay had taken the shift before dawn, so he was tired. As he settled into his chair after the noon meal, he sighed with contentment. Good food. Clean house. Pretty wife. Sweet daughters. He was a lucky man.

"Sally, you give me back my underclothes," Beth screamed.

Sally came running out of her bedroom, with Elizabeth hot on her heels. Beth dove at Sally. Sally dodged out of her reach and darted behind Clay.

"They're prettier than mine," Sally shrieked. "They've got lace on the tummy and mine don't. It's not fair!"

Beth circled Clay's chair.

A bloodcurdling scream behind his back made Clay jump out of his chair and whirl around just as Beth caught Sally and began pulling up her skirt to take the underclothes back by force. Sally slapped at her sister. Both girls were emitting such high-pitched squeals, Clay thought his ears would bleed. He wanted to shout at them, but he knew they'd cry. He wanted to run out to the bunkhouse, but he knew they'd cry.

Suddenly, something snapped inside him. All his tightly held self-control around the soft-hearted, little monsters blew away in a blaze of anger. "I—want—quiet!"

Sally and Elizabeth froze. Their eyes widened.

"Quiet! Quiet! Quiet!" Out of the corner of his eye, Clay saw Mandy stiffen with fear. Laura, in Mandy's arms, shoved her fingers in her mouth as if to make herself be quiet. Sophie looked from Clay to the girls fearfully, as if he might start shooting any minute.

It was all too much. He looked back at Sally and Beth. Their eyes were already filling with tears. He stomped his foot in the perfect picture of a man putting his foot down. "You stop that crying right now," he stormed. "There are going to be some changes around here."

"Pa," Sally quavered, "don't you. . ."

"Don't you dare ask me if I love you," Clay roared. "I don't go lovin' and stopping lovin' any time I feel like it. All this means is, I can get

purely perturbed with someone I love, and you all might as well know that now!"

A tear spilled down Beth's cheek. She nodded as if she were frightened not to agree with him. That just made him madder.

"Stop that cryin', both of you. I'm not putting up with any more of this screaming and fighting."

"But, Pa," Beth said, "we weren't. . ."

He jabbed his finger at her. "Don't interrupt me, young lady."

Beth clamped her mouth shut and shook her head solemnly as if she would never, ever, even under threat of death, interrupt him again.

"There is a right and fittin' way for folks to get along, and you girls aren't doin' it to suit me." Clay crossed his arms and got his fury under control. He pointed at Mandy and said sternly to Beth and Sally, "Get on the other side of the room with Mandy so I can talk to all of you."

The girls hurried to obey. They lined up beside Mandy, who was holding the squirming toddler. Sophie went to stand beside them. "Get over here by me, Sophie. This is for the children, and what I say goes for both of us."

Sophie arched an eyebrow at him, but she walked over and turned to face the girls.

Clay said, "Rule number one: There will be *no more crying*! No more! None! Never!"

"But, Pa, what about my. . ." Beth began.

"I'm not finished yet!" Clay snapped.

Sophie murmured, "A little child can't always. . ."

Clay turned to her. "I said no more, and I meant it. I can't stand the sound of womenfolk crying, and I want it stopped."

Sophie crossed her arms and started tapping her foot. Clay could see she didn't like minding him. Well, that came as no surprise.

She remained silent, so he forged ahead. "Rule number two: There will be no more taking things that don't belong to you, without permission!"

Beth turned to Sally and wrinkled her nose at her little sister.

"Rule number three: No more screaming!"

"Rule number four—"

"What about Laura. . ." Mandy interjected.

Clay's concentration was broken. He was kind of coming up with these rules on the fly, thinking up what would make his home a peaceful one, so he hadn't rightly decided what to say next anyway. "What about her?"

Mandy asked, "Can Laura cry? 'Cuz sometimes. . .well, she's pretty little, and she can't always. . ."

"Laura can cry," Clay decided. "Until she's three. Then that's the end of it."

"Until she's three?" Sophie shook her head and stared at Clay as if he'd lost his mind. After an extended silence, she said, "Why three?"

Clay stared at her while he thought about it. Finally, he said, "She's a baby till she's three."

He turned back to the girls. "Rule number—"

"What if we get hurt?" Sally said. "If I stub my toe or get a bee sting. What if—"

"If you're hurt, you can cry of course. . . ." Clay waved his hand at the interrupting question. "Now, let me get on with setting the rules. Rule number—"

"Why is getting a stubbed toe okay to cry over but not getting my feelings hurt?" Beth interrupted.

Clay plunked his fists on his hips. "Feelings aren't like getting hurt. Feelings—"

"Yes, they are," Mandy insisted. "Sometimes my heart hurts worse'n a hundred bee stings. Sometimes—"

"No crying over hurt feelings," Clay snapped. "Look, if it's a problem, then how about if you don't cry when you get hurt either. If you get hurt you just. . .I don't know. . .say 'ouch' or something."

Sophie said dryly, " 'Ouch'—or something?"

Clay pressed on. "You need to learn to control yourselves. If you're ever in a gunfight or get cornered by a grizzly or some such, you need to be thinking. Having feelings at a time like that can—"

"Now, Clay. . ." Sophie rested her hand on his arm, and that distracted him some from setting his house in order. In the mountains he had never been touched by women. He never quite got his fill of it now.

Sophie shook her head doubtfully. "The chances of the girls ever getting in a gunfight are—"

"That's not the point." Clay completely forgot about rule number four, which was easy because he hadn't made it up yet, although he was pretty sure there ought to be a rule against all the high-pitched giggling, and naked babies, and Sophie saying he'd been bucked off his horse while the men could hear her, and. . .

"Well, of course it's the point." Sophie smiled, distracting him some more. "Why teach the girls how to react in a gunfight if they're never going to be in a gunfight?"

"It's not about being in a gunfight." Clay patted her poor, little female hand and explained as he would to a rather slow-witted child, "It's about keeping your head in a crisis. There are lots of times they might be in a tight spot, when they need to be thinking. . . ."

"I don't want to shoot anybody," Beth said firmly. "You can't make me shoot someone, if'n I don't want to. Can he, Ma?"

Elizabeth sounded so afraid toward the end of her question that Clay was afraid she was going to break rule number one.

"I'm not going to try and make you shoot someone, Beth," Clay said in exasperation. "Don't be stupid."

"Clay!" Sophie jerked on his arm.

Clay turned to her. "What did I do now?"

"I don't want you to ever call one of the girls stupid again," Sophie commanded.

"Well, what if they are stupid? Am I just supposed to pretend to not notice?" Clay asked.

"Clay, I mean it."

"But I've called you stupid a whole bunch of times, when you've done some lame-brained thing, and you never minded."

"Clay McClellen!" She made just saying his name sound like a threat.

"Well, you didn't."

"Yes, I did!"

Silence descended on the room.

"You did?"

"Of course I did. No one wants to be called stupid—or lame-brained for that matter. It's a cruel thing to say."

"No, it's not. Not if it's the truth. It's just how to teach people to use their heads before they get themselves in trouble." Clay tried to remember how this had all started. Then he thought of his rules. He couldn't even remember them anymore, except for the crying.

"It's hurtful." Sophie lifted her skirts indignantly and walked over to stand beside the girls. "And we don't like it."

And Clay didn't like the fact that she wasn't touching him anymore. Clay looked from one of them to the next. They all had the same stormy look in their blue eyes. It panged something in his heart to see them all standing together, against him. Then Clay remembered he was in the right in this matter, and he was the head of this house. He jammed his fists against his hips. "Well, I don't like it when you all get to screaming and crying and fighting!"

They squared off against each other. Five against one. Clay figured he could take them, but it might be a close thing. And his ears would never survive.

Sophie crossed her arms. "We might agree to try and stop the crying and screaming, if you'd agree to quit calling us insulting names."

"When you do something stupid, it's not an insult to point it out. It's just the truth. And I'm not making a deal!" He jabbed his finger at the lot of them. "I'm making the rules, and you're obeying them."

"That not how it's going to be," Sophie said through clenched teeth. "You can't run a home that way. A family has to work together, everyone taking charge of what they do best. Everyone pitching in wherever they can. Your brother let me make a lot of decisions around this—"

"I'm not my brother!" Clay roared. He was tired of hearing about what a fine, brave, wise man Cliff was. He knew he'd never measure up, but that didn't mean he wasn't pulling his weight. That didn't mean Sophie had to take up the slack for him.

The girls got weepy-eyed again. In that instant, Clay was fed up. He didn't know anything about raising girls, but people were people, and the West was the West, and everybody needed to know the same things to get along.

"That's it." Clay strode to the front door, snatched his hat off its peg, and turned back to them. "Mandy, come with me. I'm going to teach you girls to behave proper."

"Behave proper? What does that mean?" Mandy asked fearfully. "Are you going to give me a whipping? I didn't do anything. It was Beth and Sally who were fighting. Give them a whipping."

"I'm not going to give you a whipping," Clay said in disgust. "Have I ever raised a hand to one of you girls?"

He almost heaved a sigh of relief when they all shook their heads. At least they agreed with him on that.

Beth wrung her hands. "But we haven't known you all that long."

Clay almost started in hollering again, but instead he said, with a strict fatherly tone that he decided he liked, "I'm going to teach you how to rope a steer. I'm going to teach you to drive a nail and hitch up the team to the wagon and work a running iron."

"Clay, there's something you should know," Sophie said. "Cliff hasn't just been gone two years. He was in the war before that. The girls and I have really been doing for ourselves—"

"Out, Mandy." Clay'd finally figured out what the whole problem was. They'd been coddled. They'd been in an all-female household for too long. All the screaming, all the fighting, all the crying—it would all end if he did what he should have been doing from the very beginning.

He'd make boys out of 'em!

"Mandy will spend the afternoon with me, Beth will have tomorrow afternoon, then Sally the next. We'll do that for as long as it takes to teach you girls the proper behavior for life in the West." Clay pointed to the door.

Mandy looked uncertainly at Sophie. Sophie shrugged at her and, after a few seconds, gestured toward Clay and the outdoors.

"Okay. Life in the West. I can do that." Mandy's expression changed, and Clay wasn't sure what she was thinking. If he hadn't known better, he'd say she almost looked sly there for a second. He must have imagined it. She gave Clay a sad, rather wide-eyed look and batted her lashes a couple of times. "I mean, remember I'm only ten, now, Pa. Go easy on me."

Clay, thrilled he was winning a fight for a change, rested a hand on her shoulder. "Don't you worry now, lil' darlin'. I'll make sure you're safe while you get the hang of things."

He paused at the door and looked back at Sophie. "If you don't like me calling you stupid, you gotta tell me. How am I supposed to know otherwise?"

He left the cabin.

"How could anyone not know it is hurtful to call someone else stupid?" Sophie asked in amazement. "Is it possible the man is really that. . ."

Sally supplied uncertainly, "Stupid?" Then Sally asked, "Why didn't you tell Pa that Mandy's been roping cattle since she was six? Why didn't you tell him we all know how to do most of those things?"

Sophie said smugly, "I did try and tell him."

Beth chided, "You didn't try very hard."

"And why didn't Mandy tell him?" Sally wanted to know. "Why did she act all sad and scared?"

Sophie grinned a little. "She probably wants to let him think he's teaching her things. It might hurt his feelings if he found out you girls can all handle yourselves as well as he can."

"So we're all supposed to act like he's teaching us stuff we already know?" Beth asked.

Sophie shrugged, "I suppose we'll have to." With some venom she added, "It's either that or tell the poor man he's stupid!"

Royce Badje set his coffee cup down with a bang. "I've been looking for you all week, Josiah. You can't go off and leave this town unprotected when there're men like that around." Royce thought about that thug who'd come to his office and shuddered.

"Nothing happened while I was away, Royce. Even the vigilantes don't come into town."

"Don't tell me nothing happened. I don't have to put up with that kind of business."

Sheriff Everett went over it one more time. "It's not a crime to kick up a fuss, Royce. The man didn't do anything wrong."

"He threatened me," Royce said indignantly.

"None of what he said—and I only know what you told me—sounded like a threat." He waved at Esther, and she came over with the coffeepot.

"It wasn't what he said." Royce fidgeted with his collar and felt the sweat break out on his forehead again. "It was the way he said it. Surely there is something you can do before he hurts someone. I'm telling you, Josiah, he is a dangerous man!"

"I told you I'd keep an eye out and I'd have a talk with him if he showed himself again. You didn't even get his name. You didn't see his brand. I've only got a description. Chances are, when he heard the place was sold, he moved on, hunting rangeland somewhere's else."

"Whozat, Royce?" Esther asked.

Esther stood beside them, her dress and apron none too clean, her body whipcord thin. As far as Royce was concerned, griminess and thinness were powerful bad things in a woman who made her living cooking. She was also the town's biggest busybody, and Royce was impatient with himself for talking in front of her. He probably sounded like a coward.

"Just some roughneck, come into the bank trying to buy the Edwards's place," Royce said. "After McClellen'd already bought it. The man threatened me, and I want the sheriff to pick him up!"

"Royce." Sheriff Everett sounded tired. "I told you. . ."

"Great big man?" Esther cut in. "Near six and a half feet tall, and weighs three hundred pounds if he weighs an ounce? Dark hair, beat-up black Stetson? A man who needs a bath and a shave even more than most of the stinkin' men in this town?"

Royce nodded with enthusiasm.

"Carrying two tied-down Colts?" Esther went on. "One of 'em with fancy carving in the wooden handle? Kinda man that makes people clear the sidewalk when he's comin' at 'em?"

"That's him," Royce said. "I particularly remember that gun. The stock was handcrafted. A beautiful piece."

Sheriff Everett glared at Esther. "I been askin' around town for two days about such a man. How come you didn't know I was huntin' him?"

Esther finished filling their cups. "I've been gone. I left on the Saturday stage to ride over to Brogado to visit my sister. I know the man you're talking about. In fact I saw him the day he came storming out of the bank."

"It was the middle of the afternoon, Monday," Royce prompted her.

"That musta been him." Esther went across the room, filled a tin cup with coffee for herself, and brought it back.

Royce thought she looked like she was settling in for a good gossip. He barely held on to his patience. "Did he come in?"

"To the diner? Nope." Esther sniffed as if any man not eating her cooking was immediately suspicious.

Sheriff Everett asked, "Do you know anything about him?"

"Heard he caused a ruckus in the Paradise a coupla weeks ago. Upset 'cuz the whiskey 'tweren't no good. Knocked Leo out cold. One of his men broke Rufus's nose."

"Why didn't someone send for me?" Sheriff Everett asked with a scowl.

"It was over before it started. Leo came around. Rufus quit bleedin'. The man who caused it all was gone." Esther shrugged. "Everybody knows the Paradise can get rough. What were you gonna do?"

Josiah didn't answer.

Royce knew Esther was right. Josiah would have done nothing. "And you're sure it was the same man who came out of the bank?"

"I'm sure." Esther slurped her coffee. "Ain't much goes on in Mosqueros I don't know about."

"Well, if someone would have called me," Sheriff Everett said, "we might know enough about him to track him down and find out what's got him all worked up about the Edwards's place. As it is, I'm stuck just keeping an eye out in case he comes back to town."

"Well," Esther drawled, "you know a bit more about him than that."

"No, I don't," the sheriff barked.

"You know his name."

"No, I don't."

"You will after I tell it to you," Esther said with a smirk.

"You know this hombre's name?" The sheriff rose partway out of his chair.

"I reckon I do. He made a big enough fuss about it to Leo."

Royce waited. Seconds ticked by while Esther sipped her coffee. The woman dearly loved to be the center of attention. He nearly squirmed with impatience. Finally, he snapped, "If you know his name maybe you'd like to share the information!"

Esther stiffened, but Sheriff Everett reached across the table and pressed her weathered hand. "It'll really help me out, Esther. If he hit Rufus and Leo and threatened Royce, you'd be doing a service to this whole town by telling us. Why, I reckon you'd be a true hero."

Esther turned away from Royce. "Well, of course I'm a-gonna tell ya, Sheriff. There just 'tweren't no call for Royce to speak to me thatta way."

Royce could almost see the old hen's ruffled feathers lay down, and he bit his tongue to keep from saying something that would make her ruffle up again.

At last, apparently satisfied she'd tortured him sufficiently, Esther said, "His name is Judd Mason."

"Judd Mason," the sheriff said thoughtfully. "Not a name I've ever heard before."

"Maybe he's wanted." Royce rubbed his hands together gleefully. They could lock this thug up and he'd be safe. "You oughta check the name against the WANTED posters."

"I know my job, Royce." The sheriff drained his coffee cup and chewed the dregs. "I'll do that, and I'll send a telegraph, with his name and description, to the Texas Rangers."

"We'd best warn the McClellens about him," Royce added.

"Don't forget to mention the brand on his horse." Esther picked up Josiah's cup and stood from the table.

"You saw the brand?" Josiah leaned toward Esther.

"What was it?" Royce could hear the cell door slamming already. "A brand's a lot harder to change than a man's name."

Esther gave him another snooty look, and Royce thought he'd pushed her too hard—again.

Finally, she deigned to answer, "J BAR M."

THIRTEEN

Adam had learned the hard way to never expect anything but trouble. As he came within a day's walk of the ranch, he faded back into the high-up country, scouting around to see why Sophie would need help bad enough that God would come, personally, to so lowly a creature as Adam Grant.

As Adam ghosted around in the woods surrounding the ranch, he began to take stock of the situation. He saw Sophie and she seemed fine. He also counted four little girls and couldn't stop himself from smiling at all the little tykes.

But he saw no sign of Cliff. Instead, another man came and went from the house as if he lived in it. Had Edwards abandoned her? Adam had always expected the man to cut and run back to the safety of the East. But he'd always expected Edwards would take Sophie with him when he went. No man was such a fool that he would have a woman like Sophie for his own and give her up. More likely Edwards was dead. The West could kill a man in a hundred ways, and—if a person was stupid—it could kill in a thousand. Despite his sharp clothes, classy education, and polished manners, Adam had pegged Edwards as stupid from the minute he'd come riding up to the Avery farm in Pennsylvania.

Adam's fear of what would become of Sophie was why he'd come West with them. Nothing in the two-plus years he'd been with the family, before Edwards drove him off, had changed his mind.

Adam wasn't close enough to see the new man's face, but he knew from the way he moved, the competent way he sat a horse, and the way he held the attention of his cowhands, that it couldn't be that worthless Cliff Edwards.

While he wondered about Edwards and worried about the voice saying, "Help me," what really had Adam upset were the tracks. Men were coming and going in the rough country above the ranch. The men were good in the woods—quiet, leaving few signs. Adam hadn't managed to spot one in person yet, but he started to recognize four different men, usually out in pairs, usually leaving during the nighttime and only scouting during the day.

Sometimes they'd follow the hands, but mainly they seemed to be keeping an eye on Sophie's man and the ranch house. Sophie's new man was savvy in the woods himself, and Adam had his hands full keeping from being discovered. He wasn't ready to come out in the open yet.

Before he could go down to say hello, he had to know why Sophie was being watched.

Sophie knew exactly why she was being watched.

They were coming—coming for Clay.

Well, she wouldn't have it! She was tired of breaking in new husbands. She was keeping this one!

Sophie hadn't survived in a confounded bramble bush for two years by being careless. She knew her property. She knew how to track, and she could read signs like the written word.

Clay rode out to check his herd every day, always scolding her to "leave man's work to men." Sophie waited until his dust settled, and she and the remaining girls that hadn't been taken off by Clay to learn how to be boys got to work.

"Ma, I finally landed a rope on a yearling yesterday," Mandy announced, as she shinnied up to the highest rafter in the barn to settle a basket of rocks on a board.

"Mandy, you didn't!" Sophie stopped prying up the floorboard she'd spent all day yesterday laying in front of the barn door.

"Pa sure threw hisself a fit when he saw you'd put a wood floor across the barn door, Ma." Sally had quit pouting because Elizabeth had gotten to go with Clay just as Sophie expected. Now that Clay was gone, there was no reason to fuss about it, because she knew Sophie wouldn't change her mind regardless of the ruckus.

"Pa and I talked about it again, Sally. I told him it'd keep down the mud, and he came around to my way of thinking once he saw I'd already done the work. His main complaint was that the barn was his territory and he didn't want me dirtying my hands with such hard labor."

Mandy giggled.

"I think that's right nice of him to want to spare you hard work, Ma." Sally said in stout defense of her beloved father.

"Kinda dumb," Mandy pointed out. "Since you haul buckets of water from the creek a dozen times a day and chop wood for the fireplace and work over the fire for hours and hunt food and clean it. . ."

"I'm not supposed to hunt anymore," Sophie reminded her.

"That's right. I remember. Pa said it was man's work, 'ceptin' he never brings in food so what are we supposed to cook?"

"I don't think he's keeping track." Sophie set the three center boards aside and began digging. "He's waiting for me to tell him I'm running low on something, then he'll go and fetch us a deer. But he's powerful busy these days, and I hate to bother him. Besides, I like to hunt as much as the next person. I hate to give it up. His heart's in the right place. He means to help."

"So now you don't just have to hunt food, you've got to do it on the sly." Mandy shook her head in disgust.

Sophie laughed. "Hunting is a sneakin' business anyway, little girl. It's no bother. And if I hadn't been hunting, I'd have never found out we're being watched. We laid traps during the years your pa was gone to war. Then we had them in the thicket. But I might not have thought to rig anything up in the barn, what with so many men around."

"You'd've thought of it." Mandy attached the braided hemp rope to the basket handle and threaded it through the notch she'd drilled in the nearest rafter. Then, she carefully eased her way out on the board twenty feet above the ground until she could reach the barn wall. She hooked the rope around a little notch left there from years back.

Sophie laughed again as she dug down to make a man trap out of the entrance to her barn. "I reckon that's so."

Mandy dropped the long rope off her shoulder until it fell to within four feet of the barn floor. Sally caught it and, careful not to upset the basket, tucked it behind the door frame so no one could pull it by accident. Mandy nimbly clambered down the barn wall and dropped to the floor.

"Anyway," Sally reminded her mother, "you'd've found out about it 'cuz Pa told you he'd seen tracks."

"True, true enough." Sophie nodded. "This pa is a fine tracker."

They worked companionably together in silence. Laura slept peacefully on a pile of straw in the corner of the barn. The hole got about shoulder deep and Sophie stopped. A man just had to fall far enough for the sharpened, wooden spikes she was going to plant in the bottom to have some poking power.

"Are you gonna tell Pa about the traps, Ma?" Sally wondered.

"I think I'd better." Sophie laid her hands on the ground and vaulted out of the hole. "I'd hate to catch him by accident."

"You know he'll have a fit," Mandy warned. "He'll figure it for men's work."

Sophie nodded and shrugged, then went to the floorboards she'd split and sanded smooth. "Still, I'd better tell him. So you roped a yearling? Already? Do you think that's wise?"

"I'd been missing for a week. It was driving me crazy!"

"Still, it took you months to learn it the first time," Sophie reminded her as she took the chisel to the floorboards. "We don't want to hurt his feelings."

"It's all right. I acted all excited and told him what a good teacher

he was. I made sure to miss three or four times, and then make one again. I did that most of the day. But toward the end I started getting right dependable." Mandy snagged a lariat hanging on the wall and whirled it around her head for a few seconds before she sent it sailing toward a post on one of the stalls. It settled perfectly in place. Mandy snapped the noose to pull it off the post, coiled it again, and lassoed the post, again and again.

"It's nice of him to work with you, but you have to go slow or he'll catch on. I just wish you could get on with learning a little faster so you could actually start helping the man."

"Oh, he's not going to let me help once I learn." Mandy replaced the lariat and started whittling on one of the spikes her mother was going to plant.

Sophie straightened from the boards she was cutting halfway through. She stood too suddenly and for a moment the barn spun around. She stepped quickly to the side of the barn and leaned, one arm out straight, until her head cleared. "What do you mean? Why would he teach you then not let you help?"

"It's men's work." Mandy looked up from her whittling and grinned at her mother.

Sophie shook her head and turned one corner of her mouth up in disgust. "Then why, may I ask, is he teaching you?"

Mandy giggled as she dropped her sharpened stick and started on a new one.

"Ah, Ma, don't let him get you all stirred up." Sally tugged on the hemp rope she was braiding. "He means well. He wants us to know just in case we ever have need of the skill, but he also keeps promising to take care of all of us forever. And that's right thoughtful of him."

"It is thoughtful." Sophie slid back into her hole and imbedded Mandy's sticks so they pointed straight up. "But how does that man think we lived without him for two years?"

"It was really more like seven years, Ma. 'Cuz Pa—I mean our first pa, you know—not the one we've got now."

Sophie said snappishly, "I'm not likely to forget the man I was married to for nine years!"

Mandy hastened to point out. "I was just trying to be clear on which pa I was talking about."

"You make it sound like there've been a dozen of them." Sophie jabbed the spike hard into the ground.

"Sorry." Mandy went on sharpening. "Anyway, my point was, our first pa wasn't around much, what with the war and all. We've been on our own almost from the first. And here we are, alive and well. How does he think we managed it?"

"I don't reckon men are supposed to think," Sally said philosophically, as the pile of hemp rope grew at her feet. "That's why God gave 'em big muscles."

Mandy tilted her head sideways for a second. "Makes as much sense as anything else."

Sophie nodded. "Men do the lifting and women do the thinking. That sounds fair. I suppose God could have planned it that way." She added, "That's enough spikes for now."

Sophie set the last one in place as Mandy laid aside her bowie knife. Sophie hopped out again.

With the girls' help, Sophie braced the boards that covered the hole much the same way they'd done to the front porch. These were sturdy enough a man could ride a horse across them, but if Sophie tripped the braces, they'd collapse.

They had a dozen other snares and booby traps set up around the perimeter of the property, not to mention a collection of clubs and sharpened sticks tossed in unexpected places so there was always a weapon close at hand.

Nope, no one was getting this husband. Sophie had become purely fond of him.

Sophie began filling buckets with dirt so there'd be no evidence of digging. "You know, I've done a fair amount of lifting to get the traps all in place, so Sally's theory about muscles isn't perfectly sound."

Mandy nodded. Sally shrugged. Laura stirred in her sleep. Sophie thought that "fond" didn't really describe how she felt about her new husband. It was a whole lot more than fond—even if he did have weird notions.

"Where do womenfolk get all their weird notions?" Clay shook his head at Beth's inept efforts saddling his Appaloosa. Why would the little mite think a horse would want to hear all five verses of "Bringing in the Sheaves"? All the girls were proving difficult to teach.

Mandy couldn't seem to twirl a rope for more than a few seconds before it would drop on her head and get her so tangled she had practically tied herself up. Her eyes had gotten all teary a couple of times, and Clay had been forced to remind her about rule number one. She'd finally gotten the hand of landing a lasso on a bored, little calf who wasn't even moving.

Sally was a trooper. She was picking things up fairly well, although she still had a long way to go, and sometimes her chatter about how brave and strong Cliff was grated on Clay's patience.

And today he had Beth. He knew she could catch up a horse. He'd seen her do it with Hector. But she was the almighty slowest little thing he'd ever imagined. She kept getting distracted by petting the horse's nose and talking about how soft the "paloose's" fur felt. She also had a tendency to giggle at things that weren't funny in the least, and that made the horse nervous. It made Clay nervous, too. They never got anything done.

And Sophie—well, Sophie had the weirdest notions of all. Clay had decided that it wasn't too late to teach Sophie a few things. So he'd started taking her out—never going far, of course, because of the girls, and setting her to practice man things. He'd needed to tell her about the men watching the ranch yard and give her orders about being cautious, both for herself and the girls.

He'd told her he didn't expect much from someone as old as she was, citing the adage, "You can't teach an old dog new tricks," but she might as well try.

She took a notion to get huffy when he mentioned her age, and all the things he taught her came a little faster. He'd have to remember a few little jabs about her being old seemed to spur her on. That might come in handy.

She was a good shot—better than good, he reminded himself, as he thought about the day she'd brought down that wild boar. And she knew how to slap leather on a horse, although to Clay's way of thinking, she spent too much time talking to the horse, too.

She started talking once about laying snares and booby traps for night riders. Clay did his best not to laugh at her, but he couldn't stop himself. He told her to quit worrying her pretty little head about man things. She worked harder than ever after that, mainly because she wasn't speaking to him at all.

But the most unusual reaction she'd had so far was when he brought the material home for her to make pants for the girls. He'd brought some other material, too, because the girls needed a spare Sunday dress, but the brown broadcloth was his favorite purchase.

Mandy hugged the bolt of flowery blue to her chest, and Beth and Sally had started a tug-of-war over a bolt of pink nonsense the lady in the general store had told him was just the thing.

"I remember once Pa brought us four different colors of cloth for dresses." Mandy nudged Beth. "Remember? He got us ribbons to match and said Ma was to make us each a matching dress, 'cept in different colors?"

Beth nodded and with a hard wrench got the fabric away from Sally. In the tussle Beth dropped the cloth, and Laura crawled over and sat down on top of it.

Clay felt his jaw tighten until it likened to break under the strain. Of course Cliff had gotten them more. Of course there'd been four pretty colors and ribbons to match. Clay felt his temper rising. He

remembered he'd made a rule about the girls taking things away from each other, but the cloth didn't belong to anyone yet, and the girls weren't screaming or crying, although they were too close for comfort. And Clay didn't want to be cranky right now. Not while they were all thinking about how much better their other pa was than him.

Laura started chewing on the material. Sally turned her attention to the bolt Mandy was holding. Beth was scolding Laura, who started to cry. Clay longed for the day Laura was three. They all ignored the brown. Clay told Sophie about his plans for the broadcloth while he was trying to think up a rule to cover this kind of racket.

"There is no way on earth I am putting my little girls in men's clothing." Sophie harrumphed. "It isn't proper! You can teach them all the manly skills you want, but it's my job to teach them to be ladies, and that means dressing as God intended!"

"Now Sophie, don't go getting all persnickety on me," Clay said. "I don't know where in the Bible it says anything against pants on a woman, so we're okay with God on this one."

Sophie stirred her soup as if her life depended on it. "We are *not* okay with—"

"We're living way out here where no one but the coyotes and the cattle see any of us."

"And the cowhands," Sophie reminded him.

Clay refused to be distracted. "No one's gonna care if the girls wear a pair of pants. It's not safe for them to ride sidesaddle. It's just a plumb fool idea. They're riding astride, and their skirts are flying all over and. . ."

Sophie wheeled away from the stove and stormed right up into his face with a steaming, heavy metal ladle. Clay almost took a step back before he found his backbone.

"You have to be mindful of their skirts, Clay." She waved the ladle under his nose. "They're out there with the hands, and I won't have their skirts flying about!"

Clay caught the ladle and relieved her of it so he could keep bossing her around without any danger to himself. He tossed it onto the table with a loud clatter and stepped up until her nose was practically pressed against his shirt. She looked up at him. The angry glint in her eye told him she wasn't going to back down. Since it was up to a man to do all the thinking for a family, especially one that had as many females as this one, Clay examined his idea for flaws. There were none.

He bent over Sophie until his nose almost pressed against hers. "Either you sew up a pair of pants for each of these girls and do it right quick, or I'll take 'em into town and buy 'em a pair right in the general store, in front of everybody!"

Sophie's eyes flashed so much fire, Clay wouldn't have been surprised if his hair was set ablaze. He held her gaze even at the risk of his charred skin. Something feral crossed Sophie's expression, and Clay got ready to catch a fist if she threw one.

Before she could attack, Mandy piped up, "Remember the schoolmarm with that split skirt she wears sometimes, Ma?"

Sophie broke the deadlock of their clashing eyes and looked at her eldest daughter.

Clay grinned. "I remember that skirt. I saw her ride by me just today in town. Why, Mrs. McClellen,"—he chucked Sophie under the chin so she'd look back at him—"are you going to stand there and tell me that Miss Grace Calhoun, Mosqueros's one and only school teacher, isn't a proper lady? Why she's the most stiff-necked, starchy female I've ever met. If she wears one of those whatchamacallem skirts, right in the middle of town mind you, I reckon my girls can, too."

Sophie jerked her chin out of Clay's grasp, looked at Mandy, then planted her fists on her hips and turned to her husband with a much more serene expression. "Yes, I hadn't thought of Miss Calhoun's riding skirt. When you showed up with brown broadcloth, I just naturally thought you were expecting men's pants for the girls, like you wear."

That's exactly what Clay had been expecting, and he hadn't once thought of Miss Calhoun until Mandy mentioned it, but since he was winning the fight, he decided to let Sophie think whatever she wanted.

162

Mandy, from behind them, said, "Pa brought us yellow calico, remember? It was mine first, but we all wore it as we grew into it."

Clay wanted to snap at Mandy, which he knew wasn't fair. It wasn't her fault her first pa had been so much nicer than her second pa. He focused his temper where it would do some good—at his stubborn wife. "Next time I give an order, Sophie, I expect it to be obeyed. We're not having a debate every time I decide the way of things. That's not how a marriage works!"

"How do you know how a marriage works?" Sophie asked tartly.

"I just do. The man's in charge, just like God intended. And that it *does* say in the Bible." Clay tried to hold on to his mad. It stung a little that Mandy had needed to jump in and convince Sophie to make the pants. But he was getting his way, and he could always go back to town for more cloth and a bunch of stupid ribbon, so he started to cheer up some.

"You've never been married before," Sophie pointed out. "I know a far sight more about marriage than you do."

"Yes, I know. My perfect brother." Suddenly it was easy to be mad again. He was sick of hearing about Saint Cliff. "Cliff, the world's bravest man. Cliff, the nicest pa who ever lived. Cliff, the best cattleman. Cliff, the world's best—"

"Who in the world ever told you Cliff was the world's best cattleman?" Sophie asked incredulously. "The man barely knew the horns from the hooves, and he didn't know how to dodge either one."

"He didn't know. . ." Clay stopped, dumbfounded. "But. . .he built this place. All these buildings. . .that herd. . .the old C Bar animals are healthier than. . ."

"Adam built the buildings," Sophie said. "For that matter, Adam picked out our cattle, bought our horses, and hired our hands."

"But what did Cliff do?" Clay couldn't get his mind around what Sophie was telling him. He'd never heard a one of these women say a word against Cliff.

"Well, he built that rickety lean-to on the barn," Sophie said.

163

It all clicked into place when she said that. He'd thought something looked familiar about the patching job she was doing. There were signs of it all over the ranch. Buildings and corrals that were well built and laid out intelligently. Ramshackle little add-ons that were almost universally falling down. Tidy little patch jobs that were holding the shoddy lean-tos and fence rows together. Adam did the building. Cliff did the adding. Sophie did the patching.

Clay suddenly quit worrying about his girls wearing pants and focused all his attention on his wife. His wife who had never had much to say about his brother. Of course, he'd never asked her about him. His wife who went around doing men's work without asking for help.

She wasn't doing it because she thought Clay was a lesser man than Cliff.

She was doing it because she thought Clay was *exactly* like Cliff!

Clay's heart lightened until he wanted to launch into a chorus or two of "Bringing in the Sheaves" all on his own.

"Girls, I gotta talk to your ma for a minute. You stay in the house." He grabbed Sophie's hand and dragged her outside, striding toward the barn until he was almost carrying her.

"Tell me!" he ordered as he pulled her around the corner of the barn.

Sophie's eyebrows arched with confusion. "Tell you what?"

"Tell me about my brother. Tell me what kind of husband he was."

"Oh, Clay," Sophie said apologetically, "I don't want to say anything against Cliff. I didn't mean to be unkind."

Clay wanted to hear every unkind thing she had to say, which caused him a second of sadness. He shouldn't want to hear ill of his brother. Even without her saying a word, she was saying a lot to admit that talking about Cliff would be unkind. Clay lifted Sophie by her waist until she was pulled hard against him and kissed the daylights out of her. He wasn't sure just when her arms went around his neck, but sure enough, they were there. He reluctantly pulled her away. "Tell me."

"Clay,"—Sophie rested her hands on his chest—"your brother was

a good man. He truly was. I cared about him, and I tried to help him the best I could."

"Help him? What does that mean?" Clay was hoping to hear that Cliff got bucked off his horse every time a naked baby went screaming past him. He didn't expect Sophie's voice to be so warm when she said Cliff's name.

Well, he'd asked for it. He braced himself as he prepared to listen to Sophie sing the praises of his brother.

FOURTEEN

Well, he'd asked for it. She braced herself as she prepared to tell Clay unflattering things about his brother.

"Do you remember me telling you, when I was saying Cliff was an only child, that I didn't think Cliff lied about it?"

"I guess," Clay said. "It sounds kind of familiar. A lot of that first day is a blur. You said something about Pa keeping the memories alive for me, and maybe Ma didn't do that for Cliff."

Sophie leaned against the barn and rested her hand on Clay's strong arm. "I believe that, Clay. I don't think he remembered you consciously, but I think he missed you all his life. Cliff was a sad man in so many ways. It was like he was always lonely, even when he was surrounded by his family. He was moody and critical, and he wasn't. . .well, I wouldn't have minded so much for myself. I'm an adult woman, and I don't need a lot of emotional nonsense."

Clay said quietly, "Maybe you needed a little of it."

Sophie smiled up at him and shrugged. "Maybe. Maybe I did. But I know the girls needed him to love them. You've noticed how they're always asking you if you've quit loving them?"

Clay nodded. "How could they think I'd just quit loving them?"

"Cliff trained them to think that way. Cliff had a way of punishing you for—I wish I could say for being disobedient or bad—but the truth was, he'd do it just because the mood struck him. If there'd been any rhyme or reason to it, we could have learned what his wishes were and

166

tried to please him, but his temper had only to do with his own feelings. We never knew when he was going to have a black mood come over him. Sometimes, he'd go days without talking to any of us."

"I can't imagine the girls letting him get away with that. They climb all over me. They never stop chattering and giggling and crying. How could anyone avoid talking to them?" Clay almost sounded envious.

Sophie had to bite back a grin. "Cliff managed it."

"It sounds like my brother wasn't a very nice man," Clay said.

"There were bad times before the war, but he was a complicated man, just like any person is. Mostly, he was all right. He could be a charmer when he wanted to be. He sure convinced me to marry him quick enough. And I'll always believe he really wanted me, not just my pa's money. But after the war, it was like he left all the softer parts of himself on the battlefield. I think it was you he was missing. It was like he didn't want anyone to be close to him. Maybe he'd learned that loving was a risk. It hurt too much."

"And what about the buildings and the herd?"

Sophie reached down to her side and patted the sturdy barn. "Adam built the barn and the ranch house with his own hands, selected the site, laid out the corrals, and handpicked good stock."

"Didn't Cliff do anything?"

Sophie said sheepishly, "He bought Hector."

Clay's eyebrows disappeared into his hairline. "What about Adam? Who is he? You've mentioned his name before."

"Adam came with me from my father's farm. He was an emancipated Negro who had worked as a hired man for my pa all my life. He heard Cliff was taking me to Texas, and after twenty years on the same farm, all of a sudden Adam announced this yearning he'd always had to go west. I never asked, but I think he saw Cliff's weaknesses better than my folks or I did, and he knew I was going to need help."

"So then, why'd Adam abandon you?"

"Cliff drove him off. Cliff was a difficult man to work for. He alienated most of the townsfolk, even before he went and fought for the Union. Fighting for the North was the last straw."

"I fought for the Union. No one's braced me with it."

"Maybe it was just Cliff. He didn't get on with people."

"Does that include you, Sophie?"

"I loved your brother, Clay," Sophie said quietly. "I loved him as much as he would let me. I won't have the girls remembering him unkindly."

"That's why you've never complained about him. That's why you do so much of what I think should be man's work. You've always covered for him."

"I guess you could put it that way. I just saw it as helping." With a deep sigh, she continued, "A few months after Adam left, my pa and ma died, leaving me a nice bit of money from the sale of their farm. Adam had always urged us to stay out of debt, but Cliff wanted to expand. He bought a lot of land and increased the herd. He even mortgaged our ranch and the cattle, so he could buy all he wanted." Sophie shaded her eyes and looked at the wooded hills above the house. "He bought all those bluffs to the west."

"But that's mostly wasteland." Clay looked at the rugged timberland.

"And he bought Herefords. He was always wanting red cattle for some reason." Sophie shook her head.

"Herefords aren't fit for west Texas. You need longhorns to survive in this dry country."

"They're expensive, too. Then he went off to fight, and I held everything together with a couple of old hands and the girls."

Sophie wondered if Clay would get the hint that they were all seasoned ranchers. Now wasn't the time to drive that point home. "Then Cliff came back, more distant and sullen than ever. He was here long enough to get his long-dreamed-of son coming along the way."

"That'd be Laura?" Clay said with a quick grin.

"Cliff would have been furious. He always was when a girl-child was born."

Clay's smile vanished. "Cliff was a fool."

"I think he was trying to replace you, Clay. Without even knowing it, he was longing for another little boy that had been lost to him. He never got his son—at least one that lived."

When Cliff gave her an astonished look that obviously asked what she meant, she told him of the son she had lost as an infant. As she finished, Sophie's voice dropped to a whisper, "And he never quit punishing me and the girls for the loss of his son."

Clay rested one arm across her shoulders, then, when she leaned into him, he pulled her close and hugged her tight. "I'm sorry, darlin'."

Sophie pulled back a bit. Clay was so close and so warm, it made her head swim. She leaned forward and rested her forehead on his chest. "I don't want you to feel sorry for me, Clay. I meant it when I said I loved Cliff. It was just that, caring about him like I did always made me sad that I couldn't find a way to make him happy. He's the one we should feel sorry for."

Clay lifted her chin. "Okay, I think I can manage to feel sorry for a man too foolish to know how lucky he was to have a house full of pretty girls all wanting nothing but to love him. And Sophie darlin'. . ."

Sophie's head swam a little more, and she hung on to Clay tight. "What?"

"You can fill that house to the rafters with all the baby girls you want, now that you're married to me. And I promise to be nothing but grateful."

The thought made Sophie dizzier yet, and her knees collapsed. Clay caught her and hoisted her into his arms. She saw the fear on his face and wondered what she looked like. She felt like all the color had drained from her face, and her eyelids wanted to fall closed.

"Sophie, what's the matter?"

In that very instant Sophie knew. Of course she knew. She was no young girl still in pinafores, after all. She'd felt this way before. Exactly five times. She said with quiet awe, "I think we might get to filling that house sooner than you think."

It took him a minute. Sophie almost smiled as she waited for him to add up all the information she'd given him.

"A baby?"

Sophie tucked her head under his strong chin. She took one arm down from where it was wrapped around Clay's neck and laid her hand on her belly. "The only time I've ever come close to fainting in my life was when I was expecting. It's the first I've thought of it, but now I can think of some other symptoms." She looked into Clay's shining eyes. "Yes, there's definitely a baby on the way. *Our* baby."

Clay swung her a bit in his strong arms and grinned until she thought his face would split in two. "You know they're all ours, Sophie darlin', but I can't help but be tickled to be adding to our brood."

The smile left his face—replaced by worry. "You can't go around riding or working outside if you might faint dead away. You've got to settle down now. You stay in the house and make sure and not overdo. You need to rest!"

Clay hoisted her a little higher against his chest and started walking toward the house so fast he was practically running. "Mandy is a right handy cook, and if she's not up to it, Whitey can make enough grub at the bunkhouse for all of us. I don't want you leaning over the fireplace. You might get dizzy and fall face first into. . ."

Clay's voice faded away, and he looked horrified. He hugged her so tight she almost squeaked, but Sophie was enjoying his concern too much to beg him to let her go for so little a thing as breathing.

"And no more riding horseback."

"Clay, I'm perfectly capable of. . ."

"If you fainted on the back of a horse, you might break your neck. You might get trampled. We'll hitch up the team for church and errands in town." Clay stopped so suddenly he almost skidded. He whirled around to head for the barn.

Sophie's head started spinning again, but it was the wild ride Clay was giving her at fault, not a baby. "We don't have to hitch up the team right this minute. We don't have church or any errands right now."

Clay lurched to a halt and stared at the barn uncertainly. "We've

got to tell the doctor you're expecting so he's ready when it's time to deliver the baby." He began striding rapidly toward the barn. He looked down at Sophie as if he were carrying some dangerous wild animal in his arms. "Maybe the doc should stay out here with us when your time is close."

Sophie patted Clay's chest. "Hush now, we don't need to go to town. I've never needed a doctor. Having a baby is the most natural thing in the world. I lived in a thicket and delivered Laura with no one around."

"No one?" Clay stopped his headlong dash for the barn. His grip loosened on her, and Sophie grabbed hold for fear he might drop her.

"The girls were there, but they slept through it, thankfully. I didn't want them to see a baby born. It wouldn't be proper. Anyway, the thicket wasn't so bad. For mercy's sake, Clay, I had Mandy along a creek on the trail west. I was alone. Our wagon had broken an axle, and Adam had gone off to the nearest town, which was forty miles away, to get a new one. Cliff didn't want to see a baby born, so he went off hunting until it was over."

That didn't seem to reassure him at all. This time he did drop her. She was ready though. She had a firm hold of his neck, so she landed on her feet. She wondered for a minute if he was going to faint. She suppressed a grin.

Her desire to smile faded as she remembered the rest of the story. "Then Cliff came back. When he saw it was a girl, he wouldn't speak to me for three days. Then Adam came back. He did everything he could think of for me, but it was all over. There was nothing for him to do. He repaired the wagon, and we continued on the trail for Texas."

Clay's pupils dilated. His cheeks flushed with anger. "If my brother were here, I'd beat him to within an inch of his life!"

"At the time, I'd have held him down for you."

"Well, it's not gonna be like that this time. There'll be a doctor, and there'll be no creek, nor a thicket!" Clay seemed to gather his wits about him. "And you're not gonna do anything that might hurt you or the baby."

171

He seemed happiest when he was issuing orders, so Sophie let him. His eyes suddenly got serious—serious to the point of frantic. He grabbed both her arms and almost beseeched her, "You're going to sit in that house and rock in a rocking chair and rest!"

"Clay, we don't own a rocking chair."

"I'll build you one." He slid his hands down her arms until he was gripping her hands tightly. "Please, tell me you'll stop working outside. I've only got two more days until we move the herd up closer to the ranch. If you'll give me two more days, three at the most, I promise I'll get to the work you've been doing."

He was squeezing her hands hard enough that she was losing feeling in her fingers. She wanted to make him happy. She really did. That's why she risked being honest. Anyway, it was high time she told him about the traps she'd set, before he caught himself in one. "The only thing is I've got a few booby traps to rig. I've hauled tree trunks off to the side of the trails up in the hills. They almost have enough rocks piled behind them to be ready. I need to find a few more rocks and get them in place and rig a trip wire and. . ."

"Booby traps? What are you talking about?" Clay shook his head, and Sophie got the impression he was trying to jiggle his brains around so they'd work a little better.

"I told you about the booby traps I was going to set. I just need a little more time. . . ."

"And I told you to forget it!" Clay commanded. "I'll see to the protection of this family, Sophie McClellen. You insult me every time you do it yourself. Now I don't want you hauling any trees." Clay's tone grew increasingly horrified, "Especially in your condition."

Sophie didn't think he'd heard her right. She'd already hauled the trees. And most of the rocks. She'd let Hector do the heavy lifting of course. She was determined to try and explain again. The man really needed to know where the booby traps were for his own good.

He swung her back up into his arms as if that was the only way he was going to let her move from now on. His strong arms around her

distracted her from pressing the point. He bounced her just a bit as he headed for the house humming to himself. Sophie wasn't sure, but she thought she recognized "Bringing in the Sheaves."

As he hoisted her up the steps, he said, "I can't wait to tell the girls."

Sophie warned darkly, "There's only two possible ways they'll react."

Clay's forehead furrowed with concern. "What are those?"

"They'll either laugh or cry. Maybe both."

"It'll be laugh," Clay said with a firm nod of his head. "They wouldn't dare break rule number one."

They cried all over him.

And with three of them on his lap at once, Clay couldn't escape. Sophie said they were crying because they were happy. Clay thought that was just a plain waste of salt and water. He reminded them that they had promised to only cry if they were stung by a bee or the like, but they cried anyway.

He went straight to work building a rocking chair, and Sophie was sitting in it by the end of the day. After some worry on his part, Clay decided it was okay for Sophie to hold Laura on her lap as long as she didn't stand up holding her. Sophie kept smiling a sweet, mysterious smile that made his palms sweat, even while he couldn't take his eyes off of her.

That look also made him want to run for the bunkhouse and the men, people he understood. But he couldn't leave her for fear she'd quit resting and hurt the baby or pick up one of the crying girls. So he kept watch of his contrary wife and took charge of the overflowing tears. He held his girls, and even though he ended up with a soaked shirtfront, it was the sweetest night of his life.

"It's all set, boss." Percy rubbed the grizzle on his chin and groaned as he sat down at the fire. Eli handed him a cup of coffee.

Judd slapped the cup out of Eli's hand, and the boiling liquid splattered over Eli's pants and shirt. Eli danced away screaming, tearing at his clothes.

"Tell me whatcha found out," Judd demanded. "You can rest later."

Percy clenched his jaw and Judd waited, almost hoping for a fight. He was keyed up from the long hours of idle waiting. He'd called off the vigilante raids for the time. He didn't want to leave the area, and he didn't want to risk being recognized, leaving him and a band of restless outlaws cooling their heels in a rough camp.

The whiskey had run dry. The coffee was low. The cards were all marked, and some of the dumber ones had gambled all their earnings away and were pushing for another strike. Judd had enjoyed beating a few of them senseless when they pushed him too hard, but he couldn't do it often. Some of the men had taken off and hadn't come back. He'd started this with twenty hardened men. Most of them had been with him for two years. Since they'd started stalking McClellen, he was down to a dozen.

It wasn't just the restlessness or the fighting that had made the men take off. It was when they'd found out Judd intended to kill Sophie McClellen. There were men who would kill their own father for a chaw of tobacco. Men who would sell out their best friend for the cash on a WANTED poster. Men who would back-shoot a preacher for the contents of a collection plate. But they wouldn't touch a woman.

Women were too rare in the West. It was in many a man's nature to protect a woman, and nothing anyone would say or do could make him go against his nature.

Eli wasn't such a man and neither was Harley. Judd had worried about that because Harley was a quiet man who kept to himself a lot. But Judd had mentioned Sophie McClellen being able to put them all in a hangman's noose, and Harley had stayed put and listened in on the planning.

Now the first part of the planning was done. Percy was back with

his report, and Judd would be hanged if he'd wait while the man had a cup of coffee to hear what he'd learned.

"He's got two men standing watch all night in such a way they can see down on the house. McClellen always takes the last shift before sunup. I've figured a way to sneak up on him and catch him flat-footed." Percy wiped the coffee away that had spilled on him.

"Why sneak up on him?" Judd asked brusquely. "Why not go in guns a'blazin'?"

Percy shook his head. "We need to do it quiet iffen we can, 'cuz the hands'll come a'boiling up that hill if there's any sign of trouble. Since we took those potshots at McClellen t'other day, the whole place is on a hair trigger."

Judd noticed Harley move restlessly when Percy mentioned the way they'd tried to dry gulch McClellen.

Jesse, one of the men who'd come from scouting with Percy, added, "There's army men among the hands and only a few that'd be called green. Even the green ones are game."

"We can't all go," Percy said. "Just a small group. Any more and we'd make too much noise."

"That whole bunch is mighty salty," Harley said. "They'll come up fightin' sure as anything."

Judd grunted. He gazed into the campfire and thought about that land. It was his. He'd claimed it in his belly a long time ago, and he didn't intend to give it up now. "Get some rest, Percy. I want you and Jesse and two others to go tomorrow night. We're gonna have this finished. I'm sick of waiting."

"I'll go along, boss," Harley said quietly.

"You're staying here." The closer they got to their goal and the tougher the McClellen outfit shaped up, the more Judd wanted Harley's quick gun and cool head at his back. "I don't want to risk being seen myself and that goes for you, too, Harley. We sit this one out. But I promise you'll be in on it when we get rid of Mrs. McClellen. I'm gonna enjoy shutting that woman's mouth for good."

Judd felt the restlessness of the men. He shouldn't have reminded them of what was in store for Sophie McClellen. No one left the campfire though, so they accepted it.

"Can I have some coffee now, boss?" Percy asked.

Judd almost sneered, but he controlled himself. By the time he was done training these men, they'd ask his permission before they so much as scratched an itch. "Yeah, have your coffee then get some rest. Tomorrow's the beginning of taking back what's mine."

FIFTEEN

Sophie was an honest woman. She prided herself on it.

Of course pride was a sin. And didn't the Bible say a sin was a sin? No difference between 'em? So telling a few lies kept her pride in check and therefore kept her humble.

Sophie found she couldn't quite let her mind make peace with that bit of foolishness. So she tried harder.

While lying was one sin, pride and the lack of humility were two. So she was ahead. She rolled a rock toward the pile and decided she was on to something.

Then she caught herself. Was a lack of humility the same as pride? Sophie shrugged and lifted the rock in place. If it was, her sins were a tie. Six and one, half a dozen of the other. Or rather, one of one and one of the other since she wasn't committing six sins after all. Why make things worse than they already were?

So since one sin was what she didn't want to do, and the other sin was what she *did* want to do, she decided to just do as she wanted.

Anyway, she didn't really consider finishing up her traps as lying. Yes, Clay had ordered her not to do it, but he'd gotten distracted by the girls' excitement over the baby before he managed to wring a "Yes, my lord and master" out of her. And since she'd fully intended to refuse to make a promise, it wasn't her fault the man issued his orders then got sidetracked.

She would have told him, straight into his teeth, that she was going

177

to go ahead and finish what she started, but she didn't bother. Silence was just her way of trying to keep her husband happy. She sighed deeply as she heaved another rock onto the stack without disturbing Laura, who was strapped to her back. It seemed like she'd spent her whole life trying to keep one husband or another happy.

Great! Now *she* was making it sound like she'd had a dozen of them.

"It's not that I don't think he'll get to it, girls," she explained carefully because the girls knew how Clay felt—in fact he'd given them a stern talking-to about taking the load off of Sophie's shoulders until after the baby came—and more and more they were taking his side in things.

"It's that I feel pushed to hurry. I can't forget the men shooting at us. Those tracks prove they're nearby, and it's riding me to have everything in place. I've been sitting in the house all week waiting for your pa to get done with the cattle, but it's driving me crazy. I just can't sit in the house stitching away on trousers of all things—for myself and you girls—while the whole family is in danger."

"I like wearing trousers." Sally tugged at the full-legged riding skirt. "I think all of Pa's ideas are good 'uns."

Sophie wasn't about to admit it, but she liked wearing pants herself. She looked down at the brown broadcloth that she'd cut wide enough to look like a skirt. She marveled at how much easier it made everything. "We'll just fill this one last trap with rocks and then we'll leave it go. I promise I won't sneak around anymore after today."

Beth snorted as she hefted a rock onto the travois they'd rigged on Hector. "You shouldn't oughta be out here, Ma. I've checked, and there's none of them varmints standing watch right now, but what if one comes while we're in the middle of things?"

"Hector will give us a warning of trouble." Sophie glanced at the stubborn old mule doubtfully while she rolled another rock in place. She dusted her hands together in satisfaction. "I'd say we only need one more load after this one and we'll be done."

"It's not just the varmints watching us. I don't think you should be carrying such heavy loads." Sally laid her smaller rock on top of the teetering pile. "Those rocks you're hefting weigh almost as much as I do, and you'd never think of carrying me around."

"Well, now, Sally honey, if these rocks would sprout a pair of legs like you have, I promise I'd make 'em walk."

Elizabeth—the animal lover, the nurse, the little girl who wanted to take care of the whole world—said, "The point is you might get hurt. Or you might hurt the baby. I never thought about lifting heavy loads being dangerous, but Pa says it is."

"Beth, your pa doesn't know the first thing about babies. He's just worried about me, which is real nice of him, and so he's trying to take care of me. But he's just guessing about me not lifting things."

"It makes sense to me, Ma," Beth insisted.

"Don't you remember what it was like when Laura was on the way?" Sophie balanced her rock on the load and decided this one was full enough.

"I remember we moved into the thicket." Beth threw the straps over Hector's head. She chirruped to get him moving to where the fallen log was resting against a brace.

"Do you remember I carried everything I could out of this house and sneaked down through the thicket on foot to stash it in the shack we moved into? I took two or three trips a night, carrying everything—even the tables and chairs—on my back because the shortcut trail we had to take was too steep for Hector. I did that for most of a month. All while doing the chores around the ranch every day and hunting and cooking for you girls. I worked ten times as hard as I am now, all with Laura getting big in my belly." Sophie walked along behind Hector, carefully concealing the travois tracks.

"I know." Beth shook her head. "You did it, and you and Laura survived it. But that doesn't mean you weren't plumb lucky. Now we got Pa here to take care of us, and I say we oughta let him. There's still plenty for us to do."

They reached the braced tree trunk and started piling the rocks behind it. Sally attached the hemp rope to the brace and ran it down the hillside. She covered it with dirt and dead leaves as she went.

Sophie looked at the booby trap with satisfaction. "We've got time for one more load before dark. Then, I'm going to scout higher up the trail and check the spots those men have been watching from, while you girls go down and get the evening meal started. I'll be back before Pa, but if he shows up, we can honestly say you girls cooked supper and I went for a walk. All honest. All just to suit him."

Beth rolled her eyes at Sophie, and Sophie knew her little girl was growing up.

They loaded rocks one last time, dragged them across the steep, treacherous face of the bluff, and unloaded them. Sophie transferred Laura to Beth's back, pulled the shotgun out of the saddle boot, and sent the girls home riding Hector.

As they walked away, Sophie heard Sally say, "It sure is a shame about men having all those muscles."

Beth was dusting out the tracks Hector left behind. She looked up from the ground. "Why's that?"

Sally's shoulders slumped, " 'Cuz we could sure stand to have some help thinking around this place."

"Ain't that the truth," Beth replied gloomily.

Sophie decided she was going to have to quit including the girls in her sneaking. She was teaching them all the wrong lessons. Since she had to keep them with her all the time, she supposed what it amounted to was she was going to have to quit sneaking altogether and rest the way Clay kept telling her to.

Rest. She had heard that word out of Clay's mouth so many times she was hearing it in her sleep. In fact, she was quite certain that she'd been awakened last night to the sound of Clay's voice whispering into her hair, "Rest, rest, rest," like some kind of chant. She hoped she'd dreamed it. Otherwise, her husband was getting weird.

It went against the grain, but Sophie knew she had to start minding

him better, for the girls' sake. And she'd do it, just as soon as all this mess with the night riders was settled. As always, when she thought of all her shortcomings as a wife and mother, all she could do was think, *Help me, help me, help me.*

As surely as he knew his name and his face and his God, Adam knew it was time.

"Buff?" Luther jumped to his feet, in front of the hat full of fire in their tiny, concealed camp.

"Huh?" Buff swigged at his coffee.

"Put out the fire. We gotta ride."

Buff didn't even ask why.

"I've been watchin' you fer days, McClellen, an' now we're to the end of it." Percy sidled from the base of one tree to the next. He knew just what trail McClellen always followed. He knew just what time of day to strike. Judd had told them to wait till just before dawn, but Percy was hankering for a whiskey and maybe a kind word from one of the saloon girls. If he could finish this now, he'd have the whole evening ahead with nothing to do. He might not even tell Judd he'd done things his own way, Judd being extra cranky these days.

McClellen always rode down to his evening meal a little after the other hands. He was easier pickings right now than when he'd be standing watch in the night.

Percy hunkered down just uphill of where McClellen always appeared, pulled his Arkansas Toothpick out of the knife sheath slung down his back, and checked the razor-sharp edge. Percy could nail a fly, dead center, from twenty feet.

He could kill McClellen quick and quiet, just like he'd been told. The other three men were lying back, waiting for the morning hours. Percy told 'em to sit tight whilst he did some scouting.

Percy had to stifle a chuckle when he thought of how he'd go awalkin' into camp, calm as you please, and say, "Let's go to town, boys. I've done in McClellen, and we've got nothing to do all night but celebrate!"

He settled in, quiet as a waiting sidewinder.

Clay enjoyed the ache of his tired muscles. He'd pushed hard today, but he'd gotten the last of the cattle rounded up. He was going to spend tomorrow branding the last of them, and then the next day he'd move them down to the lower range.

After that, he planned to spend every hour he could squeeze out of a day seeing to the chores his little wife wanted done around the place.

He grinned when he imagined how it would be when Sophie started getting round with his baby. Something caught hard right around his heart when he pictured another little girl-child to add to his brood of pretty daughters.

Then he thought of a roughhousing little boy to torment the girls and tag along after his pa, and he liked the thought of that, too. Clay didn't figure he could lose.

He began drifting down off the high bluffs toward the ranch house. As he rode along lost in thought, he thanked God for all he'd found when he went hunting for his brother. He thought of all the ways a man could mess up raising his children. The thought scared him almost as much as crying girls did.

He didn't make a sound as he prayed, *Help me be a good father to these young 'uns, Lord. Help me.*

Sophie eased her way up the hill. The bluff was so steep, it was slow going. She moved silently and slowly over a particularly slippery spot, careful not to set any little stones rolling and make a noise. She got to a level stretch and stood upright for the first time in a while.

The whole world spun around. She was only vaguely aware of falling forward into a mesquite bush as everything went black.

Percy froze when he heard brush rustle. It didn't come from where he expected to see McClellen. If someone else was around, he might not get his killin' done till breakfast.

A second passed and then another. The rustling stopped after that one slight sound, and Percy began to ease back from his spot. The sound he'd heard was fabric on brush. It wasn't a deer. He knew the woods better than that.

He shifted without making a sound, sliding from hiding place to hiding place. Sweat broke out on his forehead. Someone was out there. Someone was stalking him just like he'd been stalking McClellen. He decided waiting till morning suited him after all.

He began to rise from his crouched position when he saw McClellen emerge from the trees. Percy had moved farther than he intended, but McClellen sat there on his horse, not looking left nor right. As ripe for plucking as a sleeping goose. Percy pulled his Toothpick out of the sheath hanging in the center of his back, stopped breathing to steady himself, and let fly.

Out of the corner of his eye, Clay saw movement in the bushes. He straightened his legs to raise himself up higher. A blow hit him hard in the shoulder, and even more than the white hot pain, an instinct for survival sent him crashing to the ground on the downhill side of his horse. Facedown on the ground, he fumbled for his six-shooter, but his right arm wasn't working. A quick glance told him there was a knife lodged in his shoulder. He reached across with his left hand, but before he could grab his gun, cold steel pressed up against the back of his neck.

"Don't move, McClellen. Don't even twitch."

Clay heard the sharp *click* of the gun's hammer being pulled back. He recognized it for a rifle, and he knew he was going to die. He braced himself to fight, knowing he didn't want to die like this, flat on his belly with a gun at his back. He had to reach across the entire length of his body to grapple for the gun. He knew he was going to lose.

"It's you who doesn't want to twitch, old man." Sophie jacked a shell into the chamber of her rifle.

The pressure eased on Clay's neck, and with a single lightning move, he turned and grabbed the outlaw's gun.

Clay stood up, holding the gunman's weapon in his left hand. Sophie stood directly behind the man who'd been fixing to shoot him in the back. Her own weapon jabbed into his dirty neck.

"Clay, you're bleeding." In a voice so sharp it could peel the hide off a grizzly bear, Sophie snapped, "Back away from my husband right now."

Worried as she was, Clay watched his wife keep her senses enough to stay out of reach of the man who'd attacked him as she circled to his side.

Before she could get to him, Clay reached up and pulled the knife out of his arm.

Sophie gasped. "Be careful."

The pain of pulling the knife out almost buckled his knees, but he ignored it. There were more important things to do.

"It wasn't deep. It just caught the skin." Clay looked at the knife that had hit him. It was razor sharp and thin as a nail. "This is nice. I

reckon I've always wanted a knife like this."

The man stood in front of them, looking side to side like a wild animal hunting a bolt-hole.

"You're not going anywhere old man"—Clay aimed his gun straight at the outlaw's black heart—"except into Mosqueros to talk to the sheriff."

"We don't think that's such a good idea, Major." A second man came out of the brush. A third and fourth were just a few paces behind him. All three of them had rifles. All the rifles were pointed at Clay.

"Percy, we were getting right worried about you." One of the men stepped in front of the others.

"Right nice to see you and the boys, Jesse." A sneer twisted Percy's face. "Talking to the sheriff is a bad idea. We didn't come for naught but you McClellen, but we'da needed to see to your wife by and by. So it might as well be now."

"Yep." Jesse glanced at Sophie but looked right back at Clay, as if Sophie wasn't part of this standoff. "She's seen us now for sure. We can't let the little lady walk away."

"You may not be the ones walking away," Sophie said.

Clay realized that they hadn't been watching her, and now she had that nasty old shotgun raised and pointed straight at them. Clay felt a surge of pride in his feisty little wife. Then, in the next second, he felt sick. There was no way he and Sophie were going to get through this without getting bloody—either getting shot themselves or shooting someone else. He'd been to war. He knew what it cost a man to kill. He didn't want to do it again, and he didn't want Sophie to live with killing on her conscience. But they had to fight, or these prowling wolves would kill both of them and Clay's unborn child. Then they might turn their murderous eyes on his girls.

"She's got a shotgun, Jesse." Percy watched Sophie now.

All four men went rigid. Clay knew every one of them had seen the damage a shotgun could do at close range.

Percy stood between the three men and the McClellens. "There's two of them and four of us. And that little lady doesn't have the guts to pull the trigger on that cannon she's aholdin'."

The other men turned their attention back to Clay, which is how he wanted it. He thought with grim amusement that Percy was standing in a direct line of fire between all of them. Clay looked straight at Percy. "Whoever else dies here today, you're gonna be the first to go."

Clay didn't mean it. He had no intention of wasting a shot on an unarmed man. But Percy seemed to be giving orders, so if he backed down, they might all think twice. That was the only way everyone could come out of this alive.

"Four agin' two, and one of 'em a gutless, little female," Percy said with a cackling laugh. "I'd say that makes you purely outgunned, McClellen."

"Guess again, you low-down polecat," Adam roared from out of the trees. Adam raised his gun and took aim at the unarmed man closest to his Sophie. Fury such as he'd never known cut through his soul.

He gripped William's gun until the carved stock cut into his hands. He'd spotted horses and this rifle on a sling on the saddle. He knew he'd found the cowards who had killed his friend.

He'd taken the gun and slipped through the woods in time to listen to that murderous scum threaten his own sweet Sophie. Adam squeezed slowly on the trigger. *Revenge.* The time was now. It stood to reason that if the one man was with the lynching party, then they all were. From his vantage point, he could open up on them and take them all.

Vicious satisfaction burned low in his gut. His finger tightened. His finger trembled on the trigger. He had killed in the war. It was a horrible knowledge to carry around inside a man—the fact that he'd taken another life. Then in his mind's eye he saw William and Moses and Dinky. Swinging. Lifeless. Someone had to pay for them. These men would go on killing until someone stopped them. He aimed at the unarmed man's black heart, then he looked at Sophie.

She stood there, so fearless. His Sophie had always been tougher than any woman should need to be. Adam's devotion to her offset some of his rage when he thought of his girl witnessing the destruction Adam wanted to rain down on these brutal men.

And he thought of her call for help. The call God had allowed him to hear. Would God speak like that to a man only to bring him to this place of murder? Because killing the unarmed man would be murder. There was no other word for it.

Adam's anger still battled for supremacy, but there was Sophie. And there was God.

With a sudden jerk of his hand, Adam eased off the trigger. He'd still have his revenge. There would be other chances. But for now he would try and end this standoff without bloodshed.

His unexpected voice froze the group. "With me there's three of us. That makes us even, 'cuz you got a man without a gun. And I've got an angle on all of you. Every man jack of you is gonna die where he stands if you don't drop your weapons." Adam couldn't keep the cold amusement out of his voice when he added, "And don't you ever think Sophie don't have what it takes to pull that trigger."

Clay saw Sophie's head come up. She never took her eyes off the men who had attacked them. Her shotgun never wavered. But Clay knew from the gleam in her eyes that she recognized the voice.

He looked back at the men who had waylaid them and saw they still weren't sure. They weren't ready to back down yet.

"Make it five to three," another voice growled from the opposite side of the clearing from the first voice.

"Luther, is that you?" Clay asked in disbelief.

"It's me, boy." There was a sharp *crack* of a rifle shell being levered into a chamber. "Let me see some hands in the air. I hain't a askin' twice."

"Buff?" Clay's heart lifted. "Buff, you, too?"

187

"It's me, boy."

"We had a hankerin' to see you, so we drifted down Texas way." Luther sounded closer, and the brush rustled under his approach. "Looks like we picked ourselves a good time."

It was too much for the outlaws. Guns dropped to the ground. Clay shoved Percy toward the three men and frisked all of them for hidden guns and knives. He found a few.

A middle-aged black man, wearing only a pair of tattered trousers, stepped out of the woods. Sophie lay her shotgun aside and turned toward him. "Adam? Adam, I can't believe it's you!"

Sophie took a couple of running steps, then stopped. She turned unsteadily away from Adam. "Clay?" She sounded bewildered.

"Sophie, what in tarnation are you doing way up here all alone? I told you to stay at the house and rest." Clay saw Buff and Luther come straggling out of some brush. Clay tipped his head at the men they'd caught. "Watch 'em."

"Clay, could we talk about. . .about. . ." Her voice dwindled to nothing.

He strode toward his disobedient little wife. "Talk about what, Sophie?"

She went pale as a ghost. "Help me."

Clay caught her before she hit the ground. Adam was one step farther away, but he was at Sophie's side immediately.

Luther, busy hog-tying Percy, said to Buff, "That's her. That's whose been a-callin' me all this while."

"Figured." Buff finished off one man, bound hand and foot, and started another.

Clay turned to look over his shoulder, when Percy hollered, "Hey, not so tight!"

Luther leaned over him and growled, "Now's not the time to complain, you yellow-bellied, back-shooting, would-be lady killer."

Percy quit whimpering in the face of Luther's venom and sank against the ground.

Clay knew Buff and Luther had things in hand, so he lowered Sophie gently to the forest floor. He brushed her disheveled hair back off of her forehead. Adam knelt across from him, studying Sophie.

Her eyes fluttered open before either of them could speak. "Did I faint again?"

The fear that had burned Clay when she collapsed turned into a feeling he was way more comfortable with—rage. He roared, "Again? Again! When did you faint before? And what are you doing up here?"

"Now don't go. . ." Adam looked at Clay for the first time. "I—I—" He gathered himself. "Mr. Edwards, sir. I thought you were someone else. That is. . .I'm glad to see you. I hope I haven't overstepped myself by coming home thisaway. I know you said I wasn't to come back and make a nuisance of myself with Sophie. I'll just be movin' on through. Please don't take me being here out on Sophie or the young 'uns, sir."

Sophie rubbed her face. "This isn't Mr. Edwards, Adam. This is my new husband."

Adam looked doubtfully at Sophie. He patted her softly on the head and spoke as if she were a little child, and not a particularly bright child at that. "Why, sure it's Mr. Edwards. I can see that plain as day."

Sophie sat up, and Clay pushed her right back down on her back. The fact that she let him told Clay just how bad she was feeling.

"This isn't Cliff," Sophie said to Adam. "Cliff died a couple of years ago. This is Clay."

"You reckon this is why God's been tellin' me and Buff to come see you, Clay?" Luther had a sling on his rifle. He hung it across his back while he worked on tying up their captives. "Just to wrangle with these hombres?"

Clay looked over his shoulder. "God told you to come here?"

Luther nodded.

"Iffen this is what God wanted us to do, can we go back now?" Buff asked Luther.

"Not sure. Better keep listenin' fer a while."

"Yer hearin' voices in yer head," Percy jeered. "That makes ya crazy."

Jesse laughed, then grunted.

Clay looked around to see what caused the grunt, but all he saw was Buff busily binding him.

"Shut his mouth whilst you're at it, Buff," Luther said.

Buff pulled Jesse's neckerchief up and tucked it in.

"Adam, what happened to you?" Sophie asked.

Clay turned back at the alarm in Sophie's voice. She was reaching for Adam, and that's when Clay saw Adam had been shot—not too long ago.

Adam caught her hand and stopped her from touching his wound. "I'm fine, Sophie girl. And just so you know, God's been nagging at me, too. Something fierce. I've heard you purt near every time you've called out."

"Called out?" Sophie shook her head. "What did I call out?"

"Help me," Luther and Adam said at exactly the same second.

Clay looked at Sophie, and they both said, "God?"

Luther and Adam stared at each other for a long moment.

"The last time, it was Clay. Heard it plain as day, and we were miles off." Luther pushed his furred cap back on his bushy, shoulder-length head of hair and sniffed. "Guess God let me hear both of 'em whilst Adam only heard one."

Adam shrugged, stopped looking at Luther, and turned back to Sophie. Clay had a little dig of annoyance at the adoring way Sophie looked at Adam. She'd come close to looking at him like that a few times.

"About Cliff, Sophie, I don't know why you fell down just now, maybe from the upset or something. But I can see that Cliff is here beside you."

"No, you don't understand, Adam. Cliff died."

Adam looked worried and started inspecting Sophie's head for bumps.

"I married Clay just a short time ago." Sophie patted Adam's work-scarred hands.

"It's not such a short a time!" Clay caught Sophie's hands so she'd quit fawning over Adam. "I've had time to buy a ranch and corral a herd. Time to find out I'm a hand at running a ranch. Time to start a baby growing in you."

"A baby?" Adam smiled, but then his smile faded. "I'm right sure it'll be a boy this time, Mr. Edwards. It's just bound to be."

Clay started to tell Adam again that he wasn't Cliff, but then he remembered what he'd started to ask Sophie. "What are you doing up here? I told you to stay in the house. You could have been shot! If Adam, Buff, and Luther hadn't come along, you could have been killed."

Clay was so furious that he wanted to throttle her, except killing her would have to wait till later. Right now he was too busy keeping her alive.

"A young 'un, eh?" Luther sounded proud, like he'd arranged it himself. "Congrats, boy."

Buff chuckled, and Clay glared at them over his shoulder. "We don't have time to talk about the baby right now."

He stood with Sophie cradled in his arms. "Buff, Luther, you got 'em under control?"

There was no answer, which Clay deserved. If Buff and Luther were having trouble, they would have mentioned it. It gave him a jolt to realize just how chatty he'd gotten in the last few weeks, living with a house full of women. He looked over his shoulder and saw that they'd not only bound and gagged the varmints, they'd hunted up their horses. Luther grunted from the effort of hoisting Jesse facedown across a saddle.

"Let's go down to the house," Clay said to Adam.

"Yes, sir, Mr. Edwards, sir."

"I'm not Cliff. Sophie isn't lying to you."

"Why, I know as sure as I'm standing here that Sophie would never lie, Mr. Edwards." Adam followed Clay to his horse, as if he wanted to be handy to catch Sophie when Clay dropped her. "But I'm thinking she might be a bit overset from all this commotion, and it mixed up her thinking. Don't be mad at her for forgetting you. There's no call to be angry with her. I'm sure everything will come back to her real soon."

Clay hung on to his patience. This was the second time Adam had referred to Cliff's temper and that Cliff aimed that temper at his wife and children often enough that Adam was trying to placate him.

"I'll explain everything to you once we get home." Clay's Appaloosa stood with its reins dangling. Clay shifted Sophie around so he could catch the horse. "For right now we need to get my disobedient, little wife home so she can *rest*."

SIXTEEN

Sophie needed to get home all right. But she had no intention of resting or doing anything else Clay told her to do.

And she didn't like him calling her *disobedient* either!

Before she could tell him so, Clay asked, "Where'd you tie up Hector?"

Sophie got very busy straightening her riding skirt. Clay leaned down so he was in her line of vision. "Do you mean to tell me you climbed all this way on foot? You're miles from the cabin!" Clay looked like he wanted to explode.

Sophie sighed and braced herself.

Instead of hollering at her, he shook his head with disgust and set her up on his Appaloosa. He was very gentle, considering his clenched jaw and the bright red color of his face.

She would have explained to him that she couldn't rightly go to bed when she had company, but Clay turned his attention to getting Adam a ride.

"I'll be glad to walk down this ol' hill, Mr. Edwards," Adam said.

Clay swung up behind Sophie and pulled her onto his lap. He growled at Adam, "Call me Clay."

Adam took a worried look at Sophie, where she lay in her husband's arms. "Clay it is."

Sophie saw that Buff and Luther had led four horses out of the woods after they'd tied up the outlaws. Clay's two friends had full beards and were dressed in fur and leather. They looked like every mountain man Sophie had ever heard tell of. They'd been throwing a man over each horse, until they noticed Adam was on foot.

Buff unceremoniously tossed Jesse and Percy on the same blue roan and jerked his thumb at the sorrel. "Ride this 'un."

Adam took a couple of steps toward the now unoccupied horse then stopped. "Let's toss 'em both on the sorrel, and I'll ride the roan."

"What difference does it make which horse you ride, Adam?" Sophie asked.

"The difference is the roan is mine." Adam strode toward his horse.

For the first time, in the fading light of evening, Sophie got a look at Adam from behind. "What happened to your back?"

Adam grabbed both men by the scruff of the neck, dragged them off the horse, and let them fall to the ground with a little more force than was necessary. He didn't answer Sophie's question. He just led the sorrel over beside the men.

Adam didn't ask for help. Sophie couldn't remember him ever asking for help. But Sophie could see that Adam was taxing the limits of his strength. Clay's friends stepped in and loaded the men before Adam could get to them.

Adam went back to the roan, and the horse whickered softly at him, clearly greeting an old friend. Adam petted the horse's neck. "Missed ya, Blue."

Then Adam turned to look between Clay and his two friends. "There's a C-shaped scar under this horse's belly, and there's a ROCKING M brand on the other side of her. . .the side I haven't seen yet. She's my horse. That brand is registered to me."

None of the men bothered to check out the scar on the horse's belly, but Sophie could see the ROCKING M from where she was sitting. She could also see the look in Adam's eyes. Cold—bitter cold—and furious.

Adam had endured Cliff's constant criticism until the ranch was well started. Then, when he knew Sophie and the girls had a solid roof

over their heads and land and cattle to support them, Adam had left because Cliff had taken his sullen dislike of Adam out on Sophie and the girls. Adam, who was so politely confused over Clay looking like Cliff, was a man of patience and kindness and wisdom. The cold in his eyes didn't go with any of it.

Buff tugged on the edges of his deerskin coat. "Stolen?"

"Stolen by the men who lynched my three partners, shot me in the back, and laid a whip on me for the first time in my life."

Sophie gasped.

"Not too many black men could make that claim. But I could." Adam ran his hand over the gunshot in his side. "Till I ran afoul of this gang."

Clay's arms tightened around Sophie, or she might've jumped off the horse and gone to Adam right then. Clay whispered to her, "Leave it for now."

Adam swung up on the roan's back. "This blanket strapped on the back of this saddle is mine, and the Winchester I carried out of the woods with me belonged to my partner, William. He carved it. I just took it off the sorrel's saddle a few minutes ago."

"Reckon that makes it yours." Luther slipped a foot into his stirrup.

"These four ain't all the men. Four alone could never have taken us. There were at least twenty." Adam gave the prisoners a contemptuous glare. "Back-shootin' cowards, every one of 'em!"

"There were around twenty men in the posse that came after Cliff." Sophie twisted in Clay's strong arms to keep her eye on Adam. The look in his eyes frightened her.

Luther settled on his horse. "Four down, sixteen to go. We'd best hang around for a spell, Buff."

Buff grunted.

Adam turned to Sophie. The icy rage faded from his eyes as he looked between her and Clay. She saw concern plain on his face. She had to hold back a smile.

"Clay is Cliff's twin." Sophie patted her husband on the shoulder as if that would somehow convince Adam. "He came hunting news of his brother and stayed on to help me when he found out his brother was dead."

"Cliff never had no family, Sophie girl." Adam spoke soothingly as someone who was facing a lunatic with an ax might. "You 'member how he talked about it, what with wanting a son so all-fired bad?"

Clay tensed behind her, but Sophie didn't think much about what Adam said. Cliff's wish for a son had been a lament made long and loud with no care for who might hear. She patted Clay's arm to get him to relax and continued trying to persuade Adam. "Cliff and Clay were separated when they were very young. Cliff didn't know he had a brother."

Adam studied Clay for a long moment. "When I came into the area a few days ago, I scouted the lay of the land. I saw you from a distance. I took you to be other than Mr. Edwards by the way you sat a horse and worked the ranch, and I never got close enough to see different. Then, up close, I decided I'd been mistaken, and Mr. Edwards had just picked up Texas ways at last. But I was right all along. You're not him."

Sophie heard a snort from Adam that sounded. . .satisfied. She didn't want to think about that, so she thought of her husband. He'd been stabbed. She couldn't believe she'd forgotten.

"Let me look at your arm, Clay."

"Twenty men in a lynch mob chasing after him, and Clay has to stop to get a scratch looked at." Luther tugged on his reins and the saddle creaked as he pointed his horse down the mountain. "This might be more fun than the Rockies after all."

Buff chuckled and mounted up.

"With twenty men on our trail?" Adam asked shortly.

There was a second of silence. "Not twenty anymore," Buff said.

Adam looked at the prisoners hanging across their horses. "Sixteen."

"Sixteen to four," Luther said. "That's only four apiece."

"Fair fight then." Adam nodded.

Sophie was tearing at the blood-soaked slit in Clay's sleeve. Clay

pulled her away from it and started his horse moving ahead of the others. "I'll keep."

"Clay, don't you think we should bandage it?" Sophie tried to squirm around to see the arm Clay was using to support her back. He'd lifted her on the horse and swung on himself, never showing a bit of pain.

Luther started to laugh.

Clay glared over his shoulder, and the laugh turned into a coughing fit. Then Clay squeezed her so tight it got her attention—and cut off her air. "Hush, woman."

Sophie didn't know what to make of Clay's tone. It was very dictatorial for being so quiet. She hadn't heard him talk like that much lately, not since he'd more or less ordered her to marry him. She considered that his friends might be an undue influence on him. Still, they'd saved her life. She'd have to make allowances.

"We should at least get the bleeding stopped."

It was Buff's turn to cough, and even Adam cleared his throat for a bit too long.

"Sophie McClellen," Clay said so grimly, it got her undivided attention.

"Yes, Clay?" She was surprised she had such an obedient tone at her disposal.

"If you can't keep your mouth shut, what's say we talk about what you were doing up here when I told you to stay in the house and rest!" He'd started out whispering, but by the time he was done, he'd built to a roar.

Sophie looked around to see how Adam and Clay's friends were taking this. Clay had moved out first, so the others were strung out behind them. Clay's broad shoulders blocked her view.

She sat up abruptly, ready to put him in his place. He had no right to speak to her—to humiliate her—like this in front of his friends and Adam. And she wasn't about to lie placidly in his arms while he berated her. Clay didn't let her go, and they had a very brief tussle that she was doomed to lose from the first instant.

Finally she subsided against his chest, exhausted and slightly dizzy from the effort. She had no intention of letting him talk to her like that, and she had no intention of going down to the house to rest. And she would have made that clear to this tyrant she'd married if she could just keep her heavy eyelids from dropping closed.

"Can we please talk about this later?" She didn't mean to be pathetic. She had no respect for the tricks she'd seen women use against men. Her girls cried, but she wasn't prone to it herself. And she didn't bat her eyelashes or pout or nag. But she saw the anger leave Clay's expression, replaced with worry.

"Are you all right? You're not going to pass out again, are you?" His brow furrowed as he studied her face.

That's when Sophie decided a few women's wiles might just be the very thing. "I'm dizzy again. You were right, Clay. I need rest. I should never have gone out so far. I'm sorry I disobeyed you." She looked up at him, and without really meaning to, she was sure she felt her eyelashes bat something fierce. It didn't take much effort to make tears well up in her eyes. All she had to do was think of Clay's wounded arm.

"Please don't shout at me anymore." Sophie buried her head in Clay's chest and hugged him tight around the middle.

Clay's arms closed around her. "I'm sorry I yelled. Just please don't take such chances again. I'm glad you were there this time." He tapped on her chin, and she raised her head to look at him. "You saved my life today, Sophie. Maybe Adam and Luther and Buff woulda come in time, but it woulda been a close thing. So I'm glad you were there. But thinking you might be shot by those men. . ." His arms tightened around her. "Sophie, I—I don't think I could stand it if something happened to you. I want you to quit trying to do so much. Just tell me what you need, and I'll do it for you. I want you to take care of yourself. Please promise me."

Sophie didn't have to fake any tears. They were just there. She reached up and kissed him. She was fully aware that, while she might fail to tell him the exact, whole, absolute, entire truth on occasion,

giving a promise was something else again. She wasn't a woman to break her word. Even knowing that, she didn't hesitate to give it. "I promise, Clay. I'll only do what chores you say I can do. I know you'll take care of me."

Clay looked down at her. He was so worried, so kind. Sophie was ashamed of the sneaking she'd been doing. She was going to have to tell the girls she'd been wrong and see that they didn't learn any bad lessons from their ma. She was going to turn over a new leaf.

She turned her face up, looked at him squarely, and repeated firmly, "I'm going to do as you ask. I promise."

She was going to give the sweet man the wife he deserved.

Clay was going to give his wife the spanking she deserved.

He pulled her close up against his chest so she couldn't see his expression. He was pretty sure that what she'd see was disgust. He was disgusted with himself for tricking the poor, foolish, little female into promising to mind him by using such wily methods as sweet talk and gentle touches.

He was finally figuring it out. Women weren't really that much trouble to manage. They needed to be handled like a fractious horse for the most part. A firm hand mixed with patience, careful training, and a pat now and then.

He'd almost gotten the girls trained to the ways of ranch life. He was very satisfied with their progress working the herd. They'd been hopeless at first, but these last few days all three older girls had begun dropping their loops over running steers. They were coming along faster than he had dared hope.

Now he was starting to make some progress with their headstrong mother. At that moment, he was really glad Sophie was pulled up close because Clay couldn't keep the smile off his face.

As they wound down the steep mountain path, the sun began to drop behind the trees. The night birds sang their songs, and the soft *clop* of the horses' hooves lulled his mule-headed wife into relaxing. He glanced down and saw that avoiding her sharp gaze wasn't necessary. She'd fallen asleep. She was resting just like he'd ordered.

His smiled widened until he almost chuckled out loud as he looked down at her. Her eyelashes brushed across a faint bloom on cheeks he thought were too pale. Her pink lips were slightly pursed until he was tempted to kiss them.

In sleep she was perfect innocence, perfect peace, perfect obedience. He suspected it wouldn't last. But now he knew the trick. Now, today, finally, he'd learned how to handle her—his wife, the green-broke filly.

Clay didn't wake her when he carried her into the house. The girls gave him anxious looks, but he held his finger to his lips and walked on into their bedroom, tiptoeing so his spurs didn't jingle her awake. He lay her down and walked back out.

"We've got three extra men for supper, girls. But we won't be ready to eat for a while. We've got business in Mosqueros."

"Is there something wrong with Ma?" Beth wrung her hands and looked at the bedroom door. "You didn't—I mean, were you upset to find her up there?"

"If you mean did I give your ma's backside such a tanning when I found her on that mountainside that now she's fainted dead away, the answer's no." Clay pulled his leather gloves from behind his belt buckle. "She was just tired and she fell asleep on the ride home."

"Who were the men you brought back draped over the saddles?" Sally peeked out the window.

Mandy and Beth ran to the window and stared out.

Clay wondered why womenfolk had to talk over every little detail of what went on. "Those men tried to waylay me on the trail. The other men who road in with us helped us sort things out. Two of them are old friends of mine, and the other one is Adam. I know your ma has talked about him."

"Ma always spoke kindly of Adam." Sally turned back to Clay.

"That's him? The one with the black skin?"

"That's him." Clay tugged his gloves on.

"Was the sheriff up there with you, too, Pa?" Beth asked.

"No, the sheriff wasn't there." Clay needed to get moving to take the prisoners to town. He didn't have time for chitchat. He struggled to speak calmly because he knew the girls were prone to tears, even with the new house rules. "We'll see him when we take those men into the jailhouse."

"We might be hard-pushed to find food for all of them," Mandy said.

"You'll figure something out." Clay headed for the door.

"Do we need to feed the prisoners, too?" Beth glanced at the pot on the stove.

Clay turned back. "No, of course you don't have to feed them. We'll be leaving them in town."

Sally stared curiously out the window. "What about the sheriff and the banker?"

"What about 'em?" Clay tried to follow their winding female thinking.

"Do we have to feed 'em?" Sally asked.

"Well why on earth would you have to feed them?"

"There's more'n just them. That one's a deputy, and the other's. . .I don't know. We'd best get to peeling taters." Beth turned tiredly from the window.

"You don't have to feed that many people. Just the three I told you about. The others aren't here."

"Yeah, they are, Pa. The sheriff and his deputy and Banker Badje. And a coupla other men." Mandy pointed out the window.

Clay went quickly to the window and saw what had prompted the girls' questions. Sheriff Everett was in the ranch yard, holding one of the dry-gulcher's heads up while he studied his face.

"Why didn't you tell me the sheriff was here?"

"I thought we just did." Beth set the potato aside.

Clay clapped his hat back on his head. "I want your ma to rest, so keep the noise down."

He strode across the yard to greet the newcomers, who were talking with Buff, Luther, and Adam. His ranch hands had started straggling out of the bunkhouse as they finished eating, interested in what was going on.

The sheriff turned as Clay walked up to him. "They told me what went on up on the mountaintop."

"Only a Texan would call that anthill a mountain." Luther shook his head in disgust.

Buff grunted.

The sheriff ignored them both. "These rangers came to town in answer to a telegraph I sent about another matter."

Clay recognized one of the rangers. "Howdy, Tom, I've been meaning to get in touch with you but I haven't had a chance. I've been keeping my eyes open, but I haven't had anything to tell."

Texas Ranger Tom Jackson reached out his hand. "Looks like you been busy." He introduced the other ranger as Walt Mitchell.

"Busy don't begin to describe it." Clay shook both men's hands. "Do any of you recognize these men?"

"I think I've got posters on a couple of 'em." The sheriff studied the men. "I'll take 'em into town and lock 'em up."

Clay jerked his thumb at Percy. "That one threw a knife at me from cover when I was riding down the trail." Clay glanced down at his blood-soaked sleeve. "He was trying to kill me plain and simple. And since he had a gun on him whilst he used his knife, I've got to figure he wanted to kill me quiet."

The rangers' sharp eyes went to the wound on Clay's arm. Clay realized how much it hurt. He didn't have time to fool with it now.

"I was aiming at a grouse," Percy snarled from his awkward position over the saddle.

The whole group turned toward him. He'd pushed the gag out of his mouth, and now it rested between his upper lip and his nose.

"When you messed up my throw, I got mad for a minute," Percy growled. "I wouldn'ta done nothin' to you."

"I reckon he used his knife so they could sneak on down to the house. They said right out loud they were after Sophie, too." Adam crossed his arms and stared with cold eyes at Percy. "I heard it clear as day."

"Percy was the one doing the knife throwing," the man hanging over the horse next to Percy said around his loosened gag. "We didn't know he'd tried to kill someone. We just came along and tried to help out our saddle partner."

"Shut up, Jesse." Percy awkwardly elbowed Jesse. "You're in this just as deep as I am."

"We were there, too, Sheriff." Luther stepped up beside Adam. "It was as cold-blooded as it gets."

"Heard it." Buff nodded in agreement.

"His friends here backed him up all the way, even with Sophie. . ." Clay's voice failed him for a moment as he thought of Sophie, standing in the middle of these cutthroats. He tried again. "Even with Sophie right in the middle of it."

"Ain't too many men low-down enough to kill a woman," Adam said fiercely.

"They were planning to kill her even before I came down that trail," Clay went on. "They said they were planning to see to her sooner or later, so it might as well be now. They said those very words to me before my friends here bought into the fight."

"He"—Luther pointed toward Jesse—"said, 'She's seen us now. We can't let her walk away.'"

The sheriff looked at the men standing around Clay, and they all nodded.

Mr. Badje broke into the conversation. "None of these men was the one who wanted to buy McClellen's land."

"What do you mean buy my land?" Clay raised his eyebrows in surprise. "My land's not for sale."

"I reckon they know that, Clay." Sheriff Everett jerked his head at the outlaws. "Why else would they think they needed to kill you?"

Clay pulled his hat off his head and whacked at his pants. His nostrils filled with the honest scent of sweat and trail dust—a smell he worked hard for and was proud of—while men sneaked around in the woods plotting his death to take what they couldn't earn. "You're saying you're out here about some other man who wants to buy my land?"

"He came into my bank saying he heard the Mead spread was for sale." Badje's arms swung out from his sides. The banker's black suit was wrinkled and dirty, completely out of place with the Western dress of the other men, and in utter contrast to the rough hides and leather clothing of Buff and Luther. "When I told him it had been sold, he went crazy. I thought he was going to attack me, he was so mad."

"He tore up the Paradise about a week ago, too," the sheriff added. "Big man by the name of Judd Mason."

"Judd?" the feminine voice from the house behind them turned them all around in their tracks.

Clay groaned aloud and plunked his hat back on his head. His little filly had taken the bit in her teeth again.

SEVENTEEN

Sophie strode toward the crowd of men. With the sheriff's group and the cowhands and the prisoners, it had grown to the size of a town meeting. She wasn't sure it was safe to take her eyes off her cranky husband, but she had to. What Royce Badje had just said was too important.

"Royce, did I just hear you say his name was Judd?"

"Sophie, I told you to stay in the house and rest." Clay tugged the brim of his hat down until Sophie couldn't see his eyes. "I don't want you out here listening to talk of a man who went crazy mad and tore up saloons. It ain't fittin'."

Sophie didn't even glance his way. She said to the sheriff, "A man called Judd was chasing after Clay on the night I met him. I recognized Judd as the same man who killed Cliff two years ago. This man after our land must be the same man."

"More'n likely." The sheriff's eyes sharpened with interest. "Describe him."

"He was a big man, like Royce said. Rode a horse with a J BAR M brand."

"J BAR M," Adam exploded. "The men who stole my cattle and killed my partners had horses with J BAR M brands."

Sophie again saw the fury in her old friend. She could see it ran deep, and it scared her. She knew the look of vengeance. She'd seen it in Clay. Who was she kidding? She'd seen it in herself.

205

She didn't want Adam to be eaten alive with the thirst for revenge. Silently, in her heart, she said, *Help me.*

Luther turned and looked at her funny. He said rather tiredly, "What now?"

Sophie covered her mouth with her hand as if she could keep her prayers more private by the action. She looked sideways at Adam to see if he was still being directly connected to her prayers. He didn't seem to have heard her, and while that was normal, it worried her. She was afraid his hate was overwhelming the part of him that was open to God.

With a short shake of her head, she remembered why she'd come out here. She threaded her way through the crowd of men to Clay's side and pulled scissors out of her apron pocket. "Hold still while I bandage this."

Clay pulled away from the hand she'd latched on his blood-soaked sleeve. "Confound it woman, it's stopped bleeding now. It'll wait till later."

Sophie turned to the sheriff. "Josiah, would you mind arresting my husband until I can mind this wound?"

"Let her see to it, Clay." Josiah ambled over. "You know better'n to ignore an injury like that for long."

Clay growled under his breath, but he stood still for Sophie's nursing.

"These men we have right now are part of a lynch mob," Luther interjected. "They killed three men, and they had Adam's horse and his partner's gun."

Dead silence descended on the group. While Sophie tried to gently clean and bind Clay's arm, she was adding up all the information just as she could see everyone else was.

Luther walked over to stand beside her. He didn't speak, but she knew he wanted an explanation for her latest prayer.

Finally, into the silence, Ranger Jackson spoke. "It's gotta be the same gang who's done all of it."

Ranger Mitchell added, "It's the vigilantes that have been roaming

these hills for years. We've been looking for them, and it looks like we just swept up a big ol' handful of 'em. That means if Mason is the boss, he's got to be close around here."

"If Mason is interested in the ranch today, he might have killed Cliff all that time ago so he could have it." Clay ignored Sophie prodding at his wound.

"And now he sends men to kill you so he can get it," Royce Badje said.

"Kinda makes you wonder what became of the Mead brothers." Sheriff Everett narrowed his eyes at the bound men.

"It surely does," Ranger Mitchell said.

"It never made sense, them running off and leaving their spread." Badje pulled a white handkerchief out of his back pocket and mopped at beads of sweat that streaked his face in the late summer afternoon.

"The wound isn't deep." Sophie fastened a quick bandage in place. "It just caught the outside edge of your shoulder."

Clay reached over to pat her hand where it lay resting high on his arm. He said softly, so only she could hear, "I know, darlin'. Thanks."

Sophie smiled, and Clay looked like he might say more, maybe say something else nice. For a change. Jackson chose that moment to turn on the men tied over the horses.

With soft menace, Jackson said, "We need to know where you boys have been hiding out."

Percy grunted. "Forget it. We ain't tellin' you nothin'."

"They'll tell us," Mitchell said. "They'll tell us and like it."

"Separate 'em." Ranger Jackson started forward. "I don't want 'em knowing what their friends are saying. We'll see who talks first."

"Ain't none of us got nothin' to say to any of you." Percy struggled with his bonds until he tipped himself off the horse's back. Nobody rushed to break his fall, but Ranger Mitchell did walk over and stuff Percy's gag back in his mouth.

The sorrel pranced sideways, and Mitchell crouched down beside Percy. "The way I see it, a whole lotta things got *almost* done up on that mountain today. When we all start talking to the judge, some of you may have been innocent bystanders backing up a saddle partner, and some of you may be guilty of planning cold-blooded murder."

Ranger Jackson pulled Jesse off the sorrel and let him slump to the ground. "Just 'cuz one of you is riding a stolen horse, another is carrying a stolen rifle, and maybe a third throws a knife at a man from cover and tells a woman he's planning to kill her doesn't mean you all have to hang for it."

"I wasn't even with 'em till a few days ago," Jesse shouted. "I didn't know about no lynching."

Jackson slapped the gag back in Jesse's mouth. "Mitchell, take the one on the buckskin into the barn." Jackson gestured at the gathered ranch hands. "A few of you men go along."

Whitey nodded and took hold of the buckskin's reins.

"Sheriff Everett, I'll let you talk to Jesse. He seems eager to tell you how innocent he is. Go behind the bunkhouse. And take your deputies. We want Jesse here to know for sure he hasn't got the slightest hope of escape."

"C'mon boys," Everett said. "It's always fun to try and see how tough a man is who'll threaten a woman."

Jackson caught the bridle on a mouse gray mustang. It pulled against the firm grip. The metal hasps on the reins clinked as the horse whoofed out a fearful snort. "I'm taking this one behind the house. That way they can't hear what the others say and concoct some kind of story together."

Ranger Mitchell rubbed his chin. "Maybe they should be farther apart, Tom. Whatta ya say? They'll be able to hear if anyone starts screaming or crying or begging for mercy."

All four prisoners turned to look at Mitchell, fear evident on their faces.

Jackson said, "I think that'll only encourage the others—"

"—the ones who ain't screaming yet—" Mitchell put in.

"—to start talking sooner," Jackson finished.

Sophie started rolling up the portion of the bandage she hadn't used. She could tell this was a routine the two rangers had done many times before. But the prisoners didn't seem to think they were being conned. They looked eager to be led a safe distance away so they could start telling all they knew.

Ranger Jackson looked at Percy. "I think I'll let Adam here question you, Percy. He seems to have a powerful mad on him about you, and I don't think it'd be wrong to give him a chance to work that off. Clay can talk to you, too. Maybe it'll make that stab wound in his arm feel a little better. And there's no way you're walking away from any of this, so making you talk isn't necessary." Jackson's words could have left bite marks.

Sophie looked at the furious satisfaction on Adam's face and thought, *Help me.*

A heavy hand rested on her shoulder. She looked at Luther. For all his grizzle and trail dust, she saw kind, understanding eyes.

"We won't let Adam do nothin' what carries hard on his conscience, ma'am," Luther assured her.

Ranger Mitchell started leading the buckskin away. He slipped the gag off the man, and although she couldn't make out the words, Sophie could hear the prisoner talking fast to the ranger.

"Adam is a good man," Sophie said to Luther. "One of the best men I've ever known. But he's so angry. I can see the hunger in him for revenge."

She and Luther watched the sheriff lead another horse toward the bunkhouse.

"I know, and I'm right honored that I'm the one who hears your worries and can step in to help. But he's not the only one here that's wanting vengeance. I see it in Clay."

Sophie's eyes darted to her husband. His attention was squarely on Percy. Clay, Adam, and the remaining hired men had moved away from where Sophie stood with Luther. They surrounded Percy where he lay sprawled, faceup, in the dirt.

She saw the anger Clay had banked down. These were men who had a hand in his brother's death. They had tried to kill him and threatened to kill her. He had it under better control than Adam did, but yes, Clay was very angry.

Ranger Jackson pulled a vicious-looking knife out of his boot and slashed the rope binding Jesse's feet and hoisted him up. He shoved him away from the group.

"It's not just them neither, ma'am. I see it in you, too."

Startled, Sophie looked back at Luther. Their eyes held. After she got over the surprise, she realized there was truth in what he said—a lot of truth. She'd like very much to do some damage to these evil men. "I might feel anger, but I wouldn't do anything to hurt them."

"I know, ma'am, but hatred can burn a hole clear through a person's gut without her ever lifting a hand. Buff and me are here to make sure nothing happens. But it's a man's business, and it might be ugly before it's over. I think it's best if you go on back to the house."

"No. If I'm here they'll control themselves better."

"Or they may shame themselves deeper," Luther said. "It's a poor thing for a man to shame himself in front of a woman he loves."

Sophie looked away from Luther and stared at the ground. She knew he was right. She didn't want to go. She was eager for some revenge of her own. She wanted to see these men get hurt. She wanted to hurt them herself. She whispered aloud, "Help me."

"He is helping you, gal. But you gotta let Him."

Suddenly Sophie felt something give inside her, and she relaxed and smiled at Luther. "I'll go. I trust you to see that nothing's done to that scoundrel that'll hurt these two men of mine."

"I won't fail ya, ma'am." Luther tipped his hat, and Sophie turned and walked back to the house.

When Sophie left, Clay heaved a sigh of relief. At the same time, he

couldn't believe it. The woman had a knack for knowing what he wanted her to do and then doing just the opposite. And right now he wanted her out of the way. Bad.

So it stood to reason she'd stick like a burr to a horse's tail.

He couldn't sort out all his fury. His shoulder ached like fire, and he should beat Percy's face in for that alone. But this man had been party to killing his brother. Clay knew it just from watching the trapped look on Percy's face.

Still, the thing that kept pushing every other thought out of his head was the way they'd threatened Sophie. That's what made him clench his fists. That's what called out to his blood and made it boil.

Reacting to the growing fury, Clay leaned forward to put his hands on Percy. Before he could reach him, Adam had the man by his shirtfront. He hauled Percy to his feet and shook him like a cat shakes a rat to its death.

Two of Clay's hired hands stepped forward and caught hold of Percy's arms. Adam let go of the vermin's shirt and pulled back a powerful fist. Luther moved quickly for an old mountain man. He was suddenly beside Adam. He had the strength of the mountains he'd lived in, too. He caught the flying fist, and with a loud *whack* of flesh against flesh, Luther stopped Adam cold. Then he spun Adam around to face him. Rage flared in Adam's eyes, and Clay wondered if Adam would strike Luther.

Clay saw Adam fight for control and knew it didn't come easy to him. Adam's chest heaved, and he jerked at the hand Luther had imprisoned in his massive grip.

Clay watched Adam's black skin shine with sweat. Muscles bulged on his back and arms as Adam tried to free his hand. He looked to be over forty. His tightly curled hair was salted with gray, and his face had the weathered crow's-feet of a man who had lived all his life in the sun. But his body, bare to the waist, had the corded muscles of a man who worked long, brutal hours wrangling cattle. His expression was shot through with rage.

With all his strength and the added power of his fury, Adam

struggled against Luther. Luther was no taller than Adam, but he was twice as broad and it was all solid muscle earned carving out survival in the northern Rockies.

Adam struggled. Luther held fast. An unstoppable force. An immovable object. Something had to give.

On his best day, Adam would have had trouble besting Luther, and today wasn't close to being Adam's best day. Clay could see the lines around Adam's eyes deepened with pain and fatigue. The bullet hole, low on his right side, still oozed a clear liquid. Clay thought of the ugly stripes on Adam's back. They were a mass of scabs and puckering scars.

"Seems to me," Luther said, "before you beat information out of a man, you oughta at least ask him some questions."

Adam pulled back his other fist, his eyes fastened coldly on Luther.

"Think, man." Luther shook Adam's fist, still clenched in his massive hand. "You don't want to hit me."

Adam jerked his hand away from Luther. "You weren't there. They came onto us in our sleep. Dinky was standing guard, and they back-shot him."

Adam's chest heaved and his eyes blazed with hate. "The shot woke me up, and I saw him fall forward and try to get to his feet. By the time I'd thrown my blanket off, they were all around us. Twenty of 'em. They had whips and clubs. They didn't just hang my friends,"—Adam ran his hands through his coiled hair—"they beat 'em halfway to death first."

"I heard 'em laughing and gloating about how much money our herd would bring. I crawled away into the bushes like a worthless coward. I must have passed out, because when I woke up it was over." Adam added with bitter self-contempt, "I slept through my friends' hangings."

"And why didn't they come after you?" Luther asked quietly.

Adam shrugged. "Reckon they forgot about me in the confusion. Lost count."

Luther prodded him. "This gang has ridden these hills for two years.

No one's had so much as a hint about who they are, and that's mainly because they've never left a witness. And you're telling me they couldn't count to four?"

Adam ignored the question. "I came around and lay there, hiding, and watched my friends twist in the wind, already dead. The men who attacked us were gone. I could see they'd picked over the camp, stolen our supplies. I should have gone after them. I should have given an accounting of myself, even if it meant I died fighting."

"And why didn't you?" Clay had to know.

Clay could see Adam was so completely lost in his memories of the attack that he had to make a huge effort to think past it.

Finally Adam said, "Sophie called me."

Clay shook his head a little, hoping Adam's words would make sense. "She called you?"

"I heard her voice, clear as day."

Luther nodded. "She said, 'Help me.' "

Adam nodded. "My back was ripped open from their whips and they'd shot me. But I heard her, and I knew she needed help. I turned away, left my friends swinging. Didn't even cut 'em down and bury 'em. I started walking to Mosqueros."

"That's what happened to us," Luther said.

"You're telling me that you heard Sophie's voice asking for help, both of you, hundreds of miles from here?" Clay asked. "Hundreds of miles apart from each other?"

Luther nodded.

"Clear as if she were standing by my shoulder," Adam said.

"It was her voice," Luther added. "But I knew it was about you. I knew you needed help, boy."

"How can that be?" Clay wondered.

Adam's head and shoulders drooped as he whispered, "It was God saying I was the answer to Sophie's prayer."

"God let us hear it," Luther said. "And do you think the answer to Sophie's prayers is to beat the tar out of this man?"

Anger sparked in Adam's eyes as he looked from Luther to Percy. "Why not? God is a God of justice."

A hungry satisfaction roared through Clay as he heard Adam's words. Yes, a God of justice. Except, God was more than that. The miracle of what God had done seeped into the roiling hate in his heart and began to settle him. Reluctantly, Clay said into the moment of silence, "But this isn't justice, it's vengeance. And vengeance belongs to God."

"So are you saying we're supposed to let them go?" Adam whirled around to confront Clay. "Let them do as much damage as they want and wait for God to settle for them in the next life?"

"No." Clay didn't want to give up his revenge. "This country has a system of justice. These men have to face the law and its penalties. It's not up to us to hand out punishment for their crimes."

Even as he said it, Clay knew it wasn't what he wanted to do. He sighed. "Leave room for God's wrath. 'Vengeance is mine; I will repay, saith the Lord.'"

"If either of you killed this scum just to make yourselves feel better," Luther said, "that doesn't leave much room for God's wrath, now, does it?"

"It would speed him on his way to God's wrath." Adam crossed his arms.

Clay knew Adam didn't want to give up this chance to hurt the men who had taken so much from him.

At that moment, Ranger Mitchell came out of the barn. He yelled, "I've got the gang's hideout."

Ranger Jackson emerged seconds later from behind the house. "And I've learned most of what they've got planned."

Clay looked down at Percy's fearful expression. "It won't speed him up much. The territorial judge in this part of Texas is almighty fond of hangings."

"Yeah, they should swing from a tree, just like he done my friends."

"Just like they did my brother." Clay looked at Adam.

214

Clay could see that Adam's thirst for revenge could latch on to the vision of Percy in a noose. It wasn't a victory for God. Adam's hate was still in control.

Adam leaned over Percy. "And without me dirtyin' my hands on you one bit. I think you've just earned yourself the noose you've been handin' out to others for the last few years. Then you'll get a chance to meet your Maker and find out what kind of vengeance God has in store for you."

Adam straightened and looked sideways at Clay. "I think that's somethin' I can live with."

"Yeah, so can I." Clay turned to Luther. "Thanks."

Luther grunted. "I should hope you thank me. That's more words'n I've strung end to end in my life."

"He's gotten plumb talkative since your missus started speaking to him," Buff said drearily. "It wears on my ears."

EIGHTEEN

"M a, they're starting to clear out." Sally hung on one window ledge. Mandy was stationed at the other. Beth peeked out the door.

"I told you girls to get away from the windows." Sophie darted over to stand beside Sally. She'd avoided looking out the window, mostly. And she'd tried to keep the girls away. She remembered Luther's words about a man shaming himself in front of the woman he loved and knew that they were true.

Except for the part about love.

Why did Luther think Clay loved her? The very thought made something warm grow in her heart.

Although she was a might too sneaky to be considered truly respectful, and that husband of hers was given to grunting or yelling instead of speaking normally, Sophie thought she and Clay got on nicely enough. But love? She'd been in love with Cliff, and it had hurt. She had adored him, and he'd repaid her with coldness and criticism. No. Love was a very bad idea.

"The sheriff is loading that one on the ground onto his horse." Sally leaned until her nose smudged the window.

"Who were the other men, Ma?" Mandy asked. "The two tall ones."

"They're Texas Rangers," Sophie said.

Mandy quit spying for a second to give Sophie a startled look. "What are Texas Rangers doing here?"

"They're on the trail of the gang who shot at us the other day. The

sheriff and the rangers are hoping to find the rest of them. Then this will finally be over."

"I want things to go back to how they used to be when I was young," eight-year-old Beth said, "when we only had to be afraid of cyclones and rattlesnakes."

Ten-year-old Mandy nodded. "Those were the good old days."

Sophie was tempted to smile, except she really wanted things back like the "good old days" herself.

The remaining men stood around for a bit longer.

"Are they talking?" Sally asked.

"I reckon." Beth swung the door open just a crack wider.

"Why do you only *reckon* they're talking?" Sophie eased the door back closed a little, not wanting Beth to get them caught.

"Because you never see their lips move," Sally observed.

Sophie looked closer. They were communicating somehow. There were lots of shrugging shoulders and the occasional nod, but there was certainly no animated discussion going on.

"It's no wonder Indians can talk with drumbeats and smoke signals." Sophie's eyes narrowed as she watched closely for signs of conversation. "From a man's point of view, it must be possible to be quite eloquent."

"The cowhands are heading for the bunkhouse," Sally reported unnecessarily, since they were all watching with rapt attention.

"You know, girls, I'll bet if we were all men, Sally wouldn't have just said out loud what she said."

"I didn't mean to do anything wrong, Ma." Sally looked away from the window, worried.

"No, you didn't do anything wrong." Sophie rested her hand on Sally's silky, blond head. "That's not my point. I think, instead of saying anything, she'd have just watched silently, knowing we were all seeing the same thing."

There was a prolonged moment of silence.

"Or maybe she'd have grunted." Mandy broke into a fit of giggles.

"Or pointed." Beth closed the door and started laughing.

"And the rest of us. . ." Sally couldn't speak as she started laughing with her sisters.

All the girls started giggling until they could hardly stand up. Sophie couldn't help joining in. Finally, she finished Sally's thought. "The rest of us would have scratched ourselves and nodded while we glared at the one who had grunted, wondering why he'd gotten so all-fired chatty."

They were all laughing like maniacs when the men walked in. Clay and the other men stared silently, which sent all the girls into further fits of laughter.

Clay sighed as if he carried the weight of the world on his shoulders. Sophie saw Clay look over his shoulder at Adam, who simply shook his head. Buff shrugged. Luther harrumphed.

The girls all thought it was hilarious.

Sophie managed to get ahold of herself enough to dry the tears from her eyes with her apron. "I've got coffee."

The men all nodded. Buff scratched the back of his neck. The girls fled into their bedroom, giggling.

The men sat at the table as Sophie poured. They drank in silence. An occasional high-pitched giggle would escape from the bedroom, and the men would flinch or look over at the door as if it were dangerous. As the silence lengthened, Sophie lost whatever spark of amusement had taken hold of her, and she started to get mad. Before she could say something she'd regret, she decided to give them a chance by starting with the obvious. "Introduce me to your friends again, Clay."

Clay said, "Luther 'n Buff."

Each man nodded when his name was spoken. Sophie looked at Luther. "You're the one who said I was calling you, isn't that right?"

"Yes," Luther wrapped both hands around his tin cup. Sophie remembered cold nights in the thicket when she'd saved every ounce of heat by warming her hands that way. Out of habit she still did it, even in the Texas summer heat, just like Luther.

Sophie stifled a request for more details. She turned to Adam, who

sat at her table, battered and shirtless, but with his head up and his spine straight. He used to talk to her some. "It's wonderful to see you again, Adam. I hope you're planning to stay with us."

"Long as I'm needed." Adam took a long pull on his coffee.

Despite his short answer, Sophie's heart lifted to think of having Adam with them again. "What happened with the sheriff, and what did those men tell you? Are you going to be able to track down Judd Mason? I want to know all about it, Clay, while I patch up your knife wound better."

Clay sighed so deeply it seemed to come clear from his toes. As if it violated the Code of the West, he reluctantly said, "All right."

Sophie took him at his word and went to find her doctoring supplies. She carried them over, set them on the table, and began undoing the quick bandage she'd put on Clay's arm. "This wound is going to need stitches. And when I'm done with Clay, I want to look at your wounds, Adam."

Adam shook his head. "No need, Sophie girl. I could have used your touch a few weeks ago, but I'm fine now."

"You'll sit still while I check you over," Sophie informed him. "Then I'll get a meal on the table."

"You've been through more today than I have," Clay said. "You sit while you work on my arm, or I won't let you touch it."

"Clay, I don't need to. . ."

Luther was already dragging a chair over to the table and moving his out of the way so Sophie could sit.

Sophie decided this wasn't a fight she was going to win, so she sat.

Clay caught her hand as she reached for his arm and held it tight. "And the girls can get a meal on, or we'll go eat in the bunkhouse. I want you to rest."

"Clay, I don't need to rest." Sophie dabbed at his oozing wound. "There is nothing in the. . ." Sophie realized her fingers were going numb as Clay squeezed tighter and tighter. "The girls can do it. They have a stew already done, so they just need to mix up biscuits and set the table."

219

She was talking fast at the end. Clay released her. Sophie sighed with relief and had to control the urge to rub her hand. She arched one eyebrow at her husband.

"Good girl," he said, like she was a well-behaved horse.

"Well, I'm not too tired to listen." She pulled her needle out of its cotton wrapping and threaded it. "Now I want to hear why there were rangers out there, and what's going to happen to Judd Mason?" She pointed the needle right at her husband's nose. "And I want to hear it right now."

Clay smiled again.

Luther eased himself back in his chair. "Reckon it's a yarn I don't mind spinnin'." Luther relaxed as if he was in front of a campfire after a long day riding the range. "I woke up in the night, three weeks ago—"

"Four weeks," Buff cut in.

Luther frowned, then shrugged and continued, "To the sound of a woman saying, 'Help me.' I knew it wasn't the boy," Luther said, nodding at Clay.

"I'm father of five these days, Luth. Knock off calling me 'boy.' "

Luther grunted what might have been half a laugh. "But I knew it had something to do with him."

"We headed out." Buff slid his heavy coat off his shoulders.

The men unwound their tale, with Adam adding some and Clay filling in what had been going on at the ranch while they traveled. Sophie stitched up Clay's arm then scooted her chair around so she could stay seated while she cleaned Adam's wounds.

A warm corner of Sophie's heart, always filled by her love for God, began to expand and grow until she wanted to laugh and cry at the same time. "God heard me. He's really listening."

Clay rubbed her shoulders while she sat with her back to him, tending Adam's wounds. "He always is."

"I always pray, 'Help me,' " she said quietly.

Together, Adam and Luther said, "We know."

"And He really did. He helped me." Sophie quit talking before she

broke rule number one. She pulled her faintly trembling hands away from Adam's back before she hurt him. Clay's comforting, calloused hands stilled on her back, steadying her so she could finish with Adam.

She at last felt able to look at the three men who were sitting with Clay and her. "Thank you. You saved us."

Buff grunted.

Luther ducked his head. " 'Tweren't nothin', ma'am."

"Didn't have no choice, Sophie girl," Adam said. "A man's got God in his head, there's not much choice a'tall."

"Thank you." Then Sophie turned to Clay. "I'm really tired. The girls can get dinner on. I think I'm going to go rest."

Clay smiled his approval at her, and she wondered again at Luther's assurance that Clay loved her. It was bound to lead to hurt, but she found that she really liked the idea, especially since she was very much afraid she loved him, too.

Her eyelids almost fell closed before she found the strength to stand up and leave the room. She lay down on the bed fully clothed, planning to rest long enough to make her husband happy, then get up and help get a meal on. As she drifted off she realized it wasn't just Luther, Buff, and Adam who had been sent to her. It was Clay, too. She held sleep at bay as she thanked God.

The wonder of the words *help me* threaded through her mind, and tears pricked at her eyes. She shook her head to prevent such nonsense, but all that did was send the tears over the edge of her lower lids. She heard chairs slide around a bit in the other room, and the door to her bedroom opened.

Clay came in and sat on the bed beside her. "Adam and Luther said something was wrong."

Sophie couldn't hold back a smile even though the tears didn't quit flowing. Clay rubbed a rough thumb across one cheek. His touch was so gentle that Sophie felt as if she were made of the finest crystal. "Please don't cry, Sophie darlin'. You know I can't stand cryin'."

His sweetness and concern made the tears flow faster.

"When you cry I feel like some kind of a monster who has hurt you or scared you half to death or. . ."

Sophie lunged forward, wrapped her arms around his neck, and kissed him hard to get him to quit talking crazy. She pulled back and smiled at his stunned expression. Softly enough to ensure privacy in the crowded house, she said, "A woman doesn't always cry when she's sad or hurt, Clay. I was lying here thinking that God gave me a miracle when he sent Adam, Luther, and Buff to me."

"He did, didn't He? A true miracle."

Sophie nodded and swiped at her tears. "And He gave me a miracle when He sent you."

Clay looked confused. "It's the other way around, near as I can tell. You saved my life. You pulled me out of that creek and patched me up. You're the only one in this room who's a miracle."

Sophie kissed him again, then tucked her head under his chin and hugged him. Clay held her so tight it hurt, and it was the best hurt in the world.

At last she pulled back far enough to see him. "We are just going to have to disagree about who the miracle is."

Clay smiled and brushed the hair off her soggy face. "I reckon that's a disagreement I can live with." He offered her a handkerchief.

Sophie turned away a bit and blew her nose and clenched the handkerchief tight. "I keep thinking about how you came here and how much better my life is because of it. Then I thought about God doing a pure, real live miracle just for me, and I was so honored and humbled, it made me cry."

"Kinda like when the girls cried over the baby?"

"Just like that," Sophie said, relieved he understood.

"Waste of water and salt," Clay grumbled.

Sophie smiled and kissed him again, and only the men in the next room, who might be listening, and a twinge of old fear kept her from telling him she had fallen in love with him.

"Try an' get some rest, darlin'." Clay pressed her back against her pillow.

Sophie nodded. Clay stood and took a couple of steps toward the door. He paused and looked back at her, and then he awkwardly came back, leaned over, and kissed her on the forehead, then the cheek, then her lips.

He brushed her hair back again. "You and the girls, and this life I've got myself into, will always be a miracle to me, Sophie."

As if he'd embarrassed himself, he straightened away from her and hurried from the room.

Sophie lay there awhile and did a little more crying, but she was very careful not to think *help me*, not wanting to overtax the Lord's supply of miracles or Luther's and Adam's supply of patience. She curled onto her side and hugged Clay's baby in her arms and let her eyes drift shut, thinking she'd just rest for a second, to please Clay. The next thing she knew, Clay was pulling her into his arms, and she woke in the pitch-black room. She was just awake enough to say, "I need to make biscuits."

Clay snuggled her up close. "You just rest."

She thought how odd it was that he was so fixated on her need to rest. She had to explain to him how tough she was and how hard she had always worked. Really, her husband didn't know her at all. And she'd tell him so, as soon as she finished her little nap.

"Percy never came back," Harley said. "Something's gone wrong."

Judd threw back his blanket and started pulling his boots on.

Harley said sharply, "We're breaking camp!"

Eight of the ten men left were asleep. Harley's voice woke them as if it were a rifle shot. The two men on watch came charging into the camp. A quick glance at the heavy-lidded eyes told Judd they'd both been asleep. Judd didn't waste his lead on them.

"If they're caught, they might tell where we're hid out," Harley said.

Judd looked around the campsite. "If they'd have done for McClellen, they'd have come back into the camp hootin' and hollerin'. You're right. We break camp."

Harley was already saddling his horse. Judd noticed he wasn't particularly interested in what the rest of them did or if Judd agreed with him. Harley had lived longer than most men in his profession, and Judd trusted his instincts.

Harley said, "Let's head into the Santiagos for a few days then figure what to do next."

"What if you're wrong?" one of the men asked. "What if Percy comes back? He won't be able to find us."

"The three best trackers we have went with him. They'll find us." Judd hoped they wouldn't, since he was sure they'd have a posse with them when they came back—*if* they came back. He knew what kind of a man Percy was. A low-down, cowardly coyote who'd sell his own mother to save his skin.

"We'll drop back and come up with a new plan to get that ranch," Judd said. "We killed Edwards; we can kill his twin brother."

"We've been watching long enough to know McClellen's nothing like his tenderfoot brother." Harley spurred his horse and didn't look to see if anyone in the gang was with him.

Judd fell in behind him. As he pushed his horse into a gallop, he realized he was running. This was the second time McClellen had made them run. The defeat tasted like ashes in his mouth.

NINETEEN

The ranch settled into a routine with the capture of the four outlaws. Every cowhand did his work as usual, but all kept their guns close at hand and stayed on razor's edge. As a week slowly passed, Sophie began to hope the rest of the gang had hightailed it.

Parson Roscoe picked this Sunday to yell at them again. Sophie thought the man was on to something, changing the tone of his sermons from week to week. She certainly listened to every word he said. But why wouldn't she? He'd obviously heard how Sophie had lied by omission to her husband, and he'd written the sermon just to scold her.

She thought it was rather rude of him to pick on her, especially since she'd been trying to be more loving and a more obedient wife. But she had only decided about being a better wife after the run-in with the outlaws, so maybe the parson already had his sermon written, based on the way she used to act. Besides, it was a full month into her marriage, which was kind of late to begin behaving herself, so she figured she deserved it.

She probably also deserved to have Sally and Mandy clinging to her, one on each side, and Laura sleeping dead away on her lap. The seemingly boneless little girl seemed to gain weight with each passing moment.

"How is it that Satan has so filled your heart that you have lied to the Holy Spirit?"

Sophie didn't like to think Satan had filled her heart. She would have sunk further into her seat if she could have—she was practically slouched out of sight as it was.

"You didn't really tell a lie," a quiet voice whispered. Sophie suspected it was the voice of Satan himself, tempting her to justify her disobedience to her husband. Mentally, she told him to get away from her.

I've already decided to change, she thought. *You aren't going to convince me to keep sneaking around.*

Sophie snapped her attention back to the parson when he thundered, "Later Ananias's wife came in to the assembly and repeated the lie she and her husband had agreed on."

That's when Sophie realized the parson was reading a Bible verse, and it wasn't her heart that Satan had filled but the heart of Ananias. *Whew!*

"Peter said to Sapphira, 'How could you agree to test the Spirit of the Lord? Look, the feet of the men who buried your husband are at the door, and they will carry you out also.' " Parson Roscoe's voice kept gaining strength.

Sally and Mandy squirmed closer. Sophie, ever the mother, glanced down the row at Beth and saw that she was now sitting on Clay's lap with her face buried in his chest. Sophie wondered if the McClellen clan shouldn't start sitting nearer the back.

" 'At that moment Sapphira fell down at Peter's feet and *died*.' " The walls of the church nearly vibrated as the parson roared out the last word. Parson Roscoe stopped to take a deep breath and mop the sweat off his brow.

Sophie wondered if Sapphira wasn't Hebrew for Sophie. It was close enough to sting. *I'm done with lies, Lord,* Sophie prayed in her heart. *I am. I'm going to love everyone and be honest right down to the ground. You gave me a miracle, and I won't give back anything but my very best. Now could You please make the parson quit yelling at me?*

God had given her a miracle all right. But He didn't give her another one now. About halfway through the sermon—which stretched on so long Sophie began to wonder if there weren't more liars in the building than

just her, since God should have told the parson that she got his point right off—Sally relaxed her death grip on Sophie's arm. Sophie looked down to see her little girl fast asleep. Sophie looked sideways at Clay, who caught the glance and smiled. He reached across Sally and lifted the, by now, two-hundred-pound Laura out of Sophie's arms and settled her beside the clinging Beth. Then, with a deft move that should have required a third hand, he shifted Sally's slumbering form so it rested on his arm, instead of Sophie.

Sophie whispered, "Your arm."

Clay mouthed back, "I'm okay."

Sophie wanted to protest, but having the weight lifted off of her was too heavenly. She sighed aloud in relief and Clay smiled at her.

The parson began to wind down shortly after that. "Ananias and Sapphira died because God looked into their hearts and knew that there was no repentance and no love. There was time for both of them to change their minds and tell the truth. There is time for all of us, right now, to accept the love of God, repent of our sins, commit our lives to Jesus Christ, and accept His salvation."

The parson lifted his Bible, draped open over one hand. "It's the eternal theme. It's love. There are no lies when there is love. Can any of you imagine a more complete waste of time than lying to God?"

Several people in the congregation shook their heads, and Sophie found her head moving along.

"He already knows." The parson lowered the Bible and leaned forward. "He knows the truth in everyone's heart. Save your energy for something that has a chance of success."

Sophie reached her hand over the top of Sally's nodding head and rested it on Clay's strong, wounded arm. She didn't say anything, since they were in the front row after all. But she smiled at him and made a promise to herself that she'd tell Clay all about her booby traps and hidden weapons this very day. Why, she'd tell him on the trip home without another moment's delay. No more lies. None ever. Sophie felt a lightness come over her heart, and she knew it was the right thing to do.

With a quick prayer for forgiveness and a promise to God that she was going to start a new life this second, much as she'd promised last week, Sophie turned back to the parson and sang along to "Amazing Grace."

Just as the song ended, a loud *crash* sounded from the back of the church. It woke Sally and had both Beth and Mandy turning around in their seats.

"Is everyone all right back there?" the parson asked with a worried frown.

When he talked like that, Sophie couldn't resist looking behind her, even though it was bad manners to turn around in church. She thought the noise came from the farthest back pew, which was teeming with toe-headed little boys—the Reeves family.

"Did something get broken?" Parson Roscoe peered toward the noise.

One of the five-year-old triplets poked his head out from where he was crouched behind the pew. He said, in a tone that screamed of a guilty conscience, "No, sir."

As the raggedly dressed, dirty-faced, little boy stood up, no one could fail to see the wooden rack in his hand that was only moments ago nailed on to the end of his pew to hold the hymnal.

"Mark, you little liar." One of his older brothers elbowed the little boy.

Everyone in the church started to chuckle.

The parson walked down the center aisle and extended his hand to the little boy. "Don't worry about the book rack. It can be fixed."

Daniel Reeves stood up and took the piece of lumber out of his son's hand before the parson could reach it. "I'll repair it, Parson. A Reeves fixes what he breaks."

"I'll bet that keeps him busy," Clay murmured.

Sophie tried not to start laughing again. She was a bit surprised to see Adam standing against the back wall of the church. He hadn't ridden in with them. Luther and Buff were on either side of him, all of

them standing, although there were a few seats left. She saw Eustace and Whitey standing off to the side a little, and several others of the McClellen hands were about the room. It struck her that they were doing more than attending church—they were standing guard. It sent a chill down her spine to realize that, even in this holy place, they all needed to be on guard.

As she turned back to the front of the church to await the closing prayer, her eyes swept the cheerful congregation. She was relieved to see that the people seemed to be unconcerned about a child doing a bit of damage. Then she noticed Miss Calhoun.

Miss Calhoun sat rigidly facing forward. Sophie had the impression she'd never turned around. This was a woman who minded her manners. A look of such profound disapproval was etched on her face that Sophie wondered if it might be frozen in place.

Sophie shook her head as she considered what kind of teacher Miss Calhoun must be if she couldn't accept high spirits and a few mishaps from active little boys. Or maybe there was something more going on. Maybe the Reeveses had begun coming to school this week and proved to be too much for her to handle.

Well, Sophie imagined she'd find out today. Miss Calhoun was coming to eat with them after church. Even after the craziness of this week and the outlaws, Sophie hadn't forgotten that, and she had a wild turkey she'd snared early yesterday roasting, waiting for their return.

Sophie sighed when she thought of the meal ahead. She had to tell Clay to build them a bigger table and a few more chairs. As soon as she thought it, she cheered up. She would never have considered asking Cliff to take on such a project. And Sophie also knew it was significant that her first thought hadn't been to ask Adam to build it.

Yes, she was going to let her husband handle nearly everything that could even begin to be considered man's work from now on. And she was going to obey him, be honest with him, and most of all love him with all her heart.

"You are the sneakin'est, most disobedient wife in the whole state of Texas!" Clay snatched his hat off his head and whacked his leg with it. Sophie suspected what he really wanted to whack was her backside.

The horses pulling the wagon jumped a bit at the sudden motion behind them and picked up their speed.

Sophie looked over her shoulder at Miss Calhoun, who was riding her own horse. She was trailing along behind them far enough to avoid the dust, so she didn't hear Clay growling.

"Now, Clay, I know you're angry. But remember that I've already promised not to do anything like this again."

"Rocks! You were hauling rocks!" Clay clobbered his leg a few more times.

"I told her not to, Pa," Sally piped up from the wagon box.

Sophie glared over her shoulder at the little tattletale, and Sally subsided into a sitting position on the floor of the wagon.

Sophie just barely heard her daughter mutter, "Well, I did."

"I deserve any yelling you want to give me." She stared straight forward, fully intending to accept any criticism Clay handed her way.

Clay wedged his hat roughly back on his head. "I fully intend to. When I think what could have happened to you on that hillside hauling rocks, I want to—"

"Just know before you start with your lecture," Sophie interrupted him, "that I'm used to doing for myself. I've been on my own completely for two years, and what with the war and all, I spent most of my married life fending for myself."

"I realize that." Clay clucked to the horses to keep up their speed. "But things are going to—"

"So it's been a hard-learned lesson not to just do whatever needs doing." Sophie gave her chin a firm nod.

Laura, still asleep, began to whimper on Sophie's knee.

"I'll take her, Ma, so Pa can finish up telling you how stupid you are, without being interrupted." Mandy poked her head between Sophie and Clay, scooped Laura up in her arms, and went back to sitting.

Sophie straightened her skirt. "Yes, go ahead, Clay."

"Now, Mandy, I'm not going to tell your ma she's stupid. She don't like that, and I'd never do something she said she don't like."

"It doesn't matter." Sophie figured she deserved whatever Clay dished out. "You can call me stupid if you want to. As of today I'm going to learn a new way. If I want something done, I'm going to tell you."

"I don't think you're stupid, Sophie." Clay seemed to be sidetracked from his lecture, and Sophie really wished he'd get on with it.

"Sure you do," Sophie reminded him. "You called me stupid for going out at night when there might be cougars to eat me, and you called me stupid—"

"I only called you stupid because I know you're *not* stupid."

Sophie was unable to think of a sensible response to that, so she fell silent.

Her girls weren't speechless. "You called us stupid, too," Beth said. "Does that mean you don't think we're stupid, neither?"

"Of course I don't think you girls are stupid. I know you're a right smart bunch of children," Clay reassured her.

"So if you call us stupid when you think we're smart," Mandy asked hesitantly, "does that mean when you say you love us you really hate us?"

Clay pulled his hat off his head and started whacking his leg again. Sophie knew there wasn't a speck of dust left on his hat or his pants. She was also curious about how Clay would answer.

"If I really thought you were stupid, I'd expect you to do stupid things. But when I know you're smart and you do stupid things, then I think I've got reason to complain. Do you understand that?"

"I guess that makes sense," Sophie said. "You expect better from us. But the word *stupid* is so hurtful. . . ."

"Not if you're smart it isn't," Clay protested. "It's like if I called you ugly, when you're so pretty. You'd know I didn't mean—"

"Did Pa just call you ugly, Ma?" Sally asked from behind them. She stuck her head between them with a worried frown on her face.

Clay plunked his hat back on his head and ran one gloved hand over his face, as if he could scrub hard enough to wash the whole trip home from church out of his mind.

"No, Sally, in fact I think he just called me pretty."

"But that's not what I heard," Sally interrupted.

"And he didn't answer about hating us," Beth added with a break in her voice.

Mandy said quietly, "That's mean, Pa."

Laura bounced on Mandy's lap and said, "Mama ugwee."

"Quiet!" Clay roared.

Sophie was afraid that even the trailing Miss Calhoun could hear that one.

"I think you're all as smart as any girls I've ever known," Clay shouted. "Of course I've never known any girls, but. . .well, just never you mind that. I never heard tell of girls who could be so smart. Don't ever say I hate you. It's just a plain dirty lie to say such a thing." Clay turned to glare at the girls over his shoulder with an expression that was as unloving as any Sophie had ever seen. In a strange way, that made her believe him.

"I told you all I love you, and if that ever changes I'll let you know. So unless I've said different, I love you and that's that." Clay turned back to the horses in a huff.

"And I think you're all beautiful. Your Ma is the prettiest lady in church, in Mosqueros, in Texas, and maybe in the whole world. She's prettier than any I've seen before, and you all look just like her, so you're pretty, too. Now, could we just ride quiet the rest of the way home?" He shook the reins as if he wanted the ride to be over.

Sophie thought of her work-roughened hands and her scattered hair and her plain dresses. "You really think I'm pretty?"

Clay looked away from the horses. His expression made her wonder what he'd heard in her voice. "I think I'm the luckiest man alive to have

such a pretty little wife as you, Sophie. You have to know how beautiful you are."

If Sophie had ever thought about her looks, it had been a long time ago as a dreamy-headed teenager. She hadn't given it much notice since.

She looked into Clay's warm eyes for a long time, wishing she could be alone with him for just a few minutes. She'd tell him she loved him, and she'd reassure him one more time that she'd never lie to him again. Which reminded her, "Um, Clay, I don't think you ever finished lecturing me about the booby traps."

Clay sighed. "Are you going to quit setting your traps now?"

Sophie nodded.

"And leave the outdoor repairs to me?"

"I promise."

"And trust me to protect this family?"

"I will, Clay. I already do," Sophie said fervently.

"Then I reckon the lecture's over." Clay turned back to the horses and clucked at them again.

Sophie felt like Clay had been cheated out of his scolding. She deserved it after all. But she couldn't quite bring herself to urge him to yell at her.

As the ranch came in sight, Sophie's mind turned to the dinner ahead and the fussy Miss Calhoun. Sally poked her head between them again and turned to Clay.

He looked down at her. "What?"

Sally said with wide-eyed innocence, "I think you're pretty too, Pa."

Clay seemed taken aback for a moment, then he smiled down at Sally and chucked her under the chin with his gloved fist. "Well, thank you darlin'. I reckon that's about the sweetest thing anyone's ever said to me."

Sally grinned and pulled her head back. The last few yards of the trip were completed with Clay chuckling softly while he guided the horses.

Clay helped Miss Calhoun down off her horse just as Adam, Luther, Buff, and the others came riding into the ranch from different directions. They'd ridden out of church ahead of the McClellen wagon and disappeared to scout the trail for danger.

Sophie thought of the huge bird she had roasting. "Clay, we have plenty of turkey. Ask the men if they want to eat with us."

"That's a right nice idea." Clay went and talked to them out of Sophie's hearing. She wondered if they were talking about more than the invitation. She was a mite annoyed to be kept in the dark. But remembering her promise to herself and God, she minded Clay's obvious wish to confer privately with the men and turned her attention to Miss Calhoun.

"Did you enjoy your ride out here, Miss Calhoun? We could have made room for you in the wagon."

"I need to take my horse out when I can." Miss Calhoun neatly removed her black gloves, tugging gently on one finger at a time. "He stands idle in the stable too much of the time."

Her gloves tucked neatly away, she followed Sophie and the girls into the house. "Let me help get the meal." Miss Calhoun carried a satchel with her, and she produced a large white apron from it.

Miss Calhoun proved to be more approachable when she was working side-by-side with Sophie and the girls. Sophie was pleased when the young woman produced a carefully wrapped loaf of bread from the satchel to add to the meal.

When Sophie called out to the men that the food was ready, they all came trooping in the front door.

"There's a stew warming in the bunkhouse, too." Whitey pulled his hat off his head and twisted it in his hands. "We'll only have a bite of your turkey, ma'am. Thank you for inviting us."

Each of the men had a kind word of thanks to say as they filed through. Sophie became alarmed as she sliced away at the ever-shrinking turkey and filled the plates the men brought from the bunkhouse. The big bird lasted though, and after the last of the men went outside, she began filling plates for the women. She noticed Clay went outside with the men, and Sophie felt betrayed—and a little jealous. Then the very proper Miss Calhoun sat down, and Sophie began to think of her daughters' table manners.

They didn't have any.

Miss Calhoun sat at the McClellen's undersized table with all the dignity of a queen. She ate so neatly and cut her turkey so precisely, every move Sophie made seemed clumsy by comparison. Sophie spent the whole meal correcting the girls' manners, and from the surprised looks they gave her, she knew they'd never heard a lot of this stuff before.

"How long have you been in Mosqueros, Miss Calhoun?" Sophie asked. "Is this your first year?"

Miss Calhoun chewed thoroughly and swallowed. "I started with a winter term. I took over when the last teacher married Mr. Badje."

Sophie remembered the banker's very young wife and nodded. "How do you like it?"

Miss Calhoun lay her fork down daintily and folded her hands in her lap. "There were far fewer students for the winter term. The school is growing."

Sophie noticed Miss Calhoun didn't answer her question. "More people are moving into the area." Sophie then thought of all the men who had proposed to her two years ago. "There weren't many women here when we first settled. I know the Reeveses are newcomers." The minute Sophie mentioned the Reeveses, she regretted it. She remembered the tense expression on Miss Calhoun's face in church. She was reminded of it because that exact look reappeared.

Miss Calhoun made an effort to answer; then with a sudden fumbling movement that was at odds with her usual manner, she dragged a handkerchief out of her sleeve and pressed it to her lips. At first Sophie thought the young woman was trying to physically hold words inside herself that she thought were better left unsaid. Then she saw that Miss Calhoun was crying. There was no sobbing, but a tear ran down Miss Calhoun's cheek, and she took an occasional broken breath.

The whole table fell silent. Sophie saw the girls all stare wide-eyed at the sight of the very proper teacher losing her composure. Sophie finally got past her surprise and jumped up from the table. She wrapped her arms around Miss Calhoun's trembling shoulders. "What is it, Grace? Did something happen? Are the boys too much trouble at school?"

Miss Calhoun didn't correct Sophie's use of her name, which told Sophie just how upset she was. Miss Calhoun shook her head slightly, then shrugged, then nodded. At last the trembling subsided. Sophie thought Miss Calhoun cried more neatly than anyone she'd ever seen.

"I'm going to be fired," Miss Calhoun whispered.

Sophie gasped. She'd heard only good things about how the school was run. "Daniel Reeves doesn't like the way you handle his children?"

Miss Calhoun shook her head. "It isn't him. It's that since those boys have come, everything is in chaos. I don't seem to be able to make them behave. And now the other boys are beginning to imitate their unruliness, and the girls are being neglected. It's been pandemonium for two solid weeks. The school board made a surprise inspection on Friday."

Miss Calhoun's voice faltered. "They found everything in an uproar, and even though the children settled down once they knew the men were from the board, it was too late. I'm sure I won't be asked back after this term. And I don't have anywhere else to go." Miss Calhoun's voice broke again, and Sophie heard real fear under the tears.

"It's taking every cent I have to live," Miss Calhoun sobbed. "I have no savings and no family to go back to."

"I'm sure the board understands that it's not your fault. Anyone would have trouble making those children behave. A new teacher will be in the same situation."

"I think they're looking for a man. That's probably for the best."

Miss Calhoun made a supreme effort and made a tidy swipe of the handkerchief over her cheeks. "I'm sorry." She squared her shoulders. "I shouldn't have made such a spectacle of myself." She shook her head as if she couldn't get over the shock of crying in public. Then she moved her shoulders restlessly, and Sophie realized Miss Calhoun wanted her to move away.

Sophie obliged and sat back down at the table. Miss Calhoun turned back to her meal.

"You are not going to be fired, Miss Calhoun," Sophie said. "One unruly family shouldn't be able to drive out a good teacher. We will figure something out, and we just might start with a visit to Daniel Reeves to insist he take his sons in hand."

Miss Calhoun looked terrified. "Oh, please don't do that."

Sophie reached out to pat Miss Calhoun's hand, but Miss Calhoun jerked away. She pushed her chair back from the table. "It was wrong of me to bother you with my little problems. I've just got to try harder to manage my classroom. This is my problem, and I'll solve it myself."

She stood. "Thank you for the meal. I hope the girls can make it to school for the fall term. For who—whoever is the teacher." Miss Calhoun's voice broke. "I need to get back." She turned and ran out of the ranch house.

"Wait, Grace." Sophie dashed for the front door in time to see Miss Calhoun untie her horse and swing herself up on his back.

"We thought you'd spend the afternoon with us, Miss Calhoun," Sophie called out to her.

Grace was already guiding her horse away. She called over her shoulder, "Thank you again."

Sophie heard Clay call out from the side of the house where he sat eating with the other men, "Miss Calhoun, someone needs to ride back with you."

Miss Calhoun was far enough away she didn't hear him—or she pretended she didn't. Sophie suspected it was the latter.

"Luke, Andy, ride with her. Eustace, Miguel, Rio, get ahead of her and check the trail around her. Hurry." Clay came around the house.

There must have been horses already saddled, because there were men riding out within seconds. Only then did Sophie breathe a sigh of relief.

"Why'd she leave so fast?" Clay walked up to stand beside Sophie.

"It must have been something I said," Sophie said weakly.

Clay shook his head. "Why am I not surprised?"

Sophie thought of the promises she'd made to God the last two weeks that prevented her from replying scathingly to Clay's observation. "Clay, you are a lucky man."

TWENTY

He agreed when she told him he was a lucky man, but something about the tone of her voice warned him. "What do you mean by that?" He didn't find out because Sophie had stormed back into the house.

He shrugged and returned to the men lounging in the shade on the east side of the ranch house telling tall tales.

"It don't suit me none, Clay, to sit back and let the sheriff handle this." Whitey pulled out his bowie knife and began whittling on a whip handle he was making from cedar branch. "I say we find out where the rest of the gang is holed up and root 'em out. Let's get this over an' done."

"It's not just the sheriff, Whitey." Clay pushed his plate aside and sat on the edge of the porch. He stared at the ground between his splayed knees. "The rangers are working on it, too. They're good men. They know we're here if needed, and if we go off hunting on our own, we may get in their way. Our job is to protect this ranch and the women. I don't want to spread ourselves thin and leave this place unguarded."

Whitey nodded. The smell of cedar cut the smell of Texas dust kicked up by the departed horse.

"A few of us could go." Adam sat up straight on the porch steps a few feet down from Clay. His every moved reminded Clay of the wicked cuts on his back. "We'd leave plenty of men back here."

"Reckon I could scout back up in the hills." Luther smoothed his full, black beard in a motion Clay could remember from his earliest childhood. "I saw what direction those varmints come from."

Clay knew how good Luther and Buff were on a trail. "Waiting pits me against my own instincts. It doesn't suit me to sit by and wait while someone else takes care of a threat to my family. But I've got other instincts telling me to stay close to Sophie and the girls."

"It's a fearful thing to hear a man talkin' 'bout killin' a woman the way those polecats were." Buff shook his head.

"It was the cold-bloodedest thing I'd ever heard," Clay agreed. "And we know those men we caught weren't ramrodding this operation."

He looked from one man to the next. Every one of them got his meaning. If those men came for Sophie once, they would come again. Sure, they'd been after Clay, too, but a man learned to look out for himself. A woman was defenseless.

"I still owe those men," Adam said. "And I mean to pay 'em back every penny."

Clay heard the depth of rage in Adam's simple announcement. He looked sideways at the gaunt, scarred man and felt the echo of his own anger. Adam had lost friends. Clay had lost a brother.

"Right now we've got to concentrate on the living, Adam," Clay said. "We make sure no one else is hurt before we start taking old sins outta their hides."

Clay saw Adam tamp down hard on his anger. Adam rubbed absently at the bullet wound on his side. "I reckon it don't matter when."

Clay felt the same way.

"Hating can eat away at a man." Luther shifted his weight to get more comfortable. His boots scraped across the porch. "It can warp a man until his family don't recognize him."

Clay jerked one shoulder in a guilty shrug. "I'm working on it."

"I wonder if hatin's what turned Judd Mason into the monster he is?" Luther asked.

"I know the hunger I got in me to hurt him, hurt him bad, and all those he rides with is a powerful sin." Clay clenched his hands between his spread knees.

The men sat silently and slowly they relaxed to contemplate hate and revenge and the whereabouts of a dangerous man. All but Adam.

After a long while Adam said, "It's a powerful sin all right." Quietly he added, "It won't be my first."

With Adam, Luther, and Buff working alongside the other men, Clay expected the cattle to all be brought in closer to the ranch house by the end of the day Monday, with plenty of men left for guard duty.

Sophie had tried to get Adam to spend the day being nursed and coddled, but he wouldn't spare himself any of the hard labor. Clay marveled at Adam's knowledge of the ranch and his ideas for its development. It was plain to see that Adam loved this place as if it were his own.

Clay laid the last brand on a stray and told the men he was riding up to the house for a spell.

Sheriff Everett came riding into the ranch later on that afternoon. He rode straight into the barn where Clay was hanging up his C Bar branding iron. The man was exhausted and carried more trail dust on his clothes than Clay.

"Howdy, Josiah. You look like you've had a hard day of it."

"I've spent more time in the saddle than out of it since Saturday. The men we locked up all told the same story, and we rode straight out to the vigilante camp. They'd hightailed it."

"As long as those men are running loose, Sophie is in danger. You heard what they said about her knowing too much." Clay took off his hat, and with a dejected pass of his arm, he wiped a coating of sweat off his forehead. He'd worked up a sweat branding, but this wasn't hard-work sweat. This was fear.

The sheriff swung down off his buckskin, and Clay walked alongside as the sheriff led his horse to the watering trough.

"That was before we caught these men, though." Everett's plodding feet sounded almost as loudly as his horse's hooves. "Now that we have 'em, Mason has a lot longer list of people who can identify him. There's no point anymore in comin' after one little woman. And there's no way he can buy this ranch now, so there's no reason to go after you. My gut tells me they've started running and they won't stop. I think they've quit the country. The rangers are still on their trail."

They reached the water trough, and Clay stopped and crossed his arms. "It doesn't set right with me to stand aside while someone else takes care of my problems."

The sheriff hung his hat on the horse's saddle horn and dunked his head in the water with a rough splash at the same time his horse was drinking. Everett scrubbed at his face, then came up dripping wet and brushed both hands over his streaming hair until it was pushed straight back. The water soaked his shirt, but the sheriff sighed with pure pleasure. "You've more than made yourself clear. I know you're holding back because the rangers and I asked you to."

"That's not the only reason I'm holding back," Clay said.

The sheriff asked, "Why else?"

Clay ignored him. He wasn't about to get into a debate about the hate that ate inside him and how he was trying to battle the surge of pleasure he got when he thought of smashing Mason's face with his bare hands. "I'm not about to relax my guard just because your instincts tell you Mason is on the run."

The sheriff shrugged, plunked his hat back on his head, and threw his reins over the buckskin's neck. "No man ever relaxes much in the West. It just ain't a country that inspires relaxation."

Clay had to admit that was true.

The sheriff mounted his horse. "We're not giving up, Clay. I just thought it'd be neighborly to tell you what's going on with the investigation."

"'Preciate it, Josiah. While you're investigating, you might remember that if Judd Mason killed Cliff two years ago and waited till now to kill the Meads, then he's a planning man. He's not a man who's gonna give up easy."

The sheriff looked unhappy with that obvious bit of truth. "Nothin' worse than a patient outlaw."

"Good luck." Clay tugged on the brim of his hat.

"I wish I didn't need it so bad." Everett rode out of the yard.

Clay had been planning to go to the house, but he didn't want to go in there and have Sophie start nagging him for details of what the sheriff had said. He was mad enough to tell her everything and not soften his words, even in front of the girls. Instead he spent another hour working around the ranch. By the time he was done with the grueling work, he'd settled down.

Clay didn't like the fact that Mason had disappeared. They'd have to remain on guard. But the hard work of rounding up strays was over. He and the men would have more time to do just that.

It was time to start proving to his new wife that he was the best husband a woman ever had. Way better than Cliff. He thought she already believed that, but he wanted to make sure.

Smiling for the first time all day, he came in to supper, slung an arm around Sophie's waist, and gave her a loud smack on the lips. "The cattle are settled in the summer pasture. Tomorrow I start working around the place, repairing and adding here and there. The men will be able to help, too. I hope you didn't do all the man's work yourself, Sophie darlin'. You did leave something for me, didn't you?"

"Clay, you're filthy." Sophie slapped at Clay's chest, but he could tell by her grin that she was pleased with his attention.

"It's hard work and honest dirt, darlin'. Let me share a little with you." Clay pulled her closer, but she jumped back, grabbed a ladle off the stove, and waved it threateningly at him, failing to suppress a smile.

The girls started giggling, and maybe for the first time, Clay didn't mind it at all.

"Have you had a chance to inspect the traps I built, Clay? I don't want you or any of the men to stumble on them and set them off by accident."

"I haven't gotten to your little surprises, darlin'. I'll add it to my list of things to do tomorrow." Clay turned away from his wife to wash his face in the basin full of warm water she always had waiting for him. He sighed as he scrubbed his face and hands. He thought of the sheriff dipping his head into the cold tank. Many's the time he'd done that himself, but he hadn't considered it today, even though he was as dirty as the sheriff. He'd purely gotten a taste for warm water in a clean basin.

He marveled at the hundred ways a woman made a man's life better. He dried his face on a towel. "If I'd've only known how nice havin' a wife was, I'd've gotten married when I was twelve years old."

"Well, I would have been ten at the time." Sophie poked him smartly with the ladle. "You wouldn't have married me."

Clay grinned and lunged at her. She didn't have a chance to get her ladle up. He hoisted her in his arms and swung her around in a circle. "Well, I'm glad I waited then."

He set her down and held her steady until he was sure she wasn't dizzy, then he turned on the girls, growled at them, and charged.

They squealed and ran, but they didn't run out of the room. They just dashed around in circles, colliding with each other. Clay snagged Mandy first, and while he held her and tickled her with his whiskery face, Laura toddled up and latched on to his leg. Being careful not to shake her loose while he dragged her around after the others almost made it a fair fight.

He grabbed Beth when she danced too close, then, with his hands full, Sally jumped on his back. By the time they were done, Clay was flat on the kitchen floor, buried under three sets of petticoats and one soggy diaper.

He remembered his first impression when he'd regained consciousness in that awful shed, that he'd died and he was surrounded by angels. He hadn't been far from wrong.

Judd Mason pulled up on his black mustang, then wrenched the reins

to turn the horse around. "We're not shaking 'em. Whoever's on our trail is a bloodhound."

Eli rode up beside Judd. "It's rangers, Mr. Mason. I worked up close enough to see their stars with my spyglass. They're still a few hours behind us, but they're reading the trail like it was the written word."

Rangers! Judd had been smart enough in his life to fight shy of Texas Rangers. They were the toughest, most relentless lawmen the West had to offer.

"It's time to cut our losses, Judd." Harley reined in his horse to look back in the direction of the men hounding them. "The only way to leave a ranger behind is to leave Texas behind and not come back."

"I've heard of 'em following someone clean across the country, chasin' after 'em," one of the gang said gloomily.

"We're not quittin'," Judd roared. "I'm not leaving this country without making McClellen sorry he ever tangled with me. And I'm not leaving that woman behind to live on a ranch that she stole clean out from under my feet."

Harley rode up until his horse pressed against Judd's mustang. "Let's ride off a ways and talk this out, Judd," he said under his breath. "There's a few things the men don't need to know."

Judd wanted to refuse, but he wondered just what Harley knew that he didn't want to talk about. With a terse nod of his head, Judd wheeled the mustang around, and the two of them rode off a fair piece.

Judd jerked on his horse's reins viciously and turned to Harley. "This is far enough. Say your piece and let's get back."

"What's this really about, Mason?" Harley asked calmly. "You know there's no way you can take that land now. You're a known outlaw in these parts."

"That ain't news, Harley," Judd sneered.

"Then why hang around? You've got a lot of money in your saddle bags. You've got your whole share and the share of every member of this gang who has lit out. There's nothing for us here 'cept a bullet or a noose."

"I'm not leaving without paying McClellen back for taking my land." The mustang reared up, fighting Judd's hard hand. "I avenge a wrong done to me."

"Judd, no wrong has been done to you. *You* killed Edwards. *You* killed the Meads. *You* plotted the murder of McClellen and his wife. You've handed out all the wrong in this mess. You don't need to get revenge against McClellen. That's just your pride talking, and pride won't stop a bullet."

Judd turned red in the face and his mule-headedness kicked in full bore. He shouted over his shoulder, "Men!"

The rest of the vigilantes rode into the clearing.

"Harley wants to cut and run."

Eli rode his horse up beside Judd, showing his loyalty. One by one the men, most of them showing far less assurance than Eli, rode to Judd's side, spreading out, mindful of Harley's quick hand with a gun, until they'd formed a circle around Harley.

Judd knew Harley Shafter was nobody's fool. He wasn't about to challenge the whole gang. Harley kept his hands held loosely on his saddle horn. Judd knew it was so no one could make the mistake of thinking Harley was going for his gun.

"I see you all don't share my view." Harley watched them with cool eyes.

Seven tough men sat silently, waiting for a wrong move from Harley.

Harley kept his voice calm and his eyes flat. "If you're all still in, I'm in."

The moment strung itself out, until abruptly Judd relaxed. "I'm glad to hear you're still with us, Harley." His voice was ice cold when he spoke.

He turned to Eli, who'd been gone most of the last two days. "Did you take the horses and hide them out where I said?"

"They're waitin', boss"—Eli nodded—"right up top of Sawyer Canyon."

"Okay, then it's time for a little plan I have in mind that should settle things between me and the McClellens. Then"—he looked square at Harley—"*after* I've done for the McClellens, we'll leave this lousy country and go find us some ranch land."

Harley fell into line with Judd leading and Eli bringing up the rear.

"Ma, isn't that one of the sheriff's deputies?" Beth came in from sweeping the front porch.

Sophie hurried to the door in time to see a man come charging into the ranch yard. "Yes, I recognize him from last Saturday."

There was an urgency about the way the man rode that sent Sophie to the edge of the porch. The man ignored her. He galloped on past the house toward a pair of men herding the cattle. The deputy talked to the men, then rode off into a valley where Sophie knew there were more cattle.

"What do you reckon he wants, Ma?" Mandy tugged on Sophie's skirt.

Sophie heard the fear in her daughter's voice and regretted all the girls had been through. "I guess he just wants to talk to the men, not us." Sophie hoped Mandy wouldn't notice she hadn't answered her question.

Sophie looked around the corral and barn. There'd been someone close-up all day, working on repairs she'd been itching to get at ever since they'd moved back. Having someone else do things for her was a luxury.

"I don't see any of the men who've been guarding the house." Sally came out and went down the porch steps, looking all around.

It struck Sophie as odd. Clay had been in and out of the house a dozen times. She'd made extra coffee because Luther, Buff, and Adam had stopped in to talk more than once. She'd also offered it to the hands and had a few takers, although they had their own pot brewing in the bunkhouse.

She'd even had Clay bring in several grouse for supper when she hadn't thought to put hunting on her list. She hadn't needed to leave the house all day, and at Clay's insistence, she'd taken a nap after the midday meal, with Laura nestled at her side.

Sophie and the girls kept watching the direction the deputy had gone. After several tense moments, Clay came galloping back toward the ranch house with the deputy at his side. He swung down off his horse and strode toward the cabin.

"What is it, Clay?" Sophie expected the worst. All four girls edged up beside her to hear whatever Clay had to say.

"The sheriff has Mason cornered in the rocks a few miles south of here. The posse he has with him saw the whole gang ride into a box canyon."

"That's got to be Sawyer Canyon. It's the only dead-end canyon in that direction."

Clay nodded. "Sawyer Canyon. That's the name Deputy MacNeal used. They chased them in there last night. The sheriff has the only way out blocked, but Mason and his men are undercover. The sheriff isn't going to risk any lives staging some kind of assault. He's planning to wait them out. He wants me to send as many hands as I can spare to spell his men."

Sophie heaved a sigh of relief and hurled herself into Clay's arms. "It's over then. Finally. All but this last showdown."

Clay held her tight. "Yes, it sounds like it's finally over."

Sophie squeezed her husband tight for a long second, then released him and stepped back. "Of course we need to send help. There—there won't be any shooting will there?"

"The sheriff hopes to take the gang without anyone getting hurt," Clay said soberly. "But Mason is facing a noose."

"He won't come out with his hands up." Sophie tried to steady her nerves.

Clay pulled his leather gloves off his hands and tucked them behind his belt buckle. He brushed Sophie's hair back with one hand. "We

won't be reckless. We won't trust him for a minute."

"Do you have to go?" As soon as she said it she was ashamed. She covered her mouth quickly with one hand, wishing she could call back the words.

"Sophie, I can't ask my men to go do something I'm not willing to do."

"I know," Sophie whispered. "I know. If you could, you wouldn't be the man you are."

Clay nodded. "I'm leaving six men behind to guard the ranch. That should be plenty. We'll stay at the canyon for a while, then when the sheriff's posse is rested, we'll come back to eat and sleep. It may be awhile. We don't know what supplies Mason has. He could stay holed up for a long time."

"Like a siege," Sophie said.

Clay caressed her face again. "And like a siege, there'll be a lot of waiting but not much fighting."

Sophie leaned into his hand. "Just promise me you'll be careful."

Clay grinned at her. "I wouldn't be able to go if you hadn't said that."

The girls had lined up beside her, and now in a rush, they all said, "Good-bye, Pa. Be careful."

He gave them each a quick kiss on the forehead. "I will."

He turned just as Adam came out of the barn, leading two horses. Clay walked to the horse and swung himself up. Adam mounted his roan at the same time. Clay waved and Adam tugged the brim of his hat and they rode away, the deputy leading.

A group of the hands, including Luther, came riding around from the corral and fell into a line behind Clay.

Sophie didn't see Whitey in amongst them, but then she didn't see much through her tears. She had a sudden flash of the memory of Cliff riding off to war. It had been the saddest day of her life. He'd come back, but he'd been changed, his youthful charm forever wiped away by the brutality of war.

This was nothing by comparison. Still, Clay's retreating back brought a wash of tears to her eyes, and she sent him along with a prayer for God to protect him. She prayed it fervently and remembered how Luther and Adam had been tuned in to her prayers. "Yes, Lord," she murmured, "help him."

She saw Luther look back over his shoulder and tip his hat to her. She smiled. She pushed back the tears and waved cheerfully. Luther shook his head like he thought she was getting to be a plumb nuisance.

"Nuisance or not, I'm not about to quit praying, Luther."

He was too far away to hear her, but somehow she thought he'd gotten the message.

Whitey and Buff came around the corner of the cabin just then. Sophie looked at the two of them. They'd been forged in different fires. Buff in the bitter cold mountains, Whitey in the heat and dust of a hundred Texas cattle ranches. But they had been burned down to the same hard iron. Sophie was glad they were here, and at the same time she wished they were with Clay, watching his back.

"I'm posting Andy, Luke, Rio, and Miguel in the hills as lookouts," Whitey called out to her. "They'll all have a clear view of the ranch, and they can be down in a five minutes. Buff and me'll stay up close. It sounds like they've got all of Mason's men treed, but no one really knows how many were riding with him. There could be others skulking about. There are plenty of us to keep watch but not 'nough to do much else. The boss said to tell you we'll need a meal, ma'am. Iffen you don't mind feeding us."

"Of course I don't mind," Sophie hastened to assure him.

Whitey gave a satisfied jerk of his head. "We'll eat in shifts."

Sophie said, "Supper will be ready for the first shift in half an hour."

"Obliged, ma'am." Whitey headed back to the bunkhouse.

Buff lagged behind and turned to Sophie when Whitey disappeared around the cabin. "Prepare for the worst an' you've got a right to hope for the best. That's what we're doing here, Miz McClellen."

Sophie smiled at Buff. It was the longest speech she'd ever heard

him give. "I'll do the same, Mr. Buff."

Buff ducked his head. "Ah, Miz McClellen, it's just Buff. There ain't no mister about it."

"It's just Sophie, Buff. You're my husband's good friend, and I'd be pleased if you called me that."

"Ain't likely I'll ever call you much'a nothin'." Buff jerked one shoulder.

Sophie smiled. "Well, just in case you do. . ."

Buff nodded and almost managed a smile, but Sophie thought his face seemed close to cracking. He stopped the smile, grunted at her, then turned and followed Whitey.

TWENTY-ONE

Clay rode away, trying to make peace with leaving Sophie and the girls. He wanted to stay and watch after them himself, but he also had a powerful urge to help the sheriff clean up the mess that surrounded the McClellen/Edwards ranch.

The group rode to Sawyer Canyon at an easy lope that spared the horses, while making good time. As they drew nearer, Clay's tension increased. It didn't help that he rode alongside Adam. The black man wound tighter and tighter until Clay half expected the man to explode. He urged his horse closer to Adam's. "We're not going into this looking for revenge."

"I know that." Adam's jaw was so tense it barely moved when he spoke.

The summer breeze sifted the dust being kicked up by the riders ahead of them. "Ever since you heard they had Mason cornered, you've had the look of a man ready to go charging in, guns blazing, to get that payback you've been wanting."

Adam looked at Clay.

Clay was stunned by the cold fury in his eyes.

"I didn't come out here looking to mess up the sheriff's standoff," Adam said. "I know how this is going to go down."

"And you can live with that?" Clay drew in a long breath, as he silently asked himself the same question. The smell of the Texas dirt and the working horses steadied his temper. "You can sit and wait until

Mason gives himself up?"

"I haven't led the easiest life, Clay. I was a free black man living in the South before slavery ended." Adam gave a humorless laugh. "To protect a young girl I love as if she were my own daughter, I put up with a man who used me to survive and hated me for it."

"My brother?"

Adam didn't answer. Clay wondered how much Sophie had whitewashed Cliff's true nature out of kindness.

"I fought for the North," Adam went on as if Clay hadn't interrupted. "Many's the time I stood and fought with men who gave me less respect than they gave their horses. I rode the borders of Indian territory, rounding up longhorn cattle that were three and four generations wild and as mean as any grizzly bear you've ever heard tell of."

Adam subsided for a moment, then he added, with an icy rage that was more frightening for being spoken quietly, "I watched my friends die at the hands of thieving cowards. And I walked barefoot three hundred miles with my back lashed open and a bullet wound in my side. So don't ask me if I can live with watching a man being hanged when I want him to die by my own hand."

Adam inhaled deeply. "I've found out I can live with purt' near anything. I know what I want is wrong. I'm a man who walked halfway across an almighty big state because God let me hear a woman's prayers. I know right and wrong. I know the hate burning in me is sin."

"And yet," Clay said, "I can see the fight inside you to control your desire for vengeance."

"Yeah, I ain't doing a very good job of covering it up."

"I have my own need to hurt these men." Clay tightened his grip on the reins, and his horse whickered in protest. He forced his hand to relax. "They killed my brother and threatened my wife."

Luther rode up between them at the moment, and even though he'd been lagging toward the back of the line of riders, Clay could see at a glance that Luther knew exactly what they'd been talking about.

"Leave room for God's wrath." Luther settled into the loping pace of his horse. With his wild beard and long hair, his coarse clothing and easy riding style, Luther looked for all the world like he and his horse were a single living creature.

"What's that mean?" Adam looked sharply at him.

Clay already knew. He'd had it preached to him just a couple of weeks back.

Luther edged his horse in between Clay's Appaloosa and Adam's roan. "I think Mason's got a lot to answer for when he meets his Maker. Nothing you can do to him will begin to match that."

"But it would make me feel so much better." Clay knew that wasn't true even as he said it.

"Leave room for God's wrath." Luther dropped back.

"He's right." Clay tipped the brim of his hat back on his head with one gloved thumb.

"I know." Adam looked over his shoulder at Luther. "I'm getting purely sick of that man."

Clay nodded, and they fell silent.

The sheriff had a man waiting to bring them to the position he had fortified.

"Smart man, the sheriff." Luther swung down off his spirited bay. "Not a good idea to be riding up to a nervous, trigger-happy posse."

They were directed to safe positions, well hidden by the jumble of rocks at the mouth of the canyon, and they waited.

It didn't take long before the wait was driving him crazy, which wasn't like him. Normally, Clay was a patient man.

"I am a patient woman." Sophie crossed her arms and tapped her toe. "I am, and no one had better make me wait agreeing with me!"

Mandy said quickly, "We know you're patient, Ma."

The other girls nodded, except Laura who had fallen asleep.

"What is keeping those men?" Sophie charged over to the door and

grasped the handle for the tenth time, if she hadn't lost count.

"Ma, you know Buff and Whitey want us to stay inside." Beth dashed up beside her and laid her little hand over Sophie's on the doorknob.

Sophie held on to the knob as if it were a lifeline. At last, through pure force of will, she let it go. "Well, why aren't they in here by now? I've still got men to feed, and I can't get the dishes cleaned up until they eat. Besides, it is time for you all to be in bed, but when they come trooping through here, they'll make too much noise."

Mandy came across the room. "We'll go on to bed, Ma. It's only two more of 'em left to eat. Just warn 'em to be quiet. If we do wake up, it'll be okay. I just hate to leave you to clean up alone."

Sophie noticed her daughters were acting more grown-up than she was. "I guess you might as well. Maybe I misunderstood. Or maybe the men didn't want to take the time to come all the way in for supper. Maybe they ate on the trail somehow."

"I'm sure it's something like that." Sally, with Laura snoozing in her arms, walked over with a maternal rock to pat Sophie's arm.

When Sally reassured her so maturely, something snapped in Sophie. All of a sudden the fear that had been tangled up inside her for weeks merged into one lightning bolt of terror. She knew that terror didn't come strictly from adding up all that had her worried. That fear was a warning—straight from God. She wasn't about to second-guess the message she was receiving.

She turned sharply to the girls. "No, it isn't something like that."

"Adam, come back," Clay hissed. He had been so focused on the entrance to the canyon that he hadn't been watching the men around him. Why would he? They weren't the threat.

Adam waved one hand behind him as if to swat Clay away like a pesky fly. Adam was a hundred feet away from all of them, using every ounce of cover the terrain provided.

Ranger Mitchell sidled up to Clay, pitching his voice low so the sound wouldn't carry, "Where is he going?"

Clay said in disbelief, "I noticed him just now."

Jackson grabbed his hat off his head and slammed it on the ground where he lay on his belly beside Clay. "We have this set up so no one gets hurt. I don't want a grandstanding fool looking to put notches in his gun, charging those men."

Clay shook his head and wiped sweat off his brow. They'd been lucky the canyon opened on the east. The sheer bluffs gave the posse some much-needed shade as the sun lowered in the sky, but the day was hot and still, and keeping down to avoid a bullet warmed a man.

Clay said, "Adam's not after a reputation, he's after revenge. He's had it in him to even the score with this gang for weeks."

"I know his story, and I've seen his scars," the ranger said. "I talked to him when you first got here. He said he was content to wait."

"I had a talk with him myself. I didn't like what I was seeing in his eyes." Clay lay, watching Adam slink like a shadow between slight depressions and whisper-thin sagebrush. Adam wore a white shirt, stained brown from being soaked with sweat, as he crawled on the ground. His body was nearly invisible against the coarse dirt. "But he convinced me he had himself under control."

The two of them watched, expecting a gunshot to ring out any second and leave Adam, with his meager protection, bleeding and dying in the Texas sunset. Adam continued forward as silent as a breeze, as fluid as trickling water. As mad as sin.

"He's good, isn't he?" Clay blinked and Adam seemed to vanish. Even his black hair was coated now in the dust that came as a partner with the dry Texas heat. Then Adam moved and Clay could see him again.

"Very good," Tom Jackson replied with grudging respect.

Clay became aware of the dozen other men who had formed an impenetrable wall along the front of the canyon. All of them watching. All of them silently rooting for Adam to get through the canyon opening

alive. All of them fearing the worst.

Adam reached the mouth of Sawyer Canyon and ducked behind the first good cover he'd had.

Clay breathed a sigh of relief and looked across several other men to see Luther shaking his head. Luther looked away from Adam and caught Clay's eye. The two of them shared a moment of regret. They knew what drove Adam to do this desperate thing. It would be bad for Adam if he managed to kill the lot of them. He'd carry this act of hatred like a burning stone in his soul for the rest of his life.

"He's in," Jackson whispered.

Clay looked back at the canyon. Adam had disappeared like a wisp of smoke on the air. They waited. Clay smelled the sweat of a dozen men strung tight as piano wire. He heard someone breathe raggedly, and it reminded him he'd been holding his own breath for a while. The canyon wasn't a large one. The good place to cut a man down was right at the mouth. After that, a man had a fighting chance. The silence drew out long. Clay suddenly pushed himself to his knees. "He got through. I'm going to see if I can."

Jackson shoved Clay sideways. Only the *crack* of a gun being triggered stopped Clay from shoving back. He looked down the barrel of Jackson's Winchester. "I'm not risking another man on such a reckless attack. Don't even think about it."

Clay didn't think the ranger would shoot him, but the heat of the day and the tension of the moment were taking their toll on everyone. He didn't make any more sudden moves.

"They're gone!" Adam came running out of the canyon, no longer making the least attempt to hide himself.

"They can't be gone." Sheriff Everett jumped to his feet, leaving cover behind in a way that proved he believed Adam, even though he denied it. "This is the only way out."

Adam stormed toward the group of men then passed straight through the line, heading for the horses.

After one frozen moment, Clay started after him.

"They're gone," Adam shouted without looking back or slowing down, "but their horses are still there!"

"They climbed out?" Clay walked faster.

Adam jerked his head in agreement. "It looks like they've been gone for hours. I thought there was something too neat about this."

Adam called back to Sheriff Everett, "They set you all up. They led you to this spot so they could tie up your whole posse while they made a clean getaway."

"Whitey would have told me if his plans changed. The men were coming in to do more than eat. They needed to check in with Whitey and Buff." Sophie was the mother again. Not a fidgeting worrier who needed small children to keep her calm. "Girls, something's happened to those men. Get into the crawl space. Now!"

The girls didn't hesitate. Beth threw back the rug and pulled up the trap door. Sally dropped into the dark hole in the floor, carrying Laura. Mandy went into the hidey-hole next.

"I'll make sure the rug lies flat," Sophie said.

"Ma, I think you oughta come down." Beth looked at the front door, her face pale but determined.

"I need to keep watch, Beth. You know how we do this."

Beth hesitated again, and Sophie didn't hurry her. Sophie respected all her girls' instincts.

"I don't know why, Ma, but I've got a feeling you need to clear out of the house. If you come with us, we can work our way out to the cave and scout the men who are supposed to be standing watch. We'll know if there's any real trouble."

Sophie was torn.

"We can leave Mandy, Sally, and Laura here underground," Beth added. "They can run the porch traps. If one of our men comes, they can let 'im know where we are."

Sophie and her girls had faced a lot of danger in the years they lived alone in this house. And they'd always handled it with Sophie remaining above, guarding the house. She hesitated. It set wrong with her to leave her home undefended, but the look on Beth's face held her fast.

"Something inside me tells me that this is a good time to be afraid, Ma. Something is telling you that, too. We all need to go, Ma. Now!"

Sophie went. She left the lanterns burning to provide a little light for the underground room and to make the house looked lived-in. She grabbed the rifle and shotgun hanging on nails above the front door then followed Beth into the hole. She closed the trap door over her head. As the door swung shut, closing the five of them into the cramped darkness, she prayed, "Lord, help me, help me, help me."

Luther was beside Clay and Adam, and all at once he froze in his tracks. Adam stopped so suddenly he almost fell over.

Clay looked at both of them. "I heard her."

Luther was running. Adam sprinted ahead of him. Clay, adrenaline coursing through his very bones, tore the reins loose from the branch.

"Where are you going in such an all-fired hurry?" Sheriff Everett hollered. "We don't even know what direction they headed."

"They're at McClellen's," Luther shouted as he spurred his horse.

"How do you know?" Everett said.

The rangers were already swinging up on their horses, responding to the urgent riding of the three men.

"We heard Sophie call for help," Adam shouted over his shoulder as he kicked his horse into a canter.

Clay's only thought was to get to Sophie and the girls before it was too late. He was a mile down the trail at a full gallop before he looked back. The whole posse, regardless of the nonsense of Adam's words, had fallen in line behind him, all bent on one thing: Get to the ranch. Save Clay's family.

Sophie couldn't help being a little disgruntled. It looked like she was going to have to save her girls herself.

As usual.

What was the point of men anyway? She looked at her four precious daughters and thought of the child growing inside her. She loved her children fiercely and was glad she had them, so she begrudgingly decided men had their purpose.

"I'm going out the tunnel to the cave entrance," Beth said. "It's right above one of the best lookouts on the ranch. If they've got someone watching us, he'll be there."

"I'm going with you." Sophie started crawling toward the tunnel. It was low and dark. They would be on their hands and knees the whole way. "If we find trouble, the both of us will need to get in position to spring the traps."

Sophie left the shotgun leaning against the dirt wall of the cramped little crawl space. The only thing that kept the little cellar from being pitch-black was light coming through tiny slits between the floorboards overhead. The musty dirt smelled like safety. "Mandy, take the braces out of the porch. Sally, keep Laura asleep if you possibly can. Her crying could alert someone that you're down here. If she wakes up and starts crying, get down the tunnel about halfway. No one can hear her there."

Mandy was already working on the front porch. Sally sat back and cradled Laura in her arms.

The ranch house was built just a few dozen feet in front of the first rocky crags that grew into bluffs to the west of the McClellen ranch. Sophie had dug a tunnel in the years after Cliff had gone to war, well braced with timbers she'd cut herself, burrowing herself a little escape route. Those hadn't been particularly dangerous years, although there had been a few incidences of Indian trouble and the inevitable small-time rustling.

Sophie hadn't felt safe, and she wasn't a woman to sit by and hope for the best when there was something she could do. She'd dug her way to the cave, which had a series of caverns she could follow all the way to the top of the bluffs.

Sophie and Beth crawled through the tunnel. Sophie felt the weight of the mountain crushing down on her in the stygian darkness. They emerged in the cave and could see again, even with dusk darkening into night.

They stuck together until they reached the highest point in the underground cave system. Beth looked at Sophie, and Sophie gestured for her to go check for a lookout.

Elizabeth, at eight years, had a gift for the woods that she had honed in the thicket, sneaking up on deer because she loved to study animals. Sophie didn't like sending her daughter into danger, but Sophie knew her children's strengths. She knew Beth could do this better than she could.

Beth slipped away silently, and Sophie didn't have long to wait for her return. Beth held a finger up to her lips and led Sophie back down into the tunnel out of earshot.

"I found him right outside the cave entrance," she whispered. "He's not one of our men. He's got Rio hog-tied, lying on the ground unconscious."

Sophie's stomach did a sickening twist. Up until now she'd just been following a small voice in her head that said there was danger, but she'd had no solid proof.

Now she had it. That man could be no one but a member of Mason's gang. Adam had said there were twenty of them. They'd caught four. Clay had mentioned that several of the gang had run off. The sheriff had seen eight men go into Sawyer Canyon. Eight men.

"If Rio's tied, he's alive." Sophie made sure Beth didn't hear one ounce of fear. "If we can get him loose and he's not hurt too bad, he'll be a help."

"I wish Pa were here." Beth looked toward the cave entrance.

How had these men gotten out of that box canyon? And what had happened to the posse who had them cornered? Sophie thought, *Just once, I wish he were here, too.* Then she stiffened her backbone. "If you want to help, you'd best do some praying, Beth."

"What should I pray, Ma?"

"I haven't prayed much of anything for years," Sophie said grimly, "except, 'Help me.'"

There it was again—Sophie's sweet voice. The first time it had been laced with desperation. This time she sounded resigned and very tired. A thrill of fear cut straight to Clay's heart. He looked behind him. Luther and Adam had gotten the message, too.

In an odd way, hearing her prayer made Clay feel better. He hadn't given it much thought, but it had occurred to him that Luther and Adam had been hearing her prayers when he should have been the one God was calling to go help Sophie. Of course, up till now, he'd been on the spot, not in need of being called by a miracle since he was within shouting distance.

They had five miles to go, but it was five rugged miles, some of it up and down instead of across. They'd be an hour or more getting home. If he pushed his horse to the limit and the horse fell and broke a leg, he might not get there at all. He pushed his horse to the limit anyway. The Appaloosa was so game, Clay wondered if he hadn't heard Sophie calling, too.

TWENTY-TWO

I reckon asking God for help is about all most of it boils down to anyway." Beth squared her shoulders and started for the opening.

Sophie nodded and patted Beth on the arm.

"Then why does the parson have to go on so long on Sunday morning with his praying?" Beth asked.

"Well, we need to say thank You, too." Sophie pulled her riding skirt close against her legs to keep the fabric from rustling. "And usually when you get to counting up, we've got way more to thank God for than to ask Him for, so it can take awhile."

Beth seemed skeptical. "It's not that I mind saying, 'Help me' and 'Thank You'; it's that I mind the parson saying it so slow for so long."

Sophie didn't have anything much to say to that, so she changed the subject. "Let's get down to saving this ranch."

Beth got in position just outside the cave entrance behind the lookout.

Sophie moved through the tunnel to a lower level and slipped out to hide behind some rocks. The rocks were in a tall, jumbled pile. When she was setting her traps, Sophie had moved the pile around a bit so there was a small opening she could see through without being seen. Carefully surveying the area for others in the gang before each movement, Sophie crept up behind the rocks. She watched the man, who was only about twenty feet away from her, most of it straight up. Sophie lifted a small rock and pulled a folded oilskin paper out from under it. She unfolded the paper and took out the prettiest hanky she'd ever owned. She touched the delicate thing, all white linen and tatted lace, then she picked up a few tiny rocks and a little damp earth and slapped it into the middle of the handkerchief to weigh it down. Then she waited for Elizabeth.

Sophie couldn't hear what Beth did, but Sophie knew her little girl. She wouldn't make too much noise, nor too little. The man turned away from watching.

Sophie deftly rose from her hiding place and tossed the weighted handkerchief onto a spot about a dozen feet off the trail, in plain sight of the outlaw. She ducked back out of sight.

When the man turned around from studying the land behind him, he went back to his careful watch. It took him ten minutes to spot the hankie, and Sophie was about to explode from frustration by the time he saw it.

The man straightened. Sophie was close enough to see his eyes sharpen. Sophie had to give him credit. He was a good lookout. He didn't go down to look at the handkerchief right away. He waited, made sure there was no one around, and then started sidling down the steep trail.

He walked over to the handkerchief, and as he bent to pick it up, Sophie heard him mumble, "Was this lying here before?"

Sophie yanked the rope that released the net the man was standing on. With a startled yell, the man was jerked thirty feet in the air as the sapling sprung up straight. Just as Sophie had planned, the man ended up dangling very close to the steepest drop-off. Before he could make a second sound, Sophie stepped out from the clearing and brandished her hunting knife near the hemp rope that stretched from the ground to the tree. "If you yell again, I'll cut the rope and you won't quit falling until you've rolled all the way to the ranch house.

The man looked frantically at the knife, then he looked at the jagged rocks that covered the hillside for half a mile, mostly straight down, and didn't make a peep.

Sophie ducked back behind the rock and called out softly, "I'm waiting for your friends back here. Don't make me regret letting you live."

Sophie sat quietly behind the rock for a few minutes until she started to believe the man was actually going to remain silent. Then she soundlessly slipped back into the cave and ran up to meet Beth. Beth had Rio untied, but although breathing steadily, he was out cold. He had a good-sized welt on his forehead.

Sophie said, "We're not going to get much help from him."

Beth shook her head. "Let's drag him into the cave so no one bothers him."

It took a lot of tugging to move the burly Mexican. Sophie paused to rest several times, mindful of the unborn baby she was supposed to be coddling. They got him hidden, then they headed through the honeycomb of caves for the next most likely lookout.

"I hear someone coming in the back," Mandy hissed at Sally.

Sally lay Laura down. "The braces?"

"All out," Mandy answered. Both girls fell silent. Mandy gripped on the pigging string in her hand and two more in her mouth and waited. She'd played this game so many times with her ma that she knew exactly what to do. The only thing was, she'd never actually had to do it before. This time, it looked like it was really going to happen.

She moved to the back of the house and peeked through a hidden slit. It definitely wasn't one of the McClellen men. It was a dirty-looking man with no good on his mind, judging from the rifle in his hands. The man stepped up onto the back porch, and it collapsed under him. His head cracked with a solid *thud* on the crossbar Ma had rigged for just this reason. It left the man stunned as it was meant to.

Mandy dove at the man. She whipped the leather around his hands behind his back, then took another pigging string out of her teeth and whipped his feet together. She'd hog-tied a two-year-old steer many times, and this man didn't wiggle a bit more than that. She had him tied up tight and gagged before the dust had settled from the fall. She tossed his rifle to Sally, who caught it deftly and set it aside. Mandy dragged the man away from the hole in the porch floor with quick, practiced moves, while Sally reset the porch boards. The trap was ready again.

"I wonder how Ma and Beth are doing?" Sally asked calmly.

Mandy didn't like the way the man was staring at her, all meanlike, so she put a blindfold over his eyes from the supply of pigging strings, ropes, and neckerchiefs Ma had stored down here for just such an occasion. The man struggled as she covered his eyes, but she had him bound tighter than a year-old calf at branding time. Then she turned to her little sister.

"Ma planned this trap and it worked. No reason the others shouldn't."

"I sure wish Pa would get here." Sally settled herself to watch through the slits in the front porch steps.

Mandy checked the load in the rifle, snapped it back shut, and laid it well out of reach of the outlaw. "Me, too." She went to her lookout in the rear of the crawl space. "Someone needs to get here and save us."

"I think there's someone coming from the front." Sally backed out of the way to let Mandy through.

"Got it." Mandy caught up the pigging strings and clamped them with her teeth.

The second man Sophie and Beth snared didn't yell, because he cracked his head smartly on the trunk of the tree when he got snapped into the air and hung unconscious in the net Mandy had woven from hemp.

They freed Andy, another ranch hand, but although his eyes flickered open once, he was in no shape to help them. He had a nasty gash on his head, and when he tried to talk, he mumbled something Sophie couldn't understand. Sophie took the time to stop the bleeding and bandage him; then she and Beth left him lying in another cave to recover.

A quick but thorough check of the mountainside didn't turn up any more outlaws. "If the sheriff was right about there being eight men,

six of them might be down there right now with the other girls. We'd better get down there and help."

"Ma, look!" Elizabeth pointed to the cabin, which they could see from their vantage point. Sophie looked just in time to see a man fall through the front porch floor. In seconds, Sally was visible covering the porch back up. She wouldn't have done that if the man had given them trouble.

Sophie looked around the ranch yard to see if anyone had noticed one of their own disappearing. No one else was in sight.

"All right. That takes care of three of them. Five left." Sophie studied the terrain all around them. Frustrated, she muttered to herself, "Where are they?"

Beth was silent, also looking the land over. Finally she pressed her hand to Sophie's. "Right above us, off to the left."

Sophie turned and saw two riders. "They'll be passing right in front of one of our rock slides."

The two of them silently ducked back into the cave and ran.

Clay saw the final turn in the trail that would give way to a view of the ranch. The trail widened and flattened out. Adam and Luther caught up to him and galloped with him, three abreast.

Luther said, "No shooting."

"We'd've heard gunshots all the way to Sawyer Canyon, Clay." Adam raced his roan, bent close to its neck until he was talking into its mane. "I haven't heard a one."

"I haven't heard Sophie calling for help again either." Clay couldn't decide if that was good or bad.

They kept pushing and just rounded the corner of the trail that put them within a long uphill mile of the ranch, when they heard a thundering *crash* in the hills behind the cabin.

"What's that?" Clay sat up straight on his Appaloosa, but he didn't slacken his pace.

Luther stared at the distant hills behind the ranch house even as they charged on. "It sounds like an avalanche."

"It's a booby trap being sprung." Adam laughed over the thunder of hooves. "It's something I taught Sophie to do years ago."

"She told me about those," Clay remembered.

Luther's voice echoed with satisfaction. "That means she's alive." Luther's furred hat blew off his head, revealing a shining bald scalp. Clay glanced quickly behind him and saw the hat spook the sheriff's horse, where Josiah rode just a few lengths back.

"And she's made it through the caves into the hills," Adam said with pride. "She's got room to move in the hills. My Sophie-girl is an almighty fine woodsman. She'll be okay."

"It's one woman and four little girls facing down a gang of desperate men." The wind whipped Clay's words away as he growled, "Forgive me if I keep on worrying."

Mandy noticed Laura's eyes flickering open seconds before the little girl sat up.

"Where Mama?" Laura rubbed her eyes and stretched her chubby little arms up to ruffle her blond curls.

"Great, now we have to chase after her b'sides catching all these low-down varmints." Sally scrambled on her hands and knees over to Laura.

Mandy put a blindfold on the other outlaw. This one had knocked himself senseless when he fell through the porch, but she didn't like to think of his beady eyes on her should he happen to wake up. "I declare, the work just never ends around a Texas ranch."

Laura whimpered a little, confused by the murky crawl space. Sally lifted her into her lap. "I'd better get her up the tunnel afore she gives us away."

At that moment they heard rumbling on the mountain. Mandy's

heart lifted and she looked over at Sally. The two girls beamed at each other in the murky cellar.

Mandy gave her chin a satisfied jerk. "It sounds like Ma and Beth are all right."

Sally patted Laura's back. "Maybe, when I take Laura to the tunnel, I'll meet 'em coming back down. It's got to be Beth's turn to baby-sit by now."

Mandy checked the outlaws for hidden weapons. "You know you're in charge of baby-sitting during attacks, Sally."

Sally turned to Laura. "Why don't you grow up so you can help us fight off bad guys?"

Laura quit whimpering and stuck her thumb in her mouth.

"She'll most likely get to do most of the work with the new one Ma's having," Mandy said brightly, "now that we're working as ranch hands for Pa."

"Yeah." Sally joggled a burp out of Laura and gave her a disgusted look. "But what are the chances of us getting attacked again? Texas is getting purely peaceable these last few years."

"As long as she's quiet, why don't you stay here with me?" Mandy asked. "It's a lot quicker getting the porches put back together with your help. And with you watching out the back while I watch out the front, no one can get past us."

"Sure." She glanced at her now-contented baby sister. "I think Laura's okay for now. I'll stay as long as I can."

Sally scooted over to the lookout spot. Laura kicked her feet, seemed to decide she had all the dirt off one thumb, and switched to the other. Then she sat on Sally's lap, staring curiously at the two men who were in the crawl space with them.

Sophie quickly examined the two men their avalanche had felled. "Neither of them is dead."

"Are you sure?" Her bloodthirsty daughter sounded disappointed.

"Beth, we don't want to kill anybody." Sophie plopped her hands on her hips and turned to her daughter. "The Bible says, 'Thou shalt not kill.'"

Beth tightened the cords on the motionless man's arms then got busy on his legs. "Surely even the Ten Commandments have exceptions, Ma."

Sophie thought about it, even though they really needed to get moving before someone came to check out the noise. "That may be true, but to be on the safe side, we'd best not be killing anybody if we can possibly avoid it."

"Fair enough." Beth straightened from her work and watched the trail for trouble.

Sophie winced as she bound a leg she was sorely afraid had been broken by a falling tree trunk. "Let's get down to the ranch and see if there's any of this vermin to clear out around there."

"Should we go back by the cave and see how the girls are doing in the cellar?" Beth asked.

"I think I see someone holed up in the barn." Sophie studied the yard below.

"The barn?" Beth perked right up. "We can do some real damage to someone in the barn."

"Beth," Sophie said sternly, "quit enjoying yourself."

"Yes, Ma." Beth forced her face into a frown.

They worked their way down the hillside, avoiding the trail and keeping cover around them at all times. Sophie stopped several times to inspect the land in all directions. She saw definite activity in the barn, but she couldn't figure out why anyone would be holed up in there. Did they think they were hiding?

"They're waiting to ambush anyone who rides into the yard," Beth said abruptly.

The minute she said it, Sophie saw a group of men round the far end of the trail. She recognized Clay riding in the lead of at least a

dozen men. "By the way they're riding, I can tell they've figured out we're in danger."

Beth grabbed Sophie's arm. "He'll come charging in to save us and ride right into gunfire."

"Maybe those men expected him and that's the whole reason they're in there."

Elizabeth whispered, "I like havin' a pa, and he's been a right good 'un. I don't want to have to hunt up another."

"Then let's go try and keep this one alive." Careful to remain out of sight, Sophie led the way toward the barn.

"That sounded like an avalanche." Judd looked away from the window.

"Why would there be an avalanche?" Harley asked. "I don't like it."

Judd sneered. "I swear you're getting so's you worry just like a woman these days, Harley."

"Worrying has kept me alive this long," Harley said.

Judd ignored him.

Harley asked, "You're sure Eli got into the house?"

"I'm sure. I saw him run in." The truth was he'd been looking out the other side of the barn at the exact instant Eli had run into the house. His view of the front door had been blocked. But he'd seen Eli head for the house and now he was gone. There'd been no resistance. Where else could he be but inside? He didn't bother Harley with the pesky details.

"It don't set right, Judd, turning Eli loose on that woman and her children."

Judd looked at his partner with disgust. Harley was going soft on him. Harley had scouted the place for hours after they'd lured the posse then left 'em there guarding Sawyer Canyon like a pack of headless chickens. "McClellen's wife is uncommon beautiful, and she had four of the prettiest little girls to ever roam the hills of Texas."

271

"I don't like to think about Eli in there with those defenseless females."

Judd didn't like anyone questioning him, and Harley knew it. Judd glared at him, but Harley didn't look like he cared much what Judd thought.

Judd would have taken Harley on—he had it to do—but right now he was preoccupied with spying. "Sid's in there with him. That might keep Eli under control."

"You wanted Eli in there," Harley said with cool contempt. "You know how he treats a woman."

Judd took a second to check the two horses they'd brought into the barn with them. They were ready to ride when it was time to hit the trail. The mustang tried to bite Judd's hand, and Judd clubbed the horse hard on the head.

"Eli could have been the lookout," Harley added. "You're hoping he kills the McClellen woman so you won't have to."

"You're supposed to be keeping watch, Harley." Judd went back to his watch. He didn't look down the trail. Instead he scowled at Harley. "Don't think about what might be happening in there. Have you seen any of our men on the bluff?"

"No, but I wouldn't expect to. Do you think all the McClellen hands are dead?" Harley asked. "How much poison did you put in their coffee?"

"I put enough in to bring down a herd of buffalo. They're dead."

"You gave 'em a lot, but did they drink it?" Harley worked the action on his rifle.

"We saw the two in the bunkhouse laid out flat," Judd growled.

"They looked dead to me, too. Now we've sunk to poison. I'm a gunslinger, Judd, and proud of it. My fights used to be fair ones—they were against horse thieves. Then, at least, they were against men. We were ruthless, but we had a code. We had some honor, Judd. But where is the honor in poison? Where is the honor in turning a coyote like Eli loose on a defenseless woman and children?"

Judd looked at Harley. He didn't like the cold scorn he saw in Harley's eyes. They'd been together a long time, and what Harley said was true. They'd been hard, brutal men. Judd reveled in that. But they'd been strong. They'd taken what they wanted face-to-face, with the power of their fists and guns. It had all gone wrong along the way. And now they'd sunk to this. They were sneaks, killing women and children and poisoning honest men. Judd refused to think about it.

"As far as that avalanche goes," Harley said, "I'm not a man who believes in coincidence."

Harley quit talking. The time for talking was past. He'd never killed a woman before. He'd never even stood by while someone else did. More than that, he'd never so much as raised his hand to a child. In fact, the few times in his life he'd even seen children, he'd been fascinated by them and found pure pleasure in watching the little tikes.

He wasn't a back-shooter either. That one day, when Judd had sprung it on him that he wanted Harley to dry-gulch McClellen, he'd done it—taken his shot. But he'd had a chance to think it over since then.

Harley crouched here in this barn and knew shame.

He watched the house and thought of those little girls and the vengeful man behind him and he wanted out. He wanted out of this mess and out of this life. But how did a man turn his footsteps back from a path he'd been treading so long?

That's when Harley heard a voice. A voice he hadn't heard for years. A voice that whispered to him things his long-dead mama had told him about while she held him in her lap. About Jesus. About love. About God having a plan for his life.

Harley eased himself away from the door and forgot about keeping watch. He let all his life spin through his mind. All the little steps that, one by one, had led him to this place and this act of pure, unforgivable evil.

And that's when he remembered something else his mama had said. Forgiveness. A man was bound to do wrong because that's just the way humans were. But there was forgiveness for those who trusted in Jesus Christ. Harley reached out for it and felt years of death and hatred melt away from his heart.

Then he saw Mason tense. "Posse coming up the road," Judd called out to the man who had just changed sides. "McClellen's in the lead. He's still a ways off."

Judd lifted his gun to aim at the lead rider. Harley lifted his gun and aimed it at Judd and hesitated, torn now between his desire to save all these innocent people and his own complete unwillingness to take another human life—even a life so despicable as Judd Mason's.

A soft rustling of cloth caught his attention by a little door near a corner of the barn. Harley didn't turn to look. He knew that sound. It was soft material and lots of it. A woman.

Mason turned to the sound and with a sudden roar of rage he leapt to his feet and yelled, "I'll get that meddlesome woman myself!"

Harley turned to see her dart back outside.

Judd ran for the back door then suddenly he veered away from it. "She's not getting away from me!" Mason shouted. "You and the men in the house will have to hold off the posse!"

Mason didn't notice Harley's gun. He whirled and jumped on the back of the fiery little mustang. The horse reared and fought. Mason kicked it viciously. He didn't go toward the back door. He headed for the wider door next to it. Harley heard a soft noise that sounded fearful, and he looked straight up over the smaller door. There was a little girl. Harley was so amazed it took him a second to realize the child was holding a rope. Harley's eyes followed the rope and saw it was fastened to a basket of rocks.

If Judd went out that rear door after Sophie, he was going to get peppered with rocks. The little girl looked down from where she was perched above him, like a hovering angel. He saw the terror cross her face when she realized she'd been seen. Harley shook his head and

pointed his gun at Judd, still fighting the horse.

The little girl stared at him with unconcealed relief, then—she smiled at him. Harley was in awe. The heartfelt smile of a brave little girl fighting for the people she loved was a gift as sweet as the loving words of his mother.

God rested His hand on Harley's shoulder as surely as if He stood beside him in that barn. It was the finest moment of Harley Shafter's life.

Mason spurred his horse and suddenly the feisty, little mustang went wild. After months of abuse, or maybe inspired by its Creator, it reared until it looked to be going over backward. Then, with a squeal of rage, the horse twisted its body and landed stiff-legged on the floor. It arched its back and, with an impossible gyration, hurled Judd to the ground. He landed, almost as if the horse had aimed, right underneath the little girl and her basket.

The ground caved in under Judd. Harley heard Mason scream in pain. A basket of rocks rained down on Mason's head, and Mason was still.

Mrs. McClellen poked her head in the door and glanced up into the rafters. Harley looked up and saw the little girl grinning at her mama. Harley stood slowly and drew both women's attention. Mrs. McClellen looked at him fearfully, and he quickly tossed his gun aside. "Don't shoot, ma'am," he said to the unarmed woman. "I give up."

Clay and the posse came charging into the yard just as Harley marched out of the barn with his hands in the air.

TWENTY-THREE

"He just surrendered?" Clay asked in disbelief for the tenth time.

"He had a gun," Sophie repeated. "He didn't so much as threaten us."

"Just tossed his gun away and raised his arms? Harley Shafter?" Clay shook his head.

"If that's his name, Clay. I don't know the man!"

"Just like that? Did he think you or Beth were armed?" Clay shuddered when he thought about his little girl perched in those rafters under the rifle of a man as dangerous as Shafter. He was a known gunman and as tough as a hobnail boot.

Sophie set a cup of coffee in front of Clay, then got more cups out for the other men who had crowded into her kitchen. They were leaning against walls and sitting on the floor. All four girls had gone into one bedroom, just to make space in the cabin for everyone.

A very embarrassed Rio was leaning in the open doorway. Buff and Whitey had been knocked cold in the bunkhouse by whatever had been added to their coffee. Only the fact that they had eaten with Sophie and mostly drank the coffee she made had saved their lives. They were still too ashamed of themselves to talk. Of course, when had either one of them ever talked anyway?

Andy had the same rough bandage on his head Sophie had put on in the cave. He wouldn't let Sophie doctor him. He seemed to think he deserved to get an infection and die for letting himself be drugged

and then knocked senseless.

The wounded outlaws had been hauled away. It had been a real chore to get the two out of the trees. Sophie had answered the ranger's questions with all the men listening. Now, except for the questions Clay couldn't seem to quit asking, none of them had much to say to her at all.

In other words, everything was back to normal.

Sophie had run out of coffee cups, and Eustace had fetched all there were in the bunkhouse. And except for the silence and general air of humiliation amongst the men, it had become a party.

"What do you men want for supper?" Sophie asked into the silence.

"I can't believe you put spikes in the bottom of that pit." Clay nursed his coffee and shook his head. "That was a plumb mean thing to do."

"Sorry." Sophie served the third pot of coffee she'd made in the last hour.

"No, you're not. You're just trying to buck me up."

"I taught her about those traps, mostly," Adam put in. "But she came up with a few tricks of her own."

"Living in a thicket gives a woman time to use her imagination."

Adam nodded.

"And how many more of these traps are there?" Clay crossed his arms and scowled. "Mightn't they be dangerous?"

Sophie noticed Clay conveniently forgot that she had tried to show him the traps on a couple of occasions. He'd smiled at her "little surprises" and put her off.

"I made them so you had to trip them. No one can stumble into one. Why, you and the men have been walking over the pit under the side door of the barn all week."

Clay sat up straight and glared at her.

Sophie patted Clay on the chest as she passed him with the coffee-pot. "I'm sorry."

She wasn't, but she hoped Clay appreciated that she tried to sound sincere.

The rangers came riding into the yard. They and the deputies had taken all eight of Mason's men into town. Sheriff Everett's jailhouse was fairly bulging at the seams. Most of the men were wanted for holdups and murders all across the West. There would be enough reward money to add another valley to the ranch if they had a mind to.

Ranger Jackson strode into the house. "I want you to tell me again just what Harley Shafter did when you went into the barn."

Sophie crossed her arms and glared at him. "I've told you ten times already!"

Jackson said, "No, you've told me twice."

"You've told *me* ten times," Clay said. "But the ranger's been gone for eight of them."

Sophie sighed and repeated her story. Jackson listened, absorbing every word of it. Finally he said, "Shafter has been talking. He's confessed to everything and spared himself none of the guilt. Every member of that gang will be found guilty because of what he's said. And we found a lot of money on Mason. We'll be able to return money to the heirs of most of the men who have been killed."

"Why's he telling everything?" Clay asked. "Usually a gunman like that is mighty closed-mouthed."

"He said he heard God talking to him in that barn. He said he was ready to turn on Mason and protect the posse when it came into the yard."

"It don't sound to me like he's taking responsibility for much if he's trying to say he was on our side," Eustace said with contempt.

"No, it's not like that. He's not trying to get out of any charges. In fact, he's saying he deserves a noose, and he'll take it. He just smiles when we try and break his story. Says he knows he deserves God's wrath, but he's made his peace and he's ready."

"Leave room for God's wrath." Adam looked across the room at Luther. "Just like you said."

Luther nodded.

"I believe him." Sophie, done with her inquisition for now, began

slicing up a hunk of venison she'd put on the baking rack. "The look on his face when he surrendered was almost. . ." Sophie shrugged. "I know it sounds strange, but it was the impression I got at the time. It was almost. . .holy."

Sophie filled her fourth pot of water to make more coffee. Suddenly her knees wobbled a little, and she had to grab for the edge of the water barrel to steady herself.

Clay was beside her in a split second, lifting her off her feet. "No more questions. Sophie needs to rest."

Adam chuckled. "She's as sturdy as a Texas cottonwood, Clay, but if you want to try and slow her down, I wish you luck."

One by one the men left the cabin. Luther said as he went out, "Reckon me and Buff'll hang around Texas for a spell. It's too far to ride iffen she calls me again."

Buff grunted. As he shuffled out of the room, he said, "Sorry I failed ya, Miz McClellen."

"That's okay." Sophie blushed so prettily, Clay couldn't believe she was the same little wildcat who'd captured a gang of cutthroats.

Buff shook his head.

"Me, too, ma'am." Whitey stared at the floor as if afraid it might disappear under his feet. Andy and Rio apologized, too, on their way out. They'd each done it a dozen times apiece already.

Clay smiled as he watched the dejected group go. They were Texans. They'd bounce back.

The last one to leave was Adam. He came up to Sophie, undeterred by the stern look of *get out* on Clay's face. "Mason kept saying, when they were yanking that wooden stake out of his leg, that he'd get even with you, Sophie, if it took him the rest of his life."

"His life may not be that long." Clay tightened his grip on his wife.

"It sounded like he wanted revenge for something. But I never did anything to him." Sophie's brow wrinkled in confusion.

"It got me to thinking about the revenge I've been hungerin' for ever since my partners died. In the end, I stood by and let the law take its own course."

Clay snorted. "You went charging into Sawyer Canyon alone. I don't call that letting the law take its course."

"I know," Adam said with a sheepish shrug. "I had a real bad moment there when lettin' Mason hide out from us was more than I could bear. I admit that."

With the men gone except for Adam, the girls came out of the bedroom and sat at the table. Clay watched his family, all pretty and sweet smelling. They were soft as baby calves and tough as full-grown longhorns. He loved them.

"It's a good thing you did," Sophie said. "It brought you back to the ranch."

"Yeah, none of these outlaws would have gotten out of here alive if we'd left them to my girls for much longer," Clay said dryly.

Sophie and the girls grinned. Clay hugged his armful of a wife then set her on a chair at the table.

"Anyway, I realized that the difference between my need for revenge and Mason's is the difference between God and Satan. It's as simple as that. Mason insisted on delivering his wrath on those he was angry with, and in the end he was just a pure tool of the devil. No matter how angry I got, I could never have crossed that line and committed cold-blooded murder in an act of revenge. God has made me strong enough not to do that."

"He's made us all strong enough, Adam." Sophie reached her hand across the table to pat Adam's rugged hand. "In the end we all did the right thing."

Beth crossed her arms and tapped her toe rapidly on the wooden floor. "I think Sally and Mandy enjoyed taking those men prisoner a little too much."

"I did not! I purely hated having to catch those bad men." Sally grabbed Beth's long braid and gave it a hefty yank.

Beth screamed and backed up, pulling her hair all the more. She slammed into Mandy.

Mandy pushed her hard. "Be careful! And we did not enjoy ourselves! Not hardly none at all!"

Sally gave Beth's hair another tug, and Beth started screaming at the top of her lungs. Laura began crying in the midst of the chaos.

Sally shrieked. "And the next time we're attacked, you have to babysit. It's your turn."

"We don't take turn on attacks. Ma says—" Beth jerked her hair free, fell backward, and staggered into Clay, who threw his arms wide to keep from falling over and smacked Adam across the face.

Adam ran.

Sally and Mandy attacked Beth as a team.

Clay roared, "You girls settle down!"

The girls completely ignored his yelling, so he yelled louder. Sophie went to his side. "Aren't you pleased?"

Clay decided his wife had lost her mind.

"Can't you see the girls have decided you won't quit loving them just because you're mad?"

Clay hollered over the tumult, "And that's a good thing?"

"Sure it is." Sophie scooped Laura up as she toddled past, shrieking. "Now, if you'll excuse me." She thrust Laura into his arms. "I'm going to lie down and rest."

Clay didn't know whether to laugh or cry. She retreated to her bedroom and closed the door as calmly as if the screaming and yelling were a lullaby to her.

Clay faced his raging daughters and had a bright idea. He charged.

The screams turned to giggles as he was buried under petticoats, while his pretty wife obeyed him in the next room. Life didn't get any better.

EPILOGUE

Clifton Lazarus McClellen was born early on a bitter winter morning. All the girls slept through it, and Clay probably would have, too. Sophie was determined not to make the doctor ride clear and away out to the ranch in the cold for such a simple thing as bringing a baby.

Except there came a time during her laboring that Sophie quit trying to be brave and quiet and decided all men should die. And since Clay was handy, she might as well start with him. She was too busy to actually do him any damage before he could get out of her reach, though.

Clay panicked as she knew he would, what with him being a man and all. He started to get dressed to go for the doctor. Sophie was in the midst of a tearful appeal to not kill himself going out in the dangerous weather—ironic when a moment ago she'd really wanted him dead—when Cliff made his appearance.

His twin brother, Clayton Jarrod, was born five minutes later, while Clay was trying to wrap Clifton in a blanket Sophie had ready and, at the same time, frantically ordering Sophie to stop being in pain now, since the baby was already here.

When the whirlwind had passed and another blanket had been found, Clay finally calmed down enough to say with immense satisfaction, "We really narrowed the gap between girls and boys in this family."

"I thought you said you wanted another girl," Sophie challenged

him, still not very happy with the man who had caused her a very uncomfortable night.

"I lied," Clay announced with an unrepentant smile. "I wanted a son like the very dickens. I didn't know how much until this very second."

Sophie looked at the arms full of babies Clay held and smiled. "I didn't know how much I wanted a boy either."

"If you keep having them at this rate, we'll be tied by next Christmas."

Back to wanting to kill him, Sophie said, "Just for that, you're getting up in the night to change their diapers."

"What's a diaper?"

Sophie slumped back on the bed and started to cry. Clay sat down beside her. "Sophie, what about rule number one?"

Both boys chose that moment to start howling their heads off.

They wriggled and cried, and Sophie couldn't take her eyes off of them—until she noticed that Clay's expression had turned from insufferable pride to pure unadulterated horror.

"I didn't think boys would cry!"

Sophie forgot all about breaking rule number one because she wanted to laugh. "I'm going to enjoy watching you learn to be a pa to infants."

Clay looked up from the babies and leaned over to kiss her soundly on the lips. "I'll be great at it, just like I've learned to be a great pa to the girls."

Sophie laid her hand on Clay's cheek. "We've been through so much together this last year, Clay. I've learned as much as you have."

Clay nodded and looked back at his sons. "We're going to teach the boys to be good men. To work hard. To respect a woman's strength."

Sophie turned the edge of the blanket back on the baby closest to her. "You've never gotten over me protecting the ranch all by myself."

"Why should I get over it? I learned what a special woman I married. And I learned to trust God in everything."

"Except birthing these babies," Sophie teased him. "You wanted the doctor for them."

Clay ran his rough finger over one tiny fist, looking first from one son then to the other.

Sophie wanted to start crying again from the sweetness of it. She couldn't hold back what was in her heart. "I love you, Clay." She knew she shouldn't say it. Clay wasn't a man who wanted to talk about such nonsense.

He said very calmly, "I love you, too, Sophie."

Sophie straightened away from him. "Since when?"

Clay looked away from the babies. "Well, since always, I reckon."

"But you've never said such a thing. Why didn't you tell me?" Sophie took one of the babies from him to punish him for being such an insensitive clout.

Clay stroked the soft cheek of the baby he had left, not appearing punished at all. She nudged him sharply with her elbow. "Well?"

His eyes never moved. "Well, what?"

"Why haven't you ever told me you love me?"

"Of course I love you." Clay shook his head, still staring. "How could I not love someone as sweet and pretty as you? It'd only be news if I didn't love you, I'd think."

Sophie tried to remind herself of the lessons they'd learned about revenge, and the wildly fluctuating moods she was prone to after a baby was born. And she still almost throttled him. He was saved by the babies between them.

Sophie remembered how much he'd learned to talk in the last year and how completely he'd been surrounded by men all his life, and she decided to let him live. "It gives me a nice feeling inside to hear it said now and again."

As if he didn't know the danger he'd been in, Clay said, "Okay. How often?"

Sophie sighed deeply then decided this might be her only chance. "At least once a day is nice—at bedtime. And then throw it in out of the blue once in a while besides."

Clay nodded, rocking the baby in his arms to quiet it. Sophie thought he was getting very good at being a pa already.

He said, "Once a day and then some. That'll be fine."

Sophie shook her head. "You're hopeless."

He didn't appear to hear what she said. He was lucky she was a Christian woman—a Christian woman with her hands full. They sat together and watched their babies until the sun came up.

Then the girls came in and broke rule number one all over again.

DISCUSSION QUESTIONS

1. In *Petticoat Ranch* there is a lot of "battle of the sexes" comedy. Discuss the differences between men and women. Are they caused by society or are boys and girls just different?

2. Discuss what children as young as Sophie's daughters do. Can children this young really rope and ride? Do we ask to little of our children today?

3. The fundamental premise of *Petticoat Ranch* is, how do Christian people deal with very justifiable hate? Sophie, Clay, and Adam all hate Judd Mason for very good reasons, and yet God calls us to love our enemy. Do you have people in your life who are difficult enough that you are hard pressed to love them? How do you deal with that?

4. Do you like that Sophie acted without Clay's permission to secure her ranch? Or was she defying him against God's call for a wife to submit to her husband? How should she have handled her sweet but clueless husband who wanted her to leave everything to him?

5. Clay McClellen was so inexperienced with women. Did you sympathize with him or was he too maddening?

6. Judd Mason started out being a vigilante only chasing down bad guys, but he ended up being a law unto himself and being a criminal. Discuss why we need to be ruled by the laws. Is it ever all right to take the law into our own hands to right wrongs?

7. *Petticoat Ranch* is book one of the Lassoed in Texas Series, now a new series called Sophie's Daughter follows Sophie's girls, all grown up with love stories of their own. Talk about the three oldest girls in *Petticoat Ranch*. Were they well developed as individuals who you can see having their own stories?

8. Do you think you could skin a buck?

9. Adam's rage is white hot through this book. Did you understand his anger? Did it seem too out of control for him to be a likeable man?

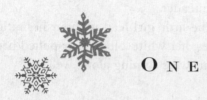

ONE

Mosqueros, Texas, 1867

The Five Horsemen of the Apocalypse rode in.

Late as usual.

Grace Calhoun was annoyed with their tardiness at the same time she wished they'd never come back from the noon recess.

They shoved their way into their desks, yelling and wrestling as if they were in a hurry. No doubt they were. They couldn't begin tormenting her until they sat down, now, could they?

Grace Calhoun clenched her jaw to stop herself from nagging. Early in the school year, she'd realized that her scolding amused them and, worse yet, inspired them. To think she'd begged their father to send his boys to school.

Her gaze locked on Mark Reeves. She knew that look. The glint in his eyes told her he was planning. . .something. . .awful.

Grace shuddered. Seven girls and fifteen boys in her school. Most were already working like industrious little angels.

Most.

The noise died down. Grace stood in front of the room and cleared her throat to buy time until her voice wouldn't shake. Normally she could handle them—or at least survive their antics. But she hadn't eaten today and it didn't look as though she'd eat soon.

"Sally, will you please open your book to page ten and read aloud for the class?"

"Yes, Miss Calhoun." With a sweet smile, six-year-old Sally McClellen, her Texas accent so strong Grace smiled, stood beside her desk and lifted the first grade reader.

Grace's heart swelled as the little girl read without hesitation, her blue eyes focused on the pages, her white-blond hair pulled back in a tidy braid. Most of her students were coming along well.

Most.

Grace folded her skeletal hands together with a prayer of thankfulness for the good and a prayer for courage for the bad. She added prayers for her little sisters, left behind in Chicago, supported with her meager teacher's salary.

A high-pitched squeak disrupted her prayerful search for peace. A quick glance caught only a too-innocent expression on Ike Reeves's face.

Mark's older brother Ike stared at the slate in front of him. Ike studying was as likely as Grace roping a longhorn bull, dragging him in here, and expecting the creature to start parsing sentences. There was no doubt about it. The Reeves boys were up to something.

She noticed a set of narrow shoulders quivering beside Mark. Luke Reeves, the youngest of the triplets—Mark, Luke, and John. All three crammed in one front-row desk built to hold two children. The number of students was growing faster than the number of desks.

She'd separated them, scolded, added extra pages to their assignments. She'd kept them in from recess and she'd kept them after school.

And, of course, she'd turned tattletale and complained to their father, repeatedly, to absolutely no avail. She'd survived the spring term with the Reeves twins, barely. The triplets weren't school age yet then. After the fall work was done, they came. All five of them. Like a plague of locusts, only with less charm.

The triplets were miniature versions of their older twin brothers, Abraham and Isaac. Their white-blond hair was as unruly as their behavior. They dressed in the next thing to rags. They were none too clean, and Grace had seen them gather for lunch around what seemed to be a bucket full of meat.

They had one tin bucket, and Abe, the oldest, would hand out what looked like cold beefsteak as the others sat beside him, apparently starved half to death, and eat with their bare hands until the bucket was empty.

Why didn't their father just strap a feed bag on their heads? What was that man thinking to feed his sons like this?

Easy question. Their father wasn't thinking at all.

He was as out of control as his sons. How many times had Grace talked to Daniel Reeves? The man had the intelligence of the average fence post, the personality of a wounded warthog, and the stubbornness of a flea-bitten mule. Grace silently apologized to all the animals she'd just insulted.

Grace noticed Sally standing awkwardly beside her desk, obviously finished.

"Well done, Sally." Grace could only hope she told the truth. The youngest of the three McClellen girls could have been waltzing for all Grace knew.

"Thank you, Miss Calhoun." Sally handed the book across the aisle to John Reeves.

The five-year-old stood and began reading, but every few words he had to stop. John was a good reader, so it wasn't the words tripping him up. Grace suspected he couldn't control his breathing for wanting to laugh.

The rowdy Reeves boys were showing her up as a failure. She needed this job, and to keep it she had to find a way to manage these little monsters.

She'd never spanked a student in her life. *Can I do it? God, should I do it?*

Agitated nearly to tears, Grace went to her chair and sat down.

"Aahhh!" She jumped to her feet.

All five Reeves boys erupted in laughter.

Grace turned around and saw the tack they'd put on her chair. Resisting the urge to rub her backside, she whirled to face the room.

Most of the boys were howling with laughter. Most of the girls looked annoyed on her behalf. Sally had a stubborn expression of loyalty on her face that would have warmed Grace's heart if she hadn't been pushed most of the way to madness.

Grace had been handling little girls all her life, but she knew nothing about boys.

Well, she was going to find out if a spanking would work. Slamming her fist onto her desk, she shouted, "I warned you boys, *no more pranks*. Abraham, Isaac, Mark, Luke, John, you get up here. You're going to be punished for this."

"We didn't do it!" The boys chorused their denials at the top of their lungs. She'd expected as much, but this time she wasn't going to let a lack of solid evidence sway her. She knew good and well who'd done this.

Driven by rage, Grace turned to get her ruler. Sick with the feeling of failure but not knowing what else to do, she jerked open the drawer in her teacher's desk.

A snake struck out at her. Screaming, Grace jumped back, tripped over her chair, and fell head over heels.

With a startled cry, Grace landed hard on her backside. She barely registered an alarming ripping sound as she bumped her head against the wall hard enough to see stars. Her skirt fell over her head, and her feet—held up by her chair—waved in the air. She shoved desperately at the flying gingham to cover herself decently. When her vision cleared, she looked up to see the snake, dangling down out of the drawer, drop onto her foot.

It disappeared under her skirt, and she felt it slither up her leg. Her scream could have peeled the whitewash off the wall.

Grace leapt to her feet. The chair got knocked aside, smashing into the wall. She stomped her leg, shrieking, the snake twisting and climbing past her knee. She felt it wriggling around her leg, climbing higher. She whacked at her skirt and danced around trying to shake the reptile loose.

The laughter grew louder. A glance told her all the children were out of the desks and running up and down the aisle.

One of the McClellen girls raced straight for her. Beth McClellen dashed to her side and dropped to her knees in front of Grace. The nine-year-old pushed Grace's skirt up and grabbed the snake.

Backing away before Grace accidentally kicked her, Beth said, "It's just a garter snake, ma'am. It won't hurt you none."

Heaving whimpers escaped with every panting breath. Grace's heart pounded until it seemed likely to escape her chest and run off on its own. Fighting for control of herself, she got the horrible noises she was making under control then smoothed her hair with unsteady hands. She stared at the little snake, twined around Beth's arm.

Beth's worried eyes were locked on Grace. The child wasn't sparing the snake a single glance. Because, of course, Beth and every other child in this room knew it was harmless. Grace knew it, too. But that didn't mean she wanted the slithery thing crawling up her leg!

"Th—ank—" Grace couldn't speak. She breathed like a winded horse, sides heaving, hands sunk in her hair. The laughing boys drowned out her words anyway.

Beth turned to the window, eased the wooden shutters open, and lowered the snake gently to the ground. The action gave Grace another few seconds to gather her scattered wits.

Trying again, she said, "Thank you, B-Beth. I'm not—not a-afraid of snakes."

The laughter grew louder. Mark Reeves fell out of his desk holding his stomach as his body shook with hilarity. The rest of the boys laughed harder.

Swallowing hard, Grace tried again to compose herself. "I was just startled. Thank you for helping me." Taking a step toward Beth, Grace rested one trembling hand on the young girl's arm. "Thank you very much, Beth."

Beth gave a tiny nod of her blond head, as if to encourage her and extend her deepest sympathy.

Grace turned to the rioting classroom—and her skirt fell off.

With a cry of alarm, Grace grabbed at her skirt.

The boys in the class started to whoop with laughter. Mark kicked his older brother Ike. Ike dived out of his chair onto Mark. They knocked the heavy two-seater student desk out of line. Every time they bumped into some other boy, their victim would jump into the fray.

Pulling her skirt back into place, she turned a blind eye to the chaos to deal with her clothes. Only now did she see that the tissue-thin fabric was shredded. A huge hole gaped halfway down the front. It was the only skirt she owned.

Beth, a natural caretaker, noticed and grabbed Grace's apron off a hook near the back wall.

Mandy McClellen rushed up along with Sally and all the other girls. Mandy spoke low so the rioting boys couldn't overhear. "This is your only dress, isn't it, Miss Calhoun?"

Grace nodded, fighting not to cry as the girls adjusted the apron strings around her waist to hold up her skirt. She'd patch it back together somehow, although she had no needle and thread, no money to buy them, and no idea how to use them.

Grace looked up to see the older Reeves boys making for the back of the schoolroom.

"Hold it right there." Mandy used a voice Grace envied.

The boys froze. They pivoted and looked at Mandy, as blond as her sisters and a close match in coloring to the Reeves, but obviously blessed with extraordinary power she could draw on when necessary. After the boys' initial surprise—and possibly fear—Grace saw the calculating expression come back over their faces.

"Every one of you," Mandy growled to frighten a hungry panther, "get back in your seats right now." She planted her hands on her hips and stared.

The whole classroom full of boys stared back. They hesitated, then at last, with sullen anger, caved before a will stronger than their own. Under Mandy's burning gaze, they returned to their seats. Grace's heart wilted as she tried to figure out how Mandy did it.

When the boys were finally settled, the eleven-year-old turned to Grace, her brow furrowed with worry. "I'm right sorry, Miss Calhoun," she whispered, "but you have to figure out how to manage 'em yourself. I can't do it for you."

Grace nodded. The child spoke the complete and utter truth.

The girls fussed over Grace, setting her chair upright and returning to her desk a book that had been knocked to the floor.

"Miss Calhoun?" Beth patted Grace's arm.

"Yes?"

"Can I give you some advice?"

The little girl had pulled a snake out from under Grace's skirt. Grace would deny her nothing. "Of course."

"I think it's close enough to day's end that you ought to let everyone go home. You're too upset to handle this now. Come Monday morning you'll be calmer and not do something you'll regret."

"Or start something you can't finish," Sally added.

Grace knew the girls were right. Her temper boiled too near the surface. She was on the verge of a screaming fit and a bout of tears.

My dress! God, what am I going to do about it?

These boys! Dear, dear Lord God, what am I going to do about them?

She tried to listen for the still, small voice of God that had taken her through the darkest days of her life during her childhood in Chicago. He seemed to abandon her today. The good Lord had to know one of His children had never needed an answer more. But if God sent an answer, her fury drowned it out. She'd been putting off a showdown with these boys all term. It was time to deal with the problem once and for all.

Sally slipped her little hand into Grace's. "Boys are naughty."

Grace shared a look with Sally and had to force herself not to nod. Seven sweet little girls stood in a circle around her. Grace wanted to hug them all and then go after the boys with a broom, at least five of them. The other ten weren't so badly behaved. Except when inspired by the Reeves.

God had made boys and girls. He'd planned it. They were *supposed* to be this way. But how could a teacher stuff book learning in their heads when they wouldn't sit still or stop talking or quit wrestling?

Digging deep for composure, Grace said, "You girls return to your seats, please. And thank you for your help."

Beth shook her head frantically, obviously sensing Grace wasn't going to take her advice.

"It's all right, Beth. I've put this off too long as it is. And thank you again."

Beth's feet dragged as she followed her sisters and the other girls to her seat.

Grace waited as the room returned to relative quiet, except for the usual giggling and squirming of the Reeves boys.

Glancing between her chair seat and her open desk drawer, Grace was worried she might develop a nervous tic. She sat down but left the drawer open. An almost insane calm took over her body. "School is dismissed except for Abraham, Isaac, Mark, Luke, and John Reeves."

Forehead furrowed over her blond brows, Beth shook her head and gave a little "don't do it" wave.

Grace could tell by the way the sun shone in the west window that it was only a few minutes early for dismissal. Good. That gave her time to settle with these boys, and then she'd have it out with their father. Things were going to change around here!

The rest of the students, stealing frequent glances between her and the blond holy terrors in her midst, gathered up their coats and lunch pails and left the schoolhouse in almost total silence.

And that left Grace.

Alone.

With the Five Horsemen of the Apocalypse.

T W O

Grace felt as if she were watching the second coming and hadn't repented.

Matching mutinous expressions settled on the Reeves' faces.

She said a prayer.

How do I reach them, Lord? Give me wisdom and patience.

Patience. She hunted through her mind for scripture about patience and remembered the long, cold years with Parrish. *"But in all things approving ourselves as the ministers of God, in much patience, in afflictions, in necessities, in distresses."*

That last part surely described her now. The Reeveses were an affliction. Getting through to them was a necessity. And her torn skirt alone qualified as sufficient distress, before she counted hunger and worry and a bruised backside. She needed to face all of that with patience.

She was fiercely determined to approve herself as a minister of God and bear whatever needed to be borne in order to reach these boys.

Exhausted, short of food, cold every night, and now wearing a ruined dress when she had none to replace it, Grace folded her hands in front of her.

With a sigh she felt all the way to her toes, she faced Mark. The ringleader. If she couldn't control him, she couldn't control any of them.

Her jaw clenched so her anger would not erupt in a tirade. "What do you think is the appropriate punishment for your actions today?"

Mark didn't even bother to feign an innocent expression. His look was far more reminiscent of "Try and punish me, teacher lady."

"We didn't do nothin', Miss Calhoun," he said. "I wonder who put that snake in your desk. That was a right mean thing to do."

A red-hot flash of temper nearly shocked Grace. She was surprised she was capable of this much rage. They always denied it. They didn't try to fake honesty. Instead, with smug disregard for any punishment she might mete out, they lied straight to her face.

"So on top of hurting me and disrupting class, you're also a liar—is that right, Mark? You can look me right in the eye and break a commandment?" Her voice rose with every word.

God, please give me patience. Please, I need a miracle to handle these boys.

Narrowing his eyes as if he didn't like being called a sinner, Mark didn't answer. He didn't mind *being* a sinner. *Just don't dare call him one.*

"You always blame us for everything, Miss Calhoun." Ike hitched up his brown, coarsely woven pants with two thumbs. The pants were short, dirty, and ragged as if he'd put them on new three years ago and never taken them off since. Red flannel underdrawers showed between his ankles and his scuffed brown boots.

"That's not very nice." John crossed his arms as if he were the injured party.

Grace clenched her hands together on the desk in front of her, picturing them wrapped around somebody's neck. She didn't care to imagine attacking children, so she settled for strangling their father. Clasping her hands as if she could physically hold her temper inside, she knew Beth was right. She should get these boys out of here and deal with them when she calmed down.

She pictured that snake striking at her from the desk and almost jumped. In that bitter cold room above the diner where the school had located her, she knew nightmares would plague her sleep tonight. No, she'd let this go on for too long. She wasn't going to back down this time. She couldn't and retain any self-respect.

She studied the little wolf pack. Mark, the oldest of the five-year-old triplets, had an inexhaustible supply of ideas. Abe, the oldest of the ten-year-old twins, picked the ideas he liked, and his approval brought the rest of the boys along. Ike always dug in and saw things through to the end. Ike had a way with animals, and he'd probably found the snake.

John did the hard work. Grace would bet John had done the actual sneaking around to put the snake in her desk and the tack on her chair. Luke was the cleanup man. Being youngest had made him tough. If they ever got in trouble as a result of their antics, Luke was the one who got revenge.

The other students left Luke alone. Grace gave him a nervous glance now, and that flared her temper more. She was actually afraid of a five-year-old.

"I go back to my original question. What would you do if you were the teacher and a student did this to you?"

"Miss Calhoun, whatever punishment you're gonna give us, you'd better hurry up." Luke's cool, level eyes sent a chill up Grace's spine. "Pa doesn't like us to keep him waiting."

"So you think you deserve punishment, Luke?" Grace thought about the ruler in her drawer. She shuddered remembering the snake that had popped out. She glanced at the drawer, still wide open. Nothing was stopping her from getting that ruler now.

She prayed silently, hating that she might need to resort to swatting their little hands. Surely there was a better way to handle them. The worst of it was she'd always known it wouldn't work. Besides her natural loathing for anyone who would hurt a child, she knew from watching these boys that they weren't overly worried about pain. The way they shoved each other around, a whack or two with the ruler wouldn't even get their attention.

But swatting them wasn't supposed to *hurt* them—she'd never wield a ruler with that much force. It was supposed to shame them into being better.

"I think you're gonna hit us whether we did anything to you or not." Luke stood, all four feet of him. "I think you're mean and you're plannin' to do whatever you want, so why waste time talkin' about it? You might as well get it over with."

The boys, all slim and wiry, stood. Luke walked to the front of the classroom, and the others followed.

Grace fought down the impulse to back away from him. She saw Luke's calculating eyes and knew the boy was up to something. Did he have a plan? Were they all in on it? Grace couldn't believe how paranoid she'd become. The boy was five for heaven's sake.

Luke stepped up on the platform that raised Grace's desk about six inches above the students'. He stood in front of her, his eyes insolent, daring her to punish him. "What's the matter, Miss Calhoun?" He sounded too polite. That wasn't like him.

Could they have more in store for her? Was there a rat in her coat pocket?

Luke gave her a wide-eyed, innocent look. "You know me and my brothers never done this to you. You just hate us and pick on us every chance you get."

"It's just the opposite, Luke. You boys hate *me* and pick on *me* every chance you get." Grace sounded like a five-year-old herself. She'd given them countless chances to change their ways, but patience hadn't worked. Firmness hadn't worked. She'd let this go on too long.

Shoving herself out of her chair, she grabbed the ruler out of the snake drawer. Facing Luke, she raised the ruler and hesitated. She'd never hit a child before—not as a teacher and not as a young girl who bore all the weight of raising her little sisters.

"I'll take the punishment for all my brothers, ma'am." Luke squared his shoulders. "We didn't do it, but I can see you're bent on blaming us. So have at it. Give me five times the whacking and be done with it."

"You did, too, do it, and not just you." She looked out at the boys, lined up behind tough little Luke.

Mark looked at her with self-satisfied amusement. All the other boys' expressions mirrored Mark's.

"I'm going to punish all of you." She raised the ruler again, staring at Luke, so fearless. It infuriated her that not even the threat of a lash on the hand with her ruler could make him back down. "Hold out your hand, Luke."

He extended his hand.

She looked into his eyes and knew she'd never be able to swing this stupid ruler.

Luke hissed at her, "Do it."

Whispering so his brothers didn't hear her, she said, "I can't."

"Why not?"

"Because I don't want to hit you."

Luke leaned closer, as eager to keep what they said between the two of them as she was for some reason. "We really did it, ma'am. I'm confessing clear as day. Have at it." He reached his hand a little closer as if worried she'd miss. He actually seemed to *want* her to hit him.

What was the little urchin up to? She almost smiled at him.

Her hand raised the ruler, planning to wave it at all of them and throw them out.

"Get away from my son, Miss Calhoun."

Grace jumped back. She bumped into her chair, and for a second she thought she'd end up on the floor again.

Daniel Reeves stood in the window to her right. The one Beth had lowered the snake through. How long had he been standing there?

She looked at Luke and saw the satisfied expression under his feigned innocence. He'd known his father was standing there. Every word he'd spoken had been planned to put her in the worst light for his father's benefit. All the boys had known their father watched.

"You boys get your things. Clay McClellen's here for the girls. Catch a ride with him to the gap then walk on home. Miss Calhoun and I are going to settle this once and for all, and it could take awhile."

Daniel left the window. The boys ran, vanishing out the front door with as much noise and shoving as they could manage. The last of them disappeared just as Daniel came in.

Grace felt her cheeks heating up. But why was she embarrassed?

These boys deserved a few sound whacks with the ruler. She'd done nothing wrong. The fact that she'd been planning to back down was almost worse than doing it.

And all of it—*all of it*—was this man's fault. This was the one she should be using the ruler on.

She stepped off her platform and practically charged. He came forward just as fast. They met in the middle of the room.

Grace barely came to his chin, and the second they faced each other, Grace wished she'd waited up front for him so he wouldn't tower over her.

But she was here, under his nose, and she was furious. Furious beat tall any day of the week. She was glad he'd shown up. This man was the problem. She'd asked him several times to speak to his sons about their behavior. His boys could do no wrong in his sight.

Grace realized she still clutched the ruler. She slapped it against the desk beside her, wishing she could use it to slap some sense into Daniel Reeves.

"You planning on using that on me, Miss Calhoun? Or aren't you so brave when you're facing an adult?"

"We have discussed your boys' behavior until I'm sick of hearing myself talk, Mr. Reeves."

"Well, I'm with you on that, ma'am. I'm sick of hearing you talk, too."

"You have to do something about them or I will. I can have them expelled from school."

"You think the school board will take your side over mine?" Daniel's blue eyes burned into her skin. They sparked with anger as he leaned over her. "I'd think a little woman who can't control a few bright, active boys wouldn't want the school board looking too close at her."

"Your boys *are* bright and active." He was trying to use his size to intimidate her, but Grace refused to back up when Daniel leaned close. In fact, she took a step forward. "Unfortunately, they use all their *intelligence* to think up pranks to disrupt the school, and they are most *active* when they're thinking of ways to harass me. Have you even *tried* talking with them?"

"Save your speeches for the school board." Daniel's nose almost touched hers. He wasn't yelling, but he spoke in his usual too-loud voice right into her face. "I saw Parson Roscoe and Zeb Morris just a few minutes ago. If we can hunt up Phillip at the general store, we'll have the whole board to hand. Then we'll see what they have to say about you picking on my boys."

"Lead the way." Grace extended her hand toward the front door. "This is long overdue."

"Oh no, *Miss Calhoun*."

Grace heard her name said with such mockery she almost regretted insisting every parent—every person—in Mosqueros call her by it. But weren't teachers supposed to demand propriety?

"You're the one who's always such a stickler for manners. I insist, ladies first." Daniel crossed his arms, practically blocking the aisle, stubborn as a mule.

Grace fumed, looking at the narrow space he expected her to squeeze through. The man was a bully. She shoved at him as she squeezed past.

She got clear of the confounded man and stormed toward the back of the schoolroom. She'd just made it to the door when her skirt fell off.

THREE

Grace had been sitting in her chair sobbing ever since the school board fired her. The straight-backed chair pressed mercilessly into her back. Tears that just would not stop had been flowing for an hour.

Opting for peace over justice, the school board had seen to it that Daniel didn't fare well either. His boys had been expelled.

They'd listened to both sides and made their pronouncement—hurried along by the freezing weather and a cow Zeb Morris had back home calving out of season. The ruling came with almost no discussion.

Grace had been too stunned to continue fighting. Penniless, hungry, and, come morning, homeless, losing her job seemed tantamount to a death sentence. Turning from that crowd of men, she'd run to her room like a coward.

Now, an hour later, amazed that there was enough water in her body to form tears, Grace lifted her hand to wipe her eyes. Her hand shook until she couldn't bear to see it. She closed her eyes and let her long tangles of dark blond hair stick on her soppy face.

She'd come here by choice, wanting the West to be uncivilized, wanting to be far removed from her trouble with Parrish. But never had she imagined anyone or anything as uncivilized as Daniel Reeves and his sons.

Sitting in her one-room attic home was the loneliest moment in her incredibly lonely life. She felt as if she were shrinking away to nothing, hiding here from the fate that surely awaited a jobless, penniless woman in the unforgiving West.

She'd had such dreams. She'd planned to help children and protect them in ways she'd never been protected. She'd planned to make enough money that, once she was sure Parrish had been left far behind, she could send for her ragtag family in Chicago and have a real home at last.

Instead, she'd failed everybody who'd ever been foolish enough to trust her.

When she'd arrived home, she'd cast her ruined dress into a heap on the floor and pulled on her nightgown. Grateful in her misery that there was no mirror in the room to reflect her emaciated body, she held herself tight in the tissue-thin, dark blue flannel gown.

"What am I going to do, Lord?" She bowed her head. She heard the words slip past her clenched jaw. It hurt to move her lips. They were chapped from the salt of her tears and the bitter cold in the attic.

The room was heated only by what crept up from the general store downstairs, and the store banked the fire at night. She had her own potbellied stove, but it cost money to buy firewood or took energy to hike out and cut it herself, energy she just didn't have.

What did it matter anyway? She could freeze to death tonight or she could starve to death next week. Grace wept, not so much for her own failure as for the way she'd failed Hannah and the other children.

All her promises rang hollow now. She couldn't even take care of herself, let alone care for someone else.

Perhaps she shouldn't have sent Hannah every penny she had to spare each payday. If she'd set a few dollars aside for a time of trouble, she could have moved on and started teaching somewhere else. But she'd never dreamed of such trouble as Daniel Reeves. Holding nothing back for herself, she'd barely kept enough to eat.

She wept, ashamed of her weakness. But what did it matter? There was no one to be disgusted by her. No one this side of Chicago cared if she lived or died. There was no way out. She'd finally hit bottom, plunged to the very deepest pit.

Her door slammed open.

The *bang* jerked her head up.

Everything that was wrong about her destroyed life suddenly meant nothing.

Parrish, with his stooped frame, hawklike nose, and cruel eyes, stepped into the room with a satisfied laugh. "Ah, Grace, have you missed your dear daddy?"

With a scream, Grace leaped from the chair. Parrish's eyes narrowed, and he rushed at her. Without making a conscious choice, Grace chose the only other exit.

Parrish tore at her nightgown. Fingernails clawed her skin as she threw herself out the second-story window. The jagged glass slit her as she crashed through. It rained around her, slashing her skin. The ground rushed at her. The icy December wind seemed to cut her skin as surely as the glass. She instinctively twisted to keep from landing headfirst.

"You won't get away from me." Parrish's roaring threats faded as she plummeted earthward.

The frozen ground hit like a fist. Glass stabbed and sliced.

"You owe me, and I'm here to make you pay!" The ugly voice overhead stung her into moving.

She scrambled to her feet, pain in every movement. The soft flesh on her hands and knees ripped on the sharp edges of frozen ruts. She was driven to survive, even when, minutes ago, she'd been ready to give up.

She darted around the corner into the alley between the general store and the diner. She tripped, falling, imbedding rock and dirt in her bleeding skin. She staggered to her feet, pressing her back against the wall. She glanced around the side of the building and up.

The broken window no longer framed her nightmare come to life. There was no sadistic, menacing man to be seen. The only way down was the back stairs.

She ran toward the front of the building, mindless of the pain in her feet, only conscious of the need to flee. She darted out of the alley in the frigid Texas night.

Mosqueros was closing down for the evening. The door banged open in the back of the store. Parrish, coming.

She saw a wagon. She scrambled in and ducked under the tarp tossed over it. She crushed her body between wooden crates, scraping new wounds in her flesh. She dragged her bare feet under the cover and stopped dead.

He'd be on Mosqueros's main street by now. He'd know there was only one place she could be. He'd pull back the tarp and put his hands on her. And then he'd make her pay for every bit of her defiance.

The wagon tilted. She heard whistling, incongruous in her terrified mind. Was Parrish climbing aboard the wagon?

A shout and the rattle of leather and chains came from the driver's seat. The wagon lurched forward with a creak of old wood.

She gathered herself to jump out of the wagon and run again. Forever running and hiding, for years, across a continent. Even in this remote Texas town, there was no place he couldn't find her. She lived like a frightened animal.

"Hold there," Parrish shouted from the walk beside the wagon.

That voice, that threatening, brutal voice. How many times had he lashed her with it? How many others had he treated the same? She'd lost count, but the faces of the others haunted her.

Grace didn't dare move. Once she was discovered, any man would hand her over. How well she'd learned that lesson.

"Whoa," the driver said, breaking off his whistling.

Grace's stomach clenched. She knew that voice. The man who'd ruined her life in Mosqueros, just as Parrish had ruined it everywhere else. The driver had seen to her firing and left her cold and hungry in a darkened room. It was the voice of a man she hated only slightly less than Parrish. Now she needed him to survive.

She didn't count on it. Daniel Reeves would probably hand her over with pleasure.

"I need to—" Parrish's voice halted.

Grace waited, trying to control her gasping breath that blew out white in the bitter cold. One move, one twitch of a muscle, and the coarse gray tarp would be thrown back.

"Need somethin', mister?" Daniel Reeves talked too loud, as usual.

"Forget it. Never mind." Footsteps clomped away on the wooden sidewalk.

"Hmm, what wazzat about?" Daniel Reeves asked under his breath.

But Grace heard him. He was mere inches away from her. She could have reached her arm out of the tarp and tapped him on the back.

There was a slap of reins on the horses' backs. The whistling resumed and the wagon began rolling, swaying side to side.

Why had Parrish left? He had to know it was at least possible she'd hidden under this tarp. It wasn't like him to quit hunting.

He didn't want a witness.

The minute the idea came to her, she knew it was right. He was still out there. Watching. He had an instinct for the hunt. How many times had he proven that to Grace?

But he'd never minded witnesses before. He'd delighted in dragging her home, screaming and crying. He'd gloated and laughed about it to anyone who watched. That could mean only one thing. He wasn't here to drag her home. Not this time.

He was here to kill her.

He would want no witnesses to tie them together when she turned up dead.

After enough time had passed to put the town behind them, the cold broke into her terror. Inch by inch so no movement or sound would draw Daniel's attention to her, Grace curled in on herself. She pulled her knees to her chest, wrapped her arms around them, and bowed her head until she lay in a tight ball among the boxes and gunnysacks. Stiff as a corpse, she hugged herself. There had never been anyone else to do it.

The cold invaded her hiding place until her bare toes went numb. As the wagon rumbled over the rough trail and Daniel whistled his mindless tune, Grace lost the feeling in her body. She fought the need to shiver as her legs, then her arms and torso, grew chilled until there was no feeling left. But she was only distantly aware of that and the bruising of the wagon box and the sliding supplies.

She closed her eyes and let the tears start flowing again. She let the cold, cruel world beat on her to its heart's content. She remembered Jesus' lament as He hung on the cross: *My God, my God, why hast thou forsaken me?"*

Why *wouldn't* God forsake her? Everyone else had.

She was surprised how much she regretted dying. Life hadn't held much pleasure for her. Clinging to it seemed at odds with the miserable existence she led.

She felt the cold wrap around her like icy hands, deepening her exhaustion, pulling her under to sleep. She didn't expect to wake.

She didn't fight it. She decided to let Parrish win.

Parrish had taught her long ago that she deserved it.

FOUR

Daniel Reeves let the winter weather cool his temper on his long drive home. The team clambered up the steep stretch of trail that twisted through the narrow mouth of his canyon home. The wind whistled through the walls of the canyon towering over his head.

The trail was so narrow in places he was tempted to suck in his gut as his sure-footed team slipped through the gap. One razor-thin switchback went almost straight sideways and straight up at the same time. A few flakes of snow drifted down on him, and he hated to think of scaling this path if it was slick.

Just as well the boys don't have to go to school anymore. Waste of time anyway. Most schooling was nonsense. Still, it burned something fierce to be told to stay away. He sucked in frigid air and shook off his anger.

Pay attention to the trail—watch the team. These are the things a rancher needed to know, not a bunch of book learning.

The snow gusted into his face as he wound around another tight switchback. A wonder they'd found this place. The boys playing around their campsite had come up with it. As far as Daniel could tell, no man had ever stepped foot in this fertile valley before he'd claimed it.

Snow sifted down from his hat, and a breeze sent it whooshing down his neck. Shivering, he thanked God it didn't snow much here.

At least that's what he'd been told. He hadn't lived through a Texas winter yet.

Good thing. If the snow came down here like it had in Kansas, this

312

gap would close up tight and stay sealed until spring.

After he'd gone a couple of hundred yards feeling so closed in the sensation almost smothered him, the canyon opened out and he caught his breath with delight. It was full darkness, but the moon glowed in the sky through gaps in the high, skittering clouds, lighting up the gentle snow flurries.

Daniel could see the wide-open spaces of the 6R Ranch. Belly-deep grass, cured lush on the stem, waved in the bitter wind as if it waved hello. Trees covered the steep edges of the canyon that disappeared out of sight. Cattle, fat with spring babies, lowed softly as he passed by them. They were all as tame as dogs from being overfed and gentled by his boys.

Home. He loved it. He loved his brand—the 6R, chosen for the six Reeves men. He'd left grief behind and begun life anew. Finally, his life was in perfect order.

A single dark thought intruded. That awful, prissy Miss Calhoun. Well, he'd gotten even today in town, but the boys still weren't welcome back. He scowled at the thought of that fussy old maid.

He shook off his temper. Miss Calhoun was gone. Spring would come soon enough, and the board had said his boys could have another chance then. Daniel was tempted not to bother. He decided he *would* reenroll them, at least for a while, just so no priggish female could take credit for stopping his boys from learning.

Satisfied to know a good teacher might take the place of Miss Calhoun, he turned his thoughts back to his idyllic life at the 6R.

He always thought of God's promises when he looked at his canyon. *"Blessed are they that mourn: for they shall be comforted."* God had indeed comforted him. It had taken time for Daniel to accept that comfort, but he'd found it in his isolated canyon with his sons.

When he was within shouting distance of the cave, he yelled, "Boys, get out here and grab a box."

Daniel hollered to be heard over the commotion that came from inside the house. It sounded as though his boys were having a fine old time. He laughed as they tumbled out of their little house, all trying to shove through the door at the same time.

"I can hear the lot of you, through stone walls, from over a mile away. It's a wonder it didn't scare the team." Daniel pulled back on the reins, but the well-trained horses knew their job and stopped without much effort from him. He set the brake.

"What'd ya get, Pa?" Ten-year-old Abraham beat his brothers to the wagon, dragging his coat on as he came, none too worried about the wicked cold.

Isaac dashed out one step behind him. The twins always moved as a team. Abe fastest and first, but Ike sticking to the end and finishing whatever Abe started.

"Did ya get plenty of taters?" Ike swung himself up on the back of the wagon beside his brother.

"An' apples, Pa." Mark, the firstborn of his five-year-old triplets, stormed after his brothers, with his two mirror images just behind.

"You said you'd try 'n' get some winter apples," John shouted.

"We heard at school Mr. Badje had extras in his cellar, 'member, Pa?" Luke came out, his blond hair a replica of his four brothers'.

The cave door stood open in the teeth of the December night.

Abe threw the tarp back.

"Get that door, Luke," Daniel yelled.

"Did'ja get us a ma?" Abe asked.

"Luke, last one out gets that door closed. I'm gonna be chopping wood all winter if—" Daniel stopped. He turned to Abe. "What?"

Adam shoved the door open, glad to be out of the wind. He wouldn't be out of it for long.

Snow blew in with him. Clay looked up from his rocking chair where he sat grinning at Sally on his lap. Sophie turned from where she laid plates on the table, her stomach so huge Adam was surprised she didn't tip over forward every time she tried to move.

Mandy stirred something that smelled wonderful in the pot hanging over the fire. Beth sat close by the fire, reading aloud to the whole family.

It was a perfect picture. One Adam had long wished for himself. He was nearing forty now, and a wife and family had never happened for him. But he'd helped Sophie have this idyllic life, and he was content.

He was also going to wreck things. "The teacher's missing."

They all turned to him and became alert. His urgency must have shown loud and clear.

"I was in town when the cry went up. Someone saw her window broken and went up to check. She's gone. Her door stood open, but from snags of fabric on the broken glass and tracks in the alley under the window, it looks like she fell or jumped out her window. They've got search parties out in every direction. I told them I'd fetch the hands."

Clay set Sally on her feet and rushed for his hat. "Don't hold dinner." He left on Adam's heels.

Adam noticed Sophie didn't try to come. She'd settled into leaving men's work to Clay and the hands. . .mostly. Being pregnant had slowed her down a mite, too.

Adam swung up on his horse. "It could have been hours ago. No one's seen her since she got fired."

Clay, striding to the barn to grab up his horse, stopped short and turned. "She got fired? What happened?"

"Daniel Reeves and his boys is what happened. Miss Calhoun and Daniel had another one of their squabbles and got the school board involved. They kicked up so much fuss the school board washed their hands of both of them. Fired her and kicked his boys out of school."

Clay got moving again. "Where'd she go? The train didn't come through tonight. Did she take her horse?"

Adam rode alongside him. "She doesn't have a horse."

Clay glanced back. "She used to."

"She came into the area on a horse, but the blacksmith said she'd sold it to him months ago. He got the idea she needed the money."

"You're sure she's not visiting one of the students?"

"We've searched every building in town, even the barns. Guess she was pretty upset after she got fired. Went to her room crying. When word got out she'd been fired and was missing, folks felt bad about it, so they've all pitched in to hunt, near tore the town apart. She's not there." Adam pulled his collar up to his ears against the cold. "No one's ever seen her with anything but her one coat and one pair of shoes, and she left them behind."

Clay wheeled and stared at Adam. "She went out her window and fell two stories then disappeared without shoes or a coat? In this weather? What's going on?"

Adam shook his head. "I've got no answers for you, Clay. I told 'em in town we'd cover the land between Sawyer Canyon and the plateau. She can't have gotten farther than that."

Clay jabbed a finger at the bunkhouse. "Go rouse the men. If she's not on a train, not on a horse, and not in town, she's in trouble."

"Bad trouble." Adam kicked his horse toward the bunkhouse. Luther and Buff were already outside in their buffalo-skin coats. The other men emerged. They couldn't know what had happened, but they'd lived long enough in a harsh land to sense danger and be ready.

"A ma." John shouted from the cave door. "We've been thinking it's a good idea 'n' all."

"You have?" Daniel remembered them saying such a thing, but he'd paid no attention. He wasn't taking a chance on another woman dying on him.

" 'Cept'n I don't know where she's gonna sleep," Luke added. "We could put the table outside at night I reckon."

Daniel looked where his son was staring. Ike was beside Abe, and Daniel couldn't see anything. Mark, Luke, and John clambered up into the wagon box and surrounded the supplies. They were all staring at something Daniel couldn't see.

"Not Miss Calhoun," Mark howled. "Take her back and get someone else, Pa. She's a grouch."

Daniel swung around on the seat and dropped into the back end of his wagon. With all six Reeves men in it, there was no room for supplies, let alone. . .

"A woman." Daniel couldn't believe his eyes. Then the shock passed and he realized she was asleep. Or dead. He bent down and swooped her into his arms. She weighed barely more than one of the triplets.

She didn't move, didn't even react when he touched her. "Something's wrong, boys." Her skin was white, and she was as cold as ice in his arms. He couldn't tell if she was breathing. "She's freezing. Let's get her inside."

"We don't want Miss Calhoun for a ma." John stomped until he shook the wagon. Daniel jumped to the ground with the little wisp of a woman in his arms and headed for the house. He saw the door standing wide open. Any heat in the little cave was long gone.

"Take her back, Pa!" Luke yelled from where he was kneeling on top of the supplies in the wagon. "Get a better ma 'n her."

Daniel strode toward the cave, trying to sort out all he needed to do to help her. "I don't have time to explain any of this to you boys." No time—and no explanation if he had all the time in the world.

"Miss Calhoun may be dying. We're going to need lots of firewood to warm her up. All of you boys scatter and get some rounded up." Daniel glanced behind him at his boys, all wearing "stubborn" like it was a winter coat. He roared, "And I mean now!"

Daniel went into the house and, with Miss Calhoun held easily in one arm, closed the heavy, dragging door he'd fashioned into the mouth of this little cave. He hurried over to the stove and knelt beside it. After a moment's hesitation, he lowered her to the chilly floor.

"This won't do," he said to himself. "She can't get warm on the cold ground." He was suddenly irritated with himself for not getting a cabin built last summer. The boys were never inside, summer or winter, and the cave was an adventure for all of them. And heaven knew it was a cheap way to live, no room for furniture or bric-a-brac and no woman to nag him for such foolishness. Still, a warm, tight house right now might mean the difference between life and death for Miss Calhoun.

He went to the bedding wadded in a heap in the corner. The furs all but carpeted the floor when they rolled them out at night. He caught up all the blankets, went back to her side, and, gently lifting her, awkwardly spread the blankets on the floor for her to lie on.

The door flew open while he knelt there, holding Miss Calhoun in his arms.

Abe came in with an armload of wood.

"Abe, close that door. We'll never get ahead of the cold with it standing open."

Before Abe could obey—on the off chance he was going to—Ike came in loaded down with sticks. The other boys were right on his heels.

"We need to get this cave warmed up. Gather more wood, enough to keep the fire blazing hot all night. Then get back in here with it fast and keep that door closed." Daniel, a little surprised that they minded him, watched them dash out, shutting the door behind them.

Daniel settled the motionless woman on the blankets. He laid his hand on her chest and, with a sigh of relief, felt a heartbeat.

Daniel stuffed the stove full of wood and heard the reassuring crackle as the new kindling caught from the old. He picked up the teacher's limp white hand and noticed how fine-boned it was. She was so thin it was like holding bone draped with skin. He meant to rub some feeling back into her, but she seemed so fragile, he was afraid he'd hurt her. Instead of rubbing, he just held her hand between both of his, trying to share some of his warmth.

Lying here, silent and defenseless, Grace Calhoun, who had always seemed like an old bat who lived for the soul purpose of terrorizing children, now looked very young. Why, she was little more than a child herself. He hadn't thought of it for a while, but he remembered now that his first impression was that she was a pretty little thing.

Then she'd opened her mouth.

Daniel thought of how painfully proper she had been when they'd met. More than proper, she was snooty as all get-out and so prissy he'd decided she lived to keep her grammar perfect and her hands clean.

He'd let her enthusiasm for schooling sway him into sending the boys. Then the trouble began. Soon enough he'd pegged her for an old maid, made of pure gristle and spite. Although, truth to tell, he'd never given her much thought beyond avoiding her at all costs.

Careful to be gentle, he rubbed her hand between his to get some circulation into her fingers and saw blood. With a gasp he turned her hand over. Her hand was scraped raw.

"What happened to you?"

For the first time he really looked at her for injuries. Her other hand had bled, too, although the bleeding had stopped. He noticed the dark blue dress she was wearing. It was flannel and thin as paper. It was torn at her knees, and he could see that she had scraped herself there, too.

Dear God, what has this woman been through tonight? Don't let her die on me, Father.

The flannel had dried to her knee in one spot. Carefully, he pulled the fabric out of the wound. She'd been in his wagon since Mosqueros. There was no other possible time she could have slipped in. He'd just loaded the wagon and thrown the tarp over the supplies, then gone back inside the general store to pay for his order. He'd only been inside a couple of minutes. She must have climbed in then.

Daniel looked at her still features. Her lips were tinged with blue, her skin as fragile as a china plate Margaret had treasured right up until the day Ike had smashed it into a thousand pieces. He remembered how his wife had cried over that stupid plate. Of course, women cried over almost everything.

Grace's naturally fair skin seemed almost translucent from the cold. He spoke to her, even though she was beyond hearing him. "I've figured out *when* you got in my wagon, Miss Calhoun. That only leaves *why*."

He realized that as soon as she was awake and able to move, he'd have to drive all the way back into town. Honestly, this woman seemed as though she'd been born for the sole purpose of pestering him.

The boys charged back in. Luke was last, and he carefully shut the door. Juggling his armload of sticks in his chubby, five-year-old arms proved to be a bit too much. He dropped half his load.

"Clumsy." Mark shoved Luke. "Be quiet. The teacher's here." Daniel noticed Mark said it at the top of his lungs.

"She's not the teacher." Luke shoved back. Mark stumbled into Ike, who dropped his bundle of wood with a clatter.

Luke clapped Daniel on the back. "Sally McClellen told me today on the ride home that Pa got her fired right after school."

"Good for you, Pa." Abe stuffed more wood into the potbellied stove. "They're gonna hafta hunt up a new teacher. A nice one this time, I hope."

"Sally said we got kicked out of school, too," Luke added.

Pandemonium broke out. The boys shrieked with joy until Daniel half expected the stone roof over their heads to raise from all the ruckus.

The jubilation wore itself out while Daniel worked on getting circulation back into Miss Calhoun's fragile hand.

Out of the corner of his eye, Daniel noticed Ike collide with Mark and then blame Mark for the crash.

"Mark, you little—" The two of them stumbled into the table and shoved it until it hit Daniel in the back. The table, the stove, two benches, and the boys, and the house was full. There was no room for a wrestling match.

"You guys, cut it out." Daniel pushed the corner of the table out of his shoulder blades. He saw that the stack of wood behind his back had grown most of the way to his chest.

By golly, those boys can work!

"That's enough wood for now. You guys go get the rest of the supplies.

Stow everything in the barn. Ike, you unhitch the team and rub 'em down. Abe, grain them for the night, hang up the harness, then all of you get back in here before you freeze. It's already past your bedtime."

Abe scowled. "Dad, we don't want to do all that."

Daniel ignored his son's complaining. He'd heard it all before. "And make sure you close the barn gate tight. If those horses get out again, you're all going to start sleeping in the barn and I'll bring the horses in here to bunk down."

Grumbling and shoving each other, the boys filed out. Ike saw to closing the door.

Daniel turned back to Miss Calhoun. He touched her face and saw that the fire had begun to warm her just a little. She still lay motionless, but she was breathing steadily under the deerskin blanket.

In the dim lantern light, Daniel leaned close enough to see an ugly scrape along one side of Miss Calhoun's face. A bruise bloomed on her forehead, and he saw several shallow slits. Inspecting carefully, he saw a sliver of glass in one cut and carefully extracted it.

With a dart of fear, Daniel wondered for the first time if she'd really climbed into his wagon. Or had she been knocked unconscious and put in the wagon by someone else? He thought of that stranger who'd hailed him when he'd climbed onto the wagon. He'd wanted something, but what? Grace?

Daniel reached for the pail of water he always kept hot on the stove. He took two rags to protect his hands from the searing tin and lowered the pail to the floor beside him.

He bathed Miss Calhoun's hands in the warm water. He washed her knees, mindful of how improper it was to see any more of her legs than necessary. Daniel finished quickly then covered her legs all the way to her toes.

He rubbed her arms and stoked the fire, planning to keep a prayer vigil into the night.

A long time later, the boys trooped back in, pink-cheeked and rowdy from working in the sharp cold of the night. They argued and shoved and fought over what blankets were left. But there was no harm in their rowdiness, just horseplay.

The boys saw to their own supper, and as they ate, Daniel could see their heavy eyelids. Even with the excitement of having the teacher in their house, he knew he'd won.

"A ma hadn't oughta take all the blankets, had she, Pa?" Luke asked, worried.

"She's s'posed to take care'a *us*, Pa," Mark whined. "Not us take care'a *her*."

Daniel didn't answer. He had his hands full controlling the urge to flinch every time the boys called this little fussbudget "Ma." What a nightmare that'd be if it were true.

The boys were exhausted. Good. That was his daily goal. Let them play hard enough and work hard enough to get them to sleep at night. They eventually settled in, piled up together like a litter of puppies, probably warmer that way than if they'd have been wrapped in a blanket.

"Boys, before you go to sleep, say a prayer for Miss Calhoun to be okay. She looks bad hurt to me and half dead from the cold. We need God looking out for her special tonight."

"We don't mind praying for her," Mark said, the spokesman for the group. "We don't want her to die 'r nothin', but we don't want her to be our ma. We talked it over, 'n' we say take her back and get another'un."

Daniel didn't bother to tell his boys, yet again, that he hadn't brought the confounded woman home to be their ma. There wasn't enough stupid in the world for him to do a thing like that.

"Well then, pray she gets well so she can get outta here. She's not going anywhere as long as she's asleep like this."

The boys all sprang to their knees and prayed with a fervor that would have humbled a fire-and-brimstone preacher at a revival meeting.

The boys finished praying and lay down, covering the floor until there was barely room for Daniel to kneel by Miss Calhoun. He was stuck—pinned in here, in the dim light of the cold night, next to the rudest woman he'd ever known. The woman who had gotten his sons kicked out of school. He'd gotten her fired from her job in return.

Here they were, she without a job and he without an education for his boys; he trying to save her life and she doing her best to thwart him, as she did in everything else.

It suited him to pray, too, because he wanted her well. He wanted her out of here. He never wanted to lay eyes on this bothersome woman again as long as he lived.

Then she began to shiver.

FIVE

The wind cut like knives through his long black duster as Sid Parrish stared at the cave. His horse, a poorly trained nag the blacksmith rented out, jerked on the reins, fighting the bit.

"I owe you, girl," he said into the frigid Texas night. Parrish wanted to hurt Grace until the wanting ate a hole in his gut. He wasn't a man who forgot a wrong done him.

But he'd seen all those kids come pouring out of the cave. And he'd seen the savvy eyes of the man who had unwittingly helped her escape. He'd have a fight on his hands if he stormed in and took her by force.

He'd be a fool to try it, and Parrish was nobody's fool. But he was tempted. His trigger finger itched, and his hand caressed the gun on his hip. He wanted to see her eyes and hear her cry out with the pain he planned to inflict. He wanted to hurt her long and slow before he killed her. He'd been too easy on her before, and it had brought him low.

The horse skittered and snorted. Parrish had rarely ridden a horse in Chicago, and he'd never carried a gun. He'd used his mind to survive there. Now he had to learn some new tricks. And the tricks of the West included horses and firearms.

He brought his hand down with brutal power on the horse's flank and pretended it was that miserable little girl who thought she'd gotten the best of him. His arm hurt before his fury was spent, and he wished for a whip and spurs to work out his rage. The blacksmith had refused to give him either, saying the horse handled fine without them.

His lips curled in cruel satisfaction as he remembered Grace's terror when he entered her room. He'd almost had her. He'd touched her for just a split second before she slipped away. His fingers still felt the warmth of her flesh, vibrating with pure horror. Knowing she threw herself out of a window to escape him satisfied his hunger to punish her. He would live on that small feast for now. But it was only temporary until he could crush her thoroughly. He was going to take her and break her. No sniveling little *girl* got the best of Sid Parrish.

He turned his horse away from the cave and headed back to Mosqueros. He was no hand for roughing it in the wilderness, and Mosqueros was a small enough town that he'd be remembered. He'd come into town on a mule skinner's wagon. The supply wagon was headed on west and had only stopped to leave a few orders at the Mosqueros general store. Parrish had slipped out into the hills around the town without talking to anyone. The townsfolk might ask questions if he turned up around the same time Grace disappeared. Parrish would pick his time and be back.

It was the longest night of Daniel's life. And he'd lived through birthing pains that produced triplets and killed his wife.

Miss Calhoun shook as if a cougar had its teeth sunk into her and wanted to snap her spine. Except a cougar would have been quick. This went on for hours. The tremors came and stayed. Miss Calhoun was never conscious through any of it. Daniel's boys slept, even when she sobbed aloud and cried out that she would perish.

Daniel pulled her into his arms and held her, trying to keep her from harming herself as the quaking went on and on. She was painfully thin, hardly an armful for him. He wondered at the sharp edges of her bones as he tried to rub circulation into her limbs. She had no cushion of warming fat to help.

After a time, the violent shivering eased and she seemed to collapse into total unconsciousness. A few moments passed; then the trembling began again. Miss Calhoun wept.

Daniel held her and prayed for her and murmured into her hair. "You'll be all right. I won't leave you. Hang on. Hang on." As he spoke to her, he sent petitions to God. However much he'd been at sixes and sevens with the snooty little teacher, he now wished frantically that she'd be all right.

And she did—hang on, that is. Her arms escaped the blankets, and she gripped him around his neck with all the strength of her convulsing arms. "Perish. No, not perish. Not again."

"You're not going to perish." Daniel kept up the comforting hum of his voice, hoping he could reach her. "You're okay. I'll keep you safe and warm. You'll make it."

The quivering she couldn't control, he knew. But he tried to ease the fear he heard in every gasp and sob. What was she so afraid of?

Miss Calhoun relaxed as the shivering passed. She lay still longer this time and made more natural movements. A pale pink flush darkened her cheeks and gave Daniel hope.

He stretched out fully alongside her. There really wasn't any other place for him in the crowded cave home. The blankets were firmly between them, but still Daniel felt an odd reaction to being this near a woman. Well, not odd exactly. Just long forgotten. He hadn't spent much time close to a woman. And, a few moments of weakness aside, that included his wife.

He tried to put a few inches between them. She clung to him, flowing toward him like warm liquid. He stayed because he had no choice, but he thought of Miss Calhoun's cruelty to his sons to keep himself from enjoying her slender arms.

And when that wasn't enough, he thought of his wife nearly dying with his twins.

And when that wasn't enough, he thought of his own stupidity to let Margaret convince him that more children were needed to make their lives complete.

And when that wasn't enough and he decided he had to get away from her, she started shaking again.

He held her through this one. Only a monster would let her face this bitter, soul-deep cold alone. And it would be an even greater evil to let her talk of perishing without trying to console her. He murmured comfort and shared his prayers with her and held on. This time the shivering didn't go on as long, and when it stopped, she seemed to drop into a true sleep.

Once he believed it, he let her go and stood away from her. He looked around the tiny cave. Why hadn't he built something? There was wood aplenty to build a log cabin in any size he chose. The work would be good for the boys.

Definitely next summer—before any more freezing-cold women happened by.

He saw her toes peeking out of the blanket and stooped to check her feet, worrying about frostbite. They had warmed considerably, and he could pinch her nails and see, in the dim stove light, that there was pink beneath them. He wrapped her again quickly.

While he crouched there, her eyes flickered open. Her eyes seemed to pick up the flickering light. They were dark golden, like her hair. Although the room was dark, the red-hot, potbellied stove cast enough light for him to see she was coherent.

"Where am I?" She sounded sluggish. Her words were slurred, and her lips barely moved.

Daniel leaned closer, trying to hear the bare whisper of her words. Not sure what she'd said, he knew what must be going through her head. "Miss Calhoun, it's Daniel Reeves. I found you in my wagon nearly frozen to death. You're at my cabin. We'll keep you warm and get you back to town as soon as you're well enough—"

"No, not town." She gripped his arm until she cut off his circulation, as well as his thinking.

"I can't go back. I'll. . .I can't. I'll. . ." Her voice faded; her grip hardened.

Daniel leaned until his ear nearly rested against her lips. He was sure she said the word "perish."

He pulled back to reassure her that he wouldn't let her perish. Her eyes sparkled. He'd forgotten how pretty she was—because he hadn't been able to see past the meanness. But the sparkle was a flash of desperation. She was beseeching him. Her nails dug into the flannel of his shirtsleeve.

Whether she knew what she was saying or not, her fear was real. Daniel knew something terrible had happened to Miss Calhoun in town to drive her out into the night in this fragile dress.

"I promise I'll protect you, Grace." He spoke her forbidden name.

She always demanded the utmost propriety. He knew that, because she'd told him. And told him and told him. Until she had, he'd never heard the word "propriety," not to mention the word "utmost." Now, with her too afraid and hurt and cold to complain, he was surprised to find out he missed her prim manners and sharp tongue. A little.

"I won't let you perish." Vowing straight from his heart, he could do no less for this frightened woman. He patted her clinging hand, hoping she was rational enough to understand him.

"Thank you." She released her death grip on his arm, and her hand went to his cheek. She caressed his stubbly whiskers for a moment. He couldn't think when last he'd shaved. He usually cleaned up for church, so it was at least once a week.

Daniel whispered into the dark of the cave, " 'Yea, though I walk through the valley of the shadow of death, I will fear no evil: for thou art with me.' "

"Yes," she breathed. "God is with me. And you. You're with me, too. Thank you, Daniel. God bless you." Her eyes fell shut. Tears slipped over her lower lashes, and she moved her palm away from his face. Her scraped and battered hand fluttered to the floor like the last leaf of autumn. She relaxed into real sleep—at last.

Six

Grace woke up in a rat hole. And the king of rats was leaning over her.

"How are you, Grace?" The rodent leaned so close to her it was...it was—*Oh, dear God in heaven, help me!* It was kind of nice.

He looked so worried, and he was so handsome.

"What am I doing lying on the floor?" Grace sat up so quickly they almost bumped noses. She didn't add "next to you." The words were just not ones she could force out of her mouth.

"Grace." Daniel studied her face so intently it distracted her from why she'd come to be here and how she'd come to be here and when she'd come to be here and...

"Where am I?"

"I'm glad you're awake. I was worried about you."

They stared at each other for a long second, and then, in Grace's muddled mind, another memory clicked into place. "Parrish."

Daniel's expression softened. "No, you'll be fine. I kept you close by the fire all night. What were you doing in my wagon anyway?"

Grace tried so hard to answer that question she could feel her forehead crinkling from the effort. "Am I... This is your...?"

She looked past his shock of white-blond hair, which he'd passed on to all his sons. She looked past his broad shoulders, which proved to be next to impossible because they seemed to block out the whole world.

Then she knew. She'd come calling when she'd started teaching. And it *was* a rat hole. The man and his family lived underground like vermin.

Still, she'd come. It was her duty as schoolmarm. She'd heard about the new family that had yet to send their young ones to school. She rode out here alone, on a rented horse she could ill afford, determined to urge the parents to educate their children.

She'd talked a skeptical Daniel Reeves into letting his boys attend school, and she'd been paying for that mistake ever since. But no mistake to do with the Reeves family made any difference to her life now. If she hadn't been fired from her job, she'd have had to leave anyway because of Parrish.

"I brought you home. Well, I didn't exactly bring you home." Daniel's eyes dropped to the space between them, which Grace noticed was minimal. He rolled up on his knees. She noticed he'd been stretched out on the bare dirt floor with no blanket while she had a stack of them. "More like I drove home, and when we went to unload the wagon, we found—"

"We don't need a ma none."

It looked for all the world as though Daniel had sprouted another head, a slightly smaller one coming out of his right shoulder.

"Good morning, Mark." Grace recognized the oldest of the triplets. She knew him by the fire in his eyes that the other boys couldn't fake and he couldn't mask. And it wasn't because the others weren't always in mischief—heaven knew they were. But this one had a diabolical bend. Grace had always been one step behind him. Oh, who was she kidding? She'd always been miles behind all of them.

Ike tended toward hard work and determination, traits he often used to cause problems, but he'd been the best behaved of the bunch. Ike had brought a kitten into the schoolroom one day and spent his noon hour fussing over it by the potbellied stove in the schoolhouse. Ike had actually talked to her a little that day as she found a soft rag to wash away a deep cut on the kitten's belly.

Abe, the oldest, was the leader, or so it seemed until she'd watched

Mark for a while. Abe gave the orders, but he very subtly looked to his little brother for ideas, not being quite diabolical enough on his own.

John was the sweetest one, but only by comparison. He was still more unruly than any non-Reeves child in Mosqueros. He was a follower, but he followed with an enthusiasm that had left Grace stunned on many occasions. He was also a good student, for some reason taking pride in doing his work quickly and well. Grace had learned not to draw attention to that fact, though, because it embarrassed John and he'd act up extra for a few days to prove what a troublemaker he could be.

Luke was the toughest. Maybe because he was youngest, he'd learned to take anything anyone handed out and return it with interest. He never cried, he never complained, but he never forgot a wrong. He had a knack for paying back anyone who crossed him that had quickly taught every child in Mosqueros, even those twice his size, to steer clear of him.

But this one, staring at her now, was the brains of the outfit. Mark Reeves was a creative genius. Grace had often thought if she could harness that brilliance, the boy could cure diseases and build great buildings and invent new wonders of the world.

Instead, he just tortured her.

"We don't *want* a ma, neither." Luke's head appeared over Daniel's other shoulder.

"I'm sure that's very interesting, Luke, but why are you telling me this?" Grace waited; all the potential heads hadn't even begun to sprout out of Daniel's shoulders.

"Because Pa brung you home to be our ma, but we don't want you." Abe appeared. "So thanks 'n' everything, but—"

"Your father *brought* me home to be your ma, not *brung* me home to be your ma." Grace thought about that for a split second before she added, "Your pa didn't bring me home to be your ma."

"You just said he did." A little furrow appeared between John's brows as he tried to make sense of her.

Grace wished him all the luck in the world, since she couldn't begin to make sense of any of this.

"Which is it?" Ike asked with a suspicious narrowing of his blue eyes.

All six men stared at her, hanging on every word. She'd never seen a single one of them be still for this long. Maybe she should grab this chance to run.

"Why're you here, then, Miss Calhoun?" Mark's eyes seemed to bore into her brain. He was no doubt reading her mind. Finding out through supernatural means what would bother her the most so he could begin tormenting her.

She couldn't tell them about Parrish. She couldn't tell anyone, or she'd be sent back.

Daniel nodded. "Go on. Answer him. I want to know, too. Why *are* you here?"

Grace sat up and pushed the foot-high pile of blankets off her body then snatched them right back up to her chin. "Oh, good heavens."

"What?" Daniel looked around the room; then he looked back at her, studying her as if he expected her to collapse at any second. "What's wrong?"

"I'm wearing my nightgown."

Dead silence fell on the room. Daniel's blond eyebrows arched up until they disappeared into the scruffy overlong bangs that dropped across his forehead. "You are?"

"I can't be out here alone with you wearing a nightgown." Grace clutched the blankets until her fingers hurt, thinking of the scandal of it all. "It's not proper."

Daniel's fair skin turned an alarming shade of pink as he stared at her. "I'll bet it wasn't proper of us to sleep together, either."

"It most certainly was not." The deep voice from behind hit them at the same instant the cold did.

They all turned to face Parson Roscoe.

The boys wheeled fully around. Daniel sat up. Grace clutched the blankets to her chest and looked into the startled eyes of the kindly parson and, just behind him, his gentle-hearted wife, Isabelle.

"Parson, it's not what it looks like," Grace said.

"Oh, thank heavens," Mrs. Roscoe said. "Because it looks like you and Daniel spent the night together in this cave."

"Then it is exactly what it looks like," John said into a silence more frozen than Grace had been last night.

"Well, yes," Daniel said. "We did spend the night together, but—"

"Daniel," Grace gasped in horror.

Daniel looked away from the parson, his skin now fully flaming red. "Well, we did. Do you want me to add lying to the parson in on top of having you in bed. . .I mean, sleeping together. . .I mean, having you here without your clothes. . .I mean. . ." Daniel lapsed into silence.

"Pa brung her home to be our ma, but he tried her out for the night and he decided to return her," Mark said.

Parson Roscoe stepped fully into the cave. "Both of you get up immediately."

Daniel stood in a single, lithe movement.

"In front of the children, Grace? I'm shocked." Mrs. Roscoe came in and shut the door behind her. The plump woman clutched her hands together in front of her chest as if desperate to get away and spend an hour in prayer just to wash the shock out of her mind.

Grace climbed to her feet. She fumbled with the blankets. There were too many of them to hold. She tried to drop a few of them and managed to drop them all. She caught at them and almost fell forward trying to keep herself covered.

Daniel caught her before she pitched over on top of him.

Every bone in Grace's body hurt. Every breath cut across her chest like a knife. Her arms and legs were so stiff she wanted to cry out with pain.

"We saw the broken window in your room." The parson produced his Bible from his coat pocket.

Grace remembered now. She'd fallen out of her window. No, she'd jumped out of her window.

"The whole town is up in arms about what happened to you, Grace." Mrs. Roscoe crossed the room, all three steps wide, and rested her hand on Grace's shoulder. "Search parties have been out all night."

"Someone mentioned Daniel being in town yesterday afternoon." The parson took up the story. "We offered to ride out and see if he knew of your whereabouts. Now I see you must have. . .uh. . .settled your differences and. . .uh. . .decided to. . ."

Grace could see the parson striving to be diplomatic when faced with the very worst possible sort of evidence of immoral behavior between two adults.

"Plan an elopement." Mrs. Roscoe's kind eyes found Grace, and the intertwined hands begged Grace to go along with this wild stab at respectability.

"No, oh no, no!" Daniel said. "We didn't plan no elopement. I don't want to marry the schoolmarm. Sure, we slept together. That doesn't mean—"

"What's 'lopement, Pa? Is that like an antelope?" John asked. "Are we gonna eat venison 'stead of dumb old steak all the time?"

"No, it's like an envelope, stupid," Abe sneered. "The parson wants to know if we've got any letters to mail."

"We don't rightly know how to fetch a letter around, Parson," Ike said. "We haven't had much schoolin'."

"And what we've had isn't much better 'n nothin'," Mark added, " 'cause Miss Calhoun was a mighty poor excuse for a schoolmarm."

Grace turned on Mark. "I was not a poor excuse for a schoolmarm, you little—"

"Do not tell me, Daniel Reeves,"—the parson stopped Grace from grabbing Mark by stepping past the boys and the table until he stood toe-to-toe with Daniel—"that you expect to keep this young lady, a *respectable* woman from *this* town and a member of *my flock*, out at your home *overnight* and not *do the right thing*."

"Right thing?" Grace forgot about Mark as she saw Daniel's Adam's apple bob up and down as he gulped.

Grace waited for the floor to swallow her up. If God really loved her, He'd just strike her dead right this minute. Then she thought of Parrish. If he found her married, would that negate any legal claim he had on her as her adoptive father?

Grace looked from Daniel Reeves and his multitude of sons to her future if Parrish caught up with her, something it now seemed inevitable he'd do.

Daniel or Parrish or death. Those were her only choices.

"Grace!" Parson Roscoe's voice interrupted her panic.

"I'm thinking!" Weighing her options carefully, she prayed, *C'mon, God. Death. I'm ready.*

The parson could be formidable without half trying. Grace saw that he was trying like the dickens right now.

In a voice that seemed to promise eternal flames, he said to Daniel, "Yes, the right thing. We'll get on with this. Call it an elopement if you will, and no one will have to know what exactly went on here last night."

"Miss Calhoun's reputation will be spared." Mrs. Roscoe scooted closer to Daniel. She laid a comforting hand on his shoulder and pleaded. "Otherwise she's ruined, Daniel. You knew that when you brought her here."

Grace wondered what the parson and his wife were imagining happened in the tiny cave with five children as chaperones. She felt her cheeks heating up as she considered what might be going on in their minds. Although truly she didn't have a clue what might be going on in their minds, because she had no idea what went on between a man and a woman.

"Well, Daniel, will you do the right thing by this young lady?" the parson asked in a hard voice. "Answer now, in front of God, your pastor, and your children. Think well before you speak."

Daniel looked at the parson. He looked at his boys. Grace saw him look at the stone roof only a couple of inches over his head. Then he looked at her. It was the look of a wild animal caught in a trap.

He appeared for all the world to be considering the pros and cons of gnawing off his foot.

He turned back to the parson. "Nothing improper went on here last night."

"I won't hear another word," the parson thundered. "She's ruined, and well you know it."

"I don't mind being ruined," Grace said. "Surely it's better than being stuck with him!"

The parson turned his eyes on her, and Grace remembered his roaring sermons, all aimed straight at her. She was suddenly afraid to go to church on Sunday. And as soon as she spoke, she realized she *did* mind being ruined. She'd lived close to disaster for a long time, but she'd always clung to the highest level of respectability. With her background, it was terribly important to her.

The parson looked away from Grace, having silenced her. Grace took just a split second out of this living nightmare to envy the parson that glare and wish she could look at her students like that. Of course, she didn't have any students. She'd been fired, thanks to the King of the Rats, here.

"Daniel Reeves, don't make me ashamed of you." The parson gripped his big black Bible in both hands as if he needed to physically hang on to his faith in the face of this indignity. "You will stand side by side and make right this grievous wrong you've perpetrated on this innocent maiden."

"What's *per potato*, Pa?" John tugged on Daniel's sleeve. "Does the parson want to stay for breakfast? I'm hungry, and I'll be glad to start cooking if you—"

"As long as Pa brung us a ma for one night, don't it seem like she oughta do the cookin'?" Luke asked. "It's the least she could do after she and Pa shared the blankets overnight."

"That's *perpetrated*, idiot." Abe shoved John into Mark. "It's like Methodist and Baptist and Perpetyrians."

"What's an innocent maiden?" Luke asked.

Daniel jerked his thumb at Grace, in a gesture Grace found shockingly rude. "It's her."

The parson narrowed his blazing eyes. "Until last night."

"I been around her long enough to know she's not innocent at all," Mark said. "Why, she's a cranky old—"

"Answer me right now, Daniel!" The parson glowered.

Daniel looked at her again.

Grace looked back.

Mrs. Roscoe cleared her throat. "There is no decision to be made here. Begin the service at once, Irving."

"Do you, Daniel, take this woman—"

"Now just hang on a minute there, Parson." Daniel talked over the top of the parson, holding up both hands, his palms flat in front of him as if trying to calm a nervous horse.

Grace quit listening to the parson as she considered what seemed to be going on in this cave this morning. Forget nervous horse: Try runaway train. This situation was definitely out of control, and Daniel's flat hands didn't have a chance of stopping anything.

She leaned forward to stare at the boys. "You're confusing *perpetrated* with *Presbyterian*, Abe." Grace believed in teaching, and none of the boys had been more stiff-necked about learning than Abe. If she taught this boy one word, she'd call her entire life a success, because he seemed stubbornly averse to learning of any kind. "*Perpetrated* means—"

"Daniel Reeves, speak!"

Grace pulled her attention away from Abe. Daniel was staring at her, his eyes so wide Grace would swear the man had seen a ghost.

Daniel shook his head.

The parson started yelling again. He seemed prepared to call down lightning on all of them if Daniel didn't speak, and now.

"I don't even know how I got here." Grace flung her arms wide, narrowly missing backhanding Daniel in the face.

"I do." Daniel grabbed her hand to protect himself. "It's like this. I needed supplies. . . ."

Grace almost smiled. Finally, she'd hear the whole story.

"About time." The parson turned his fire-and-brimstone eyes on Grace and scared her into paying attention.

"No, I didn't mean—" Daniel dropped her hand as if it had sprouted cactus bristles.

"Silence, Daniel."

Grace ran that tone of voice quickly through her head. She had to practice. How she'd love to be the proud owner of a tone of voice that could silence Daniel Reeves.

"Do you, Grace, take Daniel—"

Mark shoved between his father and the parson. "We told you we aren't keepin' her for our ma." Mark appeared to be the only one in the room with no fear of Parson Roscoe's close ties with the heavenly Father. He turned on Grace. "You want out of here as bad as we want you out of here, don't you?"

Grace nodded frantically. "I do."

"Hallelujah!" The parson raised his hands to heaven, reciting a blessing that Grace couldn't quite understand because she was too afraid to take her eyes off of Mark.

"I now pronounce you. . ."

Mrs. Roscoe threw herself, weeping, into Grace's arms, whispering something. Grace could only make out "Congratulations."

"What?" Grace turned back to the parson.

But what was there in this mess to be congratulated for?

The parson finished with a prayer that nearly shook the solid rock cave; then he tipped his hat. "I'll expect you all to be sitting in church together when I announce your good news."

Grace thought immediately of Parrish. He would hang around Mosqueros, trying to pick up her trail. "No—"

"Yes," the parson retorted. "You will be there. You'll accept everyone's congratulations and put this episode behind you decently and in order."

"Congratulations for what?" Grace then realized the parson and his wife could give her a ride back to town. Then she thought of Parrish.

Mrs. Roscoe clutched Grace's hand. "I've always had a feeling about you two. That's why, when you were missing, I insisted Irving and I be the ones to come out here and check."

"You've had a feeling about Mr. Reeves and me?" Grace had a feeling, too, every time she'd spoken to the man. Quite a few feelings, honestly: contempt, fury, disgust.

The parson, who Grace had always liked, and his wife, who seemed like such a sweet-natured woman in the normal course of things, swept out of the cave home. The door slammed shut on the seven of them.

"But I need a ride back to town," Grace called after them.

"You're not getting a ride back to town, woman. You're married!" Daniel might as well have been a cougar trapped in this cave with her. She'd have felt no safer.

"I'm what?" Deafening silence followed her question. She thought of what had just happened. She'd heard no such talk of marriage. Had she?

"She's what?" Abe and Ike asked together.

Mark shoved himself to the front of the pack of boys. "To who?"

Grace looked at Daniel, and it hit her like that imaginary runaway train Daniel had tried to stop. She was the mother of five—including two ten-year-olds. And she was only seventeen.

She'd be in all the medical textbooks if word got out.

"I can run after the parson and catch him," John offered with frantic eagerness.

"There's no need, boys." Daniel's shoulders slumped as if all five boys had just jumped on his back.

"Why didn't the parson give her a ride back to town, Pa?" Luke asked.

All the boys turned to their father with curious expressions.

In a voice so tired Grace would have felt sorry for him if she hadn't had her hands full feeling sorry for herself, Daniel said, "Because I brung her home to be your ma."

Grace sank onto the floor and pulled all six blankets over her head.

"Irving, I'm ashamed of you." Isabelle Roscoe folded her hands over her ample middle and tried to look severe.

Her husband started laughing. "You played right along, Belle. Now don't try and deny it."

"We could have taken that poor girl home and no one would have been the wiser."

"Something needed to be done." Irving chirruped to the horses, unable to feel any remorse. "Miss Calhoun had nowhere to go, and the good Lord knows Daniel Reeves needed a mother for those poor children."

"Yes, something did need to be done. But I'm not sure forcing them to get married, right there on the spot, was for the best. That sweet girl could have lived with us for a while until she found another job."

"Yes, she could have. But why, when this solution is so obvious? Anyway, it was necessary. They'd been together for a full night. Nothing else would have suited the situation."

"Alone with five boys? Nothing sinful happened in that awful cave, or everyone would have known it. Those two don't get along, Irving." Isabelle shook her head; then a grin escaped.

Irving chuckled. "You're the one who said you'd always had a feeling about those two. Where'd you come up with that?"

"Well, I did have a feeling she'd left town with him. I just figured things had finally come to a shoot-out and we'd find Daniel's body somewhere along the trail."

When they stopped laughing, Irving clucked to his horses. "They're not going to have an easy time of it."

She waved away his worry. "What newlyweds ever have an easy time of it?"

Irving nodded. "Well said, Belle." They eased through the gap, out of the canyon, their team already wading through knee-deep snow. "This trail is going to fill. They'll be stuck in there together awhile. That'll help them sort things out. What do you suppose possessed Daniel to build in here anyway?"

Isabelle shrugged. "I've heard talk in town that no one knew this canyon existed until Daniel turned up living in it. Look at this narrow entrance. Why, I wouldn't be surprised if this canyon closes up so tight they'll be locked in here solid until spring."

"They'll be settled in by then. Maybe we'll have a baby to baptize before they get snowed in next winter. It'll all work out fine." The two exchanged a fond, if conspiratorial, look as the horses plodded toward home through the narrow gap, snow drifting heavily down on their heads.

SEVEN

Adam staggered against the wind howling through the mouth of Sawyer Canyon. He clung to his Stetson, his belly protesting his hunger. He'd been out all night and most of the day searching for Grace Calhoun. The sun had long since dipped behind the rugged hills, although a dusky light made it so he could still see. The cold wind blew all day, but only in the bottleneck of this canyon had it grown teeth.

Remembering Judd Mason and the standoff at this canyon that had almost gotten Sophie killed, he prayed again for forgiveness of his sinful heart, knowing God had saved him from hate during that dark time.

He caught the reins of his horse and turned his roan toward home, knowing he had to go in and get some rest before he collapsed.

Where is she, God? Where did the schoolmarm get to?

Crackling brush had him wheeling his horse toward the rugged incline that guarded the canyon, his eyes narrowing on an area strewn with rock and scrub mesquite.

He pulled his Winchester and jacked in a shell. With a cluck of his tongue, he urged his roan forward. He saw nothing, but he wasn't a man to dismiss an out-of-place sound. Could the schoolmarm be hiding from him? Why would she do such a thing?

He considered firing a shot to summon Clay, but the hands had fanned out wide, and it'd be a distance for Clay to travel. Anyway, as a black man who'd lived free all his life, and now ran his own Texas ranch, he'd learned to saddle his own broncs. If he really needed help, there most likely wasn't time for it to get here.

"Miss Calhoun, you in there? I'm here to help. No harm will come to you."

He heard a tiny squeak of fear that was human for sure. If she really was out here with no coat or shoes, she might be beyond responding. He swung down off his horse and inched forward in the gathering dusk. The bushes rustled just enough for him to know he was on the right track.

He reached for the winter-killed branches of the waist-high scrub and pushed it aside. He looked into a woman's wide brown eyes so awash with terror they made his heart clutch. Then she screamed and leaped for his throat.

Daniel wondered if he hadn't ought to drag Grace out of there.

He'd fed the boys breakfast. They had beefsteak and eggs and potatoes and biscuits and milk. They'd gone out and fed the horses, milked the cows, gathered the eggs, and checked the herd. Grace had stayed under the blanket.

He'd made dinner, beefsteak and eggs and potatoes and biscuits and milk. And Grace stayed under the blanket.

He would have asked her to join them, except he couldn't get his throat to work. Not when it came to the woman huddled in the corner of his house.

They went back to work in the blowing snow, dragging windfall trees closer to the house to cut up for firewood. They took an ax to the ice that had backed up behind his spreader dam and threatened to overflow. They tracked down a cow that had calved out of season and took the pair into the barn, hoping the little one would survive the winter weather.

Daniel's boys toiled alongside him, doing good work the way he'd trained them. And getting tired for bedtime, he hoped.

A heavy snow became blinding by midafternoon. The wind picked up, and as night came, the snow fell more heavily, and Daniel thought they might be looking at a blizzard. This far south?

The gap they drove through to get to these highlands might close them in tight, but surely these harsh conditions wouldn't last. He'd heard Texas winters just weren't that cold. At any rate, Daniel had supplies. He didn't need to go running to town every time he turned around.

He set the beefsteak and eggs and potatoes and biscuits and milk on the table for supper. And Grace stayed under the blanket.

"Well, so far she ain't no trouble." Ike held on his lap the cat he'd brought home from school. Daniel knew Ike wouldn't sneak the cat so much as a bite of steak. A cat needed to catch his own supper.

"Nope." Mark looked at the pile of blankets. "No help, but no trouble."

"Do we have'ta sleep without blankets again tonight, Pa?" John asked. "Is that what havin' a ma means? No blankets?"

Daniel sighed all the way to the soles of his feet. With a dejected shrug of his shoulders, he said, "So far."

"Maybe she's dead under there." Abe stared at the unmoving lump.

Daniel had lived twenty-eight years in a hard land. He'd worked for everything he'd ever gotten. None of it came by luck. So he figured he wasn't going to get lucky now. "Reckon she's alive."

"Well, I want my blanket back." Mark got up from the table and turned to his new ma.

Daniel braced himself to see her. He could almost stand her if she'd just stay under there.

Ike grabbed Mark and held him back with wide-eyed fear. "Don't touch her."

Mark jerked his arm away. "I'll touch her if'n I wanta touch her. She's my ma. I get to touch my own ma."

"But what if she starts talking and fussing like she does at school?" Luke said. "We're better off with her under there."

Grace pushed the blanket off of her head. Daniel could see that she'd been asleep most of the time. Or the shock had knocked her insensible, maybe.

"You can have your blanket, Mark." Grace pushed all the blankets away then looked down at herself, saw that blasted nightgown, and pulled them all back. Daniel had the feeling he could have somehow saved himself from getting stuck with her if she hadn't been wearing that nightgown.

"What in the world were you doing in my wagon wearing a nightgown anyway, Grace?"

"That's *Miss Calhoun*, Mr. Reeves." She pulled her knees up to her chest and wrapped her arms around them.

Daniel thought if she stayed that way and never ate, she wouldn't be much trouble. But he'd been married. He knew women were *always* trouble.

"No, Grace, it's *not* 'Miss Calhoun.'" Daniel had heard her say those words many times. They'd always set his teeth on edge. "It's *Mrs.* Reeves." Daniel added with angry triumph, "And guess what? I'm calling you Grace and the boys are calling you Ma."

Daniel pushed back his chair, and all the boys stood from the two benches that lined the sides of the table. Abe and Ike were on one side; Mark, Luke, and John on the other.

"And I'm the head of this house. Someone as proper as you should know that's the God-given way to run a family. And the first order I'm giving is for you to tell me *what you were doing in the back of my wagon.*"

Grace clenched her jaw and pursed her lips. Her hair flew around, as wild as a litter of wolf pups. She jammed her fingers into it, making it even worse. Her eyes looked swollen from sleep.

So she'd been sleeping all day while he and his sons worked their fingers to the bone. He wanted to cut her down to size. He wanted to blast her for mucking up his life. He wanted to shake her until she wasn't his wife anymore, and she wasn't here in his home with her cool manners, and her snooty nose wasn't in the air, and her yammering mouth never again criticized his boys.

A tear ran down her cheek.

Daniel froze. He'd forgotten about crying. The boys all inhaled sharply and took a step back.

"What's'a matter with her, Pa?" John hugged up against his leg and whispered, even though Grace was only three steps away and could hear every word.

The cave was a single room, roughly ten feet by ten feet. *Everything* was just three steps away.

"I'll tell you what I was doing in your wagon, Mr. . . ." Grace lapsed into silence. She dropped her head onto her knees and clutched the top of her skull with both hands. Her shoulders shuddered violently. He heard her breathing become rough and unsteady. Crying.

Daniel had to fight the urge to give her the house and the herd. He'd take the boys and make a run for the border. He wondered if Mrs. Roscoe ever cried. Surely the parson would understand.

He and his boys stood absolutely immobilized.

The wind moaned around the house, and Daniel wondered if he'd have to dig them out in the morning. They lived on fairly high ground. They got a beauty of a snowstorm once in a while, he'd heard. A blizzard might cut them off from civilization for a spell, if Mosqueros could be called civilized.

Then he realized there was no way they were going to get to church in the morning. Daniel liked church. He did. But once he showed up with Miss Calhoun in town, his marriage was a done deal.

And that's when he realized he was still trying to think of a way out of this. But Daniel Reeves was no fool. He could dream all he wanted. He was tied to this woman.

John whispered again, "Is she supposed to get all sad like that, Pa?"

"Yep, in my experience with wives, they're supposed to fuss about something all the time. I've never had me one that didn't cry up a storm at the drop of a hat."

Grace lifted her head and scowled through her tears.

Daniel was surprised at his urge to laugh. She really was a mess. The oh-so-tidy Miss Calhoun kept getting herself slopped up more and more. He wondered when she'd gather her wits together enough to care about that.

"Did it ever occur to you that you might be doing things to your wives that make them cry?" She pushed her hair off her soggy face with shaky hands.

"Nope." Daniel shrugged. "Never was nothing I did."

"Is she gonna cry all the time, then, Pa?" Abe edged closer. " 'Cause if'n she does it *all* the time, then I reckon it don't mean nothing. Reckon girls just leak."

Grace gave Abe a dark look, then lifted a blanket and handed it to him.

He snatched it and dropped onto the floor and wrapped up.

One by one the boys all got a blanket. And then the boys spread out along with the blankets, except the one wrapped around Grace and that blasted nightgown.

Daniel was looking at a long, cold winter.

He turned his back on her and lay down as far from her as the room would allow. They only missed touching by inches.

She tapped his shoulder, and knowing he'd regret it, he turned around. "What?"

"I'll tell you what I was doing in the wagon, but I wanted to tell you privately. That's why I waited until the boys were asleep."

Daniel felt all the boys' ears perk up. They were all playing possum. Not a one of them was asleep. Daniel decided right there and then that he'd wait until a very private moment to hear Grace's story.

It suddenly occurred to him that Grace might have been up to no good. Maybe, just maybe, she was *already* ruined and not the proper young lady she'd led the town to believe.

And Daniel knew what ruined meant. Babies. His stomach clenched as he thought about having another child. The first two had almost killed Margaret, and the last three *had* killed her.

She'd begged him to have another child. He'd absolutely refused. But his wife had done her best to tempt him, and he'd been weak. His weakness had killed his wife. And now he might have another wife with a child, and through no doing of his own. He'd vowed to God there'd be no more Reeves babies to come in packs and finish off some poor woman.

Daniel sat up and leaned as close to her as he could. Her eyes got wide, and he wondered what in tarnation she was thinking. He whispered into her ear, "The boys are still up. We'll talk another time."

He pulled back, and she nodded. Her hair bobbed and swayed like a tumbleweed blown along before the wind. Surprised by the little corkscrew curls, he couldn't resist the temptation to push a couple of them away from her eyes. She'd always had her hair pulled neatly back. Unable to stop himself, he touched her curls again, just to test their softness. Then he looked at her for a long time. The tears had etched their way down her face. Her eyes were swollen almost shut. Red veins traced their way across the whites of her eyes, and the strange sparkling golden color, an exact match for her hair, was shining with tears. She hadn't been sleeping all day. She'd been crying.

But crying because of a mix-up that had left her married to a man she didn't want? Or crying because she was ruined and in despair over how to explain a baby that came too soon? The bruise on her face had darkened to purple. Had she told some man the bad news and he'd laid his hands on her? Was that why she'd run?

There was one question he knew would haunt him if he kept it inside. "Just tell me one thing."

Her puffy eyes widened a bit at his severe tone. She nodded and silently waited, acting like an obedient wife should.

"Is there a baby?"

Her eyes went blank, as if he'd spoken the question in Apache.

"A baby," he repeated, "on the way. Is that why you hid out in my wagon? To trap me?"

She gasped.

Daniel heard the boys gasp, too, though he doubted they knew what he was really asking. She knew all right, because she unwound from the little ball she'd curled herself into and slapped him hard across the face.

The boys all jumped, but they stayed under cover.

Smart boys.

She packed quite a wallop for a little thing. His face burned. His temper rose.

Her chin began to quiver. The sparkle in her eyes blazed into fire. She pulled her hand back to paste him again.

He caught her hand with a smart slap of flesh on flesh, surprised at how furious he was. He should have been sorry. He should have been begging her pardon for asking such a thing. But he wasn't. And her anger might be over getting caught rather than being insulted.

"Sorry, Mrs. Reeves, but that's no answer." The sting on his cheek came out in his voice.

She jerked against his grip.

He held fast.

She raised her other hand—this one clenched in a fist—and he caught that, too.

He leaned close. "You are well and truly trapped, *Mrs. Reeves*. Just like I am."

Daniel tried to think of the men in Mosqueros. His stomach twisted to think of such a thing passing between this proper young lady and one of the rough-and-ready types who lived around here. There were decent men, of course, but none of them would have dishonored her.

Maybe he was wrong about her problem, but there was something here, something behind her eyes. She was definitely hiding something. What else could it be? Why else hide in his wagon? What else couldn't she say in front of his boys?

"We'll talk when we can have a private moment." He let her arms go and lay down with his back to her, cold, blanketless, and looking likely to stay that way for the rest of his life.

349

Let her pound on him all she wanted. He felt only contempt for this ruined woman. By dragging him into this mess, she'd ruined them both.

She didn't attack. He didn't know what she did. He ignored her and looked at the tense shoulders of his wide-awake boys. He loved them fiercely. He was so proud of them he'd like to burst when he thought of how fine they'd turned out, raised only by him.

She'd ruined them, too, and *that* was something he couldn't forgive.

E I G H T

Adam fell backward more from surprise than from the impact. He landed flat on his back, and the woman shrieked and scrambled forward as if she'd try to flee. He tried to regain his feet and grab her, and then something hard swatted him in the face. He fell flat again, and a boot caught him in the chin.

Adam grabbed at the worn dark leather encasing her wildly swinging foot, got smacked in the hand by what felt like iron, then noticed her ankle wore a shackle, and blood dripped from around the metal binding. He let go, not wanting to deepen her scrapes. Blood glistened against skin nearly as black as his.

A black woman. His heart clutched; he hadn't seen a black woman in years.

In the dark night, he only knew it was blood because of the damp sheen glistening in the sliver of moon peeking out of the scuttling clouds. And there was the smell of blood to confirm his suspicion. She was hurt, the poor, helpless little thing.

She sprang backward, screaming so loudly his ears hurt, and something hard and fast-moving whizzed past his face and caught him on the shoulder.

"Ow!" He stumbled to his feet. "Miss, please. I won't hurt—"

"No!" She slammed the heel of her hand into his nose.

He hit the ground again, and blood splattered down the front of his buckskin coat. He'd have just left her alone, except her arms were bare, and she trembled visibly from the cold. He had to help her. He advanced on her, trying to trap her flailing hands without doing any injury. Finally, he gained a firm grasp on one arm.

"Let me go, please!"

A dull clink of metal on metal pulled his attention to the fetter that dragged several links of chain. Chain she'd used as a weapon.

She wrenched against his hold like a wild animal.

To Adam, it appeared her fear had a grip on her mind and she wasn't capable of hearing.

She twisted frantically. "Leave me alone. Let go. Please don't hurt me." Her terror was punctuated by thin, high-pitched cries of pain.

Adam knew he was bruising her. Then he saw more bruises. Even in the dark he could identify them against her mahogany skin. Old bruises, yellow and purple. Not the kind of bruises a person got in an accident. She'd been beaten. Equal parts compassion and fury nearly overwhelmed him. The one thing he couldn't do was add to her injuries. His heart thudding, he released her, not sure what he'd do if she ran—because he couldn't let her go.

He stepped away, his hands in the air. "I won't hurt you. I'm not restraining you."

"Don't make me go back." Stumbling over a mesquite bush, she flattened her back against the wall of rock behind her. She buried her face in her hands and began to weep, sinking to her knees.

She wore a drab brown dress hanging in tatters and button-up boots, her toes visible through holes. With her head bowed low, he could see her long, tight curls, tangled with sticks from the bushes.

"I can't leave you out here, ma'am. You're freezing. Let me take you to the ranch."

"No!" She looked up. Tears cut through dust on her face. She staggered to her feet. "Just ride on. If you really want to help, just leave. I'll die before I go with you."

Regret, deep as grief, cut through Adam's heart at her panic. She was beyond rational thought. He was going to have to force her to come along. Then he felt blood drip off his chin and swiped at his broken nose and *hoped* he could force her. He spoke as gently as he could, hoping he could penetrate her fright.

She cringed and dodged his attempt to urge her toward his horse.

"I'm sorry, ma'am. I won't hurt you, I promise. And I won't let anyone take you anywhere you don't want to go. But I can't leave you out here." Flinching to prepare for her next attack, he reached for her.

Instead of fighting, she sank to the ground, screaming as if he were driving a knife into her heart.

Adam swung her up into his arms. Her hopeless tears hurt him worse than the beating he'd just taken.

Grace lay awake, numb from staring sightlessly at his back. His back. Her husband's back. Daniel Reeves. Her husband.

She was going completely out of her mind. She was trapped. He'd used those very words. Trapped. Both of them. All of them.

She heard the wind and knew there'd be no church tomorrow. That was a blessing.

She cut off the thought. *No, forgive me, God. It's not a blessing that there's no church. It's just a blessing that. . .*

No, it was *not* a blessing that she was trapped in a house with six men, all of whom hated her. All of whom were completely out of control. Rude, sloppy, ignorant.

And here she lay married to the rudest, sloppiest, most ignorant one of the bunch.

So what did that make her? No well-mannered, tidy, brilliant choices had brought her to this place. That meant *she* got the prize as the most ignorant one of all. No contest.

Of course, if they couldn't get out, Parrish couldn't get in. She knew the man. *Tough* was not a word she'd use to describe him, and facing a Texas blizzard took all kinds of tough.

So she was safe and in the middle of a complete disaster at the same time. No wonder she couldn't sleep.

She finally noticed another reason or two she couldn't sleep. She started to cry when she thought of it. She needed to go to the outhouse. And she was starving. How could her body make such mundane demands of her at a time like this?

She didn't even know where the outhouse was. She didn't even have shoes. She had to wake Daniel. She had to ask him for help and take the first step to being a functioning human being in this household. She wasn't going to be able to stay curled up in her ball forever. That was the only plan she'd come up with today.

Her body wouldn't let her ignore its discomfort anymore. Her arm fighting every inch-by-inch movement, she stretched out her hand and—shuddering all the way to the soles of her feet—touched her husband.

Daniel rolled over. His eyes were open, fully alert.

Grace thought of the sluggish way she woke up every morning and almost jumped at Daniel's reaction. Forcing the words past reluctant lips, she said, "I. . . That is, can you. . . Is there a. . . I need directions to the. . .the. . ." She was pretty sure it was too dark in the minuscule cave for him to see her cheeks go flaming red.

Daniel must've been used to the question. Of course he would be. The father of five would know about nature calls in the night. "I'll get the lantern and go with you."

"No, just directions, and. . .a. . .a coat."

"The snow's too deep for you to go alone." Daniel didn't discuss it or try to change her mind. He got up, lit the lantern with a piece of bark he touched to the fire in the stove's belly, and pulled on his shoes.

He glanced at her. "You're about the size of a ten-year-old boy, I'd say." He rustled around in a pile of clothes by the door and tossed her a shirt, a pair of boots, and—

"I can't wear a pair of pants."

Daniel's eyes narrowed in the lantern light. He said with grim humor, "Wade through the snow barefoot in your nightgown for all I care." He turned his back to give her privacy.

Grace wanted to start crying again. She thought of the years with Parrish, and the recollection steadied her. She'd survived that. She could survive anything.

She turned her back on Daniel and slipped on the clothes. She pulled the pants on under her nightgown. They were too short, but they buttoned comfortably on her waist. The boots fit perfectly. She *was* the size of a ten-year-old boy. She just pulled the shirt on over her nightgown, unwilling to undress further in front of Daniel. She tied the boots, and he handed her a heavy coat, which she pulled on.

"Ready?"

She nodded.

He swung the door open the smallest slit possible, and they slipped through into the biting cold and driving snow.

When they got back, Grace was shivering all the way to her bones. The snow had come in over her boots, and sharp needles of ice had cut through her clothing to her skin.

She trembled as Daniel closed the door behind them. He hadn't asked her any questions outside, thank heavens. The weather was just too brutal for anything like that. But she was well aware that she'd just had her chance to explain things to Daniel and she'd passed it by.

She at least could have told him there was no baby. But she was still so insulted she couldn't bring herself to deny his charge. She was tempted to let him wait nine months and figure it out himself.

If they continued living like this, it might even be possible never to tell him. When would they ever have a moment alone? The thought cheered her considerably.

Now they were back with the boys, who surely had been awakened by the noise and the blast of cold air, though none of them moved.

"I would like a biscuit, please," she whispered. "I'm hungry."

"Suit yourself." Daniel lay down on the bare dirt floor.

Grace wanted to kick him, but what had she expected? That he'd serve her then stand at her elbow while she ate? She neither expected nor wanted that.

She grabbed the single remaining biscuit off the kitchen table. She had to move carefully because the boys' sprawled bodies covered the floor. How could they live like this?

She thought of Parrish and the conditions she'd lived in with him. She thought of the litany of work Daniel had ordered his children to do. Had she stumbled onto a family that ran much like hers? The boys were little monsters, but that didn't mean she was going to stand by and watch them be treated like slave labor.

She thought of Hannah and wondered if her sister was safe. Surely Parrish had focused all his rage on Grace. But without Grace's money, how long before Hannah and the children began to go hungry? And how long before timid, nurturing Hannah came up with one of her harebrained schemes to rescue her missing sister?

Grace knew she had to get a letter to Hannah as soon as possible so she wouldn't go crazy worrying. As the wind whistled outside the door, Grace knew it wouldn't be tomorrow.

Grace closed her eyes and prayed that God would tend to Hannah and the little ones. Grace knew it was a sin to ask. God cared for his children. He knew the number of hairs on Hannah's head. She was distrusting God when she didn't put her faith in His promises. But where was God when she and Hannah and all the others had been in Parrish's clutches all those years?

Distrust came easily.

She found a few inches of milk in the bottom of the pail. One tin cup sat in the center of the table next to the biscuit and the milk. She poured herself the milk, finished it and the biscuit, and went back to bed. She rolled up tightly in the coarse woolen blanket. She should share it with Daniel, she knew.

Instead, she ignored him. And comfortable, fed, and warm, she found herself once again staring at Daniel's back. Her husband's back. Daniel Reeves. Her husband.

She fell asleep before she could start crying again.

"My name is Adam."

The words pulled Tillie awake.

"I'm taking you home with me."

A black man held her. She hadn't seen a black man in years, not since the war was over. And Master Virgil had kept only Tillie as a slave long after all the other slaves had been freed by law. Of course, she hadn't known the war was over and the slaves had been freed until just recently.

"No one will hurt you at home."

No black man would send her back to that nightmare, would he?

"You're too cold. You have to get warmed up. I can't leave you here."

She felt the world shift steadily along and realized she was on horseback, held by a man—a black man—with arms like iron bands. Those arms tightened in a way that told Tillie he knew she had roused. She looked up into the full dark. Barely able to see his face shrouded by the brim of his hat, she tested his grip and found no escape.

Black eyes gleamed in the night. He watched her. She could tell even with his face in shadows darkened by his ebony skin.

Panic soared in her stomach like a flock of frightened birds. If only the wings were real and could carry her away.

Maybe if she convinced him she was all right, he'd let her go. She stiffened her spine and forced herself to speak calmly. "Thank you for helping me. I was frightened at first. That's why I fought you. I apologize for hurting you."

"I'm fine. You didn't hurt me."

"Your nose is bleeding, and one eye is swollen shut. I'm sorry. I don't know my own strength sometimes."

He tilted his head so the moonlight revealed his astonished expression. "You'd have never touched me if I hadn't been so careful not to hurt you."

Tillie controlled her expression, though a soft sniff of disdain might have escaped. Still, he wouldn't have noticed it. She hoped. "Well, for whatever reason you *let* me hit you, I do apologize. Now, I really need to be on my way. Please let me down, sir."

The man—Adam—didn't even slow his horse. "It's Adam, not sir. And I'm not letting you walk away from me in the snow and cold. I'm taking you somewhere safe. My boss's wife and daughters will see to your injuries. We will protect you from whoever hurt you. I promise."

"I don't need protection. I can take care of myself. And no one hurt me."

"Uh...so that metal cuff on your ankle is...jewelry of some sort?"

She'd forgotten about that horrid binding. She couldn't get it off no matter what she tried. It made her explanations sound weak. She looked up at Adam. His voice and the strength of his arms could be a sanctuary, but trust was foreign to her.

A horse snorted, and she realized she was being carried along on its back at a ground-eating pace. The animal's feet crunched on the snow, its bridle jingling when it tossed its head, white breath whooshing out of its nose as it hurried along.

She became aware of a coarse blanket surrounding her. She wasn't so cold anymore. She'd been cold for so long that this blanket qualified as luxury.

"The McClellen place is just ahead, miss. You'll be safe and warm there. We'll tend your wounds, get you a hot meal and some warm clothes, and give you a soft bed for the night."

It sounded like heaven, back when she believed there was such a place. What choice did she have anyway? Since her escape attempt had turned to this disaster, she hadn't eaten, hadn't slept, hadn't been warm for days and days.

"What's your name?"

The chain on her ankle clinked, an eternal reminder of where she'd been, what she'd left, what awaited her if she was taken back.

"I won't tell you."

358

He made a sound, soothing, maybe prayerful. One strong hand held the reins while the other supported her back and gently caressed her shoulder as if she were a fretful child. But he was a fool if he prayed to a God who had forgotten one of His children. A God she'd believed in for so long, only to be betrayed. The knowledge that all of her years and years of prayer had been whispered into nothingness—because no God could have heard her prayers and left her with that madman—was worse than finding out the war had been over for years. It had nearly destroyed her.

Adam suddenly pulled his horse to a stop. "We're here. You'll be fine. I'll carry you into the house."

Tillie had vowed when she ran from Virgil that never again would someone tell her where to go and what to do. That vow had lasted less than a week, because now Adam was taking charge of her life. But not for long.

"Clay, get over here and take my horse!" Adam swung down to the ground with her still in his arms, his gentleness in vivid contrast to the brutality of Virgil.

His last beating had come with words that cut her to the heart. Virgil had sneered at her that there'd been a war. The slaves had been freed. But not her, never her.

She looked away from Adam to see a cabin, tiny compared to where she'd lived, but neat, with smoke pouring out of the chimney and lights glowing in each window. She saw a looming barn to her right. Wooden corral fences stretched away from the barn, and in the moonlight she saw grazing horses and other outbuildings.

A man strode toward them from the barn and caught the horse's reins.

Adam immediately started for the house as if he was afraid she didn't have much time.

"I heard they found the schoolmarm eloped with Daniel Reeves," the man called after them. "Did you catch up with Mrs. Reeves making a break from Reeves Canyon?"

"No, it's someone else. She's hurt. Sophie, open up." Adam strode along, taking her somewhere against her will.

Her whole life had been lived against her will. "I can walk."

Adam smiled down at her as his spurs clanked. "I've got your feet all wrapped tight. I'll put you down when we get out of the snow." He climbed a few steps to a porch, and a door opened and swung wide.

"What happened?" A very pregnant blond woman stepped back to let Adam in.

He entered the house as an equal, not submissively.

Tillie looked away from the woman by reflex. She'd learned well not to look a white man or woman straight in the eye.

Children filled the room. A bevy of little girls came up to Adam, trying to take a peek. Tillie turned her head so they could see her and felt the fear ease. The pretty smiles, bright lantern light, and warm home were so different from where she'd been.

"Bring her into the back room, Adam. It's the warmest. Mandy and Beth can share a bed tonight."

"I don't want to share a bed with her! She kicks!" the oldest girl screeched.

There hadn't been children in Master Virgil's house. She stopped herself. No, she wouldn't think of him as "master." But the name was branded into her mind.

The girls bickered, full of life and energy and courage, as Adam laid her on a feather bed. The chain on her ankle clinked against the wooden frame.

"What in the world is that?" Sophie reached for the chain, then stopped and looked sharply at Adam. "What's going on here?"

Adam would drop his gaze now. He'd back down and start saying, "Yes'm," and "No, ma'am," in the face of the lady's upset.

Adam didn't blink. Instead, he actually glared at the lady. "I don't know. But it's coming off." He wheeled and headed out of the room.

"Wait. Her ankle is cut up from this thing." The lady—Sophie—looked at Tillie. "What happened to you? Adam, go for the sheriff. He can be out here in an hour. They can arrest—"

"No!" Tillie hadn't meant to shout, and she had to fight not to cringe. But her cringing days were over. "Please, don't call the sheriff. Please."

A tense silence stretched out. Sophie stood with her hands on her hips, obviously unsettled. Adam was holding on to the doorknob, looking eager to go for the law. Tillie was hoping, even praying, until she caught herself and stopped, that they'd let it drop.

Adam stepped back to the bedside. "Whoever did this broke the law. The days of chaining up another human being are gone." Adam's jaw clenched until Tillie wondered if he'd grind his teeth down.

Sophie patted Adam's arm and spoke quietly. "Get the tools and tell Clay to quit fighting with the girls and get in here to help. While you're finding the tools, I'll talk to her."

"Thanks, Sophie."

Tillie's mind almost couldn't wrap around the way the white woman touched Adam without landing a blow or issuing a harsh command. And Adam's response was even more astonishing. Respectfully, he'd backed off, but there was no bowing or scraping.

His eyes met Tillie's, and a thousand questions wanted to rush from her lips. Who was he? How had he found this life? Was he truly considered an equal by these people?

The girls screamed in the background, and a man who must be Clay hollered at them to be quiet. It sounded like the same man who'd taken Adam's horse, almost as if Clay served Adam. Except the girls were calling him Pa and they'd called Sophie Ma, so this must be their home and their family with Adam as a guest.

The fighting changed to giggling.

Sophie sat on the side of the bed and looked up at Adam. "Ask Clay to bring in some of the stew for her. It's still warm. Then go eat a bowl yourself. You've been out all day. It'll be a few minutes before I'm ready to have you work on the shackle."

Adam nodded then looked at Tillie. "I'll be right in the next room if you need me. Sophie won't hurt you. Promise me you won't try and run away again."

Tillie hesitated, but Adam looked as if he wasn't going to leave unless she gave her word.

Sophie looked at Adam, and her eyes narrowed. "What happened to you?"

Adam jabbed a finger at Tillie. "She fought me when I found her."

Sophie looked back at Tillie, her eyes wide with amusement. "You really gave him a pounding. Good girl."

"Hey!" Adam's chin came up, and his eyes blazed bright as if his very manhood had been questioned. "I was being careful. I just didn't want to hurt her, so I didn't defend myself."

Sophie laughed then took Tillie's hand. "You're my kind of woman."

Tillie felt a spurt of amusement that shocked her. She couldn't remember the last time she'd been tempted to smile.

Adam snorted. "I'll get the soup. But watch her like a hawk, Sophie. She doesn't seem to have the sense to realize she can't go walking in the middle of a Texas snowstorm with no food and no horse and no coat."

Sophie waved her hand at Adam. "Shoo! She needs to eat, and you do, too. Get her some stew; then get something in your own stomach."

NINE

A foot landed in Grace's stomach.

Her eyes flew open as her. . .son?—Mark—tripped and landed smack on top of her.

If she could have breathed, she'd have breathed a prayer of thanks. There were bigger feet than Mark's in this family. And she imagined it was only a matter of time until they all stomped on her one way or another.

"Hi, Ma!" Mark shouted like a banshee.

Why did this family say every word at the top of their lungs? He scrambled up off of her, then tripped and toppled toward the red-hot stove. She lurched up to rescue him, but he managed to evade disaster at the last second.

Hollering all the while, he leaped toward Luke, who skidded to a stop and missed stepping on her by inches.

The front door—the only door—hung wide open. Snow gusted in, pushed by a wicked, moaning wind.

"One of you boys shut the door," she said in her teacher's voice. She recognized it plainly.

So did they. They ignored her just like always.

Luke dived at Mark's ankles. They crashed to the floor, slamming up against the cast iron legs of the stove, which weren't as hot as the belly, thank heavens. Luke pounded a huge fistful of snow into Mark's face as Mark howled loudly enough to bring down the rafters.

Grace looked up. They had no rafters.

Mark crawled and rolled until he could regain his feet. The shrieking and threatening never paused. The two of them disappeared out the door.

"I told you boys to close that door."

Grace had been about to say that, but Daniel saved her the trouble as he came in, dragging snow inside with every step. The boys ignored him, too. He set a bucket down. Grace could see it was brimming with milk. He yelled, "Breakfast in just a minute," out the door that was swung inward, hanging from leather hinges. Daniel shoved it shut across the frozen ground.

Grace had just a glimpse of the swirling white world outside. The snow was scraped back from the cave a few feet, and footprints had battered it down somewhat past that.

Grace heard the whoops and hollers of a thousand marauding Apaches outside.

"Those scamps." Daniel shook his head and laughed as he picked up his bucket and turned to the stove. He saw her and froze as surely as the cold winter world outside this gopher hole. "You're awake."

Grace didn't point out that he was stating the obvious. She started to push back her blanket and then clawed it back, remembering her nightgown. And that's when she realized she was dressed. Brown broadcloth pants—of all things—stuck out from under blue flannel. A heavy brown and white shirt buttoned down the front. She even had boots on.

She'd crawled back under her blanket last night without giving her attire a moment's notice. Now she noticed. She felt her skin burn with embarrassment as she saw the way the too-short pants hugged her ankles.

"You're going to wear those until I can get to town and buy you something else. And they're the only spare pants Abe has, so you'd better appreciate 'em," Daniel ordered.

"So you've taken up mind reading, then?" Grace snapped. She held tight, for one last precious second, to any thought of modesty. It showed in the clinging grip of her hands on the blanket. She looked at her white knuckles sunk into the coarse gray deer hide; then, sick with humiliation, she thrust her cover aside.

She stood up, looked at the ridiculous sight of herself in a long nightgown, pants, and a shirt, and said, "I'll need you to step outside while I remove my nightgown."

Daniel glared at her. "I've got breakfast to get on. I'm not going anywhere. I'll look away for exactly one minute." He wheeled around. "Sixty, fifty-nine, fifty-eight. . ."

Grace opened her mouth to protest and just generally scold the man for his very existence.

"Fifty, forty-nine, forty-eight. . ."

He meant it. Grace whirled away from him and dragged the shirt off. She tore the nightgown off over her head and thrust her arms back into the shirtsleeves.

"Thirty-seven, thirty-six, thirty-five. . ."

Grace buttoned the shirt with scrambling fingers.

"Twenty-three, twenty-two, twenty-one. . ."

The pants were indecent. Tight all over. After a shaky moment of indecision, she left the shirttails hanging out in hopes of maintaining a shred of decency.

"Ten, nine, eight, seven. . ."

The shirt covered her nearly to her knees. It had to be Daniel's. She couldn't walk around dressed in a strange man's clothing. She couldn't. . . .

"Three, two, one." Daniel turned around and started plopping steaks directly on the cast-iron top of the stove.

Grace gasped, "I am horrified that you wouldn't give me a moment of privacy. It is completely inappropriate for you to—"

"D'ya know how to make biscuits?"

"Your manners leave me speechless. I cannot live in a place where—"

"Speechless ain't as quiet as it used to be, that's for sure. How about the biscuits, wife?"

Grace did *not* know how to make biscuits. She braced herself for the ridicule when she admitted it. "No, Mr. Reeves, I'm afraid I don't. . . ."

He didn't disappoint her. "So I got stuck with a wife who's so worthless she can't even make a biscuit. Looks like my luck is holding. You ever heard tell of a woman giving birth to *four* babies all to onest?"

"Four babies at once?" She didn't even try to keep the horror out of her voice.

"If it can happen to anyone, it'll most likely happen to me. No need to concern yourself. We won't be risking young'uns, no way, nohow. Get over here and keep an eye out for these steaks. I'll mix up the biscuits."

Grace edged between the table and the stove.

Daniel thrust a fork her way and, without giving her so much as a look-see, slipped by her and went to a canister sitting by the front door. He began scooping out flour onto the table.

Grace looked away from him when a flame jumped up from inside the stove through a slit in the lid. It flared nearly to the ceiling. Grace screamed, jumped back, and dropped the fork.

Daniel placed both hands on her waist, shoved her none too gently aside, and sneered under his breath, "Consarned woman'll manage to burn down a house made'a rock and dirt."

He stooped to pick up the fork. The tines had stabbed into the packed dirt floor so that the fork stood straight up. Daniel plucked it off the floor, swiped it front and back on his pant leg, and expertly flipped seven steaks with fire dancing madly all around his arm. He turned, still not looking at her.

She jumped back to keep him from tripping over her.

He went to the door, flung it wide open, and roared, "Ike, get in here and help with breakfast." Daniel left the door open and went back to the table and his biscuits.

Finally, a job I can handle. Going to close the door, she leaned outward into a world that was pure white: ground, trees, mountains, air all around, and sky up above.

Ike jumped down—from on high apparently—and almost took her

arm off. With a shout of raucous laughter, he stomped into the house, making a damp floor even worse.

His cat raced in on his heels. Had the cat, no longer the skinny animal Ike had rescued, come down from overhead, too? Grace didn't have the courage to ask. The unflappable cat, as wild as the Reeves boys, seemed content to live the rough-and-tumble life.

"I thought Ma was gonna do the cookin' now. Why in Sam Hill'd'ya git 'er if'n she weren't gonna do nothing? You done mighty poor by us, Pa."

Grace wanted to point out that it was rude to talk about people as if they weren't there. Honesty prevented her from actually denying Ike's words, though, because Daniel *had* done mighty poor by his boys when he'd gone and gotten himself married to her.

"Mind the steaks." Daniel's voice shook the room. He always seemed to talk at a near shout, except when he shouted, which was extremely loud, so Grace knew the difference.

Grace went back to the door just as all four boys still outside came flying down from above.

Mark first, then Abe, then Luke, with John right on his heels. Each landed on a snowdrift and rolled out of the way so the brother plummeting down next wouldn't crash-land on him.

The boys wallowed in the snow, kicking a drift back into Grace's face. She paused long enough to make sure they were all alive. Wrestling, pummeling each other with snowballs, shrieking through mouths full of snow, she judged them to have survived. Fine. They plunged from the sky and lived. She slammed the door.

Ike played in the fire behind her back. "Pa, why're we cooking? Why're we doin' women's work now that we've got us a woman? Pa, I wanna go back outside 'n' play. It don't snow much, an' this is our chance to. . ."

"Can you get over here, Grace, and pay attention?" Daniel didn't seem aware that his son was talking to him.

And Ike didn't quit carping or insulting his new mother, even when his pa talked over top of him.

"You may not know a lick about cooking, but maybe we can learn you something. You just take five or six fistfuls of flour. Boys have appetites. . . ." Daniel threw flour around until the air in the cave turned as white as the world outside. "That jar there,"—Daniel jerked his head at the floor in a direction so vague Grace wasn't sure if it was a lame effort at pointing or if he had a crick in his neck—"you put a glug or two of that. . ." Daniel quit throwing flour, grabbed up the milk pail, and glugged away, slopping some milk straight onto the pile of flour on the table.

"If she's not going to cook, what's'a use of her, Pa? She's just hogging up the blankets near as I can see."

The door slammed open, and John charged in. He hurled a snowball at Ike, then whirled and ran out, whooping and hollering every step of the way. Ike roared like a rebel charging down the slopes at Gettysburg and ran outside.

"Get back here!" Daniel kept mixing while he yelled.

Grace covered her ears against the pain of Daniel's thunderous bellow, afraid for her hearing. The flour was now a lump of dough.

Daniel went back to talking in his normally deafening tone. He didn't seem to notice Ike was gone. Well, he noticed. He'd yelled loudly enough, but he didn't do anything when Ike ignored him.

Grace pulled the door shut again. She'd found her place in the family. Door-shutter. She'd be busy from morning till night.

Daniel set the bucket of milk aside. Had he said something about some unknown number of glugs again? Daniel went to the stove and flipped the steaks through the roaring flames. Then he quickly stacked an enormous mountain of meat and reached for the lump of dough. He tore off knots of the white goo and dropped them directly on the stovetop, beside the steaks. He flattened each with his hands, adding dough until the stovetop was covered.

Daniel flipped open the small stove, and with a long-handled ladle he'd snagged from behind the stove—Grace was fairly certain it had been on the floor—he fished around inside the roaring fire until he began pulling out blackened lumps that looked like coal. He tossed them on the table and they rolled, but none went onto the floor.

Grace decided whatever he was doing, he was an expert at it.

He clanked the stove door shut, used the fork to prod the biscuits around until he could turn them, shoved them to one side, pulled a bucket from under the table, and began cracking eggs onto the stovetop. When he had a dozen or so broken, he went to the door, pulled it open, and bellowed, "Breakfast!"

By the time the ringing in Grace's ears subsided, the boys came charging in, skidding through the wide-open door on the packed snow. Abe got there first and slammed into the table. The coal started rolling, and before Grace could react, Abe and Daniel caught the lumps and held them down, corralling them with their forearms. Ike came swooping in next. He careened into Abe, who shoved him. Ike nearly crashed into the stove.

"Watch the food, Ike. You're eating 'em whether you knock 'em on the floor or not." Daniel set the milk bucket in the center of the table.

John came next, with Luke right on his heels. The two of them knocked into the bench that sat alongside the table. With deep-throated laughter, they dived out of sight then popped up on the other side of the table, clambering onto a bench and reaching for the coal.

Daniel whacked at their hands with his fork.

They ducked the slapping utensil, snagged the coal, and began chewing on it.

Mark came in last. "You better not've eaten my share."

Grace backed as far as she could from the earsplitting child. She pressed up against the wall and stayed there.

Daniel threw the fork at Abe.

Abe caught it in midair. He stabbed a steak from the top of the tower of meat and handed it to Mark. Mark took it off the fork with his bare hand and started gnawing on it as he rounded the table, making sure to stomp on Ike's toe. Mark got shoved toward the bench. He sat down next to his brothers.

Ike took the next steak for himself and started eating as he stomped to the bench seat directly across from his triplet brothers. Abe handed a steak to Luke and John. He was getting near the bottom of the pile. Abe forked the next one and threw it to his father, who caught it. Abe took one for himself then stopped short.

"You made too many, Pa." Abe looked at the steak with pure greed shining in his eyes.

"Nope, had to make Ma one." Daniel pulled the single tin cup forward and poured it full of milk directly from the bucket that sat in the center of the table. He downed the milk then poured again. He handed the cup to Ike, who was sitting next to him.

The cat landed in the middle of the table and made a dash for the milk.

"Scat, you." Abe swatted at the cat.

The cat, obviously a master at self-preservation, leaped off the table with a yowl.

"Don't you hit my cat," Ike raged as he punched Abe in the shoulder.

Grace prepared for an all-out fight, no goofing around this time.

Abe shoved him back. "If I'd'a wanted to hit that cat, he'd've been hit."

That seemed to satisfy Ike, or he was starving. For whatever reason, this once the twins didn't end up tussling on the floor.

Abe gave Grace a glowering look, as though he was considering fighting her for the meat. Grace would have backed up more, but the wall held her in place. With a shrug of disgust, Abe forked up a steak and took it for himself, then poked the last one and raised it, stuck on the utensil, in her direction.

"I. . .I don't eat. . ." Her voice started to fade. She hadn't seen the smallest sign of plates or silverware, besides the fork and ladle of course. The fork that had been sticking straight down into the dirt floor just moments ago.

"She don't eat?" Abe looked from her to Daniel, his eyes shining with hunger. "If she don't want that steak, I claim it."

"She's eating it." Daniel jabbed at Abe with a half-gnawed steak bone. "Put hers on the table. It was on the bottom of the stack, direct on the stove. It'll need to cool."

Abe turned from Grace and plopped the sizzling meat directly onto the tabletop. Then Abe began breaking biscuits in half, shoveling a hard-cooked egg into the middle of each, and handing the biscuits to Ike. Ike passed them on around. Each of them got two biscuits with eggs inside and one plain biscuit, besides the enormous steak.

Grace could see now that the coal was really baked potatoes.

Abe was almost finished when he looked at her. His surprised expression told her he'd forgotten his brand-new ma again. He tossed two egg biscuits beside her rapidly cooling steak. Blood ran off the steak and onto the floor, and fat began to congeal on the table.

The milk kept getting passed. After everyone had a drink, the tin cup would start another circuit. Grace gulped when she saw Mark fish around in the milk with his unwashed index finger, snag something, swish it out and flick it onto the floor, then guzzle down the rest of the milk.

"We coulda stood some'a them apples, Pa. Didn't he have none left?" The din of conversation, all at full volume and all with mouths stuffed full of food, went on only briefly. The food—meat to the equivalent of half a cow, a small mountain of potatoes, a whole. . .stovetop full of biscuits and eggs, and an entire bucket of milk—vanished.

The boys shoved and pummeled each other as they ran back outside.

And Grace still stood, stunned, against the back wall of the tiny cave, with the door wide open to the bitter winter wind.

"S'pose it's beneath your dignity to help clean the kitchen up." Daniel scowled at her and began clearing.

Except Grace noticed that there was nothing to clear. The boys hadn't made a mess. They'd barely let the food cool and certainly never let it sit on the table. They'd even taken their steak bones out with them.

Daniel scooped the empty milk bucket full of snow and set it on the stove. He picked up another bucket half full of water that was tucked behind the stove, poured a little water into the milk cup, swirled it around, and then tossed the water out the door. Daniel shut the frigid day outside and set the milk cup back on the table—the table that was now perfectly clean except for Grace's cold, bleeding meat, with its pair of biscuits standing by its side.

"Eat when you want. Warm it up if you've a mind." Daniel grabbed the bucket of water and went outside without a backward glance.

 T E N

"Ain't she *never* gonna do *nothin'* but stare or hide under a blanket, Pa?" Mark tugged at Daniel's sleeve while he fed some grain to the four milk cows. Mark seemed the most determined to return Grace.

"As long as she keeps outta the way, we'd better count our blessings, son." Daniel watered the cows with the bucket he'd carried from the house; then he went to the chicken coop to scatter cracked corn.

Mark carried his own, smaller bucket of corn and slogged along behind, setting his small feet in the tracks as Daniel broke a trail in the deep snow, trudging through the snow back to the barn. Mark nagged him every step of the way.

Abe and Ike had taken off on horseback to ride herd. Luke and John were in the woods that climbed the hill behind the cave—the one the boys liked to slide down on their bellies and go flying past the front door. It was Mark's turn to stay close to the place and help with the barnyard chores.

Daniel climbed up into the haymow and grabbed up the pitchfork. "Couldn't you've done a better job of pickin' a ma?" Mark shouted from down below where he wrestled all three baby calves into the pens with their mamas.

After the Reeves family got their milk, the babies got to suckle the rest out for their own breakfast. The calves bawled and rushed for their mothers, who crooned deep in their throats to their babies. Then there

373

was silence as the calves started feeding, their little tails jerking in time to their feasting.

" 'Tweren't no big rush about it." Mark trailed Daniel up the ladder and grabbed armloads of hay to throw down to the fat cows below.

"When we told you we wanted a ma, none of us never said you had to go off half-cocked and bring home the first ma you run across."

The kid hadn't stopped yapping since he'd come outside. Daniel pitched hay down, trying to work fast enough that— Daniel shook his head. Fast work wouldn't make him go deaf, and that was his only escape from Mark's harping about Grace.

The cows started crunching away at the hay, but the noise didn't drown out the boy. "Maybe if we took her back and told the preacher real nice that she weren't good for *nothin'*."

Mark's prattle was wearing on his ears to the point Daniel was tempted to leave the rest of the chores to Mark and go inside. Except "inside" was plumb full of that useless, prissy woman. She was most likely still standing there, holding up the consarned wall.

"Just tell him that she hasn't done nothing, 'cept'n sleeping with you. . . ."

Daniel cringed and forked faster.

"Maybe he'd take back your I do's. Just kinda erase the whole stupid thing. I'd be glad to tell Parson Roscoe that so far going to bed with you is the only thing she's good for. If the parson knew that—"

"Don't try and help me out with this, son. It ain't a job for young'uns." He worked beside his carping son in the dry, sweet-smelling hay. After he had the milk cows' feed bunk full, he moved to the opening above the hogs and gave the sows their share. They rustled their snouts into the growing pile in their low manger, their babies squealing and nudging the sows' fat udders for milk. Then he moved on to the pen with one older calf. The little heifer was weaned but too young to go out with the herd. He finished with the pen of older pigs from last summer's farrowing. The greedy little beasts squealed and bit at each other as if they were starving to death. Last he pitched some hay down to the cow with the new calf he'd found yesterday. They seemed to be doing well, but Daniel knew he'd have to keep them inside until the cold weather broke.

The barn was bitter cold, but the doors were tight and the frigid wind stayed outside. It was about a thousand times nicer place to be than that dark, musty cave. Daniel wondered again why he'd never got around to building a house. He craved the thought of having a bedroom for his new wife. She could hide in there forever if it suited her.

Daniel would just shove a steak under the door three times a day and be done with it. And he would build himself a room, too—as far from Mark's nagging and Grace's finicky manners as he could get. In fact, for a moment, Daniel toyed with the idea of just moving himself out to the barn. Sure, he'd freeze to death, but that was the only flaw he could see in the plan.

Mark kept pestering. He wasn't driving the boy hard enough. He'd never get too tired to talk at this rate. The work his other boys were doing would half kill them, Daniel thought with satisfaction. They wouldn't get all the way killed. He'd trained them up right. Another ten or fifteen hours of hard labor mixed with wild, reckless play, and his boys would sleep like the dead. Now he only had to wear out this chatterbox.

"Mark, brush the horses when you're done here; then start fetching pails of snow into the house. Leave 'em long enough to melt; then water the animals. I gave the cows some, but I shorted 'em, so you're gonna need to—"

"That's right. With this much snow, we won't have to chop a hole in the crick er nothin'." Mark beamed at him. "It'll be fun feeding the stock snow."

"Don't forget the chickens. I'm gonna saddle up and see to dragging windfalls in closer for the night. John and Luke can't gather enough wood to last for long."

"I'll be ready to chop it for you by the time you're back."

Daniel jammed his fists on his hips and turned to face his son.

"What'd I tell you about the ax?"

Mark's eyes narrowed.

Daniel held his gaze. It was a showdown. He had one about twice a day with Mark.

Finally, his son caved. "All right, Pa. You think I'm too young for chopping."

"I don't *think* you're too young for chopping. There's no *I think* about it. You're *too young for chopping*, period. You're only five. I keep that ax as sharp as an Apache tomahawk, and it's every bit as dangerous. I've only been letting the older boys work it for a couple of years."

Mark glared.

Daniel had to hold his frown firm. He was mighty proud of all his boys, but Mark was the biggest handful. Maybe not the smartest, because all of them were smart, but the craftiest for a fact. Daniel loved that about him. It'd take Mark as far as he wanted to go in life—as long as it didn't take him to the ax. "Your chance'll come. After the watering, you can fetch around sticks with John 'n' Luke then break up the ones you brung in." Daniel held Mark's gaze for as long as it took.

Finally, Mark kicked at the nearest mound of snow, sending a plume of white into the air to be swirled about by the wind. "All right. I'll leave it be."

"You know better 'n to lie to me, boy. Right?" Daniel waited. Mark might cut a corner time to time and mislead a body with vague words, but his son knew not to lie straight to Daniel's face. Mark had learned that lesson over Daniel's knee.

"I know." Mark stomped his foot hard. "I promise."

"Good boy." Daniel ran his gloved hand over Mark's heavy fur cap, almost knocking it off his head. Daniel leaned close.

Mark gave him a suspicious look, the one he got if Daniel ever did something so foolish as hug him. Daniel stooped quickly, grabbed a handful of snow, and smeared it into Mark's face. Mark shrieked and dived toward the ground, caught up a ball of snow, and threw it back. Daniel laughed, and the fight was on.

By the time they were done, Daniel was almost too warm in his fur-lined buckskin coat and his long scarf, wrapped five times around his neck. His already-battered Stetson had been knocked off his head and trampled. Snow pounded onto his head had turned him halfway into a snowman. And he knew from the burn that his cheeks were glowing red with cold every bit as much as Mark's. Slapping his son on the back, Daniel said, "Get to it, boy."

Daniel glanced at the door to the cave. Normally about now, he'd go inside and slice more steaks. He brought a hank of meat in every night to thaw for the next day. They went through a cow and a pig about once a month, and he had the better part of a cow carcass hanging in the barn right now. He was glad he'd cut it down to size, because it was frozen solid.

He didn't want to go inside. "Bringing a new ma home for you boys was kinda an accident. But we're stuck with her now. There's no way back."

Mark sighed.

Daniel knew exactly how he felt.

"Reckon we'll just have to make the best of it, huh, Pa?" Mark crossed his arms and shot a hostile look toward the cave.

Daniel well remembered Grace's scathing comments about his sons when she'd been their teacher. And she'd been particularly hard on Mark. He didn't blame his boy for being unhappy. Daniel said, "Remember last summer when the McClellens were attacked and almost killed by those murdering renegades who were running the hills?"

"Yep, 'twere a mighty close thing."

"Well,"—Daniel picked up his hat and whacked the snow off it against his leg—"having Grace come live with us can't be any worse than that."

"The McClellens got to solve their problems by shooting folks." Mark gave their home a contemplative look.

"No, they didn't. No one got shot in that mess, although it looked to be shooting trouble for a while. They solved their problem with their smarts. They worked it out. Grace. . .uh. . .that is, your ma. . .is here to stay. So we'll use our smarts to figure out a way to get along with her."

"And Miss Calhoun is smart, too, or leastways she kept acting like she was."

Daniel shrugged his shoulders. "She might be smart. No sign of it anywheres I can see. And besides, there's smart and there's smart."

"What's 'at mean, Pa?" Mark scooped up a handful of snow and seemed to be studying the house.

Daniel had to bite back a smile. "It means. . .smart is what you do with it." Daniel nodded his head at the house. "I've known a few real educated men, got through high school 'n' everything, who didn't have a lick of sense. And I've knowed some men who couldn't read nor write, who didn't have a day of book learning, but I'd trust 'em with big decisions about real important stuff, like my cattle, even."

"So we'll just see what kind of smart Ma turns out to be."

Daniel sighed again, and this time the sound seemed to come all the way from his toes. "Yep. The good news is, since we're stuck with her for life, she's got a lot of time to learn."

Mark hurled the snowball at the cave door. It splatted harmlessly against the rough wood. "She's got the rest of our lives."

Daniel nodded, thinking that the menfolk in his family leaned toward long lives. He envied the boys getting to grow up and move away.

Then Mark perked up. "You know what?"

"What?" Fear skittered down Daniel's spine like an eight-legged creepy crawler. He'd seen that wily look on his son's face before.

"She don't have the rest of *our* lives. She's only got the rest of *her* life." Mark tipped his head sideways in a way that was purely cheerful. "Gotta get to the chores."

Mark went off toward the barn whistling, almost as if he knew Grace's life wasn't necessarily going to be very long.

ELEVEN

She was going to die. If she was lucky, it would happen soon.

Grace pushed herself away from the wall. "And when in my life have I ever been lucky?" The whispered words echoed in the burrow she now called home. She might as well plan on making a hundred years old. She moved hesitantly toward the steak—expecting the bloody thing to make a run for it.

It just lay there, taunting her. It turned her stomach, but she was hungry. After a dozen or so nervous looks at the door, which she expected to crash open any second, she got tough. The one thing Grace knew how to be was tough.

She picked up the fork Daniel had washed up and set aside, speared the steak, and tossed it on the stovetop. The steak sizzled and sent a savory plume of smoke toward the roof of the cave, all of twelve inches over her head. Grace picked up the egg and biscuit sandwiches and began gnawing on them as the steak turned to a more edible color. The dry bread and cold eggs stuck in her throat, but they tasted like heaven.

Daniel and the boys had downed all the milk, and Daniel had left the bucket, now filled with rapidly melting snow, on the stove.

She looked at the communal tin cup, remembered how she'd lived with Parrish, and decided this wasn't so bad. She dipped herself a drink of cold water to wash down the crumbling biscuits. When the biscuits and eggs were gone, she used the fork to lift the brown steak, now dripping clear juice. Unable to find a more ladylike way to dine, she proceeded to eat it hanging from the fork with all the manners of a hungry wolverine.

Grace ate the whole steak, which was at least an inch thick. She'd been hungry for a very long time, eking out a living on the two dollars a month she kept from her teacher's salary. She thought enviously of the blackened potatoes. She could've had one if she'd been on her toes.

She licked the fork clean, considered what to do with the steak bones, pitched them out the door as the boys had done, and washed the fork. She found a rag and wiped the blood from her steak off the table and looked around her home with satisfaction. There wasn't going to be a lot of housekeeping to do. That was for sure.

As she tried to wrap her mind around her current circumstances, she remembered the foul accusation Daniel Reeves had made last night. Equal parts fury and humiliation flooded through her as hot as the blood in her veins.

She had learned how to walk and dress like a lady. She'd learned how to speak correctly, remember her manners, and always behave properly—all without help. To be caught in this compromising situation by the parson then accused of flagrant sin by that worthless Daniel Reeves—Well, it was as if the last two years of struggle for respectability were for nothing.

With a pang of fear that overrode her anger, she suddenly wondered if the condition of being poor and unwanted clung to her like an odor. Perhaps she'd fooled no one. Maybe the whole town had turned up their noses at her from the first. Maybe the school board had been looking for an excuse to fire her when Daniel came to them with his complaints.

The door crashed open. Daniel filled the doorway then came inside carrying a huge knife.

He might be planning to kill her, but again she remembered that she'd never been lucky.

Daniel closed the door and set a bucket on the stove. He went to a dark corner of the tiny room.

In the shadows, Grace noticed half a beef hanging by one skinned leg. How odd that she hadn't seen it before. Of course, she'd been in a daze since she'd awakened in this house. "Daniel. . ." Grace figured there was no point in putting this off. They definitely needed to talk.

"Huh?" Daniel hacked away at the meat without so much as glancing at her.

"Umm, I. . .I think—that is, we need to. . ." Grace had no idea what to say.

Daniel turned to face her with a stack of meat in his hand. "Talk? We need to talk? Is that what you were going to say?"

Grace nodded, her tongue as frozen as the world outside. She saw the fury in him. She saw the despicable suspicion clearly written on his face. She wanted to deny his accusations. She wanted to demand he treat her with respect. She wanted a different husband. Or better yet, no husband at all.

Into the silence, Daniel said with a sneer, "We could talk about the fact that you are now my wife, even though I neither want nor need a wife."

They probably really did need to talk about that. "Well—"

Daniel cut her off as if she were just another steak. Of course, he didn't use the knife. His sharp tongue was enough. "We could talk about the fact that you hate my sons. Not a good thing when you're now their ma."

"I don't—" Grace stopped. Daniel had a point. She wouldn't have gone so far as to say *hate*. Hate was a little harsh. It wasn't Christian to hate anyone. Sure, she thought they were crude, grimy, smelly, noisy, rowdy, and rude. But hate? No.

Daniel snorted at her silence as if she'd just admitted to hating his boys. "We could talk about the fact that I've got no time for you, no place for you, and no interest in you."

Grace wanted to say, "Same here," but Daniel didn't give her a chance.

"Or we could talk about the really interesting question. The one that really might answer all the others." Daniel glared at her. The silence stretched. He finally said in a voice that could have blown in on the icy wind, "What were you doing hiding in the back of my wagon? Were you hiding from someone? Or were you planning exactly what happened? Did you need a husband and you heard I owned a nice stretch of land?"

"As if"—finally he'd asked a question she could answer, so she crossed her arms and lifted her chin and glared right back—"I'd pick *you*."

Daniel's fair complexion mottled with red. "You might. You might if you found yourself. . .needing to be married right quick."

Daniel's blue eyes flashed bolts of lightning. "Desperate times call for desperate measures. What's his name, Grace? I'll deliver you and his"— Daniel glanced significantly at her stomach—"*mistake* to his door."

"Daniel Reeves. . ." Grace jammed her fists onto her hips. The coarse cloth that touched her hands reminded her she was wearing pants. She was embarrassed, vulnerable, and so insulted she wanted to slap him. "There is no man. That is a dirty lie you made up to shame me. Don't you ever—"

The door flew open. Didn't anybody ever open and close the door slowly in this place?

Mark came in carrying a bucket of snow. He stopped short and looked between the two of them, reading their expressions.

Daniel relieved him of the bucket and handed him the other one, the snow inside now melted.

Grace had to step back to let Daniel pass her.

"Mark, get back outside and stay there. Your ma and I have to talk a few things over. Don't come back in here till I tell you to."

"Are you fixin' to return her now, Pa? I can hitch up the team for you whilst you get her out of Abe's clothes and back into the nightdress. It'll be plumb nice to have her gone. You won't have to share your blanket anymore, nor lie with each other. I'll be glad to tell the parson she did nothing but sleep with you the whole time she was here."

"Quit helping me!"

Mark pointed to the floor. "There ain't no room for her. The two of you was so crowded you 'bout had to lay right smack on top of her. Now that you've tried her out, you can tell Parson Roscoe and the whole town she just weren't no good."

"Mark!" Daniel's roar made Grace jump.

"I'm only trying to chip in and return her. It's what we all want. Her, too, I reckon." Mark glanced at Grace.

She remembered those eyes. This one was *always* thinking.

Mark swung the bucket of water.

"Get out. Get your chores done," Daniel ordered.

Grace didn't like the tone of Daniel's voice. She felt sorry for the little boy. No wonder he was so difficult.

Parrish had been able to scare children into submission with just his voice, too. Although he didn't always confine himself to yelling.

"Get to work and stay busy until I call you in for dinner. Go!"

Mark glared at Daniel then turned his eyes on Grace. With enough stubborn grumbling to save himself from being obedient, he finally turned and marched out of the cave, leaving the door wide open.

Daniel shut it without comment.

"You leave that little boy alone." Grace surprised herself. And she wasn't done yet. "How hard do you make him work?"

"Until he drops over if I'm lucky." Daniel gave her an unreadable look. He was probably trying to decide how much hard work he could get out of her.

"Children aren't slave labor." Grace stepped right up to his face and wagged a finger under his nose. "It's no wonder they acted up in school. They're used to this kind of treatment. They think this is normal to be worked like dogs from morning to night. When I treated them decently, they probably—"

"Do not"—Daniel brushed Grace's scolding finger aside and leaned down until they were nose to nose—"tell me how to raise my sons."

"Well, somebody needs to. You have them shoved in this"—Grace waved her arms in a wild gesture that took in the tiny cave as Daniel ducked so she didn't catch him on the chin—"hole-in-the-ground. You feed them on a table with no plates or silverware as if you were throwing scraps to a pack of dogs." She jabbed him in the chest. "They have no clothes, no privacy, no manners, and no hope of ever getting any with you for their father."

Daniel grabbed her wrist so she couldn't poke him anymore. "You're about one wrong word away from sleeping in the barn with the animals."

"And that would be different from living in here, how?"

"That's the word." Daniel jerked her forward.

She jerked back.

They tripped over a stack of bedding that stuck out from the side of the wall and fell over in a heap.

He landed on top and knocked the wind right out of her. She gasped for air, but catching her breath was impossible with his weight. She shoved at his shoulders, but he was already scooting off.

As if he refused to do anything that she thought of, he stopped moving and settled down. His eyes flashed. His hands sank into her hair. "Tell me what you were doing in my wagon."

Grace felt something close to panic at being so controlled by Daniel. She'd sworn never to be under anyone's thumb again. But for all his fury, she didn't fear Daniel's fists. She wasn't sure why; probably just bad judgment on her part.

She looked in his eyes and knew she couldn't tell him the truth. He hated her. He'd hand her over in a heartbeat. But she could tell him enough, maybe, to stop his horrid accusations. Maybe if she did, he'd get off.

"I was hiding. A man. . .a man frightened me. I didn't choose your wagon. I was running—"

"Some man in Mosqueros was chasing you?" Daniel's eyes changed. The fury faded, replaced by worry. "Why didn't you go to the sheriff?"

Because the sheriff would have sided with Parrish. He would have held her until Parrish got there. "I didn't have time. He was coming. I just saw your wagon and climbed in. I didn't know it was yours. I didn't *choose you.*" The very thought made Grace shudder.

Her trembling caught Daniel's attention, and he seemed momentarily distracted. His hands, which had held firm in her hair but never pulled, loosened now until her head rested on his flexing fingers as if they were a living pillow.

Grace swallowed and tried to remember what they were talking about. Oh yes—terror, hiding, freezing nearly to death. "I was afraid to move, and I was afraid to tell you I was there because you'd take me back to town and leave me where he might find me."

"I'd have found him and taken him to the sheriff for you." Daniel removed one hand from her hair. His eyes were concerned.

Grace was surprised to realize he meant it. He would have protected her. If this story she was telling him was true.

"I would have, Grace. We may not agree on my boys, but I wouldn't have let you come to any harm. Surely you don't think I'm that much of a low-down skunk."

Grace almost did believe him. She couldn't let herself. "I just stayed quiet, thinking to wait until you were out of town where it was safe. The cold was too much. I. . .I guess I fell asleep or passed out. I didn't t-trap you. There's no man with whom I have been. . .dallying. I'm not. . ."

Suddenly it was all too much. The fear of Parrish and this stupid marriage she'd been thrust into. Daniel's awful accusations. She felt the tears burn in her eyes. This man had reduced her to tears twice now. And Grace hardly ever cried. She'd learned long ago that it just didn't do a lick of good. "How could you think that of me? I am not a woman who—" Her voice broke.

"Don't cry." Daniel sounded a little desperate.

She tried to stop. She breathed raggedly. "I'm sorry. I don't blame you for thinking the worst of me." She reached for her cheeks to wipe the tears away.

Daniel's rough thumb got to the tears first. He wiped at her cheeks with surprising gentleness. She looked up to thank him.

Their eyes caught. Their breath caught.

Daniel rolled off of her as if he'd been burned. He jumped to his feet, threw some potatoes into the stove, tossed the steaks on next, and asked, "Can you make biscuits?" He didn't look at her. In fact, he kept his back squarely to her as he worked around the kitchen.

She could tell her tears had disgusted him. Parrish had always punished her for crying. She quickly dashed them away. Then she thought to breathe again.

She'd seen Daniel mix the biscuits up for breakfast. She thought she remembered. How hard could it be? "Yes, I'll do it."

"Make a lot. Watch the steaks. If they catch fire, be careful. Hold back on the eggs until we show our faces." Daniel grabbed the bucket of now-melted snow off the stove and opened the door.

Grace saw another bucket heaped with snow sitting there.

"I wonder how much of that Mark heard?" Daniel muttered. He put the bucket on the stove and crossed to the door. As he left, he turned back toward Grace. "Maybe you didn't trap me a'purpose, but we're well and truly trapped just the same. But there's trapped and there's trapped. No woman's ever gonna die giving me another child. That's a kind of trapped I won't be a part of." He walked out, slamming the door behind him.

Grace wondered what on earth he meant by that. It wasn't for the first time she realized that she knew nothing about men or marriage— or being a woman, for that matter.

And she set out to prove she knew nothing by making biscuits for the first time in her life.

Twelve

"Come for supper." Hannah Cartwright whispered out the door into the bitter cold of the dusky Chicago afternoon. They just had to survive until spring. Everything was easier when the weather didn't try to kill them.

She didn't hear the children, but she knew where they were. Trevor huddled next to Libby near a grating, a warm spot they'd discovered across the alley from their little shed. The little boys sometimes found the energy to play hide-and-seek or toss a rock back and forth between them, but not today.

The children liked to be outside. Hannah didn't blame them. The little shed was dreary, and it smelled terrible, as if the owner had used it to store rotting potatoes at one time.

Hannah only came inside when the cold was too much to bear. The wind cut through her thin dress, and she stepped in to save as much of the precious warmth from the burning barrel as she could.

Stepping back from the shed door, her hands quivering with cold, she opened the letter from Grace. Pulling out eighteen dollars, in weary-looking one-dollar bills, she asked the empty room, "How much do schoolteachers make anyway?"

Afraid the answer was twenty dollars a month, Hannah stared at the cash. Grace was holding back two dollars for herself. That wasn't enough to buy food.

Hannah knew teachers didn't make much, and this must be the lot of it—again this month. "Grace, how are you living?"

Grace's letter spoke extravagantly of the meals she ate with her students' families and the warm, cozy room she'd been given as part of her salary. Even with little or no money, she should be able to get by, but she'd have nothing left for a proper schoolteacher's dress or any other necessities.

Trevor came into the shed behind the blacksmith's shop, helping Libby, with Nolan ahead of him and Bruce bringing up the rear.

The boys were all thoughtful and too quiet for Hannah's peace of mind. They didn't have food enough in their bellies to laugh and play.

Always so careful of Libby, who never spoke a word, they took their time walking beside her, supporting her as she limped on her slow-healing ankle. The instant they got inside, they carefully closed the rickety door to preserve the heat.

It was so different having brothers. Parrish had always preferred girls for some reason. Hannah and Grace believed he enjoyed terrorizing girls more than boys. Maybe they cried more easily when he laid the belt to them.

"It's time to eat." Hannah waved them toward the bucket of water to wash. "Mr. Daily set the bread out."

"I found this, Hannah." Nolan pulled a dented can out of his pocket. The label was gone, but there would be food of some kind inside.

Trevor went to work on it with a rusted can opener.

Bruce's hands were full of trash to burn. When he set it beside the barrel, to be fed in slowly all night, he shoved his hand deep in his pocket and pulled out a penny.

"A lady over by the train station gave me this." Bruce reached over to set it behind the barrel. From his other pocket, he produced a good-sized rag. When he spread it out, Hannah could see it was a shirt the right size for Libby, with an arm torn away.

Bruce glanced up at them with defiant eyes. Only six, he'd come into their shed one night and crawled up to the heat, looking at them as though they might attack him. Instead, Hannah had given him a full share of their bread and let him join the family. Bruce brought a wallet home with him the next day with five dollars in it.

Grace's money had run out early that month and the boys were starving on the bread. Hannah had a talk with Bruce about God and sin and what the police did to children who were caught stealing. But, though she'd never picked anyone's pocket, she'd swiped a few apples off a grocer's cart when they were starving. She was no innocent.

The eighteen dollars from Grace each month should have been enough to buy good food for all of them, with enough left over to rent a room and buy warm clothes. Hannah had written to Grace just once and never hinted that they were anything but comfortable. But paying off Libby's doctor bills to treat her ankle used every penny of it. Thank heavens they'd found this empty shed, or they'd have been sleeping on the street.

Every day Mr. Daily, who owned a diner three blocks over, watched for Hannah, and when she came, he slipped outside and gave her two loaves of bread. A generous, Christian man, he was careful not to let his wife catch him.

Hannah could hear Mrs. Daily shouting from inside the diner anytime she happened into the back room. Carefully Hannah would crouch in the alley near the back door, knowing Mr. Daily would leave the food whenever he could.

"What's for supper?" Trevor smiled.

She couldn't smile back at her fourteen-year-old brother. She lifted the envelope so Trevor could see inside.

Lips curling down into a frown, he asked, "What's she living on? Did she write? Does she ever mention buying herself a new dress or shoes? Is she eating?"

Trevor had never met Grace, but Hannah had told stories of her brave big sister until they all felt as if she were out fighting the world for them.

"You know Grace. According to her letter, everything is fine. All she talks about is how comfortable she is and how bad things are for us here. Of course, she doesn't know about you boys, and she's dead set against adoption, so I didn't tell her I found homes for the little girls, but she's adamant that none of us work. I'm too old for school now, and maybe I could get a job, but I don't think Libby can stay at home alone while I work yet."

Trevor gave Libby a long look. He had been the one to find her, curled up in an alley, living alongside the rats, fighting them for food thrown in the trash, dragging her broken foot behind as she hopped or crawled after food. He'd brought her home, and because the little girl didn't speak and was too little to write, Hannah had taken to calling her Libby. Libby was tough, and Hannah and Trevor both well knew that the painfully thin three-year-old could survive alone in this shed all day. But neither of them wanted it that way.

"Grace hated seeing children put to work. She trusted me to look after the little girls when we got them away from Parrish. The one promise she demanded of me was that they'd stay in school and never be put back into that mill. They've all found homes now, but the same promise applies to you boys and Libby. Protecting us from the mill and from Parrish matters more to her than a new pair of shoes."

Trevor dragged his ragged woolen hat off his head. "The eighteen dollars would rent us a room, except—" He glanced at Libby for a split second then looked away before the tiny girl noticed.

Hannah thought about the doctor bills. They could pay them only because of Grace's money. And Libby needed to keep being doctored until her foot healed, if it ever would.

Bruce went straight to the barrel and threw in paper and other burnable trash he'd dug out of the alley. Kneeling by it, he reached out his hands to soak up the meager warmth. The elbows of the gray sweater he wore hung in tatters. Hannah saw the holes in the soles of his shoes. She'd found both in the trash and been grateful for an actual pair. Nolan's were mismatched.

"Yes, Trevor, 'except.' That about says it all." Hannah thought the last operation on Libby's leg had finally fixed the problem, and Hannah wasn't above cheating the doctor out of his money—she'd done worse things to survive. But they had to pay him because they might need him again.

"Well, since that money is all spoken for and we're eating bread—only bread—for the fourth day in a row, I'm not listening to Grace or you anymore. I'm doing things my way."

"Not a job, Trevor." Hannah caught at his arm. "You need to stay in school. Just three more years and you can get a real job, something good that will be safe. That mill is a trap that you'll never get out of without schooling. I'll gladly let you work for the rest of your life once you're graduated."

"It's not child exploitation if I do it to myself."

Hannah flinched when she heard Grace's most hated words—*child exploitation*. Grace had taught those words along with reading and writing. Wanting to argue with her brother, who had come sneaking out of an alley a year ago and joined the family, Hannah instead remained silent.

At last she said, "I think I'm going to exploit myself, too."

"No, Hannah." Trevor shook his head. His dirty brown hair hung too long on his forehead, and he shoved it aside impatiently. "You need to be here for the little ones."

Libby hovered near the burning barrel, turning her hands back and forth to warm both sides.

"I can earn money, too." Nolan slumped beside Libby, his face lined with the defiant expression all street kids had, acting as if they didn't care about anything. "If all three of us work, we'll earn enough to be comfortable."

Nolan had never worked in the mill. He'd been on the street from his earliest memory. It was hard to explain to him the difference between Grace's schoolteacher job and work at the carpet mill. He'd never seen what it was like. The bitter cold in winter, the vicious heat in summer, and the roaring, deafening noise. Hannah still cringed when she thought of dodging the huge, dangerous machines, the cruel foremen wielding rods to whip slackers, always yelling and pushing them to hurry, work faster, work harder.

Hannah could see the determination on his thin, pale face. Nolan, ten years old, looked as though he was starving. No matter how Hannah tried, she could never fill the growing boy's belly. She knew Trevor went hungry, too. And heaven knew she did.

Libby backed away from the bit of warmth from the barrel and looked at Hannah with big, sad eyes capable of breaking Hannah's heart. The doctor had treatments for Libby's leg, but he didn't know what to do about her silence. He didn't think she'd had an injury to her voice. Instead, he thought Libby had seen something awful.

The doctor said that sometimes when people experienced something so dreadful their mind couldn't deal with it, they reacted in this way. He said that the words were locked inside her, and until she could face what had happened and speak of it, she would remain silent. There was nothing he could do. He warned Hannah that her little sister might never speak again.

Turning her freckled nose away from the meager heat, Libby limped to Nolan's side. Nolan pulled the little girl, hardly more than a toddler, into his lap and hugged her close.

Hannah shook her head. "Grace will hate it. She's sacrificing everything for us. Going to work instead of school is the thing she would hate the most."

"It'll be different for us," Trevor insisted. "We'll keep all the money we earn. You said Parrish always took every penny. I can't make twenty dollars a month like Grace, but I can make something."

"You'll be lucky to make a dime a day, Trevor. And you'll work seven days a week."

Trevor's eyes narrowed. "Well, that's ten cents a day more than we have now. Ten cents would buy us a little meat."

Nolan carefully lowered his eyes to look at Libby, but Hannah saw them light up at the thought of meat to add to their bread.

"With what Grace sends, we can save up and go find her. The five of us and Grace can make a home together."

Hannah smiled even though her heart was heavy. Grace didn't know what a change had overtaken the family. Hannah hadn't told her about how hard she'd worked finding families for the little girls. Sneaking around, peeking in windows at night, Hannah had inspected each family to the extent she was able to make sure the girls would be safe.

Grace hated the whole idea of adoption because of Parrish. But Hannah knew there were good people in the world, and she'd set out to place the little children in homes. The only trouble was, as quickly as she found a home for one child, she found another on the street who needed her.

Grace had never stayed in one place long enough for it to make sense to write a letter. Now she seemed settled in Mosqueros, and Hannah had spent a few precious pennies to write and tell Grace that everything was okay, but she'd given no details. If Grace had heard Hannah was putting the little sisters up for adoption, she'd have quit her job and come rushing back to Chicago, trying as always to mother all of them.

For that same reason, Hannah didn't tell her about the new children. Grace would only worry.

Once Grace settled in Mosqueros and looked to stay there, she'd write for them to come. She'd send eighteen dollars a few more times, and no doctor would make a claim on the money. They'd always been an all-girl family, but Grace loved all children. She'd be happy to see the boys, too.

"I'm going to pound the next boy who comes slamming through that door." Grace piled flour on the table and used the family fork to mix up the first batch of biscuits in her life. There hadn't been much time to develop womanly skills when she worked twelve hours a day in a carpet mill.

The steaks blazed away happily. She went to them and turned them, doing her best not to catch herself on fire.

Back to the biscuits. "He put. . ." She tried to imitate the amount of flour Daniel had thrown into the bowl. His hands were bigger, so she threw in a couple of extra fistfuls.

"Then there was milk. . ." Grace looked at the bucket on the stove. Water. They'd finished the milk for breakfast. Daniel knew that. She shrugged. "If I'd needed milk, he would have said something." She poured water into the flour.

She looked around. He'd added something else.

The steaks waved flames at her. She awkwardly shifted them away from the fire, except the fire seemed to follow the meat.

She spotted the jar on the floor next to the flour canister. She unscrewed the lid. She jerked her head back and almost dropped the jar. "Ewww."

Switching over to mouth-breathing, she held the jar as far away from her nose as she could. It wasn't far enough. She set the jar down on the table with the dull thunk of glass on wood and backed across the room. She stared at the foul mixture of rotten. . .goo.

She looked around the cave. "He must have used something from another jar." There were no other jars. She closed her eyes and tried to picture Daniel's quick, efficient movements. She opened her eyes again and stared at the strange bubbly concoction. "He used that."

She tried to sneak up on it. It seemed to be staring at her. She lifted the jar, breathing through clenched teeth, and poured—she didn't remember how much. But it was so awful, the less the better. She quickly clapped the lid back on the jar and returned it to its dark corner where it could fester in peace.

The steaks, looking far less bloody than they had this morning, thank goodness, shot fire most of the way to the ceiling. She took a moment to be grateful that her home was made of dirt and rock—nothing flammable.

She decided it was time to stack the steaks the way Daniel had.

She stirred the biscuits. The dough was too thick. She added water.

It was too thin. She added flour. The dough stubbornly refused to settle on the right consistency. By the time she hit a thickness she could live with, she had a huge supply of biscuit dough and the table was coated with a sticky layer of it. Daniel had left the table as clean as when he started. The dough smelled like that nasty jar of stuff. She didn't remember the biscuits smelling bad when she'd eaten them.

Daniel had picked up the dough in his hands, but it was a bit too runny for Grace to make that work. Instead, she picked up a small handful and turned to drop it on the stove before it oozed out between her fingers. The blobs of dough ran together slowly—not as if the dough was really liquid, but more as if it was just being uncooperative—until they formed one big biscuit instead of a dozen small ones. She watched it, not sure what she'd do when it was time to turn it. She armed herself with the fork and waited.

At first the dough threatened to run down the side of the stove, but Grace was quick and kept scooping. The dough eventually hardened and stayed put next to the steak mountain.

After what seemed like forever, she lifted the corner of the monster biscuit. It was dark brown on the bottom. Very dark brown. She poked at it and struggled to flip it, and it broke apart.

She was inspired. "You know, why does it have to be whole anyway? I actually *want* it to break. She sawed little biscuit-sized sections loose and flipped them. The first ones fought her, but by the time she was done, she was getting to be handy at it. There were crumbs everywhere, and the biscuits had gone from brown to black about halfway through, but they were all flipped and cooking along nicely.

She saw that the bottom steak was on fire again. Her forking arm was exhausted, the stack of steaks was teetering a little, and no room was left on the stovetop, so she decided she'd eat the bottom one herself if it was overcooked.

The door slammed open.

As if a dam had burst, a flood of males rushed in. All six of them filled the room. The triplets and Ike made straight for the table. Grace shut the door, almost catching the cat's tail, and waited for them to thank her for making them dinner.

Daniel fished the potatoes out of the stove's belly and barked, "Abe, fetch the steaks from your ma."

Grace decided she wasn't going to put up with his abuse of the children. That was the first change she was going to make around here. "Before we eat, I want to—"

"What'd you do to the biscuits?" Daniel backed away from the stove.

Abe grimaced at all her hard work. With a grunt of disdain, he started grabbing steaks and pitching them to his brothers.

Grace backed out of the line of fire.

"You made a mess of the table, too." Daniel grabbed a rag and swiped at the layer of clinging dough until it was gone.

"Ick, what is this?" Abe finished with the steaks and, with a look of disgust, began tossing biscuits across the room.

The boys howled as they caught the biscuits.

"Are they safe?" Mark bit into one and said, "Bleck." He took another bite.

"They'll likely break my teeth." Ike gnawed away, risking his teeth with abandon.

John gagged as he alternated a very black steak with his burned potato, which was mealy and white inside. He choked—loudly—swallowing his hardened biscuit.

Luke waded through the food, occasionally crashing his shoulder into John or Mark on either side of him. Grace found herself holding up the back wall again.

"Where'd you learn to cook a mess like this?" Daniel complained around a mouthful of food. He said to Ike, who was gulping milk with an air of desperation, "Hurry with that milk. I'm choking on this."

She might have answered, except the other boys were talking and choking, too—far more than was called for in Grace's opinion, even if the biscuits and steak were a little. . .tough.

"No eggs, Pa." Abe kept handing out biscuits. When the stovetop was cleared, except for a thousand crumbs that he scraped onto the floor, he cracked a dozen eggs onto the cast-iron top. "I'm cooking 'em hard. I don't think these biscuits'll break apart for a sandwich."

The cat dashed over to the scattering of crumbs then, after a few cautious sniffs, turned up its nose and went to sit by the door.

"Cat's lucky," Mark said.

"Why'zat?" Ike turned to look at his pet.

" 'Cause he can gnaw on a live rat 'stead of having to eat this."

All six of them nodded together, looking with blatant envy at the cat.

"Burn 'em good," Daniel said, gulping down a cup of milk and handing the cup on to Mark on his right. "It'll go with the rest of the meal."

The boys howled with laughter. Abe threw a hardened little circle of egg. They were coated with burned biscuit crumbs that had stuck to the stove, but at least the cast-iron stove top was clean now. Abe set an egg beside a black biscuit for Grace and snagged the last one for himself. Sitting down on Daniel's left, beside Ike, he began eating.

Luke, in the middle across from the twins, dropped out of sight, and his big brothers almost tipped over backward on their bench.

"Luke, leggo my boot." Abe made a concerted effort to kick Luke in the head, from what Grace could see going on under the table.

All five children laughed.

"Knock it off," Daniel roared. "Finish eating. We've got a long afternoon of work."

The boys ignored him. He didn't seem to mind. The chaos went on for about fifteen minutes. They insulted her and ignored her as she cowered in the same place she'd stood at breakfast. Her heart crumbled worse than the biscuits as she listened to them mock her hard work.

They all got up and left, taking the bucket with them.

Daniel said, as he left the room, "Next time use more sourdough and less milk. And for Pete's sake, don't burn them steaks up like that.

The triplets still have their baby teeth. They'll break 'em off. I'll be back to cut the supper steaks later in the afternoon."

Somewhat amazed, Grace realized that Daniel, who'd enjoyed getting her fired as a teacher, wasn't going to fire her from cooking. She wanted to let him go. If she would just keep silent for another minute, he would. "Daniel, wait!"

He had the door almost closed. She saw him freeze. She could almost feel his longing to ignore her.

But she couldn't let him. Some things were just necessary.

He came back into the room. Standing in the doorway, letting the snow swirl in, he asked, "What?"

"Last night, when you. . .uh. . .led me outside." She fell silent, waiting for him to get it.

He didn't.

"I don't know where we went. I mean, it was dark, and I just trailed behind you to find. . .the. . ."

"It's an outhouse, Grace. Is the word too crude for you to say?" Daniel seemed very tired for some reason. She didn't know how he could be. He was making the boys do all the work.

"Come on, then. I'm in a hurry." Daniel stepped out the door. "Got to get the boys to work on windfalls."

Grace wanted to scold him. She looked at his impatient expression and decided to postpone it. She trailed him to the outhouse.

When she got there, Daniel said with heavy sarcasm, "Can you find your way back?"

Since it was only about twenty feet from the front door, she didn't bother to answer. She just went in the little house and shut the door with a sharp click.

When she came out, he was gone.

She hadn't seen where she lived before. When she'd been inside, it had seemed like a cave.

That's because it *was* a cave.

All she could see from where she was standing was a wooden door set into the side of a snow-covered mountain. A plume of smoke curled out of the hillside where the stove's chimney emerged.

Even with the snow still falling, she could see where the boys had left tracks sliding down this morning. Her heart quavered at the long, reckless ride they'd taken. Then, at the end, they'd become airborne for another ten feet before landing in a deep drift. She could see the battered-down drift just in front of the door. Daniel had trampled the snow back a bit and broken a path to the outhouse, but everywhere else it was standing in fluffy drifts higher than her head. The cave door swung inward, or they'd never have gotten it open.

This wasn't like a Chicago snowstorm. There the snow came heavily, and the weather was viciously cold. Wind battered the tall buildings endlessly in that big, dangerous city. The snow was dirty and flattened by the clattering wheels of countless delivery wagons and carriages.

It was bitter cold here, but it didn't cut through her clothes and into her skin as it had there, at least not today. And this Texas snow was pure white, almost blinding—beautiful.

Reluctantly she went back to the house. The door was closed because she'd been the last one to use it. She went inside and wished she could stay out. The dark cave didn't appeal to her. There was nothing to do. The boys had taken their steak bones and potato skins with them. A new bucket of snow melted on the stove. And there was a neat little pile of food at the end of the table closest to the stove. Her dinner.

She noticed they'd left her a potato this time and almost smiled. She washed her hands with water she scooped out of the bucket on the stove, ate her lunch with no utensils. . .and enjoyed the quiet. She actually went so far as to sit on Daniel's stool. The biscuit was so awful she didn't finish it, and she wondered how the boys could have.

"Use more sourdough." She looked down at the ugly little jar pushed up against the wall beside the flour and a bucket of eggs. Sourdough, huh? That sounded about right.

Enough light sneaked in through the stovepipe hole and the edges of the door that she could see, although the room was murky. She looked around, remembering she'd missed the hanging beef this morning. The stove was in one corner, but small as it was, it took up most of one wall. The ladle she'd used to pour water out to wash her hands hung on the wall behind the stove. There was a stack of clothing and blankets beside the stove.

The door was in the wall opposite the stove. The beef was in one corner beside the door, and the table was in the other, although they couldn't exactly be called corners because the walls were uneven and the room was more round than square. The table took up a quarter of the room. A lantern sat on the floor beside the table. There was nothing else. No more surprises.

She was tempted to do a practice batch of biscuits, but she didn't dare waste flour. She threw her scraps outside, lingering in the crystal clean world. She wondered how long this snow would last. With a little smile, she decided at least it would keep Parrish away. She enjoyed the cold and soaked up the purity of the white world. She couldn't help but be glad she had on boots and pants. Her legs had never been this warm before.

The cold finally drove her back toward the house. She wondered how the boys and Daniel stood it all day. Of course, Daniel was driving them with hard work. She looked over at the nice barn. A building five times the size of the house. She saw a little chicken coop, too, but the chickens must have taken refuge from the cold and stayed inside.

If hard work kept Daniel and the boys warm, it might work for her. She was tempted to go see if there was any work she could do outside, but there was no one to be seen around the place. Her. . .family—she could hardly make herself think the word. Her husband and. . .children—her stomach swooped as she forced herself to face facts. They were nowhere to be seen. She went back inside reluctantly and sat down to wait out the afternoon.

THIRTEEN

Sally sat on Adam's shoulders, and a giggling Laura hung from one ankle as though Adam were nothing but a tree to climb. He'd had Laura in his arms most of the way, but that hadn't suited her and he had the broken eardrums to prove it.

Mandy and Beth tagged him, yammering up a storm and kicking the snow out of the way with their boots. The girls were all red-nosed and buzzing with energy from sledding. He tried not to pick up the pace any more as he headed for the porch steps. He was next thing to trotting now.

Clay had as good as thrown him out of the house because his hovering was driving Sophie crazy. But the woman he'd rescued was Adam's responsibility. He'd found her and brought her home. No reason all the work should fall on Sophie.

He swung Sally down headfirst over his shoulder, pretending to drop her just to make her scream. Her head would knock on the low porch roof if he left her perched up there. Then he hoisted little Laura into his arms. Sally dashed inside. Mandy snatched the tyke away from him as she charged into the house. He stepped back to let Beth pass then walked in.

The injured woman sat at the kitchen table, quietly slicing a hank of venison into steaks while Sophie kneaded bread and talked. Both women looked up. Sophie smiled. The other one frowned.

"You're feeling better, then?" Adam flinched at his stupid question.

MARY CONNEALY

Of course she was feeling better. She was awake and sitting up. Sophie had her wrapped in a warm shawl, and though the woman was a sight taller and a whole lot thinner than a very round-bellied Sophie, she wore one of Sophie's riding skirts.

Adam could see a flash of her ankles swathed in thick red socks. The ankle where she'd been bound was thicker because of the bandaging Sophie had done. The bit of red showing in the toe holes of her boots reminded Adam of how close she'd come to real danger in last night's cold. But not so close she hadn't managed to slug him solidly. His nose was swollen to double its normal size, and one eye opened only a slit.

The woman nodded then focused on the venison as if the job were a matter of life and death.

Adam took a second to stare at her. She was skin and bones, but under Sophie's blouse and riding skirt, he saw strength, too. Her hair was streaked here and there with gray. Last night he'd judged her to be a young woman, considering her strength. He rubbed his aching nose tenderly. Now he thought she was older, maybe close to forty, only a few years younger than his forty-five.

She'd pulled her hair back and pinned it into a knot low on her head. He could see the long and graceful curve of her neck. Her hands worked with steady competence, every move so feminine and dainty he could almost hear music.

After her staunch refusal to talk about how she'd come to that remote place, Adam knew it was a waste of time to question her, but he had to try. "Can you talk about what happened to you?"

The woman's hands paused. She looked up, shook her head, and went back to slicing.

"Now listen here. . . ." Adam jerked his Stetson off his head and crushed the brim beneath his buckskin gloves.

"Leave her alone, Adam." Sophie waved a hand towel at him as if she were shooing away a pesky fly. "She'll talk when and if she's ready, and she doesn't need you badgering her."

Adam slapped his thigh with his hat and saw snow sprinkle down

402

onto Sophie's floor. "I want to know—"

The girls picked that moment to erupt from the bedroom, their warm sledding clothes shed. The girls started chattering and giggling.

Mandy had Laura on her hip and went to sit down by the newcomer. "Want to trade jobs, Tillie?" Mandy offered Laura to her.

"Tillie?" This was the first time Adam had heard her name. Maybe she'd confided in Sophie about everything.

"Let me take your coat." Beth came up beside him, always the caretaker.

Sally gave him a huge hug around his waist.

The woman's eyes widened as she looked between the baby and the girls tending Adam. She looked stunned and almost broken. He thought he saw tears brimming in her eyes.

"What is it?" His question was between the two of them. The girls were too busy chattering to notice, though he suspected they and their ma didn't miss much.

"They. . .touch you." She shook her head as if she was dazed then dashed the back of her wrist over her eyes. Tillie stood from the table. "I'll be glad to hold the baby. Let me wash up."

Mandy giggled. "You'll be sorry you said that soon enough. I'd rather chop on a dead animal any day than have to look after Laura. She weighs a ton!"

Tillie's full lips curved into a smile. She went to the dry sink, and Sophie handed her a bar of lye soap and poured warm water over her hands. Tillie gave Sophie a startled glance. "You don't have to wait on me, Miss Sophie."

Adam figured it all out then. He'd never lived as a slave, but he'd known men who had. Of course, Tillie had spent time as property to someone else. His life as a freeman from birth was the exception rather than the rule among black folks. She was stunned that white children would touch a black man. She couldn't believe Sophie was helping her wash up.

And that shackle told the rest of the story. Oh, it was possible she was an escaped prisoner, wanted for some crime, but that didn't seem likely. Adam suspected her own war for emancipation had just been waged, and she didn't trust anybody to back her should the man who owned her come hunting.

Tillie washed her hands and took Laura as if she'd been handed a pot of gold.

Adam smiled. He could see her uncertainty with the condition of freedom. She needed guidance and help.

And he was just the man to provide it.

Parrish looked at the gap. He'd ridden through it just a day ago, following Grace cowering in the man's wagon. Parrish was sure the man had no idea he'd been carrying a stowaway. Parrish had camped out in the nasty weather so no one in town would see him so soon after Grace's disappearance. He'd had to talk to the blacksmith to rent a horse, but he'd kept away from folks otherwise.

Now he was back to finish his business with that snip of a girl so he could get out of this wretched country. Solid snow packed the gap straight up a hundred feet. Absolutely impassable. He was so furious that his rage threatened to choke him.

He took his temper out on the worthless nag he was riding. The blacksmith hadn't given him the same horse he'd rented Friday night. This one was balky, even more uncooperative than the last. The blacksmith had given Parrish a harmless look and said the other horse he'd rented was spoken for, although that same horse stood right there in the stall, plain as day.

That young punk Mike O'Casey stood coated in filth and sweat from working over his stinking forge, with no respect for his betters. Parrish wanted to beat the arrogance out of him. But the Irish trash, with his freckles and red hair, had arms like corded steel. He weighed a hundred pounds more than Parrish, and he looked as though he'd welcome a fight. And even if Parrish won, which he figured to do if only by using the revolver he carried, he'd still not have a horse.

Parrish had gritted his teeth and taken the nag.

And now here he was. Grace as far from him behind this snow-filled pass as if she perched on the moon.

He knew he should just ride away. Texas didn't suit him. He missed the anonymity of Chicago and the street urchins who made such easy prey.

But his temper goaded him. He hungered to make her sorry for what she'd done. The image of her cowering under his fists kept him awake at night and rode him like a spur all day. He'd been out of prison for a year, and he'd yet to sleep a full night through. And when he did fall into a fitful sleep, he had brutally satisfying dreams of making her bleed and crawl.

"There has to be a way into that canyon." He rode to the left and the right, but not trained in the ways of the wilderness, he couldn't think of how to get past that solid wall of rock and snow.

He looked back at Mosqueros. If he showed up there acting as though he was passing through, he could scout around and find a way in, but it would take time. He shivered from the wind-whipped snow and ached from the rough ride on the slow-moving nag.

How could he stay in Mosqueros? He was down to his last few dollars. If he *was* passing through, he'd steal something and hightail it as he had in a string of towns as he followed Grace's trail. But he'd found her now, and he had to stay put until he got his hands on her.

Then he laughed. His laugh turned into a snarl. His fists rose in the bitter wind. *Mosqueros needs a schoolteacher!* He'd driven the one they had into the hills. There'd be no one else to handle the job. He'd been a schoolmaster in his youth before he'd found children to make his money for him.

He turned the horse back toward Mosqueros. He'd keep an eye on the gap and scout the land on Saturdays and Sundays looking for another entrance. And the rest of the time, he'd bring a little learning to the children of Mosqueros. He might not be able to get this stupid horse to mind him, but he'd always had a knack for instilling fearful obedience in children.

All but Grace.

He might even find a few children who'd be likely members for the new family he'd need to start once he worked his fury toward Grace out of his system.

He kicked the horse savagely to make it move. The hag crow-hopped and kicked up its hind legs. Nearly unseated, Parrish didn't kick the animal again. Nothing in Texas acted the way it should. Nothing!

The cave was warm—she'd give Daniel that. The door slammed open. She had already realized she needed to give the door a wide berth in the tiny house. She braced herself.

Ike came dashing into the house, bent double as if he was in pain. He actually closed the door, which sounded an alarm to Grace.

"Ike, is everything all right?" Grace stepped back so he didn't knock her over.

"I gotta get warm." Ike dropped on his knees in front of the stove. Grace knelt beside him, worried that his hands were frostbitten, since he'd tucked them inside his coat.

Slowly, on a soft breath, Ike pulled out his hands.

Before Grace could see what he'd done to himself, the door slammed open again and Luke rushed in, carrying the cat. It yowled and wriggled until Luke dropped it.

"Close the door, stupid." Ike pulled her attention back.

He opened one hand, and Grace saw two tiny furry things; his other hand opened, and there were two more. Kittens. So tiny they still had their eyes closed.

"Where did you get them?"

The cat came up to Ike on the side away from Grace. Rising up on her hind legs, she sniffed at Ike's hand. A much smaller cat than she'd been just last night.

"Your cat had kittens?"

"Out of season. She should have had 'em in the spring." Ike lowered his hand so the cat could see her four babies. "She must have just birthed 'em last night. I found them in the barn, but it's too cold. They'll freeze to death."

Ike glanced up, and Grace remembered the day the two of them had doctored the cat at school. Despite the fact that none of the boys wanted her for their ma, accord passed between her and Ike.

"They'll be okay." Grace patted Ike's shoulder. "You'll take good care of them, and their mom will feed them. Before you know it, we'll have five cats in this family."

Luke shoved himself between Grace and Ike. He jostled Ike's arm.

"Watch it, stupid." For the first time in history—as far as Grace knew their history at least—one of the boys got bumped without hitting back. Ike held the kittens too carefully. He didn't even yell, out of deference for the babies.

"Sorry, Ike. Can I help?" Luke leaned down until he almost touched the kittens with his nose. He reached his hand toward one.

"Just one finger, Luke. They're really fragile. You shouldn't touch a baby kitten at all. Their mother might abandon them. But I had to bring 'em in." Ike looked sideways at Grace for a second, a furrow cutting between his brow. "I know I shouldn't have touched them. But she born-ed 'em right out in the middle of the barn. It must be her first litter. I reckon she don't know how it's done yet. You think they'll be all right?"

"I think you had to take the chance." Grace silently prayed they would survive, hurting for Ike if they didn't. He'd blame himself. "They'd never have made it if you'd left them there. You had to do it, Ike."

Ike nodded, frowning but with an assurance that Grace had seen before when he tended animals. Ike said to Luke, "Touch it on its head and draw your finger gentle-like down toward its tail."

Luke did as he was told. "It's so soft. Softest thing I've ever felt."

Ike's expression lifted as he smiled at his brother. "Yeah, it is. Let's see if we can get the cat to feed 'em."

Ike glanced at Grace. She nodded and knelt beside the fretful mother cat. She petted the cat, gently urging her down on her side. Ike laid all four kittens on her belly.

The mother, her yellow fur soft and thick with winter growth, twisted her head back to study her babies. The babies started a high-pitched mewling, and the mother's purr sped up.

Grace had no trouble keeping the cat on her side. She seemed to know that was where she needed to be. The kittens' tiny paws waved and pushed at the fur. Their bellies were on the ground, and their feet could only inch them along.

Ike and Luke—who still used but one finger—nudged the kittens toward food. One by one they found what they were looking for and their heartrending cries quieted. It was only moments later that all four babies were eating.

The mother cat kept looking at them, giving them an occasional lick with her pink tongue or caress with her quivering nose. The babies drank steadily. Their paws, tipped with claws so fine that they were translucent, kneaded at their mother's stomach.

Grace knelt there stroking the cat's fur in a moment of peaceful joy with two of her sons. Ike and Luke just watched, looking up at Grace to smile every now and again.

Finally, Ike broke the silence. "They're gonna make it, aren't they, Ma?"

Grace smiled back. "You know, I think they are. Now there are enough cats so everyone can have his own."

Ike said, "Nope. They're all mine."

Luke nodded without comment.

"You know, I just thought she was fat." Grace sat back on her knees.

Ike snickered. "Me, too."

Daniel came in carrying an armload of wood. He kicked the door shut. "What ya got there, boy?"

He dropped the heavy pieces of split oak in one corner then crouched down beside the cat. "Kittens, great. They'll keep the mice down. But they should be in the barn. No room for five cats in here." Daniel sounded strict, but he pulled one glove off his left hand, reached out, and rubbed the cat's shoulder. His heavy hand rested gently on the new mother.

"I'll move 'em out just as soon as I can, Pa. She didn't even make a nest for 'em. She had two in one spot and the other two just laid out alone. Reckon she's too young to be a ma yet."

Daniel thought about it. "How hard did you hunt, boy? A mother cat has six kittens most times."

Ike jumped to his feet. "I looked pretty hard, but maybe I'd better go over the barn again."

Daniel nodded. "Just to be on the safe side."

Ike rushed out with Luke on his heels. Ike took a second to close the door.

"That young'un is the animal doctorin'-est boy I've ever seen." Daniel kept petting the cat. "Luke's got the talent for doctoring but not the same soft heart for animals as Ike has. That soft heart of his will get him in trouble."

Grace couldn't help but smile. "I wonder where he got that soft heart?"

Daniel jerked his head up and scowled as if he'd forgotten Grace was there.

Well, to whom had he been talking, then?

"I'm not softhearted."

The cat stopped purring at Daniel's disgruntled tone.

Grace just barely kept from rolling her eyes. "No, of course not. . . excuse me. You're just as hard-hearted as they come." She glanced at the cat, which Daniel still petted.

With a heavy sigh, Daniel said, "I reckon we just got ourselves four more house cats. When Ike brought that kitten home, I told him, 'No cat in the house.' That didn't even last an hour."

"Five house cats. You ever have a mouse in this house, Daniel?"

"No, but what self-respecting mouse would want to move into this place?" Daniel's mouth turned up on one side, nearly a smile.

Grace grinned.

"We did have a badger pop out through a hole in the ground in that corner." Daniel pointed to a spot right behind Grace.

With a squeak not much different than that of a hungry little kitten, Grace wheeled around on her knees toward the corner.

Daniel was still laughing when he closed the door on his way out.

The kittens moved into the tiny cave with the rest of them. When they survived through a couple of nights and the mama cat seemed to catch on to just how to mother them, Daniel insisted they be moved back to the barn.

The mother, in full power as a parent now, moved them back to the cave, carrying them by the napes of their necks, one at a time.

Daniel declared war with the mother cat and moved them back.

They'd been fighting it out for three days.

The snow started melting. The winter blizzard had come and gone, leaving cool but tolerable weather.

Grace's biscuits showed meager improvement, or else the menfolk were truly starving. Either way, the people survived just as well as the kittens.

As she stood, wondering how to pass this afternoon in the dark little home, even the kittens were currently, if temporarily, outside. She, on the other hand, had been made to feel decidedly unwanted outside.

The door slammed open. She braced herself for the onslaught.

It was only one small onslaught—John.

"Hi, Ma."

"Close the door, John."

John stopped short. He stared at her.

"The door," she said again.

He still looked.

"What's the matter?" she asked.

He shut the door.

A surge of triumph went through her. Suddenly she realized that it didn't take much to make her happy. A burned steak, warm clothes, an occasional split second of obedience from her son.

"How'd you know I'm John?"

The question surprised her. "How could I not know? You boys are nothing alike."

"We're exactly alike. Everybody says so."

Grace shrugged. "You're John. You sit in the middle at meals. You're a good reader." She leaned down and whispered, "And I think you're the nicest one of the bunch."

He gave her a look that made her wonder if she'd just insulted him.

"Am not. Mark's best."

"At some things he's best," Grace agreed. "At other things Luke is best. You've all got talents."

John studied her as though she had just sprouted a second head. "No, we all know Mark's best, then Abe." John looked down at the floor and kicked at it.

He was so overly nonchalant that Grace knew what he was going to say next was very important to him.

"I'm worst at things. It's okay."

Boom! An explosion shattered the quiet of the cave.

FOURTEEN

Something slammed into the roof so hard the whole mountain shook.

Grace screamed and stumbled into the back wall. John shouted in terror. His fear hurt worse than her own. He fell against her, and they crashed to the floor in a heap.

Rocks from the ceiling pelted her back. John jumped up. Instinctively Grace grabbed him and sheltered him with her body. A sharp stone ripped her shirt with a loud tearing sound.

The door blasted open. One leather hinge at the bottom of the door snapped. Snow erupted into the opening. The door wedged into the ground and stayed standing.

The red-hot stove shook. It tipped sideways onto one leg, falling straight toward them. Grace shoved John against the far wall, mere feet away from the stove. With a sharp rending of metal, the stovepipe shattered into pieces and tumbled to the floor, rolling toward Grace. She flung her arms around the boy. Glancing over her shoulder, Grace saw the blazing stove teeter.

She lifted her feet and braced them on the wall as a piece of metal clattered toward her, keeping her body between the pipe and John. When the pipe stopped rolling, she kicked it away. The stove tilted back, rocked twice more, and stayed upright.

The outside rumbled and exploded around them. Dirt and stones from the ceiling continued to crumble, filling the house with choking grit. The savagery went on and on. Minutes passed. The cave went pitch-black except for the fiendish red glow from the fire.

Grace felt as if she were being swallowed, gulped down into the deep, dark belly of a monster. The noise became muted. Snow cascaded through the hole in the roof left from the broken pipe. The snow sizzled on the stove then clogged the small opening and stopped.

John sobbed in her arms, and she whispered comfort to him without knowing just what she said.

As suddenly as it began, it stopped.

The silence filtered into her mind. She slowly lifted her head. Dirt and rocks fell away from her back. The air she breathed was thick with dirt. She glanced overhead. The ceiling hadn't collapsed. The stove still burned. She looked down at the frightened boy in her arms. "John, it's over."

His face was buried against her chest.

"It's really over, John."

John lifted his tearstained face and looked into her eyes. His expression beseeched her to say they were all right.

He said between trembling lips, "Wh–wh–what happened?"

"I don't know." She lifted herself to a sitting position, and slashing pain tore across her back. She wanted to cry out, but John's terror forced her to be calm. "But we survived it, whatever it was."

She moved slowly, afraid the world would erupt again. John clung to her. She pulled him with her as she brushed the dirt and rocks off her back. Her back protested. A stab of pain ripped across her chest. One of her shoulders didn't want to move. She suppressed a groan of agony.

She got to her feet, John's arms sliding from around her neck to around her waist as she stood. She was too unsteady to do anything but stumble to the nearest bench. Careful to avoid the hot stovepipe, she lowered herself onto a seat and pulled John onto her lap.

He hurled himself the few inches between them and wrapped his sturdy arms around her. Her bruised body protested, but he felt so good—so solid and healthily and miraculously alive—that she hugged him back fiercely. She buried her face in his soft blond hair, and when he started to cry, she couldn't hold back her own tears.

The emotional storm passed, and John's shoulders ceased their shuddering. He lay exhausted against her for long minutes.

She had no idea what had happened. She wished John were safely away from this living tomb. But she was treacherously glad she had him with her in the awful, cramped, dark little world.

At last his arms loosened from her a bit. She lifted her head from his white-blond curls, and they looked at each other.

She wasn't ready for his question. "Are Pa and my brothers all right?"

Grace caught herself before a cry of fear could escape. She'd only had time to think of herself and John. What *had* happened?

Grace looked down at John's frightened little face. The stove lit up his eyes. The slits in the stove door glowed like devilish teeth, bared in an evil smile. They were trapped, buried alive. She had to take care of him. She squared her shoulders, straightened her aching spine, and began taking stock.

"Hop down. Let's see what's going on."

John got up, but he caught hold of the baggy shirt Daniel had given her and stayed tight up against her side.

She went to the door and pulled. It dragged against the floor and reluctantly swung open. They were faced with a solid wall of white. Even in the darkness, the white was so vivid they couldn't fail to recognize it. Snow. The door was buried in a snowdrift.

"There must have been an avalanche," Grace said. "Has this ever happened before?"

She looked down at John. He shrugged. "We just moved here this spring. We've never had a winter before."

"Well, I suppose your pa is just going to have to dig us out." Grace had a vision of a mountain of snow burying them hundreds of feet deep. Had Daniel and the other boys escaped the avalanche, or were they out there somewhere under this snow, crushed and dead?

She turned her mind away from such dreadful thoughts. She kept the fear out of her eyes as best she could. "I guess we can help. Let's start digging."

John seemed to become calmer when she suggested a job for him to do. She was a little steadier herself. They went to the door and began pawing through the snow.

They pulled the snow inward and shoved it off to the side. At first they felt a feverish rush as they dug, but after a while the hard work began to tell on them, and they calmed down and worked steadily. When their fingers got too cold, they went to the stove and warmed them.

As she and John stood side by side at the stove, Grace realized that the crimson teeth weren't so bright as they had been. "We're going to need to add kindling. The fire is going out."

John bent down to the woodpile beside the stove while Grace, using her shirt to protect her hand, turned the squeaking little knob and lowered the cast-iron door. Burning wood nearly tipped out into her hands.

Grace realized that the stove didn't need more fuel. So why was the fire going out? She slammed the door with a sharp clank of metal and said, "Let's don't add wood yet. It's still got enough and we're warm."

John looked at her. "Okay." With perfect trust, he dropped the sticks back onto the woodpile.

The fire was dying. Grace looked up at the sealed opening where the stovepipe belonged. Where a fire couldn't live, people couldn't. They were running out of air.

A light sweat broke out all over her. She steadied herself and looked down at John's trusting eyes. She had to think of something, for him.

"I'll tell you what, let's say a prayer." Since she'd escaped from Parrish, she'd attended church as was proper. But right now she needed more than proper. She needed a miracle.

"Okay," John said. "But don't be all day about it like the parson."

In her heart she prayed, *God, what do I do? I need help. Not for me, God, but for John. He's so young. He trusts me.* She stared at the stove, aware of John's chubby little hand catching hold of hers.

"God, take care of us and take care of the rest of the family." She smiled down at John. "How was that?"

She backed up, thinking to sit and hold him again. Working made you breathe hard, and that *must* take more air. They needed to save it for as long as they could.

As she stepped back, Grace tripped over the stovepipe. She looked at the snow-packed hole. It dripped steadily onto the stove. If it was melting slowly now, maybe it would melt faster with the stovepipe carrying hot air directly to it. She didn't know if she'd thought of it or God had told her, but she thought the timing of her "idea" was directly related to her prayer.

"We'd better see if we can get those pipes back into the hole." She bent to pick up the first cylinder. "The stove won't burn well if it doesn't have an airhole."

John went right to work. They gathered four pieces of the cooled pipe and fitted them together in a column about as tall as Grace. As the hollow metal clinked, Grace heard John whimper softly.

Trying to keep both of them encouraged, she said, "You know, you're wrong about Mark being better than you, John. I think you're terrific." She wasn't saying it to make him feel good. She had always thought John was the best behaved of the rowdy Reeves boys.

"Nah, I'm not. I'm dumbest and smallest and slowest."

"You did really well in your classes, John. Better by far than Mark. You weren't dumbest."

"Yeah, I was, 'cause Mark knows how to do everything. He just doesn't do it, if'n he don't want to. I wanted to do it, 'cause I thought it was fun, mostly. But if he'd'a wanted to, Mark woulda beat me for sure."

Grace shook her head as she settled the pipe into the hole in the center of the stove. "That's not how it works, John. Smart is as smart does."

John helped her brace the stovepipe. "What's that s'posed to mean?"

Grace smiled in the fading red light. She could imagine the little furrow in John's forehead. He and Ike were the only ones who ever doubted themselves for a second. "It means if you're smart inside your head but you never act smart, then you're not so smart after all."

"Mark acts smart."

"Not in school things," Grace pointed out. "He got bad grades."

"But in other things," John insisted. "In real things that matter, like hunting stray calves and handling the horses."

Grace's jaw tightened as she thought of such young boys doing so much work. They needed a chance to be children, and they needed to respect education. She wanted to shake Daniel.

Then she thought of him out there somewhere and realized if she could get her hands on him right now, she'd be so glad to see him— because it would mean he was alive and she was unburied—she'd give him a hug instead of shaking him. And she also had to admit that she was glad she had a steady little worker like John beside her in this tight spot. And who had trained him to work but Daniel?

Metal scraped on metal as she raised the pipe to the ceiling. She struggled but couldn't get it to go into the snow-clogged hole. The fire dimmed now until there were no flames at all, only glowing embers. Grace knew they didn't have long.

"John, what you're saying is making my point. Mark is better at some things, and you're better at others. That's just what I said."

"Yeah, but school is dumb and animals are important."

Grace fought down her panic as she wrestled with the stubborn pipes. Goaded to hurry, she lifted the whole thing off the stove and set it on the table. "I've got to clear some of that snow and stick the pipe out first, then set it on the stove hole."

John worked beside her. He pulled up a bench and held it steady.

She clawed at the snow and let it fall with a hiss on the stove. Her arms reached up higher and higher into the hole. The snow burned at her hands as they became encased in the bitter cold. If the hole was just a bit bigger, maybe she could squeeze through and dig them out through the roof, but the hole was so small now that not even John could wriggle through. When she'd cleared it as high as she could reach, she said, "I'm ready for the pipe now."

John handed the awkward tube to her.

This time, fitting the pipe into the hole overhead first, she got the whole thing put together neatly. As she climbed down off the bench, she heard water begin running down the pipe.

The fire in the stove sputtered wildly.

She had latched onto the fire as proof that there was still some air to breathe in the cave, and her heart fluttered with fear at the thought of its going out and leaving them in the pitch dark. Then, as the embers hissed, it occurred to Grace that putting out the fire might be a good thing. That might leave more air for them.

"Let's build the fire up some more," John suggested. "It looks kind of low."

Grace wondered how far the pipe had to melt before the smoke could escape and let fresh air in. She knew if she threw in more wood, it wouldn't burn. "Not yet. There's plenty for now until the snow stops melting." Grace sank down onto the bench.

John sat on her lap without being urged.

They sat there and listened to the water run. The embers continued to fade. There was plenty of wood for a roaring fire.

Please, God, help us.

"We should pray again, Ma." John turned from the captivating red and looked at her.

Grace couldn't help but smile. "I was already praying in my heart. But let's pray out loud."

John bowed his little head, and Grace remembered the unruly Reeves boys tearing around in church every week. She'd judged them very harshly for their behavior. But they'd been there, worshipping. She should have given Daniel credit for that.

"Help Pa to be okay. Bless Abe, Ike, Mark, Luke, and John." He reeled off the names, including his own, as if he'd done it a thousand times. "And God bless Ma."

He was silent, so Grace spoke into the darkness. "Take care of the whole Reeves family." John had prayed for himself. She opened her mouth to add, "And me," then realized she'd already done it. She was part of the Reeves family.

Suddenly she didn't have to forcibly keep her fears to herself or her spine straight. She wrapped her arms tightly around John. "You just did something wonderful for me, John."

He looked up at her. "You mean praying for you?"

That pulled Grace up short. No, she hadn't meant that. But maybe, just maybe, praying was what it all came down to. She settled John firmly against her. "Praying for me was wonderful. Thank you. And you did something else for me, too."

"What's that?" John rubbed his head against her neck when he looked into her eyes.

She glanced at the dying fire and heard the dripping of the melting snow. She felt a pang of regret that she hadn't been able to do more to save this precious little boy. She felt even worse to think that she would never have the pleasure of being his mother. Her chin quivered, but she held it steady. "You reminded me of who I am."

"The teacher?"

Grace shook her head. "No, before I was a teacher."

"You worked somewhere else?" John shifted his weight around as if getting comfortable for story time.

"Oh yes. I worked very hard somewhere else. But I'm not talking about what I did. I'm talking about what I was."

John shrugged and looked confused. "What were you?"

"I was brave."

FIFTEEN

John tilted his head and frowned. "Brave?"

"Yes, I was so brave when I was growing up." Grace nodded. "I had to be very strong for the work I did and for the children I took care of."

In a voice laced with fear, John asked, "You didn't cook for them, did you?"

Grace smiled. "You ate it."

"Yeah," John admitted. "But it helps if you're *real* hungry."

Grace laughed out loud. "Well, the truth is, I didn't cook for them. I worked at a really hard job, and when we'd get home—"

"Who's 'we'?"

"My sisters and I."

"Did you have a lot of them?" John bounced on her knee and swung his dangling legs.

Grace was glad he was relaxing. "I had more sisters than you have brothers. About twice as many."

"There were ten of you?"

"Yup, at least."

One corner of John's mouth curled up in confusion. "You don't know for sure how many?"

"No, it wasn't that. I lived with a man who adopted me. I was an orphan. And he adopted a lot of other kids, too. The older ones would grow up and go away." Run away—like she had. "And younger ones would come and take their places at the carpet mill."

420

"What's a carpet mill?"

"It's a big, noisy factory where they make rugs." Grace cringed when she thought of the deafening weaving machines, clacking hour after hour. "It's too hot in the summer and too cold in the winter. We worked long hours at hard labor and didn't get much to eat. Then we'd go home to our father, who took all our money and fed us. . .well. . .not much."

"And when you were doing that, you were brave?"

"Oh yes. I took care of all my little sisters. I had to be tougher than all of them, and some of them were really tough because they'd been orphaned and lived on their own. And I had to be tougher than the other kids at the mill who picked on us. And I was. I could face down anyone." Honesty forced her to add, "Except my father." She'd always been scared of Parrish. For good reason. But she'd stepped in many times to draw Parrish's beatings onto herself to protect a little sister. "Sometimes I was even brave with him.

"And I was a teacher to my little sisters. I didn't learn to cook, but I knew how to read before my own mother died, and I taught my adopted sisters how, late at night when our light was supposed to be off."

"Boring," John groused.

Grace ignored his all-too-common opinion. "Then when I was old enough, I got to leave my father's house and be a teacher for a real job. For you and your brothers."

"Till Dad got you fired," John reminded her.

She shrugged. "What's done is done."

In Chicago, she'd left Parrish by running away. But unlike her older sisters, she couldn't just go off and leave all those little ones in his brutal hands. No one would have cared if she'd told the police, "My father adopts children to force them to work like slaves."

But they'd listened when she said, "My father is stealing from the carpet mill."

With grim satisfaction at the memory, Grace said to John, "Oh yes, I used to be brave, but I forgot how. . .until just this minute."

Grace and Hannah had come up with the plan of making a home

421

for the six younger children. Grace had lived with Hannah for nearly ten years. They knew each other too well. Grace had the nerve to run and lead Parrish on a wild-goose chase. Hannah had the natural mother's heart and would do best with the children. Besides, Grace was old enough to be a teacher. She could find work and send money.

"And now you've remembered?" John asked.

"Yes, I have." When the police came, thanks to Grace's anonymous information, she and her sisters had been ready. The minute the police took Parrish away, Grace and her little family of girls had run.

Grace had no intention of putting the children in danger by returning them to the orphanage where they might again be adopted by some parent as cruel as Parrish, so they'd vanished into the streets of Chicago. Grace had seen to it that Hannah was settled then set out to find work. Always in the back of her mind, she knew Parrish would come after her.

Grace had heard that mother birds sometimes pretended to be wounded, letting a wing hang awkwardly, when a predator came too near. The hungry coyote would come after the wounded mother, leaving the nest of babies safely behind. She had no wing to dangle, only herself, but Parrish was a coyote. If he got free, he'd come.

She'd stowed away on a train that took her to Kansas City. At first she'd cleaned houses and served in diners, sending money home to Hannah. Then, after only a few months, she'd caught sight of Parrish walking down the Missouri street. He'd either escaped from jail or used his connections to escape justice.

She hopped another train, weaving her way across the country, changing names and jobs as she went, trying to lose herself in the western lands. . . .

John nudged her out of her thoughts. "What made you remember?"

At last she'd seen the ad for a teacher in Mosqueros. Teaching—it was what she'd always wanted to do. By that time, she hadn't sighted Parrish in months and she was tired of running. She had no schooling, but she didn't mention that when she asked to be tested. She'd educated herself thoroughly while she studied with her little sisters, so she fortunately passed with ease and was hired by Mosqueros to teach at their school.

One bright spot Grace thought of—if Parrish was still hunting her, he wasn't adopting more children. She didn't tell John any of this. Instead, her eyes fell on a Bible, tucked into a corner of the room, on the floor like everything else. "I just had the strangest thought come to me, probably because we're trapped in here."

"What thought?" One of her sons was actually listening to her.

Grace had been blessed by having children listen to her all her life, with the exception of her brand-new sons. She hoped she had something worth hearing. "I remembered that God is faithful."

John's brow furrowed with concentration. "What's 'at mean?"

" 'It is of the Lord's mercies that we are not consumed, because his compassions fail not. They are new every morning: great is thy faithfulness.' It's from Lamentations. I used to read that one to my sisters."

"What does it mean that God is faithful?"

"Don't you ever feel like God is far away?"

John shrugged. "He *is* far away. He's up in heaven with my first ma. Pa says so."

Grace smiled. "Yes, God is up in heaven, but He's right here, too,"—she tapped John on his chest—"inside your heart."

"How can an old man be inside your heart?"

Grace controlled the urge to laugh. "Your picture of God as an old man is a common one, but that's not the picture I have of God. I think God looks like the wind."

"The wind doesn't look like anything," John protested.

"You can't see it, but no one doubts it's there. He has power like wind has power. You've seen the trees blowing in the wind, right?"

"Right."

"So you believe in the wind because of what it does. No one sees God, but everyone sees what He does. And the wind is air and the air is inside our chests when we breathe, just like our hearts. God is everywhere. And God never leaves us. God is faithful to us, even when we aren't so faithful to Him."

"Even if we're bad, God is still with us?" John asked with fearful eyes.

Grace knew her son. He had indeed, in his short life, been very bad. "Everyone is bad sometimes. 'For all have sinned, and come short of the glory of God.' That's why Jesus came and died. God sent Him to die in our places. Jesus sacrificed His life to save us."

John nodded with a serious face. "That's what Pa says."

"And what can be more faithful than that?"

"So God loves us and is faithful to us, even when we don't deserve it?"

Grace hugged him until he squeaked. The pain in her back and shoulder didn't seem important anymore. She pulled back and, in the dim light, saw a little boy who desperately wanted a mother.

Grace fell in love. She knew a fraction of how God felt because she knew she'd die for John. "God loves us *especially* when we don't deserve it, honey."

She gave him a noisy kiss on the cheek, which he wiped off with a growl of disgust, but he leaned closer to her. The disgust was all for show.

She didn't want to give him an excuse to climb down off her lap. She badly needed to hold on to someone she loved right now, when she might not be on the earth much longer. Every minute the stove dimmed.

"Let's read." The meager light from the stove would be enough. There was only one book in the house. John hopped off her lap and was back instantly with the family Bible.

She and John sat together, and she helped him sound out words. Slowly they worked their way through a sentence. She chose the book of John because her son liked knowing his name was from the Bible.

" 'In the beginning was the Word, and the Word was with God, and the Word was God.' "

John had taken to schooling. He'd picked up his letters and numbers right from the first. Now he read all but the hardest words. " 'The same was in the beginning with God.'"

And he kept improving. " 'In him was life; and the life. . .' " His reading slowed; his head nodded. " 'Was the light of men.' "

Grace knew they didn't have much longer.

She jerked awake when the Bible hit the floor. She realized it wasn't light in the cave anymore. John had fallen asleep in her arms.

With a nervous glance at the stove, she saw that the grating had become so dark that only the faintest glow of red still showed. The water hissed against the hot coals. She tried to stir herself to stay awake, but her muscles were heavy, her head cloudy and confused. She wanted sleep.

"This is it," she murmured. "The air is running out." She looked down at the sweet, sleeping boy in her arms. *God, forgive me for the coward I've been. Once I started running, I turned into a scared rabbit instead of the fighter I used to be. I thought. . .I guess I thought proper manners and the loneliness I've been living with were how respectable people behaved. Now I see I just held people away out of fear. I'm sorry.*

She used her waning strength to lift the Bible onto the tabletop. A loud splatter of snow dimmed the red glow until it was barely visible. With one hand holding her son and another resting on the Good Book, she prayed into the dark room, *Now that I remember how to be brave, if I had more time, I'd make You proud, Lord. Forgive me. Take John and me to be with You.* Her head fell forward.

A loud thud from the stovepipe startled her awake. Her heavy head lifted, and John stirred. A puff of white steam exploded from the grating.

"The snow must have put it out." John's voice quavered.

His fear was too much for her to bear. Yes, she'd been brave, and she was still brave. And she was married and the mother of five sons, even if just for another few moments. She refused to sit here and die without a fight.

She didn't like the idea of staying still and doing nothing while they both suffocated in this dark pit. Her words sounded thick and stupid. "Let's throw some kindling on the fire. Maybe we can keep it going."

She and John tried to stand. She had to force her body to obey. John swayed and would have fallen if she hadn't steadied him. They both stumbled to the stove. Grace opened the grating door in the stove's belly. The wet wood in the stove mocked them.

Grace grabbed the fork and poked at the sodden black mess. She uncovered glowing embers. They tossed in kindling. Grace leaned down and blew gently on the smallest pieces of wood. And the stove blew back.

Grace jerked upright. "I felt wind."

She also realized her thoughts had cleared. "John, let's get some more wood on the fire. I think we've melted our way out through the stovepipe."

A little coaxing and patience and the first bit of dry wood caught. A curl of white smoke, full of steam, rose straight for the stovepipe, and then the shredded kindling burst into flames. Sizzling in protest, the wet wood even grudgingly dried and burned. The flame danced higher.

A draft from the stovepipe blew cold and fresh.

Shut in as tightly as they were, the cave was very warm, and working on the stove had made their fingers nimble. That gave Grace the energy to turn to the door again. She stared at the solid wall of white. "I wish we had a shovel."

"Wishin's a pure waste of time, Ma," John said.

Grace thought John sounded a little too old, but in this instance he was absolutely right. She held the ladle up in front of her and studied it against the heavy snow. Setting it aside, she said, "Let's get back to work with our hands."

Grace and John scooped at the snow. With a steady supply of fresh air, they had the strength to work steadily, pausing to warm themselves as the fire leaped up and burned with a white flame.

John talked about his family and school and ranch life.

Grace was surprised at how much advice the little boy had for her about cooking. "Your pa taught you all how to cook?"

John shoved snow to the side. The pile grew until it reached the tabletop. It melted on the side nearest the stove, and the floor of the little cave became muddy. "I don't know about teachin' us, Ma. He just makes us do it an' we've had to learn or we starve, simple as that. We all started out cookin' kinda like you."

"Um, you eat it," she reminded him again. She'd eaten it, too.

"Like I said, eat it or starve."

"So how do you make the biscuits stay separate, like your pa does? Mine all run together."

"First you take the flour and—"

Grace noticed the stove had stopped sizzling and the fire burned brightly. "Look at the pipe, John."

John turned away from the hole he'd been digging so diligently. "There's light coming in from around the edges."

"Grace, are you down there?" Daniel's voice echoed through the stovepipe.

She felt tears of relief burn behind her eyes as she ran to the stove and shouted to the ceiling, "Yes, John and I are trapped in here."

There was absolute silence. For a second she began to think she'd imagined hearing Daniel.

In a strangled voice, Daniel finally said, "John is in there with you?"

"Yes, we were in here when the whole world seemed to explode. We've been trying to dig our way out."

An explosion of another kind came from above the pipe. Daniel shouted, "John's in there, boys. He's okay."

Shrieks and hollers of glee rattled the pipe.

"Where'd you think I was, Pa?" John yelled.

Daniel's shouting turned to laughter. "I was worried about you, boy. I didn't know where you'd gotten to. There was an avalanche, and. . ." Daniel's voice broke.

Grace heard everything. He'd thought his son might be buried in the snow, just as she and John had worried about the rest of the family. Her heart turned over, and the tears spilled as she imagined what Daniel had gone through. "Are all of you all right?" Grace yelled.

"Yeah, sure. We were above it. I was afraid. I've been praying and working full steam ever since it happened, trying to get to you. Hoping John. . ." He fell silent.

"Are you going to stand up there and talk all day, or are you going to get us out of here?" John demanded.

Daniel spoke again, steady now. "We'll have you out in two shakes, son. I've been digging out front. When I saw smoke coming out of the stovepipe, I ran up here to see if you could hear me. We were dragging windfalls down, and they got away from us on the steep slope. I didn't think. . .I mean. . .an avalanche never occurred to me."

There was silence again. Then Daniel roared, "Get back to work on that diggin', boys."

Grace turned to John. "They made it through. They're coming for us."

John smiled. His lips wobbled, but he held them steady. "I was powerful worried about 'em, Ma."

She dashed the tears away with her wrist then hugged John's shoulders. "We'll be out in a minute," she said. "Let's scoot up to the stove and take a break until our fingers get warm."

Without waiting for him to agree, Grace sat down and pulled John onto her lap. He seemed to fit there comfortably. She hugged him close and thanked God for her family, even though they still scared her to death.

Parrish had always scared her, but that hadn't stopped her from being brave. Well, it was time to remember how to be brave again.

"We've rested enough, John," Grace said with a firm jerk of her chin. "Let's get back to digging."

 S I X T E E N

A fist, delicate and lily white, punched out of the snow and smacked Daniel in the nose.

He jerked backward, his feet slipped, and he landed on his backside. He looked at the hole in the snow made by the fist and saw Grace's cherry-red nose poking out of the snowdrift. He suspected his nose was now the same color, and not because of the cold.

"Well, it's certainly nice to see you boys." Grace smiled and pulled her nose back out of sight.

"We got through!" Mark dived at the hole and began clawing with his mittened hands.

The other boys plunged in.

Daniel scrambled around on his hands and knees and began digging. The hole grew wider. He saw little boy hands and big girl hands digging from the inside.

"We didn't think you guys were ever going to get here!" John shouted.

The sound of his son's voice gave Daniel such a thrill that his heart almost pounded right out of his chest. He'd been so scared. He'd been fighting off the urge to begin mourning. Then he'd heard Grace and then John through the stovepipe.

"We're sick of being stuck in here!" John yelled as if he were disgusted.

They all laughed as if that was the funniest joke they'd ever heard. John and Grace laughed, too. All of their spirits were so high that,

429

although Daniel was exhausted from hours of hard work in the sharp cold, and he knew the other boys were, too, Daniel could feel them bursting with energy.

Daniel heard Grace's gentle laughter from under the mountain of snow. He didn't think he'd ever heard her laugh before. The music of it warmed him as much as the hard work.

Before long, John poked his head out of the widening hole, then dived forward and tumbled through into the outside.

"Hey, don't leave me behind." Grace's good-natured voice—something else Daniel had never heard before—was full of mock indignation. Nowhere did he hear the prim, overly polite schoolmarm.

Grace scrambled out next, laughing. She jumped to her feet, threw her arms around John, and hollered, "We're free! We made it!"

John slung his arms around her waist, and she whirled him in a circle. Then, as John's legs flew out, she let go deliberately and tossed John into the feather-soft snow. She turned on Mark and did the same thing to him.

Mark landed in the snow beside John, who grabbed a large ball of snow and slammed it into Mark's head. Ike got tossed next as Grace wrestled with him.

The reunion turned into a riot. Grace tackled every one of the boys. They ran wildly away from her, screaming, only to turn and attack. John joined her side and lunged at anyone who got close to them.

They were all shouting and shoving at each other when Grace turned from the chaos. Daniel caught the wicked gleam in her eye just before she charged him. She ran smack into him with her shoulder and slammed to a stop. Daniel looked down at her, feeling her arms around his waist and seeing her upturned face just inches below his. She weighed just slightly more than the average feather.

"You're a moose," she pouted. "How am I supposed to knock you into the snow?"

Daniel couldn't help grinning down at her impish exasperation.

"Boys, how about a little help?" Grace shouted.

In a split second, all five boys pounced. With a shout of protest, Daniel went down in a flurry of arms and legs and snow.

They continued the battle until they had nearly turned themselves into a family of snow-people.

Finally, Grace plowed a huge armload of snow into Daniel's face. "Give up, big man. We've got you. Admit it."

Daniel lay flat on his back with Grace straddling his stomach. Two of the boys were on his legs. John and Mark were clinging to his arms. Somehow Abe was halfway underneath him, with his arms wrapped around Daniel's neck. They were all laughing like loons.

Daniel made one more Herculean effort to throw them all off, chuckling through the mouthful of snow. He managed to knock Mark loose and tip Grace forward until she almost smacked face-first into him, eating a mouthful of the snow that she'd smeared on him.

"Mark, hang on. He's getting away." Her golden eyes sparkled inches from his. Her cherry-red lips curved in laughter and glistened from the gleaming snow. She filled his sight. For a moment the weight of her filled his whole world.

Then his boys were back in the fray and pinned him down again. He quit fighting them from pure exhaustion. "I give." He let all his muscles go lax and lay flat on his back, panting for air. "I give. You win."

Grace began giggling. "We beat him, boys."

All five of his sons cheered and jumped off him. They began dancing around in the snow like a tribe of Indians at a medicine dance.

Grace scrambled off him. Aware of every move she made, Daniel studied her. She didn't seem to notice what she was doing to him. Leaping up, she celebrated with the boys.

Daniel lay there trying to cool down. Then he remembered his son, and the long, frightening day, and the victory over death. He staggered to his feet, his energy returning, and he joined the riot, only occasionally noticing Grace's long, snow-soaked tendrils of hair and the glitter of gold in her hazel eyes. Only now and then, when she sassed him or laughed in his face, did he wonder how her smile tasted.

The snow had buried an overanxious prude. He'd dug up a little spitfire.

At last, with a final laugh, Grace sat right down in the snow. "That's it. I'm tired. Party's over."

The boys all collapsed beside her, and Daniel dropped down on his knees in front of the line of them. They all breathed hard for a time.

"Say, how'd you know it was me Pa threw off his arm?" Mark asked, breathing hard.

Daniel braced himself for whatever trouble Mark might cause, such as telling Grace to go away and putting out that pretty spark in her eyes.

Grace laughed and pushed Mark backward in the snow. Mark just flopped back. He didn't even try to fight.

They'd sleep good tonight, Daniel thought. As long as they didn't have nightmares about John being buried alive. John and their ma.

"Okay, boys, here's how it is." Grace got to her feet. Snow stuck to her front and back, head to toe. She turned to face them.

The boys were in a straggly row in front of her, sprawled back on their elbows while Daniel knelt in the pounded-down snow at Grace's right. He watched as she nodded her head at the boy farthest left and went down the row without hesitation. "Ike, Mark, John, Abe, and Luke." The she jerked her head sideways and looked down at him. "And this big one, who's so hard to get down, is Daniel. Am I right?"

Abe crossed his legs at the ankle and sat forward, plopping his elbows on his knees. "No one knows us apart. Pa's the only one who's mostly always right, but we fool him from time to time."

"You do not." Daniel tossed a handful of snow at his oldest son.

Abe smirked, and Daniel wondered what tricks these scamps had pulled on him over the years.

"Well," Grace said, studying them, "if you set your mind to it, I'm sure you could fool anybody, because you're a smart bunch. But when you're just being yourselves, I never have to think about it twice."

"But what's the difference in us?" Luke set his face into such stubborn lines that Daniel knew they'd turn into wrinkles before he was thirty.

Grace crouched down in front of Luke. "You've got a line right here." She drew a finger down between Luke's eyes. "It's there because you're always thinking, planning. You're the best planner of the bunch, I'd say, always keeping in mind what you've got in front of you to do."

Daniel knew the exact line Grace was talking about.

She turned to Abe. "You and Ike are as alike as two peas in a pod, but right here,"—Grace touched the corner of Abe's mouth—"when you smile, this corner of your mouth curls up first; then the other corner follows."

"With Ike,"—she turned to him and reached past John and Mark—"both corners turn up together."

She put her left thumb and index finger on Ike's mouth and pushed his face into a grin. She smiled at him until he smiled back. She leaned away. "Two great smiles, but as different as your pa is from me."

When Daniel thought of the differences between his wife and himself, it wasn't their smiles that came to mind.

"Now John I know because he's. . ." Grace hesitated.

Daniel knew why. John was the best behaved, the most polite. His son would die of embarrassment if Grace said that out loud, and his brothers would torment him about it forever.

"John's got this little arch in his eyebrow, right here." She touched him, and Daniel watched John enjoy that touch, leaning closer to Grace to make it last. She rested her cold, snowy hand on the side of his face.

Every touch she bestowed poured over the boys like water in the middle of a parched Texas summer. He saw them, each and every one, drink in the pleasure of her touch.

She'd left Mark until last. Daniel covered a grin, wondering what Grace would have to say about this rapscallion. He didn't think Mark's heart was tender, so she couldn't hurt him when she described him. But he could dig in deeper in his wish to have her gone.

"And Mark. Let's see—what do you think, Mark?" She dropped to her knees so she knelt beside Daniel in the trampled snow.

He felt as if they were together. Them against the kids. With Margaret, he'd always felt as though he was parenting mostly alone. Margaret had never been strong. Despite being large and looking hearty as a lumberjack, she'd spent a lot of time in bed, before and after the babies were born. They'd been married only six years, and the first babies had come along quickly. She'd been sick more than not that whole first year. For a year after the twins came along, she'd taken to her bed, mending from the birth. They'd had a couple of good years with the boys mostly tagging him around their Kansas farm. That had been a good time, and Daniel had been firm in his wish for there to be no more young'uns.

He hadn't been strong enough to resist his wife, though. She was a warm, generous woman, given to a lot of laughter and far and away too many tears, especially in the year after Abe's and Ike's birth. One night of weakness between them after nearly three years of holding firm and he'd given her another child.

Looking at Mark, Luke, and John, he corrected himself. He'd given her *three* more children.

"Just one this time, though, Daniel," Margaret had joked, but underneath she'd been serious. Who could have known they'd get three?

Then another year with Margaret either sitting in her rocking chair or staying in bed altogether. Daniel tended the twins, who were four at the time and starting to be real helps around the farm, doing his best to keep them away from their ma, who was more prone to tears than laughter when she was brooding with young'uns. And then the triplets came.

And Margaret went.

He was grateful when Grace interrupted his unhappy memories. It was Grace's fault he'd started thinking of Margaret. Because he could see that if he wasn't careful, there'd be babies between him and his new wife, too.

"The truth of it is"—Grace laid her hand on Mark's cheek—"I just know you by the fire in your eyes. Luke's the planner, figuring out how to make things work."

Daniel noticed she didn't mention planning revenge. That was Luke's greatest talent. But come to think of it, he did have a practical streak. Daniel knew that. He'd just never put it into words.

He watched Mark pretend to ignore Grace's soft hand. But he didn't pull away, and Mark was a boy who didn't put up with anything he didn't like.

"You're the idea man. You come up with one great idea after another." Grace arched her eyebrows at Mark, and he grinned at her, not a repentant bone in his body.

"You come up with them." She jabbed a finger at Mark.

She turned to Abe. "You throw in."

"Ike and John do the hard work to make sure your scheme of the day gets done, and you"—she turned to Luke—"make sure nothing gets missed, no detail is overlooked, and no poor, defenseless teacher or mother is left untormented."

With an indelicate snort, she shook her head. "My word, if General Grant had you boys on his side, the Civil War would have ended the first weekend. How could I not know you apart?"

Daniel looked at his boys. Yes, as alike as peas in a pod. Yes, as different as day and night.

Ike studied her. "No one else can tell between us."

Abe sat up straight. "You know, you've been telling us apart since the first day we came to school, haven't you?"

"She has," Luke said, nodding. "I didn't think much of it—figured you knew where we sat or something—but you've always gotten it right."

Grace shrugged. "It's easy."

"It's hard," Mark insisted.

"Not for me."

Luke said quietly, "For everybody."

Grace grinned at them all. Daniel thought she looked like a child herself down in the snow teasing his boys.

"Well, I'm not apologizing for it. You're as different as can be and that's that."

The boys stared at her with a mixture of fascination and fear, as though maybe she had some magic power that let her know who was who.

As he studied them, his boys so alike, he remembered how this whole snowball fight had started—a celebration of life.

Daniel reached for John and pulled him onto his lap. "I was mighty worried about you for a fact, son. I'm so glad you're all right." He wrapped his arms around John, and although it was completely against their family's view of proper behavior, John hugged him back.

"I'm sorry you was worried, Pa."

"I love you, son. I was so afraid the avalanche had got you." Daniel held his son and marveled at the mass of wiggling, lively, unhurt boy he had in his arms.

And Grace had kept him safe. She'd been there for John in that dark one-room cave. He'd have come out of there terrified if he'd been trapped in there alone. She'd protected his boy. Thinking about it shook him deep and hard. He had a wife now, a wife he didn't want and wished he could get rid of. And God had used her to protect one of Daniel's precious sons.

John, alive and chipper and snug in his arms. Grace, full of sass and vinegar from cheating death and so pretty it hurt to look at her. For just a second his eyes stung, and he caught his breath at the force of his love for his children and what a miracle they were.

Then he remembered who he was and, worse yet, where he was. He'd die before he let the boys see him crying. He broke the spell that had spun itself around him as he relished John's hug.

He pushed John away to arm's length and grinned at him. "Let's get the rest of this snow out of the way so we can get into our house."

He jumped up. With a laugh, he dumped John, none too carefully, in the snow. He turned to the cave and began digging with the shovel he'd brought from the barn.

Grace stood behind him, and he forgot she existed for the most part. But she was a woman, so of course she didn't let him forget for long. "We're not living in this cave. You are building us a proper house, Daniel Reeves, and you're doing it starting today."

Daniel quit digging and turned around.

Abe took the shovel away from him and kept working while the other boys pushed at snow with their hands.

He looked into Grace's sparkling eyes. "Did I just hear you right? Did you just *order* me to build a house?"

Grace plunked her fists on her slender hips, wrapped in those silly-looking pants of Abe's. "Of course I didn't. Because you are a smart man, and you have already seen that we cannot continue to live in that cave."

Daniel wanted to argue with her. It seemed almost required, considering they'd done nothing but argue since the day they'd first clapped eyes on each other. Then Daniel looked over his shoulder at the steep, snow-covered hill above the door.

He turned back to her. "We haven't been here that long. I didn't know snow could bury the place like this. I. . .I'm so sorry, Grace." He took a step nearer to her, conscious of his snoopy sons and their sharp ears. He caught her upper arms, and she lifted her fists away from her hips in surprise. "Thank you for taking care of John in there. I'm sure it must have been dark and frightening. . .and. . .I just. . .I never thought. . . I dragged those windfalls right above the house. You could have been. . . John could have been. . ." Daniel thought he might disgrace himself.

She smiled and arched her delicate brows. "We made it out, Daniel. We're all right. Don't think up things to worry about that didn't happen."

Daniel nodded and returned her smile with a sheepish one of his own. "Heaven knows there's enough that *does* happen out here, we don't have to make stuff up."

"I'll bet that's right." Grace shook her head. "Now how about that house?"

Snow flew past him from the fast-moving shovel, burying his feet.

"I don't see any reason we should wait another day to start building."

The boys, listening just as he suspected, began whooping and hollering loudly enough to raise the dead. The snow flew all the faster, as if they could begin building as soon as the door was clear.

He turned to them. "I didn't know you boys wanted a house."

Mark yelled, "Neither did we, Pa!"

"But it's a great idea." Ike jerked the shovel out of Abe's hands and started digging.

Abe yelled and dived at Ike, and the two of them rolled into Mark and John.

"Should the boys be playing right underneath where an avalanche just came down?"

"Reckon not." Daniel shook his head at the horseplay and left his boys to their wrestling. "We've got a nice thick stand of trees to use for lumber. In fact, we brought so many windfalls down that hill with the avalanche that we've got a good start on the logs."

"And since we've just had the snowslide and a nasty storm," Grace pointed out, "you'll have a real good idea of where to build out of the wind and drifts and away from the danger of a future avalanche."

Daniel was struck for the first time that he'd married a schoolteacher. She was a right smart woman.

He glanced over his shoulder at the mountain looming overhead of his front door. The hillside looked swept clean of most of the snow, but he'd never again allow his children to sleep in there.

"I don't like the look of that hill even now. We're not spending another night in that cave."

Luke jumped out of the cloud of snow he and his brothers were stirring up. "Are we gonna sleep outside, Pa?"

Daniel noticed the sharp-thinking furrow between his son's white eyebrows that Grace had pointed out.

"Nope, tonight we sleep in the barn with the horses. It'll be cold, because we can't build a fire in there, but the night isn't bitter and we'll cuddle up." He turned away from the treacherous hill above his home and looked back at Grace. He froze as surely as if he'd been turned to ice by the now-faded blizzard.

She smiled, her expression playful and warm.

And he thawed under the golden fire in her eyes.

He thought of the weight of her on his body, and he remembered earlier in the week when he'd fallen down on top of her. He had a wife. One who needed him to cuddle up to her in the night. How else could he keep her warm? He smiled back.

Then he remembered the price he'd paid for giving in to a man's weakness. He'd killed his first wife. He'd die himself before he'd kill another one. The smile faded from his face.

She looked confused and hurt when he backed up a step.

He tore his eyes away from her, the effort as painful as tearing his own flesh. He turned toward the cave. "That's enough, boys. Since we're not moving back in, all we gotta do is get our things out. Let's start by moving the table and benches to the barn. Everybody grab something."

He charged into that hole in the ground feeling as if he were running away from the devil himself. As he grabbed the table, he realized that he was doing exactly that. Temptation. Straight from the devil himself. He'd given in before.

Margaret had been too warm and giving to be resisted. But only a fool reaches into a fire after he has been burned. Daniel Reeves had been burned badly, and he was no fool. He began dragging the table. Ike and Abe got the other end and lifted. The three younger boys were wrestling over the benches, arguing and laughing.

Daniel walked backward, glancing just once at Grace's uncertain expression.

As he passed her, she said, "Daniel, did I do something wrong?"

"There're things in there you can tote, Grace," he said as he passed her, looking anywhere but at her. "Make yourself useful."

Abe and Ike looked at him and frowned.

Grace lost all her sass. "Of course, Daniel. I'll be glad to help." She gave him one last unhappy look and turned to the cave.

They moved the rest of their meager belongings in a matter of minutes.

Daniel made supper that night. He went in the cave and cooked it, then brought their steaks and eggs and potatoes and biscuits and milk to the barn for them to eat. Everything was cold.

Especially Daniel's heart.

SEVENTEEN

She didn't know what she'd said or done to make him mad, but Grace's stomach twisted when she looked at Daniel's angry eyes. She let it bother her for about an hour, about the length of time it took for them to sit down in the waning light to eat their cold supper of steak, eggs, potatoes, biscuits, and milk. The meal was a vast improvement over the wretched meal she'd cooked at noon. Then she remembered what she'd learned today.

"Great is thy faithfulness." God had been faithful to her. She could only be faithful in return. For Grace, being faithful meant being brave, having the courage to trust God with her life.

Her bravery didn't extend to grabbing Daniel by the ear and twisting until he told her what was the matter. But it did mean taking charge of the boys. "All right, this corner of the barn is farthest from the wind. Let's pitch some straw onto the floor. No reason the animals should have it better than we do."

The boys, subdued by their father's sudden bad temper and their own hard work, obeyed instantly. Daniel helped, too. They built a comfortable little bed for themselves and worked up a nice glowing warmth in their muscles.

Grace lay down, not willing to put on her nightgown and wear it in front of the boys. She had no way to wash anything out, either. She wondered how long she had to live in the same clothes night and day. Pulling John into her arms on one side and with Ike up against her on

441

the other, she tried to relax.

She didn't look at Daniel, who had slept at her side until now. She had no desire to cuddle up to the cranky old bear. As they all cuddled together, they barely noticed the cold weather. The sun having long since set, they were all heavy lidded from the long day's tension and labor.

Lying awake, Grace heard the breathing of her sons all around her and the heavier breathing of her husband, about two children away. She gave a mental shrug. She didn't know what to make of the heat in his eyes, and she didn't know how to speak of it. The ways between men and women were a mystery to her.

The only man she'd really known was Parrish, and Daniel was certainly a step up from him. She'd done poorly being on her own as a teacher. She thought of going to bed cold and hungry every night. At least she'd been earning money for Hannah.

How would Hannah manage without her? She'd received one letter since Grace had sent the first money. Hannah had insisted she stop giving away every dime she made. She said they had found a safe place to stay and that generous people gave them food. All the children were in school and doing well. Grace hoped that meant Hannah could manage without eighteen extra dollars a month. Since she could do nothing about it, Grace committed Hannah and the little girls to God and forced herself to quit fretting.

All in all, moody husband or not, she decided she'd made an improvement in her lot in life.

She prayed before she went to bed, but her prayers were different than they'd been since she'd run away from Parrish. She returned to the prayers of her childhood.

Give me courage, Lord. Help me be brave. Give me wisdom. Give me strength. She thought that about covered what she needed to survive. She added, *Help me love these boys as my own children.*

As she said it, she smiled into the night. Sleep pulled her into the cold darkness. She didn't need to ask for that again. God had already given her an abundance of love for the little monsters. *Thank You, God.*

They awoke the next morning to the sound of dripping. Grace burrowed her way out of the straw in the murky morning light and realized that it was almost too warm buried in blankets and children.

She gave John's shoulder a playful shove. "Get up, sleepyhead. We've got a lot to do today."

John mumbled and rolled away from her. Then he sneezed and shoved a stick of straw out of his nose and sat up with a big grin on his face. "Mornin', Ma. Why's it a big day?"

"It's a big day because, starting today, your pa's going to build us a house." She announced it loudly, and by the time she was done, all her boys—all six of them, considering Daniel was acting like a child—were sitting up rubbing their eyes, and most of them—five to be exact—were grinning.

Scowling, Daniel shoved the straw away from his legs. The boys began climbing out of their makeshift bed, scattering straw far and wide, yelling and pushing at each other for no reason Grace could imagine.

Mark tripped over her stomach and raced, shrieking, out of the barn.

Grace looked at Daniel, who calmly stood up out of the cattle forage. "Why did he yell like that? He sounded like a wolf was chasing him out of the barn."

Daniel shrugged.

"He's getting first turn at the outhouse," Ike grumbled. Stumbling over feet that had started growing ahead of his body, he ran out of the barn, too, hollering loudly. The rest of the boys were on his heels.

Grace shook her head and stood up. She whacked at the straw clinging to her then looked Daniel in the eye. He didn't seem to have eaten vinegar for breakfast; his face wasn't all twisted up and sour. Cautious, so as not to set off his temper again, she asked, "How do you build a house, Daniel?"

Daniel cocked his head to the side with a little one-shouldered shrug. "Hard work, long hours, lots of slivers in your fingers."

Grace narrowed her eyes at him. "That could describe half the jobs on the earth."

"Why don't you let me show you? Talkin's a waste of time." Daniel walked to the wide-open barn door and shouted until her ears rang, "First chores, boys, then breakfast. Then we cut down a passel of trees; then we build a house."

His announcement was met with more yelling.

Grace thought it sounded as though the boys were unhappy, but maybe the high-pitched racket was joy. She couldn't tell much difference in the sounds they made. Maybe she'd pick it up in time.

He looked back over his shoulder. "I'm gonna get the fire going in the cave and throw in the taters. Then I'll milk the cow. I don't want you going in there. I'm afraid of all that snow clinging to the hill overhead. You and the boys stay well away."

"I should be the one to go in," Grace said, striding toward him. "If another avalanche comes down, you need to be outside digging."

Daniel shook his head. "I'll go in prepared to dig from the inside. I'll be in and out quick. What I don't want is any of you stopping near the door. I can come out quick and get myself clear of the base of that hill, so I'll be safe. But no one is to hang around near the entrance in the meantime."

"I could go in and out quickly just as well as you could," Grace said in exasperation. "And I could be cooking while you're doing chores. It'll save us time starting on the house."

"No, it won't," Daniel said flatly.

"Yes, it will. How can you say it won't?"

" 'Cause it'll slow us down trying to chew on those burned biscuits of yours."

Grace gasped and looked up at him, her feelings hurt.

He laughed in her face.

"You're just lucky I'm in a hurry, then." Grace spun around before she could smile back at him. His handsome smile did strange things to her insides—made parts of her melt while the rest of her shivered. She didn't understand it. She only knew that she'd felt this way yesterday, right before he'd gotten surly as an old grizzly bear. She decided she didn't want to risk that again. Odd that her being happy seemed to make him decidedly unhappy.

She said over her shoulder as she walked away, "Well, if you have to do it yourself, then I suggest you get a hustle on, Mr. Reeves. The sun's already lifting high into the sky." She marched away then stopped short and turned back to him. "I thought you said the boys were racing to the outhouse." She pointed to the little building, standing alone.

Daniel snorted. "No, Ike said Mark was getting first turn at the outhouse. The other boys just—" Daniel stopped talking.

Grace watched his cheeks turn red on his fair-skinned face. His blond hair, badly in need of a trim, hung down his forehead and to his collar from under the Stetson he always clamped on his head.

"What's the matter?" She took a curious step toward him, amazed at the blush that colored his whole face.

Staring at the ground, he said, "Um. . .nothin'. It's just. . .well. . . uh. . .boys can, well they can use an outhouse or not." Daniel peeked up at her for one second, then turned and headed for the cave at a near run—a handy place to hide until he quit blushing.

Grace looked around. None of the boys was visible. It finally dawned on her what he meant. She turned and headed for the outhouse at a near run—a handy place to hide until she quit blushing.

EIGHTEEN

"G ood news. They've hired a new teacher in Mosqueros." Clay rode in from his trip to town.

Adam paused with his load of sloshing water buckets.

"Wash day?" Clay nodded at the bucket.

When had Clay gotten to be so long-winded? They were water buckets. What else could they be for? Adam shook his head in disgust and didn't comment further on the obvious. "A teacher already? That was fast. Last I heard, they figured to close the school down until spring at least, while they hunted up a new instructor."

"A guy came through figuring to settle in for the winter. He's educated, so Royce convinced him to take over the school."

Adam lowered the buckets to the ground. This was his fifth trip back and forth to the spring on this cold winter afternoon. He was keeping ahead of Sophie, so a break wouldn't hurt a thing. "They just hired some drifter?"

Clay shrugged. "Surely the school board checked him out."

"How?" Adam crossed his arms.

Clay jerked one shoulder. "I'd like to talk to him myself before I let him take charge of all those children. I'll ask Royce about it at church."

Adam nodded and picked up the buckets. "If he don't shape up, we could just turn the girls loose on him."

Clay's hearty laughter followed Adam into the house.

The door swung open before Adam had to set the buckets down to grab the knob. Tillie greeted him with her shy smile and downcast eyes. She sure was a pretty thing.

He tore his eyes away from her and saw Sophie at the cookstove hoisting a steaming pail of water with a thick towel protecting her hands. Sophie was busy, but she still found time to smirk at him. He rushed over and relieved her of the pail.

"I can get it, Adam. It doesn't weigh a thing."

"Just behave yourself. I'd leave you to it if I wasn't here, but as long as I'm nearby, let me do some lifting for you."

Sophie sniffed in disdain, but she let him have his way.

Mandy knelt in front of the fire with a wooden tub and the washboard, scrubbing away to the sound of splashing water. Her fine blond hair escaped from its braid and hung bedraggled around her damp brow.

Beth hefted a basket, woven out of slender branches, off of the kitchen table. It was filled with damp clothes to take out in the cold to line dry.

Sally stood by the table, wielding a hot flatiron on the stack of clothes Beth must have just brought in. A steaming tub of water took up the rest of the table.

Beth went out the door.

Laura giggled as she dashed around them all; then she toddled her way toward the fireplace. Adam set the pail on the floor and rushed to grab the baby. Sophie would have gotten to her in plenty of time, but maybe she'd worry and that'd wipe the smirk off her face.

He caught Laura high against his chest and bounced her until she started shrieking with joy. "Clay just came home from town and said the school will be starting up again right away. They found a new teacher."

The girls all groaned. "Ma, we don't want. . ." All three of them set to whining until Adam thought his ears would bleed.

"They found someone already?" Sophie, despite a belly that looked far bigger than normal to Adam, took Laura and walked to the hearth to scold the little girl about the danger of fire.

Between the whining and the scolding, Adam almost had Tillie to himself. He stepped up close to her and whispered, "I'd like to go riding with you, Tillie."

She'd been staring at the girls and him in the way she had, as if the whole family struck her with a sense of awe. When he spoke, she lifted her chin and started shaking her head.

Before she could say a word, he added, "I'd like to talk to you about my life here and the changes this country has seen since the war ended."

A quick glance around the room told him no one was paying attention. "I think I can put your mind at ease about someone coming after you and taking you back as his property. There are decent men hereabouts. None of them would stand by while someone abused a woman or took her somewhere against her will, no matter the color of her skin."

Her eyes widened, and her expression was equal parts doubt and hope. "Oh, if only that were true."

"Come riding. There is a lot you've missed and maybe a lot you need to say, especially to a man who knows some of what you've been through. Anything we talk about would be private. You have my word on that."

Tillie hesitated until Adam was sure she'd say no. Then her shoulders squared and her chin lifted. Adam had seen her do that before, as if she was having a talk with herself and reminding herself to be brave.

"I'd like that. Yes. You look cold. We could do it another time."

"I've been carrying water buckets for a couple of hours. I'm warm from all the exercise. There's no need to wait."

"Right now I need to rinse the next load of clothes."

Sophie came up beside them, stomach first. "No, you go ahead, Tillie. The girls and I can finish. Having all your help has put us hours ahead."

Adam looked at Sophie, and there was no teasing smirk this time.

Only the kind eyes of a woman who was like a daughter to him.

Tillie insisted on staying. She could have stood up to him, but Adam knew she didn't have a hope of changing Sophie's mind once it was made up.

Sophie had her convinced in no time. She patted Tillie on the arm. "Take my coat."

Adam was careful not to look Sophie in the eye as he held the door for Tillie. He never could abide a gloating woman.

Adam led the way toward the barn, with Tillie fussing with the fur bonnet Sophie had provided.

Finally, as they entered the barn, Tillie looked up. A black woman couldn't blush so anyone would notice it. But Adam was sure Tillie had pink under those dark cheeks by the wariness in her eyes.

"I'm really sorry I beat you up, Adam. I hope you're feeling better."

His pride pricked at his temper. "You only got a hit in because I was being careful of you."

"But your eye was barely open."

"You didn't hurt me a bit." Adam stalked into the first stall and threw a bridle on the gentle mare the girls sometimes rode.

"And there was a bruise as clear as day on your—"

"I'm fine!" Adam forced himself to unclench his jaw before his teeth broke.

The mare widened its eyes and danced sideways. He worked on getting both horses ready then went to boost Tillie into the saddle.

She swung herself up so effortlessly he had to reassess everything he'd thought of her. Except he hadn't thought of her. . .much. Well, some. A lot, honestly. Constantly.

They rode single file out of the wide barn door and headed up the trail.

"I've got something I'd like to show you." Adam set a brisk pace, hoping the woman wouldn't have enough breath to spare to apologize yet again. He skirted along the bluffs north of the house, right along the tree line in the general direction of Reeves Canyon.

When he came to an arroyo that cut down out of the hills, he followed it, noticing with relief that it hadn't filled in with snow like Reeves Canyon had. He hadn't been up this way in the winter before. He wasn't sure just what to expect.

They rode up the mountainside through the gap, smoothed by runoff water, and entered a pretty valley slanting upward for several miles.

Adam stopped and stared at the snow-covered beauty. He still slept in Clay's bunkhouse, but come spring this would be his home.

"I've homesteaded this land." He swept his arm to encompass the whole valley.

Tillie gasped. "They let a black man homestead?"

Adam looked away from the site of his dream for the future. His own land, near his beloved family, the McClellens. "Yes, they did."

"I can't imagine." Tillie looked from the land to Adam and back.

"There's a lot you've yet to imagine, Till." Adam turned his horse so he faced her, their legs nearly touching. "You're not the first slave that wasn't set free when the war ended."

Tillie's gaze locked on his. "I never said such a thing."

"They can't take you back. The law is on your side. But the best protection you've got is to tell me about it. What if they did try and take you—"

"They will."

Adam ached when he heard the fear in her voice. "If they did, I'd come and get you. I'd bring a posse along. Clay would come—a lot of men would. You'd better tell me about it so I know where to come look."

"If no one knows I'm here, Master Virgil—" She lifted her head, her neck stretched as elegantly as a swan. "I mean *Virgil*." She spat the name. "I won't call that man master ever again. He can't find me."

Adam nodded. "I think you'll be safer if I know, but that's your decision. When you trust me enough, you'll tell me."

"I. . .I do trust you, Adam. It's not that."

"It's just a habit to keep things to yourself. And it's a habit not to make yourself vulnerable. I know the feeling." Adam nodded. "But maybe someday you'll be ready. And in the meantime, if something happens to you, even if you don't tell me where to hunt, we'll still find you. There are some first-rate trackers at the McClellen place, so we'll find you."

Adam leaned closer to her. "You're safe, Till. You're free. I've never been a slave, but my best friends in the world were. I ranched with them for ten years. I know the difference between slave and free. Once you begin to trust it, you won't believe how sweet the air smells."

Tillie's mouth curled down, and a breath caught in her throat. "Free. I've never really thought about it. I only knew about a month ago that the war had ended. He always kept me chained. I knew that the chain wasn't strong. I was sure with work I could break one of the rustier links. But I could never figure out what the point of running was. Run where? To what? Then he told me about the war." Tillie's hand went to her face.

Adam could still see the slight swelling.

"He needed to hurt more than my body for once, and Mas—I mean Virgil—gloated about it. I bided my time; then I broke a link in my chains and ran. I hid out in a baggage car on a train and rode a long, long way. I had as much food as I could carry, no money, and only the clothes on my back. I just found a spot and tucked myself away. Then they found me and threw me off. I walked until I found a wagon train with a big line of supply wagons and hid in there for days on end. They found me, too, and threw me off again. I've been walking ever since. I've been out of food for days. I. . .You saved me, Adam. I wouldn't have lasted through the night in that storm. And I thanked you for that by giving you a beating."

"You didn't give me a—"

"I'm so sorry."

Her apology was so kind Adam decided to let her have her way. For now. "Apology accepted then. Just don't make a habit of pounding on me, okay?"

Adam smiled, and Tillie smiled back. A glorious smile that lit up her whole face.

"How do you like my valley?"

"I love it."

"What do you like best about it?"

Tillie's smile widened, and Adam could sense that she was really having the first moment of understanding what it meant to be free.

"I love that it's yours."

And that about summed it up for Adam, too. "Let's head for the ranch."

Daniel pointed to the canyon gap, visible in the distance, as he and Ike prepared to chop down another tree. "It's filled almost all the way to the top."

Ike turned and looked where Daniel pointed. He dropped his ax, missing his foot by an inch. "We'll never get out of here."

Daniel felt his stomach sinking. "I reckon not. We're socked into the 6R solid till we've had a good long thaw."

"But the rest of the snow is almost gone." Abe came up beside them, not watching where he walked as he stared at the canyon mouth.

Everywhere Daniel could hear the sound of running water. The steep mountainside where they were chopping trees was clear except on the north side of the trees where the sun never hit. When it melted, it ran off because, Lord have mercy, it was steep. Daniel found out that cutting down trees wasn't much work if gravity worked alongside you. All he had to do was pick the right tree and hack away. The tree fell all the way to the building site.

He'd been chopping trees for two days solid, barely taking time away to eat and sleep. By now the land around the cave and barn was clear; the bulk of the melting snow had run off instead of soaking in because the ground was sloped.

The house site was one of the few level spots on Daniel's property. It had taken a woman and an avalanche—to Daniel's way of thinking, one and the same—to make him carve out a real home for his family. The 6R was going to be a bona fide ranch once this house was up. He was glad she'd thought of it.

"Will we starve, Pa?" Ike picked up his ax.

Daniel wondered if he should be letting ten-years-olds handle something so dangerous as that well-honed ax. "Nope. We've potatoes and flour to last the winter and eggs, milk, and beef to last a lifetime."

Daniel waved at the longhorns that grazed far and wide in the vast canyon. "God's been good to us, boys. We're wealthy men. We've all we need to last forever. The only thing town has for us is luxuries, like apples until we can grow our own. But we can get along without anyone else, and that's something a man can take satisfaction in."

Daniel looked down over his valley and felt rich as a king. He had found this place while scouting the area, looking for good grassland.

"Remember when John found this place for us, Pa?"

Daniel pulled his head away from daydreams. He smiled down at Ike. It took young'uns to keep a man honest, it seemed.

"Sure I do. He'd got up to foolishness as usual."

"We were just playin', Pa. No harm in a little hide-and-seek."

"There's harm in it when one of you hides so well he can't find his way back to camp."

Abe and Ike laughed. Daniel grinned then laughed along with them. "John getting lost was the luckiest day of my life. Because when I trailed him in here—"

"Into what looked like a solid wall of stone," Abe reminded him.

"Yeah, I didn't see that notch in the wall until I was ten feet from it. Even then I'd'a missed it if John hadn't left footprints."

"It's still hard to see," Ike added. "Half the people in Mosqueros can't figure out where the 6R is because of the way the one side of the rock juts out farther than the other and the two sides blend together to look solid."

"And you tailed him into that cut and found our home," Abe finished with satisfaction.

The hidden gap had opened into this lost paradise in the rocky west Texas plateau country. Daniel had hurried to town, homesteaded one hundred and sixty acres, and then bought ten thousand more acres for pennies from the state of Texas. His home was registered as a mountainous wasteland on the surveyor's map. He'd registered his 6R brand, bought a small herd of longhorns, and still had most of the money he'd earned selling his Kansas farm.

"So God and this rich land He created gives us all we need and more besides." Daniel nodded his head. He breathed deeply of the cold pine-scented air. The damp soil and fresh-cut wood were better than the rarest perfume.

"An' you brought a heap of supplies with you when you brung Ma. It's a wonder you could manage to fit her in with the flour sacks."

Daniel wondered again exactly what Grace had been doing in his wagon. Had a man really chased her? "Yep, it was a tight squeeze, all right." He thought of how pretty she'd looked yesterday, wrestling with his boys, trying to tackle him, and sitting on him.

Daniel jerked his thoughts away from trouble and looked at the stand of trees. "We've got about another two hours of chopping, boys; then we'll have us enough to build a house." He glanced at his sons, still transfixed by the snow-packed gap. It scared him a little, too.

He looked on up the mountainside. He could climb out of here if he needed to, but it would be a couple of days of hard climbing on loose rock with hundreds of feet to fall if he missed his footing. Then if he got out, it was a fifteen-mile walk to town, which he could manage in a day, or about ten miles to the nearest ranch, where the McClellens lived. Then what help he found would have to make the dangerous trek back with him. If an emergency cropped up—say, if the boys needed a doctor—it would take a minimum of three days to get out and back in. He couldn't get help in time.

Daniel looked at his boys and the sharp axes, and his gut clenched.

He almost ordered them to leave the chopping to him and go do the animal chores. He clenched his jaw to keep from saying the words of caution. He couldn't live his life like that.

Then he thought of Margaret dying. A doctor couldn't get there in time to help her, either. He breathed a sigh of relief that he didn't have to worry about Grace and a baby. He believed her that there wasn't one on the way. He still thought she'd run from a man because she'd mixed herself up wrongly with him. But that didn't mean a baby.

Then he thought of her sweet smile and knew what his husbandly rights were. The Bible was clear about that. A woman was to meet her husband's needs. And since a woman inspired most of those needs, it was well and good that she met them. The way she smiled at him made him wonder if she wouldn't even welcome a child from him. Temptation made him shudder.

The Good Book said Jesus was tempted of the devil for forty days in the wilderness. So Jesus knew just how Daniel felt. He breathed a prayer for strength to withstand the temptation.

He looked back up the steep cliff and thought of the doctor and how far he lived from town. He looked at his boys. They weren't in nearly as much danger with those axes as he was with his brand-spanking-new wife.

"Let's get these trees down, boys."

Abe and Ike looked away from the gap and lost themselves in hard work. Daniel did his best to sweat every ounce of temptation out of his body. Or at least make himself so tired he didn't have the strength to give in to it.

Daniel thought ruefully that he was a very strong man.

NINETEEN

As the sun set on the third day of chopping, Grace served supper to the usually riotous group. Their eyes were heavy with fatigue, and they could barely chew their food—and that was due to exhaustion more than her cooking.

Trying to hold her tongue in front of her sons, Grace wanted to berate Daniel for pushing them so hard. When she'd announced so boldly he was going to build the family a house, she hadn't meant to add yet another burden to the boys. She needed to put a stop to it.

She squared her shoulders. If Daniel avoided being alone with her all day, every day, they'd just have to have it out with witnesses.

"Mark, you little rat!" Grace covered her ears as Ike shrieked as if he were being murdered. He ducked under the table and almost tipped it over.

Daniel steadied it without so much as a pause in his eating.

She had to get Daniel to let up on the boys, and she had to teach these little monsters some manners. "Daniel, we need to talk."

No one heard her over the shouted insults being tossed back and forth between Ike and Mark.

Grace clamped her mouth closed. There was no point in discussing anything now. The boys were hungry and tired. They didn't have enough energy to listen—only enough to yell and fight. Or maybe she didn't have enough energy.

She forced herself to say nothing as Mark dropped from his bench

The room in her shirt—or rather Daniel's shirt

458

and disappeared under the table for the third time during the meal.

The barn proved to be a more pleasant place to live than the cave. And now that the temperature was more moderate, they had gladly remained here even though enough snow had melted and no further danger of an avalanche existed.

None of them suggested moving back into the cave. The boys didn't show it, but fear haunted Grace, and at least John had to feel a bit of it. She'd lay awake at night and remember that glowing ember fading, dying from lack of air. Then she'd shake herself and remember to be brave.

Thinking she might calm the riot and then be able to bring up more important subjects, she tried to engage Daniel in polite conversation. "Well, have you picked a site for the cabin?" She'd learned about pleasant talk while waiting on people at the railroad diner. She'd mainly worked in drab, dirty little restaurants, moving from one cow town to the next. But that railroad diner was a clean, refined establishment. She'd stayed there until she'd found a place that would give her a job as a teacher.

Luke yelped with pain and jumped and knocked his stomach against the table so hard it upset the milk cup. Fortunately, it was empty.

Daniel set the cup to rights without comment.

Mark stuck his smirking face out from under the table and growled at Luke.

Grace breathed through her nose so the threatening words wouldn't explode.

John patted her on the knee and tilted his head toward his brother and sighed.

Grace smiled.

"There's only about one level place in this whole canyon," Daniel said. "It's just to the uphill side of the barn."

"Right by the stack of trees you've been letting fall down the mountain. Daniel, you won't have to worry about dragging them a long way."

"Yep, that's why I cut 'em there. Didn't you know that? The mountainside is covered with trees. I could have cut them anywhere."

"Well, you never said. I guess I was thinking you decided to let them fall there because it was well away from the ranch yard where the trees could come crashing down and kill us or the animals."

Daniel shrugged.

Ike screeched in pain and punched at Mark under the table, who laughed uproariously and popped up into his seat again beside Daniel.

"Gotcha," Mark said with a smug grin.

Ike seemed about to throw his steak bones at Mark.

Grace grabbed them and laid them out of his reach.

Ike didn't seem to notice or care about her displeasure.

"A man hadn't oughta hafta say everything out loud that goes on in his head, Grace. You should figure what I'm thinking and save us some time." Daniel began scooping white, mealy potato out of his charred, black potato skin with his fingers.

Grace tried to imagine a better way to cook the poor charcoal-colored spud. If only she had a pan. Of course Daniel wasn't even letting her cook much, which rankled her. He refused to start the stove in the cave unless he was there to do the cooking. He carried the only matches they had in his shirt pocket, and she didn't know how to light it without them. John said he knew, but his pa had forbidden him or any of the other boys to teach her.

She shook her head. "So we're building it on that level spot. I want to help, Daniel. I'll do anything you say." She looked at him.

"Anything?" He looked back, and after he'd looked too long, she shivered.

He suddenly turned rapt attention to eating his potato.

Grace tried to figure out what about the word "anything" had bothered him so much. She mentally shrugged her shoulders. As long as he let her help build, she didn't care. "You know, Daniel, the trouble with expecting me to read your mind is sometimes you aren't really thinking what I think you're thinking."

Daniel looked back at her.

The collar on her shirt—or rather Daniel's shirt, because she still

He almost ordered them to leave the chopping to him and go do the animal chores. He clenched his jaw to keep from saying the words of caution. He couldn't live his life like that.

Then he thought of Margaret dying. A doctor couldn't get there in time to help her, either. He breathed a sigh of relief that he didn't have to worry about Grace and a baby. He believed her that there wasn't one on the way. He still thought she'd run from a man because she'd mixed herself up wrongly with him. But that didn't mean a baby.

Then he thought of her sweet smile and knew what his husbandly rights were. The Bible was clear about that. A woman was to meet her husband's needs. And since a woman inspired most of those needs, it was well and good that she met them. The way she smiled at him made him wonder if she wouldn't even welcome a child from him. Temptation made him shudder.

The Good Book said Jesus was tempted of the devil for forty days in the wilderness. So Jesus knew just how Daniel felt. He breathed a prayer for strength to withstand the temptation.

He looked back up the steep cliff and thought of the doctor and how far he lived from town. He looked at his boys. They weren't in nearly as much danger with those axes as he was with his brand-spanking-new wife.

"Let's get these trees down, boys."

Abe and Ike looked away from the gap and lost themselves in hard work. Daniel did his best to sweat every ounce of temptation out of his body. Or at least make himself so tired he didn't have the strength to give in to it.

Daniel thought ruefully that he was a very strong man.

NINETEEN

As the sun set on the third day of chopping, Grace served supper to the usually riotous group. Their eyes were heavy with fatigue, and they could barely chew their food—and that was due to exhaustion more than her cooking.

Trying to hold her tongue in front of her sons, Grace wanted to berate Daniel for pushing them so hard. When she'd announced so boldly he was going to build the family a house, she hadn't meant to add yet another burden to the boys. She needed to put a stop to it.

She squared her shoulders. If Daniel avoided being alone with her all day, every day, they'd just have to have it out with witnesses.

"Mark, you little rat!" Grace covered her ears as Ike shrieked as if he were being murdered. He ducked under the table and almost tipped it over.

Daniel steadied it without so much as a pause in his eating.

She had to get Daniel to let up on the boys, and she had to teach these little monsters some manners. "Daniel, we need to talk."

No one heard her over the shouted insults being tossed back and forth between Ike and Mark.

Grace clamped her mouth closed. There was no point in discussing anything now. The boys were hungry and tired. They didn't have enough energy to listen—only enough to yell and fight. Or maybe she didn't have enough energy.

She forced herself to say nothing as Mark dropped from his bench

456

wore the same outfit—suddenly fit too tight. Grace unbuttoned the top button so she could breathe and maybe cool off a little. And she wasn't reading his mind worth anything, because she wasn't conjuring up a single thought about the house.

"So do you start building tomorrow?" Excitement rose in her that didn't seem reasonable. *Of course, every woman wants a house,* she imagined. But the thought of its imminent construction made her breath come short and her heart race as she looked into Daniel's eyes. She remembered her promise to God to be brave, and somehow, returning Daniel's look took true courage.

Daniel flashed a look at her hot enough to cook the potatoes with neither pan nor fire. "I can work up the dirt on the house site for a while before dark."

He got up so abruptly he knocked his seat over. Snagging his coat and hat, he almost ran out of the barn. "I can use a hand, boys."

The boys bolted what scraps of food were left on the table, yelling as they gobbled and ran out after him.

Since it was already full dark, Grace didn't have any idea what he planned to do. Maybe he could work by starlight.

She sighed and cleaned up the supper dishes—that is to say, the cup and fork. It took thirty seconds. Then she followed after her family.

"So you've done a lot of teaching in your life, Mr. Parrish?" Royce Badje asked.

Parrish watched the banker puff out his chest. The arrogant little man looked as though he thought the world rose and set at his command. Parrish assumed his humble teacher's voice, even though it was all he could do not to jeer at the pompous little pigeon of a man. "Yes, sir. I've been a teacher all my life. After my wife died, I couldn't stay in Chicago anymore. I decided to go west. I've traveled around some and planned to spend the winter in Mosqueros. I wasn't thinking of finding work here, but the teacher's job being open seems providential. I'd like to settle and begin a new life."

Parrish already had the job, but he'd been asked to visit with a few folks after church, and he'd played his part and agreed easily. He'd led everyone to the schoolhouse.

"You'll have your hands full, Mr. Parrish." Clay McClellen sat a bit slumped in the undersized school desk. He should have looked ridiculous, but McClellen had watchful eyes. Parrish concealed his contempt even though McClellen was obviously a crude piece of western trash. This whole land was filled with the dregs of humanity as far as Parrish could see. But not by so much as a sideways glance or the least twist of his lips did he reveal his disdain for the coarse clothing or the uncultivated manners.

Sophie McClellen sat next to her husband. This should have been man's work, but she'd come along and no one had told her to leave. "The last teacher left because the children were unruly. They'll keep you on your toes."

The way Mrs. McClellen talked, Parrish knew she spoke of Grace. *So Grace quit, eh?* Did no one in this town even know she'd been fleeing when she left?

"She ran off and got married is what she did," Badje said, pulling his black greatcoat around him in the cold little schoolroom.

Clay and Sheriff Everett grinned.

Parrish sat up straighter. Grace, married?

McClellen, even though he was amused and sharing a joke with the sheriff, never quite stopped watching. The slovenly cowboy had noticed Parrish's reaction and narrowed his watchful blue eyes. Parrish forced himself to relax.

Sophie shook her head. "Those Reeves boys will eat her for dinner."

How had Grace gone into that gap, hidden in a wagon, and ended up married? Parrish considered how a husband would complicate his taking of Grace. His legal claim had just been severed—that was for dead certain.

Parrish's blood ran as cold as the winter wind. Everything would be more complicated now. He should just ride on. Then he thought of his night dreams and daydreams. He thought of Grace, begging and crying and promising, under the thud of his fists, never to disobey him again.

Parrish closed his eyes for a second and fought for control. He opened his eyes, wiping every expression from his face.

McClellen's humor had evaporated. "Where is it you say you've taught before?"

Parrish was prepared for this question. He produced five letters of recommendation from his pocket. A passing good forger, Parrish had been mindful to carry them with him at all times. Some of them were years old and showed it. Some were fresher. They were written in different kinds of ink on different types of paper. Most were from Chicago, where he'd been careful to use names of people who were dead. One he'd written himself only yesterday, dated for last spring, from a town far enough away that it would be impossible to check the authenticity.

He ruthlessly controlled a smile as he thought of how his former prison warden would feel about having his name listed as a proud school board member, recommending Parrish highly.

"I don't know anybody in Chicago. And I've never heard of this last town. There's no way to check these letters." McClellen tossed them to the sheriff with little more than a glance, as if to say they weren't worth the paper they were printed on.

Parrish saw Mrs. McClellen pick up on her husband's attitude. Her expression mirrored her spouse's.

He forced himself to smile. "Well, that's true enough. If you wish to test me, I'm sure I can pass any exam you have." He knew he could do it. He'd been a good student. And what he couldn't do honestly, he could cheat his way through. "That's the way most teachers are hired, isn't it? Do you often have someone with any experience take the job?"

McClellen and his wife exchanged looks. McClellen turned back to him. "No, that's true enough. Miss Calhoun was young."

Badje said, "The one before her, my wife, was young, too. This was her first job."

"Well then, gentlemen and lady." He nodded to McClellen's wife, the only woman present. "Test me if you like, or perhaps just give me a chance. If you like the way the school is run, you can keep me on. If not..." Parrish shrugged, careful to keep the look of a lamb amid lions.

"Sounds good enough to me," Badje said. "Any school is better than no school at all."

Three other school board members nodded. The McClellens didn't, but they didn't protest, either.

Parrish shook hands all around with the fools. He wanted to laugh out loud when they told him part of the miserable pay was the same room the former teacher had. He wished Grace would come home and find him there.

Welcome home, Gracie.

Daddy's here.

TWENTY

Daniel scraped a ditch the width of a tree trunk into the ground to set his biggest logs for a foundation. He glanced back and saw pretty little Grace coming out to help. He turned back to his digging. He was going to make the house big. If he had his druthers, he'd keep building day and night for the rest of his life. It helped to be exhausted.

A bedroom for the twins.

"You get down from there. Pa doesn't want us up there."

Daniel didn't even turn around when Luke started shrieking. He sounded jealous. Probably Mark had gotten to the top of the woodpile ahead of his brothers.

A bedroom for the triplets.

Ike and Abe were digging straight toward him. Mark, Luke, and John were fighting over which log was the biggest as they climbed over the tippy stack of lumber. They found one that teetered, and with a whoop of joy, they invented their own seesaw.

It rolled on them, and they had to scramble to get out of the way. Daniel heard Grace gasp.

A bedroom for Grace.

"Boys, be careful," she scolded.

The boys climbed around like monkeys, escaping death by a whisper. It was what boys were good at, after all.

Why was she out here?

"If you break a leg, we can't get out of the canyon to get to the doctor."

Daniel glanced over his shoulder and saw her with her hands fisted and planted on her slender hips. Hips encased in Abe's outgrown pants. He needed to get her a dress somehow, a big, loose-fitting dress. He looked long enough to see she had fire in her eyes. A fire that hadn't been there before the avalanche.

What about being buried alive could spark such a fire in a quiet, prissy woman? Because there was definitely a fire. It burned him hotter every day. He turned, half desperate, back to the trench.

And definitely a bedroom for me.

"Big. Build it big," he muttered and dug and dug some more. "I don't ever want to run across her by accident."

He worked until he was ready to drop, which was his plan. He and the boys dragged themselves back to the barn. Grace slept curled up in a ball to keep herself warm. She'd asked today about heating water to wash clothes and have baths.

Daniel almost turned back around to dig some more. Instead, he collapsed on the ground with the boys firmly between him and his very own God-approved wife, the one to whom he'd pledged himself.

He fell asleep dreaming about baths. He'd always hated baths. But his dream wasn't a nightmare, far from it.

He did the chores before first light because he was up and out of the barn early anyway. He made a quick breakfast of steak, eggs, potatoes, biscuits, and milk and was building by the time the sun came up.

"It seems kinda big, Pa," Abe said, scratching his head and staring at the immense rectangular foundation and all the smaller trenches that split the house up into rooms.

Daniel had to admit the boy was right. And he'd been toying with the idea of adding another couple of rooms. After all, the boys might want their own someday. And besides, if the house was huge, he could keep busy for the rest of his life chopping firewood to warm it. He'd never tried to build an upstairs any fancier than a crawl space in the rafters. He could do that here. That'd take awhile.

"It just looks that way now. Once we get the walls up, it'll be normal size. Besides, we're a big family. We need a lot of room."

"One bedroom for us boys and one for you and Ma oughta be enough," Ike said dubiously. "There're a lot more 'n two."

"Yep, we need two." Abe looked at the neatly arranged trenches dividing the house up into a kitchen, dining room, sitting room, pantry, and four obvious bedrooms.

"Well, I thought you two could have your own room, without the triplets in it to bother your stuff."

Ike looked at Abe.

Abe shrugged. "We don't have any stuff."

Daniel knew that to be the honest truth. "Well, maybe if we have enough room, we'll get you some stuff."

Abe looked intrigued.

Ike looked confused. "We got everything we need now, Pa. 'Cept'n I'd surely like an apple now and then. But the apples won't take up that much room."

"I'd kinda like to have my own ax," Mark said.

"No ax, Mark, and you know it." Daniel turned on his son. Stubborn kid. Smart, too. Daniel didn't want him to start reasoning out bedrooms.

"This is enough digging." Daniel changed the subject before the boys could count the trenches again and ask about the other bedroom. The one on the far end of the house, as far from the bedroom Daniel had planned for Grace as he could get it.

In fact, he was thinking of putting a door to the outside of the house in that bedroom, and no door to the rest of the house. Maybe he'd be able to sneak in late and leave early and never see her again. He was from a long-living family of men, but he was almost thirty. He could keep up long workdays and full-time sneaking for fifty years or so.

He jabbed his shovel at the tree pile. "Let's strip the branches off those trees so they'll line up neat."

Mark jumped to his feet. Running eagerly to Daniel, he skidded up, slammed into Daniel's legs, and almost knocked the both of them over. "Let me help, Pa. Let me take a turn with the ax. I'll be careful. I'm getting on toward six now, and you know I'm smarter 'n every one of the rest of the kids. I'll be careful."

"You turned five in November. You're not getting on toward six. And anyway, you need to be ten. Don't ask again." Daniel held Mark's stubborn gaze. "And don't you ever let me catch you playing with that ax."

"Aw right." Mark kicked the ground with the toe of his boot.

Daniel noticed the top was tearing away, and he could see some of Mark's sock peeking through the worn leather. And Grace was wearing the pair of boots set aside for the next triplet who needed shoes.

Daniel wondered if he could fetch home a deer and make moccasins tight enough to keep the snow off Mark's feet. He'd never done much boot making, but he could certainly tan a deer hide. He reckoned he'd put in some time practicing and learn that just as he'd learned everything else—by doing. Plus it'd keep him extra busy.

He and the boys tore into branches. He set Mark, Luke, and John to work dragging the scrub branches away to be saved for firewood and furniture and whatnot. Grace helped.

Daniel noticed that John stayed near her, talked to her, and seemed to side with her when the other boys got too rambunctious.

When they had nearly a mountain of logs stripped, Daniel hitched up his calmest horse to start dragging the trees into place.

"A few more steps, boys." Daniel waved Mark and Luke ahead. Abe and Ike walked on each end of the log to give a tug if it started plowing too much ground as it slid along.

Grace tagged along, holding John's hand. Daniel caught himself glancing at those joined hands more than once. He remembered his own ma and how much he'd liked holding her hand when he was a youngster. He couldn't help being glad for John that he'd found himself a nice mother.

Grace was treating the other boys well, too. She looked the same on the outside, but inside, the fussbudget schoolteacher had changed into a laughing, sweet lady. A very pretty lady. Of course, he'd noticed from the first that she was pretty. Even when she was so grouchy about his boys, he'd been able to see that her hair was a pretty dark blond and her eyes had the shine of pure gold. Her waist was slender and her ankles trim. . . .

He jerked his attention back to the log. "Hold up there, boys. That's far enough."

The boys gave him a funny look. He realized they'd already stopped the horse. He wondered how long he'd stood there looking at his bona fide wife. She was his, after all. God and Pastor Roscoe had said it.

"All right, let's get this log notched. Abe and Ike, come here and I'll show you how to do it."

"Pa, can't I—"

"Forget it, Mark." Daniel chipped away a squared notch in the top of the log. It was slow, tedious work. He glanced at the vast number of logs he'd cut down and the huge house he planned for his family. Building it would most likely wear him down to the bone.

Good.

With his jaw set in a grim line, he finished the second notch on the first log and said, "Okay, boys, let's get this log into the trench."

"Can I help, Daniel?" Grace stepped close, and even bending over to lift the log as he was, he could see her ankles plain as day with those stupid short pants of Abe's.

"Sure, grab ahold down at that end." He pointed to the far end of a long, heavy tree without looking up.

She sighed, and he wanted to stand up straight and find out if anything was wrong. He had to fight himself to keep from dropping the log and seeing to her happiness.

Working himself to death was the only way to save his sanity. . .and her life.

TWENTY-ONE

Grace had married a crazy man, and that was that.

"How can you see to build this thing in the dark? Come down from there, Daniel." The noises from on top of the house sped up. What was the man thinking?

The boys were all asleep, collapsed from exhaustion. They ate more and yelled more and, in general, just lived life as they always had—only more since they'd been building this house.

"I'll be down as soon as I lash these logs into place. Don't want them collapsing in a high wind."

"Daniel, this is the most sheltered spot on the face of the earth, let alone on the 6R. And you've built this house solid as a rock. The wind is not going to blow the house down."

"Until the roof is on, I'll worry. But lashing the top of the walls to the crosspieces of the roof will brace her up."

"Daniel Reeves, you get down here, or by all that's holy, I will drag you off that wall by your ear." She used her schoolmarm voice. "Now quit risking your fool neck by working in the pitch dark when you're so tired."

"It's not that dark. The moon is high and the stars—"

"Daniel," she barked. She really did bark. She was starting to sound like the coyotes that wandered these hills and howled at the moon. Since he was acting like a stubborn child and she was treating him like a stubborn child, she went ahead and added, "Don't make me come up there."

Her schoolteacher voice had made many a tough young man mind. True, it had never worked with the Reeves boys, but some almost as wild. She wondered if her tone would work on the biggest and, right now, wildest Reeves boy of all.

She heard Daniel grumbling as he climbed down. She had to force herself not to grin. He might see it and become mulish again and climb back on that roof. There was, after all, considerable moonlight.

She picked her way across what would one day be her front yard to meet him. Chunks of wood from Daniel's notching and limbs from a thousand sword fights and shoot-outs lay scattered around the yard.

Daniel scampered down the corner of the house where the ends of the notched logs stuck out like interwoven fingers. He had to be worn to a nub from his hard work, and yet he seemed as strong and energetic as ever.

When he got to the bottom of the wall, she was waiting. "The house is—"

Daniel yelped like a scalded cat. He whirled to face her. "What are you doing here?" His eyes practically burned her skin.

"I just talked to you. Of course I'm here." Grace crossed her arms over her chest. She chanted to herself, *Be brave.* She could handle anything with God at her side. She thought about reciting the Twenty-third Psalm, but really, a cranky husband wasn't exactly "the valley of the shadow of death." Surely that wasn't called for.

"Get to bed. I'll be in after a bit." He turned away from her.

She grabbed his elbow and pulled him around to face her. She was surprised she could stop him. He was, after all, huge. Over six feet to her five feet six, he outweighed her by sixty or seventy pounds, and his muscles felt like iron. She could feel the corded strength of him just by gripping his arm. His shining white hair caught the moonlight and glowed almost as if a halo had settled on his head. But Daniel was no angel. She could see the fire in his blue eyes even in the moonlight.

"Why are you so mad at me? What is wrong this time?"

"I'm not mad at you." Daniel jerked free of her grip. She expected him to storm away, but he didn't. He stood facing her, his shoulders heaving with temper and exertion and who knew what else.

"Well, that is just so obviously a lie that I can't even believe you said it." Grace stepped right up under his nose. "Are you mad because I wanted a house? Are you mad because John likes me a little?"

He probably was. *Be brave.* She jabbed him in the chest with her index finger. "Maybe you're just mad because I'm *here*. I didn't plan it, but I'm here now. I'm sorry if my presence inconveniences you. I'm sorry if I couldn't be polite enough to die in the avalanche. I'm sorry if you're stuck with me, but I'm stuck with you, too." She poked him again.

"Stop that." Daniel shoved her finger aside.

Her temper flared. He should stand there and take his poking like a man. "I'll do exactly as I want. That's what *you* do. You storm around and work yourself and the boys to death and ignore me or yell at me." Poke.

It occurred to her that this might be her only chance to talk to Daniel about the way he worked the boys. But somehow that didn't interest her at all. She dug her fingernail in a little the next time she poked him.

Daniel shoved her hand again. "Don't touch me, Grace. Get out of here. Go to bed."

"Not without you, Danny boy." Poke. That really bothered him. Good.

His breath heaved faster, and he moved closer.

She could see the flushed cheeks and the narrow eyes that had locked onto hers. She felt a thrill of satisfaction that she could goad him like this. Now, she thought with a surge of power, she was being brave.

"You're coming in, Daniel Reeves."

He leaned down closer. "Get away from me. I'm not some tame dog to be kept on a chain."

He was upset about the house. He blamed her for all his hard work. But they needed it, and that was the truth. She had no intention of letting him make her feel like this was her fault.

"I may have been the first one to talk about this house, but you know it had to be built. You don't need to take your temper out on me." She really needled him with her finger with the next poke.

Daniel's huge, work-roughened fingers closed around her wrist. His voice sounded husky. "I told you to stop touching me, woman."

"Why are you angry at me?" She jerked her hand loose and poked him again, even though she had the strangest feeling that he wasn't angry anymore, and she wasn't exactly angry anymore, either.

"I'm warning you." He caught her hand again. This time when she pulled against him, he didn't let go. He tugged her by her forearm until she bumped up against him.

"Answer me, then." She poked him with her free left hand. "What is the matter with you?"

He caught her left hand. He pulled her closer. He leaned over her. "Why are women like this? Why do they torture a man? Dear God, why?"

Grace had a second to think Daniel didn't sound angry at all. He sounded confused and desperate, and his question to God was a genuine prayer.

Then he lowered his head, and the stars and moon blinked out, hidden behind his burning eyes and his glowing halo of white hair.

She opened her mouth to demand he be nicer to her.

And he kissed her and pulled her hard against him and lowered her to the cold ground.

It was the nicest thing he'd ever done.

Grace awoke when she felt Daniel stir then stand and walk away from her. "Daniel?"

"Get out of here, Grace." He strode into a shadowed corner of the house.

The moon had set, and clouds must have come in, because the stars were blotted out. She couldn't see him in the dark interior of the roofless cabin. She saw him sink to the ground in a far corner and lean against the house's log wall.

"Come back here, Daniel." Slipping into her clothes, she wanted him to hold her again. She wanted to tell him she loved him. She wanted him to say it back.

"No."

She saw barely visible motion from the corner, and she could make him out as he stood.

"No, I won't come over there. Leave me alone."

Grace's heart clenched at the cruel rejection she heard in Daniel's voice. Earlier he'd been gentle, loving as he helped her understand what it meant to be truly man and wife. Now all that tenderness had vanished in the dark.

As an orphan abandoned by her parents, then as the adopted daughter of a man who made a mockery of the word *father*, she'd had plenty of practice being rejected. She expected it. She hadn't ever known much else. And now she found there were more ways to hurt. The pain of Daniel's rejection sliced through her not-so-tough-after-all heart until she wondered if when she looked down at her chest, she'd be bleeding.

"Daniel, what's the matter?" But she knew what the matter was. It was her. Something was missing in her. She wasn't a woman anyone could love. Why hadn't she realized that before and protected herself better?

"Get out of here, Grace."

Her real parents, her adoptive father, her husband, her children—none of them wanted her.

Except John.

"Be brave."

She didn't think it. She wasn't strong enough to think that right now. It had been a whisper on the wind that flowed inside her and all around.

John loved her. And Ike was a little nicer these days. She got an occasional smile out of Luke. And one night the cat had sat on her lap.

She turned to her husband in the open doorway of their half-built house. She wanted to hurt him. She wanted to cut him as deeply as he'd cut her.

"Be brave."

Again the still, small voice. Not her own. Not her thoughts.

God.

She didn't hurl at him the awful words that came to her. True bravery wasn't spiteful and petty. God wanted her to be brave. She knew the brave thing she'd say to him if she could: "Daniel, I love you."

But she wasn't that brave. And it might not even be true, because she hated him right now just as much as she loved him.

"Yea, though I walk through the valley of the shadow of death. . ." Now that verse seemed appropriate, because she felt as if she were dying inside.

The bravest thing she had the power to do right now was say, "I won't bother you again. I'm sorry."

She turned and left the cabin.

From behind her, Daniel's anguished voice said softly, like a prayer, "I'm sorry, too. Dear God, I'm so sorry."

Beth hung her cloak on the nail where it always went. Feeling just a touch shy, she waited while Mandy set down the lunch pail so they could go inside together. Miss Calhoun had been prickly, though kind underneath. Beth wanted to get off on the right foot with the new schoolmaster. She'd never had a man teacher before, but Ma had said it was normal enough.

She exchanged a glance with Mandy, and it helped to know her big sister had some jitters, too. They went through the little entry area into the classroom and headed straight for their seats. Her eyes widened at the old man who stood up front slapping a ruler in his hand. Wrinkles cut deep at the corners of his down-turned mouth in a way that told her Mr. Parrish spent far more time scowling than smiling.

Nervous, Beth settled silently in her desk and noticed Sally whispering to one of the two other students in her grade, a boy.

"Sally." Beth kept her voice to a whisper even though several children were talking in normal voices.

"What?" Clutched against Sally's chest was the slate that Ma always sent from home.

"Sit down and be quiet," Beth hissed then glanced up at Mr. Parrish. He was staring straight at Sally, and his scowl had deepened.

Sally looked at the new teacher. A furrow appeared between Sally's brows at Parrish's glare. She fell silent and settled into her seat. The other children were soon settled and silent.

"My name is Master Parrish. You will remember that." He slapped the ruler against his hand. Beth's spine straightened almost instinctively. Her feet flattened on the floor. Her eyes were fixed on the teacher.

"My rules are behave, be quiet, be warned." He slapped the ruler with each rule. "No second chance will be given. Behave—I expect my rules to be followed instantly and completely or you will be punished. Be quiet—you are silent from the moment you're called back into class unless called on. That means the silence begins on the playground when I ring the bell. Be warned—this is your first and only warning. You will be punished for disobedience immediately. I assure you I have discussed my rules with your parents, and they assure me that they want order as much as I do. This school was run in complete disorder with your last teacher."

Beth had to admit that was the truth, but only when the Reeves boys were here. No one could make them behave. With a flash of loyalty to poor Miss Calhoun, Beth remembered how well the school had run before the Reeves. She wanted to defend her former teacher, but one look into Mr. Parrish's eyes scared her out of any thought of speaking up.

"That will not be the case in my school." His eyes seemed to come back again and again to Sally. Beth wondered why he would focus on the littlest girl in the room. She wasn't likely to be any trouble.

"And your parents have also agreed with me that if you come home complaining about school or about being given lashes, they'll back me and hand out double the punishment." He slapped the ruler on his hand again with a loud crack.

Beth knew that was true. Her parents had always said whatever punishment the girls received at school, they'd find awaiting them at home. Of course, Beth couldn't remember ever being punished at school—scolded a bit from time to time, but never given lashes with the ruler—so that rule had never been tested.

"Very often I've found children to be both stupid and naughty, and they need a lesson to see that I mean what I say." Mr. Parrish's eyes narrowed on Sally. "You, little girl, what's your name?"

"S-Sally McClellen."

"Sally, you were noisy entering this classroom. That's one lash. Come forward."

Beth looked at her sister and saw that Sally's eyes had gone wide with fear. "B-but, Mr. Parrish—"

"And now you're disobeying me. That's a second lash. Do you wish to continue disobeying me?"

Sally slowly rose from her desk. Her usually pink cheeks white, her chin tucked against her chest, she walked to the front.

"It is *Master* Parrish."

Beth thought he said the word as if he savored it, as if he were feeding on something delicious.

"You will speak my name as I order you to, or you will be punished."

Sally opened her mouth, then stopped herself and nodded.

Beth was afraid if Sally spoke, she might be breaking the quiet rule, and obviously Sally had thought of that.

"Extend your hand, palm up." Parrish stood on the raised floor at the front of the room beside his desk. He towered over Sally. She raised her hand as ordered.

The moment stretched. Beth held her breath. Master Parrish stood like a looming vulture.

Please, God, help me be good. Help us all be good. Please, God, don't let Ma and Pa find out Sally's been bad.

The ruler crashed on Sally's soft skin.

Beth saw tears well in her little sister's eyes, but Sally was good. She took the thrashing with complete and utter silence.

TWENTY-TWO

The house was going up with lightning speed. Daniel worked until he wanted to drop every night and got up hours before dawn the next morning. He couldn't sleep anyway.

What if there was a baby? What if she died? He prayed long and hard as he worked the punishing days. *Please, God, please, please, I can't stand to bury another wife.*

By the end of the week, he'd finished the roof and the fireplace could be lit.

He laid a wooden floor. Splitting all those logs was a useless frippery, but it was hard work that took a long time, so Daniel insisted on it. When he got the floor done in the main room, the family moved in. He planned to put flooring down throughout the house, but since the boys only had blankets to sleep on, they could clear out of their rooms in half a heartbeat and he would work in there during the day. Grace avoided him, thank heavens. But as she carried a flour sack from the barn to the ridiculously large cabin, he knew he hadn't built it big enough. She was ignoring him, but he knew the ways of women, and now he didn't have anything to do to keep busy.

It took about ten minutes to settle into the house. Once they had a real home, Daniel realized that they really had nothing.

"Pa, aren't there some boxes up in the barn loft left from back home?" Abe asked one day.

Daniel had forgotten them. He'd wanted to forget. He hadn't wanted anything in Texas that reminded him of Margaret.

Grace heard Abe. "You've got things for a home stored away?"

"Sure. Let's go get 'em." Abe jumped up from where he sat on the floor in front of the fireplace. "I think there are some dishes in there and other stuff left from our first ma."

"Grace, I don't—" Grace was gone before Daniel could protest.

Daniel watched her go. She was too thin. Her ribs stuck out almost sharply. She was underweight and had a tiny frame. Margaret had been big-boned and built from sturdy Irish stock. And childbearing had been too much for her. He decided then and there Grace needed to fatten up.

He stared out the door after them and saw them enter the barn to collect Margaret's things. Daniel wanted to call out that they were to leave those things alone. They were his, not to be toyed with or used or even seen.

He didn't because he would have had to speak to her, and he hadn't in nearly two weeks.

All he needed to make his life into perfect torture were Margaret's fussy belongings spread out all over this house.

The other boys went whooping and hollering after Abe and Grace. They liked Grace, all except Mark. He delighted in tormenting her. Mark didn't follow her like the other boys did.

Daniel looked down at his son. An expression had settled over Mark's face that Daniel suspected was an exact reflection of his own.

"We have to get rid of her, Pa."

Daniel didn't speak for a long moment as he looked out the open door. He wanted to agree. *God, there's no getting rid of her. What am I going to do?* He ached for her.

It was part of Satan's plan to bring mankind down. Daniel had to be strong. That was God's will.

Daniel glanced at Mark. His heart turned over at the anger and rebellion on his son's face. Daniel knew he was responsible for that. The other boys were giving in to their longing for a mother, but not Mark.

Mark followed his father's example. And while Daniel didn't need a wife, Mark needed a ma.

The gentle ways of a woman were so pleasant to a child. He had loved his own mother fiercely. He could still hear the gentle way she sang a lullaby and feel the soft touch of her hand when she tucked him into bed at night. Yes, children needed a mother. So why did God let a woman die giving birth? It made no sense.

Daniel wrestled with his own dangerous feelings. He had to be a better example for Mark or the poor boy would grow up twisted inside. "Well, let's go help drag that old stuff out of the hayloft."

"We don't need it." Mark crossed his arms.

Only then did Daniel see his own crossed arms. He let them drop. "Sure we do. We didn't have room for anything to spare in the cave, but here we're rattling around. Let's get that house stuff out and use it. It's dumb not to."

Daniel headed for the barn, knowing he had to set an example for Mark.

They met Grace backing down from the hayloft, balancing a small box in one arm. The boys were coming right after.

Grace turned to him and smiled. "There's a lot there we can use, Daniel." She always spoke nicely to him, considering he never spoke back.

"There are even some women's dresses. I can get out of these ridiculous boy's clothes." She sailed past him, not waiting for a response that he'd trained her would never come.

He caught sight of one of Margaret's dresses poking out of the box Grace carried. He thought of Margaret, bleeding and dying and begging him to save her. Her strength ebbing away as Daniel pulled child after child from her body. He was overwhelmed by three wriggling babies and two frightened five-year-olds.

Margaret's weak pleading had come close to breaking him. He'd tried everything, knowing nothing to try.

Do something, Daniel. Help me.

His hands had been soaked in blood. It coated his clothes. He watched Margaret die by inches. The blood, the pleading, the fear, the hungry infants, and the crying toddlers had kept him awake every night for months. After she died, all he'd done was stay alive and keep the boys alive and his livestock alive so he could get milk for the babies. It took a pure miracle from God to keep the babies alive.

Now, five years later, he'd begun to forget. He hadn't jumped awake in the night, feeling Margaret's blood on his hands, for a long time. Until two weeks ago.

His nightmares were back, and he might have to live through it all again if Grace had a baby.

The rest of the boys followed after Grace, their arms full. He thought of Mark and the example he knew he needed to set and turned to climb to the hayloft. He had to treat her decently while the boys were watching.

On his way back to the cabin with his arms loaded with bits of fussy lace and cloth that he didn't remember from their other home, he said to Mark, "We're in the house, but we aren't gonna be settled for a long time. I need to build some furniture." He stepped inside. "You boys need beds."

With a sigh of relief, he realized he'd thought of a whole new big job to keep himself busy.

Sophie McClellen was delivered of twin boys in the middle of a cold winter night, and after that, Tillie worked so hard she quit feeling guilty about putting Beth out of her bedroom.

Tillie heard the whispers coming from behind the chicken coop and almost went back to the house so as not to disturb the girls' privacy. She could collect eggs later. The days were getting longer as the winter wore down, and she'd come to fetch eggs without bothering with a wool coat she'd made, bought with money Sophie had paid her for nearly running the household since the twins had been born.

"You didn't deserve that thrashing." Tillie recognized Beth's voice and stopped her retreat.

"I'm telling Pa what Master Parrish did to you." Mandy's angry voice rose past a whisper.

Master? What was this? And thrashing? The schoolteacher had thrashed one of the girls? A shudder ripped the whole length of her body as Tillie remembered thrashings. She'd grown nearly to womanhood with her parents on the plantation in Virginia, and she'd never received one of the beatings the field slaves had endured.

And then she'd been sold south to Louisiana. She was the sole slave to a miserly man who lived in a decrepit, isolated mansion just outside New Orleans. Virgil was brutal, and nothing she did pleased him. She toiled all day in the thick heat, her legs cuffed with a short length of chain between them. Then she slept shackled in the cellar at night. He delighted in finding a reason to reach for the whip or a cane. When those tools weren't handy, he'd used his fists or a boot. And then to find out she'd been freed by President Lincoln years ago. The injustice of it infuriated her.

And the injustice of someone striking Sally set a torch to that fury. She'd never seen the McClellen girls receive more than a quick swat on the seat at home. They were lively but bright, with hearts as good as gold. She didn't even make a conscious decision. She marched around the chicken coop and saw the three older girls sitting on the ground.

"Your teacher makes you call him Master? Master Parrish?"

They all gasped, and their matching blue eyes shone with fear. Their reaction reminded her so much of herself that her throat nearly swelled with a sob.

"Y-yes," Sally said.

"I *hate* the word *master*." Tillie jabbed a finger at the three of them. "No schoolteacher is going to thrash one of my girls. You tell me what's going on."

"No—you'll tell Ma, and then we'll get in real trouble."

Tillie knew just how it was to be in trouble not of her own making.

She felt such a kinship with the girls she wanted to go fight the schoolteacher for them. Sophie and Clay were good people. But Sophie was so busy with her baby boys that she barely stirred from the house. And schooling seemed like a woman's business.

She briefly considered telling Adam. But he might tell Clay, and if her actions somehow resulted in the girls getting a beating from their pa, Tillie would never forgive herself. Before she decided what to do, she had to find out what exactly the trouble was.

Despite her doubts about the girls keeping this from their parents, she nodded firmly. "I won't tell unless you give me leave to. Now what is this man doing to you?"

They all relaxed. Mandy eased back from the circle of bright-colored gingham to make room for her. "Okay. Let us tell you about the mean man they hired to be our schoolteacher. Maybe you can help us figure out what to do."

TWENTY-THREE

Grace washed the supper dishes and caught herself humming. She had dishes. A whole set of china. Plain white clay pottery to be sure, but pretty enough, especially compared to a bare tabletop. A couple of pieces had chips here and there, and a fine mesh of cracks covered all of them, but they were beautiful just the same.

She might have a husband who didn't love her, but that was pretty much the same as her life had always been. At least now she had a roof over her head and a cloth for the kitchen table and one to spare. She had a nice set of silverware, enough so everyone could have his very own fork, and four spoons in case she ever learned to make soup out of steak and eggs and potatoes and biscuits and milk.

She even had a soup bowl, although only one. But since she had no idea how to make soup or porridge, it hardly mattered.

Washing carefully, Grace enjoyed the smooth sides of her very own paring knife. Daniel had used his whetstone to put an edge on it as sharp as a razor. She'd already nicked herself with it a dozen times, but she still loved that knife.

There were pots and pans so her potatoes didn't have to look like coal, although she was having a little trouble managing the heat and had a tendency to scorch the poor potatoes. But she'd learn. And her steaks could be cooked without being laid directly on top of the cookstove, although they seemed drier and there was no way to get six in the two skillets she owned. So she fried away on the stovetop much the same as always.

She had a stack of sheets that needed beds to go with them and tatted lace that she planned to drape over the backs of the chairs the menfolk were making.

There were several little combs and a necklace from which dangled a golden heart that misted Grace's eyes when she looked at it. A gift of love from Daniel to Margaret certainly, the most beautiful thing she'd ever seen. She set it aside immediately. Not for a second had she considered wearing the pretty necklace.

And best of all, she had clothes.

Women's clothes. They were far too big, but with the thread and needles found in the boxes, she had plans to alter them, if only she could figure out how to sew.

Life was good. She'd married an idiot—but a woman couldn't have everything.

Feeling as though her life was at last in order after a lifetime of one kind of desperation or another, she now had time to fix things with Daniel. And she needed to fix more than his attitude. She didn't like the way he worked the boys.

Until now she'd stood by while Daniel drove them like slaves to build this house. But the way he pushed them reminded her too much of Parrish. She wanted to tell him children should be children for a while, not slave labor. But Daniel, although outwardly polite to her, avoided her like a leper unless the boys were around. So how was she supposed to straighten out his crooked thinking when she could never get a minute alone with him?

With a long yell of pure frustration, Abe shook the chair he worked on. "Pa, help me fix this blasted thing."

"Abe, watch your language," Grace admonished.

Abe ignored her, which Grace expected, and held out the lopsided results of hours of toil. It had no back yet, but the seat and four legs were together.

The other boys had gone outside to play in the dusk, but they rushed to see what Abe had hollered about.

Daniel, sitting by the fireplace sanding a board to be used as a seat, turned from his work and picked up Abe's chair. "That's nice work, son."

The four boys fought each other to be the first one inside the door, plugging up the doorway until none of them could get through. Yelling threats at each other, they shoved and punched.

Daniel and Abe didn't look away from the chair.

Grace noticed Mark had a bloody nose. "Mark, what happened?" She rushed toward the clog of boys.

Ike crushed his little brothers enough that he finally got through. The rest of them came through like a gusher. They almost knocked her over, but she'd learned to be nimble since she'd become the mother of five.

"What happened to what?" Mark went to Abe's side.

"You're bleeding."

Daniel looked up from the chair then went back to work.

"Eww, get away." John shoved him. "You're getting blood and snot all over everything."

Mark swiped the back of his hand under his nose, coating his hand up to the wrist in mostly dried blood. Grace could see that the bleeding had already stopped.

"No, it's not nice work, Pa." Abe finally acknowledged his father's comment. "The legs wobble."

Grace had to admit the boy was right. The chair didn't look safe to sit on. She didn't say anything, but she vowed that if her son made a chair, she'd sit in it and say thank you with never a word of complaint until the day it collapsed under her. Then she'd sit on the floor and pretend she liked her chairs that way.

She firmed her jaw as Daniel inspected the job. She knew he'd never let up until Abe got it right. Of course, by then Abe would be able to build a proper chair, and that was a good thing. But the boy was only ten. Did Daniel have to push so hard?

Daniel, holding the chair with the legs sticking up, turned it over and set it on the floor. Sure enough, it teetered drunkenly.

Abe ran his hands through his white hair, leaving bits of wood shavings behind. "I've tried to cut 'em off even, but I can't get it."

"You've gotta be mighty careful with that." Daniel smiled. "If you keep trimming one leg after another, before you know it, you've got yourself a footstool."

Abe blushed a little, and Daniel clapped him on the shoulder. "I'm not saying you'll do that, boy. I'm saying I did that the first time I built a chair. You've been smart enough to quit before that happened."

Abe smiled.

Grace wondered if Daniel knew how much his approval meant to the boys. She wondered if he knew they would work themselves to death trying to please him.

Daniel pulled up the wood stump he'd dragged into the house from the cave.

He looked at his boys. "Gather around and we'll have a chair-making lesson. We've gotta make enough chairs for all of us, so we'll be plumb good at it before long."

The boys all dropped to the floor and listened with rapt attention—until Luke screamed.

Grace looked immediately at Mark, who held up a bent pin he'd found among the household treasures in the attic. Unrepentant—in fact, eager to admit what he'd done—he waggled the little pin in Luke's face.

Luke launched himself into Mark, who tumbled backward and grabbed Luke around the neck, jabbing at him with the pin.

Daniel somehow reached into the middle of the ruckus and snagged the pin away from Mark, then ignored the boys as they rolled around on the floor.

A solid smack of a fist earned a yell of rage from Mark. He tossed Luke hard away from him, and Luke rolled into Ike. Ike would've smashed the half-built chair to bits, except Daniel swept it out of the way of the tumbling bodies and kept talking to Abe and John as if the other boys were still listening, too.

Ike jumped to his feet and took a dive straight at Mark. Mark ducked sideways, and Ike hit the floor, rolling straight for the fireplace.

Grace took a half step toward her son's certain death before Ike caught himself. Stopping inches from the flames, he charged toward Luke, roaring like the Chicago train that had taken Grace west. He shook the sturdy new house like those trains had done, too.

Daniel didn't seem to notice Ike's brush with death or the racket. He talked in his usual too-loud voice to Abe and John as they whittled away at the chair legs.

Grace raised her hands helplessly toward heaven, then turned to tidy up the kitchen and play more with her new dishes.

Sophie rocked one of her fussy sons in front of the fire while the other—Tillie thought it was Jarrod—lay fidgeting in the cradle, close enough for Sophie to nudge it with her foot and keep it rocking. "I would never get by without you, Tillie."

Sophie was strong, and Tillie knew she'd be going full speed if necessary. But Tillie's presence allowed her generous hostess to rest, and Tillie felt as if she earned the roof over her head.

Serving Sophie and Clay and their children was similar to being a slave in the work Tillie did. But there was no comparison. Just Sophie's constant thank-yous made a world of difference. But there was more to it. The freedom of knowing she stayed by choice rather than by force was heady to the point Tillie felt almost as if she could sprout wings and fly if she wanted.

"God sent you to us, as sure as can be. I thank Him for you with nearly every breath I take."

Tillie sliced through the last eye-stinging onion for tonight's supper as she opened her mouth to tell Sophie, "I thank God for you, too." But Tillie couldn't say the words. It wasn't true. She hadn't talked to God since Master Virgil had told her the truth about the War Between the States. If God was up there, He was cruel. If He wasn't up there, then what was the point of praying? Either way, Tillie didn't have the breath to waste on such a God. But talking to God was an old habit. One she'd learned at her mother's knee. Now in this pleasant house, Tillie had to fight the urge to return to her old ways.

Tillie added the last of the savory onions to the stew meat that had been simmering to perfect tenderness all afternoon. Then she stooped over the fireplace to settle the pot of beef stew onto the hook. The ranch house door swung open, and all the girls crowded in, home from school. They rushed to peek at the babies and giggled. "Hi, Ma. Hi, Tillie." Their chorus of greetings was as nice to her as to their ma. Such sweet girls.

Tillie loved being part of this happy family. Suddenly her eyes stung with the realization that her separation from God created a separation from all believers, however kind they were. That wasn't of the McClellens' making but of hers, because they talked of God often and with much sincerity. Tillie couldn't join in.

Sally had left the door ajar, and when Tillie went to close it, she caught a glimpse of Adam shaking the reins with a soft slap of leather on the broad horses' backs as he headed the buckboard toward the barn. Tillie knew Adam had gone for the girls; he did it often. She still marveled at the way the McClellens trusted Adam and her with the children. Mas—Tillie caught herself—*Virgil* had taught her no slave would be given a moment's trust. And thoughts of Virgil and the word *master*, brought thoughts of the nasty teacher they'd hired in Mosqueros.

She looked the girls over. They seemed fine, but Tillie knew better. No one, slave or free, was fine who had to live under a brutal taskmaster. She needed to talk to them again, but it was so hectic lately that she hadn't had a chance.

Tillie stirred the thick broth, the smell making her mouth water. She'd been short on food for a long time after her escape, and before that, what Virgil had given her had been skimpy and often spoiled.

Bread was baking in the oven, its smell enough to weaken Tillie's knees even after a long stretch of having enough to eat. A cobbler Tillie had contrived with dried apples and brown sugar sat warming on the cast-iron top, sweet juices oozing up through the fluffy biscuit top. The bread needed a full hour to bake, but it would be fresh and still hot from the oven when Clay came in for supper.

The whole house was overflowing with love and good food and the sweet laughter of happy, healthy little children. But were they happy? Tillie's smile faded to a worried frown as she wondered.

Tillie went to pick up Jarrod before his fussing got out of hand, but Mandy beat her to him. Beth wheedled Sophie until she got little Cliff. Laura picked that moment to come out of her bedroom, rubbing the sleep from her eyes, and Sally went to help the little girl slip on her shoes.

After a very busy day, Tillie suddenly had time on her hands, and she considered beginning the cutting for a new set of clothes for the babies.

Adam swung the door open before she could act on the idea. "You need water or more wood, Sophie?" he asked.

"No, Clay brought everything in earlier. We're fine."

After making a proper fuss over the twins, Adam tickled Sally and Laura until they screamed and ran wildly around the room.

"Thanks for getting them all wound up," Sophie said dryly.

"My pleasure, ma'am." Adam grinned, his white teeth flashing in his dark face.

"I'm glad I've got someone to make that trip to town. They wouldn't be in school if it was up to me."

The girls all froze, the smiles drying off their faces.

Sally said with casualness Tillie could tell was false, "Ma, we'd be glad to stay home if it makes things easier for you."

Sophie just smiled.

Tillie knew Sophie suspected Sally just didn't like school, as so many children didn't. But it was more. Tillie had to bite her lip to keep from saying something.

Mandy gave her a nervous look as if afraid Tillie would betray their trust.

"I was glad to make the trip. I needed to get some supplies. I'll be starting work on my cabin in another couple of weeks." He turned to Tillie. "I need to ride out and pace off the cabin so I can get a few things ordered. It'd take an hour or more."

"I really need to help—"

"That's a great idea." Sophie spoke over the top of Tillie. "You've been working day and night since the twins came. It's cold out, but the wind is low and the trail is sheltered. I think you should go."

Tillie had lived here long enough to recognize that look in Sophie's eyes. When the woman made up her mind about something, there was no stopping her. Tillie didn't even bother to try. She found herself bundled in a heavy cloak, fur bonnet, and gloves and thrust out the door.

"That is one strong-willed woman," Tillie muttered as the door shut firmly behind her.

Adam grinned. "I guess that describes my Sophie pretty well."

Tillie glanced at him, startled. The close relationship between Adam and the McClellens amazed her.

Adam walked beside her to the barn and had two horses saddled before Tillie could offer to help. She'd done some work with the animals for Virgil and could hold her own slapping leather on a horse.

They rode out of the yard in the direction of Adam's claim, the sharp cold making talk difficult. Their breath froze white in the air. The soft plodding of the horses' hooves was the only sound save the singing of the breeze overhead.

When they reached the shelter of the canyon, Adam guided his horse toward a sunny southeastern slope and swung down. "I'm putting the house right here."

Tillie slipped to the ground and Adam tied the horses to a low shrub.

"A perfect spot, out of the wind, with good sunlight all day long." Tillie nodded as she looked at the grassy valley sweeping for a mile before the canyon walls sprung up, rugged and majestic. The sky was white. Wind brushed across the waving grass like the hand of God. A sharp cry far overhead drew Tillie's gaze. A bald eagle soared the length of the valley, free and strong and beautiful. "This must make you so proud, Adam. To own this, to have a place of your own."

Adam nodded. "It's a dream come true. I owned a herd before but lost it to rustlers. It was in Indian Territory, and I could never call the land my own. Now I'm ready to settle down, and being this close to family makes it the next thing to heaven."

"Family?" Tillie looked away from the panorama. "What family?"

Adam smiled, his white teeth making his skin seem darker, the strong lines of his face sculpted as if carved from shining black marble. "I mean Sophie and her young'uns. Clay, too, come to that. I consider Sophie my next thing to a daughter. I worked for her pa when she was growing up. Then when her first husband headed toward Texas, I came along to see that everything was taken care of in order."

"First husband?"

Adam nodded. "She was married to Clay's twin brother, Cliff. Cliff is the girls' father."

"I've never imagined Clay wasn't the girls' father. They all seem to love each other so much."

"Yep, it's worked out mighty well. Cliff was long on dreams but short on backbone, to my way of thinking, and I knew before she married him, Sophie'd need help."

"But how does that make her your daughter?"

Adam pulled his Stetson off his head and ran a hand into his tight curls. "She was always underfoot in the stables as a child. I found her tagging me almost as soon as she could walk. She was an only child, and her pa couldn't deny her a thing, so she ran like a tomboy from the first. He liked having her around when most men would have shooed her off to the house to keep her skirts clean. Her pa trusted me to take care of her, too, and it was a good thing, because it took us both to keep up with her. Between us, she learned horses and cattle and she worked the fields as much as we'd let her. I taught her carpentry, hunting, and tanning hides. You should see that woman shoot. It's a humbling thing to know she's bested me in nearly everything I taught her."

Adam curled both hands around the brim of his hat and looked away from the land to Tillie, his kindness shining from his dark eyes. "I do think of her as a daughter. God has given her into my care, and I'm thankful for finding land that will keep me near her."

"You credit God with giving you a white woman as a daughter? And yet He left me imprisoned in Virgil's house for years." Tillie shook her head. She had to clear her throat to speak the heresy that she'd accepted in her heart. It sounded horrible, but Tillie refused to live with the lie. "There is no God, Adam."

Adam's smile returned so brightly it reflected the sky. "Oh yes, there is, Till."

Adam's reaction startled her. She'd expected shock or maybe an argument.

"I believed all that once, but no more. Let's pace off your house and head home."

She took one step before Adam's hand descended on her forearm and pivoted her gently but firmly.

"I know there's a God because He spoke to me."

Tillie opened her mouth to brush aside Adam's nonsense, but there was something alive and vital in his expression.

"He came to me and called me here, home, when Sophie needed me." Tillie shook her head.

Adam pulled Tillie closer. "It happened. As real as I'm standing here in front of you. I knew Sophie needed help and I headed out. No one can ever tell me there's not a God, because I *know*. Do you hear me? I heard His voice. I had my own miracle."

Tillie wanted to challenge him, but his voice filled with a conviction that seemed to break the chains that had bound her soul ever since she'd found out the depths of Virgil's evil.

"Really?"

Adam nodded, and his hand relaxed on her arm. "There's a God, Till, and He loves you."

"He forgot me."

"He never forgets His children."

"He left me in chains."

"Virgil left you in chains, not God. God was with you the whole time, keeping your soul safe."

"No."

"We're from a people that have known chains for centuries, and yet I've seen a powerful faith in slaves, captured or free. Our people have always been too wise in the ways of hardship to believe God exists to make sure the world treats us fair. Instead, He comes to us in the midst of great misery and ministers to our souls. Don't tell me He waits until we're free any more than He waits until we're happy or healthy. God comes all the way to you, wherever you are, and all He asks is for you to accept Him."

"What about what I ask, Adam? What if I ask more of God than just to be in my soul? What if my prayers are ignored and my abuse is ignored? Why do I want a God like that?"

Adam was silent for too long, looking off in the distance. Tillie saw contemplation in his eyes. She'd spoken the truth to him, and now he'd have to admit that her truth was the correct one. But God had spoken to Adam. Was it possible? Tillie felt the wonder of it.

Finally, his eyes focused on her, and that shining smile returned. "What kind of world have we got if you don't have God? Your suffering on this earth is for nothing. Your living is for nothing. You live, you die, they throw dirt over you—is that all life is? God put a yearning in everyone's soul, crying out for more. You feel it—I know you do."

The eagle screamed again. The beauty of creation surrounded her. She did yearn for God. She'd been heartbroken—no, soul-broken—ever since she'd given Him up.

"He really spoke to you?"

Adam nodded. "Not just me, either. If it was just me, we could call it my own desire to see Sophie again. But he spoke to Buff and Luther, too."

Tillie had met the gruff old mountain men who worked with Clay. They seemed to be unlikely men to receive a miracle. "Really?"

Adam nodded. "This life is hard enough without giving up our only unshakable source of comfort."

Comfort. Odd he should use that word. How many times in the darkness of Virgil's cellar had she thought she could bear the loneliness no longer and a Comforter had come to her in the night, giving her the strength to face another day?

God's own Holy Spirit. She'd forgotten about that in her rage over Virgil's injustice. "I want to believe, Adam."

Again that easy smile. There was no doubt in Adam. Not one tiny shred. He lifted his hand from her arm and nodded at the piece of flatland where they stood.

"I'll tell you the whole story while we pace off the house. How Sophie spoke a prayer to God and He carried it on the wings of the wind to my ears, hundreds of miles away."

Tillie sighed from the wonder of such a thing. "I'd like to hear it."

Adam turned her toward his plot by resting his hand on her back. "Which side should we put the kitchen on? The east or west?"

She felt his strength, and though no man had touched her in kindness before, she didn't flinch away. In fact, she leaned a bit closer. And it seemed very logical that he'd ask where she wanted the kitchen.

"Ma, come quick!"

John's voice. This was it. She'd been terrified of it since the beginning. One of them had managed to break a leg or otherwise permanently damage himself with the doctor out of reach.

Grace flew toward the door, tearing off the oversized apron she'd found among Margaret's things. "What happened?" She ran out into her front yard.

"We've got the first new calf of spring, Ma."

The triplets fussed around the new calf and the cow, thankfully one they milked, because the rest of the herd didn't like the boys hanging around them.

Grace marveled at the competent way the five-year-olds handled mama and baby.

There was plenty the little boys could do. Daniel wouldn't let them near an ax, which Grace approved of. But all three had wickedly sharp pocketknives and were talented whittlers.

Later Daniel set them to making spindles for the backs of the chairs and even let Mark, who had a knack for fine work, turn his hand to carving fancy curls and whatnots on the wood he'd use atop the spindles.

"There has to be something I can do." Grace plopped herself onto the floor in front of the fireplace, her legs curled up under a bluish dress dotted with yellow flowers.

"These legs need to be braced." John scooted next to her, holding a chair seat with the legs attached. "Here, I'll show you how to tighten these strips of bark. It keeps the legs from spreading."

Grace loved working right alongside them.

They had three chairs done by bedtime.

"Time for bed, boys."

The groans of protest were so predictable Grace couldn't hold back a grin. She looked up and caught Daniel's eye. He looked disgruntled at the whining. She smiled and one corner of his lip curled up.

"No sense getting upset about it, Grace. Boys just naturally don't wanta go to bed."

"Nor girls, either, as I recall."

Mark jumped up from the floor with fire in his eyes. "I forgot my pocketknife in the barn." He dashed out the door.

"Mark, wait," Daniel called.

"I'll help him hunt," Abe hollered.

"Boys, you get back here." Grace's voice nearly echoed in the empty cabin.

As quick as a flash of lightning, all the boys disappeared from the cabin.

Daniel shook his head.

"What are they up to?"

Daniel shrugged. "Maybe Mark's really looking for his knife. Maybe they've got something else up their sleeves. Don't worry about it. They've run these hills since we moved in last summer."

Grace got up from the floor.

She saw Daniel watching her.

"You sat on that floor as long as the boys. You're as limber as a child, Grace." Daniel gathered up wood shavings to throw in the fire.

She stared after the complaining boys. "I am most definitely *not* a child. I'm seventeen now."

Daniel dropped his wood curls. "*How old?*"

The boys came dashing back in at that instant and froze at the sound of their father's voice.

Grace turned, shocked at his outburst.

"S-seventeen," she repeated.

"Seventeen? And you were a schoolteacher, alone out here in the West?"

"Well, actually, I was sixteen when I got the job. But that doesn't mean I'm a child. Sixteen is old enough—"

"What were your parents thinking to let you come out here?"

"Ma don't have no parents, Pa."

"John," Grace said quickly, "don't—"

"She's an orphan." John charged on without hearing the warning in Grace's voice.

She looked at Daniel, who was glaring at her for no reason she could understand.

"Chalk up another secret for my wife. How many more do you have?"

"She didn't have no ma." John looked at his brothers, fairly bursting with pride that he'd known something no one else had.

"Just like us?" Mark asked, his eyes wide with amazement.

"I don't want to talk about—"

"And she was raised by a mean man who 'dopted her and made her make rugs while he starved her and her ten or twenty brothers and sisters."

"Ten or twenty?" Daniel looked at her.

"O-only sisters," Grace corrected. "It's not like it sounds."

"And you're only seventeen?" Daniel's eyebrows met between his eyes as they furrowed. "Did the school board know your age when they hired you?"

With a weak shrug, Grace said, "It was no secret. I don't recall them asking, exactly. Girls start teaching school young."

"Boys, go to bed."

Grace recognized the voice Daniel kept in reserve for when he wanted the boys to mind.

The boys didn't utter so much as one "I'm not sleepy." They disappeared into their separate rooms like a flash.

Daniel could almost see them pressing their ears to the doors.

He marched over to Grace, took her by the hand, and dragged her into the bedroom she'd been sleeping in alone. It was empty except for a bed on the floor that was little more than a couple of tanned cow hides sewn together and stuffed with hay, then covered by a white sheet and a blanket.

He glared over his shoulder at the boys' rooms, slammed the door, turned on her, and hissed, "What is that all about? Is what John said true?"

She backed away from him. "Daniel, it's not important."

"So it is true." Daniel, speaking under his breath, advanced on her. "You had a father who worked you half to death. Rugs, Grace? He means a carpet mill, doesn't he? I know what they're like. The children who work in them are treated like slaves."

"Don't make more of it than it was." Grace backed up until she bumped up against the wall and had to stop.

"What else don't I know, Grace?" Daniel wished he had a voice for Grace like the one he used on his boys. She was the most stubborn woman he'd ever met. "You've never told me why you were hiding in my wagon. You've never told me about being adopted. You've never told me your age. Are there any more secrets you'd like to get out in the open"—Daniel leaned down until his nose almost touched hers—"before I learn them from the boys?"

Daniel saw the second Grace's temper caught fire. "And just when was I supposed to tell you about this, Daniel? At the beginning when you were accusing me of—"

Daniel clamped his hand over her mouth and pressed her head firmly against the cabin wall. "Keep it down," he growled. "The boys can hear every word you say." He lifted his hand from her lips and rubbed his palm on his jeans.

Grace glanced at the door, then did her best to whisper and yell at the same time. "You know the vile things you accused me of. And then after the avalanche you were mad all the time. And you avoid me as much as you can by working all the hours God made in a day. And ever since..." Grace's voice lowered even more, and her cheeks flamed red.

Daniel knew exactly "ever since" what.

"You won't even speak to me. Just when was I supposed to tell you all about myself? You've never asked because you don't want to know. You just want to stay away from me, and when you can't, you want to hurt me because you regret being saddled with a wife."

Grace stuck her nose right up to his. "And now I know just what you were accusing me of. And I think. . .I think. . ." Grace's mouth wobbled. Her eyes filled with tears.

Not tears. Dear Lord, why did you make women cry? It's not fair.

"I didn't even know a man and woman could. . .could. . .do such together. And to think I'd be with a man that way who wasn't my husband. . ."

Her tears overflowed her eyes. Her throat clogged until she couldn't go on. She tried to slide sideways to get out from between him and the wall.

He stopped her.

She covered her face with both hands, and her shoulders shuddered with suppressed sobs.

"I know. Everything you say is the truth. I've never asked you anything." He fell silent, his hands drawing her close, her face buried in her hands between them. He'd do anything to make her quit sobbing. He'd do anything to keep her safe. He wondered if there was a baby as the result of their night together, but he was terrified to ask.

Grace's shoulders finally quit shaking, and she looked up. "What?"

He leaned close and whispered, "Are you carrying my child?"

Grace dropped her hands. In the darkened bedroom, moonlight streamed in through the cracks in the shuttered window. Her tears ran unchecked down her face.

"Quit crying. I can't abide a woman's tears." He tightened his grip on her shoulder.

"How could I know such a thing?" she whispered. "I wasn't even aware that. . .well, what I mean is, I've never had a mother to explain things. And. . .for a child to begin. . .I've never given it a thought."

"You'll know because your. . ." Daniel fell silent. He had to force the words past his throat. "Y-your. . .uh. . .lady's time—" He lapsed into silence.

She gasped. "I'll not discuss such with you, sir." She tried to step away from him.

He held on doggedly, his eyes closed tight so he wouldn't have to look at her while he discussed such an embarrassing subject. "A lady's time. . .doesn't. . .come when a woman is with child. Has yours come?"

"It doesn't?"

Daniel shook his head.

"But that will take months to know."

"No, it doesn't. It only takes a month."

"Why is that?" Grace asked, her eyes wide with confusion.

Nearly in physical pain from the topic, Daniel growled, "Because it comes every month, so if it doesn't come that month, then you know."

"Mine doesn't. . .come. . .every month." Grace licked her lips as if her mouth had gone stone dry. "I mean, it never has. I had no idea it was supposed to." With a sudden flare of temper, Grace added, "Every month? That will be a nuisance."

She exasperated Daniel past his embarrassment. "You're a woman grown, Grace. You're supposed to have one per month."

"Well, I've only had a couple of them in my whole life."

Daniel glared at her. "How old did you say you are?"

"Seventeen."

"I was married at seventeen. My wife was the same age. She told me it started when a woman was twelve. Every month. You're not doing it right."

Grace looked angry for a moment, then her mouth formed itself into a straight line and her brow wrinkled. "I'm s-sorry." Her eyes filled with tears again. She looked down at her skinny body.

"It's okay. I reckon you can't help doing it wrong." He patted her on the arm with his big clodhopper hands.

"I doubt if I'm carrying a baby. I've never been much good at any woman things. I can't cook."

"You're getting better."

"The potatoes were awful tonight."

Daniel shrugged. No truer words were ever spoken. "We could go back to cooking in the belly of the stove. Then they were only black on the outside instead of all the way through."

"I can't sew." She looked at her pretty but gigantic dress.

"We've got growing boys. You really do need to figure that one out. Maybe Sophie McClellen could help come spring. We don't have any goods for you to sew anyway. I'll teach you how to make moccasins if you want."

"I'll probably fail at this baby-having business, too."

"It's not a failure if you're not expecting. It would be for the best."

Grace shook her head. "You've got five children. You must love them. Of course you want more of them."

"No, I don't."

Grace looked up at him, her heart in her eyes. "Why don't you want to have babies with me?"

Daniel looked at her and ached with the loneliness of married life. "Why has God allowed such a wicked temptation to exist? He has to know how dangerous it is."

"Dangerous? What do you mean?"

"It is if you have a child—especially my child. I seem to make them in batches. Margaret barely survived the twins. She felt sickly for months before and after they were born. We never should have risked another child. Never!" Daniel gulped and felt his Adam's apple bob much as Adam's must have when he swallowed that tempting fruit in the Garden of Eden.

"I was weak. I let Margaret convince me."

"Well, Daniel, God probably made people that way."

"No, it's not God." Daniel shook his head. If he could just convince her, then she'd help him resist. It would be so much easier with her help. Margaret had worked against him. "It's the devil himself that lays this temptation down before me. I figured that out as soon as the twins were born."

"Why would you think that? God created man. He wanted children to be born so the world could go on."

"If he wanted the world to go on"—Daniel caught her by the upper arms and held her so tightly his hands shook—"then why did he make Margaret die?"

Grace was silent.

Daniel's grip loosened; he knew he must be hurting her. "The Bible says, 'And thy desire shall be to thy husband.' It was part of the punishment of Eve. I've read it over a hundred times. Eve got desire for her husband and pain in childbirth. Adam got hard work and weeds in his field."

"I have no idea what you're talking about, but I would love to have your child."

"No! I don't want to lose you. I can't lose you." Then he lowered his head and captured her lips with his own.

She grabbed hold of him and hung on like a buffalo burr. "You're not going anywhere."

"I have to get out of here."

Grace caught two handfuls of his golden hair in her fists and glared. "You are the most stubborn man who ever lived. This is why you've been angry at me all this time?"

Daniel couldn't stop his hands from sliding up her sides. "You're too thin. You have to eat more."

She twisted his hair. "Don't change the subject. I have always been thin. I have survived very well with no meat on my bones. Now answer me."

Daniel closed his eyes. "Yes," he admitted. "This is why."

"Well, stop it." Grace pulled his hair tighter; the pain must have gotten his attention, because his eyes popped open. "This family is going to start getting along, and that includes you and me. And every time you're rude to me, I'm going to know why, understand?"

Daniel nodded. On a sigh he said, "But what if you have a baby? What if you die? I can't stand to—"

"Daniel?" Grace yanked his hair until he quit talking.

"What?"

Grace drew his head toward her. "I'm counting that kind of talk as rude."

A woman leaned heavily on her husband, pale and thin, shaking, near collapse. She was weeping into her hands. The husband, as sad as his wife, supported her. Hannah could see that he fought his own tears.

"The doctor says we don't dare to try again, Virginia."

"I don't mind, Phillip." The sight of Virginia, her eyes red and teary, made Hannah wonder what could leave someone so devastated. "I'll be all right."

"No, I almost lost you this time. I won't do that. No babies, Virginia—no!"

Hannah's breath caught in her throat. All this grief over a child? All she knew about children was that people threw them away. Oh, to be wanted like this. Tears welled in her own eyes at the bittersweet dream.

She studied the couple, looking at how neat and clean their clothes were, no worn seams or faded fabric. They weren't dressed like wealthy people, but their cheeks weren't hollow and their eyes, though sad, weren't sunken with hunger. She wasn't even aware of standing or moving until the man nearly bumped into her.

She preferred to look more closely at a family before she approached them, but she felt God nudging her, telling her to speak. She had time to wait until the doctor was done checking Libby's ankle; then her little sister would stay overnight. God had brought Hannah to this office at this moment.

With her voice trembling, Hannah said, "I am trying to raise three boys I found living on the street. They are good boys, smart, polite, and honest, but I can barely afford to feed them. They aren't babies, and I know people want babies. . . ."

The look in the woman's eyes, the dizzying swing from despair to hope and longing, almost broke Hannah's heart. Her chest heaved with a sob, but she kept it inside. She would live on the kindness in this woman's eyes for years.

The man looked down at his wife. "Children who have lived on the street might be difficult, Ginnie. I don't know. . . ."

"Would it hurt to meet them, Phillip?"

Hannah, with all the skills of a master beggar, manipulator, and liar, said, "If you don't want them as your children, maybe you could put them to work. They are fourteen, eight, and six. They could live in your barn, and they'd want nothing but food. They're used to the cold. The rags they wear are all they need."

Hannah didn't mention Libby. No one would want a mute child who limped. Just finding someone to take the boys would be a miracle. Yes, they would lose Trevor's three dollars a month—the only money they had—but she wouldn't ask God for more.

"They're hungry, Phillip." Virginia's hand clutched at her husband's arm until Hannah thought either her hand or his arm would break. "I want to meet them. So do you—you know it."

Phillip held his wife's gaze for a long moment; then a smile broke out. He turned to Hannah. "Yes, we do want to meet them."

She left the couple waiting near their shed, not wanting them to see how the family lived. Then Hannah went to her brothers.

Trevor sat on the floor next to the trash barrel, reading a book to Nolan and Bruce. Elation raised her spirits as she looked at the three of them.

"How is she?" Trevor closed the book. All three boys looked at her. Libby would be home tomorrow and in need of constant care.

Hannah pulled her scarf off her head, her arms almost too heavy to lift. "The doctor said she'd be okay."

Hannah looked at Trevor. She saw the answer to her question in his eyes. No letter from Grace. She slumped into the only chair they owned.

Nolan looked at her with wide, worried eyes. "I got the bread, Hannah. Mr. Daily let me have it, and I was real careful to hide from his grumpy wife."

Despite her best efforts to protect the children from grim reality, they knew how bad things were.

Hannah smiled at her brothers. Trevor had been killing himself working for a pittance at the carpet mill. Nolan, growing fast, hungry all the time, such a bright boy, hated going to school when he could be earning money. Little Bruce should have had baby fat still; instead, he was lean and far too quiet. And he had a gift for thieving that would only get more pronounced if he kept living on the street.

"I talked to someone who would love to have children." Her heart lifted as she thought of the lovely couple who had come out of a room beside Libby's.

Hannah knew her brothers. Trevor understood what she meant, and he looked wary. Nolan, smart as a whip, was wondering if they'd feed him. Bruce turned his trusting eyes on Hannah, too obedient for a six-year-old. She knew he'd do as he was told. Nolan and Bruce would go, but Trevor needed this home, too. He needed to get out of that mill and back into school. And he wouldn't want to leave her and Libby.

Hannah prayed. She knew God would have to make it all work out, and she had no doubt He would. "They're waiting in Daily's Diner to meet you. I didn't want them to see us in the shack. If they like you, they'll take you home tonight."

Trevor opened his mouth to refuse.

She nailed him with a glare. "I want you to go with them, Trevor. To make sure the boys are okay."

"What about you? What about Libby?"

"Grace's money will come. We'll be okay."

"What kind of people are these who would take three of us and leave you and Libby in the cold?"

"They don't know about Libby. I saw no point in telling them." Hannah's hand closed hard over the wobbly latch that pinned the little door closed. "I'm sixteen. Grace got a job teaching school when she was sixteen."

"You can't teach school. You haven't been to school yourself." Trevor stood, trembling with anger. "You need me. Let the boys go."

"I haven't been to school, but that doesn't mean I'm uneducated. I can read and do my numbers. I can teach. I'll find work. You kids"—she waved her hand as if she were annoyed with them—"have made it impossible for me to work. And now, with Libby getting better and three less mouths to feed, I won't have to earn that much. As soon as I can find a teaching job, I'll take it. Libby might start talking when her foot is better, and then maybe someone will adopt her, too."

Except Libby's foot was never getting better. And that probably meant she'd never speak, either. The doctor had done all he could. She didn't tell her brothers that. She'd pick her up tomorrow, give the doctor the last bit of money she had, and bring her little sister home.

"You need me, Hannah." Trevor stepped away from his brothers and glared at her.

"The boys need you more. Please, Trevor, go."

Bitter and angry, Trevor stared at her. She prayed he'd relent as she fiercely controlled her tears. She had to get him out of here, out of this life. Even though his mill money was all they had, continuing to work there would destroy him.

And if he went to this meeting angry, the couple wouldn't want him. Just the chance that they could want a fourteen-year-old was slim.

"Trevor, do this for me. This couple seems very nice, but I'll feel better if you're there to make sure nothing like Parrish happens to Nolan and Bruce. Don't think of it as being adopted. Think of it as the two of us splitting the family in two so we can take better care of them. You see to the boys; I'll care for Libby."

Trevor hadn't been one of Parrish's children. Parrish only wanted girls. But he'd heard all about the hard work, cruelty, and hunger.

After a long second, Trevor said, "Promise you'll find me if you need anything. I'll get a message to you so you'll know where we are."

Hannah's exhausted eyes dropped closed with relief. Now if only the couple would take them. Now if only Grace would send money one more time. It had been too long. Grace had never been a day late before. Hannah knew her sister was in trouble, but she didn't speak of it. Hannah held her breath, waiting, praying. She'd have said anything to get Trevor to grab this chance.

"Promise me, Hannah."

She would never disrupt their lives. She would never see her little brothers again. She prayed for forgiveness and said, "I promise."

The couple grabbed onto the boys as if they needed them to survive. They bought them supper, including Hannah. She waved her brothers off with a smile and a full belly then returned to her empty shed, her empty cupboard, and her empty life. Adding Libby to it tomorrow would only emphasize the emptiness.

The boys had left everything behind—and that wasn't much. But Hannah had three tattered blankets to roll up in. She lay by her barrel and cried until her heart was as empty as her life.

Her house was full of furniture.

Her boys were full of laughter and food.

Her heart was full of love.

Grace kept coming back to it. For the first time in her life, she was truly, fully, joyously happy.

She had no idea about the baby, but from what Daniel said, with her body being abnormal, she doubted she could have a child.

She wanted one. It was amazing how fiercely she wanted one. She pictured a tiny baby—a girl, she wished fervently, especially when the boys were rampaging through the house, slamming doors open and leaving them that way. Only one, not a set all coming at once.

But God had already given her so much, she didn't dare ask for more. If she asked for anything, it was for Hannah. There would be no money coming from Grace. How were they managing?

She thought of her promise to be brave. God's faithfulness to her deserved her best efforts at being faithful to him.

"It is of the Lord's mercies that we are not consumed, because his compassions

fail not. They are new every morning: great is thy faithfulness."

Be faithful to Hannah and the children. Grace smiled as she prayed it. God was so much more faithful to His children than His children ever were to Him. Grace clung to that promise and attended to her new family.

"Great is thy faithfulness." The verse echoed in her head as she saw the life she had literally fallen into. It could only be God's will that she be here with Daniel and the boys. How could God have found her in that awful house with Parrish? How could He have led her to this place and, through the work of her fear and Parrish's cruel obsession with her, driven her into Daniel's home? How had God arranged for Parson Roscoe to drop by and insist on a marriage? Even the snowfall that had kept Parrish out and kept Grace from escaping in those first unhappy days were part of the pattern God had set for her life.

Oh God, thank You. Help me give back to You with my own faithfulness. She thought it when she woke. The words sang in her heart throughout the day. She remembered it while she talked with the boys and her husband. She fell asleep in Daniel's arms with that prayer on her lips. God would care for all His children.

Great is Thy faithfulness, Lord!

Whack! "We're going to go over this again, Miss McClellen."

Whack! Parrish lifted the ruler and held it ready over Sally's trembling hand. The raised welts on her palm gave him vicious satisfaction. He glanced up and saw the rage and fear on her sisters' faces. They didn't like it, but they wouldn't do anything.

He knew how children were. They didn't tell their parents about punishment at school. Parents sided with the teacher and doled out a second punishment at home. The ruler sang as it whizzed through the air and landed on soft flesh. By nightfall, the welts would go down, and palms didn't show bruising. Even if a bruise or two showed, a few lashes with a ruler were acceptable punishment.

Whack! If Parrish wielded his ruler with more force, more often than might be called for, who was to know? The other children studied, their heads kept carefully bowed. He had them well trained. Mandy and Beth did their best not to glance up, but he saw them sneak a peek once in a while. He'd make them regret that.

Whack! He sometimes let the ruler fall almost until he drew blood, especially with the girls. He would work out his anger on those little hands and imagine Grace and what the future held in store for her.

He heard Sally's stifled sobs and felt a thrill of savage pleasure. That was four. He usually gave five, but Sally McClellen was unusually stubborn. One more.

Whack! She would know better than to jump to the defense of her slow-witted kindergarten classmate. A boy. He much preferred punishing girls. One more.

Whack! He had to force himself to stop. The sound of wood striking flesh made his mouth water, and he wanted to go on all day. He saw a line of blood welling on the side of Sally's hand. He reined himself in before he marked her any more. It wouldn't do for her father to get upset. Clay McClellen had the kind of eyes Parrish didn't want looking at him.

"Go back to your desk, you stupid child. I'll be glad to give you your little classmate's punishment anytime you want."

Trembling and bleeding, Sally went quietly to her desk. She flinched every time he called on her. He made her stay in for morning recess and sit at her desk through dinner. She folded in on herself when she was in the schoolroom alone with him. He thought finally she was learning.

"We've got to do something about him," Beth hissed as she and Mandy shared their lunch pail.

Mandy looked at the schoolroom. Her eyes burned. Beth knew that

510

look. Mandy wasn't one to sit back when the family needed protection, no more than Ma.

"We can't tell anyone," Mandy whispered back. "Master Parrish says Pa would stick up for the teacher. He says we'll get a thrashing at home worse than the one at school."

"We told Tillie, and nothing bad happened." Beth chewed on her sandwich. It tasted like sawdust. "She said she'd figure out a way to help us. And Pa might not stick up for Master Parrish, either. He might see how mean Master Parrish is and beat him up and fire him and everything."

Mandy stared at the building as if she could see through the walls if she tried hard enough.

"I don't like Sally being in there alone with Master Parrish. He's cruel, and he likes making her cry. You can see he likes hurting her." Beth looked nervously at the school. Even from across the yard, she worried that somehow Master Parrish would know they were bad. He liked lashing Sally the most, but he didn't spare the rod for the other students.

"I wish the Reeves boys were here."

Mandy gasped. "Why would you want those awful Reeveses around?"

"Because no one can control them. They'd figure out a way to make Master Parrish's life miserable, maybe even get him fired like they did to poor Miss Calhoun." Beth figured out that the Reeves boys might be pure trouble on ten running feet. But after all, they were only boys. Since when did a bunch of boys hold a candle to a girl when it came to plotting? It was time to take action.

"True enough. They'd never put up with him."

Beth needed her sister to agree. Mandy was the organized one. She'd have to help. She decided making Mandy even more upset might be just the right thing to do. "Sally wasn't bad today. She just tried to explain about Clovis being young. She didn't do anything wrong."

"Nope, she didn't." Mandy kept eating, but she swallowed as if the sandwich was stuck in her throat.

"She was bleeding." Beth added that just in case her big sister wasn't 100 percent mad clear to the bone.

"I saw." Mandy turned away from the school.

Beth snatched the biggest apple out of the tin pail.

Mandy didn't fight her for it, so she knew Mandy was serious about setting Sally free from the man who seemed to delight in picking on her.

"He wasn't like this at first. He's getting worse as the year goes on. And he seems to especially like to pick on Sally." Beth had felt the lash of those six whacks with his ruler. They all had. Six-year-old Sally, the littlest girl in school, seemed to earn the brunt of his temper, and Beth couldn't help believing it was because she was so small and defenseless.

Mandy looked away from the building. "Ma and Pa might not agree that we need protecting from Master Parrish, but I'm not going to sit quiet while he hurts my sister."

Beth nodded in complete agreement.

"I say we take care of it ourselves."

"But how?" Beth asked, thinking of the power of a teacher.

Mandy looked around the school yard. All the other children lived in town in Mosqueros. They had gone home for lunch while the McClellen girls lingered over their tasteless food.

Mandy leaned close to Beth and whispered, "I've got a plan. But we might need help."

Beth felt her heart beating with excitement. Mandy was almost as good at setting a trap as Ma. "Tillie hates that he makes us call him Master. She'll help."

"She will for a fact." Mandy smiled a mean smile.

Beth crunched into her apple, and it almost tasted sweet—like revenge.

"The weather is almost springlike, but that gap is still packed to the top with snow. What if it stays forever, Pa? What if we have to just live in here by ourselves for the rest of our lives?" Mark tugged on Daniel's pants as they trekked through the woods.

Daniel had a surprise for the family and decided to let Mark in on it. Mark was still openly hostile to Grace, and Daniel blamed himself for it. He needed to unteach the lessons the boy had learned at his side.

"There wasn't any snow in it when we bought the place in June. So it figures it melts sometimes. And anyway, that snow we got was a freak blizzard. I don't reckon we'll ever get snowed in here so rock solid again." He laid his hand on Mark's shoulder. "It hasn't been so bad, being stuck together all winter. We got the house built and all that furniture. If we'd been running to town for schooling and such all winter, we'd'a never gotten half as much done."

"But now Ma is trying to make a school for us out here. I don't wanta hafta study all the livelong day." Mark kicked at the rotting leaves and fallen branches that littered the woods.

"It comes in mighty handy to know some figuring. And reading is just plumb useful. We should count our good fortune to have a schoolteacher of our very own, right here."

Mark snorted. "If she's so good, why'd you get her fired from her job in town?"

Daniel flinched. "I think she's changed some since then." He thought of his warm, generous, playful wife. Nothing like the fussy, impatient schoolteacher she'd been. "I know she's changed."

"Well, she still comes at us with the Bible, trying to make us read it. I'm already a good reader. I don't need no more schoolin'."

Daniel tried not to smile at his five-year-old son. He remembered school. He'd spent more time fighting it than he ever had learning anything. He'd missed every day possible, and he'd quit the first second his pa had let him.

"Look up ahead. That's the surprise I was telling you about."

Mark stopped. He looked around the woods.

Weak winter sunlight filtered down through the bare branches. A light cold breeze made the treetops sway, but tall, thin saplings blocked the wind near the ground. It was a pleasant day for a walk.

"I don't see anything." Mark turned left and right.

"Look up." Daniel lifted Mark's chin.

A grin broke out on his son's face. "A bee tree."

Daniel chuckled. "Yep. And where there's bees. . ."

Mark chimed in, "There's honey."

Daniel nodded, and he and his stubborn son shared a smile. Everyone back home would love this treat. "We're taking it. The bees will be sleeping because of the cold. They won't give us a bit of a fight."

Daniel pulled the sack off his shoulder. He'd collected every jar and crock in the house and brought them along. Mark and he would fill them all then take back what they could carry. Daniel could already taste honey on his biscuits.

Daniel and Mark were greeted like heroes. Mark even endured a hug from Grace. Daniel did more than endure one. He gave her one right back.

They ate their lunch with their biscuits smothered in honey. Daniel showed Grace how to sweeten the sourdough and add extra flour and eggs to make a cake. They all spent an afternoon in the crisp mountain air fetching more of the sticky sweet treat.

When Grace made the boys settle in for lessons after supper, Mark went along willingly.

"Daniel, it wouldn't hurt for you to do some reading along with the boys," Grace said sternly. "You're never too old to learn."

Daniel's mouth dropped open. Then he saw Mark staring at him and quickly controlled himself. He said with mock obedience, "Yes, ma'am."

His boys snickered, and Daniel let them. In fact, he did a fine impression of them for the fun of it. He slumped over to sit in front of the fire in the rocking chair he'd built for himself to match Grace's. Grace handed him a piece of bark and a chunk of coal.

"Do the multiplication tables. Your stubborn sons think they're too hard. You need to set a good example for them. Start with the ones, and when your slate is full, let me check them. If they're all correct, you can rub them out and do more."

Daniel was stunned at her bossy voice.

Ike's giggle turned to out-and-out laughter, and the rest of the boys joined in.

Grace, her eyes shining, couldn't keep a straight face.

Daniel gave up and laughed along with them. And he did his multiplication tables swiftly. The little woman might as well know he had some book learning.

When Grace said, "Daniel, I'm impressed," his heart turned over and he kissed her.

Then she thanked him for the honey just as warmly. She thanked Mark, too.

They finished their lessons together, with Daniel reading to them out of the big Bible.

 **T W E N T Y - F I V E**

Tillie heard the whispers from behind the chicken coop. This time it was no accident that she'd stumbled on the girls. She'd seen the welts Sally had tried to hide. The girls were still determined not to tell their parents, but they'd confided in her before. Maybe they would again.

When they got home from school on Friday, the girls made quick excuses to go outside, either to hide Sally's wounds or to commiserate.

Tillie watched them slip behind the little building and followed them as soon as she could, leaving two sleeping babies and Sophie with Laura on her lap.

Tillie heard Sally's little voice break. Mandy and Beth made cooing sounds of comfort. Comfort. That was what Tillie had come to give to the girls. She stood straighter as she remembered the comfort God had sent to her when she was young and afraid.

God, I'm sorry I turned from You. I am truly sorry. Thank You for Adam's miracle. It called me to my senses. Only now that I see children trapped in their own prison of fear do I remember the comfort of Your saving grace.

Tillie felt God's own arms wrap around her and protect her. Tears nearly bit at her eyes as she realized all she'd given up. The only One who would always be with her.

Forgive me.

She walked around the shed.

The three girls, sitting in a little huddle whispering, straightened and looked fearful. It cut at Tillie's heart to think she'd added fear to these little girls' lives.

"Now then, young ladies, what are we going to do to rid this town of that nasty *Master* Parrish?" She made sure to sneer his name.

Three sets of bright blue eyes hardened with determination.

Mandy said, "I told Sally to make sure you saw her hands."

Tillie realized that it had been a little too easy, especially when an observant mother like Sophie had missed it.

"Why did you do that?"

"Because we've got a plan that might need a little adult help."

Tillie had planned her escape for months. She approved of plans. "I'll be glad to help."

"Good." Mandy's eyes sharpened in a way that made Tillie glad she was on the same side as these little rascals. "Because we've got some work to do before Monday morning."

"And what happens Monday morning?"

Beth put her arm around Sally and lifted her little sister's palm so Tillie could see the cuts and welts. "Come Monday morning, we're breaking free of things like this."

A hundred less-than-Christian thoughts flooded though Tillie's mind, all centering around that awful man who'd hurt these girls. But she saw their courage and knew how smart they were.

Tillie didn't get mad. Instead, she smiled and dropped down on her knees, joining the girls' circle. "When it comes to breaking free, I'm just the woman you want."

Parrish's cruel hands reached for her. They grabbed her, and his fists landed. And then it wasn't she they were hitting; it was Grace.

Hannah jerked awake with a scream.

Parrish had Grace. Hannah knew it. Nothing less than terrible danger could have kept Grace from sending the money. But finally, after months of silence, Hannah had to give in and admit it. Grace was in trouble. Which meant she and Libby were on their own.

Libby had healed more slowly than ever this time, too laid-up for Hannah to leave her and find work, not that anyone would hire her anyway for anything but mill work, not dressed in rags like these. She'd moved the two of them to a deserted cellar because she didn't want Trevor to come hunting and see how much trouble they were in and maybe give up his new home.

Mr. Daily always remembered the bread, and there was more for her and Libby now, without the boys sharing, but that was all. For a month, except a few scraps Hannah had dug out of the garbage and a few bites she'd bought with money begged from strangers, they'd lived on nothing but bread. It took good food, meat and vegetables, to knit broken bones, and their meager fare had kept Libby from healing.

They were warmer here than the shed because of the approaching spring. But still their cellar became sharply cold at night, even with the two of them snuggled up.

The house, less than twenty steps away, had a single man living in it. He'd never noticed them. His scraps, thrown out in the alley for stray cats, had helped keep them alive.

No one showed any interest in this hole in the ground.

When Libby came down with her third cold of the winter, Hannah sat next to her, fighting back tears as she longed to give her little sister suppers of warm broth full of meat and vegetables and hearty breakfasts of oatmeal and honey.

They lay together in the pitch dark of the cellar. Hannah's nightmare had awakened Libby. Hannah could see her little sister's eyes silently worrying. They were able to see each other only because moonlight had found its way through the cracked cellar door only inches overhead.

Hannah put her arm around Libby. "I've been thinking about Grace. I'm worried about her."

Libby had never met Grace, but Hannah talked of her often.

Hannah considered all that was involved in her plan; her main worry was for her silent little sister. Libby would agree to anything if it meant helping others. She'd never make a demand for herself.

Hannah brushed her chapped, calloused fingers down Libby's hollow cheeks. "Grace and I are sisters, just like you and I are sisters. We just found each other and hung on."

Libby watched her with wide eyes. Her eyes shone with love when Hannah talked to her or read her stories.

"I was six and Grace was seven. She'd already been with Parrish for three years. He adopted her out of the orphanage when she was three. That's how old I think you are right now."

Hannah held up three fingers and counted slowly, "One, two, three."

Libby touched each one of Hannah's fingers, copying the motion but not saying the words. Hannah hoped that, inside her head, Libby was learning. Soon she'd teach her to write. Then maybe Libby would find a voice through the written word.

"By the time she was four, she was picking lint off the carpet under the presser."

Hannah suspected Libby had been doing that when she'd been hurt. Children as young as three were often forced into the mills. She still wanted to cry when she thought of the shape Libby had been in when Trevor had found her.

Trevor had carried her home, dark rage in his eyes as he demanded that Hannah take her in. As if Hannah would have refused.

They'd taken her to the doctor for her broken ankle, Hannah pretending to be her mother so no questions would be asked. The ankle had to be rebroken before it would heal. Grace's first envelope of money had come the same day as the doctor's bill.

"How would you like to get to know Grace?" Hannah considered all the complications. But Hannah was out of ideas. Hunting down her big sister tempted her beyond her ability to resist.

The three-year-old brightened and sat up, looking at Hannah with eager eyes. With a sigh of relief, Hannah could tell that Libby was going to get over this cold without it going into her chest. A rugged little girl who'd lived through three operations and been thrown out onto the street with less regard than that given to a wounded animal, Libby was tough.

I wonder if maybe Libby isn't tougher than I am.

"I think we ought to go visit Grace."

The hope in Libby's expression ate at Hannah's heart. *No one should want to leave their home this much.* But Chicago hadn't been kind to either of them.

A flush tinted Libby's cheeks that made her look almost healthy.

Hannah decided then and there to act on the notion playing around in her head. They were getting out of here. "We're going really soon, and we're going on the train."

A gasp of excitement shook Libby's little body.

Hannah hugged her tightly. A train meant change. It meant getting away and starting over. To Libby, a train must sound like a dream come true. "We do have a couple of problems."

Libby's eyes narrowed, and her brow furrowed.

Hannah almost smiled at the childish determination. There was a problem. They'd overcome it. That's how children of the street survived.

Hannah almost trembled, she was so afraid of what had happened to Grace. She kept thinking that Parrish had finally found her.

Libby tugged on her dress as if to ask, "What problems?"

"Well. . .the. . .uh. . .the main problem is. . ." Hannah looked down and smiled at this sister of her heart. "We can't afford tickets." Hannah remembered Grace's plan to stow away in the baggage car. That was what she and Libby would do.

The other problem Hannah didn't speak of. What would they find when they got to Mosqueros, Texas? Hannah wanted out of the city for Libby, but she also had an overwhelming urge to go rescue her big sister. Wherever Grace was, she must be in terrible, terrible trouble.

Grace snuggled under the covers, thinking of her blissful life. A rumble of thunder had jarred her from sleep. She shifted position, disturbing Daniel, who had been holding her close in his arms.

"Rain." She gave Daniel's shoulder a good jostle. "Wake up. It's spring."

"It's the middle of March. It's not spring yet." Daniel rolled over, grumbling.

"This is Texas. Spring comes in March." Grace laughed and gave him a solid poke in the ribs with her elbow.

He sighed deeply. Then the thunder sounded again and he sat up beside her. He ran his hand over his rumpled blond hair. "Rain'll speed things along, melting us out of here." He looked sideways at her and smiled.

"Still trying to escape from this marriage, Mr. Reeves?" she sassed.

Daniel grabbed her and hugged her tight. "I reckon I give up. I am well and truly caught." He left to start the kitchen fire.

Lying in bed still, nearly humming with the pleasure of her new life, Grace watched him leave. It was more than she'd ever dreamed possible. Oh, the boys were pills, especially Mark. And Parrish might still be out there somewhere. But what could he do now? She was a married woman. Any claim of fatherhood was dissolved by her marriage. The law wouldn't stand by while she was handed over to him. And neither would Daniel.

And what about Hannah and the rest of the sisters who had escaped from Parrish? If only all her sisters could know the joy of having a family. She was suddenly glad that Parrish had chased after her. Yes, she'd been hounded nearly into the ground, but at least her sisters had been safe. And now she was, too.

She said quietly to the ceiling, "If Parrish did show up now, Daniel would protect me. Daniel loves me." He'd never said it, but Grace knew with heart-deep assurance it was true. She threw back the covers, excited to think about the coming of spring.

When her feet hit the floor, the room lifted up off the ground, spun around over her head, then turned on its side. She fell face forward, scrambling to grab the bedpost. Her hand slipped, and she crashed to the floor.

TWENTY-SIX

The children ran screaming across the playground, enjoying their morning recess. What little beasts they were. Parrish went to the door and rang the school bell, ending their fun with relish.

He'd dreamed about Grace again last night, about hurting her. And he'd awakened so hungry for his revenge that he needed to work it off on someone.

Parrish stood just inside the door as the children trooped into the schoolhouse. They were instantly silent. He'd trained them well. The littlest McClellen girl hung back with her sisters. She was just a bit older than Grace had been when she'd first come to him. Grace's hair had been this same white-blond color. He'd been too easy on Grace.

Sally McClellen was finding out how he should have acted. He knew just what he was going to do when he got his hands on Grace this time.

Spring was slow in coming. The weather had turned warm, but not warm enough to melt the snow in that gap. He'd heard talk around town about the Reeveses. He'd listened but had been careful not to show any interest. No one knew if that gap had ever snowed closed before. Until Daniel Reeves had moved in there, no one in the area had even realized the canyon existed.

Several times he heard men talking at church—which he faithfully attended to pick up gossip and impress parents with his piety—about scaling the sides of the canyon and checking to see if the Reeveses were faring well.

They talked, but the consensus was Daniel had beef enough and supplies to last all winter and he'd be fine. There was no need for someone to risk his neck climbing in there. Parrish learned that Daniel was a Kansas farmer with five little boys. He also knew the man hadn't been in the war, spent time in the frontier army, or been on a cattle drive, things that would have made him tough.

Luther, an old hand on the McClellens' ranch, said he might make the climb just to spend time in the mountains again. Buff, his saddle partner, snorted and said there was no such thing as a Texas mountain.

"These hills wouldn't be foothills in the Rockies," Luther agreed. Luther discussed a way across the top of the bluff, where a man could go most of the way with no trouble if he went afoot.

Parrish heard every word. He'd spent enough time scouting the area that he knew the exact place Luther meant.

Parrish was running out of patience. His dreams were coming more often. Sleep was eluding him. The children were grating on his nerves. If that fat old Luther could get in there, then so could Parrish. He could handle Daniel Reeves and his whelps, and he could haul one little woman back out with him. He slapped his ruler on his hand, hungry just thinking about what he'd do to Grace.

"Adam!" Tillie slammed through the barn door.

Adam looked up from the roan that he'd taken back from vigilantes who'd been gunning for Sophie. He straightened and smiled. He looked at her pretty face and knew he needed to talk to her, too. He gave his horse a soft slap on the rump and laid the brush aside. Swinging the stall gate closed behind him, he walked right up to Tillie. She looked excited about something, but he decided he needed to go first, before she said something that got him off the subject.

He forced himself to say what had been on his mind from the first minute he clapped eyes on her. "You are the prettiest little thing I've ever seen."

Tillie's open mouth stopped yammering as if every thought had fled from her mind.

"Yep, and you're not the same woman I found out in the hills that first night."

"I—I'm not?" she stammered.

"Nope. That woman was afraid of her own shadow."

"Did you decide that before or after I beat you up?"

Adam felt his brows slam together. "I've told you a dozen times I was trying not to hurt you. Now don't start that. You've been so busy with Sophie and those babies that we haven't even been able to go on another ride. And I need to find out more about how you want the house laid out. I'm ready to start building."

Tillie crossed her arms as if he'd just insulted her. "Why on earth would I care how you lay out your house, Adam?"

Adam wondered if women were born so scatterbrained or if it was something they learned at their mamas' knees. He figured the trait must be inborn, because his Sophie hadn't spent much time at her mama's knee, and she had that same twisting-turning way about her thinking.

"You need to like it."

Tillie's eyes narrowed. "Why?"

Another dumb question. But Adam didn't point that out. He'd learned a lot from watching Clay chase his tail around his women-folk. He knew there was a fitting way to talk to women. At least fitting to their way of thinking, dumb as it seemed. He relaxed and smiled, though his stomach twisted in a way that made it mighty hard to keep the corners of his mouth turned up.

"Because..." Adam fished around in his head. He'd read some books. He'd heard talk. He knew what she wanted. He sank to one knee on the straw-covered barn floor and took her hand.

Her eyes widened until white showed all the way around, like the eyes of his roan when it had a bad scare. That wasn't what Adam wanted to see. Still, he floundered on. "Because I want you to marry me."

Her jaw dropped open. Adam was grateful it was still early spring, or bugs would have flown into her mouth.

"Since when?"

Adam's heart sank a bit, and he stood, thinking this might go better if he was standing over her a bit. "Why, since almost forever, I guess." He held her hand tighter and pulled her close. "I've never given much thought to getting married. And since I've met you, I haven't been able to think of much else."

"Really?" Her eyes turned from scared to interested.

Adam's heart quit pounding so hard, although it still seemed as if it might knock clear out of his chest. "You're a fine woman, Tillie. I think we'd get along well together. Please, will you marry me?"

Tillie stared at him a long, long time. At last, as if her neck became weak, her head dropped down and she looked at their joined hands. "We don't know each other very well, Adam. I am so honored by your proposal, and"—she looked up, scared again, but a different kind of scared—"a woman likes to hear of love when a man asks for her hand. But I don't think we know each other well enough to call it love."

Adam nodded. "But we do know each other well enough to believe love could come with time." Adam looked at her work-calloused hands, so competent and still so soft. He smiled. "And maybe not that long a time."

Tillie smiled back. "I believe I'd like to be married to you, Adam."

Adam laughed and grabbed her around the waist. He lifted her off her feet until she looked down into his eyes, almost as though he'd knelt again. Then he lowered her until her lips met his, and she came halfway to meet him.

When the kiss ended, he settled her on her own feet again. "Maybe not that long at all, Till. And how would you like a cabin and a barn and maybe even a few children running around our ankles, like Sophie and Clay's?"

Tillie jumped as if she'd been stabbed by a hat pin. "I didn't come in here to get proposed to."

Adam's heart twisted. Was she taking it all back? Was she changing her mind? "Well then, why did you come in here?"

She grabbed Adam by the collar of his shirt with both hands and shook him.

"Master Parrish?" Sally turned wide eyes on Parrish.

He looked at the youngest McClellen. "I've told you many times to go quietly to your seat, Miss McClellen."

"But I brought you a piece of cake, Master Parrish."

Parrish knew the ways of children. He saw something in the unpleasant child's eyes that didn't sit right with him. Catching her chin, he took a moment to consider it.

No fear. That was what was missing. The McClellens had always been a strangely stiff-necked brood, harder to cow than some. But why wouldn't she be afraid after she'd defiantly broken the rules?

The brat held out a neatly-wrapped napkin. She unfolded the edges, and he saw that a slice of white cake lay on her hand. Could she really think a piece of cake would save her?

"To the front of the room, Miss McClellen."

The girl's confident eyes wavered.

The power to make her afraid rushed to Parrish's head like strong liquor. He could live on it instead of food.

Sally walked slowly to the front and stood beside his desk. Her shoulders trembled.

Parrish followed along, enjoying every slow step that brought him closer to her.

"Master Parrish?" Mandy McClellen rose from her desk, another child speaking when she was supposed to sit quietly.

Parrish would have found an excuse to punish someone, most likely

Sally, but he was thrilled that the children made it so easy. "Join your sister at the front."

"Master Parrish, I want to take Sally's punishment for her." Mandy strode forward and planted herself in front of her sister.

"You'll get your own punishment. My ruler is strong enough to last through many lashes." Parrish approached the older girl. The girl stood fast between him and Sally.

"Sally's hand hasn't healed up from Friday, Master Parrish. Don't hit her again. I'll take double the lashes." Mandy held out her hand.

"You can have that indeed, but your sister will still take hers, as well." Parrish noticed Mandy's hand was steady. He wanted it to tremble. He wanted fear. He kept coming. His ruler rested on the desk behind the girls.

Beth McClellen stood from her seat. "If you won't let Mandy do it, let me. I'll take Sally's punishment." Beth joined her sisters in the front of the schoolroom. "Sally's hand is too sore. You could really hurt her, Master Parrish. You can't hit her again so soon. You punished her every day last week. That's wrong of you."

Parrish froze. The three girls faced him defiantly. Not even little Sally was shaking now. Her sisters, blocking him from her, seemed to give her courage. They were brave little girls but foolhardy. Parrish smiled. He came forward.

The littlest boy in school came forward. Clovis Moore. He was nowhere near as steady as the girls, but he stood beside Mandy, in front of Sally.

"No, Clovis, sit down," Mandy hissed at him.

"I'll take Sally's punishment, sir. I'm the reason she got such a whipping Friday. You made her bleed, Master Parrish, just because she stuck up for me. I tripped and fell. I made all that noise 'n' misrupted class. If you have to punish someone, punish me."

Clovis extended his quivering hand, palm up, ready to take Sally's lashes.

Sally's first-grade classmate Linda O'Malley stepped forward. Her cheeks were flushed as red as her hair.

"Sit down, Linda," Mandy ordered.

Linda shook her head as she bravely extended her hand. "I'm in Sally's class. If her hand is too tender and you want to punish a really little girl, then I'll take her lashes, Master Parrish. It's wrong to hurt her again when she's still sore. Sally's a good girl, sir. She don't deserve all the whacks you've been givin' her."

"Do you think I won't punish you all?" Parrish asked.

Three more children, the oldest boys in school, stepped to the front. They lengthened the line that blocked his path to Sally. Another child stood, and another. The classroom desks emptied as the children all rose and filed quietly to the front. Each one extended his or her hand and offered to be the one to take the punishment.

"It seems everyone in here is anxious to be punished today," Parrish said. He had a lot of anger. He could accommodate them all.

Parrish roughly shoved past Mandy and Beth. He loomed over Sally. "Your defenders are going to wish they hadn't stepped in. Tomorrow they'll let you take your punishment on your own." He lifted the ruler from the desk.

"Are you going to hit me because I offered you cake, sir?" Sally asked. Her blue eyes met his, her fear palpable, her courage, too.

Parrish wanted to beat that courage out of her. It was the same courage he'd always seen in Grace, and it infuriated him that he'd never broken her. Sally wouldn't be so lucky. And as soon as spring came, Grace would find herself broken, too.

"You talked. You are to remain quiet when you're in the classroom. But it doesn't matter what my reasons. You're nothing. You are an urchin who is little better than an animal. If I beat you,"—Parrish glanced at the children surrounding him, all with one outstretched hand, all holding his gaze—"I will hit you because I say you deserve it, and no one will tell me different. I'm your teacher. When you are in this classroom, you will submit yourself to me in any way I say."

"My parents never hit me, Master Parrish," Sally said. "I don't think they'd like you giving me so many lashes."

"Your parents will thank me for beating some manners into you. They will take my word over yours that you are a bad, bad girl. They will probably take you and beat you more when they get you home." Parrish lifted the ruler high, planning to make this one—all of them—sorry.

"Her parents don't beat her, Parrish." The deep voice from the window turned the whole classroom around. "And they sure as shootin' aren't about to start on your say-so."

Parrish froze, the ruler suspended cruelly in the air as he looked into the eyes of the black man who had accompanied these children to church.

Daniel came running into the room as she lay there, dazed. Grace looked up at him. He seemed to be standing upright with no problem.

"What happened?" He knelt beside her and eased her onto her back.

She shook her head, and the room swooped. She held her head carefully still. "I don't know. I—I guess I swooned."

Daniel's eyebrows knitted together. "Why'd you do that?"

"I was wondering the same thing."

John's head poked up beside Daniel's shoulder. "Why's Ma on the floor, Pa?"

"Should she be down there, Pa?" Luke asked. "Now that we've got a bed 'n' all, it don't seem right that you still make her sleep on the floor."

Mark stumbled into his brothers, who stumbled into their pa.

Daniel almost fell over on top of Grace.

With a sudden fit of panic, Grace pictured all four of them collapsing on her. She reached her hand up and grabbed at the deerskin mattress.

Daniel crouched lower, eased his arm behind her shoulders, and slowly raised her to her feet.

She stood beside him and grabbed her stomach. "I don't feel so good." She breathed in and out, trying to steady her rebelling stomach.

Daniel said, with a voice so faint it drew her attention, "You think you're gonna be sick?"

The boys all took a quick step back.

Grace wasn't about to admit such a personal thing. Not when she hoped to avoid doing it. "No, I'm okay."

Daniel helped her sit on the edge of the bed then knelt in front of her.

"Did'ja say she was gonna toss her cookies, Pa?" Ike asked.

"I can get a bucket in here for her, if'n you want me to," Abe offered. But he stayed in place, and none of the others offered to get the bucket. They were all here.

She wanted to be alone. If she got sick to her stomach, she didn't want them all watching. She'd throw them out if she thought for a second they'd obey her.

Six blond-haired, worried men had their blue eyes riveted on her. She could have sworn all of them, except Daniel, thrilled at the prospect of her disgracing herself completely.

"If I could just lie back down for a few minutes." Grace began sinking onto her side.

Daniel jumped up and helped settle her onto the bed. "You want to throw up and you're dizzy. What else is different, Grace? Are you having any other symptoms?" Daniel hadn't blinked since she'd grabbed her stomach. He looked terrified.

"Symptoms? What are you talking about? Symptoms of some sickness?"

"No, Grace." Daniel sounded wound up as tight as a pocket watch. She could almost hear him ticking with tension. "Symptoms of carrying a baby."

"A. . .a b-baby?" Grace was stunned. "Does fainting come with that?"

"And a sour belly first thing in the morning." Daniel dropped to his knees beside the bed.

"What're we gonna do with a new batch of babies?" Mark groused.

"I remember what it was like when you guys were born. You cried all the time." Abe shoved Luke sideways; then Luke slammed into John. "They're not sleeping in me 'n' Ike's room."

"And the diapers for three babies made the house stink like an outhouse, all day, every day for years." Ike shuddered and pushed his way past Daniel to stare at Grace. "Do we have to have three again, Pa? Can't we just have two like normal?"

Daniel didn't answer. He stared at her, still not blinking.

Grace hoped his eyeballs didn't dry out.

He had braced his elbows on the bed and clutched his hands together close to his chin.

Grace thought he looked for all the world like he was praying. Well, prayer wasn't a half-bad idea. Three? Two?

"Babies don't have to come in batches, d-do they, Daniel?" Grace started praying, too.

"Yep," Mark said with solemn certainty. "In this family they have to."

"So far," Luke said. "I want three again. Three's been fun, hasn't it, guys?"

John wormed his way past Ike and Daniel and plunked himself down beside Grace. "You can have one if'n you want to, Ma, but bunches are more fun. Us guys'll help you with all three of 'em. We don't mind helping out with little brothers, and they can all sleep in with me 'n' Mark 'n' Luke if'n you want. We were sleeping six to a room when we lived in the cave." John looked at Mark. "Weren't we?"

Mark asked Ike, "They really stink?"

"Well, *you* sure did." Ike gave Mark a hard slug in the arm.

Mark fell onto the bed on Grace's feet.

She pulled her feet up out of his way and almost kneed Daniel in the nose.

Daniel didn't seem to notice that the bed was fast filling with wrestling boys.

"Daniel, say something," Grace demanded.

His face seemed to be frozen. His knuckles were white where he clutched them together like one huge fist. Daniel's voice scraped against her skin, low and hoarse and full of despair. "I was weak." He breathed in and out as if he were consciously making his chest work. He stopped staring straight forward and looked at Grace. The detached shock was gone, replaced by fury.

"You tempted me, and I was weak." Daniel lurched to his feet. Two more of the boys, who were practically hanging on their pa's back, stumbled and fell on top of Grace.

Daniel backed away from her and the bed full of boys. "I was weak, and now you're gonna die." Daniel whirled and ran out of the room.

His announcement stunned the boys into complete silence.

The door to the outside slammed.

"Adam, you're here. You came," Sally whispered.

Beth turned on her little sister, surprised but relieved. "You told Adam to come?"

Sally shook her head.

"No, Beth—I did." Tillie appeared in the window.

"But you promised not to tell." Beth was traitorously glad Tillie had broken her promise.

"I did promise, and I meant it when I said it." Tillie gripped the windowsill so tightly Beth saw her black knuckles turn white. "But after I thought about it awhile, well, I admit free and clear I broke my promise. I didn't think you girls could take him."

Mandy snorted. She pointed at the floor. Everyone looked at the spot where Parrish stood, still frozen, his mouth agape as he stared at Adam.

Mandy jerked on a cord that came up through a knothole in the floor and hung inconspicuously from a hook attached under the top of Master Parrish's desk. The floor collapsed under Parrish's feet. With a shriek, Parrish dropped out of sight with a loud crash.

Tillie stood on her tiptoes and looked through the window at the hole where Master Parrish had just stood. "Sorry, I never should've doubted you."

Mandy sniffed.

Beth giggled.

Adam and Tillie disappeared from the window. Clay McClellen came in the front door. Luther was only a couple of steps behind him. Adam and Tillie appeared seconds later.

Clay came to the front of the schoolroom and looked down at the hole in the floor.

Beth saw Parrish glaring up, rage etched on his face.

Sally leaned against Pa's leg. He rested a hand on her shoulder, and she seemed to soak in his strength.

Beth wondered why she hadn't tattled on Parrish the first time he'd punished her little sister for nothing.

"Did you dig that hole?" Pa turned to look at Mandy.

"I dug it, Pa." Beth stepped forward. If there was punishment, she'd take her share.

"I fixed the braces and rigged the trip line so we could make the floor fall in," Mandy admitted.

"I carried buckets of dirt outside and hid 'em in the woods," Sally added.

Tillie stepped up, her head bowed. "I helped them smuggle tools to town, Clay."

Adam came up beside her. "You didn't tell me all that. You just said the girls needed help."

Tillie shrugged. "They did need help. . .this morning. Yesterday digging the hole, they were fine on their own."

"When did you do all this?" Pa lifted his cowboy hat with one gloved hand and rubbed his hair flat as if soothing his brain.

"Uh, we, uh. . .we snuck out of church yesterday morning." Mandy arched her brow as if asking how much trouble was coming her way.

"You were sitting with us. You weren't gone long enough to—"

"I left with one of the twins, 'member, Pa?" Beth said. "Right away at the start of the service. Tillie had the tools hid in the wagon so we could pry up the floorboard and dig."

"And I left with the other baby," Mandy confessed.

"I took Laura out when she started into hollering." Sally stared at her toes peeking out from under her dress.

Beth didn't blame Sally for being a bit nervous. This had always been the weak part of their plan. Missing church was a no-no. She tried to be helpful. "We watched the little ones real careful, though, whilst we dug."

"Laura even helped carry dirt a little." Then guilt clouded Sally's eyes, and she looked at the floor. Beth swallowed hard, worrying. What now? Maybe they'd all get a beating out of this yet.

Pa sighed. "What did you do, Sally?"

"I, uh, pinched Laura to make her cry to begin with, 'cause she was behaving herself right proper in church."

"Well, that was a plumb mean thing to do, girl." Luther bent down, grabbed Parrish by the back of the neck of his black suit coat, and pulled him out of the hole. Luther tossed him onto the floor like a landed catfish.

The children gathered around, enjoying watching their teacher get his comeuppance.

Pa leaned over and looked down into the hole. "You girls didn't put spikes in the bottom of that, did you?"

"Nope." Mandy sounded as though she regretted skipping the spikes.

Beth nudged her.

Clay looked at Sally and crouched in front of her. "Let me see your hand, darlin'."

Sally held her palm up. The bruising was dark, and there were several cuts in her tender flesh.

Pa gave her hand a kiss then lifted her into his strong arms as he rose and hugged her tight. He pulled back far enough to look her square in the eye. "You could have told me. I'd've listened. You're not a little girl to tell lies, and I'd've trusted you."

Sally's eyes filled with tears, and she flung her arms around her pa's neck. Beth thought Sally might squeeze the life out of him.

"Now you know better 'n to cry, Sally." Pa patted her on the back. "Remember rule number one."

Mandy tossed herself against Pa's leg.

Beth hugged him, too. Somehow he had enough arms to hug them all.

When they let go, Luther said, "Drat. I was plumb distracted by your caterwauling womenfolk, and Parrish lit out of here."

"No matter," Pa said in a mild voice that gave Beth the shivers. "I'm in the mood for hunting varmints."

There'd been a time not so long ago when there'd been only Ma and her sisters to stick up for her. Not that they needed a man, but a good one could make himself purely useful.

Pa's eyes swept over all the students. "I saw what you all did, standing up for Sally. I'm proud of every one of you. I'm sorry we didn't get Parrish taken care of sooner."

Solemn faces turned to smiles all around.

"For now, school's out until we hire a new teacher. You can all go home."

He looked at Sally, still perched in his arms. "Your ma is waiting for you in the wagon."

"How'd you get her to wait outside, Pa?" Beth asked.

"When Adam told me there was trouble, I told her I was riding to town, but I didn't say what for. She thinks we need supplies. I also left her holding both twins and Laura on her lap."

"That'd slow her down some," Beth said. "I hope she didn't hurt Master Parrish."

They all ran outside.

"Parrish must have sneaked out the window," Tillie said.

"Yep," Mandy agreed. "Because Ma would've caught on that something was wrong if she'd've seen him sneaking out, and she'd've had him."

Luther tugged on his fur cap. "You'd better see to your young'uns, Clay. Adam and I'll head after him. Send Buff out to pick up our trail. Adam 'n' Buff 'n' me'll hunt up Parrish."

Adam slung his arm around Tillie and said, "If you boys can handle one measly schoolmaster alone, Tillie and I have a few things we need to do before the wedding."

"What wedding?" Clay, Luther, and the girls all asked.

Adam grinned.

"What wedding?" Tillie asked.

Beth noticed Adam's eyes narrow as he looked at Tillie, and Beth knew what wedding. Now all he had to do was convince Tillie.

Staring at Tillie, Adam said, "I can see we definitely still have some planning to do." He snugged Tillie's waist tight and dragged her away from the schoolhouse.

Beth heard Tillie's soft laugh as they disappeared.

"The young'uns are fine with Sophie, Luth." Pa's words drew her attention back. In a voice that thrilled Beth because this was *her* pa, protecting *her* and *her sisters*, Pa said, "Reckon I want in the hunt for any man who puts his hands on my girls."

Luther asked, "How are we going to get Sophie to stay out of it?"

"That's gonna be harder than tracking down that varmint Parrish." Pa's shoulders slumped, and he walked toward the wagon.

T W E N T Y - S E V E N

Grace looked at the empty doorway then reluctantly glanced at her sons John, Ike, and Mark on the bed with her. Luke and Abe stood beside her. All of them stared after their father. As if their necks were all controlled by the same muscles, they turned to look at her.

"You're gonna *die*?" John asked.

"I—I don't think so." Grace looked at her stricken son, the one who loved her first and most.

"Pa seemed pretty sure." Mark sounded as though he was prepared to face facts and not get overwrought about it.

Mark's calm acceptance—so calm it bordered on eagerness—John's teary concern, and the bed wavering as if it might collapse under the squirming weight of four people, helped settle Grace's stomach and clear her head.

She swung her feet over the side of the bed and carefully stood. The room behaved. "Now, boys, whatever your pa said, I'm not going to die. Your ma did, but there are lots of women who have babies without dying. Why, Sophie McClellen has had a whole passel of young'uns and she's fine."

"Yeah, but. . ." Mark looked as if he was going to insist the family settle on Grace's dying.

"Enough, Mark. I'm living and that's the end of it." Grace hadn't heard that tone of voice from herself before. It was more fearsome than her teacher voice. She decided she would use it often. "Now scoot on out of here so I can get ready for the day."

The boys headed for the door. John was slow climbing off the bed, and Ike tried to pass him with a hard shove. A bare foot whizzed past Grace's face as the two of them ended up in a tangled heap on the floor, twisted up in blankets. Mark stepped on them as he climbed out. Ike yelled out in pain, loudly enough to hurt Grace's ears. He twisted his body when Mark stepped square on his back. Mark fell forward into Abe. They left the room, yelling and shoving each other.

Grace realized their antics didn't even bother her—that was just the way they moved from one place to another. She closed the door and turned to get dressed without seriously considering telling them to quiet down.

She had a worrywart husband to find. First she'd give him a big hug and tell him not to worry—she wouldn't leave him. Then, if that didn't work, she was going to hammer some sense into him.

And if she had to, she'd use a real hammer!

Parrish had learned the hard way that you needed to know where you were going and how you were getting there because you might have to leave town quickly. He always had an escape plan. He hit the ground running when he ducked out of the schoolhouse window, and he hadn't stopped yet.

"Stupid hicks are probably still there talking," he muttered gleefully. He slipped between buildings, coolly asked to rent the blacksmith's horse with no intention of returning the nag, and headed south out of town.

He rounded a curve in the trail, looked carefully around to make sure he wasn't being watched, and rode into rough country following a game trail that would take him north. . .to Grace.

"He went up the hillside, Ma," Abe yelled, pointing at the obvious tracks in the muddy ground.

Grace plunked her fists on her hips as she stood in the pouring rain. "Your pa is the most stubborn man I've ever known. Why would he go up that slippery trail this morning?"

"Reckon it's 'cause you're gonna die." Mark sounded a shade too chipper. A crack of thunder sounded as the rain soaked them to the skin.

"I'm not going to die." Grace ignored the rain to glare at Mark. "Now stop that foolish talk."

"Pa said." Mark didn't sound as if he was hoping for it. He just wasn't all that upset.

"Don't die, Ma. I love you." John threw his arms around her legs and almost knocked her over. A wave of dizziness swamped her, and she was glad the sturdy little five-year-old held her steady.

She turned and hugged him close, his sad face buried in her soaked skirt. His rain-slicked hair was cool under her hand. "Now, John, your pa's just being foolish. He's worried about me because of your ma, but lots of women have babies and live through it just fine. Your own ma did it once."

John lifted up his face and looked at her. His eyes were filled with tears.

Grace did her best to buck him up. His brothers would torment the living daylights out of him if they caught him crying.

"And how about Sophie McClellen?" Grace ran her hand down John's head and rested it on his rosy cheek.

John nodded, sniffling a little. He glanced behind him and saw all four of his brothers. He buried his face in Grace's stomach again and discreetly blew his runny nose on her dress. Grace grimaced, but she willingly sacrificed her dress to the cause of manliness.

John looked up again, looking much steadier. "You're right. And there are some kids from big families in Mosqueros. And they've all got mas."

"That's because it's real unusual for a lady to die having a baby." Grace tipped John's chin up, and after giving him a long look, she glanced at the other boys gathered around her. "It was your ma's time, boys. God is faithful to us. That's something I learned when I came here."

The thunder rumbled again, but it didn't frighten her. She only heard the rumble of spring. In it was the rumble of new life. Grace loved the sound, just as she loved Daniel and her boys and this tiny new life inside her.

She reached out a hand and caressed Abe's worried face, then Ike's. Then she turned and smiled at sassy Mark and quiet Luke. "I came here purely by accident, not planning to be your ma, and you not wanting me for the job."

"That's for sure," Mark muttered.

Grace smiled at him. "But God is faithful, Mark. God knew what He was doing. God knew you needed a ma, and more than that, He knew I needed a husband and five sons."

"You needed us?" Mark's brow furrowed.

"I needed you so much." She grabbed him and gave him a hard hug as he tried to squirm away. She let him go with a little laugh. "Having you to take care of and having you to take care of me is the finest thing that ever happened in my life. The Bible says, 'It is of the Lord's mercies that we are not consumed, because his compassions fail not. They are new every morning: great is thy faithfulness.' "

"God is faithful to us?" Abe asked. "I thought it was the other way around. I thought we were supposed to be faithful to God."

Grace smiled and pulled John toward the house. All the other boys followed. She stepped inside, out of the rain. "We *are* supposed to be faithful to God. We are supposed to trust Him to take care of us, trust that Jesus died so we won't have to."

"We do have to die, Ma," Ike said. "Everybody dies."

"No, they don't. They live their lives out on this earth, and then they go to heaven and live with God. Jesus died in our place."

"So you don't think our ma is really dead?" Mark asked.

"I know she isn't. She was a good woman who put her faith in God.

He's got her right now in a safe, happy place. And He was so faithful to you that, knowing you wouldn't pick me for a ma and knowing I'd never have picked you for my sons, He stuck us together. He even sent the parson to do the marriage ceremony. And He snowed us in together so we had the whole winter alone to get to know each other."

"God did all that?" Luke sounded awestruck.

Grace nodded and gave Luke a quick kiss on the head. He hunched his shoulders as if the gesture of affection bothered him, but he stayed and took the kiss. He even grinned shyly at her.

"God is faithful. His loving-kindness never ceases. His compassion never fails. Great is God's faithfulness. He knows how to take care of us long before we do. And He is sending us this baby. So we have to trust that God is being faithful to us in this, too. He knows what He's doing."

Mark shrugged. "God oughta know what He's doing."

Abe nodded. Ike joined in. John hugged Grace one more time then backed up and knocked into Luke, who stumbled sideways and fell against Abe, who shoved him away.

Grace caught hold of Luke before all five boys ended up tumbling to the floor. She hugged him, and he relaxed enough to hug her back.

Grace asked, "So who is left in this family who doesn't know this baby is a gift from God?"

All five boys looked between each other; then they looked at Grace and said all at once, "Pa."

Grace smiled. "Your pa needs to learn a lesson about being faithful to God, boys. Let's go find him and drag him back down here and convince him God is faithful."

The boys all turned.

"Hold it," Grace ordered. "You get coats on and boots and we split up so we can cover the most area. We saw which way he went, but his tracks will disappear once he gets off the trail."

The boys scrambled into their coats with a maximum of noise.

Grace pulled on Abe's old buckskin jacket. "Ike, you take John and go up and to the north toward the sapling stand. Abe, you and Luke go straight up the hill. Mark, we'll go south toward the cave. He's just up there worrying. He's not hiding. We'll find him in a few minutes."

They smiled, eager for a chance to run out in the spring rain. They turned and went outside on a pa hunt.

# TWENTY-EIGHT

Parrish spent the whole morning pushing his nag as fast as he could. He cut a switch from a low-hanging branch and whipped the beast until it trotted steadily. Parrish bounced in the saddle, taking the beating of a lifetime. As his backside took a pounding, he grew more and more irritated with Grace. He'd been mad when he'd gotten out of bed this morning. The need to slake his temper had been building steadily. If he could have knocked the sass out of that littlest McClellen girl, it would have taken the edge off, but that pleasure had been denied him, and now he burned.

"It's high time we had this out, girl," he yelled at the dripping sky. "You sent me to prison, and now you're gonna pay."

His horse snorted and looked over its shoulder at Parrish. They climbed steadily, following the trail Parrish had scouted a dozen times through the winter. They neared the steepest part, where that hillbilly Luther had said a man afoot could make it. Parrish sneered. This horse would take him all the way over this canyon wall and like it.

The horse balked at a particularly steep stretch of the trail. Parrish whipped the horse soundly. Fighting the bit, the horse charged at the slippery rocks. Parrish could see footholds large enough for a horse, even though the trail disappeared and the canyon wall swooped steeply enough that he could have touched the mountainside with his left hand while his right foot dangled over thin air.

The horse plunged up a step, then another. It slipped in the drizzling rain, regained its footing, and lurched forward again.

"You stupid brute. Get up there. Get up!" His whip lashed with all the strength in his arm. A rock dislodged under the horse's hoof, and the horse reared up and back, sliding and rolling on its haunches. Parrish saw the horse coming over backward. He grabbed the steep edge of the cliff. The horse slid out from under him. The coarse grass and shifting rock Parrish grabbed caved under his weight, and he fell after the horse. Parrish landed on a narrow ledge in the soft mud. He saw the horse fall a few feet farther, then hit a level spot and stagger to its feet. The horse looked up the hill at Parrish. With a whinny that sounded like mocking laughter, the horse turned tail and ran down the slope it had just been forced to climb.

Parrish sat in the mud, screaming his rage as the animal raced away down the trail, heading for Mosqueros. Aching joints punishing him, Parrish staggered to his feet. His fury boiled over. He shook his fist at the dripping rain, howling with fury, then remembered whose fault this really was. He turned to look up the hill and, a burning need to punish riding him, continued on his mission to find Grace. He couldn't get her out of here now, not on foot.

"So I won't try to take you with me. I'll settle with you here, girl. I'll pay you back for doing me wrong. And I'll make it hurt until you know what I suffered those months I spent in jail. Then I'll get out of this miserable state of Texas."

"Look, there's Ike, way over on that rise," Grace said to Mark.

Mark looked over and saw Ike and John waving at them. "Find him yet?" Mark's voice echoed across the canyon.

"No!" came the shout back.

They waved at each other and kept searching.

"Where do you think he's got his self off to, Ma?" Mark asked.

Grace looked down at her most difficult son. "I'm not too worried about him, Mark. He's all upset because he thinks I'm going to die."

Mark shrugged and glanced sideways at her. "Reckon you're gonna, if Pa says. He knows everything."

"Well, he doesn't know this. Why, I can think of lots of women who have had children and not died."

"Never three at onest though, Ma. That's what'll probably finish you off."

Grace stopped and took hold of Mark's shoulders and turned him to face her. "You don't have to sound so happy about it." She glared at him.

One corner of his mouth curled up as he smirked at her. He was worried about his foolish pa, who'd just gone for a walk and would be fine. But he wasn't upset in the least about her dying.

He pulled against Grace's grip, but she held on. "Mark, is this how it's always going to be with us?"

"Whaddaya mean, how's it gonna be?" Mark's face was far too blank and innocent.

"Whatever else you are, Mark," Grace said, "you're not stupid. Well, guess what? Neither am I. I can tell you don't like me. I want us to get along."

Mark stared at her, his eyes cool, his expression faintly amused. It was an expression Grace could imagine hardening into real trouble as the years went by. But for now, this little scamp was only five. She could handle a five-year-old. She hoped.

She pulled him over to a fallen tree and had him sit down. The rustle of branches and the rain, now just a faint sprinkle, were the only sounds as she sat beside him and prayed for wisdom. *Lord, how do I make a child love me?* She meditated on it.

No still, small voice gave her an easy answer. And then she remembered.

"When John and I were trapped in that avalanche, we were really scared."

Mark's expression softened a bit as he seemed to think about the danger his brother had been in.

"It made me realize that I hadn't been faithful to God the way I should be."

"Now, Ma,"—Mark patted her on the hand—"I'm sure you're not all that bad. I'm sure God'll let you into heaven after you die having my next three brothers."

Grace forced her eyes to remain straight forward even though she wanted to roll them in exasperation. "You're not listening to me, young man," she said sharply.

Mark's eyes grew cool again. She'd never had any luck reaching him with stern words or threats. Confound it, why couldn't this child be just the least bit afraid of her?

"It made me realize that I had to start living bravely for God." That caught his attention. Bravery evidently appealed to him.

"How do you live bravely for God?" Mark asked, scooting just a hair closer to her on the tree trunk.

"When I was a child, I was really tough. I faced down bigger kids and even some grown-ups who wanted to hurt me. But then I got away from my—" Grace never had been able to call him her father. "From the man who adopted me."

"You were an orphan, like us? I remember John saying that."

"Except you aren't an orphan. You always had your pa, but you know what I mean." Grace nodded. "Then, once I got away from the man who adopted me, he chased after me. I spotted him in a town where I ran to. He was supposed to go to jail, but he must have wiggled out of it somehow. I saw him on the street before he saw me and sneaked away that very night, hiding out on the train."

Mark's eyes grew wide. "That sounds really brave." He sounded impressed.

"Well, it was brave of me in some ways. But the thing is, from then on, I started running." Grace turned Mark, her hands resting on his shoulders. "I learned to always be on the lookout. I watched behind me all the time. I saw him once in a while, too. I thought I'd gotten away for good in Mosqueros. It was so far from Chicago."

"And then he got here, right?" Mark's eyes narrowed.

Grace thought the boy looked as though he might be willing to fight Parrish for her. She didn't know if it was because he liked her at least a little or because he just wanted an excuse to fight, but still, it was something.

"Yes, he got here, and I hid from him in your pa's wagon, and the parson caught me with the lot of you, and it's improper for a man and woman to stay together without being married."

Mark piped up, "So the parson made you get hitched."

Grace nodded. "And that's okay, because I love being here with you. I love you boys and I love this canyon and I love your pa."

Mark said in amazement, "You love us boys?"

"Yep," Grace said, smiling.

"Not including me, right?" Mark looked a little guilty. "I haven't been too nice. I don't expect you to love me."

"Well, you *have* been a handful, young man. But you're smart and brave. You love your brothers, and you've got a good, honest heart." Grace lifted one hand and rested it on Mark's cheek. "How could I not love you?"

Mark was tough and stubborn, but he was, after all, five. Grace saw the longing in his heart for a mother to love him. She knew that longing because she had lived with it all her life.

She said gently, "We've talked about the Ten Commandments when your father reads the Bible to us at night, haven't we?"

Mark nodded. He let her hand remain where it was. He even leaned into it a little.

"Well, Jesus said, a long time after Moses brought the Ten Commandments down from the mountain, that He had two new commandments. He said if you followed these commandments, then you would always follow all the others. Do you remember what they are? We've read those verses."

Mark said, " 'Thou shalt love the Lord thy God with all thy heart, and with all thy soul, and with all thy mind.' "

Grace said, "Right, that's the first. Then Jesus said, 'And the second is like unto it—' "

" 'Thou shalt love thy neighbour as thyself.' " Mark sat quietly. His forehead furrowed as he thought about the new commandments.

"That's it. Love. God says, 'Love Me, and love each other.' It's simple. And so I love you. I love you because God tells me to."

"You didn't love me when I was your student and you were getting me thrown out of school."

"Yes, I did. I wanted your pa to understand how unruly you were in school. I'd tried to talk to you, but you still wouldn't mind. I'd tried to talk to your pa, and nothing changed. You boys were making it so the other students couldn't study." Grace left her hand on Mark's cheek. With the other, she waggled her finger right under his nose.

"Loving you doesn't mean you get to be naughty. I hoped by going to such lengths with your pa, he'd see reason and insist you boys behave. If I didn't love you, I wouldn't have cared how you acted. I wouldn't have cared if any of my pupils learned or not."

Mark reached up and caught Grace's scolding finger. He lowered it away from his face. She wondered if he was going to start fussing at her again, as he always had in school.

Then the unhappy look on his face lightened, and he began to glow from within. "You love me?"

Grace nodded once, firmly.

Mark held tight to her hand and whispered, "I love you, too, Ma." Then his very young blue eyes filled with tears. "I don't want you to die." His voice broke on the last word. He flung himself into her arms and squeezed the breath out of her and cried.

"I'm not going to die, son." Grace caressed his blond hair and murmured nonsense to him until he'd worked himself through his upset.

He finally lifted his head and dashed his hand across his tear-streaked face. He looked around carefully. "Um. . .you won't tell the others I cried, will you?"

"It'll be our secret," Grace said. "And, Mark. . ."

"What, Ma?" Her name had never sounded so good.

"We'll find your worrywart pa and convince him I'm okay, and then this family can get back to normal."

Mark nodded. "Yep, we're finally going to be a real family."

Grace gave him a sound kiss on the cheek and straightened away from him. "Everything is going to be just fine."

Just then a hard arm grabbed Mark and pulled him backward off the log.

TWENTY-NINE

Grace screamed as that filthy arm wrapped around Mark's little neck. She didn't think. Desperate to protect him, she lunged for Mark.

A brutal hand slapped her aside. She fell on her side to the ground and whirled around on her hands and knees, braced to attack again.

Then she saw his face.

Parrish.

"Get up, little Graceless." Parrish lifted Mark by his neck.

Mark grabbed Parrish's strangling arm with both of his little hands, squirming and trying to shout.

Parrish cut off the noise.

Mark kicked him.

Parrish shook Mark viciously. "Stop fighting me, you little—"

"Let him go." Grace shook off the paralyzing terror that Parrish had trained into her so well. She scrambled to her feet and advanced toward this beast who had hurt so many children for so long.

Parrish's arm tightened, and Mark coughed and yanked desperately against the vise around his neck. He began to fight less frantically, and Grace saw his eyes begin to glaze.

"Let him go. I'll do anything you want. You came here for me."

Parrish smiled. Fear like a cold Texas wind chilled Grace's backbone. He loosened his grip slightly. Mark, still conscious, sagged against Parrish's arm and dragged air into his lungs.

"Come over here, Graceless. When I have you, the boy can go."

Grace felt the bite of tears. She looked at Mark and didn't hesitate for a moment. She rounded the tree trunk she and Mark had been sitting on. A deep, coarse laugh erupted from Parrish as Grace came within his grasp. Parrish threw Mark aside. Mark rolled on the ground and hit the fallen tree hard.

Grace turned to help her son. Parrish grabbed her arm and jerked her upright.

Mark moaned, turning over sluggishly on his back. Blood streaked down his forehead from a nasty gash. Mark faltered as he tried to sit up, and then he collapsed, completely still.

Parrish dragged Grace toward the top of the canyon wall.

"No, I've got to help him. You hurt him, you—"

Parrish spun her around to face him. He slapped her across the face. She'd have fallen if his grip hadn't been so tight. He raised his hand again. "The only reason to go back for that boy is to make sure he's dead. Shall we do that, Graceless? You want me to go back?"

A wasteland of cruelty and sadistic pleasure glowed in Parrish's eyes. He'd do it. He'd kill Mark and enjoy every minute of it. His huge, hard hand cut into her right arm until she wanted to cry out from the pain. He'd like that.

She refused to give him the satisfaction now, just as she had in the last years she'd been with him. Her back bore testament to how long and hard Parrish had lashed her with his belt, trying to break her spirit.

His grip tightened. A step above her on the steep hillside, he towered over her. "Your choice, darling daughter. We go quietly, or we stay and see to the boy."

Grace looked back. She took one long last look at her son. The boy who said he loved her. She'd repaid that love by bringing Parrish down on this family. She never should have tried to face Parrish all those years ago. She never should have fought him. It had led to this.

Feeling like a coward after her high-minded talk of being brave, she turned away from Mark. "Let's go. I'm ready for my punishment."

Parrish jerked on her arm until it felt as though it would be torn off. That pain was nothing compared to the pain of seeing Mark lying behind them, hurt and bleeding.

"You knew the cost of going against me." Parrish's fingers dug deeper, and her arm began to go numb. "Yet you did it. You thought you could fight me." Parrish laughed again.

Grace had heard this laugh a thousand times as he used his belt on her or the other children. But there was an edge to it now. Something shrill and furious echoed behind the laughter. She looked at him as he dragged her at a rapid pace up the slope through the thick woods.

He had always been clean cut, polished, even fastidious. Now he was filthy. His face coated with dirt, his suit torn but also worn paper thin. Parrish had changed. He'd been a sadist before, enjoying the pain of others, but he'd gone beyond that.

He looked down at her, and it cried out from his red-rimmed eyes. He was mad. She'd fallen into the clutches of a raving madman, and the only way to save Mark was to stay and let Parrish have his revenge.

Parrish twisted her arm as he dragged her upward. Farther every step from the only happiness she had ever known.

She'd left Daniel on an unhappy note. That was how he'd remember her. John loved her completely, and this would break his heart. It occurred to her that Daniel had been right all along.

She was going to die.

The minute they disappeared into the trees, Mark jumped to his feet. He looked after them, thinking hard but not long. He rubbed a handful of blood off his forehead.

"Blood!" Thrilled at the nastiness of the injury and how much bragging he could do, he wiped the blood on the front of his shirt where it'd be sure to show. He plotted just where that awful man would take his ma and the lay of the land. Then he turned and ran in the opposite direction.

He needed his brothers.

Parrish gasped for breath by the time they reached the halfway point up the canyon. The wall began to get steeper. The trees fell away. Grass grew, but the land was too full of stone for anything larger to thrive.

His grip never relaxed, but Grace didn't try to fight him regardless. The boys were in danger as long as Parrish was close. That kept her moving. No matter what happened to her, she had to get Parrish away from this canyon for the sake of her sons.

Sweat stained the ragged black suit Parrish wore. He inched his way up, looking for footholds in the canyon wall. Grace looked upward. Daniel had said if they needed to go to town he could get out this way. But it was rugged and slow. Parrish stumbled on the rocky ground. He didn't let her go, so she fell with him. She landed hard, flat on her belly on the hillside, right beside the vile man.

That's when she thought of her baby. She suddenly realized that it wasn't only her sons who needed protection. She had a baby that deserved better than dying before it had lived.

"Great is thy faithfulness."

The words came to her, whispered on the wind. Her prayer for courage. She'd thought going with Parrish to protect Mark was the right thing to do, and it had been at that moment when Mark was so vulnerable. But what about now? Where was her courage? Parrish was an old man, exhausted and not in his right mind.

Grace thought of her boys wrestling in their bedrooms, knocking each other off their new beds, playing King of the Mountain. Well, they were on a mountain right now. She lifted her knees up to her chest and kicked Parrish in the belly.

"Aaahh!" Parrish's fingers clung to her arm, but her dress ripped with a hiss and the sleeve tore and jerked the buttons loose in the back; the dress was pulled halfway off her shoulder as he slid backward. He held on to Grace and pulled her with him. They tumbled a few yards before Grace came up fighting. She caught a handful of mud in her hand and threw it into Parrish's ugly, snarling face. He swallowed it and began choking.

"You lousy little. . ." He lunged for her. "I'll teach you some respect if it's the last thing I do."

Grace jumped aside, reached out her foot, and tripped him, just as Mark always did to John. Parrish caught her skirt as he fell past her, and she fell again, head over heels, down a long stretch of the canyon-side, into the grove of trees.

She landed with a dull thump against a loblolly pine. The blow knocked the wind out of her, but she ignored her pain and staggered to her feet, fighting for each breath. She saw a tree branch and remembered the boys' sword fights. She snatched it up, the sleeve of her dress hanging from her wrist, and swung with all her might.

Parrish, charging, ran right into it. The branch smacked him in the belly with a hollow thud. It stopped him cold. He sucked in air on an inverted scream, dropped to his knees, and stared stupidly at her. Grace lifted the branch again. She owed him another one for the time he'd thrashed her and her five little sisters for reading after dark. *Whack.*

She owed him for the times he'd made her sit on the floor and fed her thin oatmeal, while he sat at his fine table eating roast beef. *Whack.*

She owed him for the little girl he'd whipped so hard she was never normal again, and as soon as he saw she was permanently damaged in the head, he sent her back to the orphanage. *Whack.*

She owed him for the blow she'd taken just now, which might have hurt her unborn baby. *Whack.*

And she owed him for the blood on Mark's head. Her son might be dead even now. She lifted her arms high for this last solid blow. Then she had to go to Mark.

Mud splattered into Parrish's face. Then a hail of mud balls pelted him.

A shrill scream from overhead whirled Grace around.

Mark swung down out of the tree, hanging from a vine. He plowed, feet first, into Parrish's chest, knocking him on his back onto the ground.

Abe and Ike charged out of the woods, roaring like Johnny Reb charging into battle, armed with sticks and stones.

Luke and John were right on their heels, screaming like banshees. Mark, out of control on his vine, swung back and slammed into all of them, knocking them down like dominoes.

He fell off the rope, bounced a few times, then turned, along with his brothers, and charged at Parrish, who sprawled flat, too addled to notice all the little feet kicking him.

Grace dashed forward to get the boys to stop.

Then. . .she didn't.

She pulled her dress back onto her shoulders, looking at her dangling sleeve and thinking she had no idea how she would sew it back on. With a shrug, she left it there and dusted her filthy hands. After an unsuitable length of time, she said, "All right. That's enough."

The boys must have worn themselves out, because they stopped almost immediately and turned to her, grinning.

"You really pounded him, Ma," Ike said. He dropped a heavy hackberry branch and ran over and threw his arms around her, nearly knocking her farther down the hill.

Abe slammed into her from the other side, thus balancing her again.

The rest of the boys swarmed her.

"Wow, Ma, we saw you beating that man up. I never knew you were tough like that." Mark looked up at her, his eyes shining with admiration.

Grace thought of all the times she'd tried to get this little scamp to respect her when she was teaching school. Apparently all she'd needed to do was get in a fistfight on Mosqueros's Main Street and he'd have behaved.

Parrish groaned from where he lay on the ground.

"Who is he, Ma?" Ike asked.

"Yes, Grace. Who in the world is that poor man you and my boys have beaten into the dirt?" Daniel stepped out of the woods.

"Where did you come from?" Grace tried to think back, a thousand years ago, to this morning. Daniel had declared her as good as dead and walked off in a snit. The big dummy.

"The woods." Daniel shrugged, looking between Parrish and her as if he might be the slightest bit afraid his turn came next.

She planted her hands on her hips. "Have you by any chance noticed what is going on in your canyon, Mr. Reeves?"

She spoke in the voice she'd always used when she was the schoolmarm and he was the father of unruly students.

"I heard the screaming."

"Pa," Mark said, "you should've seen Ma whacking this guy in the head. It was really something."

John ran up and slammed into Daniel's leg. Daniel stood still, solid as a tree.

Grace wondered where he'd gotten such good balance. Practice no doubt.

"Pa, I've decided Ma's not gonna die having that there baby." John jabbed his thumb at Grace.

"John, it's rude to point." Grace noticed Parrish trying to get to his hands and knees. She walked over and whacked him once with her branch, still to hand. He fell back face-first in the mud.

"Speaking of rude, it might be rude to beat that man with a stick, Grace."

John tugged on Daniel's leg until Grace was relieved her husband had equipped himself with a good, tight belt.

"What is it, John?" Daniel asked, still looking at Parrish and Grace and the stick.

"I don't know about our other ma, but I think this one's pretty tough. I reckon she can kick out babies galore and not let it bother her none."

Daniel asked hopefully, "You think?"

Grace asked nervously, "Galore?"

"You gonna tell me who that man is, Grace, honey?"

Grace stuck her nose straight up in the air. "Are you going to quit scaring us all to death with your talk about babies killing their mother?"

Daniel tilted his head as though he was thinking. "I'll try and buck up."

"That's my father." Grace jabbed her thumb at Parrish. She saw herself point and tucked her thumb into her fist and tried to look innocent.

All six of her menfolk turned to look at the man Grace had just walloped.

"Uh. . .you weren't close, I'm guessing," Daniel pushed his hat back and scratched his head.

"I ran away from home, and on my way out of town, I told the police he was a thief and turned over his account books that proved it."

"He tried to strangle me, Pa," Mark said, obviously thrilled to have had a brush with death.

"He what?" Daniel's brow furrowed in anger.

"And I played possum while he drugged Ma away. Then I went for help."

"It's *dragged*, Mark," Grace corrected. Just because they'd had a life-and-death struggle was no reason to let their grammar slip.

Daniel pointed at Parrish. "He drugged you?"

She flinched when Daniel pointed but held her tongue.

"Mark showed us where he hightailed it with Ma. He was kidnapping her, toting her off the 6R right over the canyon wall," Abe added.

"And we've gotten plumb used to having her for a ma and we don't wanta break in a new one," Ike added.

"They are mighty hard to train," Mark said with a sigh. "We've got this'n just how we like her."

"We don't just like her, Mark,"—Luke whacked Mark in the shoulder—"we love her."

"You love me, Luke?" This was the first time Luke had said such a thing.

Mark shoved Luke back. Luke stumbled into Abe.

"That man hit you, Mark?" Daniel stepped toward his son.

"Get off'a me, sissy-baby." Abe knocked Luke backward, where he stepped on Mark's toe, who jumped sideways with flailing arms and swatted John right in the face. John slugged him, but because his eyes were closed from the blow he'd just taken, he missed Mark and punched Ike.

Ike grabbed John around the chest and lifted him in the air.

"Will you boys cut it out?"

They all froze and turned to Grace. John's feet dangled in the air. Mark, holding his foot, howling with pain, was cut off in midscream.

She smiled. "Thank you. Please don't make me shout again."

They nodded fearfully.

"Yes, that man hit Mark." Grace studied her temporarily subdued children. She turned to Daniel. "He didn't drug me." She glanced at Mark. "That's poor grammar, son. He *dragged* me."

"He dragged you?" Daniel's voice rose as if his patience was falling by the wayside.

"He came here looking for me. He found me in Mosqueros last—" Grace was blank for a moment. It seemed as though she'd lived here always with these men she loved and with whom she had a perfect, tranquil life—except for the screaming and punching.

"January," Daniel supplied immediately. "The twelfth. It was a Friday. We got home at about six in the evening."

Grace glared at him. Apparently he remembered to the minute.

"What?"

She continued. "He's been trailing me for the last two years. He must have gotten out of jail in Chicago somehow. And he isn't a man to let a young girl do him harm without getting revenge."

Daniel looked at Parrish, moving slightly, groaning occasionally, lying on his belly. "He did a bad job of getting revenge this time."

"After he tookened Ma,"—Mark jumped into the space between Daniel and Grace—"I went and found the guys. And we set up a trap for him. We was gonna corner him and I swing-ed down outta that tree." Mark pointed up but was too busy telling the story to make it clear.

Abe stepped between Mark and Daniel, adding to the number of people between Grace and her confused and sweet and stubborn-as-an-ox husband. It would always be like this.

"Ma saved herself." Abe jumped up, swinging an imaginary club in the air.

He clonked Mark on the head with his arm. Grace caught Mark by the shoulder before he could retaliate.

Ike jumped in between Abe and Daniel. "We had to hurry or she'd've polished off clobbering him before we got here."

Daniel looked over the long line of children at Grace. His eyes suddenly narrowed and focused on her. He rounded the boys and had her by the shoulders. "What happened to your face?"

Grace lifted her hand and realized her right cheek was swollen. "Mark's bleeding. He had it way worse than me."

She saw the effort it took Daniel to tear his eyes away from her and glance at Mark. It was purely encouraging.

He looked down at Mark, who had done his best to keep himself coated in blood.

Daniel let go of Grace and crouched down in front of Mark. "Are you all right?"

Mark shrugged and stared at the ground and kicked at a clod of dirt. "Aw, shucks, Pa. It ain't nothing."

"It *isn't* nothing, Mark," Grace corrected by reflex, tugging on her wrecked dress to keep herself decently covered. "I mean, it isn't *anything*." Grace shook her head. "It is *too* something."

"Are you folks doing okay here?"

All of them whirled around at the new voice.

THIRTY

Clay McClellen walked down the last stretch of the steep slope. Three men were right behind him, one of them the sheriff. All of them were armed and determined and looking right at Parrish.

Grace could feel Clay taking in Mark's bleeding face, her bruised face and shredded dress, and Parrish's inert form.

Parrish groaned loudly and pushed himself to his hands and knees, wobbling all the while.

"You folks have some trouble with this feller, too?" Clay jabbed his index finger at Parrish.

Grace had to clench her jaw to keep from telling him it wasn't polite to point.

Daniel stepped forward, showing he was head of the family.

Grace harrumphed. "About time you took charge, Daniel." She realized that Daniel had indeed seemed to become more in charge as she'd come to know how the Reeves men worked.

Daniel heard her and glanced back. Then he turned to Clay.

Parrish stumbled to his feet.

"Hang on to him this time, will ya, Luth?" Clay asked.

A man Grace remembered from church, wearing fur and leather and a full beard, stepped over and grabbed Parrish by the shoulder. Another man, looking much the same, stood on the other side of the unsteady prisoner. He went by the name Buff, and he resembled a buffalo somewhat.

Daniel turned back to Clay. "This varmint knocked Mark out and tried to kidnap my wife. I want him arrested."

"I'm not going to be arrested." Parrish fumbled in his pocket.

Grace gasped.

"Watch him, Luth," Clay said. "He might have a gun."

Luther grabbed Parrish's hand and pulled it up. It contained a piece of paper.

"I'm hunting her." Parrish burned her with his eyes, but Grace noticed he didn't point. At that moment she discarded a lot of what she considered proper manners. She had no desire to live by rules that appealed to the likes of Parrish.

Luther took the paper out of Parrish's hand and unfolded it. He studied it for a moment then looked up at Grace. He turned the paper so everyone could see it. "You know anything about this, Miss Calhoun?"

A wanted poster. With her picture on it. Her picture, saying she was wanted for stealing money in Chicago. The silence was deafening. Grace felt the group study her likeness on that poster. She'd never seen it before. She looked up at the sheriff. His eyes, cool and detached, seemed to measure her for a jail cell.

She looked over at Clay McClellen. His expression didn't show much at the best of times. She had only to imagine what he was thinking.

Clay's other friends were just as remote. She looked at Parrish, greedy for her to be turned over to him. It had happened in Chicago the first time she'd tried to run away.

Parrish had found her, and she'd fought him. She'd been too small, eleven years old, to fight very hard. He'd been lashing her soundly with his belt on a cold, snowy street, when a policeman had come by. She'd run to him for protection.

Parrish had told the policeman he was her father and she was getting the beating she deserved.

The policeman had told her, straight into her bruised and bleeding face, to go home quietly and behave herself from now on.

Grace had gone home and taken her beating. There had been many more through the years.

She waited now for the same thing to happen. When she'd married Daniel, she'd hoped a husband's rights overrode a father's. But she hadn't known about being wanted by the law. Parrish expected his word to be taken over hers. Finally, nearly choking with fear, she looked to the one person here whom she expected to support her, even though the law would most likely side with Parrish.

Daniel.

His expression was as cold as ice. His eyes cut through her like a frozen blade. He was going to side against her. Her lips trembled. She closed her eyes against the tears and the terror of what lay ahead when she was again in Parrish's power.

The sound of paper crumpling brought her head up. Sheriff Everett had grabbed the paper, wadded the wanted poster into a ball, and tossed it down the hillside. "You no-account varmint, what kind of skunk tries to shake the blame for his own wrongdoing by accusing a sweet little woman like Grace Calhoun of being a thief?"

"Grace Reeves," Daniel reminded the sheriff.

"Grace could no more rob someone than she could fly." Clay McClellen marched straight up to Parrish. "What kind of fools do you take us for? She taught our children. She lived among us for months. We know her, and we know you."

Clay grabbed Parrish by his shirtfront in a way that made Grace wonder for the first time why they were here. Following Parrish, of course. It was no coincidence that they'd all come at once.

"You're just the kind of man who'd hide behind a woman's skirts." Clay gave Parrish a good shake then shoved him backward. Only Luther and Buff held him up.

"Low-down coyote." Buff shook his head. He said with contempt, "It's 'bout what I'd'a expected from such as you, Parrish. You hit little girls."

"He hit little girls?" Grace gasped. "When did he do that?" Grace balled up her fist and took a step toward Parrish. "He used to make up excuses to hit me and my sisters."

Daniel grabbed her by the arm and held her back.

"You got sisters, Ma?" Mark asked. "Does that mean we got us some aunts and uncles somewheres?"

Daniel pulled Grace up against him so he braced her from behind. Just as he pulled her close, her dressed sagged off one shoulder again.

"Grace, what happened to your back?" Daniel's voice was barely audible, as if he were speaking around a huge lump in his throat.

Grace shoved at her dress and tried to turn away from him, but if she did, all the other men here would see the marks, not to mention entirely too much of her skin.

She tried to whisper, but she knew every man there heard every word. "Parrish had a taste for working his children over with a belt. There are marks on me that will never heal, Daniel."

He pulled her against him, as if he could protect her back from ever being injured again. With both arms around her waist, he said, "My wife is the most honest, upright woman I've ever known. Hanging is too good for anyone who says such things against the mother of my six children. And anyone who puts marks like this on his child needs to be locked away for good."

Grace's heart swelled with love as she leaned back against Daniel's strength. Looking over her shoulder, she saw Daniel's eyes burning with the cold fury she'd seen before. But now she knew it was all aimed at Parrish.

She folded her arms so she could hold his hands tight against her and realized she'd only begun to know the faithfulness of God. He'd brought her to this time and place for His purpose, and she'd do her best to be worthy.

"You stole a horse before you left town, Parrish," Sheriff Everett said.

"Can our aunts and uncles come to visit, Ma?" Abe asked.

"Only aunts, Abe," Grace said. "And I don't know. I've kind of lost touch with them." She wondered about Hannah and the little girls. Maybe Hannah could come. She'd write the second she could get a letter to town.

Clay McClellen scratched the side of his head. "Six children?"

"And horse thievin' is a hangin' offense in the West, Parrish." Luther looked at the group of children.

Grace could see Parrish's lips moving as he counted.

"Yeah," the sheriff said, "but the horse bucked him off and it was heading toward home when we passed it. Don't rightly know if we can hang him on that."

"He needs hanging. I say we go ahead and call him a horse thief," Luther said.

"Anyway, it don't matter about our horse—he's done a sight more 'n horse thievin'." Sheriff Everett pulled some papers out of the pocket of his white shirt. He unfolded them, and Grace saw more wanted posters. "I've got posters here hunting for Parrish all over the West. You stole and cheated your way here, then lied your way into a job."

"Why didn't you notice them when he was working at the school?" Buff grumbled.

The sheriff looked sheepish. "It don't look that much like him. And whoever thinks the schoolmaster is a swindler?"

"You hurt our children." Clay's voice was as cold as the grave. "You threatened Miss Calhoun."

"Mrs. Reeves," Daniel said.

"Now you're going back to Mosqueros to face Texas justice," Clay said with satisfaction.

"That's if we can keep Sophie away from him until it's time for a hanging," Luther pointed out.

"She'll mind me." Clay said it with utmost confidence, but Grace thought his eyes wavered a bit.

Luther caught Parrish by the left arm. "We've got a long hike outta this canyon."

Buff caught him by the right. " 'N a long, hard ride home."

"Parrish!" Grace shouted. Buff and Luther paused and turned so her father faced her. "You've spent your life hurting children. You, the father to so many, don't know a thing about fatherhood. God is the perfect Father, Mr. Parrish. I commend you into His hands and hope you'll give Him a chance to make the rest of your life a better one."

Parrish glared at her as if she'd slapped him.

The two men dragged Parrish, limping and bleeding, up the hill.

"I'll be over as soon as the pass is clear with Sophie and the girls for a visit," Clay said. "It oughta be passable in another month or two." Clay reached out his hand and shook Daniel's firmly. "And congratulations about the baby."

"Thanks kindly, Clay." Daniel smiled.

A burn climbed up Grace's cheeks at such a personal thing being discussed in front of these men. The embarrassment, combined with the fear, Parrish's hard hand, and Daniel's kind words, caused tears to fill her eyes.

Clay took one look at her watery eyes and ran.

The sheriff trudged after the others.

Grace wiped her eyes and turned to her family.

"He was your pa?" Ike asked.

Grace nodded.

"He was a mighty poor one," John said. He came up and threw his arms around Grace's legs, nearly knocking her over.

Daniel held on and kept her on her feet. "Amen to that."

Luke came up and threw himself against Grace's and Daniel's legs. He hit a little too hard, and they staggered sideways down the hill.

"Watch out, stupid." John turned and tried to club Luke with the back of his closed fist. Luke ducked and John hit Ike instead.

"Hey, you little runt." Ike charged John.

Daniel tightened his grip on Grace and, with a fast swoop, spun her out of the way of the collision.

Grace's stomach was left behind. She breathed quickly to control her nausea and stave off humiliation.

Ike slammed into John and Luke. They fell, sliding downhill. Shouting and threatening each other, they slid into Abe, who went down amid the flailing arms and kicking feet.

Mark started laughing uproariously. He bent over and grabbed a clod of muddy earth and heaved it onto Abe's head. Abe shouted and jumped to his feet. Mark ran screaming toward the cabin.

"Daniel,"—Grace poked him in the stomach to get him to stop laughing—"make them stop. Someone's going to get hurt."

The shrieks were deafening.

"Oh, let 'em play, Gracie. It keeps 'em quiet."

All five boys whooped like wild Indians. A scream that sounded like real pain made Grace jump. Daniel held on and firmly turned her around to face him.

She saw the love in his eyes and forgot all about the madhouse in the woods behind her. "I'm not going to die, Daniel. I'm a strong woman. Having babies is going to agree with me. I know it."

Daniel's eyes closed; then, after a moment, he opened them. "God has been faithful to us, to bring us together."

Grace realized he'd been praying when his eyes were closed. "It's a pure miracle is what it is. To think Parrish made me hide in your wagon, and it all led to this."

Daniel pulled her close. "I don't think of it as a miracle, I don't reckon. I think of it as how everything was meant to be. God worked all the twists and turns. He was watching out for us, caring for us, without us even knowing."

"He was faithful," Grace said thoughtfully. "And remembering God's faithfulness was what gave me the courage to fight Parrish. I knew that if God was with me, Parrish couldn't stand against me."

"And God *is* with you, Grace. He wanted you to come here and make our family whole again. He's not going to take you from me now."

Grace laid her hand on Daniel's chest. "And even if He does—"

Daniel's arms tightened on her waist. "Don't say that, Gracie. I love you. It would kill me to lose you."

Grace said firmly, "Even if He does, it will be His will, His time. He will still be faithful to us and we will be faithful to Him in return, whatever this life holds."

Daniel shook off the sadness of her words and nodded. He lowered his head. Grace closed her eyes and stood on her tiptoes, reaching for him.

A crash from behind them sounded as though the boys had brought a tree down on their heads.

"We'd better go see," Grace said.

"I can tell by the screaming it's nothing serious." Daniel pulled her back and kissed her.

The boys kept screaming, but now Grace was happy for it because it kept them busy while she kissed her husband fervently.

He was right.

The screaming did keep them "quiet."

DISCUSSION QUESTIONS

1. Who was your favorite character in *Calico Canyon* and why?

2. Do you think the book looked unfavorably on men considering the unruly Reeves boys and Daniel's hostility, or was the treatment fair and were the men given sufficiently good qualities? Could the ill behavior of the male characters have been a cover for their emotional scars?

3. Are the boys treated fairly in *Calico Canyon*? Have you known little boys this rowdy? How can their extremes be managed?

4. Did you find Daniel loveable despite his fairly uncivilized manners and opinions? What were his most endearing qualities?

5. Discuss the way boys and girls are different by what is taught to them and what is natural to their sex. How can we nurture our children and demand discipline while respecting their fundamental differences?

6. Have you ever noticed that most of the great child rearing books are written by people with only one kid? How does having more than one child awaken you to a new understanding of how a child reacts to discipline based not just on whether they're boys or girls but also based on their individual personality?

7. Discuss childbirth in earlier times and how dangerous it was.

8. Family trees are full of grandfathers and great-grandfathers who remarried after losing a wife in childbirth. Do you have ancestors who died in childbirth?

9. How does facing her cowardice change Grace? How does her courage make her more appealing to Daniel?

10. Discuss how Daniel was struggling just as much from a lack of courage as Grace was.

11. Grace makes an attempt in the end to reach out to Parrish—not as a daughter but as a child of God. How do you deal with forgiveness in your life when the one you need to forgive doesn't ask for it, want it, or admit wrongdoing?

12. What does Jesus demand of us when it comes to forgiving people who want no part of our forgiveness?

13. Does Tilly's struggle for freedom from slavery reflect Grace's struggle against child labor? How so?

14. In your opinion, is Tilly's attitude a fair representation of how a person who has been enslaved would act? Discuss the impact of physical slavery upon emotional slavery.

15. We all know how hard it is for people raised a certain way to truly change their outlook. Becoming a Christian is a life-changing event, but it isn't a personality change. It's a soul change. In the case of Grace's childhood of abuse and Tilly's enslavement, could these women overcome the emotional scars of their upbringing through new life in Christ? Did the author lay a good foundation in the story for these characters' change?

16. Does the comedy of *Calico Canyon* pull you deeper into the faith story, or do you think Christian fiction needs more solemnity to honor God?

"Pure religion and undefiled before God and the Father is this, to visit the fatherless and widows in their affliction, and to keep himself unspotted from the world."
JAMES 1:27

ONE

Sour Springs, Texas, 1870

Martha had an iron rod where most people had a backbone.

Grant smiled as he pulled his team to a stop in front of the train station in Sour Springs, Texas.

She also had a heart of gold—even if the old bat wouldn't admit it. She was going to be thrilled to see him and scold him the whole time.

"It's time to get back on the train." Martha Norris, ever the disciplinarian, had a voice that could back down a starving Texas wildcat, let alone a bunch of orphaned kids. It carried all the way across the street as Grant jumped from his wagon and trotted toward the depot. He'd almost missed them. He could see the worry on Martha's face.

Wound up tight from rushing to town, Grant knew he was late. But now that he was here, he relaxed. It took all of his willpower not to laugh at Martha, the old softy.

He hurried toward them. If it had only been Martha he would have laughed, but there was nothing funny about the two children with her. They were leftovers.

A little girl, shivering in the biting cold, her thin shoulders hunched against the wind, turned back toward the train. Martha, her shoulders slumped with sadness at what lay ahead for these children, rested one of her competent hands on the child's back.

Grant noticed the girl limping. That explained why she hadn't been adopted. No one wanted a handicapped child. As if limping put a child so far outside of normal she didn't need love and a home. Controlling the slow burn in his gut, Grant saw the engineer top off the train's water tank. They'd be pulling out of the station in a matter of minutes.

"Isn't this the last stop, Mrs. Norris?" A blond-headed boy stood, stony-faced, angry, scared.

"Yes, Charlie, it is."

His new son's name was Charlie. Grant picked up his pace.

Martha sighed. "We don't have any more meetings planned."

"So, we have to go back to New York?" Charlie, shivering and thin but hardy compared to the girl, scowled as he stood on the snow-covered platform, six feet of wood separating the train from the station house.

Grant had never heard such a defeated question.

The little girl's chin dropped and her shoulders trembled.

What was he thinking? He heard defeat from unwanted children all the time.

Charlie slipped his threadbare coat off his shoulders even though the wind cut like a knife through Grant's worn-out buckskin jacket.

Grant's throat threatened to swell shut with tears as he watched that boy sacrifice the bit of warmth he got from that old coat.

Stepping behind Martha, Charlie wrapped his coat around the girl. She shuddered and practically burrowed into the coat as if it held the heat of a fireplace, even as she shook her head and frowned at Charlie.

"Just take the stupid thing." Charlie glared at the girl.

After studying him a long moment, the little girl, her eyes wide and sad, kept the coat.

Mrs. Norris stayed his hands. "That's very generous, Charlie, but you can't go without a coat."

"I don't want it. I'm gonna throw it under the train if she don't keep it." The boy's voice was sharp and combative. A bad attitude. That could keep a boy from finding a home.

Grant hurried faster across the frozen ruts of Sour Springs Main Street toward the train platform and almost made it. A tight grip on his arm stopped him. Surprised, he turned and saw that irksome woman who'd been hounding him ever since she'd moved to town. What was her name? Grant'd made a point of not paying attention to her. She usually yammered about having his shirts sewn in her shop.

"Grant, it's so nice to see you."

It took all his considerable patience to not jerk free. Shirt Lady was unusually tall, slender, and no one could deny she was pretty, but she had a grip like a mule skinner, and Grant was afraid he'd have a fight on his hands to get his arm back.

Grant touched the brim of his battered Stetson with his free hand. "Howdy, Miss. I'm afraid I'm in a hurry today."

A movement caught his eye, and he turned to look at his wagon across the street. Through the whipping wind he could see little, but Grant was sure someone had come alongside his wagon. He wished it were true so he could palm this persistent pest off on an unsuspecting neighbor.

Shirt Lady's grip tightened until it almost hurt through his coat. She leaned close, far closer than was proper to Grant's way of thinking.

"Why don't you come over to my place and warm yourself before you head back to the ranch. I've made pie, and it's a lonely kind of day." She fluttered her lashes until Grant worried she'd gotten dirt in her eye. He considered sending her to Doc Morgan for medical care.

The train chugged and reminded Grant he was almost out of time. "Can't stop now, miss." What *was* her name? How many times had she spoken to him? A dozen if it was three. "There are some orphans left on the platform, and they need a home. I've got to see to 'em."

Something flashed in her eyes for a second before she controlled it. He knew that look. She didn't like orphans. Well, then what was she doing talking to him? He came with a passel of 'em. Grant shook himself free.

"We'll talk another time then."

Sorely afraid they would, Grant tugged on his hat brim again and ran. His boots echoed on the depot stairs. He reached the top step just as Martha turned to the sound of his clomping. She was listening for him even when she shouldn't be.

Grant couldn't stand the sight of the boy's thin shoulders covered only by the coarse fabric of his dirty brown shirt. Grant pulled his gloves off, noticing as he did that the tips of his fingers showed through holes in all ten fingers.

"I'll take 'em, Martha." How was he supposed to live with himself if he didn't? Grant's spurs clinked as he came forward. He realized in his dash to get to town he'd worn his spurs even though he brought the buckboard. Filthy from working the cattle all morning, most of his hair had fallen loose from the thong he used to tie it back. More than likely he smelled like his horse. A razor hadn't touched his face since last Sunday morning.

Never one to spend money on himself when his young'uns had needs—or might at any time—his coat hung in tatters, and his woolen union suit showed through a rip in his knee.

Martha ran her eyes up and down him and shook her head, suppressing a smile. "Grant, you look a fright."

A slender young woman rose to her feet from where she sat at the depot. Her movements drew Grant's eyes away from the forlorn children. From the look of the snow piling up on the young woman's head, she'd been sitting here in the cold ever since the train had pulled in, which would have been the better part of an hour ago. She must have expected someone to meet her, but no one had.

When she stepped toward him, Grant spared her a longer glance because she was a pretty little thing, even though her dark brown hair hung in bedraggled strings from beneath her black bonnet and twisted into tangled curls around her chin. Her face was so dirty the blue of her eyes shined almost like the heart of a flame in a sooty lantern.

Grant stared at her for a moment. He recognized something in her eyes. If she'd been a child and looked at him with those eyes, he'd have taken her home and raised her.

Then the children drew his attention away from the tired, young lady.

Martha Norris shook her head. "You can't handle any more, Grant. We'll find someone, I promise. I won't quit until I do."

"I know that's the honest truth." Grant knew Martha had to protest; good sense dictated it. But she'd hand the young'uns over. "And God bless you for it. But this is the end of the line for the orphan train. You can't do anything until you get back to New York. I'm not going to let these children take that ride."

"Actually, Libby joined us after we'd left New York. It was a little irregular, but it's obvious the child needs a home." Martha kept looking at him, shaking her head.

"Irregular how?" He tucked his tattered gloves behind his belt buckle.

"She stowed away." Martha glanced at Libby. "It was the strangest thing. I never go back to the baggage car, but one of the children tore a hole in his pants. My sewing kit is always in the satchel I carry with me. I was sure I had it, but it was nowhere to be found. So I knew I'd most likely left it with my baggage. I went back to fetch it so I could mend the seam and found her hiding in amongst the trunks."

Grant was reaching for the buttons on his coat, but he froze. "Are you sure she isn't running away from home?" His stomach twisted when he thought of a couple of his children who had run off over the years. He'd been in a panic until he'd found them. "She might have parents somewhere, worried to death about her."

"She had a note in her pocket explaining everything. I feel certain she's an orphan. And I don't know how long she was back there. She could have been riding with us across several states. I sent telegraphs to every station immediately, and I'm planning on leaving a note at each stop on my way back, but I hold out no hope that a family is searching for her." Martha sighed as if she wanted to fall asleep on her feet.

Grant realized it wasn't just the children who had a long ride ahead of them. One corner of Grant's lips turned up. "Quit looking at me like that, Martha, or I'll be thinking I have to adopt you so *you* don't have to face the trip."

Martha, fifty if she was a day, laughed. "I ought to take you up on that. You need someone to come out there and take your ranch in hand. Without a wife, who's going to cook for all these children?"

"You've been out. You know how we run things. Everybody chips in." The snow was getting heavier, and the wind blew a large helping of it down Grant's neck. Grant ignored the cold in the manner of men who fought the elements for their living and won. He went back to unbuttoning his coat, then shrugged it off and dropped it on the boy's shoulders. It hung most of the way to the ground.

Charlie tried to give the coat back. "I don't want your coat, mister."

Taking a long look at Charlie's defiant expression, Grant fairly growled. "Keep it."

Charlie held his gaze for a moment before he looked away. "Thank you."

Grant gave his Stetson a quick dip to salute the boy's manners. Snow sprang into the air as the brim of his hat snapped down and up. He watched it be swept up and around by the whipping wind then filter down around his face, becoming part of the blizzard that was getting stronger and meaner every moment.

Martha nodded. "If they limited the number of children one man could take, you'd be over it for sure."

Grant controlled a shudder of cold as he pulled on his gloves. "Well, thank heavens there's no limit. The oldest boy and the two older girls are just a year or so away from being out on their own. One of them's even got a beau. I really need three more to take their places, but I'll settle for two."

Martha looked from one exhausted, filthy child to the other then looked back at Grant. "The ride back would be terribly hard on them."

Grant crouched down in front of the children, sorry for the clink of his spurs that had a harsh sound and might frighten the little girl. Hoping his smile softened his grizzled appearance enough to keep the little girl from running scared, he said, "Well, what kind of man would I be if I stood by watching while something was terribly hard on you two? How'd you like to come out and live on my ranch? I've got other kids there, and you'll fit right in to our family."

"They're *not* going to fit, Grant," Martha pointed out through chattering teeth. "Your house is overflowing now."

Grant had to admit she was right. "What difference does it make if we're a little crowded, Martha? We'll find room."

The engineer swung out on the top step of the nearest car, hanging onto a handle in the open door of the huffing locomotive. "All aboard!"

The little girl looked fearfully between the train and Grant.

Looking at the way the little girl clung to Martha's hand, Grant knew she didn't want to go off with a strange man almost as much as she didn't want to get back on that train.

"I'll go with you." The little boy narrowed his eyes as he moved to stand like a cranky guardian angel beside the girl.

Grant saw no hesitation in the scowling little boy, only concern for the girl. No fear. No second thoughts. He didn't even look tired compared to the girl and Martha. He had intelligent blue eyes with the slyness a lot of orphans had. Not every child he'd adopted had made the adjustment without trouble. A lot of them took all of Grant's prayers and patience. Grant smiled to himself. He had an unlimited supply of prayers, and the prayers helped him hang onto the patience.

Grant shivered under the lash of the blowing snow.

The boy shrugged out of the coat. "Take your coat back. The cold don't bother me none."

Grant stood upright and gently tugged the huge garment back

around the boy's neck and began buttoning it. "The cold don't bother me none, neither. You'll make a good cowboy, son. We learn to keep going no matter what the weather." He wished he had another coat because the girl still looked miserable. Truth be told, he wouldn't have minded one for himself.

Martha leaned close to Grant's ear on the side away from the children. "Grant, you need to know that Libby hasn't spoken a word since we found her. There was a note in her pocket that said she's mute. She's got a limp, too. It looks to me like she had a badly broken ankle some years ago that didn't heal right. I'll understand if you—"

Grant pulled away from Martha's whispers as his eyebrows slammed together. Martha fell silent and gave him a faintly alarmed look. He tried to calm down before he spoke, matching her whisper. "You're not going to insult me by suggesting I'd leave a child behind because she has a few problems, are you?"

Martha studied him, and then her expression relaxed. Once more she whispered, "No, Grant. But you did need to be told. The only reason I know her name is because it was on the note. Libby pulled it out of her coat pocket as if she'd done it a thousand times, so chances are this isn't a new problem, which probably means it's permanent."

Grant nodded his head with one taut jerk. "Obliged for the information then. Sorry I got testy." Grant did his best to make it sound sincere, but it hurt, cut him right to the quick, for Martha to say such a thing to him after all these years.

"No, I'm sorry I doubted you." Martha rested one hand on his upper arm. "I shouldn't have, not even for a second."

Martha eased back and spoke normally again. "We think Libby's around six." She swung Libby's little hand back and forth, giving the girl an encouraging smile.

All Grant's temper melted away as he looked at the child. "Hello, Libby." Crouching back down to the little girl's eye level, he gave the shivering tyke all of his attention.

Too tiny for six and too thin for any age, she had long dark hair caught in a single bedraggled braid and blue eyes awash in fear and wishes. Her nose and cheeks were chapped and red. Her lips trembled. Grant hoped it was from the cold and not from looking at the nasty man who wanted to take her away.

"I think you'll like living on my ranch. I've got the biggest backyard to play in you ever saw. Why, the Rocking C has a mountain rising right up out of the back door. You can collect eggs from the chickens. I've got some other kids and they'll be your brothers and sisters, and we've got horses you can ride."

Libby's eyes widened with interest, but she never spoke. Well, he'd had 'em shy before.

"I can see you'll like that. I'll start giving you riding lessons as soon as the snow lets up." Grant ran his hand over his grizzled face. "I should have shaved and made myself more presentable for you young'uns. I reckon I'm a scary sight. But the cattle were acting up this morning. There's a storm coming, and it makes 'em skittish. By the time I could get away, I was afraid I'd miss the train."

Grant took Libby's little hand, careful not to move suddenly and frighten her, and rubbed her fingers on his whiskery face.

She snatched her hand away, but she grinned.

The smile transformed Libby's face. She had eyes that had seen too much and square shoulders that had borne a lifetime of trouble. Grant vowed to himself that he'd devote himself to making her smile.

"I'll shave it off before I give you your first good night kiss."

The smile faded, and Libby looked at him with such longing Grant's heart turned over with a father's love for his new daughter. She'd gotten to him even faster than they usually did.

Martha reached past Libby to rest her hand on the boy's shoulder. "And Charlie is eleven."

Grant pivoted a bit on his toes and looked at Charlie again. A good-looking boy, but so skinny he looked like he'd blow over in a hard wind. Grant could fix that. The boy had flyaway blond hair that needed a wash and a trim. It was the hostility in his eyes that explained why he hadn't found a home. Grant had seen that look before many times, including in a mirror.

As if he spoke to another man, Grant said, "Charlie, welcome to the family."

Charlie shrugged as if being adopted meant nothing to him. "Are we supposed to call you pa?"

"That'd be just fine." Grant looked back at the little girl. "Does that suit you, Libby?"

Libby didn't take her lonesome eyes off Grant, but she pressed herself against Martha's leg as if she wanted to disappear into Martha's long wool coat.

The engineer shouted, "All aboard!" The train whistle sounded. A blast of steam shot across the platform a few feet ahead of them.

Libby jumped and let out a little squeak of surprise. Grant noted that the little girl's voice worked, so most likely she didn't talk for reasons of her own, not because of an injury. He wondered if she'd seen something so terrible she couldn't bear to speak of it.

The boy reached his hand out for Libby. "We've been together for a long time, Libby. We can go together to the ranch. I'll take care of you."

Libby looked at Charlie as if he were a knight in shining armor. After some hesitation, she released her death grip on Martha and caught Charlie's hand with both of hers.

"Did I hear you correctly?" A sharp voice asked from over Grant's shoulder. "Are you allowing this man to adopt these children?"

Startled, Grant stood, turned, and bumped against a soft, cranky woman. He almost knocked her onto her backside—the lady who'd been waiting at the depot. He grabbed her or she'd have fallen on the slippery wood. Grant steadied her, warm and alive in his hands.

TWO

"Excuse me." He said it even though it was all her fault he bumped into her. She'd obviously been eavesdropping. He'd thought she was pretty before. Now she just looked snippy.

The woman looked past Grant like he was dirt under her feet and said to Martha, "You can't put these children into a home without a mother."

"Don't worry, Miss. . .Miss. . ." Martha came to stand like a bulwark beside Grant.

He appreciated her siding with him, especially when common sense would tell anyone that, in the normal course of things, this busybody was right.

"I'm Hannah. . .uh. . .Cartwright. Surely there are laws against a man simply sweeping up children to take them home for laborers. If there aren't, there should be."

"Laborers?" Grant went from annoyed to furious in one fell swoop.

He had the sudden desire to wipe the superior expression off Hannah Cartwright's face. "This isn't any business of yours."

"Now, Miss Cartwright, that's not—"

The train whistle blasted again, drowning out Martha's words even though her lips kept moving.

"It's very much my business if children are being exploited."

"Exploited?" Grant erupted, but then he caught hold of his temper.

585

He didn't calm down for the prissy female. He did it for the children. They didn't need to start out their life watching their new pa throw a pitched fit at a young woman, no matter how bad-mannered and misinformed that woman might be.

With exaggerated politeness, he said, "You don't know what you're talking about, so I'll forgive your rudeness."

He turned to Libby and Charlie. "Let's go. We need to get back to the ranch in time for the noon meal."

Libby backed away from him a step and peeked up at the nagging woman behind him. Out of the corner of his eye he saw Miss Priss take a step forward—to keep an eagle eye on him, no doubt.

"Why don't the children stay with me until we can find a suitable home for them?" Her voice had a nice quality to it, all smooth and sweet. At the same time, it rubbed on him like a rasp, burning him until he felt all raw and tender inside. He wished for just one second she'd use it for something besides giving him a hard time.

"Oh no, that would never do," Martha said. "We can't let an unmarried woman have a child. That's out of the question."

"Why is it out of the question for a single woman but not a single man?"

Grant glanced over his shoulder. "You really want to adopt these children?"

Dismay crossed Miss Cartwright's face, as if she'd spoken without thinking. Grant decided the look was fear that she'd be saddled with two kids when all she wanted was to be a troublemaker.

"Well, a single man probably would be out of the question most of the time," Martha said in her brisk, stern voice that concealed a heart as big as Texas. "I know orphanages sometimes place their children with bachelors or spinsters, but I've never approved of it. Children need a family, a mother and a father. Grant is a special case. We make an exception for him."

The pest pushed past Grant to face Martha directly. "Mrs. Norris, you know I've been on the train with you for a while now. I've taken a liking to the children. I don't want them...that is...can't they..." The lady frowned at Martha, her blue eyes shining in the swirling snow, her dirty face going pink under the grime. "Can I at least talk to the children before you decide? I want to make sure they really want to go with him. They might be so tired from the train that they're desperate. And they might still find families elsewhere if we—"

"Miss Cartwright, please," Martha cut her off. "This is the last town we have appointments in. No, if they don't find a home at this stop, Charlie and Libby will have to ride all the way back to New York. The children will be better off with Grant."

Grant and Martha exchanged a look. He reached for the children's hands and felt a small but firm grip on his arm. Exasperated, he wheeled around and faced Miss Cartwright.

"I'm not allowing you to leave with these children. I know how this works. You take them out to your ranch, virtually stack them in inadequate space, and press them into being little more than slaves. I'm not going to allow—"

Libby made a little sound that sounded like pure fear. She started crying, dry sobs escaping her otherwise silent lips. She hurled herself into Charlie's arms, and Charlie staggered backward a step but held on and looked angry, his eyes darting between Grant and Miss Cartwright.

Grant gave Miss Cartwright a furious look, which she returned in full measure, shooting flaming arrows from her blue eyes that liked to stab him to death on the spot.

The whistle blasted and the train began inching out of the station.

Grant turned away from the nag, feeling like a spinning top going round and round from Martha to Hannah to the children. Speaking louder to be heard over the chugging engine, he said, "Hurry up, Martha. You're going to miss your train."

"Grant, I don't want to leave this woman with the impression that—"

Grant caught Martha's arm and firmly guided her to the platform, leaving the children and the irritating meddler behind. "If you miss your train there won't be another one along for days. You've no doubt got appointments scheduled for the return trip and you'll have to cancel them. We'll be fine. I'll handle that little pest back there."

Martha smiled at him through the soot on her face. "Now Grant, be nice."

"Nice?" Grant yelled as the train started moving faster. "I'll be nicer'n she deserves."

Martha quit protesting and hurried toward the nearest car. She jumped on board like the seasoned traveler she was and turned to yell over her shoulder. "I'll send the paperwork for the adoptions through the mail just like always."

Grant waved good-bye and turned to see Miss Cartwright fuming. He wondered how mad she had to be before she'd melt all that snow off her bonnet. Her temper didn't bother him much. What upset him was Libby's fear as she clung to Charlie.

Grant strode over to the children and, ignoring the cranky little woman who stood there looking at him like he was 180 pounds of stinking polecat, he hunkered down again. With a gentle chuck under Libby's chin, he said, "Don't worry about what she said about slaves. She is shaping up to be a very silly woman who doesn't know what she's talking about. My home is a nice place."

"Mr. Grant"—Hannah's hand closed on his shoulder so tight he wished for his coat back for protection from her fingernails—"how dare you call me names?"

Grant stood up, stretching to his full six feet as he turned, making it a point to look down on her. "You call me a slave owner."

Trying to keep his voice down so the children couldn't hear every word, he narrowed his eyes at her and spoke through his clenched teeth. "You frighten these innocent children who are already going through such a tough time."

He leaned closer. "You insult me with every word that comes out of your mouth." Their noses almost touched. "And then you have the nerve to take offense when *I call you silly?*"

With a snort he didn't even try to make sound friendly, he said, "I'd think, tossing out insults the way you do, you'd have grown a hide as thick as a buffalo by now." He leaned even closer. "I'd think you'd've been called silly a thousand times in your life and be used to it."

He spoke through gritted teeth. "I'd think the only single, solitary chance you have of getting through a day without someone calling you silly is if the world plumb goes and turns flat and the rest of us fall off the edge."

Grant glared at her for a long moment. She glared right back. He had one tiny flash of admiration for her guts. She might insult the stuffing out of him, but she didn't back down when she thought she was right. Too bad she was wrong.

Sick of the staring match, he turned back to the children. "You'll have some chores to do, but there'll be a lot of time for fun."

Libby stared at him. The only sound she made was her teeth chattering.

Grant saw the hurt in the little girl. He knew having a mother was the dearest dream of every orphaned child's heart. A father came in a poor second. But a poor second still beat having nothing, which was what Libby had now. He rested a hand on her too-thin arm and answered the question he knew she wanted to ask. "No, little one, there's no ma. But I've got a couple of nearly grown daughters who will love you like you were their very own. I think you'll like 'em."

Libby watched him in silence for a moment then stared forlornly after the rapidly disappearing train. She looked at Miss Cartwright again, and Grant decided the two must have struck up a friendship on the trip because so much passed between them with that look. At last Libby squared her tiny shoulders, as he could tell she'd done a thousand times before in a life that didn't offer much good news.

That was the best Grant could hope for—for now.

"Mr. Grant," Hannah repeated.

He stood. He needed a few more moments to reassure the boy, but he had to get this nagging woman off his back. "What is it, Hannah?"

"Well, first of all"—her eyes flashed like summer lightning—"it's Miss Cartwright to you."

Grant noticed they were very pretty blue eyes. Too bad they were attached to a snippy woman who seemed bent on freezing him to death or nagging him to death, whichever came last, because he had no doubt, if he froze here, solid in his boots, Hannah would go on snipping at him long after he'd turned to an icicle.

Grant crossed his arms over his chest. He knew it made him look stubborn, which he wasn't. He was a reasonable man. But the truth was he was cold. He tried to look casual about it. Charlie hadn't wanted to take his coat in the first place. It wasn't right to suffer visibly right in front of the boy. "All right, Miss Cartwright, what awful thing do you want to accuse me of now?"

Hannah seemed prepared to launch into a list of his shortcomings.

Grant braced himself for a blizzard of cold, critical words to go with the weather.

Libby tugged on Grant's arm. He turned to her and waited to see what she wanted to tell him. All she did was tug and squirm around, doing a little dance Grant had seen thousands of times before.

Bending close to her, he whispered, "There's an outhouse behind the depot. Let's go. Then we'll head on out to the ranch and get you two out of this cold weather."

Libby nodded frantically and hopped around a bit.

"Come on, Charlie." Grant swooped Libby up in his arms.

"Now wait just a minute, Mr. Grant." Hannah jammed her fists onto her waist.

Grant noticed she wasn't wearing gloves and her teeth were chattering from the cold, just like Libby's. She was skin and bones, too, and her coat was worn paper thin. He had a moment of compassion for the little pest. She didn't deserve the compassion, but Grant knew she had to be suffering.

Libby looked back at Hannah.

Deciding he was right about Libby and her friendship with Hannah, Grant, spurs clinking, headed for the edge of the platform. He glanced over his shoulder. "It isn't *Mr.* Grant. It's just Grant."

"Well, what *is* your last name?" The woman kept nagging even as he left her behind.

Grant wondered who was supposed to come get her. "I don't have a last name."

"No last name?" She seemed frozen with shock, but Grant considered the possibility that she was actually frozen. The temperature was dropping as fast as the snow.

Grant and the children started down the clattering wooden steps of the train station. "Libby, what's your last name?"

Libby shrugged then clung to his shoulders as they bounced down the stairs.

"Charlie, what's yours?"

"I don't have one." Charlie waved good-bye to Hannah.

"Me neither." Grant glanced back at Hannah as he got to the ground. "It's just one of the facts of being an orphan, often as not. I did finally get adopted when I was almost grown, but after my folks died, I decided I'd live my life without one so I'd never forget what it feels like to need a family. I don't expect you to understand, Hannah Cartwright. No one can who isn't an orphan."

He jerked his chin down in a terse nod at Hannah that said good-bye more clearly than words. He disappeared around the corner, leaving her with her mouth hanging open.

THREE

I t cut like a razor to be left standing in the bitter January cold wondering what her last name might be.

The wind whipped Hannah, lashing her like Parrish's belt. She understood exactly what it felt like to be an orphan. And she knew exactly what Libby and Charlie faced now that they'd fallen into Grant's clutches. Fists clenched, she wanted to scream at the unfairness that forced her and Libby to pretend that they didn't know each other. They were sisters, of the heart if not the flesh. They belonged together.

Hannah stared into the cruel blizzard winds, fighting tears that would only freeze on her cheeks if she let them fall. Libby—she had to save Libby. She'd never considered the possibility that Libby would be adopted. No family stepped forward to accept a child who wasn't perfect.

No one had wanted her in Omaha when they'd stowed away on the orphan train the first time. Of course no one would want her now. So why had that awful man taken her?

Had Libby limped in front of Grant? Libby had walked off the train, so of course she'd limped. But he hadn't been here yet. Maybe he hadn't noticed. Or maybe the work he had in mind for her might be done by a girl with one badly broken foot. Maybe, once he got her home, he'd realize what he'd done and throw her out, maybe this very night in the middle of a blizzard.

Libby had been thrown out before. She'd been around three, living in a Chicago alley, fighting the rats for bits of food, when one of the boys who made up Hannah's ragtag family had found her and brought her home to the abandoned shed they slept in.

Hannah and Libby had been sisters for nearly four years now, and Hannah had yet to hear Libby speak a word.

There were no limits to how cruel people could be. Someone had thrown Libby away as if she were trash. The scars on Hannah's back attested to the lengths to which her own adoptive father had gone to wrest obedience from his daughters.

The instant Grant knew Libby wasn't perfect he'd get rid of her. Throw her out or keep her for hard labor, starving and beating her. Either was a disaster for frail, little Libby.

She rushed after Grant, but she stopped, almost skidding off the slippery station platform. The snow slashed at her face and the wind howled around her as she tried to decide what to do.

Hannah had to stop Grant. But what could she do alone against him? It was more than obvious that he had no intention of letting her stop him. Making off with two more indentured servants put speed in his step.

She thought of how awful he looked, like an outlaw. Long stringy hair and a smell that Hannah thought belonged to an animal and not a man. Eyes flashing gold at her like a hungry eagle swooping down to snatch away youngsters and carry them off to his nest. Captivating eyes that sent a shiver through her when she thought of how they shined out of his grimy, whiskered face.

The shiver wasn't exactly fear though. It wasn't normal that she hadn't feared Grant. Her fearful reaction to men was something she'd been fighting all her life, at least since Parrish.

Her shoulders squared and she lifted her head as she remembered confronting Grant. Never for a moment had she considered cringing or dropping her eyes. Why wouldn't Grant have that effect on her, when he was so much like Parrish?

A feeling of power firmed her jaw. She'd been taking one daring chance after another in the last few years. Maybe she'd finally built herself a backbone.

She couldn't defeat him physically, but she and Grace had outsmarted Parrish. And Grant struck Hannah as none-too-bright. She'd have to outthink him.

She rushed back to her satchel. It held her and Libby's few possessions in the world. Then she marched herself straight across the wide Sour Springs street, stepped up on the boardwalk, and went into a building with the words STROBEN'S MERCANTILE painted on the front window.

Shuddering from the delicious warmth and the smell of food, she ignored her frozen fingertips and empty stomach and dodged around bolts of cloth and barrels of nails toward the whipcord lean woman standing behind the counter.

Another woman, unusually tall, painfully thin, and nearer Hannah's age, stood in the corner of the store feeling a bolt of cloth. She looked up when Hannah charged in, but Hannah barely spared a glance.

Pointing back toward the street, Hannah said, "A man just took two orphans off a train and is planning to take them home. He has no mother for them. I tried to stop him, but he ignored me. I need help. He said his name is Grant."

The shopper drew Hannah's attention when she jerked her head around. Setting the fabric down, she turned toward Hannah, opening her mouth as if to ask a question. Then her teeth clicked and she went back to browsing.

The lady behind the counter looked up from a scrap of paper in her hand and stopped in the middle of setting a jar of molasses into a wooden box. "Lord'a mercy, that Grant. Another two kids?" She started laughing, loud braying laughs that would have set a donkey's heart into an envious spin.

"It's not funny." A noise from the street snagged Hannah's attention and she spun around. Through the storefront window, she saw Grant driving out of town in a rattletrap wagon, with Libby barely visible, sitting squished between Grant and Charlie on the seat.

Hannah ran to the door just as Grant disappeared into the swirling snow. With a cry of anguish, she ran back to the lady in the back of the store. "He's leaving. We have to stop him."

"Harold." The lady turned away from Hannah and hollered into the back of the store, "Grant took two more kids out to the Rockin' C."

Laughter came from the back room.

Desperation making her furious, Hannah snapped, "If you won't help me then direct me to the sheriff."

Turning to Hannah with narrowed eyes, the storekeeper smoothed her neat gray braid, curled into a bun at the base of her skull. Her woolen dress was as faded as Hannah's and patched at the elbows, but the work was done with a skill Hannah admired. A couple of missing teeth, a beak of a nose, and round, wire-rimmed glasses gave the lady a no-nonsense appearance, and Hannah thought at first she'd made the woman angry.

Then the woman started laughing. "The sheriff don't have no call to go chase Grant down. Ned and Grant are friends. Ned's not going out in this storm just to meet two more of Grant's young'uns. Ah, Grant and that crowd of his. Just thinkin' of it fair tickles me to death."

Hannah turned to storm out of the store, aware that she'd done more storming around in the last few minutes than she'd done in her entire, meek life.

Before she could move another step, the woman asked, "Hey, who are you anyhow?"

Hannah stopped, not sure where she was storming to anyway. "I'm Hannah. . .Cartwright." She stumbled over the name she'd made up so she could get general delivery mail from Grace. She'd never used it much, avoiding people for the most part except for Libby, and Libby certainly never spoke Hannah's last name.

"What are you doing in Sour Springs?"

"I. . .I am. . ." Hannah drew a blank. There was one thing that was the truth. She was staying until she could save Libby and all the other children Grant had absconded with. And she couldn't afford to stay because she had no money. "I'm looking for work."

The storekeeper jumped as if she'd been poked with a hatpin. "Really, can you read and cipher? Because we need a new schoolteacher."

The storekeeper pointed a thumb at the other woman, now moved on from the dress goods to a stack of canned vegetables. "We offered Prudence the job, but she's come to town to take up as a seamstress. Not a lot of sewing around these parts. But she's bent on it, aren't you?"

Prudence nodded her head.

"It's a respectable enough business for a woman, I reckon, but you're apt to starve. Still, that's your business and no one else's."

Prudence's silent response reminded Hannah of Libby. She had to save Libby.

Hannah gave a friendly nod of hello to Prudence then opened her mouth to admit she'd never spent a day inside a classroom. She caught herself. That wasn't the question. "Yes, I can read and cipher."

"Harold," the storekeeper bellowed into the back of the building, "get out here."

A huge, unkempt man ambled out from the back room, wearing a union suit that might have been white years ago and a pair of brown broadcloth pants with the suspenders dangling at his sides.

"We got a young lady here, huntin' work. She'd make a fine schoolmarm, I'd say."

Wiping his hands on a dingy cloth as he plodded in, Harold said, "Great, we weren't going to be able to open up on Monday, since the last teacher ran off." He caught sight of Hannah and tilted his head to stare at her as if he was reading her mind, hunting for intelligence.

Hannah knew this might well be the only job in this tiny town. And she had to feed herself until she could get Libby back. "I have some experience teaching."

She didn't go into details—that she'd taught her little sisters after

Parrish went to bed at night. Then she'd taught the street children who had teamed up with her after she'd escaped Parrish's iron grip.

Harold headed for the front of the store. "I'll get the parson and Quincy Harrison. We can vote on it right now."

Harold grabbed his coat off a bent nail by the front door as he left the store, letting in a swirl of snow and frigid wind. He pulled the door closed firmly with a crack of wood and a rattle of its window.

Hannah turned to the storekeeper. "Uh...Mrs....uh..."

"I'm Mabel Stroben and that's my husband Harold. Call me Mabel. Do you have a place to stay? A room goes with the job. It's the room above the diner."

Hannah had no place to stay and only a few coins left in her pocket. "A room would be wonderful."

"Great, then it's settled, all except getting you hired."

That sounded like a really big "except" to Hannah.

The door squeaked like a tormented soul when Harold came back. He shed his coat, dusting snow all over the room. Before he'd hung up his coat, a man wearing a parson's collar and another man, dressed a lot like Harold but half as wide, came in.

Mabel pointed at Hannah. "Here she is."

"Well, that's just fine. I'm Parson Babbitt." The parson turned kind eyes on Hannah. "Let's sit down here and have a nice chat."

There were chairs pulled up around a potbelly stove in the front corner of the store, opposite that lone shopper.

Hannah knew this wasn't going to work. She had no idea what being a teacher required. She was fairly certain she had the ability to teach, but she had no schooling or experience and she wasn't about to lie. She relaxed as she gave up this pipe dream. She'd only had a couple of minutes to consider the idea anyway. It's not like she had her heart set on it. She took a seat and folded her hands neatly in her lap.

Prudence was now leafing through a book of fairy tales.

Hannah had learned to be suspicious to stay alive, and she had the distinct impression the woman was eavesdropping. But why? Maybe she had children and wanted to know if there'd be a school. Except, no, Mabel said they'd offered Prudence the teaching job and no married woman would be allowed to work.

The parson settled on her left; the other man sat on her right. Harold perched his bulk on a chair on past the parson and. . .the chairs were gone. Mabel moved down the counter that stretched the length of the small store and leaned on it to listen.

"I'm Quincy Harrison. I'm president of the school board. The parson and Harold are the other board members."

"Hello, Mr. Harrison, Parson Babbitt." She smiled calmly, completely sure this farce would soon be over. Her insides were gnawed with worry over Libby, but she had no worry about getting hired. They'd say, "No thanks"; then she'd go rent a horse and chase down her little sister, hide out somewhere with Libby in this dinky town, and stowaway on the next train coming through.

But what about the other children? Hannah had to save them, too. She would listen for a few minutes then decide what to do next.

Quincy Harrison said, "Can you read and cipher?"

Hannah nodded. "Yes, very well in fact."

"Do you want the job?" the parson asked.

"Yes, I'd like it very much." No lies necessary yet.

"It's settled then." Harold stood up. "You're hired."

Hannah's jaw dropped open. This was the interview? "Uh. . .don't you want me to take some tests? Show you what I know?" Hannah could pass those tests, she had little doubt.

"No need." Quincy stood next. "If it turns out you can't read or cipher, reckon we'll just fire you." He headed toward the door.

"Wait for me, Quince. We'd best stick together in this weather."

Hannah was distracted from needing to save Libby and that sweet little boy for just a second. She had a job. As a teacher, of all amazing things.

"Did you leave your things over at the station, Miss?" Harold started to pull his coat on.

The door slammed as the two men went out.

"Yes...I mean no." How did she explain to this man that she didn't have any *things* except her satchel. "Everything's been taken care of already."

Since everything she owned in the world was on her back or in her satchel, that was true. She went back to what was important, possibly life and death. "What about that man? We can't just stand by while he steals two children."

"Steals children? Grant?" Mabel started laughing as she headed back toward the center of the counter.

A bit slower to react, Harold started in, too. "I think I'll box up some of the extra pumpkins in the cellar. They aren't gonna make it to spring anyhow." Harold seemed to accept Hannah's statement that her things were dealt with.

Mabel nodded. "He's got a sight of mouths to feed."

Hannah remembered about the girls Grant had told Libby would love her. "How many children has he made off with like this?"

"Don't rightly know." Mabel looked at the ceiling as if only God could count fast enough and high enough to keep track. "Over the years... maybe twenty or twenty-five. Some of 'em're done growed up and gone nowadays."

"There's half a dozen or so of the older ones married and living around Sour Springs, and that many again scattered to the wind." Harold grabbed his heavy coat off the nail where he'd tossed it a few short seconds earlier. Hannah's whole life had changed in less time than it took the snow on Harold's coat to melt. "I'd say he's only got five or six out there."

"Four, I think," Mabel said with an unfocused look that made Hannah wonder if Mabel could read and cipher herself. Of course, Mabel wasn't the new schoolteacher. "Until today. Now he's up to six."

"Twenty or twenty-five?" Hannah exclaimed. "*Twenty-five children?*"

At his very worst, Parrish had kept six. All crammed into one room while he had a nice bedroom all his own. The children were stacked into one set of bunk beds, three on the bottom, three on top, with no more regard than if he'd been stacking cordwood.

"All together, give or take," Harold said, satisfied with the estimate. "Not all at one time. Lordy, that'd be a passel of mouths to feed, eh, Mabel?"

Hannah pictured a hovel filled with underfed children gnawing on raw pumpkin while they were forced to work from dawn until dusk to make money for the man with no last name. She also realized that the town accepted this wretched state of affairs and she'd get no help—at least not from these two.

She should have enlisted the parson's help. It didn't matter. The parson had to know and had done nothing to stop it. If they wouldn't help her save those children, she'd do it herself. "Someone has to put a stop to this. Why, the man is no better than a slave master."

Mabel didn't seem capable of being riled. "Now, Miss Cartwright, it's not that'a way with Grant. Don't go getting your feathers all in a ruffle. Just let us explain how things work here in Sour Springs, and you'll see that you just need to be reasonable."

Hannah balled up her fists. "I have no intention of being reasonable!" Mabel blinked.

That'd come out wrong. Hannah heard the door open and close and glanced back to see the other shopper leave without buying anything.

She looked back. From the set looks on Mabel's and Harold's faces, they were supportive of the miserable way Grant treated his children. Well, maybe some people could live their lives like this, but she wasn't one of them.

Rather than waste another second arguing with these two, she decided to handle this situation herself. She had a few meager pennies left. She'd see where she could hire a carriage, ask directions, and take care of Mr. . . .Grant herself.

FOUR

She turned to Harold. "I'd appreciate it very much if you could direct me to my room."

"I'll guide you over, miss. It's the room over the diner."

Hannah sniffed in disgust as she turned to walk out. As she left the store, she heard Mabel say to herself, "Steals children. . .Grant? Imagine." Then Mabel started laughing all over again.

Pulling on his coat as he walked, Harold led Hannah through the cutting snow, down the wooden sidewalk, toward the town's only diner. Harold led her down an alley that seemed to catch all the wind and shove it through at top speed. He rounded the back of the diner, went through a door and up a narrow flight of creaking steps.

Hannah clutched her satchel and followed.

It was exactly what she expected, but at the same time she was dismayed at the cramped space. A single room not more than ten-feet-by-ten-feet, with a sloped roof that made the place even smaller. A narrow cot, a row of nails on which to hang her clothes, and a rickety stand with a chipped white pottery washbasin and pitcher. The only heat radiated off a stovepipe that came up through the floor from the diner below. "Do all the teachers stay in this room?"

"The last four have. We've had a sight of trouble keeping a teacher in this town though. The women tend to up and get married or run off for one reason or another. I remember one that got kidnapped,

I think. Or no, maybe she ran off with a tinker. Or was that two different teachers? It's hard to keep track."

Kidnapped? Who got kidnapped? Hannah thought of Grace, teaching in a small town in far west Texas. Could she have met such a fate? That would explain why the letters quit coming. Hannah wondered if she'd ever see her sister again.

Harold crossed his arms and screwed up his face as if thinking were painful. "Or did she get kidnapped by a tinker then marry him? I can't rightly remember. And I think we had one once that turned to horse thievin'. Bad business that one was. They all kinda fuzz together in my head." Harold shrugged as if willing to make up a story if he couldn't remember the truth.

"Mabel and I have seven boys, but they're all grown now, so even though I'm on the school board, we don't have much to do with the school. We've been known to run through three or four teachers a year."

This town obviously chewed teachers up and spit them out. It occurred to Hannah that she could be the next in a long line.

Afraid more thinking might make Harold's brain explode, Hannah said, "We can discuss the other teachers later." She moved to the door, thinking to shoo him and his body lice out.

"Oh, little advice, miss. Think long and hard a'fore you go walin' on any of the kids. Some of the town folk don't take kindly to it."

Hannah stiffened. "I don't intend to *wale* on any child, for heaven's sake. I'd never strike a child."

"Now don't go making promises you can't keep. The Brewsters've moved on, but their like've come through town before 'n more'n likely'll come again. Need a good thrashin' real regular, those young'uns did."

"No youngster needs a *thrashing*. Children need love and understanding. Now really, I must ask you to leave. I've got things to do."

Harold must have been long on mouth and short on ears because he apparently didn't hear her and kept talking. "No figurin' people near as I kin figure. But the likes of the Brewsters'll be back. Two boys and a girl. The lot of them Brewsters could stand a good thrashin' to my way of thinkin'."

Hannah bristled up until she could have shot porcupine quills at Harold. *Thrash a child indeed.* Why, she'd be no better than Parrish.

She had to get Harold out of here so she could go save Libby.

Swamped with stubbornness she didn't know she was capable of, Hannah decided then and there she'd neither thrash a child, nor steal a horse, nor let herself be kidnapped, nor marry any man. She'd had her fill of men, first Parrish and now that awful child-stealing Mr. . . . Grant. She planned to have no man in her life ever. In fact, squaring her shoulders, she vowed right then and there she'd start a new tradition and stay at the school forever—unless she had to steal Libby away from her new father and save the other children out there and run. She tried to imagine twenty-five children stowed away on a train. Or was it six or four? She'd heard several numbers. Hannah got a headache just thinking of all she had to do.

As Harold finally ran out of chatter and turned to leave, Hannah, now sworn to her job for the rest of her life, asked, "Who do I talk to about the school? I want to know all of my pupils' names, and I hope to visit them in their homes before the start of the winter school term." Grace had written that a teacher must visit, and Grace was the best teacher Hannah had ever known. Although, honesty forced Hannah to admit that Grace was the only teacher Hannah had ever known.

"No time for that. School starts Monday."

Already she was failing. "Well then, I'll visit after school starts."

"Try asking Louellen downstairs. Running the diner the way she does, I reckon she knows about everything that goes on around here. I know there are a dozen children in town and maybe that many again in the surrounding ranches. Oh, and Grant's young'uns? That's another dozen." Harold broke down and laughed until he had to wipe his eyes.

Hannah's jaw clenched as she waited the man out.

Tucking his handkerchief back in his pocket, Harold shook his head. "He doesn't usually send 'em in 'cuz he hasn't liked the teachers we have. So don't count them. They'll be here for a few days most likely, and then he'll just take 'em home and school 'em hisself like always. Were I you I wouldn't even let 'em sit at a desk. They'll be gone afore you need to bother."

"He don't. . ." Hannah stumbled then corrected her grammar. Honestly, she'd only been here an hour and she already sounded like Harold. "He doesn't send his children to school? Well, we'll see about that. Could you direct me to his ranch?"

That question seemed to amuse Harold because he began chuckling and shaking his head. Of course Hannah was beginning to believe that a rabid wolf would amuse Harold so she didn't put much stock in what struck him as funny.

"Gonna get after Grant, miss?"

Hannah crossed her arms while she waited for directions.

"That I'd like to see."

"Directions?" Hannah tapped her toe.

"You can hire a horse at the livery stable or the blacksmith shop. But Ian O'Reilly is the blacksmith, and I think he's gone for the day, so don't waste your time goin' there. He wouldn't like you scolding Grant anyway, because he's one of Grant's kids."

"The blacksmith? How old is he?"

Harold shrugged. "About Grant's age, I 'spect."

"Mr. . . .Grant adopted children *his own age*?"

"To get to the Rocking C, go straight out'a town west for about five miles. The woods clear out for a spell, then there's a thicket of bright red sumac and huckleberries that's been cut back so's a trail'll go through it. Take that trail and go south a spell. The woods'll start up again and the bluffs'll rise up on both sides. Gets might rugged. Grant has an old wagon wheel by his place, with a piece of bent iron hooked on it in the shape of a C. Turn east and that trail'll take you right up to the cabin."

Hannah tried desperately to remember everything he'd said. West five miles. Trail through a thicket. South between some bluffs. Wagon wheel. East.

Harold gave her a jaunty wave and went out. He was back the next second. "There's a shorter way, but it's kinda confusing."

Hannah shuddered at the thought of directions more confusing than the ones she'd already been given. "No, thank you."

He said good-bye and exited her room. He came back in. "Turnin' into a mighty mean day, miss. Not fit for a ride by my way'a reckonin'. If you can wait till tomorrow, Grant'll be in to Sunday services so you could ride back out with him."

When Harold said Grant would bring the children to church, Hannah doubted herself for the first time. That spoke well of the man. Parrish had certainly never let her or the other children attend church. But she couldn't overcome her first impression of Libby and Charlie being taken off into a dangerous situation. And if her instincts were right, she didn't think it could wait until tomorrow.

"I believe I'll go on out myself." How well she remembered her first night in Parrish's clutches. She wanted to save those children before Grant had time to frighten them into submission.

Harold shrugged.

Hannah had heard this was the way things worked in the West. People minded their own business. Indignantly she thought that was the very reason Grant had been allowed to abscond with so many children.

Harold went out, then he came right back. "If'n you get lost just start heading south. You'll run into the spring. Sour Springs we call it. Named the town for it. Stinks like a herd of polecats. Can't miss it. Upstream'll lead you right smack into town." He tipped his hat and left.

Hannah sighed in relief to have the bad news bearer gone.

He popped his head back around the corner. "Oh, and don't touch the sumac. It's poisonous." He left again.

Hannah stared dolefully at the empty doorway where the man

bobbed in and out like a sneaky prairie dog.

He rounded her door again. "But the sumac'll be buried by snow more'n likely, so forget about it."

He'd told her to turn at the sumac. If it was buried, how was she supposed to use it as a landmark? She waited for the voice of doom to return so she could ask him. He appeared to have given it all to her at last. She pulled her worn-out coat tight around her and headed for the stable before she could second guess herself.

A mountain of a man forked hay into feed bunks for a half dozen horses. He introduced himself as Zeb Morris. He was as hairy as his horses, nearly as big, and he smelled none too much better. Hannah knew that even though she stayed well away.

"Hey, missy. Heard you're the new schoolmarm." Zeb grinned, showing more teeth missing than present.

Word did get around in this town.

"Welcome to Sour Springs. My pappy founded this settlement."

Sour Springs was named after a spring? Or the way his father smelled? Then she thought of a town that would ignore the plight of orphans and wanted to sneer at his pride. Instead she said politely, "I'd like to rent a carriage for the rest of the afternoon."

The man looked doubtfully out the wide open door. "No day for pleasure ridin', miss. I wouldn't stray six feet from town if'n I didn't have to."

"Well, I have to. So, if you'll please do as I ask?"

The man hesitated. Then, just as Harold had done, he let her go about her own business. "Don't rent carriages, only saddle horses."

That wasn't what Hannah wanted at all, but her fear for the children overruled her fear for her own safety. "That will be fine."

She rented a horse that seemed as unhappy to go to work as it was swaybacked, but Hannah had grown up in the Wild West, or the next thing to it—Chicago. So she'd ridden a horse a time or two. Actually she thought carefully and decided exactly a time, not two. Well, there was no help for it. The children needed her.

She was tempted to ask for directions again from the man who rented her the horse, but she thought she had Harold's advice memorized and didn't want to muddy the waters.

Zeb saddled the horse. He—Zeb, not the horse—got far too close for her nose's comfort when he boosted her on its back. Then he led her out the door.

Taking up the reins, she kicked the horse and the horse kicked back. Since she sat on top of the beast, it didn't hurt her but it bounced her around some. Finally, with a slap on the backside from the hostler, she got the beast moving at a snail's pace in the right direction.

She hadn't ridden five minutes on the lazy, uncooperative creature before she admitted to being hopelessly lost. The skittish horse twisted around and pranced sideways. If there'd ever been any trail, it'd been well and truly buried under the snow. Once she'd left the meager shelter of town, the wind whipped harder until the snowstorm became a full-fledged blizzard.

Looking desperately, she searched for the prints of her own horse in the snow to make sure she hadn't left the trail. The snow around her was trampled down in all directions by the nervous horse, and his prints were filling in fast. She gave the animal its head, hoping it would start for the barn, but the horse just let its head sag as if it didn't have enough energy to move another step.

Hannah kicked the horse, and it moved a few steps forward then stopped again. Her heart pounded as the snow drove itself through her thin coat. Fighting down panic, Hannah realized she'd become hopelessly lost in a Texas blizzard. She should have left Libby to Mr. . . . Grant for one night, because now Hannah would freeze to death in a blizzard and not be around to save her from her nightmarish fate.

FIVE

Libby snuggled up on Grant's left knee and, with a smile, rested her head on his shoulder.

Grant eased his toes closer to the fire with a blissful sigh and opened the book.

Benny scrambled onto Grant's right knee. Charlie sat on the floor with his back leaning against the stones that edged the fireplace. Joshua leaned on the other side of the fire playing "Silent Night" softly on his mouth harp. Christmas was just over, and the whole family still felt the glow of the holy season.

Sadie and Marilyn sat at the table doing the studies Grant had set for them, but he wondered if the girls were really reading. Josh's playing was too sweet to ignore. He could coax music out of that harmonica that could break a man's heart or make him laugh out loud.

When the music ended, Grant opened his well-worn copy of *Oliver Twist*. He produced it every time a new child came into the house. Grant had found it helped start the new young'uns talking about where they'd come from.

Of course Charlie had that hostile look. Children with that look rarely talked about their lives before they came to Grant's home. And Libby wasn't likely to start in talking. But they could at least hear that a book had been written about some of what they'd been through. It was Grant's way of letting them know he understood, and they weren't alone.

Grant looked up from the book before he began. "Dinner was good, girls. Thanks for having it hot and ready when I got in from chores."

Marilyn, his oldest daughter, her blond hair curly and fine as a cobweb, nodded. "You're welcome, Pa."

Sadie grinned, her white teeth shining against her ebony black skin. "We all cooked together whilst you, Joshua, and Charlie worked with the cattle. We had the easy part of this storm."

"Knowing we'd have a hot meal kept us going." Grant pulled Libby closer, his arm around her, holding the book.

Six-year-old Benny, supposedly near Libby's age but about twice her size, snuggled closer, his head resting on Grant's shoulder. He glanced up through the shaggy hair that had flopped onto his forehead. "Want me to hold the book, Pa?"

"Thanks, Benny. I just remembered I hadn't said a proper thank you to the girls." He let the book settle in his youngest son's hands. Grant wasn't the only one in this family who needed a haircut. "Let's get started reading."

Grant looked around the tiny room. Yes, it was a tight squeeze for them all, three bedrooms—if those tiny spaces could be called bedrooms—for seven people. And yes, he'd be sleeping on the kitchen floor for a while. But he'd done that many times to make space. The kitchen was warm, and he didn't mind being cramped.

He loved this tiny house, these children. He loved his whole life. God had given him the family he'd dreamed of while he shivered in the New York City alleys. Here they sat with full bellies thanks to the girls' dab hand with a skillet, a warm, crackling fire, and a roof over their heads no one could take away from them.

He gave Libby a gentle hug, and she looked up and smiled her quiet smile. That smile meant more to Grant than if a million dollars had rained down on his head. He had everything in the world that mattered. He was a happy, contented man.

His contentment was broken by the memory of that snippy woman at the train station. All she'd accused him of, all her insults. The smile faded from his face for just a second. Why would she come to mind now? It's like she meant to ruin his night.

Maybe it was because she looked cold and hungry.

And why had she gotten off the train and let it leave her behind? What business had brought her to Sour Springs? She must have family here. Grant hoped she finished her visit lickety-split and got back on her way before he ever had to see her again. How dare the little meddler accuse him of mistreating his children?

He could picture her right now, sulking, judging him and his orphaned children while she sat somewhere warm and fed and comfortable.

Driven snow slit at her skin like a million tiny knives. The wind lashed her.

Disoriented, Hannah thought of the times she'd been lashed by Parrish, his belt punishing her for something or nothing.

God, no, don't let Parrish get me. Protect me.

How often had she prayed that prayer as a child? How many nights had she been jerked awake by nightmares and been punished for screaming out in her sleep? How often had Hannah clung to God, even when Parrish came and God let the worst happen?

As the storm assaulted her, Hannah thought of how Parrish dragged her out of the bedroom she shared with her sisters. How Grace tried to turn Parrish's anger away from Hannah. Sometimes it would work. More often Parrish would laugh at Grace and slap her aside, then whip Hannah until she collapsed.

Now, in the wind, Hannah heard her father's sadistic laughter ringing in her ears.

And then Grace had done the unthinkable. She'd fought back. She'd had Parrish arrested. Drawing Parrish's fury on herself, Grace had run like a mother bird faking a broken wing. . .with Parrish in pursuit. Hannah had taken the other children and hidden away in Chicago's streets until Grace could send for her.

Despite Grace forbidding it—Grace had a deep horror of adoption—Hannah had found homes for the four little sisters left in her care. And then, before Hannah had set out to join Grace in Mosqueros, Texas, she'd found more children.

Trevor, who tried to rob Hannah and ended up sharing what he'd already stolen. Nolan, who crept into the shed she and Trevor lived in and defiantly slipped up to their tiny bit of heat, expecting to be thrown out but willing to face danger to escape the killing cold of another winter night. Other children had come and gone and Hannah had found them homes, all but Libby with her broken body, silent lips, and heartbreaking, beseeching eyes.

Now Libby was gone. Grace was gone. Hannah, alone, shouted into the teeth of the blizzard, "God, they're all gone."

The horse jerked forward, startled by Hannah's screams.

Hannah broke down and wept into the bitter, driving, merciless wind. Shuddering with sobs, holding her arm up to shield her face, Hannah blinked and, as if God himself had pulled back the veil of driven snow, she saw a blurred object. She clung to her horse's reins with one hand and dropped her shielding arm to clutch the collar of her coat. Peering into the storm, trying to make out the shape, a strange peace settled over her.

As she calmed, she realized it was a building she'd passed just moments ago on the edge of town. She could find her way back. She could save herself.

But what about Libby? Who would save her?

Hannah knew she could do nothing tonight. Wiping the already freezing tears from her face, she headed quickly back toward Sour Springs, leaving Libby to her fate for one night. But Hannah promised it would be one night only!

She left the horse with the smug hostler, who kindly returned her two bits, only saying, "I told you so," six or seven times. Then Hannah trudged through drifts to her room.

As she battled the storm, she saw that all the businesses were closed and shuttered. It was late enough in the afternoon that the sun had set and there'd be no customers in this weather.

Then as she passed a building near the mercantile, she saw one lone light flickering in a window. Through thin curtains, Hannah saw a tall, reed-thin shape pass the light. Prudence, maybe, the seamstress she'd met in the general store. Hannah paused, drawn by the light and life of that building, even as she knew she didn't dare pause on the way to her own dark room.

As she watched, a second shape moved in the same direction as Prudence. A man, a giant of a man, bigger even than Harold, was in Prudence's room with her. They'd offered Prudence the job as school-marm, hadn't they? Only a single woman would be offered that job. And Mabel had definitely said Prudence was new in town. So what man was with her on this bitter cold evening?

True, it wasn't very late, just after suppertime most likely. But people would want to get home and tuck themselves in safe for the night. The aching of Hannah's feet prodded her onward. She had almost no feeling in them as she hurried home.

The diner was closed but the back door was unlocked, and Hannah got to her room without trouble. She spent the rest of the bitter night clutching her worn coat and the single thin blanket she'd pulled off the narrow cot around her. Leaning into the stovepipe with its meager warmth, she trembled with cold in the wretched room and thought of the glowing letters she'd gotten from Grace about her comfortable situation in Mosqueros. Hannah, with no food and no dry clothes, shivered and her stomach growled.

Hannah wrapped her arms around herself, missing all of her sisters. If Libby were here, the two of them would snuggle in bed, share their warmth, and survive the night by being strong for each other. They'd done it many times in Chicago and Omaha and other places.

Hannah vowed to God, as she stared into the ceiling of her black room, that she'd save Libby. She'd save all those children Grant had taken. Then she'd show this town there was such a thing as a teacher who stuck, no matter the provocation.

Barely twenty, she felt like she'd been old since the day she was born. She was so tired of always having to be strong, beyond tired of all work and no play. Grim experience told her what Libby and Charlie were going through tonight and she wept. From the deepest part of her heart, she cried out to God through her tears.

Forgive me for failing them and subjecting them to that hard, miserable life.

SIX

"Let's go sledding!"

Grant was jerked out of a restless sleep when Benny tripped over his stomach.

Benny fell with a terrible clatter against the kitchen table, hitting so hard he should have broken every bone in his body. The six-year-old bounced back to his feet and grinned down at Grant, who lay on his bedroll on the kitchen floor. "Can we get the sleds out, Pa? Can we, huh? Can we, please?"

Benny'd been on the orphan train when it turned around here three years ago. He'd ridden all the way from New York with Martha and never been adopted because he was too young. Three when Grant got him, Benny was the closest to a baby Grant had ever taken, and Grant couldn't have loved him any more if he'd been his own flesh and blood.

Trying to shake off a lousy night's sleep, he massaged his head to clear it. Grant rubbed a hand over his face. No bristles. *Oh yeah, I shaved last night.* Why had he shaved? Normally he'd do that Sunday morning not Saturday night. For that matter, what was he doing sleeping on the floor?

Grant sat up straight. *I adopted two more kids yesterday.*

Benny didn't wait for an answer. He dashed to the little window beside the front door and pressed his nose against the frosty pane. "This is the bestest snow I've ever seen." Benny glanced over his shoulder and gave Grant a sly look. "I mean, this is the worstest snow I've ever seen. We can't get through it to church. No way! It'd be"—Benny paused for dramatic effect—"dangerous!"

Grant grinned at Benny. Then he laughed out loud.

The other children came pouring out of their rooms wearing their heavy nightgowns or union suits—depending on whether they were girls or boys. Even the older girls rushed to the window and crowded around fighting for a square inch of glass.

Libby was right behind them, still as silent as a tomb. He wondered what it was the little girl couldn't say.

Marilyn turned and scooped Libby up in her arms so the little one could see the snow outside. Their two heads together, Libby's dark and Marilyn's fair, the expressions of joy and excitement matched until they looked almost like sisters.

Before they'd covered the window with their rampaging herd of bodies, Grant had seen that the sun wasn't even up yet. Only the faintest light glowed in the eastern sky. Grant couldn't resist saying, "If the mountain pass is snowed in, we can still make it through the valley."

Grant heard Benny groan, which made Grant grin all the more. "I think there's time for a couple of quick trips up and down the hill before church."

There was a collective gasp of joy, and the children vanished out of the room so quickly Grant might have thought he'd dreamed the whole thing if Benny hadn't stepped on his stomach again in the stampede.

If he let them go, he'd be stuck with all the morning chores. But in New York City, where Grant had grown up, there had been plenty of snow but never time for sledding. And here in Texas, it got cold, but the snow didn't come this deep very often, and it never lasted for long. He wasn't going to deny the children this pleasure.

Thinking of the fight on his hands to get the young'uns ready for church, he heaved himself up off the floor and groaned. He was getting too old to sleep on a hardwood floor. He quit his groaning to smile at himself. He was twenty-six. Not too old for anything. Although, raising twenty children on his own, starting from the time he was seventeen, might have made him an old man before his time.

He got to his feet and laid more wood on the fire before he did another thing. Then he adjusted his suspenders onto his shoulders and pulled on his boots over the thick socks he'd worn to bed. With a couple of quick scrapes of his fingers, he gathered his hair at his nape then tied it back with a leather thong to keep it out of his eyes, wondering if one of the older girls would mind whacking some of his mane off for him. Pulling on his buckskin coat, he grabbed the bucket to go for water.

Benny beat him to the door, shouting with glee and running for the barn and the ragtag sleds Grant had collected over the years.

By the time Grant hauled back the first bucket of water, all six kids were long gone sledding. He poured water into a pot for coffee and a basin for washing. He hustled to milk both cows, gather eggs, and make sure the livestock in his barnyard had gotten through the blizzard in one piece. Hefting an armload of firewood inside, he stoked the stove then reached for the boiling coffeepot to pour himself a cup before he went to wrangle with the children about coming back in to get ready for church.

Then something snapped. He poured his untouched coffee back in, shoved the pot to a cooler spot so it wouldn't burn. . .and ran.

He got to the bottom of the sledding hill just as Marilyn and Libby sailed down the slope on the little toboggan. They upended the sled in a snowdrift and came rolling out of the snow, giggling hysterically.

Grant shouted, *"My turn!"*

The kids started shrieking and jumping up and down, yelling encouragement to him.

Grant grabbed the rope of Marilyn's sleek wooden toboggan, one that Grant had built himself last winter, and plunked Libby down on it. He trudged up the hill, giving his newest daughter a ride.

Joshua passed him on a runner sled going down. Benny, Charlie, and Sadie were next on the big toboggan.

He got to the top only a few paces ahead of Joshua.

"I'm faster'n you, Pa," Joshua taunted in his deep, adult voice. His black skin shone with melting snow, and icicles hung off his woolen cap. "I was way behind you when I went down."

Grant laughed at his seventeen-year-old son. "I gave Libby a ride. You made Benny walk. All the difference."

Joshua shoved Benny sideways, and the little boy plopped over into the snow. Benny came up hurling snowballs, and Joshua whooped and ran.

Grant turned Libby around to face downhill. "Let's get out of here, Lib, before we get attacked!"

Libby laughed out loud, and Grant's joy was so great to hear this solemn little girl laughing he wanted to dance. He jumped onto the back of the sled, tucking his long legs around her, and pushed off. Just as he started moving, he felt something heavy hit his back, and he glanced behind to see Benny tackling him. Grant pulled Benny over his shoulder while the boy laughed and wrestled. Libby started giggling again.

Grant glanced sideways to see Charlie riding in front of Sadie and Marilyn, laughing. Charlie's laughter meant the world to Grant. He knew the boy would be a tough nut to crack. Hostile and suspicious, Grant understood that the boy expected every moment in this house to be his last. He didn't trust anyone. All of the new brothers and sisters hadn't gone down well. He had especially hated sharing his tiny loft room with Benny.

And now Charlie laughed and played. Grant's heart danced even if he was too buried under kids to do it for real.

The sled soared down the hill, completely out of control because Benny had a boot in Grant's face. The wreck came as it always did against the drifts that had formed at the base of the slope.

By the time Grant got the snow wiped out of his eyes, all six of his children were scattered around beside him, buried at all different depths. All of them laughing like loons.

Grant knew he was pushing his luck, but he couldn't make them quit yet. "Once more down the hill."

All the laughing stopped and the complaining began.

"Pa," Benny wailed, "it's already warming up."

Charlie kicked at a clump of snow in front of him. "It'll be gone by the time church is over."

"Two more times down the hill," Grant amended. "If we hurry!"

He caught the sled rope and planted Libby back on the sled and raced Joshua, pulling Benny, to the top of the hill. Charlie was right beside him. The girls beat the rest of them to the top and jeered at Grant for being slow.

The kids nagged him into four more times down the hill. Then they had to skip breakfast and head for church with their coats still wet and their hair straggling around their faces. Grant knew they were all a mess, but laughing was something none of them had known how to do when they'd first come to him. Enjoying family life was as much a kind of worship to an orphan as sitting in the Lord's house.

"The gap is filled up to the canyon rim."

Daniel's announcement nearly broke Grace's ear drums as he slammed the door open to their cabin. To knock the snow off his broad shoulders, he shook himself like a wet dog.

"Daniel!" Grace held up both hands to ward off the flying snow. She risked a peek through her fingertips and saw him grinning at her.

"No school till spring! The canyon's snowed shut for sure." Mark launched himself at Luke and the two of them slammed to the floor. "I thought it'd never happen. I thought we'd be stuck schoolin' all winter."

Grace closed her eyes so she wouldn't see the breaking bones and blood. She peeked again. Of course no one broke. A Texas cyclone couldn't play this rough, and yet the boys stayed in one piece more often than not.

A cry out of the bedroom pulled Grace's attention away from the riot in front of her.

"I'll get him. Your little brother's up, boys!" Daniel ran toward the room with all five boys charging after him. Daniel beat the crowd through, but the boys clogged in the doorway and fought each other to be second.

"*Be gentle with him!*" Grace used to be soft-spoken, but no one seemed to hear her. Now she hollered, and they still ignored her for the most part. But at least they now ignored her because they were rude, not because of any failure on her part to let them know what she wanted. So she could blame them fully when they didn't mind her.

Daniel appeared from the bedroom with Matt, still droopy-eyed from an unusual afternoon nap. The boy wasn't inclined to unnecessary sleep. None of the men in this family were.

Her three-year-old son was bald as an egg, but Daniel said all of his sons started out that way. He claimed it was real convenient to have no hair on a baby because it made mopping the food off their heads easier. Grace had found that to be the honest truth.

Abe and Ike shoved through the door next. They'd shot up in the last year. Fourteen years old now, soon to turn fifteen, they were within inches of Daniel's height but not nearly as broad. Their shoulders and chests hadn't filled out yet, and they had a gaunt, hungry look, no matter how much food Grace poured down them.

The boys were eating the herd down so fast, one of these days Grace expected to see the cattle making a break for it.

Abe and Ike did the work of men, but they still played like kittens. Big kittens. One hundred-fifty-pound kittens who would sooner knock the furniture over than go around it.

Mark, Luke, and John, the nine-year-old triplets, came in next. Luke tripped Mark because Mark dodged in front of him to get out of the baby's bedroom. Mark smacked into his older brothers. As long as they were within reach, Mark made a point of knocking them sideways as he fell. The two of them turned and attacked. John, a step behind Luke, jumped on the pile of wriggling, screaming boys.

Daniel ignored the ruckus, as did Grace to the extent she was able. They met in front of the fireplace, and Daniel handed little Matthew over. Grace settled into the rocking chair Daniel and the boys had built. Matthew lasted all of ten seconds on her lap, then he yelled and squirmed until she let go. He launched himself at his brothers. His high-pitched screams were deafening, so his brothers howled all the louder and proceeded to grab Matt and toss him in the air between each other. It was the baby's favorite game.

Grace covered her eyes.

"What's the matter, honey?" Daniel leaned down, resting one hand on the back of her rocker while he pressed his forehead to hers.

She loved it when he touched her. She loved the way he smelled. On the rare occasion when she could get a sweet word out of the big lummox, she almost melted into a puddle at his feet. She breathed him in.

Luke fell over the kitchen table and broke one of the legs off.

Daniel yelled, "*You boys go outside and fight!*"

Grace, her ears ringing, looked up at her grinning husband as the boys stormed through the outside door. She could tell that he was already planning to repair the table. He was good at it, thanks to all the practice.

Thanks to the moment of silence, Grace could concentrate, and she realized what Daniel had said. "The gap's snowed shut?" And oddly, her throat seemed to swell shut at the news. "We're trapped here until spring again?"

"Yep, but it held off a long time this year. We got in to Mosqueros for Christmas. But I'm tired of the run to town for school. Glad to be shut of it for the year. And it don't matter none. We have supplies for the winter. I stocked up good and early. Plus, I married me our own private teacher." Daniel grinned at her then took a step away toward the table.

Grace caught his arm, choking on the idea of being trapped for months. "You're *sure* it's all the way snowed shut. Have you ever tried to shovel a path through? Just wide enough to walk out?"

"Naw, it's packed in tight, fifty feet deep. No gettin' out. I s'pose we could get an early thaw, but that don't usually happen. You know how slow that gap is to melt. Spring will have been here for a long time before we can get out."

Grace's finger sank deep into Daniel's sleeve. "Daniel, I think we're going to have to get out of here once or twice this winter. You got a lot done on that high pass, didn't you? We can get out of here once in a while, can't we?"

"We could, but why should we?"

Something hit the front door so hard one of the hinges snapped. Grace saw Ike and Luke through the splintered wood before they fell to the ground.

"Because I get a little. . .oh"—her fingers tore little holes in the fabric—"restless, I guess, not seeing another woman all winter. If we could just go to the McClellens every month or so. . ."

Daniel went over and lifted the door back into place.

"I'd go alone," she offered. "I could just jump on a horse and ride up to the pass. I'd let the horse go and he'd come right home. Then I'd walk to Adam and Tillie's. It can't be more than five miles. I'd be fine on my own."

"You can't get over that pass alone."

"Sure I can." Grace felt her throat shutting tight, not unlike the gap. "Scaling that last cliff isn't so hard."

"What do you mean it isn't so hard?" Daniel set what was left of the table upright using the broken-off leg to prop it then came back to her side. "Even after all the work we done, we have to hang on by our fingernails. John fell almost a hundred feet when he went over the edge last summer."

Grace decided the sleeve hadn't gotten his attention nearly enough. She grabbed Daniel's skin beneath the cloth, picturing her hand on his neck. That wasn't like her. "But he rolled most of the way. It's not like it's a dead drop. He had hardly a scratch. And besides, he was wrestling with Abe. I wouldn't be reckless like the boys are."

Normally the winters didn't bother her all that much. But for some reason, right now, it was driving her to panic. Her fingers sank into a hunk of Daniel's skin. And speaking of claws. . . "I would just claw my way up and out. I'd be glad to go alone if you didn't want to come along."

Mark screamed like he was being stabbed to death.

Grace flinched. "In fact, I'd *insist* on going alone. I'd go see Sophie. I might stay for a day or two, just once a month."

Grace heard someone roll off the roof, shrieking like a banshee.

"Once or twice a month, for two or three days each time." Grace gave him her most fetching smile. The one that often got her what she wanted, or rather got her Daniel, which was often what she wanted. "You could manage without me."

Daniel leaned down and kissed the tip of her nose. "No, we couldn't, honey. What would we eat?"

"You could have steak and eggs and biscuits and potatoes and milk?"

He caught her hand and removed her fingers from his skin. "It's good, but it has an extra sweetness when it's made by your pretty little hands."

Grace heard more racket on the roof. Her pretty little hand formed a fist. A puff of soot whomped out of the fireplace and the flames danced wildly. She waited to see if one of the boys would fall through.

"Oh." Daniel slapped his forehead then reached for the back pocket of his broadcloth pants. "There was another letter for you in Mosqueros. I forgot. I've been carrying it around for a few days. It's from your sister who writes from time to time."

"What?" Grace launched herself to her feet. "Hannah wrote and you forgot to tell me?"

Daniel held the letter out then backed away as if a Texas cougar had just popped into the kitchen.

Grace snatched it out of his hand, tore it open, and read. "She's in Texas." She read more, faster. She'd reread it a thousand times, savoring every word, but right now she just wanted to make sure her sister was alive and well.

Grace looked up, her heart racing. "She's just a short train ride away." Well, most of the whole state, but still, only one state. . .a large one, granted.

"That's nice, honey." Daniel turned his attention back to the table.

"Daniel, she says she's working. She can't come the rest of the way. But we could go."

A vicious, half-wild longhorn stormed past the window, bellowing in terror. Three blond heads zipped right along behind it, as if they were after dinner on the hoof. Yes, her boys could scare a longhorn to death.

A break from that might be nice. For Grace. In fact, the more she thought of it, the more she decided the rest of the family didn't need to go at all. "I think, maybe, if I don't get out of here a few times, I might. . . uh. . .kind of. . .go crazy." Grace was surprised to realize how much she meant it. She furrowed her brow as she tried to figure out why hearing about that sealed-up gap was making her feel so trapped.

"You'll be fine, honey. Best to avoid the cliff. Winter doesn't last long." Daniel patted her like he was taming a fractious horse and smiled. "Three or four months, tops."

"But this would be such a great chance to go see Hannah. Visit my sister. You know how worried I've been about her. She's written several times, but she's told me she's never gotten but one letter from me in all these years." She heard herself wheedling and was ashamed.

Then, to her surprise, she decided she'd quit begging and punch Daniel in the nose. Curling up one discontented corner of her mouth, she paused. The need to sock her husband wasn't like her. She had only wanted to punch Daniel once in their married life.

Honesty forced Grace to admit that wasn't purely true. In the very beginning she'd wanted to punch him pretty regularly. But lately only once. Exactly three years and nine months ago.

A body hurled past the window. The glass in the window rattled, but it didn't break for a change.

She lowered her hand to her stomach, did some quick figuring, and raised her eyes to her husband. And by golly she almost did punch him then.

She narrowed her eyes at him.

"What?" He straightened away from her, alarmed.

"This is your fault."

He arched his eyebrows. "Most things usually are."

"It had better be a girl this time."

Daniel froze, staring at her as if she'd grown a full set of longhorns. Then he screamed and ran out of the house.

Which was only what she expected.

He left the door open so she could watch him as he vanished into the trees. How long would it take him to calm down this time? She also apologized to her little unborn daughter for the torture that was in store for her from her brothers.

The table, teetering on three legs, crashed over on its side. Grace sank back into her rocker, and her eyes fell shut. No way would this baby be anything but another unruly little boy. There was something wrong with Daniel that he could only make boy children.

A stick flew in through the window, shattering the glass. The stick landed near her feet and shards of glass rained down on her. She didn't bother to get up. She could brush the glass off later.

She unfolded Hannah's letter and read it again, more slowly this time. There was no denying that her sister was in reach for the first time in years.

She had to get out of here a few times this winter. Going to see Hannah was the perfect solution.

She looked down at her stomach and conjured up the only voice she had that the boys obeyed. With a jab of her finger straight at her belly, she said, "And there'd better only be one of you in there!"

S E V E N

They were still a merry band when they got to town.

Grant thought they'd made it just in time. Benny ran ahead and as good as erupted into church. Grant saw the minute he followed his last child in that services had already started. Grant, with Libby hoisted in his arms so she could keep up, immediately began shushing the kids to settle them down and let Parson Babbitt go on with his prayers. But Grant had his hands full curbing their high spirits, especially with the two youngest boys.

The parson gave him a kind smile and moved along with his preaching.

Grant had learned to expect a strong shoulder and a kind heart from Parson Babbitt. And the rest of the congregation spared Grant quick glances and smiles. Not all of the citizens of Sour Springs were kind, but the people who worshipped in this little white church on Sunday were good to the orphaned children in their midst.

Grinning down the two rows his family filled, he settled in with his squirming, whispering family and had almost relaxed when he caught the snippy woman from the train depot looking over her shoulder at him. Glaring her disapproval, she might as well have shouted at him from across the room.

Grant realized that his sons all still had their hats on. He reached over and pulled them off Benny's and Charlie's heads. Joshua caught on and tugged his off. As Grant dropped Benny's snow-soaked wool hat onto his lap, Grant realized he still wore his own battered Stetson. Feeling his cheeks heat under Miss Cartwright's glare, he tugged it off, looking straight forward. Miss Fussbudget oughta keep her eyes to the front, too.

About that time, the parson announced that Hannah was the new schoolteacher in Sour Springs and that school would start Monday.

Grant's heart sank. He'd dealt with teachers many times who thought orphans somehow didn't deserve to be given the education that other children received. Try as he might to control his rising temper and listen to the sermon, the devil gnawed at his good nature, and Grant kept looking back at the stiff-necked Miss Cartwright, rehearsing the set-down he'd like to give her. He knew already that his children wouldn't last a week in her school.

Settling into a slouched lump of irritation, he knew they wouldn't last two days. No matter what happened that first day, even if Miss Prim-and-Proper Hannah didn't throw his kids out, some parent would get in a snit about some story a child brought home from school and there'd be a group before Grant got there the next day. Of course, the Brewsters had moved, so it wouldn't get as nasty as most years, but he'd still end up schooling his young'uns at home.

When it came time for music, Josh went to the front by the parson and played his mouth harp for the whole church. It was the only musical instrument in Sour Springs. It lifted Grant's spirits briefly, but once the music stopped his mind went back to being snappish.

By the end of the service, the kids were fairly writhing in their seats as they looked fearfully out of one of the windows, afraid their precious snow was melting while they sat. When the parson said his last "amen" the children fell over themselves dashing outside to the buckboard.

Grant managed to thank Parson Babbitt for the service and apologize for the noise. "It's the snow. They're crazy to get their sleds going."

The parson laughed and clapped him on the arm. "I was young

once, Grant. I well remember the sound of a sledding hill calling to me during church. Don't keep them waiting."

Harold hollered, "I put a bunch of pumpkins in your wagon, Grant. We had more 'n we knew what to do with."

"Thanks, Harold, Mabel." Grant nodded at the couple.

"We're getting more eggs than we can eat, Grant."

Grant turned to nod at Priscilla Denby and her husband. He knew they were sharing their meager supplies, but to save his pride they acted as if they had plenty. "God bless you, Priscilla. We'll eat 'em up fast enough." Grant had chickens of his own, but they could always use a few more eggs.

Grant saw several people setting boxes in the back of his wagon. He never got to church without having people send things home with him. He never asked for help, and he'd have managed without all the gifts, but the clothes and extra vegetables really helped.

"I put a bolt of fabric in your wagon, Pa." Megan, one of his girls, married and soon to have her third child, waved. Before Grant could say hello, Megan was dragged by her five-year-old son, Gordy, toward her husband, Ian, and their wagon. Grant heard the boy yammering about sledding. Ian was one of Grant's, too. That made Gordy Grant's grandson.

"Let me go talk to Grandpa, Gordy."

Twenty-seven and already a grandpa to a five-year-old. Grant had to smile.

Gordy kept tugging, yelling about the snow melting.

Soon to be three children in Ian and Megan's family, the two they had had bright red hair like both their folks. Grant looked at his grown children, the O'Reillys, and saw their young'uns looking exactly like them.

Something caught in Grant's throat a bit to know he'd never have a child who might have eyes the same strange color of light brown, speckled with yellow and green, as his. The odd color of his eyes always made him wonder if, somewhere out there, there might be an older woman with eyes like his, or some other orphan child, deserted just like he'd been. Or could there be a man who never knew he had a child, who lay awake some lonely nights and wished for a son with greenish-yellow eyes?

Benny ran past, storming into the crowd of redheaded O'Reillys, and Grant shook off the silly feeling. *There's nothing about my eyes I'd wish on a child.*

Ian came up with Catherine, his toddler daughter perched on his hip. He clapped Grant on the shoulder. "Two more, huh, Pa? Heard about it."

Grant nodded. Ian, only two years younger than Grant, had lived only a short time in Grant's home. But he seemed to like the sound of the word Pa, even though Grant had told him to stop calling him that several times.

Pointing, Grant said, "The boy is Charlie. He's already helping with the younger kids. And Libby is the little girl." Grant watched as Joshua boosted Libby onto the back of the wagon. "She hasn't talked since we brought her home. She's gonna need special care."

"You're up to it, Pa." Megan came up, winning her tug-of-war with Gordy. She tied her no-nonsense wool bonnet on her head. "Let me know if you need anything."

Megan, his daughter, now gave him advice. It was pretty good advice, too. "Thanks. Appreciate it."

Ian rested a hand on Megan's waist, and she smiled a private smile at him.

That look made Grant's stomach a little twitchy, but he wasn't sure why.

"How'd you get them off the sledding hill this morning?" Megan asked.

"It wasn't easy, especially since I didn't want to quit either. And now we've got to run. They're scared to death that the snow'll melt out from under 'em."

"It probably will." Ian settled his Stetson on his head.

Gordy started jumping up and down, yanking on Megan's hand. "Let's go!"

Ian interceded. "You're wearing your ma out. Dangle yourself from my hand for a while."

Gordy giggled and dived at his father's hand.

Megan rested one hand on her midsection and gave Ian a grateful smile.

"Pa, we've got to go!" Benny barreled into Grant's leg, knocking him sideways.

Grant rested one gloved hand on Benny's shoulder and grinned down at his son.

"Gordy was sledding before first light himself." Megan laughed. "And he's itching to go back. We'd better get a move on."

Grant nodded good-bye as Benny grabbed his hand and dragged him toward the wagon. He plunked his hat onto his head and jogged along with his son. Benny let him loose, obviously convinced his pa was going to do the right thing.

Someone caught Grant's sleeve. He recognized that insistent tug. His heart sank into his scruffy boots. He rolled his eyes but got them under control before he turned around to face Hannah.

"Mr. . . .Grant, I'm coming to visit you this afternoon." She released his coat as if he might infect her with some disease born in filth. "I want to meet all the children I'm going to have in school."

"We've got a busy afternoon, Hannah." He used her first name just for the pleasure of annoying her. "We've got chores, and the children want to spend any spare time sledding. We won't have time for company."

"Mr. . . .Grant, I'm not asking permission," she snapped. "I'm telling you I'm coming out. I want to see exactly the conditions these children are living in on your ranch. Why, you have them dressed in the next thing to rags. Their hair hasn't seen a comb in days and—"

"We didn't take time to change for church is all. They were sledding, and I let them go until we didn't have a second for breakfast or cleaning up." Grant was annoyed with himself for explaining. He didn't have to justify his actions.

"You haven't fed them yet?" Hannah's eyes flashed, and Grant wondered if she'd snatch the whip off his buckboard and thrash him with it. He was sure he could take her, but she had a lot of rage so he didn't want to put it to the test.

"I feed my children, Hannah. And they have decent clothes."

Benny came dashing back to Grant's side, the brim of his woolen hat ripped halfway off the crown. His coat, a hand-me-down through a dozen boys, hanging in rags off his back.

"Can't we go, Pa?" Benny danced around frantic. "I'm cold and hungry."

Heat climbed up Grant's neck. He looked down at his own coat, which was no better. He noticed the tip of his bare toe showing out of his right boot, a hole in the leather opening up to a hole in his sock. Of course they hadn't worn their Sunday best to go sledding, and Benny's coat might be ugly, but it was warmer than his good one, the one handed down through only about four sons.

Grant had to force himself to stand still and listen when his wildly impatient children dashed back and forth begging for him to come. He thought of all the cutting comments he'd rehearsed when he should have been worshipping, and the fact that he'd spent his church time wallowing in the sin of anger was all her fault.

He drew himself up to his full six feet. She wasn't a tiny bit of a woman, at least five-six, but he still towered over her, mainly because his anger made him feel a lot bigger. "Miss Cartwright, I have had enough of your—"

"Pa." Marilyn stood beside the two of them.

She diverted Grant's attention from the scalding comments he wanted to make. Grant had spent the last ten years putting children ahead of himself. It was second nature to set aside what he was doing and listen when Marilyn talked.

"What is it?"

"I'd like for Miss Cartwright to visit. Maybe if she waited a couple of hours, let the children run off some of their steam on the sledding hill, she could drop in for a while this afternoon. The snow will be gone by then anyway."

Grant's teeth clicked together in frustration. He saw the children almost bouncing with impatience and felt the vibration of Hannah's acute disapproval. It was too much pressure coming from all directions. He caved.

He turned with exaggerated politeness. "It would be a pleasure to have you drop by and visit. Come around three."

Marilyn frowned a little at his tone then, with a half-amused shake of her head, went on to the wagon.

"You can stay for an hour. Interview the slaves. . .uh. . .I mean the children. Inspect the prison. . .that is. . .our home. Maybe we'll give you a bit of gruel and some stale bread to eat before you set off for home."

Hannah jammed her fists on her slender waist. "Mr. . . .Grant!"

Grant turned away and jumped up on the wagon seat without letting her finish. He turned back to her. "Are you deciding whether we're worthy of the fine school here in Sour Springs, Hannah? If you are, don't bother. I've already decided that your school isn't worthy of my children."

He released the hand break and slapped the reins against the horses' backs. They snorted, tossed their heads, and jingled the traces, then pulled the creaking wagon away from the church. Grant left her standing in a swirl of snow. He knew he shouldn't have been so rude. Why was it all right for her to be so nasty to him, but somehow he wasn't supposed to be mean back?

"She's just worried about us, Pa." Sadie spoke as if she'd read Grant's mind. "Maybe she's seen orphans mistreated before. If she's really trying to rescue us, then she's not such a bad person. Having her out to visit will make everything better."

"You're right." Grant shook his head slowly, wondering at himself. "But that woman does have a talent for bringing out the worst in me."

Sadie patted his shoulder. "Your worst is still real good, Pa." Sadie sank back to sit on the floor of the wagon box to wrangle with her brothers and sisters about who got first turn on the toboggan.

Grant let go of some of his bad temper. Fine, he'd let Hannah come out and inspect.

Then he thought of the home she'd be inspecting. If she came out to inspect, she'd see his tiny house and his hodgepodge of clothing and furniture. She'd see the scanty food he had on hand and find how many chores he asked his children to do.

His hands tightened on the reins to turn his team around to forbid her to come. Then, with a sinking heart, Grant let the horses go on. He could forbid till he was blue in the face, the stubborn woman would still visit. And whether her problem was disapproving of orphans or disapproving of him, she'd still do one or the other. So what difference did it make?

He sped the horses along and planned on another term of schooling his children himself.

"There he goes." Prudence watched until Grant disappeared, then dropped the curtain and turned to Horace.

Horace sat at the kitchen table scooping stew into his mouth. Prudence looked at him with envy. He got to stay out of sight. He dressed in comfortable clothes and didn't have to take a monthly bath. He had the easy half of this cheat.

"You should'a gone to church." He spoke through a mouthful of food. "Good chance to meet him."

Prudence rolled her eyes and sighed. "*I know!* You don't need to tell me what I already know. I'll go. I figured the storm'd be a good enough excuse to miss this mornin'. I can't stand sitting there all morning listening to that preacher go on and on."

Horace nodded as he shoved a biscuit into his mouth. "I've got the worst of it though." He swallowed hard. "Digging in that stink hole."

"It pays better'n sewing." Prudence paced, her arms crossed, as she tried to figure out how to corner a man who barely showed his face in town and, when he did, was surrounded by that gaggle of children.

"Yeah, but I'm gettin' real sick of it. Can't you get your hooks in that man? You're losin' it, Prudy. Losin' your looks. We've gotta make this score a'fore you're an ugly old crone."

"Shut up!" Prudence picked up a plate off the sideboard and was tempted to throw it at him. Anything to stop his mouth from telling her what she already knew.

"I've had a couple of people in LaMont ask me where I'm finding the oil. Mostly people don't know what it is, or I s'pose they know and just don't recognize its value. And I just put it on the train and ship it out fast so no one pays much mind. But a few have noticed. Last time I had to ride the wrong direction out of town then circle around before I lost a man tailing me. Digging that black gold out of the ground is hard work, and I hate it. But much as I hate it, I don't want to lose it. This is our big score. We need to own it then sell it. We can go to California, buy a hacienda, and settle down for good. No more slavin' our lives away. But it won't happen if you don't get your hooks into that man. You're gonna lose everything for us."

Prudence nodded. "I'm working on it. I may have found a way in, too. The man needs clothes—anyone can see that just by looking at the rags he and his children wear. I'm watching to catch him alone and that's the tricky part. I've already offered to do sewing for him, but so far he keeps refusing. I suppose he's got no money. But I'll offer to work cheap. I'll get him. My business is getting a little better. A few men want me to sew them a shirt from time to time. No more women than there are in town to sew, I'm making a slim go of it. But Grant's never come in with an order."

"Make it quick. You're gonna have to come up with somethin' better than sewin' pretty soon. If you can't get next to the man, how're you gonna get him to marry with you?"

"Yeah, and how am I gonna be a widow who inherits his land if I can't get him to marry me?"

"You've never had trouble before, Prudy. Use your head, use your body, use what's left of that pretty face, and figure out a way to compromise that cowpoke. He don't look like he'll be any trouble to fool if you just once get your chance at him."

"I am using my head. Why don't you use yours? You shouldn't be in here today. Someone's gonna see that I've got a man staying with me. We'll either have to lie about you being here or explain who you are, and then there'll be questions we don't want to answer."

Horace stood from the table, swiping his sleeve across his mouth. "Too bad."

"Well, when you're found out, you'll ruin everything."

"Watch your mouth. I'm holding up my end of the bargain." He strode across the room and shoved her back. "You hold up yours."

"You dig in the dirt and keep your head down. I take all the risks. When he turns up dead, they'll look to me, not you, you stupid oaf." Prudent felt the thrill of fear that came when she goaded him, knowing how he'd react. "And now you're ruining it by being in here. You're a fool, Horace. A lowdown, half-witted, old coot."

Horace backhanded her.

She slammed into the wall. Stars exploded before her eyes. Her tongue touched the blood pouring from her split lip.

Grabbing the collar of her dress, he drew back his fist.

"Not my face, you stinking pig!"

Ruthlessly, he squeezed until he cut off her air.

She clawed at his strangling hand. Her nails drew blood on his rough knuckles.

Wrenching her to her tiptoes, he went for her stomach.

Eight

"Humpf! Take those children right out from under my nose, will you?" Hannah set out in the same direction she'd taken yesterday. Only this time she wasn't blinded by a blizzard. Instead she was blinded by her temper.

All through the ride she talked to herself, working up her indignation. It helped to keep her mind off the unfriendly horse.

She'd barely taken the time to write her usual letter to Grace. Hannah made a point of mailing off a letter to Mosqueros every time it looked as if she'd be in one place for a while. But she'd always moved on before a letter could come, assuming Grace even got it. Assuming Grace was alive and could write back.

In her heart, Hannah knew Grace would never have had time to receive Hannah's letter and write an answer. That gave Hannah hope for the sister who seemed to have vanished off the face of the earth almost four years ago. Had Parrish caught her? Was Grace, even now, back in Parrish's clutches, living as a prisoner, forced into hard labor?

She had a few pennies left. Hannah wanted to send the letter quickly so Grace could have the news if the letter ever reached her.

The horse jumped sideways at its own shadow and Hannah almost fell off. She went back to paying attention to the horse.

And thinking of one ornery beast led her thoughts directly to another. Grant.

"Refuse to send them to my school?" Hannah found the thicket. The horse wanted to nibble.

"Say my school isn't worthy?" She found the wagon wheel. The horse stopped to scratch his backside against it.

Prodding the old nag she'd rented, at last a tiny cabin appeared a mile or so in front of her, tucked in front of a ragged line of mountains. The ramshackle building was about a fourth the size of the barn that stood beside it.

Screaming erupted ahead.

Frantic, Hannah kicked her horse to get it moving. It reacted poorly to that and crow-hopped. It left Hannah behind on the second hop. She landed hard and broke through the rapidly melting snow to an impressive stand of buffalo burrs. Hannah heard her dress rip. The sound almost made her heart skip a beat. It was the only dress she had.

The horse, showing more energy than it had demonstrated up until now, took off running back the way it had come.

Hannah wanted to rub her sore backside and scold her horse and generally cry her eyes out, but the screaming kept her from doing any of that. She leapt to her feet and ran.

Grant dropped the reins on the horse he'd been leading in from the corral and ran.

He got inside the barn in time to see Benny reel backward and land on the seat of his pants.

Rushing past the other children, Grant grabbed Charlie's upraised arm and wrenched the tree branch out of his hand.

"Give it back!" Charlie lunged at the branch.

Grant held it overhead, out of reach. Charlie clutched Grant's arm and used it for leverage to jump at his weapon. Grant grabbed hold of the boy's arms, and Charlie proceeded to kick him.

"Joshua, put my horse up." Grant grunted with the impact of Charlie's flailing hands and feet and glanced over his shoulder at his oldest son.

Marilyn rushed into the barn, carrying Libby. Sadie was right behind them.

"Yes, Pa." Joshua was as tall as a man. Right now his intelligent brown eyes were grave. He went outside to round up the pinto gelding Grant had let loose on account of the screaming.

Marilyn, sixteen and as pretty as she was sweet—and relatively new to the family—said, "Let's go in the house, Benny. We need to wash that cut."

"Not just yet, Marilyn." A sharp kick on the ankle almost made Grant let Charlie go, but he hung on doggedly and the boy finally quit fighting. "We have to settle this."

Grant looked down at Charlie's belligerent face. "There's no call to be so upset. There's room for everyone at the Rocking C."

"I've been on my own before." Charlie resumed his struggle against Grant's hold. "I'm not staying squashed into that stupid house."

"Settle down, son." Grant's heart ached as he caught Charlie's shirt collar to further subdue him. He hated putting his hands on his children with anything other than complete kindness.

"I'm not your son!" Charlie jerked against Grant's hold. "Don't call me your son!"

Benny, too courageous for his own good, climbed to his feet and faced Charlie. "I'll help you hold him, Pa."

Charlie threw himself at Benny and would have hit him if Grant hadn't restrained him.

Grant shook his head. "I've got him, Benny. Thanks."

Libby edged up beside Marilyn. Grant could see Libby was already adopting the oldest girl as a substitute mother, but she had an attachment to Charlie from the train, and worry had cut a crease in Libby's smooth brow.

"Stop it, Charlie." Joshua returned, leading the pinto into a stall alongside the line of well-fed horses. "We've got room for everyone."

"Yeah," Sadie snipped. "Everyone was good to you when you came home with Pa last night. You gotta be good to us back."

Charlie didn't look at his brothers and sisters. He kept glaring at Benny.

Grant spoke quietly in Charlie's ear. "I don't blame you for being angry. It wouldn't be normal if you weren't."

Charlie struggled. Benny wiped at a trickle of blood dripping into his eyes.

"I can see how badly you want a family, Charlie. I know I'm too busy to pay you the kind of attention you'd hoped for from a pa. And you're going to have to share everything. It's not the family you dreamed of."

Some of the fire cooled in Charlie's eyes.

"I can sleep in the barn for a while, Pa," Joshua offered. "Charlie can have his own room. I know how he feels. If it gets too cold, I can get a bedroll and sleep by the kitchen stove like you."

Grant shook his head. "No child gets brought into this home and then gets shoved out into a cold barn."

"But right at first, to Charlie, it's important to have his own space." Joshua came and stood at Grant's side. Grant realized he could look straight into his son's eyes. "I don't need much."

"He don't want you in the barn." Charlie renewed his wrestling against Grant's firm hold. "He wants you inside with him. I'm the one he'll heave out into the cold."

Grant saw the burn of tears in Charlie's eyes. But Grant knew Charlie wouldn't cry. There'd been enough pain in his new son's life that nothing could shake tears loose anymore. Add to that the real fear that a show of weakness would set the other children on him like a wounded animal chased by a wolf pack and there's no way the boy would cry.

"How long have you been here?" Charlie snarled at Benny.

"I've been here almost three years."

Charlie quit struggling. Grant saw his surprise. "You must have been just a baby. They put babies on the orphan trains?"

Benny shrugged. "Pa says I was so young it didn't make no sense. That's why no one chose me. But Pa did."

Benny nodded at Marilyn. "Marilyn's just been here a few months."

Charlie looked at Pa. "The orphan trains come through that often?"

"No, Marilyn was living in an alley in LaMont. I found her there when we drove some cattle in to sell."

"The orphan train doesn't come through this route more than once every year or two," Sadie added.

"But whether we came on a train or some other way, we've all been through this." Joshua wiped the sweat from his shining black brow. He'd been cleaning stalls. "Pa brings new kids home all the time. Sadie 'n' me were with the first group of kids he adopted. We've been here ten years and we've seen lots of new brothers and sisters. He doesn't throw the old ones out or love the new ones more. He has enough love to go around."

"God has given Pa a heart that has more room in it than this whole wide Western land," Sadie said.

Grant's heart ached at hearing Sadie's kind words.

Charlie glanced at Grant, then at his other brothers and sisters, then back at Benny. He scowled.

"We're all orphans," Grant said. "Me included. I know exactly what your life has been like because I've lived the same one." Since the boy hadn't taken a swing at anyone for a full thirty seconds, Grant took a chance and released Charlie, then came around and hunkered down to his eye level.

"All of us have," Marilyn assured.

"We know how it is," Sadie nodded.

"That's why I can't let Joshua live in the barn." Grant silently prayed that Charlie would understand. "I have to treat Joshua right, and I'm going to treat you right, too. Can't you see that a parent who loves one child more than another hurts the child he loves as much as the one he doesn't love? If I treated you better than Joshua, I'd be hurting you both. I'll never desert you, no matter how angry you get. I know what it's like to hate the whole world just because it hurts too much to hope for something good."

"It's all right, Pa." Joshua said. "I can sleep in the barn. No matter where I am, I know you love me and I know God is always with me."

Grant focused on Charlie. "When you're alone in the world, God is a really good idea. It's the best lesson you'll ever learn. God will never fail you. He'll go with you wherever you end up." He smiled at the confused, angry little boy.

A deep longing appeared on Charlie's face then was wiped away by rage. "Why would God love a kid when his own parents don't?" Charlie gave Benny a violent shove, knocked him down, then whirled and ran out of the barn.

The whole family watched Charlie go.

"You think he'll run away?" Joshua crossed his arms.

"Maybe." Grant sighed. "But he can't get far. I'll talk to him. He'll get over being mad."

"I think I'd better go after him, Pa," Benny said. "I'm the one he has a problem with."

"No, he might hurt you again. I don't know all he's been through." Grant frowned and rubbed at the deep furrows that cut across his forehead. "But I can imagine."

"That's okay. I can take it. I'll watch out for branches, and if he wants to take a swing at me, well, I don't mind if he works off a little temper on me."

Grant shook his head, "Benny, thank you, but—"

"You let these children work their tempers off with fistfights?" Hannah rushed into the barn and hurried over to Benny. She immediately pulled a handkerchief out of her sleeve and began fussing over Benny's bleeding temple.

"What kind of a madhouse do you run here, I'd like to know?"

NINE

If this was a madhouse, Grant was the man in charge when he should have been an inmate.

Hannah had a good mind to shove him into a straitjacket right here on the spot.

She dropped to her knees and dabbed at the blood-soaked cut on Benny's head. "This looks ghastly! We need to get him to town to a doctor." Hannah felt her sleeve drop off her shoulder in the back. It was still stitched on the front, hanging by a few threads. She ignored it, too worried about Benny's cut to care about her dress.

"I'm okay, really, Miss Cartwright." Benny patted her hand. "I think it's already quit bleeding."

"You're very brave." Hannah comforted him. "But you're just a child. You can't see how serious this is."

At that moment, Grant caught Hannah's hands and pulled them away from Benny's head, then lifted her to her feet until their noses almost touched. "Quit fussing over him. He's all right."

"He is *not* all right." Hannah wrenched her hands against his steely, work-roughened grip. "He's hurt and bleeding. You can't just stand by and do nothing while these children harm each other."

Grant didn't even seem to notice her pathetic efforts to pull away.

"It's a head wound, ma'am," a black boy nearly as tall as Grant said politely. "Everyone knows they bleed like crazy."

As she jerked against Grant's hold, the last stitch on her sleeve gave up the ghost and the fabric fell the rest of the way down to her wrist. Grant's eyes zeroed in on her bare arm, and humiliated, she looked over at the boy who had spoken to her then looked at all the children who stood behind Grant as if they were lined up against her.

She was making a fool of herself fighting Grant's superior strength. She quit struggling and drew herself up to her full height. She came to Grant's chin.

Grant said with mild menace, "Do I have your attention?"

"You do." She spoke through gritted teeth.

Grant, without looking away from Hannah, asked, "Sadie, what work do you do around here?"

Hannah identified Sadie by the way she stood straighter and took a step closer to Grant. Her dark eyes glowed out of the ebony skin on her face. "I cook the meals with Marilyn and now Libby."

Hannah had been so upset about Benny's bleeding that she hadn't even given her little sister a look yet. She noticed Libby clinging to Marilyn, but when Sadie said Libby helped with the cooking, Libby beamed.

Sadie took the bloody handkerchief out of Hannah's confined hand and pressed it against Benny's head while she went on. "I wash a couple of batches of clothes a day and I keep the cabin straightened. I sew for the family and I ride out with the herd in the afternoon if I have time."

"Do you ever get any time to rest or have fun?" Grant asked, still staring into Hannah's eyes, holding her secure.

A flare of heat climbed up Hannah's cheeks.

Benny took over tending his wound.

Sadie stepped back beside Grant, tugged at her tightly curled black hair that had escaped from a bun, and tucked it behind her ear. "Well, sure, Pa. I go along when there's a church social. And I spend time every evening reading."

"Marilyn, how about you? Miss Cartwright is the new schoolteacher. She thinks I work you children too hard. What do you do around here?"

"The same as Sadie." Marilyn was as fair as Sadie was dark. Her fine hair was pulled into a flyaway braid that hung down nearly to her waist. Every hair that had escaped curled. Her eyes were blue under slim arched brows. Her skin was deeply tanned, and she was almost a foot taller than Sadie. "I'm also working on a patchwork quilt and I help with the younger children, see to their baths and help them with their studies and such."

"Do you have any fun, ever?"

"Since Wilbur's been sparkin' me, I have him over of an evening, and sometimes we go for a buggy ride or the whole family goes to a church social. And I spend time reading, too."

"Miss Cartwright seems to think you're a slave," Grant said in a voice so acid it nearly burned Hannah's skin.

Hannah jerked on her wrists, but Grant didn't loosen his hold.

"A slave?" Marilyn gasped.

The older black boy stepped forward. "Only a person who's never been a slave and knows nothing about slavery would make such a comment."

"That's Joshua." Grant pulled Hannah a little closer until her arms bent at the elbow and pressed against Grant's chest. "He spent the first few years of his life on a plantation. His father was sold when he was too young to remember him. His mother died after a beating from her master when Joshua was five. He escaped with some other slaves running away and ended up living on the streets in New York. Eventually he came here. How about it, Sadie? Do you think this silly woman should be throwing the word *slave* around?"

Sadie, short and black with very old eyes, crossed her arms. "My parents were emancipated before I was orphaned. I was four when they died. Joshua and I and four others lived on the street for a year. Then we found out we could hide on a cargo ship and get out of that cold, awful city. We ended up in Houston."

Grant shuddered visibly. "Sadie and Joshua, living on the street, behind Confederate lines during the war."

"How long did you live on the street?" Hannah's earliest memories were of a Chicago orphanage. Then she'd been under Parrish's thumb. But the last few years, Hannah had been little more than living on the street.

"About a year in New York before we got the idea of stowing away. We'd only been in Houston a little while when Pa found us there and—"

"Yes," Grant interrupted, "one of the boys they were running with tried to pick my pocket."

"Will," Joshua said with a fond smile.

"He was a mighty good thief," Sadie added.

Grant shook his head. "No, he wasn't, or he wouldn't'a got caught."

"He just didn't know who he was dealing with." Joshua shoved his hands in his pockets. "He didn't know he was taking on someone who'd been a hand at thievin' himself for a time."

Hannah knew how it was to be hungry or cold and see something you needed. Things had found their way into her hands, too. She'd never picked anyone's pocket, but a pie left on a windowsill or a dress hanging on a clothesline had come home with her now and then.

She'd known it was wrong and she'd gone right ahead. What's more, to survive, she'd do it again, maybe not for herself. She liked to believe she could put herself in God's hands and even face death from cold or hunger before she'd break another commandment. But if she had children in her care, she wouldn't stand by and let them starve. She couldn't. She asked for forgiveness to God and hoped the day never came again that she was forced to make such a choice. She waited for Grant to make excuses and pretty it up.

He didn't.

Joshua continued, "It's how I survived. It was wrong, and I knew it, but I did it anyway." He nodded at Sadie. "She's fifteen. Sadie is one of the few of us who knows her last name."

"Sadie Mason." The black girl tilted her chin up with pride. "My pa named himself after what he did for a living in New York. Then he and Ma died in a diphtheria outbreak. They were both born into slavery, and they were separated from five children, all sons. Their owner sold my brothers off when he needed a little spending money. I wasn't born until later, after Pa and Ma had escaped north. They told me what it was like, and even though I was mighty young when they died, I remember the scars of lash marks on both of their backs. You're a mean lady to come in here and tell Pa he's treating us bad. You don't know what bad is if you can say such things."

Hannah knew exactly what bad was. She'd lived it herself when she'd been in Parrish's hands. She had lash marks of her own, and she knew a person didn't have to be black to be a slave.

Every breath she took was for the purpose of helping and protecting children. Her heart ached to see these young spirits broken to the point that they'd defend this man. She remembered the times she'd said what Parrish expected her to say and put her whole heart into the lie, because she knew punishment awaited her if she didn't defend her pa.

She looked at the little boy who was standing beside Libby. The bleeding *had* stopped. Freckles sprinkled across his nose, and lank hair drooped across his eyes. His ears stuck straight out from his head, and his brown eyes didn't shoot pellets of rage at her. Stepping nearer to her, he watched her like he was afraid she'd vanish.

"I'm Benny, an' I'm six. Pa isn't a bad man. And I don't think you're a bad lady neither. You came out here because you were worried about us. I think that's nice. We're fine, but you can worry about us if'n you want to." He edged closer.

"You're right, Benny." Marilyn stepped up beside Grant, her blue eyes level with Hannah's. Hannah wondered if Marilyn wasn't almost her age. "She's not bad. She just doesn't know us very well yet. She doesn't understand how things work on the Rocking C."

Marilyn looked sideways at Grant and added with a teasing lilt to his voice, "You seem to have latched on to Miss Cartwright for good, Pa."

Grant looked away from Hannah and arched an eyebrow at Marilyn. Hannah saw the sassy way Marilyn grinned at him and knew for a fact that she'd never grinned at Parrish in such a way. Grant returned the smile, then let loose of Hannah's wrists and stepped away.

Hannah rubbed her wrists distractedly and noticed her sleeve dangling. She pulled the fabric up to her shoulder, but it drooped back down. Ashamed of her arm being bare, she pulled it back up and clamped her arm to her side to hold it as best she could.

Looking from one child to the next, Hannah balanced their obvious contentment here against what she knew their life must be like. She noticed Grant rubbing both his hands on his pant legs, as if touching her had gotten his hands dirty.

She finally ignored the rest of them and said to Benny, "I'm not a bad person. You're right about that, Benny. I didn't like Charlie and Libby coming here when Mr. . . . Grant said there was no mother and not enough room. I still don't think he should have all of you out here."

Grant snorted, clamped his arms across his chest, and shook his head. He opened his mouth, but before he could speak, Joshua said, "So what would have been better, ma'am? All the folks that wanted kids had already chosen. Sour Springs is the end of the line. The only thing ahead for Charlie and Libby was a long train ride back to the orphanage. You really think they're worse off here?"

Hannah glanced doubtfully at Benny's bleeding head.

Suddenly Grant's eyes gleamed. "What is it you'd like to inspect, Hannah?"

That's when Hannah remembered she was usually afraid of men. Up until now, even with his grabbing her and looking at her with that narrow-eyed predator look, she'd forgotten to be scared.

"Why don't you come on into the house and help us get an evening meal on the table?" Grant said it so sweetly the hairs stood up on the back of her neck.

Hannah knew she was being tested. . .or maybe used. After all, there was no woman around to do chores. It was just the worst kind of dirty shame that she had never spent much time in a kitchen.

She wasn't going to admit that. "I'd be glad to stay and help. In fact, I insist upon it."

Grant jerked his head toward the barn door. "This way."

He scooped Libby up in his arms and walked past Hannah without another look. Libby looped her arms around Grant's neck and stared over his shoulder, smiling at Hannah.

Falling into line with the other children, Hannah scowled at the way they trailed after Grant. She decided to catch up and prove herself his equal. Before she could, Benny's hand slipped into hers. She looked down at the little boy.

He was watching her with wide, adoring eyes. "You smell good, ma'am."

Hannah was sorely afraid she smelled like a horse, but Benny didn't want to hear that. "That's very sweet. Thank you."

Benny crowded closer and walked slowly as if he wanted the time with her to last. Hannah's heart melted as she felt his hand cling tightly to hers. As Hannah neared the awful, undersized house, she felt even more that she had to protect these darling children.

With Parrish it had been an apartment, the children confined to their one room nearly all the time while Parrish lived in the other four rooms. This wasn't just about Libby anymore. With Benny pressed up against her, she knew she'd just fallen hopelessly in love with another one of Grant's children.

Her spine stiffened as she watched that awful man walk toward that awful house.

No matter how hard you try, Grant, until I'm sure everything is as it should be, you're not going to get me out of here.

TEN

I've got to get her out of here.

Grant strode toward the cabin, stunned by the way the kids were looking at Hannah. He didn't have to be a genius—he didn't even have to be particularly bright—to get what Benny was thinking.

Mother!

It's a good thing he didn't have to be bright because he was the dumbest man who ever lived. He'd had this little moment of insanity and thought it would teach Hannah a lesson if he made her come in and help make dinner. She would see how great the girls were as cooks. She would see the other children pitching in with a cheerful attitude, and as a bonus, he'd get a little free labor.

Now he was letting the confounded woman into his house, and she was going to see how crowded it was and how sparse and rickety the furniture. She'd see the bedrooms crammed with beds and that there really wasn't enough room for Charlie and Libby.

With a sigh, Grant admitted it didn't matter that he'd invited her. He'd have never kept her out anyway.

After one look at Benny practically wrapped around her, he didn't look back again. He should have looked sideways, because if he had he might have headed off the next question.

"Is that the only skirt you have for riding?" Marilyn asked. "I have a split skirt, and it's way handier." Marilyn tugged on her riding skirt.

"Where did you get that?" Hannah's voice sounded envious. "I've never seen one before."

"I made it." Marilyn smiled. "It's much more modest on horseback."

"You know how to sew?"

"You don't do any sewing, Miss Cartwright?" Marilyn dropped back to walk closer to Hannah.

Grant was sure that the older girls had been annoyed with Hannah just a few moments ago. Now he was feeling deserted. At least Sadie didn't—

"We could show you how, and then we could give you a pattern for a riding skirt." Sadie turned and walked backward so she could look at Hannah, since Hannah was out of sides to walk beside.

Marilyn adjusted Hannah's torn sleeve slightly. "We'll help you get this sleeve put back on. And there's a tear partway across the back. We can mend that, too."

"Oh, thank you. I was worried about getting my dress patched back together in time for school in the morning."

Grant shook his head in disgust. It looked like it was Joshua and him against the women.

"What happened to your horse, Miss Cartwright?" Joshua gave Hannah a concerned look. "I don't see it tied up anywhere."

"It threw me."

"That's how you tore your dress?" Marilyn asked.

Hannah was silent so Grant had to turn around to see her nodding and fiddling with her sleeve.

"You fell off your horse?" Grant snorted a manly snort and exchanged a look with Joshua.

Joshua's eyes were fixed on Hannah. "Are you all right?"

"I was upset when I heard the screaming coming from the barn. I kicked the horse to hurry him up, and he tossed me off his back. I'm afraid he's long gone by now."

"Don't worry about it." Joshua dropped back to walk closer to

Hannah, too. "If you rented him from in town, he'll go back. I'll hitch up the team and give you a ride home after supper."

"Why, thank you, Joshua."

That left Charlie. Grant had no hope. Charlie had taken off somewhere, and if he was here, he'd probably throw in with Hannah just to prove how much he hated his new family.

Grant thought of all the places there were around here to hide. Usually the young'uns picked a favorite, and Grant got onto it and could find them in a pinch. But Charlie hadn't been here long enough for Grant to know where he'd hole up.

"I'd better go find out where Charlie took off to."

"Leave him be, Pa." Joshua looked around. There was no sign of the boy anywhere.

Grant shook his head. "I'd better go."

"I've got a feeling about Charlie, Pa. I think he might be better after he's had some time to cool down." Joshua held Grant's gaze, clearly expecting Grant to listen.

Grant all of a sudden realized that while he wasn't looking Joshua had turned from a boy to a man. Then he counted and realized Joshua would be seventeen in a couple of months—based on the age and birthday Grant had urged Joshua to pick when he'd come here so they could have a special meal for his birthday. For all Grant knew, Joshua could be twenty by now.

Grant had been on his own by that time. In fact he'd adopted six kids the year he turned seventeen. One of them was Joshua, and the boy was a son to Grant in every way imaginable without being flesh and blood.

Grant's older girls talked sewing with Hannah. Benny and Libby had found a new ma. And Joshua had just grown up right in front of his eyes. For the father of six, Grant didn't have much to do. He slumped his shoulders and wondered if he hadn't oughta adopt more kids as soon as possible.

They got to the house, and he remembered why he shouldn't have taken the two he'd just gotten. He shifted Libby to one side while he held the door open, thinking he could at least serve some purpose manning the door. He let the whole family troop past, minus one troubled young boy, plus one interfering female.

He noticed Hannah having trouble getting in the door with her little vine, Benny, clinging to her. She veered a bit too close to Grant while she went in sideways, and Grant got something else in his head to worry about.

Benny was right. Hannah did smell good.

He had a notion to tell her. For some reason it reminded him of that strange, secretive look that had passed between Ian and Megan at church this morning. With only the vaguest idea of what it meant and why he'd think of it now, Grant fought down a surge of restlessness that he'd rarely felt before, being exhausted half to death most of the time.

But somehow that restlessness erased his impatience with Hannah, and he didn't mind her staying around quite so much. His mind swirled with a lot of confusing thoughts he couldn't pin down. And he considered how nice Hannah would look in a split skirt as he followed close after her.

Then Hannah gasped.

He stepped well away and focused his eyes elsewhere. Before she could start in on him, he said defensively, "It's the house my folks left me when they died. I've been meaning to build on, but money's scarcer 'n hens' teeth and time is scarcer yet. I've got three bedrooms. The girls, Marilyn, Sadie, and now Libby, sleep together."

"Parents? I thought you were an orphan." Hannah hoisted Benny up in her arms as if she'd done it a thousand times.

"My folks adopted me off an orphan train when I was fourteen. I lived with 'em for a couple of years before they were killed when their team ran away with their wagon. They left me this house, and it was so quiet I couldn't stand it. I went to enlist in the Confederacy, went as far as Houston and found six kids living in an alley. I just turned around and brought 'em back home."

"You adopted six children when you were sixteen?"

"I was seventeen by then. And later, after the war, I got more young'uns that were leftovers on an orphan train."

Hannah settled Benny more firmly on her hip as if she planned on taking him with her. "That's ridiculous. Who allowed that?"

"Martha was riding with the children even then."

"What was the matter? Did you need help on the ranch?"

Grant stepped close to Hannah. He knew he should back off, but he didn't quite have the self-control. "I had a home. Those children needed it."

"A seventeen-year-old boy isn't a parent. What were you doing? Adopting *playmates*?"

"I'm not saying I was a good parent, but I could put a roof over their heads."

"Children need more than a roof. Mrs. Norris should have been reported for allowing such nonsense."

"Martha will be given jewels in her crown in heaven for bending the rules and letting me take those kids."

"I may report her yet." Hannah tore her eyes away from Grant and stroked one hand over Benny's hair, still soaked from after-church sledding and tinged with blood. "Isn't she answerable to anyone?"

"You leave her alone." Grant's eyes narrowed. "She's the finest woman I've ever known. If you cause her one second's trouble, so help me, Hannah, I'll—"

"Don't you threaten me." Hannah stepped right up into his face. "If my complaint causes her trouble, then what does that say about her actions? If she's got nothing to hide, then—"

"What was the point of me living in a house by myself while they had nothing?" Grant leaned down toward the stubborn woman. "I didn't plan it, but I couldn't let them go all the way back to New York."

Hannah's chest heaved and her eyes flashed fire. She clung to Benny as if she'd be willing to fight and die to protect him.

This little spitfire was as alive and spirited as anyone he'd ever known. Grant couldn't look away.

"If you were adopted, why didn't you take your parents' name? Then all these children would have names."

"My parents' name was Cooper. I can use that if I need to. But I want to remember what it's like to not have a name."

"Why? Why would you cling to that memory? By not claiming a legitimate last name, you're reminded every second of every day of your hardships. That has to be. . .exhausting." Hannah shuddered as if she herself had burdens that rode on her shoulders and never let her rest.

Grant wondered what those burdens were, and if she'd had any luck forgetting. He didn't think so. He thought his way was more honest. "It's who I am. It's *what* I am. Why try and forget something that is unforgettable?"

Her eyes narrowed as she studied him. She glanced at Libby in Grant's arms, and the two females exchanged a long, secretive look.

Grant tightened his hold on his newest daughter. He'd have to keep a sharp eye out or this lady might go to stealing his children. "The second I forget what it's like to be alone, maybe I'll forget there are children in this world who need me. I'll never do that." Grant held Hannah's gaze.

He saw her waver between compassion for the children and maybe some compassion for him. Her eyes hardened and she hugged Benny closer.

His shoulders slumped. He'd picked a life that was one long fight— wonderful but troubled children, unkind townspeople, and contemptuous teachers. He looked at the bedroll he'd shoved under the kitchen table. He didn't even have a room to sleep in anymore.

Disgusted, he shook his head. "I'm through wasting my breath on you. Why'd I think for even a minute you might understand?"

He turned away and set Libby in a chair by the stove. "Just finish your inspection and go, teacher lady. I told you where the girls sleep. Joshua has the back bedroom, and Charlie and Benny sleep in the loft. That's not too crowded."

"You forgot to mention yourself, Pa." Sadie pointed out helpfully. "You're going to sleep where it's warm by the fire. So the off side of the kitchen is your bedroom. That makes four bedrooms."

Thanks a lot. Grant knew Hannah wouldn't let that pass. He shook his head and braced himself.

"A four-bedroom home," Hannah said with a surprising amount of sarcasm for a woman holding a child so gently in her arms. "Why, it's the next thing to a mansion."

Of course Grant's house wasn't a mansion. The kitchen was just barely big enough to contain one long thin table, two benches on each long side, a stool on each short side, a potbelly stove, a dry sink, and a fireplace. When he'd started, he had the cabin, the land, and a few dozen head of cattle left to him by his parents, but not a penny in cash. He'd scrimped and saved, living off the land for years. These days, with his herd growing and a couple of cattle drives under his belt, he had some cash money, but counting pennies got to be a habit and it was a good lesson to teach his kids. So what if they'd never gotten much that was fancy? What furniture wasn't left from his parents' time, Grant had made by hand, like the extra long table.

I know how to make things sturdy, but no one would accuse me of makin' 'em pretty.

The girls' bedroom was on the east side of the house. It had its own door and stretched half as wide as the little kitchen and as long as the bunk bed it contained—the room's only piece of furniture.

Joshua's room was a lean-to on the back of the house that had been meant as a place to hang coats and kick off muddy boots. The loft overhead dropped down a scant few feet from the peaked roof. Benny and Charlie had to shimmy in on their bellies, and it was barely long enough to stretch out in. It had been Grant's bedroom while Benny slept with Joshua, until last night.

Grant saw Hannah inspecting through the wide open door to the girls' room. The orphanage Grant had grown up in had bunks, and he'd done his best to build his own version with no advice or pattern.

And every spare inch of the house—of which there were few—was jammed to the rafters with children and fabric and clothes set to be handed down. Grant couldn't help being embarrassed about the shabby little house. Hannah's disapproval rolled toward him in waves.

Dragging his Stetson off, he hung it on one of the dozen racks of deer antlers lining one wall, coats and hats hanging from them all. "Look, I know it's not much," he began before she could start in on him. "I've been meaning to build on. But the kids need things like books and shoes and we've got a lot of mouths to feed. I'm not spending my money on lumber, and the only available wood to cut is on a slope too dangerous to tangle with. We need to eat and sleep and we've got it. We spend most every minute of the day outside anyway, tending the herd and doing chores."

Grant snapped his mouth shut. He hadn't intended to start listing off the work the kids had to do, but there was nothing wrong with a young'un having chores!

Hannah looked rather helplessly around the little house until Marilyn distracted her by saying, "Let's get started on supper."

Hannah bit her lip and looked uncomfortable. "I. . .I'm not a very good cook."

"We can handle it," Sadie said. "You're company. You just sit and watch."

"No." Hannah removed her bedraggled bonnet and found a spare antler.

Grant really looked at that limp, tattered bonnet for the first time. Of course he'd noticed how Hannah looked. He hadn't done much *except* notice her anytime she'd been within a hundred feet of him. But for the first time he looked beyond the flashing blue in her glaring eyes and the pretty pink of her insult-spouting lips.

The ride out to the Rocking C had been hard on her. Her horse had thrown her. He'd barely registered that when she'd said it, even though Joshua had thought to express concern. There was dirt streaked on her fair skin, and the neat bun she'd had at church was gone. Buffalo burrs clung to the back of her ripped-up dress, the same dress she'd had on yesterday at the train station and at church, although it was travel-stained. It was faded as if it'd been washed hundreds of times and the seams looked nearly worn through. The cuffs and collar were frayed. Grant knew enough about not having that he was abruptly, absolutely sure that this was the only dress Hannah owned.

Marilyn rested a hand on Hannah's arm. "Sit down, Miss Cart-wright. While Sadie starts supper, I'll baste this sleeve back on and put a patch on the back of your dress. It'll only take a minute."

"Thank you so much, Marilyn." Her eyes said thank you a hundred times more than her words.

How had she learned the children's names already? Half the people in Sour Springs didn't even bother to learn them. Of course they were as different from each other as night and day, but it took a bit of time and effort to learn someone's name. The good folks of Sour Springs seemed to have no interest in exerting either.

As Marilyn fussed over her, Grant noticed the dark circles under Hannah's eyes. The long train ride she'd finished only yesterday—the same one that had worn Libby and Charlie to a nub—had beaten her down, too. But even exhausted, she hurried out here to check on some orphaned children.

Grant thought again of that look between Ian and Megan. He knew nothing about what passed between men and women, and he had the unnerving notion that maybe Hannah could explain it to him.

Marilyn turned Hannah to face the lantern, and while Marilyn threaded a needle, Grant caught himself studying a chunk of Hannah's bare back that showed through a gaping hole in her dress. His eyes narrowed as he realized what he was seeing—scars.

With a quick, unplanned step, he was behind Hannah, pulling the fabric aside. "What happened here? Did you do this falling off your horse?"

She froze while Grant's hand traced the jagged furrow that disappeared behind the fabric. Then with jerky, uncoordinated movements, Hannah pulled away from him. He hung on until he heard a tear in the threadbare fabric. Not wanting to ruin what must be her only dress, he let go. Furious at that mark, a mark he bore himself, he wanted to see how deep it was and how long and if there were others. And how old it was. No fall off a horse this afternoon put this mark on her.

She turned so her back was away from him—out of reach, out of sight. "It's nothing Mr. . . .Grant. I insist you keep your hands off me." Her tone could have turned water into ice and her eyes were colder still.

But her trembling lip wasn't cold. She was obviously afraid of his question.

"Hannah, tell me what—"

Pleading with her eyes, she said, "Leave it alone."

"Please." Grant took a faltering step toward her in the tiny cabin. No one was far apart, but even so Grant was far too close to Hannah.

Marilyn came up behind Hannah and, after a quick glance at the scar, looked up and shook her head, warning Grant off.

He clenched his fists and saw Hannah look at that sign of anger as if afraid he'd use those fists on her. And that stopped him when no words would have.

He thought of her spunk yesterday and today. But those marks had been put there by someone laying a whip or a rod to her back. Far too many of the children he adopted bore them. So how had she gotten them?

He'd have the answer. . .but not now.

Sadie sneaked a peak at Hannah's back from where she peeled potatoes at the table. She looked quickly away, running a damp, trembling hand up her own arm, which had been scarred by boiling water. A man who caught her stealing food out of the garbage in his alley had thrown it at her.

Joshua came to Sadie's side, gave her a quick hug, took the potatoes and sharp knife away, and started peeling.

"I'll go get us a chicken." Sadie rushed out of the cabin.

Grant looked after her. She needed a few minutes when she got to thinking about her days on the street, more so than the other children. There was a lot she'd never told and probably never would. He let her go.

Marilyn took quick careful stitches on Hannah's dress as the room fell silent. Each of his children lost in his or her memories. Grant had plenty of his own.

Fighting the need to punch somebody, Grant noticed Libby stand from her chair by the stove and limp into her bedroom.

He remembered a job that needed a father's hand. Glad for an excuse to leave the room and break the spell that had settled on Hannah, his children, and himself, he followed Libby into her room. "Let's have a look at your shoe, Lib."

Libby sank onto the bottom bunk and looked at him with wide, scared eyes. Trembling all over, she stretched her little foot out toward him.

It was wrong to hate, Grant knew it all the way to his soul. He was a believer in God and had read the Bible clear through several times. He knew, above all else, God called His believers to love and forgive. But right that minute, Grant hated every person who'd ever made any child fearful. Hannah sat in there not willing to talk about the marks on her back. Sadie shook with the memories that burned more deeply than boiling water. Grant thought of a woman working in his orphanage who had taken the job, he was sure, to have access to defenseless children and feed her hunger for inflicting pain.

And here sat this little girl feeling like her broken ankle made her unworthy of love. Grant knew her silence was rooted in her fear. How many times had she been hurt for speaking the wrong words? What made her hide inside herself this way? What had she seen that was unspeakable?

Grant sank down onto his knees in front of his new daughter and took her tiny shoe in his hand. "I want you to know, Libby, that having a foot that's hurt doesn't make you any less of a wonderful little girl."

Libby dropped her gaze to the floor.

Grant barely fit in the space between the bed and the wall as he slipped off her shoe and inspected. "Does it hurt, honey?"

Shaking her head, her lower lips trembled.

Setting the shoe aside on the lumpy mattress, Grant studied the thickened ridge around her ankle and the thin scars that spoke of medical treatment that helped ease Grant's temper and shake him loose of his memories. At least someone had cared enough to try and help her.

He let loose of her foot and said briskly, so his voice wouldn't shake, "Now, get up off 'a that bed and stand straight in front of me. I think I know a way to help your leg."

Libby stood straight, looking at the wall over his head as if she expected him to hurt her. Grant suspected she'd been hurt plenty in her life. As he reached for her leg, Libby looked away from the wall and out the door to the kitchen. The way Libby's eyes lit up, he knew only one person could be there.

Hannah was inspecting him again.

He wanted to turn on Hannah and order her out, but the mule-stubborn woman didn't obey orders worth a hoot. Instead he ignored her and studied the way Libby stood and experimented with lifting her foot a bit. "Lib, I think your leg must have healed shorter than it was before. I can make the sole on your shoe thicker and maybe you won't limp anymore."

Libby looked skeptical, but Grant knew she was out of practice at hoping.

Grant took Libby's worn-out little lace-up boot and went with it to the kitchen. Gathering his razor sharp hunting knife, he pulled a piece of thick leather from one of the untidy mounds of clothing and fabric. Next he hunted up several tack nails. Settling himself at the kitchen table, since that was where the only chairs in the house were, he went to work.

Joshua set the potatoes on to boil. "I'll have a look around for Charlie. He might have cooled off by now."

"Thanks, son." Grant turned his attention back to the shoe.

Once her dress was repaired to the best of Marilyn's ability, Hannah donned an apron and hesitantly offered to help cook supper.

While Grant repaired Libby's boot, he got to watch the show.

ELEVEN

"I thank you for all your help making my home run better, Hannah." Grant lifted the reins and started the wagon moving.

Hannah sighed and wished like crazy that Joshua had been allowed to drive her home. But the supper had been late—thanks to her. Night had fallen early as it did this time of year, and Grant had declared the trail treacherous. Hannah thought of the long, flat trail to town and wondered where the treachery was—being tormented to death by Grant maybe?

"Ignoring the last two hours was too much to hope for, I see."

"Yep." Grant's gloved hand settled his Stetson more firmly on his head as the wind threatened to whip it off. His dark hair, a ridiculous length for a man, had escaped its pony tail again and now whipped around his ears and collar. "You definitely made it clear to me why I mustn't take a child without first having a wife."

Hannah thought he might be rolling his eyeballs at her. She thanked God for the darkness.

The wind blew her poor battered dress across Grant. Delicately—for a lummox—he pushed her skirt off his leg. He briefly fingered the charred spot around her knee.

Hannah just barely resisted the urge to slap him. "As long as you insist on talking, why don't we discuss sending the children to school?"

As her eyes adjusted to the night, she could now see Grant give her a sideways look. "They'll be there until I decide they shouldn't be."

And what was that supposed to mean exactly? "Why on earth wouldn't you want your children in school?"

"It's not the schooling. I'd love to have some help with that. I know there are some gaps in my own education, since I never went to school myself."

Hannah gasped and turned on him. "You don't know how to read? Is that it? Mr. . . .Grant, I can help you with that. I'd be more than glad to—" Hannah snapped her mouth shut when she remembered Grant reading a chapter of the Bible before they'd started eating.

"As I was saying," Grant said with exaggerated patience, "my children have had some bad experiences with both students and teachers. It's mainly the other children, but some of the teachers have been cruel, and there are people in town who don't want my children mixing with theirs. After all, orphanhood might be contagious."

"I'll see that none of that goes on." Hannah almost liked the man for a second. If only she could be sure he treated them as well when no one was watching. She knew how good a front Parrish had put on.

Grant gave her a long look. "You say you'll do it. I suppose I believe you. We almost always give a new teacher a chance, although one comes and goes so fast sometimes, we don't even get in before she's gone. The Brewsters, the family that treated the kids the worst, left town."

Although he spoke quietly, Grant's tone changed until it was as grim as death. "But the first time one of the kids comes home asking what some ugly word means, and I have to explain it means his daddy wasn't married to his mama, well, I'll just keep 'em home."

Hannah could feel the fury in Grant. It exactly matched hers. She'd been called that word. The main person to call her that had been Parrish, the man who insisted she call him pa.

"There will be no crude talk like that in my school, Mr. . . .Grant."

"Maybe you'll try, Hannah." Grant took his eyes off the trail and met her gaze. "Maybe you will. But you can't watch all of them every minute."

Hannah knew that was true, and she wouldn't make a promise to Grant she couldn't keep. Grant fell silent and seemed to concentrate on his driving. They got to the end of the first stretch of trail and, instead of Grant turning and going the way she'd come, he followed a trail that was nothing more than a pair of wagon tracks. In the moonlight, the trail seemed to head directly for an impassable mountain.

"This isn't the way back to Sour Springs." She looked at the trail they were slowly leaving.

"Thank goodness you're here, Hannah," Grant said with mock relief. "I've only lived here for twelve years. I might not be able to find my way back to town without your able assistance. After all, you've been a resident of Sour Springs for. . .how many hours now?"

Hannah fairly vibrated with annoyance. She was really tired of Grant's overly polite chiding. "I *demand* to know where you're taking me, Mr. . . .Grant."

"That's not my name, you know." Grant hi-upped to the horses and slapped the reins gently across their backs. The traces jingled; the horses picked up speed. He didn't turn back.

Hannah looked at him. "Grant isn't your name?"

The corner of his mouth turned up in a smile as rude as it was unamused. "No, Mr. . . .Grant isn't my name." He greatly exaggerated the pause between Mister and Grant.

"Excuse me for having manners, Mr. . . .Grant." Hannah could feel that one coming, but she couldn't stop herself. "If you don't want me stumbling over your name, then you should pick a proper one." Hannah settled in her seat prepared, now that she'd spoken her mind, to ignore him all the way to town.

"You're very brave for a woman who is probably being taken out into the wilderness to be abandoned." Grant rested the reins on his ragged pants, the knees patched and the patches worn through. The calm, cooperative horses seemed to know the way without much guidance from him. Maybe he dumped people off in the wilderness regularly, especially unwanted children.

Hannah grabbed the seat and whirled to face him. "I knew this wasn't the way to town!"

"Well, that's a nice surprise." Grant shoved hair out of his eyes. "There *is* something you finally know. What a relief."

"I'm sorry about the potatoes." Hannah should have been more afraid, but for some reason the only feeling Grant seemed to stir in her was anger. She clenched her fists in her lap. "How many times do I have to say that?"

"How about once for every one of my kids who didn't get a full belly because of you."

"Marilyn made more!" Hannah knew she was out of line, but he kept goading her and she'd apologized nearly once per child already.

"That's good then. We grew enough potatoes to feed the whole family several times over. It's probably best to burn some of them up. If it weren't for the stink—"

"I'm sorry! I'm sorry! I'm sorry! That's three. How many children did you have again? Too many for a mere schoolteacher to count at a glance. Was it six? I'm sorry, I'm sorry, I'm sorry."

"At least you chased down the ones you spilled all over the floor. Having you crawl around under the table was kind of like having a pet. The kids have been wanting a dog."

Hannah didn't hit him, and he was too dense to know what a lucky man he was. "Not everyone was born being at home in a kitchen, Mr. . . .Grant." Okay, she was going to stop doing that. It went against the grain, but she was going to have to start calling him Grant without the mister.

"Yes, Missssss. . .Cartwright, I could see that cleaning a chicken was a mystery to you. I believe you ended up wearing the few feathers you managed to separate from the poor bird."

"I have skills. . .Grant. They just don't extend to gutting chickens." She could thread a weaving loom so fast no eyes could follow her fingers.

She hoped to never have to thread one again.

"No need to point that out, Hannah. I got that plain as day."

Hannah sniffed at him. "Cleaning a chicken is disgusting. I refuse to be ashamed of not having such dreadful knowledge."

"You do admit the hypocrisy of *eating* a chicken when you can't bear the thought of getting it cooked."

"I admit no such thing. I'm not stupid. I'm just untrained. I could learn to clean a chicken and boil potatoes without scorching them and—"

"And to stop slicing the bread just one tiny, little second before you get to your hand."

Hannah looked down at her throbbing thumb. Why had Grant insisted on bandaging it himself? Surely his daughters usually handled the nursing. She had the clumsy knotted rag on her hand to prove Grant didn't know what he was doing. And she was left with the warmth of his hands on her—a warmth that lasted long after he'd quit touching her. Of course Grant had been obnoxious the whole time he'd done his crude doctoring, but Benny had pressed against her side and murmured comforting words.

And all of that might have been forgotten, since the girls took over and did the meal with her safely settled out of the way, if she hadn't tried to redeem herself by pulling the pot of coffee out of the coals and—

"How exactly did you manage to set your skirt on fire?"

Hannah was done with being badgered. "You were right there and you know good and well how it happened!"

The team slowed as it began pulling them slightly upward. The trail didn't go right up the side of the hill; it slanted across the face of it. They were sloped sideways with Hannah on the uphill side, and they skidded occasionally on spots left slippery with melting snow. Hannah couldn't stop herself from leaning hard against Grant, despite her struggle to keep her distance. Grant's shoulder was like solid iron beside her. Warm, solid iron.

Grant seemed supportive of her efforts to stay away from him because he gave her the occasional strange look that she imagined must mean, "Get over."

But now she understood what Grant had meant about the treacherous trail. The good side of that was Grant was too occupied driving the team to torment her.

With a sigh, Hannah wondered how she'd come to a point in her life that she had to choose between hugging up against a man who delighted in insulting her or rolling off a cliff. One prospect was as unpleasant as the other. In the end she just clung to the seat.

Just when she thought her spine had taken such a beating that she'd be permanently tilted to the left, they came out on top of the bluff, and Hannah could see the brightly lit windows of the little town of Sour Springs right at the bottom of the hill in front of them.

"I rode that horse nearly ten miles!"

"Zeb at the livery gave you directions?" Grant's brow furrowed, and though his expression held its usual grouchiness, for the first time it wasn't aimed at her.

"No, Zeb didn't tell me. It was Harold at the general store. He said there was another way, but it was confusing."

He pressed down on the wagon brake and sent the team over the crest. Now they were tilted sideways in Hannah's direction.

"Ah, Harold." Sawing the reins with one strong hand encased in a worn-out glove, he leaned hard on the brake and kept his eyes strictly on the trail ahead. "He's easily confused."

After a brief pause, Grant added, "But it was Zeb who rented you Rufus?"

Something in his tone made Hannah glance at him. "Was that the horse's name? We were never introduced."

Grant turned away from the crazy trail and grinned at her. It was definitely the first time he'd done that—of course he'd laughed at her quite a bit, but that wasn't the same thing at all.

"A swaybacked, gray horse with a white blaze, one white front leg, and a bad attitude?"

"There are, no doubt, several horses in the livery that fit that description." Hannah had the sudden urge to protect Zeb, and she didn't know why.

"Nope. I think Zeb saw an easy two bits and landed old Rufus slap on top of you." Grant added in a grim tone that didn't bode well for Zeb, "He hadn't'a oughta done that."

The trail canted. Grant leaned against her, and she didn't think he was making the least effort to prevent the contact. She braced her arm against the seat and held them both on the wagon.

After far too long of brushing hard up against him, they reached the bottom of the bluff and within minutes were at the edge of Sour Springs.

"You can probably get the worst of that scorching out just by washing the skirt." Grant paused while he straightened the team out and headed for the diner as if he already knew where she lived. Most likely he did. It was a small town. "You do know how to wash clothes, don't you?"

Hannah would have given her first month's salary, all twenty dollars of it, to have a washboard and a few minutes of freedom with Grant's head at that moment. She glared at him, and he laughed in her face as he pulled the team to a halt.

He swung down and came around to help her. Hannah hurried to arrange her skirts and climb down before he got there. She didn't so much climb down off the buckboard as she fell. Grant caught her.

He steadied her feet under her and said with a smug grin, "Thanks for the help with dinner, ma'am." He deepened his Texas drawl and did his best, Hannah knew, to sound as dumb as a post. "Shore am glad we had a woman around for a change."

Hannah didn't have the energy to hit him. She stiffened her spine and became aware that Grant was still holding her up. He was so strong she could imagine leaning on him forever.

Just because she'd made a fool of herself didn't mean she wasn't right about Grant and his children. "You have to do something about the conditions those children live in."

Grant dropped his hands from her waist, far too slowly to Hannah's way of thinking. He kept up the dumb act. "So you're gonna let me keep 'em now? You just want me to keep 'em better. I reckon that's progress."

His comment surprised her because he was right. Somewhere in the middle of the girls mending her dress and making dinner in such a competent manner she *had* changed her mind. She had no intention of admitting that.

She also noticed Grant rubbing his hands on his pants leg again. Touching her must be repulsive. No doubt he'd wash his hands for an hour as soon as he got home. . .that was assuming the untidy man washed at all.

"Surely it doesn't cost that much to add on a couple of bedrooms." Hannah walked toward her boardinghouse wishing he would leave so she could go upstairs and be alone with her humiliation.

"It doesn't cost much, just more than I have," Grant said. "As I already told you, I could cut down the timber to build on, and it wouldn't cost me nothing but time and a few aching muscles, but the stand of trees fit for building is on a slope so steep I'd have to risk my neck to get at 'em. My children have a roof to keep the rain off their heads and plenty to eat. Well, 'cept for today. Today was kinda slim pickins, what with you burning most of it to a cinder. I never knew how tricky all this woma stuff could be. Guess that's cuz it all came so easy to me and it being easy to teach to all my many mistreated children."

Hannah whirled on him at his last dig. "I know I don't have wom skills! I accept that about myself."

Suddenly Grant's teasing smile faded, and he spoke so sof it was almost a whisper. "When are you going to tell me how those scars, Hannah?"

A dog barked, breaking the silence that lay like death between them. Grant's team shifted as they stood, and the hardware of the traces clinked together.

"That's none of your business, Grant. I'm never going to talk about it and you shouldn't have seen my. . .uh. . .shoulder uncovered."

Grant's eyes narrowed and Hannah prayed he'd let it go. He studied her, waiting, thinking, wondering. She saw his frustration. He wanted answers, but she wondered if maybe he also *didn't* want to know. If he'd been an orphan, he knew children had stories they didn't want to relive, either by speaking of their own experiences or listening to someone else's. She thought of all she'd suffered at Parrish's hands, and the words wanted to flood out. Her throat clogged shut with anger and pain and heartbreak. She understood all too well how Libby could choose to not talk. Sometimes the words were too awful to be spoken aloud.

"I know it's none of my business." Grant tugged off one glove and ran a finger over the seam Marilyn had sewn in Hannah's dress. "It's just that—"

"Go home, Grant." She could do it. She could be tough and resist the temptation he offered to lean on his broad shoulder. She needed him to go away. This day and the kindness of his children was all she ould handle. "Make sure you have your children in school tomorrow. If keep them home, I'm going to—" Her voice broke.

rprise flashed in his eyes, and she turned and marched toward door of the diner. He wasn't allowed up, thank heavens. Tears ind her eyes and she hurried all the more. Hard fingers arm before she got inside.

ack only because he made her. She stared at the second fighting back the unexpected tears and waiting in ckening pity.

hin until she lifted it and met his eyes. He said can teach school better'n you can cook."

Hannah's mouth gaped open on a gasp, and she made a fist that she would most likely have used on his smirking face if he hadn't headed back for the buckboard, laughing like a maniac every step of the way.

He drove off with a jaunty wave.

She watched him go and noticed he went to Zeb's livery instead of heading back up the steep trail. It took her a moment, but she realized she was standing in the alley behind the diner staring after the man. She whirled around and rushed inside. It was only as she climbed the stairs to her tiny, lonely room that she realized Grant had headed off a bout of tears by deliberately insulting her. It was by far the nicest thing he'd done so far.

And anyway, she desperately hoped she *could* teach school better than she cooked because she'd never done it before, either.

"Is the gap melting down at all?" Grace thought her throat might shut up completely.

"Nope, sky-high and no getting out of it. It's been too cold for a thaw."

Grace stepped away from Daniel as if he were aiming a gun at her. She didn't rest her hand on the baby in her belly because Daniel tended to run screaming when she made any reference or gesture that reminded him of the young one.

"So, how about the pass?" Grace twisted her hands together as if she were wringing a wet dishcloth. Or Daniel's neck.

"The high pass, Ma?" Mark looked up from the fireplace. He and his brothers were thawing out after they'd ridden out to inspect the cattle. They'd be warm and back outside in a matter of minutes. Grace had a strange urge to beg them to stay inside and talk to her. She felt so alone, trapped, strangled, desperate.

Okay, calm down!

She pulled a long breath into her lungs. "Well, what would you boys like for dinner? I've got a mind to make a cake."

The boys cheered and beamed at her. She had their undivided attention.

"We're well stocked with honey and flour and eggs."

She thought of the high pass. In fact, she thought she heard a voice whispering to her through the tall pines that lined the canyon. Calling her to come up, come over, go see Tillie or Sophie.

Go see Hannah.

That letter had been driving her close to mad, knowing Hannah was so near. She'd calculated that it would be a three-day train ride only. Simple.

She shook her head before she raced outside to follow that voice.

"Maybe one or two of you boys would like to stay in with me and help me mix the batter."

A chorus of groans almost deafened her.

"You stay and help her. You're a baby!" Mark shoved Matthew straight toward the fire. Matthew lurched to the side and toppled into Abe, who slugged him. Matt did a sideways dive that would have made a circus acrobat proud then fell over backward into Mark, who screamed as if he'd had an arm severed.

The whispering outside grew louder. Grace smiled. She felt almost insanely calm as she decided it was wrong of her to be the only one in control of herself in this family. Why, it was almost a sin. If she really loved her boys and Daniel, she'd be out of control, too. It was the right thing to do.

Her smile fixed firmly. "I need some fresh air."

Grace snagged her coat and boots as she dashed outside. No one noticed her leave, being involved in a riot as they were. A foot, or maybe a body, slammed into the door just as she swung it shut.

She slipped on the boots then pulled on her coat as she started walking toward the high-up hill. She didn't bother catching up a horse.

It was only a mile or so.

Then she got to the part that was mostly straight up, with icy ledges and treacherous toe holds buried in snow. She should probably wait for a thaw, but that thought didn't even slow her down. She reached the first clump of trees and began singing as if the trees were a chorus of angels and she was lead soprano.

Daniel didn't catch her until she was up and over and within a mile of Adam and Tillie's house. He grabbed her arm. "What in the world are you doing, woman?"

Grace's ears had quit playing with her mind—or was her mind playing with her ears—as soon as she'd topped the high pass. She turned and smiled at her husband, not wanting to punch him at all. "I believe I mentioned that I'd like to get out and see Sophie once or twice this winter. Being snowed in is a bit—" Grace quit talking before she told him the truth. That it was possible she was losing her sanity. That it was possible she'd start screaming or maybe beating on him while he slept. She rubbed the back of her neck while she stood there facing her husband.

He pulled his hat off his head. The wind whipped through his overlong blond hair, and Grace tried to remember the last time she'd made him sit for a haircut. She'd thought of it a few times, but her hand had gotten a bit shaky at the thought of standing behind Daniel's back with a sharp object. She brushed her hand over his hair.

"Grace, I've got chores."

"I'm over the treacherous part, Daniel. You should have just gone on back to your chores and not worried about me."

Grace saw Abe, a mile or so behind them, dropping down the cliff with reckless speed. She didn't even cringe when she saw Matt strapped on Abe's back. They'd be fine.

"No, it's a long walk to Adam's. There're dangerous animals out here, Grace. What kind of husband would I be if I didn't protect my family?"

With a loud snap, a branch Abe was using for support broke. Her oldest son fell forward and slid on his belly the rest of the way down the cliff. Matt screamed and laughed and slid for about a hundred feet as if he was on a sled and Abe had fallen specially, just to make the trip fun.

Daniel glanced backward but didn't react. Fine job he was doing protecting any of them.

"Uh, Daniel, the whole bunch of us Reeves seem to have a knack for survival. I think I'll be okay."

"The boys are sturdy enough, but wives are puny, sickly things, and I think I'd better stay close."

Mark topped the canyon wall.

Grace felt her lower lip begin to tremble. "So, are all the boys coming?"

Daniel settled his Stetson more firmly on his head. "Once we figured out you'd cleared the canyon rim, I sent 'em back to do the chores and told 'em to come on along once they were ready."

Abe picked himself up, and Matthew shrieked and kicked his brother's sides and yelled, "Giddup!"

John's head popped up atop the rocks.

"Let's go then." She turned and strode toward Adam's, planning to make a better headstart for herself next time. Maybe if she snuck out in the night—

"You know there are mountain lions in these parts. It shore were a stupid idea for you to set out on your own." Daniel fell into step beside her and rested an arm along her shoulders.

Grace nodded. "Not the first stupid thing I've done." She gave him a significant look, but he smiled and didn't seem to get the hint that *he* might qualify.

"Reckon that's true enough." He pursed his lips and pulled her a bit closer. "And reckon it won't be the last."

Grace picked up the pace, but the boys still caught them before she was even close to Tillie. Somehow she didn't mind. Now that she was going visiting, she liked having her family along.

When Adam's neat cabin came into sight, Adam was outside tending his livestock and he straightened and waved. He was too far away from them for Grace to see his face, but she could imagine his pleasure at having company.

Adam, a black man who was good friends to the Reeves and a right hand man to the McClellens before he started his own ranch, waved again, then walked briskly toward the house, telling Tillie the good news no doubt. By the time Adam vanished inside, the boys had whooped at the sight of their friend and started racing toward the house.

Grace made only the barest notice of Adam stepping outside and shuttering the windows. He'd barely closed one when Mark sent a branch he'd been using as a walking stick straight at Ike's head. It missed Ike and slammed up against the shutter.

Adam finished securing the shutters and turned to face them. "Well, hello there, neighbors. Didn't figure to see you again until spring."

Tillie came outside, and Grace saw that Tillie's stomach got out the door well ahead of her.

"You're expecting a baby?" Grace gasped and ran toward Tillie.

Bright white teeth flashed in Tillie's dark-skinned face as she laid one hand on her belly. "Yes, I am. We haven't been to town in a spell, and of course Adam never thinks to mention it, so the word is just now getting out."

"I'm so glad to s—see you." Her voice broke and she launched herself into Tillie's arms.

Tillie hugged Grace closer. Tillie was enough older than Grace that Grace almost felt mothered. Tillie turned, Grace still in her arms, and walked with her toward the cabin. "I'll make us a nice cup of tea."

Abe opened the cabin door.

"Hey!"

Adam's voice startled Grace. She noticed the boys stopped in their tracks to look at him.

Once he had the boys' attention, he said, "Uh. . .sorry, didn't mean to yell. Uh. . .I was just thinking, I could saddle you boys each a horse, and we could ride out to look at my herd. We could let the women have an hour or so of hen talk."

Grace thought Adam seemed on edge, but she could imagine why. The boys whooped and charged toward the barn.

Tillie dragged Grace inside and shut the door quick. She settled Grace at the table then reached up to a padlocked cupboard and opened it to pull out a heavy pottery coffee cup.

"Why do you keep it locked? No one would steal glassware."

Tillie bustled about filling the kettle with tea. "Uh. . .*Adam* has on occasion been known to break a bit of glass. Clumsy men, you know."

"Oh my, do I ever know."

Tillie came and sat down straight across from Grace. "So, tell me what brings you here."

Grace felt like wings sprung straight out of her heart. These were the exact words she wanted to hear from some woman, any woman. Maybe she wouldn't have to go all the way to Hannah's after all. Not on *this* visit.

TWELVE

Horace sneaked out of Prudence's house before first light. He didn't like getting up early, he didn't like hard labor, and he didn't like Prudence being a stand-up citizen while he went slinking around in the dark alleys like a rat. He was sick of it all. This plan needed to work, and soon.

He slipped out of town on foot. He'd left his horse nearly two miles away. Horace chained it overnight in a stand of scrub pines. The horse didn't like it, but the nag had all day to graze.

After the long trudge in the cold, Horace rode the rest of the way to the oil seep. The closer he got, the worse the stink. He had to fill another couple of barrels today if he wanted to keep up the rent on Prudence's store, but he couldn't stand it so early in the morning.

He got to his work site, tucked into a canyon behind the Rocking C—this whole area was Grant's property. Knowing he should go straight to work, instead he veered his horse toward the rocky game trail that led to the top of the bluff surrounding the reeking, oily waters of the spring. The sun was up enough to look down on the world.

He reached the top and saw, a mile away, the shack full of children ruining his plans. He saw Grant emerge from the hovel and head for the barn. Two of his boys tagged him, a familiar little boy that looked barely school age and a new one, a skinny blond Horace had never seen before.

Where was the bigger boy? Horace sneered at a man taking in one of *that* kind. Grant was trash and his whole family was trash.

The black-skinned boy, more man than child, was always along with Grant. Working as if he'd never been freed from slavery. Of course Grant worked like that, too. Fools, when there was a living to be had on other men's sweat. Horace could only feel contempt for the mess of a family.

Horace climbed down off his horse, chained the beast up good and tight, and walked to a better spot where a steep, rugged trail led down the bluff on the Rocking C side. Horace had never gone down. No sense leaving a track for anyone in that family to find. The whole bunch of them ran wild in these hills, but the smell of this area and the rancid water kept them and their herd away from this black spring.

As he neared the overlook, Horace heard rustling just over the rim. He ducked behind a boulder. Deer most likely, but no sense being caught by surprise.

The black boy topped the trail. Prudence had found out about the family. This one's name was Joshua. The boy crawled up the last sheer stretch using finger and toe holds.

Horace watched and knew the instant Joshua'd seen the horse. The boy scrambled to the top and took a step forward. Horace's hand closed over the butt of his revolver. The boy walked toward the nag. He'd go straight past Horace.

Joshua stepped alongside Horace's hiding place. Horace lunged and smashed the gun over the boy's head. The dull thud was satisfying. The boy staggered backward. A trail of blood gushed down the side of his face, the red vivid against Joshua's dark skin. His dazed eyes fixed on Horace and focused.

The boy had seen his face. Glad for an excuse to dispense more pain, Horace realized he couldn't let a witness go.

Horace lunged to grab Joshua, but his fingers slipped on the slick, blood-soaked shirt. Instead of catching hold, Horace shoved him backward, and the boy reeled over the edge of the cliff.

Horace dashed to the drop-off and watched the body tumble and bounce. It slid nearly a hundred feet then landed in a thicket of mesquite. Horace didn't like the way the boy had landed—flat on his back and with that thicket breaking his fall. The impact wasn't hard.

With a long look at the climb, Horace dismissed going down. He took careful aim with his revolver. It was a long shot, and Horace wasn't the best marksman. He liked living by his wits, not his gun. Besides, he didn't want to shoot. A gunshot would draw attention. And a bullet hole in the trash at the bottom of this cliff would be proof positive this wasn't an accident.

In the growing sunlight, Horace eased off the trigger and watched the still form. Blood coated the boy's face and shirt. Seconds ticked past, then minutes with no movement, not even the rise and fall of the boy's chest. Finally, with a satisfied grunt, Horace decided the job was done better if there was no gunshot, no bullet to explain.

A boy, playing, taking a fall. No reason anyone would question things. If there was any blame it would land on Grant. Any father worth his salt would make sure his young'uns stayed well away from this area.

"What were you doing up here anyway, kid?" Horace asked the motionless young man.

Horace'd best not be in the vicinity if they came hunting the boy. He had most of a load of barrels. He'd planned to finish filling the wagon before he took them in, but now it seemed like a good day for a ride to LaMont.

A movement caught his eye. Horace looked overhead and smiled. A vulture.

Watching the flesh-eating animal circle high above, Horace laughed. "Well, there's proof."

Horace made his way down the steep trail, gloating at getting rid of the first of those worthless ophans. Glad for an excuse to quit working and get away from the stinking springs, he untied his horse, hitching it to the buckboard and headed for LaMont.

He carefully wiped out his faint tracks on the rocky ground as he left. He'd earned a break with this day's work.

"Where's Joshua?" Grant went into the cabin for breakfast. "I sent him to scout for that stubborn roan longhorn. The one who thinks she's a mountain goat. She's probably wandered off to have her calf."

Marilyn shrugged as she stirred the oatmeal. "He must be late, Pa."

Sadie, picking up a stack of bowls, paused. A furrow cut between her brows. "He wasn't going far. He should have been back."

Grant nodded and realized he had an itch between his shoulder blades that made him feel like someone had a rifle trained on his back. "I'll ride out and check. I've got the wagon hitched. Marilyn, can you and Sadie drive yourselves to school?"

"Sure, Pa." Marilyn looked up from her steaming pot. "But don't you want us to help hunt?"

"No, he probably just found that stubborn old cow and he can't get her in. I'll meet him coming home, trying to drive her. I'll let him ride the buckskin into school. He'll probably catch you before you get to town."

"No, I don't think so, Pa." Sadie set the stack of bowls down with a hard crack. "Joshua isn't one to be late. You know him better'n that."

Grant knew a person could get held up working cattle, but Joshua was a boy. . .man. . .who was always ahead of time. It wasn't something Grant had taught; it was just part of the boy's character. A niggle of worry grew to about ten times its size. Grant's calm snapped.

"Set the breakfast aside, Marilyn." Grant raised his voice. "Kids, I need help."

Charlie poked his head out of the loft above. Benny came running in from the back bedroom. Libby limped into the kitchen. Grant couldn't leave her and he couldn't let her hike. He plucked the child up and wrapped her coat around her.

"You'll ride with me." He looked at the other children. "We're gonna hunt down Joshua. If we find him along the trail with no trouble, we can all enjoy pestering him for being late. If there's trouble, I might need extra hands."

Marilyn shoved the pan of oatmeal off the heat and efficiently stripped off her apron. All of the children scrambled into their outer things with Marilyn helping.

Sadie strode toward the door, pulling on her coat. "I'll start saddling the horses."

"Libby and I'll head out now in the buckboard. Benny, you ride along with us." Grant followed Sadie out the door, fear goading him to hurry. Sadie was right. Joshua wouldn't be late.

There was trouble.

Standing in the entrance to the little schoolhouse, Hannah hesitated. This mess in Sour Springs had sidetracked her from her plan to move to Mosqueros and search for Grace.

When Chicago had gotten too cold and miserable for Hannah to bear, she and Libby had begun their odyssey to save her sister. First stowing away on a train headed to Omaha, they'd found themselves on a car carrying orphans. Hannah realized that rather than hide for the whole trip they could move around the car, pretending to the conductor that they were with the orphan train and pretending to the orphans that they were passengers. They'd mixed with the huge unruly crowd of children, even so far as sharing their food. The first stop to meet prospective parents was in Omaha. Then, because the train was going on west and Grace was south of them, they slipped away.

There was no opportunity in Omaha to hitch a train ride south.

The security was too tight, especially because nothing like that orphan train came through again. Hannah and Libby lived in cold alleys and tried to earn enough for two tickets.

Libby had stood on street corners wearing a sign asking for money. Hannah had carried groceries and washed clothes. She'd swept sidewalks and washed windows. None of the jobs lasted. None of her bosses were interested in Hannah's problems, and she learned to keep them to herself. Hannah was none too clean, and she knew there was a desperate gleam in her eyes that she couldn't quite suppress. . .and that didn't inspire many to give her a chance.

Hannah and Libby wore rags and starved themselves trying to scrape together cash enough for tickets. They lived in alleys and sheds rather than spend their precious earnings on themselves. It had taken them a year.

Finally they got to Kansas City. The money was harder to come by, and it took them a long time to raise a few pennies. Despairing of paying their way, with luck and a ridiculous amount of risk and with a determined sheriff on their trail, Hannah and Libby snuck onto a train and made it to St. Louis. It was a step in the wrong direction, but they'd needed to get out of Kansas City.

In St. Louis, after working and struggling until it looked as if they'd never afford the next step of their journey, they ran into another trainload of orphans, this group headed for Texas—a giant step toward Grace. They fell in with them, and it went well until Martha identified Libby as being an orphan. She'd pulled Libby in with the group. Hannah had stood by and let her because Martha was feeding the other children, and for the first time in years, Libby ate well.

No one would adopt Libby, of course, not with her limp and her unnatural silence. She had planned for Libby to slip away from the train in a bigger town, much as she'd done in Omaha on the first leg of their arduous journey to find Grace. From there, they'd plan the final journey to Mosqueros.

Then Grant had done the unthinkable and adopted a little girl who wasn't perfect. They'd made it this far, after all these years, and there was no way to get Libby away from Grant and head on toward west Texas.

And now Hannah had a school to teach. She took one step into the school and almost turned around and ran. She'd been teaching children all of her life, but she didn't have the slightest idea how a school worked since she'd never been in one.

Before she completely lost her nerve, she hustled to the front of the room. She started the stove going first, pleased to see that the school was supplied with plenty of wood. When the fire was crackling cheerfully, she found a stack of books on the teacher's desk.

From her own satchel, she produced careful notes she'd made for her Easter pageant. It was the dearest dream of her heart to watch the children singing and acting out the parts of the Resurrection story. She'd heard a new name for such a pageant, a passion play, and she'd always wanted to be part of telling the story of Jesus' victory over death. These notes and papers, which she'd written so carefully for children, had stayed with her as she'd traveled across the country.

She laid the papers aside and studied the room. There were fourteen desks in two neat rows of seven, with a center aisle between them. Each desk held two children, although three students could be squeezed in a two-person desk if the students were small.

If Mabel's estimate was correct, this room was going to overflow. Hannah spent the next hour looking through each book, knowing she'd have to find out where all of the students were in their studies before she could set their lessons.

She had the school warm and her confidence fully in place an hour before the first child came in the door.

She said a prayer that Grant would let his children attend school. If they didn't show up, she'd go after them. There was no reason good enough to excuse them from being here.

THIRTEEN

"Josh!" Grant yelled over the roaring in his ears. He dragged the team to a halt, locked on the brake, leapt off the high buckboard seat, and ran.

His son.

Joshua had been with the first children Grant had adopted.

Now here he lay, coated in blood. Broken. Dead.

"Josh, can you hear me?" Grant skidded to his knees beside the boy. Pressing his ear against the boy's chest, Grant prayed. Nothing, no heartbeat.

Grant tore Joshua's coat and shirt open. The acrid smell of blood sent Grant's stomach churning.

Benny dropped to the ground on the opposite side of Joshua's inert body. He reached to help Libby down to her knees.

Grant listened to Joshua's chest and finally caught a faint noise. "He's alive." Grant looked up. "Josh is alive! His heart's still beating." Grant looked at the steep bluff looming overhead and knew the boy must have fallen. He'd been trailing that agile, wild cow, or possibly looking for a high spot to study the terrain. Most likely the latter. The boy loved to climb.

Grant jerked off his gloves and tucked them under his belt, threw off his coat, tore at the buttons on his shirt, and then dragged it off. He ripped the shirt in half and pressed the worn fabric gently against Joshua's bleeding head.

The cold bit into Grant through his tattered union suit and he shuddered. But it wasn't from cold. So much blood. Grant's makeshift bandage was soon soaked.

"What'll we do, Pa?"

"Can you run back for the girls? We need— No, wait." Grant looked straight at Benny. For the first time ever, Grant was scared to send one of his children off on his own. Something had happened out here. Something bad. No way did his nimble son fall off a cliff. A bird had a better chance of forgetting how to fly.

"What, Pa? I can help."

Think. Think. Think. Grant's heart pounded. He couldn't catch his breath, driven by fear he needed to control now of all times.

He inspected Joshua's battered body. His head and neck were scraped badly, his clothing cut to ribbons. The gash on Joshua's forehead bled crimson against his son's coffee-dark skin. It looked like Josh'd been struck over the head. Joshua's left arm hung at an odd angle. The boy's heartbeat was weak but steady.

"I know you can help. There's just no point telling the girls to go for bandages. We'll have to get Joshua back to the house." Grant nodded at the rags of his shirt. "Can you hold this bandage?"

Benny reached his small hands in and held the cloth.

"Something else you can both do." Grant staggered to his feet.

Benny and Libby looked up.

"Pray. Joshua needs all our prayers."

Libby clutched her hands together and closed her eyes. Her lips moved silently.

Stomach twisting with dread, Grant eased the broken arm across the boy's chest. Binding it with remnants of his shirt, Grant jostled his son as little as possible.

Once the task was done, he dared to breathe again. "Okay, Benny, Lib, I'm going to lift him into the wagon box. I need you to step back." Grant took over with the bandage.

Benny put his hand on Libby's shoulder and the two of them rose to their feet and stepped away.

Grant bent down. His son was reed thin but muscular from long hours of hard work on the ranch. And he was as tall as a grown man. Grant said a prayer for strength, then slid his arms under Joshua's shoulders and knees and lifted the boy, grunting with the effort. Doing his best not to disturb the arm, it took every ounce of Grant's strength to lift him. Grant eased his son onto the wagon bed.

He turned to the young'uns. "Benny, Libby, hop in. I'm going to start for home. You watch Joshua."

Benny boosted Libby up over the side of the wagon. Grant stepped over and hoisted the little girl the last few inches while Benny practically took flight over the edge of the box.

Grant fastened the tailgate, the hinges creaking as he lifted the flat slab of wood, the metal sounding rusty as he shoved the five-inch-long pins into the iron hooks that held the gate closed. He'd left Joshua close to the back end, to avoid moving him one inch more than necessary.

Grant vaulted to the wagon seat and gave a tiny shake to the long leather reins, holding the horses to a slow start. They headed toward the Rocking C. The horses had caught Grant's terror and tried to speed up. Pulling them to a walk, Grant feared every jounce might shake something inside of Josh and kill him. Grant glanced over his shoulder every few steps.

They met the girls riding toward them. Charlie peeked out from behind Sadie.

"We found him." Grant jerked his head toward the wagon. "He's been hurt."

Both girls gasped. Charlie scowled. They rode up beside the wagon. "Is he alive?" Marilyn asked sharply.

Sadie cried out, covered her mouth with one hand, and began to weep softly.

"He's alive." Grant kept driving and praying. "Marilyn, ride to town for Doc Morgan. Tell him to bring his plaster. Josh's arm looks broken. And get Will and Ian. I may need some help."

Marilyn whirled the horse in a tight circle, slapped her reins against the animal's hindquarters, and tore off, bent low over the roan's shoulders.

As she dashed off, it struck Grant again that he shouldn't let her go off alone. There was danger out here. But the thought came too late. Marilyn was out of sight and out of earshot.

Sadie rode close, her eyes riveted on Joshua, but Grant had other ideas for her. "Head for the cabin and get some water hot and tear up a sheet. We'll need to sterilize his wounds, and the quicker the better. The doc will need to sew him up and put a cast on his arm."

The look of stubbornness on Sadie's face surprised Grant. She'd been with him as long as Joshua, and she'd always been the first to lend a hand. Before Grant could repeat his order, Sadie looked away from Joshua. Grant caught sight of the tears streaming down the girl's face. She yelled to her horse and went for the cabin at a full gallop, with Charlie holding on for dear life.

The wagon took the rest of them slowly home.

As they finally arrived, Marilyn was just riding up with the doctor.

Grant pulled up as close as he could get to the front door. Grant saw Ian coming fast up the trail. Other horses came behind him.

"Benny, get up here and hold the reins." Grant put on the brake then jumped to the ground.

Benny scrambled over the front of the wagon box to the high seat.

Grant came around to the back just as the doctor swung down off his horse. Grant opened the tailgate.

Ian pulled his horse to a stop.

Will rode up and dismounted. Will was another of those first six children. Joshua was his brother in every way that counted. "What's happened?" Will's gaze was riveted to Josh's still form.

"Thanks for coming." Grant couldn't think clearly enough to answer Will.

"Let me look at him before we move him." The doctor edged in between them.

Grant realized he'd blocked the man away from Josh.

The doctor leaned close.

Ian joined them. Grant's heart eased just knowing his family was gathering to lend a hand. He had a lot of trouble with the folks in Sour Springs, but not everyone was unkind. In fact, most of them were generous, decent people. But a few could make a lot of noise.

Another horse drew near, ridden by Parson Babbitt.

The sudden tightening of Grant's throat caught him by surprise. He hadn't cried since he was five years old, but these men coming to help meant a lot.

The parson came to look over the side of the wagon, and Grant saw his lips moving. As soon as he assessed the situation, Parson Babbitt gave Grant a serious nod of his head then went around the wagon to stand with the children. He picked Libby up, rested a hand on Benny's shoulder, and spoke quietly to the youngsters.

"The shoulder's dislocated, not broken." Doc Morgan stepped closer and leaned over Josh, touching the gash, checking his heartbeat and breathing, running his hands over his legs. A firm push on Josh's ribs forced a moan out of the boy.

Grant's heart raced. It was the first sound out of his son.

"There could be internal things but, barring that, it looks like he's going to be okay once we patch him up." Dr. Morgan looked over his shoulder at Ian, whose arms were thick from working his anvil. "I can use your strength here. I'll show you what to do. We'll put this shoulder back in place before we move him. I'll bind it up good and it'll heal fast. Then I want him inside for the stitches."

"Kids, make sure the kitchen table is clear." Grant looked up.

"I already checked, Pa. It's good." Marilyn stood with her arms crossed, watching the doctor with wide eyes.

Grant noticed Charlie's usually furrowed forehead was smooth. A look of wonder had settled on his face as he watched the family hover around Joshua. Grant suspected the boy had never seen so many people worried about an orphan.

Ian followed the doctor's orders and grasped Josh's hand. Grant saw the sheen of sweat break out on Ian's forehead, not from effort but from worry. Resetting a joint was going to hurt Josh bad. But it had to be done.

The doctor explained what he expected. With a hard pull from Ian, a cry wrung out of Josh and the joint snapped audibly into place.

Grant's knees sagged, and Will was there with an arm to support him. Grant ran both hands into his hair, slick with cold sweat. He knocked his hat off his head. "I was fine handling Josh until someone took over."

Will nodded. "Tell me what happened."

"Not now," the doctor interrupted as he rested Josh's limp arm on his chest and then moved aside. "We need to get him in and I don't want him bumped around. I suspect he's got broken ribs, and there are other things inside that could be busted up. He might have broken his neck while he was at it. Ian, you pick him up. Be real smooth about it."

The doctor jabbed a finger at Will. "When Ian gets him up, come over to the other side and steady him. Grant, help ease his feet off the wagon when Ian lifts him away. Hold them straight all the way stretched out until we get him laid down inside."

With Ian's strength and Will on hand, they moved Josh inside easily. Ian stretched the boy flat on the table. Everyone moved inside. All but the doctor stepped to the far side of the room, which wasn't all that far.

Parson Babbitt just poked his head in the door. "You youngsters come on with me to the barn. They haven't got room to move in here."

Grant saw mutiny on his children's faces, but they did as the parson asked. Libby, Benny, Charlie, and even Marilyn minded the man of God.

Sadie gave Grant a beseeching look. "I want to stay, Pa."

The doctor looked up. "I might need a hand."

Grant nodded and settled in to endless, silent prayer for God to hold Joshua in this side of heaven.

Minutes stretched as the doctor bound Josh's ribs, moving him as little as possible, then put a sling on his arm. When that was done, he cleaned Josh's cuts, taking pains to make sure there wasn't a speck of dirt left in the head wound. Half the morning was gone before he straightened. "All right, Sadie, I could use a nurse here if you're willing."

Sadie stepped up. The doctor began issuing orders. Sadie pulled threads, ointments, and bandages out of the doctor's bag, whatever he asked for.

The doc was just clipping the last thread when Joshua's eyes flickered open.

Sadie inhaled sharply and leaned down. "Josh, you're awake."

Grant was struck with another unlikely burn of tears. He rubbed the heels of his hands across his eyes to ensure no embarrassment. When he finished, he noticed Will doing the same thing.

Doc leaned down over Joshua and lifted one of the boy's eyelids. "Can you hear me, Josh?"

Josh nodded once then gasped. A moan escaped his lips, but even that was cut off quickly as if even using his vocal cords hurt.

"Lay still. You took quite a tumble. I've got you patched up, but you're going to have to give yourself time to recover."

Josh didn't so much as nod his agreement.

"I'm going to give you some laudanum for the pain. Not much, just enough so your pa and brothers can get you moved to your bed. Then you'll have a long sleep. You're going to feel puny for the next few days, but you'll heal."

Sadie handed the doctor a brown bottle and a spoon.

The doctor administered the laudanum, and Josh shuddered from the taste, winced, and then slowly let his eyelids fall shut.

Doc straightened and turned to Grant. "Be as easy as you can with him. Let's get him to bed."

"Can I talk to him for just one second, Doc?" Grant moved up beside Josh.

Doc nodded and stepped back. "Make it quick. That drug will kick in, and he won't be making any sense for a while."

Grant bent over the table. "Don't try to talk, son. Don't nod your head or so much as budge. Just blink your eyes, once for yes and twice for no. Do you understand?"

Josh's eyes blinked once.

"I know you didn't fall of that bluff, Josh. Did someone push you?"

Sadie gasped.

Will stepped closer behind Grant.

Ian asked from behind them, "You think he was pushed?"

Josh opened his eyes.

Grant saw the hesitation. "Do you know?"

Josh blinked his eyes twice very deliberately. Then the dark brown pupils dilated.

"No. Okay." Grant leaned closer. "Did you hear anything? I'm going up there to scout around, but do you remember—" Grant stopped, frustrated by the inability to really talk to the boy. "Do you—"

Very slowly Josh's lids slid closed.

"Josh, wait. I need to know. . ."

"No more, Grant." Doc's hand settled on Grant's shoulder. "He's asleep. Even if you could get him to blink, you couldn't be sure he'd know what he was doing. The drug can make you mighty confused. Pretty common after a knock on the head to forget what happened just before the blow, so he probably wouldn't answer you anyway. After he gets some rest, you can question him again."

Grant straightened and looked in Sadie's eyes.

He was surprised by the flowing tears. . .and the fury. She asked, "You think someone deliberately pushed Josh?"

Will moved closer to Josh. All the protective instincts of a big brother shone in his eyes. Looking between his two children, Grant said, "Josh is like an antelope on those hills, surefooted and careful. He didn't just fall off that mountain."

"I'll go with you to do your scouting." Will jerked his chin. Ready to fight for his brother, just like he'd been fighting for him ten years ago when they'd been living on the street. Will had realized the peril two black children were in on Houston's streets, and he'd been ready to fight and die then for Josh and Sadie. When Grant had taken them to a diner to feed them, Will was the one who wouldn't let his little brother and sister go in. Will was the one who stood his ground and made Grant understand the consequences.

"Me, too." Ian hadn't lived with them long. He was nearly a man grown when Grant took him in. But his wife, Megan, had been part of the family for five years before Ian had swept her off her feet. Ian was one of them.

The three of them exchanged a long look. Then Grant turned back to the doctor. "I don't think we should mention this in town. I'll have a talk with the sheriff, but if whoever was up there lives in Sour Springs, we don't want him to know we're onto him."

"You're jumping to conclusions, Grant." The doctor busied himself rolling down his sleeves. "Anyone can take a fall. Rocks slide unexpectedly, the dirt crumbles on a trail."

"Maybe it happened that way, Doc. But I know my boy. I'm going to go have a look. Would you mind not talking about my suspicions in town?"

"I'll keep my mouth shut. Nothing to tell anyway, as far as I can see." The doctor slipped his arms into his black suit coat then added a heavy sheepskin on top of that. "I'll be back in the afternoon to check on Josh. If you need me before that, send someone running. Everyone in town's going to know he's hurt. I'll just let it out that he took a fall."

When the doctor said everyone, for some reason Grant thought of

Hannah. He wondered what that little snip would think about this. He'd promised to have his children in school and he'd failed. Now Josh was hurt, and she'd probably find a way to blame Grant for that. She'd be riding out here, scolding and insulting him before the end of the day. She'd probably try to take Josh and the rest of the children home with her.

A twinge of regret that she was always going to find him wanting as a father twisted his heart. He *was* wanting as a father. He did his best, but it was true he didn't have enough room for them. He knew they all worked hard, maybe too hard. Their clothes were torn and patched as often as not. He knew all of that. But he'd never gone to beating up on himself for it. He was better than nothing, which is what these children had before.

At least he'd never gone to beating up on himself till Hannah. He wished she were here to worry alongside him.

Grant's eyes widened and he straightened his spine. He did *not* wish she were here. He wanted the woman to stay as far away from him and his young'uns as possible.

Grant shook his head to clear it of notions that he didn't have time for. It didn't matter what the woman did or said. He managed as best he could. Grant knew that for the honest truth. And no amount of nagging could change that, whatever his shortcomings as a father.

And Grant prided himself on being an honest man.

He was a shameful, lowdown, lying polecat. None of Grant's family had come. He'd promised they would.

Hannah looked at her mostly empty room. She'd expected thirty or more children here today. There must be others missing, too. "Children, take your seats, please." Hannah stepped to the front of the room.

Five children, most fairly young, looked up with wide eyes.

Hannah honestly didn't know quite what to do about her absentees.

"I thought there would be more students here today. Was I mistaken?"

One little girl with two dark braids hanging down nearly to her lap shook her head. "Lots of kids didn't get here cuz of the trouble."

Hannah gasped. "Trouble? What happened?"

Another young boy, this one buck-toothed with serious eyes, said, "Someone came riding in for the doctor. They both tore out of town so fast no one had a chance to ask her what happened. Ian from the blacksmith shop tore out next in the opposite direction. Then he come back through town with Will, Ian's brother. So we knew it meant trouble. Will would'a brought his family to school. But Will lives a ways out so, without him, his kids couldn't come."

Another child chimed in. "And the doctor's got four in his family, but his wife keeps them to home when there's a ruckus. My ma says Mrs. Doc gets notional and we all just have'ta let her do what she wants."

"And the blacksmith's wife is getting on with a baby," the dark-haired girl added. "So like as not she won't try and get Gordy to school on her own."

The children added new names, all kept home because of the trouble. Several said their fathers had headed out of town after the doctor.

"Why would everyone follow after the doctor? Surely he doesn't need that much help."

"Can't never have too much help, Miss Cartwright," the dark-haired girl said.

The serious boy said, " 'Sides, they're mostly all family. I mean not all, but those that ain't connected still might want'a ride out and see what's what. So it's not likely they'll send their kids if they're busy waiting on news."

Hannah kept the scowl off her face by pure will power. "School should be a priority." First the town had no school. Then it hired her with no care. Now they didn't send their children. She started working up a nice head of indignation.

"Well, they've all made a mistake. This town needs to realize that education is important. Where did the doctor go? Who exactly is it that's more important than school? I intend to tell them that they've got their values all wrong. They need to change their ways and make sure that nothing short of God comes between children and schooling, and that's that!" Hannah's voice rose as she worked her fury up to a full boil. "Where did the doctor go? Who exactly is it that's more important than school?"

"One o' them orphans from out to the Rocking C."

"Class dismissed!" Hannah slapped her hand flat on her desk.

The children erupted from their desks, gleefully screaming in delight.

Hannah barely noticed, her heart thumped until it pounded in her ears. She hurried after them. What had happened? "Libby!" Hannah broke into a run. What if Grant had finally realized fully what it meant that Libby couldn't talk or do heavy work? What if he'd done something to her? Maybe Grant had gone too far with a thrashing.

Hannah dashed toward the livery. She needed to save her little sister and all of those other poor children!

FOURTEEN

Grant, Will, and Ian left the cabin and found half the town standing outside waiting for news. Someone had set up a makeshift table, and ladies had brought food and were serving the children breakfast. Several men came forward to see if Grant needed any help. Grant noticed a new pile of food, clothing, and supplies in the back of his wagon.

Harold Stroben from the mercantile lumbered over. "What happened?"

"The boy had a fall. He's badly battered, but the doc says he's going to be all right. Thanks for checking, Harold."

Grant waited until the first flurry of questions and concern had passed, not wanting to raise suspicions. Impatience beat against his chest, but he waited until everyone seemed satisfied.

"I need to ride out to where he fell." He pulled his gloves on with hard, jerky motions. He only held his temper through years of practice.

As he, Will, and Ian walked to the barn, Will said, "Joshua didn't trip and fall off that north bluff."

Ian snorted. "Not possible. My little brother could scale a greased rainbow."

Grant took a second to note Ian's bright red hair and the freckles so thick on his face it was hard to tell where one stopped and another started. Ian and Josh, brothers? Only at the Rocking C. But this *was* the

Rocking C and they *were* brothers, as close as blood. Grant would have smiled if he had one ounce of humor left in his body. "I'm gonna scout the trail up that hill."

Will untied his chestnut gelding from a mesquite bush. Ian swung up on the back of his paint mare. They met Grant as he emerged from the barn on his roan.

Grant looked over his shoulder to see two more of his sons riding up. Several folks were heading back for town. Sour Springs had a lot of good people, Grant decided. A few bad apples had forced him to stay isolated. With the Brewsters gone—they'd been the source of so much trouble—maybe he needed to give the whole town another chance. Including the school.

Will set out at a gallop for the bluff, Ian hard on his heels. Grant fell in behind and he heard more hoofbeats following. His family. He'd created it out of his desperate loneliness. But created it he had. He'd done a good job.

He never had to be alone again.

"Just wait until I get that man alone!"

Trying to dismount, Hannah swung her leg over the horse's rump. She'd been pleasantly surprised at the amiable nature of the horse she'd gotten from Zeb Morris. A far nicer mount than Sunday's. Zeb had acted nervous when she'd come in. He'd apologized for her trouble with Rufus and given her the use of the horse for no cost. He'd also boosted her on.

No one was handy to help her down. Her boot heel hung up on the back of the saddle and she shrieked as she toppled backward and landed with a dull thud in the dirt. She blinked her eyes and looked up at people rushing to her side.

"Are you all right, miss?" A man carrying a doctor's bag crouched by her side as if ready to examine her.

She gave her head a brisk shake to clear it and sat up. Everything seemed to work. "I think I am."

Several smothered giggles drew her attention to Charlie, Benny, and Libby. Libby laughed behind her hand. And her little sister was also, obviously, not hurt. The panic cooled inside of Hannah, and her cheeks heated up with a flush of embarrassment.

If Libby was safe, then what had happened out here that needed the doctor? There were a lot of children Grant could have been too harsh with. Hannah sat up.

"No, wait, we should check for broken bones before—"

Hannah was on her feet looking down at the crouching doctor. "Before what?"

"Never mind." The doctor stood. "You seem fine."

"Of course I am." Hannah gave one fast jerk of her chin in agreement. "What happened? Who was hurt?"

The doctor looked back at the cabin. "Joshua. He fell off a bluff this morning. He's pretty beaten up."

"You're sure it was a cliff? He wasn't hurt by someone. . .you said beaten."

Several people gasped.

"Grant actually—"The doctor cut off whatever he was going to say. "He fell. Yes, he was found at the bottom of a steep bluff. He was out chasing strays."

Hannah could tell the doctor had started to say something. Would he lie for Grant? She well remembered people ignoring her plight. "Who found him?"

"Grant."

So there was only Grant's word for it that Joshua had fallen. Hannah thought of Grant's teasing last night. She'd decided he wasn't so bad. It hurt her heart now to consider that the man, although certainly not a proper father, might have that cruel side. But Hannah knew she couldn't let her feelings rule. "Where is he?"

"Grant?"

"No, Joshua." Hannah resisted the urge to roll her eyes. Why would she want to see Grant?

"He's asleep."

"I'd like to take a turn sitting with him if I may."

The doctor nodded. "Sadie's with him now, but I shooed everyone else outside. I'll bet she'd appreciate the company."

"Thank you, Doctor." Hannah brushed at her dirty dress, wondering if she'd ever dismount a horse without it leading to disaster.

She headed for the house, taking one long look backward to reassure herself Libby was alive and well. Libby grinned at her, waggling her fingers in such a lighthearted way Hannah had to believe her little sister was reasonably well treated. Libby turned to chase after Benny. Hannah noticed that with her boot fixed Libby hardly limped at all.

Hannah went inside, not to sit with Joshua but to guard him. And she wasn't budging until she'd gotten the truth out of someone in this strange family.

"That's blood!" Will rushed past Grant.

Grant jumped aside as Will charged past him. They'd just now topped the cliff, and immediately his eyes had gone to a red splash on a large rock.

Ian crouched by the man-sized boulder and touched the still damp blood splattered on the stone. As he knelt, he flinched and held up a harmonica from under his knee.

"Josh's." Grant recognized the prized possession. "He was playing it just last night. That proves he made it to the top. It proves he somehow started bleeding up here, not from the fall."

"What it proves is," Will said, his mouth a grim line, "someone hit Joshua and shoved him over the cliff."

A tense silence fell over the threesome as they looked at the evidence of attempted murder.

"If someone pushed Josh over that cliff, he'd expect the fall to kill him." Ian rose and handed the harmonica to Grant.

"And when he learns it didn't kill him," Will said with a scowl, "he may worry about Josh turning him in to the sheriff."

The words burned. So furious he barely trusted himself to speak without raging, Grant said through clenched teeth, "Ian, you're in town all day. Put out the word that Josh lost his memory. Talk to anyone who comes into the blacksmith shop then stop at the diner, the mercantile, Zeb's livery, anywhere you can think of. Tell 'em all Josh doesn't remember a thing. Maybe that'll keep him safe. The doc needs to know so he can back our story. Ask him to spread the word, too." Grant turned the metal and wood instrument that had meant so much to Josh over and over in his hands. "I want everyone in Sour Springs to know about this before the day's out so whoever tried to kill him loses his reason for finishing the job."

"I'll talk to Doc Morgan," Ian offered. "Megan was going to have to see him one of these days because of the baby, so we'll use that as an excuse."

Grant's eyes strayed from the mouth harp to the blood-splattered stone, and his boys turned to look at the grim evidence of treachery.

Grant broke the silence first. "You can do that later. For now, we don't leave here until we trail this varmint to his lair."

Grant and his sons rode to the ranch house, exhausted, demoralized, and furious.

The ground was too rocky for a trail to show anywhere around that bluff. There was nothing to identify Joshua's assailant. They'd climbed all the way down the other side of the hill, past the stinking oily water of Sour Springs, and found nothing.

Will and Ian had stuck with him well into the afternoon. His boys headed on home while Grant rode up to the cabin, saddle sore, filthy, and starved.

He recognized another horse from Zeb's and barely suppressed a groan. Soon he'd be praying for a return to this blissful condition.

Hannah.

He had no doubt the woman came to snipe. He fought the temptation to ride back out. Maybe snare a rabbit, do some fishing, live off the land for a week or two. She'd go away eventually.

Resigned to a few hours of nagging, he stripped the leather off his horse, brushed it down for far, far too long, and then gave it a bait of oats. He headed in feeling like he was taking that long, last walk to a gallows.

Maybe it wasn't her. Someone else could have rented a horse. He swung the door open daring to hope.

Inside, instead of hope, he found Hannah.

Sitting in the one and only rocking chair reading *Oliver Twist*, she held Libby and Benny on her lap. Charlie leaned against the stones of the hearth. Sadie worked next to Marilyn at the stove.

Despite his daydreams—he was a realist, he'd known it was her— Grant was caught by how right the family looked with Hannah in the center. His eyes burned. He blinked away the shocking desire to cry. Hannah would think he'd gone soft. And he was only acting like this because of the upset of Josh.

The thought of Josh snapped him out of the emotional weakness. His injured son was nowhere to be seen.

What if. . . Could he have. . . Grant nearly panicked. "Where's Josh?"

A movement brought Grant's head around to the back entry–turned bedroom. Joshua stepped through the little door that led through his room and out the back of the house. His arm in a sling, his face haggard,

Josh had a tidy bandage on his forehead. The gauze glowed white against his black skin. But he was standing.

Grant's knees almost buckled. "You're looking a sight better, Josh." Grant had his hands full keeping his voice steady. "You're gonna be okay then?"

"Yep." Josh didn't so much as shake his head. "I'm still seeing two of everything. Doc Morgan stopped by this afternoon and said that's normal. My ribs feel like I've been kicked by a mule and my shoulder's on fire. It's nothing that won't mend."

Grant could tell the boy still hurt. . .and badly.

Hannah stood carefully, mindful of easing the children to the floor. "Here, take this chair."

"No thanks, Miss Cartwright. I think I'll go back to bed. I just heard Pa ride up and decided if he could see me standing he'd quit worrying." Joshua smiled then turned back to Grant. "I woke up in there awhile ago and lay listening to her reading to the young ones. I was awhile working up the nerve to try and stand, but I did."

Grant managed a half smile and hooked his fingers through his belt loops. "You know me well, son. It does put my mind at ease to see you up. But I wouldn't have made you get to your feet." Grant felt the harmonica in his pocket and produced it for Josh. "We found this."

Josh lit up then flinched in pain.

Grant was at his son's side in an instant. "I'll put it by your bed."

With a heavy sigh, Josh said, "Thanks. I'm not up for much. I didn't get up just for you. I needed to prove to myself that I could stand on my own feet. I'll go back to bed now though. I ache like I took an all-day beating. Sorry I won't be able to help around much for a few days. But if you'll give me some time, I'll be back at it." Josh quirked a pained smile at Grant, and they both acknowledged his weak effort at a joke. Of course he'd have all the time he needed.

Grant noticed Hannah's eyes narrow at the word "beating." Grant glanced at Hannah, and those narrow blue eyes were aimed right at him. He wanted to exchange a look of concern with her. Instead, she as much as accused him of beating his son.

His jaw tensed, and Grant had to force himself to smile and speak easily to Josh. "You'll have all the time you need."

"I'll bring your supper in as soon as it's off the stove, Josh." Sadie flashed him a smile. Grant could see the worry on her face, but she did her best to cover it.

"Thanks." Joshua turned slowly and made his way back to bed with as little jostling of his battered body as he could manage. Grant set the harmonica close, and as Josh settled on the bed with as little movement as possible, Grant spoke low enough no one could hear him. "Have you remembered what happened out there?"

Josh closed his eyes. "No. I remember setting off to track that cow, but nothing after that."

Grant knew Josh was in danger until he could name his attacker. "Doc says that's normal. It'll most likely all come back to you soon."

Josh's eyes slid closed and he didn't respond.

Grant whispered, "Good night."

As he left the room, Marilyn spoke up. "Miss Cartwright, you asked if you could help. Would you mind setting the plates and forks around?"

Throwing a quick prayer of thanks to his Maker that Marilyn was smart enough to only let Hannah handle things made of tin, Grant went to the washbasin and scrubbed his face and hands. He took his time. He straightened as Sadie disappeared into Josh's sickroom with a plate. Marilyn called the rest of the family to dinner.

Hannah, it appeared, was staying for another meal. Grant was tempted to charge her room and board. The light was failing; that meant he'd need to ride beside her into town. Stifling a groan, Grant headed for the table, hoping Hannah didn't burn anything to the ground before he got her out of here.

F I F T E E N

Hannah had to ask. She wouldn't respect herself if she didn't.

She'd seen the way the children interacted with Grant. It was almost impossible to believe they harbored an ounce of fear of him. But he had barely spoken to her during the meal and now he sat beside her grim and stiff, frowning as if she smelled bad. . .which she no doubt did.

Still, she had to ask.

Struggling to be diplomatic, she said, "So what exactly happened to Josh?" There, that was nice. Of course she'd like to know. She was only a caring neighbor. She was proud of herself. Grant was a decent man. He'd be polite.

"You mean did I thrash him within an inch of his life for not working an eighteen-hour day? Did the boy ask for a crust of bread and I took a belt to him? Just say what you're thinking."

He had the manners of a warthog.

Grant gave the reins a hard shake and the horses picked up their pace. His jaw was so tense Hannah expected his teeth to crack.

"I am not thinking that." She was, but she had no interest in admitting it. "The children seem very content with you. I apologize for being unhappy about all those children without a mother. It sets wrong with me, but I can see they need a home. I don't think you've got any right to hate me for worrying about them." She felt her temper

704

climbing and clamped her mouth shut. She'd break a few teeth of her own before she spoke to the surly man again.

Then she thought of something else, and since she hadn't told Grant about her plan to give him the silent treatment, she felt no compulsion to live with that decision. "And I didn't force my way into a dinner invitation. The children wanted a story. Sadie and Marilyn were upset, and at first they were caring for Josh. Then they had to catch up on chores, and Libby and Benny were acting up, probably because they were so fretful about Josh. You should have been there with them when they were so upset. But no, you were off doing who knows what! I stayed because I thought I could help, you. . .you big. . ." She snapped her teeth together again.

They were coming up on the steep climb over the hill and down to Sour Springs. Grant suddenly pulled back on the reins, and when the horses came to a halt, he turned to her. "I'm sorry. You're right. Having you there did help out."

He couldn't have surprised her any more if he'd sprouted a full white beard and left her a sack of Christmas presents.

"Well. . ." Speechless, because she had a hard time thinking of anything to say to Grant that wasn't rude, she fell silent. She wanted to rub his nose in his rudeness. She looked, glared probably, at Grant and saw how tired he was. She remembered the worry on his face when he came in and didn't see Josh.

It hurt a bit, but she managed to say, "Thank you."

Grant nodded then turned to look between his horses' ears. "It helped *me* having you there, too, Hannah."

Hannah should have corrected him and insisted on "Miss Cartwright." Everyone in town needed to treat her with the dignity due a teacher's station, to set a good example for the children. But he sounded too weary and kind.

"When I saw Josh lying there—" Grant's voice broke. His chin dropped to his chest, and his shoulders rose and fell as if he hadn't taken a breath in hours and was only just now remembering how. He whispered, "I thought he was dead. I thought my son was—" Grant's gloved hand came up and covered his eyes.

Hannah didn't know what to say. She wanted to hold him, comfort him. But it was completely improper. His shoulders trembled.

Her arms went around him. "I'm so glad he's going to be okay."

The touch must have helped because he lifted his head and glanced down at her. They were too close. The silent night, the bank of endless stars, the gentle cold breeze, her warm arms, their eyes. . .

She jerked away. Faced forward. "We'd better get home. I've got school tomorrow." Because something had stirred in her, in a deep place, a place she didn't know she had, she spoke brusquely, "And your children had better be there. No excuses."

Out of the corner of her eye, she saw Grant give his head a shake and scrub his face with his hands. "They'll be there, Hannah."

Hoping to regain the distance she wanted between them, Hannah did her best to annoy him. "It's Miss Cartwright."

There was an extended silence. Hannah refused to look sideways to see what Grant was waiting for. She was afraid she knew.

At last he sighed so deeply the air might have come all the way from his toes. "Fine!" With a slap of leather, he set the team trotting. They started the ascent up the mountain at a pace far faster than the last time.

The snow was melted mostly away so possibly this was a normal speed for the horses, but Hannah suspected it had a lot more to do with getting rid of her. For the next few minutes, Hannah had her hands full keeping her seat.

They came down the other side, and as they leveled off, Grant said in a voice that sounded like he had to drag the words out of his throat, "As to your none-too-sneaky hint that I might have given the boy a beating, I didn't. I was gone because I spent the afternoon hunting for answers. Josh isn't a boy to go falling off a mountain. He's agile and quick. The trail was one that'd make a mountain goat think twice, but Josh scaled it all the time. What happened to him was no accident."

"You mean someone attacked him?"

"Yes, that's exactly what I mean."

"But who?" Hannah's breath came in shallow pants as she remembered so many experiences with violence in her past.

"I don't know, but I intend to find the truth. But I should have stayed with the children. You're right. They needed me."

Grant sighed as the wagon pulled into Sour Springs. "Please don't repeat what I've said. For now, until we can figure out what happened, we want everyone to believe Joshua fell by accident."

As Grant stopped the horses in back of the diner, a swish of skirts drew Hannah's eye. The seamstress who had been in Stroben's Mercantile that first night came out of her shop and headed for them like she was a magnet and Grant was true north. Grant saw the woman—Prudence, Hannah remembered—and jerked as if he'd been bee stung. The woman must mean something to him.

His shoulders slumped, and he swung himself down off the high seat. He made a move to round the back of the wagon, but the tall, slender woman cut him off. A trained cow pony couldn't have done it better.

"Grant, I saw you coming into town. I wondered if you'd like to come over tonight. Last time the weather stopped you."

"Uh. . .hi there. . .uh. . . ."

There'd been a last time? They must be seeing each other. That moment on the drive, when their eyes caught, flared to vivid life—if he was seeing Prudence, he shouldn't be looking at Hannah that way. Heat crawled up her neck, and she was thankful for the dark that covered her blush. Of course someone as handsome as Grant would be thinking of finding a wife. But where in heaven's name did the man intend to put her in that tiny house?

Prudence rested her hand on Grant's arm in a way that Hannah found far too familiar for a public street. Of course there was no public, only Hannah, and she quite obviously didn't count.

All Hannah's haranguing about having no mother for his children now echoed like pure foolishness in her ears. But why hadn't he told her? Why had he let her go on and on if he was already thinking to take a wife? And a tall wife, graceful and beautifully dressed, too. Nothing like Hannah in her rags.

Hannah realized she was staring. She also realized she'd expected Grant to help her down off the wagon. He had last night. Well, she'd fall down before she'd stare at the couple a second longer.

She heard the murmur of voices, which she studiously ignored. She reached the ground with just enough clumsiness to feel even more foolish than she already did. Her skirt snagged on a step and she pulled it quickly free. But there was no reason to be embarrassed; the couple never glanced her way.

She took a quick peek and saw Prudence snuggled up against Grant. Hannah hoped he didn't behave like this in front of his children.

Hannah's temper rose. She squashed it. And she wasn't going to just run away. She lifted her voice so Grant could hear her over the sweet nothings he was no doubt whispering to Prudence. "I'll expect your children at school tomorrow, Grant. If they're not there, I'm coming out to get them."

Grant lifted his head and took a step toward her, dragging Prudence along as if she'd forgotten to take her claws out of him. Prudence was enough of a drag to stop him, and he didn't seem inclined to fight her off. "I'm planning on them being there."

Hannah jerked her chin up and down—which he might not have even seen in the darkness, especially with Prudence as a distraction. Then Prudence closed any gap that there was between her and Grant.

Hannah turned and rushed inside—which was completely different than running away.

Feeling pure envy, Grant watched that pest Hannah run away.

Sure, she was running from him, but she had the extra treat of getting far away from Shirt Lady. Grant wanted to run himself. If he could only dislodge the woman's fingernails. He gave a second of thanks to God that he was wearing a coat or she'd leave scars.

Her grip reminded him of last Saturday when he'd had to practically fight her off to get Charlie and Libby. It also reminded him of his bucket of eggs and the impression he'd had of someone lurking around his wagon that night. His chickens were doing well, and he'd planned to do some trading in the general store. He didn't think much about the eggs. But the bucket hadn't turned up along the trail, so they hadn't fallen out of his wagon. Right now he'd rather be talking with an egg thief than dealing with this woman and her fingernails.

He endured Shirt Lady's brainless chatter for as long as he could, worrying about getting home to Josh and thinking about what a nuisance Hannah was and how nice it was that she'd brought her little nuisance self out to watch his children today. Now the young'uns were home alone while Grant stood here trying to be polite to a woman whose name he'd made a deliberate effort to not learn. All he knew was the lady was always and forever talking about making him a new shirt.

Grant glanced down, remembering he'd torn to shreds his best shirt to make bandages for Josh. That now-destroyed shirt was little better than a rag before he'd taken it straight off his back but a lot better than the one he now wore.

The woman finally took a breath, and Grant near to knocked her over taking possession of his arm. He thought she might have left scratch marks, even through his buckskin coat.

"I've left the young'uns alone too long." He vaulted onto the wagon seat. It occurred to him that Shirt Lady hadn't come out to check on things today. Half the folks in town had come. They'd offered food, their strength, their support, their prayers. Shirt Lady hadn't so much as asked after Josh, even now. No possible way she could have missed what happened with all the effort Ian and Will had made to put the word out Josh had amnesia. Any decent person would now ask which boy was hurt and inquired after his health. She just hadn't cared.

He saw that same sour expression on her face that had been there before when he'd talked about his children. She looked up at him on the high seat. "But Grant, what about coming over?"

"I've got to get home." Why would she even want to pass a moment of her time with him if she didn't like children? It just didn't stand to reason. It was on Grant's tongue to say something mannerly about "another time," but he feared if he started talking something rude might come out. The best he could manage was, "Evenin', Miss...." He jerked on the brim of his Stetson and slapped the reins on his horses' backs so hard he owed the poor critters an apology. Well, too bad. They weren't gettin' one. Helping him escape was part of their job.

He saw Shirt Lady jump back. She dodged the wagon. Good, if he'd run over her toes he'd've had to stop and take her to the doctor.

Grant promptly dismissed What's Her Name from his thoughts and quarreled inside his head with Hannah all the ride home.

S I X T E E N

"You may close your books, children. Class dismissed for recess."
The children dashed out the door.

Hannah waited until the last one left, then buried her face in her hands and wept. She did her best to muffle the sound, but she couldn't control the shuddering of her shoulders and the quiet, choking sobs. She gave herself up to it completely, knowing these tears would just have to run their course. She'd be fully recovered by the time her students came back.

A hand rested on her shoulder, and she jerked her head up, mortified. Marilyn looked down at her with a kind smile.

Hannah had a split second to wonder if this particular student was older than she. Then she took another split second to wonder just how old either of them was. Chances were no one really knew.

"Don't cry, Miss Cartwright. You should be happy. You're a wonderful teacher."

Hannah really needed to cry for just a few minutes, but with Marilyn watching, she got a grip on herself. Her shoulders stopped quivering. She sniffed and blew her nose with the handkerchief she clutched in her hands. She wiped her eyes and struggled with the last few tears. Her lower lip trembled. "You should be outside playing."

With a smile, Marilyn said, "I'll leave in just a minute."

The stern look Hannah tried to muster was ruined by the hiccups.

At last she managed a weak smile. "It's really going well, isn't it?"

"You know pride is a sin, Miss Cartwright." Marilyn straightened and showed no sign of leaving.

Since she was caught anyway, Hannah decided she was glad for the company to interrupt her foolish tears of joy. She dabbed at her eyes. "And why do you mention pride?"

"Because you're so proud of yourself for the way things went this morning." Marilyn's smiled broadened, her blue eyes flashing with pleasure as she gently teased. "I don't think it's a sin for *me* to be proud of you, though."

"Are you proud of me?" Hannah leaned forward. "Did it go as well as I think?"

Marilyn nodded. "I've just come to live with Grant recently. Before that, well, there was never much time for schooling, but I did manage to do some learning. I think you have a rare gift for working with children. I'd say you've done it before a lot, haven't you."

"I've never taught a school before. This is my first time."

"There are other ways to work with children, other ways to teach besides in front of a classroom." Marilyn sighed. "I've done some teaching myself in the orphanage where I lived before I ran off."

Needing to get on with preparing for the rest of the morning classes, Hannah said, "You'd better go on out. Charlie isn't one to let anyone push him around. Maybe you can keep the peace."

"I'll go. I just thought you looked a little wobbly, and I wanted to make sure you were all right."

"I am now. I'll come out and watch recess in just a minute."

"No hurry." Marilyn pulled a sandwich wrapped in a square of fabric out of her coat pocket. "Pa sent way too much food with us today. He must have packed it thinking Joshua was still going to school. Sadie and I pack the lunches, but he came in after chores and threw a few more things in. I can't possibly eat three sandwiches, two apples, and six cookies. I don't want Pa to feel bad if I don't finish it though." Marilyn laid the sandwich on Hannah's desk.

Hannah felt her stomach growl. She'd had no breakfast. She wouldn't have money to eat until her first pay came. It frightened her when she dared to think of it, because that might be a month away. The only food she'd had since she arrived at Sour Springs had come from eating at Grant's. But Hannah would never take food out of a child's mouth. And Marilyn was thin already. "Uh. . .I don't think I should."

"It'd help me out if you took it."

Hannah realized that part of the reason she'd broken into tears was because she felt so shaky from hunger. Marilyn set the food on her desk, holding Hannah's gaze. Hannah didn't look at the sandwich because she was sure Marilyn would see hunger. Marilyn no doubt had plenty of experience with the feeling.

"Take it. There's plenty more for me. I wouldn't lie to you, Miss Cartwright."

"Thank you." Hannah noticed the faint trembling of her hand as she reached for the sandwich. "That's really generous of you."

"I can handle whatever trouble comes up outside. You should eat your lunch early. You'll need the energy for class. You look like you skipped breakfast this morning."

Hannah couldn't even control her hunger long enough to let Marilyn leave the classroom. She bit into the hearty roast beef sandwich and chewed slowly to make it last. She didn't know where her next meal might come from.

As soon as her hunger eased, Hannah reflected on the morning. She had worried that Grant's children might be well behind others their ages, but all of them were quite well educated. The older girls, Marilyn and Sadie, stepped in so willingly and helped with the younger ones—all of them, not just their own brothers and sisters—Hannah nearly had two other teachers in the room.

Sadie had a voice that would stop a naughty little boy in his tracks. She must have had considerable practice making little brothers and sisters mind. Hannah was distracted by envy every time Sadie verbally cracked the whip.

Marilyn had a comforting touch that made children turn to her like flowers turning toward the sun. If anyone cried, whether from hurt feelings or a scratch, Marilyn went to the child before Hannah could so much as move.

She had thirty-two students; many had to sit three to a desk so everybody would fit. But they shared with good spirits, listened when she taught, and studied quietly when she worked with others. She'd spent the morning quickly dividing them into classes and starting their lessons.

Learning was the important thing. If only she could educate them so they'd never be forced into mill work or, because of illiteracy, have no prospects of any jobs. She believed giving them an education could be the difference between life and death for some of them. It might be the difference between keeping their own children or sending them off to orphanages. With a kind of desperate urgency, Hannah taught them words and numbers to put them one step further from the awful fate that could await the uneducated.

The morning had gone wonderfully. Once her sandwich was finished, she went out and observed the playground. There was lots of running and shouting, but everything looked peaceful.

Emory Harrison, a first-grader in the same class as Benny, sidled over to Sadie and, wide-eyed with curiosity, asked, "Why do you have black skin?"

Hannah froze, afraid that this could bloom into trouble.

Sadie pointed to a big, dark freckle on Emory's arm. "I've got that kinda skin all over."

The boy stared at his arm a moment then nodded and went back to playing.

Hannah found an apple on her desk when she came in from watching the children during the noon recess. She found two cookies after the afternoon recess. She knew Marilyn had left them, except once she caught a gleam in Sadie's eyes that made her wonder about the apple. And Libby grinned at her impishly when Hannah asked about the cookies. No one would admit to leaving the food. Not knowing what to do, Hannah slipped the treats into her desk drawer for later.

The rest of the day went well, and Hannah went back to her cold room. There'd be no supper, but her stomach wasn't painfully empty as she'd expected.

The sun set early in the Texas January, and with no time wasted preparing an evening meal, and no light from a lantern because she had no oil, she looked out the single narrow window overlooking Sour Springs. She saw again the window in the living quarters of Prudence's sewing shop. And again she saw a second figure, just as she had on the night of the blizzard. Of course it wasn't late. Anyone could have dropped by for a visit. Anyone. . .including Grant.

Even after such a brief acquaintance, Hannah had a hard time believing Grant would go out on a date the day after Joshua was so badly hurt.

The curtains were drawn, but they weren't heavy enough to block out the pair of silhouettes. Hannah turned her back on the sight and on her roiling emotions.

SEVENTEEN

Hannah got to school early the next morning. She had a complex arithmetic problem she needed to explain to her older students and she wanted to review.

Hannah was distracted from her studying when four ladies and two men, looking grim, stormed into the schoolhouse.

"Can I help you?" Hannah smiled, rising from behind her desk, but her stomach sank as she studied the somber crowd. She recognized Quincy Harrison from the interview for her job. The others were familiar faces from around town, but she didn't know them by name.

The six people approached her desk and stood without speaking for a moment, until one particularly sour-faced woman poked the man beside her. "Get on with it, Quincy."

Hannah braced herself.

Quincy looked uncomfortable, but he stepped forward. "We need to discuss the trouble here at school yesterday. We're concerned that the children won't be able to learn in these conditions."

Mystified, Hannah asked, "What trouble? The children all worked hard, and they seemed—each one of them—bright and eager to learn."

"Of course they're bright," the woman who'd poked Quincy said. "Did you expect our children to be stupid?"

Another woman interrupted, "Let Quincy speak for us, Gladys. We agreed."

Hannah opened her mouth to apologize. Of course she hadn't expected her students to be stupid, but caution kept her silent. Instead of talking she began to pray. She waited to hear what the problem really was, terribly afraid she knew already.

"It's not that our children didn't learn." Quincy looked from his toes to Hannah and back. "It's just. . .we don't like the idea of them uh. . .uh. . ."

Gladys lifted her nose even higher in the air. "Mixing with the wrong sorts."

Hannah remained silent. Her empty stomach twisted with dread. This was what Grant had been talking about. These people had made it impossible for the children at the Rocking C to attend school. Her prayers flowed to God as she wondered how she was going to feed herself. Because if these people insisted she send the black children home, or for that matter the orphan children home, she was quitting.

Gladys elbowed Quincy in a way that made Hannah guess he was her husband. "Get on with it."

"It's just that. . .that. . ." Quincy fell silent.

The other man was thin and nervous looking. "I'm Theodore Mackey, Miss Cartwright. We got together last night and decided we needed to meet with you. We all just want what's best for our children."

Hannah finally had control of herself enough to speak calmly. "School went very well yesterday. I don't see the need to change a thing."

"We saw that older girl. . . ," Theodore said.

"Which older girl?" Although Hannah knew which quite well. Sadie.

"The Negro." Gladys said it as if she were spitting.

"Well," Quincy said, "she was playing with the other children and sitting right with the other girls."

Another woman spoke up. "They're all part of the orphanage that man runs on his ranch."

"His name is Grant, Agnes. And well you know it. I'm Ella Johnson," the third woman said. She looked at Hannah while she introduced herself then turned back to the crowd she'd come in with. "Now being orphans doesn't make those children bad. They had no say in how they came into this world."

Hannah immediately focused on Ella Johnson, hoping she'd found an ally.

"You're just saying that because your sister married one of Grant's brood," Gladys said.

"That's right, Gladys, that's exactly why I'm saying this. I know what a decent man Will is, and Grant raised him. It's not right to deny those children a place in this school just because they came out here on a train."

"It's more than that," Gladys snapped.

"Then it's about that girl being black?" Ella stood her ground

Gladys turned toward her. "It's about more than their skin color."

Ella might be better able to absorb any cruel words Gladys jabbed at her, but this was Hannah's fight. "Ella, if you don't mind, I'll handle this."

Ella looked at her then with a nod said, "Yes, ma'am."

"What's going on here?" Grant's voice, far harder than usual, broke into the conversation.

All of the people confronting Hannah turned to the back of the schoolroom.

"Glad you're here, Grant," Ella said. "I'm planning to see that your children get the education they've got coming."

At Ella's announcement, dead silence fell over the group.

"Obliged, Ella." Grant stayed near the back of the room, looking over the rows of desks at his neighbors. "But this is my fight."

Ella fidgeted but didn't say anything.

"No, it's not, Grant. It's mine." Hannah rested her hands on her waist. "I'm the teacher of this school, and I'll be the one to talk with parents who have a problem with the way I run things."

"This isn't about you, Hannah. It's about my children." Grant pulled his hat off his head in a reflex show of manners. But there was nothing polite in his expression. Grant stared at the group for a long awkward minute, then he turned from them to Hannah. "I most always accompany the children to school the second day and come in ahead of them so I can attend this meeting. It waited until the third day this year because my young'uns didn't come in on Monday. Three whole days in school." Grant laughed bitterly. "A new record. 'Course they missed the first and are being kicked out before the third begins."

"This happens every time?" Hannah fought to control her temper. If the angry words that pressed to get out escaped, she'd say things that, no matter the provocation, she shouldn't say.

"I'm here, aren't I?" Grant went back to staring at the group. "And they're here. As dependable as the rising sun."

He opened his mouth, then clamped it shut and shook his head. "What's the use? I'll just take them home," he said to Hannah, as if the others weren't there. "They really liked school. They really liked you for a teacher, Hannah. But I won't subject them to this treatment."

"They were treated well." Hannah pushed past the crowd and ran to catch hold of Grant's arm as he turned to leave.

"So I heard. And they really felt like they could learn things from you that I'm missing. Marilyn talked about becoming a teacher. She said you let her help, and she really enjoyed it. Maybe if you recommended the right books for them, I can do better."

She refused to let go of his wrist. "They're not quitting school!"

Grant looked at Hannah, and she felt his kindness and the regret he had over taking his family out of school. But she could see how fiercely he wanted to protect them.

Whispering for only Grant to hear, she said, "I don't know how I could have looked in your eyes a single time and doubted that you'd take good care of your children."

Grant's eyes lost some of their wintry sadness. "Thanks, Hannah. I'd best be going."

Hannah held on tight. "I'm not letting you go anywhere." Still latched on to him, she turned to the group of complainers. She knew if she said what needed saying, she'd be fired. She didn't have a spare penny to feed herself. Still, she couldn't stand by and let Grant's children be cast out while she stayed safely employed. "If you don't allow orphans in this school as students, then I'm sure you wouldn't want one as a teacher," she said politely. "I'm afraid you'll have to fire me. I'm an orphan myself."

Fear, disgust, and surprise crossed the faces of the people in front of her, all but Ella. Then Grant tugged on the hand she had latched onto him, dragging her attention back.

"Why didn't you tell me?" he whispered.

She couldn't meet his eyes, and she spoke low to keep their conversation private. "I don't like to talk about it. It. . . M–my childhood. . . was awful."

"That's why you were so worried about the children. That's why you expected the worst." Grant fell silent for a second. "That's how you got those marks on your back."

Hannah nodded.

"That's why you care so much."

Hannah lifted her chin and almost fell forward into the understanding in Grant's eyes. He'd know how it was. She'd spent all her life being strong for her little sisters and Grace, never adding her misery to the weight anyone else had to bear. But Grant was strong. He could bear a lot. He'd lived much like her. Like a yawning chasm, the dangers of sharing everything about herself opened at her feet. Tempting her to take that step.

"My years as an orphan weren't pleasant. Too much work, too little food, not enough love. Then I got adopted and things got worse. I escaped from the man who adopted me, and I have been looking over my shoulder since I left, wondering if he's searching. He's the type to want revenge."

Grant rested a strong hand on her arm, as if could take all of the bad memories away. . .or at least replace them with new ones that would outshine the bad. Hannah wanted to tell him more, tell him everything.

"There was certainly no mention of you being an orphan when you applied for the job of teacher." Gladys scowled, striding toward the back of the classroom. "You have lied to us, Miss Cartwright."

Applied? Hannah remembered her interview and almost smiled. She turned away from the offer Grant made with a kind touch and understanding eyes and faced the lynch mob. She'd just handed them all the rope they needed to hang her. "I didn't lie. I'm a twenty-year-old woman." Hannah wasn't all that sure, but it was a fair guess. "And how I was raised had nothing to do with whether I could do this job."

Furious, she ruthlessly suppressed her temper, knowing they would chalk up any bad behavior on her part to dreaded orphanhood. "I just didn't tell you everything about my childhood. The full truth is I've been teaching children all my life. When I was adopted, I was taken to a home where the man pressed all of us into work at a carpet weaving factory. I was six when I started working sixteen-hour days. I and my older sister taught my younger sisters how to read and write and cipher late at night when my father wouldn't catch us and punish us for it."

"Still, you should have been more forthcoming, Miss Cartwright." Gladys sniffed and began pulling on her gloves as if the meeting were over.

Hannah suspected it was. "The only lie I told you was my name." Hannah glanced up at Grant and tears filled her eyes. "I made up the name Cartwright. I don't know what my last name is."

"Orphans can't be trusted," Gladys went on. "And I believe your lies have proved that to us."

"They learn bad ways that have to be taught out of them," Agnes said. "Maybe Grant does all right when he has them for a long time to train them, but he keeps getting new ones and—"

"You can fire me if you want, but I will not listen to you speak ill of Grant's children. They are good, hardworking children who were a wonderful addition to this classroom."

Ella shoved herself between Hannah and Gladys. "Hannah is not fired, and Grant's children are welcome in this school. You do not make the decisions here, Gladys. I've already talked with the parson and Harold at the general store. They both heard good things about the school and want Miss Cartwright to stay."

Gladys's lip curled. "You went behind my back to talk to them?"

Grant stepped in front of Ella. "Stay out of this, Ella. You've got to live in town with these folks. I don't want trouble stirred up that's going to bother you, or your sister and Will."

What Hannah heard in Grant's voice humbled her. He was worried about someone else. Nothing she'd felt had come close to the depth of Grant's kindness. How many times had Hannah longed for a father to care this much?

It inspired her to be kind herself, when her temper wanted free rein. She walked around Grant and Ella and faced Gladys. "I know how much you love your children, Mrs. Harrison. I know you only want what's best for them."

Gladys's mouth clicked shut.

"Did any of your children come home upset about school?" Hannah looked right at Gladys, but her question was for everyone.

Quincy said, "It was just the opposite. I've never had my young'uns so excited about learning. Why, my littlest one even read a few words out of the family Bible and he wrote his name, after only one day of school."

"That's Emory," Hannah said. "He was so good yesterday. So eager to learn. He's a really special little boy, Mr. Harrison. I'll have to work hard to keep ahead of him."

Quincy fairly glowed with pride.

Even Gladys's dour expression softened. "He's always been quick. He keeps the two older boys working on their studies, afraid their little brother will catch up and pass them."

Hannah laughed, and several of the group who had been so disapproving before smiled. "And your twins, Agnes, they are so pretty. They tried to fool me about their names once yesterday, but I had them figured out from the first."

"You could tell Samantha and Emily apart?" Agnes shook her head. "Are you sure? They even manage to trick me and their pa part of the time."

"I counted the freckles on their noses the first minute I saw them."

"Their freckles?" the twin's father exclaimed. "I'd never thought of that."

"I knew a set of twins when I was young, in the orphanage, and they liked to play twin tricks, but I could tell it meant the world to them if someone could tell them apart. So I suspected your girls would feel the same. Samantha has ten freckles and Emily only has eight. Emily and eight, both start with E. It was easy after I figured that out, if they just gave me a second to count."

Agnes and her husband smiled.

Grant said to the parents, "Miss Cartwright, having so much experience with children, knew a way to touch your daughters' hearts. Being an orphan is the reason she's as good at teaching as she is."

Gladys looked long and hard at Hannah.

Ella's hand rested on Hannah's shoulder. "Say all you want about this being someone else's fight, Grant's or Miss Cartwright's, but I've got the backing of the school board. Two against one, Quincy. You'll have to persuade them to change their minds in order to fire Hannah."

Hannah wanted to weep at Ella's generous courage. Hannah hadn't planned it, but she had come to be standing between Grant and Ella as if they were guarding her.

The parents had come in here with their minds made up, and it didn't sit well, especially with Gladys, to change. But Gladys was proud of her boy, Emory.

Finally Gladys relented, relaxing her shoulders. The rest of the group took their cue from her and exhaled silently.

"It's true that you did a good job here yesterday, Miss Cartwright. And it's true that Ella's brother-in-law is a good man. I can see that with my own eyes. And Grant, your son Ian is a good blacksmith, honest and hardworking. I'm just. . ." Gladys hesitated.

"You want your three boys to grow up to be decent men." Hannah nodded as she spoke. "You're watching out for them and trying to protect them from being hurt or being led astray. That's what any mother would do. You were right to come in here and get your questions answered. You come back in any time you are concerned about the school, Gladys. I will work with you to give your boys the best education I can."

Gladys seized on Hannah's offer as if she'd gotten exactly what she'd come in for. "I'll just do that, Miss Cartwright. You won't be doing anything in this school of which I disapprove."

Hannah had a sudden inspiration. "You know what would be really good? If you would take control of part of the Easter pageant I'm planning."

Gladys's eyes gleamed. Hannah thought the use of the word "control" was inspired. It looked like Gladys thought she should control the whole world.

"I'm going to teach them songs, and there'll be a speaking part for every child. There'll be songs and Bible readings. I've written it to be appropriate for children. We'll need simple costumes, and I'd like the parson to say a few words and maybe the parents could bring in cookies so we could have refreshments afterwards." Hannah heard the enthusiasm in her voice, and she thought she saw a corresponding reaction of interest from the parents.

"Gladys, you could be in charge of organizing the whole thing. The children will need help learning the songs and their parts. I think we should insist that they memorize everything."

Now Gladys was really excited. Hannah surmised that she was a woman who was all for "insisting."

"Why, I'd be happy to take charge, Miss Cartwright," Gladys said.

"I'll help," Ella offered. The other parents chorused their willingness to get involved, although Hannah noticed Grant stayed silent. Hannah wondered if they realized yet that they'd just agreed to let her keep her job until spring and had quit trying to get Grant's children expelled. She didn't point it out.

"We haven't ever had an Easter pageant in Sour Springs. I think it's a great idea." Quincy turned to his wife. "Now, we'd better let Miss Cartwright get on with her preparations for school."

The angry little mob of parents disbursed in a flurry of cheer.

Ella patted Grant on the shoulder. "Will wanted to come, but I thought he might make things worse."

Grant nodded silently and Ella left.

Hannah heaved a sigh of relief.

EIGHTEEN

Grant heaved a sigh of despair.

"They'll never leave my family alone." He turned to face Hannah. "They were this mad after yesterday, and yesterday there was no trouble. Just wait until one of your students goes home crying because Sadie beat him in a spelling bee. That bunch will be back."

Grant noticed Hannah's hands were trembling as she crossed her arms.

"I can't believe they let me off as easily as they did. I thought I was done for from the minute they showed up because I was going to quit before I let them drive your children out of the school."

"Don't sacrifice your job, Hannah." Grant put his hat on with a rough jerk of the brim and turned to go. "I don't expect you to do that for me."

"I wouldn't cross the street for you, you idiot." She grabbed his arm and spun him around.

She only managed to manhandle him because he was turning back toward her anyway in surprise. Grant had one split second after she exploded to marvel at how well she'd kept her cool with that posse of orphan haters. Then she attacked.

"If you think I'd side with that mean-spirited, selfish bunch of vigilantes over your children, you don't—"

Grant held up both hands to ward her off. "Look, Hannah, I didn't mean—"

Hannah grabbed the lapels of his flannel shirt. "—have any idea who I am. Why, if you think—"

"It's not that. I didn't say—" Grant backed up a step.

Hannah followed him all the way to the wall. "—I'll stand by and let Sadie get thrown out of school because of the color of her skin—"

"I'm sorry. Really, Hannah. I wasn't suggesting—" Grant caught her hands where they were shaking his collar. She seemed determined to strangle him to death.

She tightened her grip. "—or slam the door in the face—"

Grant stopped trying to placate her and leaned over her, "Listen, I didn't mean to imply you had anything against orphans. If you'll—"

"—of any child—"

All his tension uncoiled like a striking rattler. "—just shut up for a second—" He pulled her hands off his throat.

She yanked away from his grip. "—orphan or not, who wants to learn—"

He just needed her to shut up for a minute so he could tell her how much he appreciated her standing by him, and how sorry he was she had to face down a mob, and how annoying she was, and how pretty, and sweet— He turned her around and trapped her against the wall. "—and let me apologize, I'll—"

She turned her face up, her eyes flashing with fire and spirit, her cheeks flushed. "—then you're the most insulting man I've ever—"

He couldn't think of any other way to close her yapping mouth.

He kissed her.

It worked.

She shut up.

He jumped back so fast he tripped over a desk. "I shouldn't have done that."

"You shouldn't have done that." Hannah covered her mouth with her hand, her eyes wide, watching him like he'd grown rattles and fangs and attacked her.

Grant shook his head and felt his brain rattle, so maybe he *was* close to growing the fangs, and he was very much afraid he might attack her again.

Hannah ran her tongue over her lips as if she wanted to wash the taste of him away. "That can't ever happen again!"

"That can *never* happen again." Grant couldn't back farther because of the desk. That's the only possible reason he went forward instead. And kissed her again.

"Let go of me!" Hannah wrenched away from Grant, which was hard with her arms wrapped around his neck. But she managed, with Grant helping, to pry her hands loose where they'd gripped the hair curling down the nape of his neck.

Grant looked aghast. "That never should have happened."

"Never, not ever."

"It's never going to happen again." Grant turned his back on Hannah and figured out that if he moved sideways he could get away from her. Why hadn't he thought of that before? "We don't even know each other," Grant added.

Hannah smoothed her hair, which Grant noticed was messy.

He remembered running his fingers through it. How long had he spent kissing her? Her lips were pink and a bit swollen. He looked closer. He moved closer.

Those lying pink lips said, "We don't even like each other."

Shaking his head to break the spell Hannah had cast over him, Grant pushed his hat firmly on his head and looked straight at her out from under the low brim. "Oh, maybe we like each other a little."

"Some." Hannah's eyes found his. . .and held.

"But it was wrong." Grant turned away to prove he could.

"Oh yes, it was."

"Very, very wrong," Grant agreed, suddenly furious with her for being so certain, because in his whole life he'd *never* felt anything so right.

At that moment, three dozen children flooded into the room.

Grant saw Hannah's knees give out, and she caught herself before she fell by leaning against the wall. It was a good thing she saved herself from collapsing because Grant wasn't capable of moving.

If they'd been a few seconds earlier, the whole school would have walked in on them. By nightfall, all of Sour Springs would know he'd kissed the new schoolmarm in front of all her students. Something like that had to be followed immediately with a wedding, or Hannah would immediately be fired. And if they announced an engagement, Hannah would be fired with everyone's best wishes for happiness, and Grant would be saddled with a wife—a meddling, potato-burning wife. He looked sideways at her, leaning against the wall, both hands clapped over her bright pink cheeks. An annoying, nosy, beautiful, kindhearted wife who'd offered to sacrifice her job to fight for his children.

That wasn't going to happen since Grant had promised himself and God a long time ago, on a cold Texas morning in Houston, that he'd never marry. The day he took six children home with him, he dedicated his life to caring for children nobody wanted rather than having even one speckled-eyed child of his own.

Besides, he didn't have room for her. He'd have to put her on the kitchen floor.

Next to him.

"Gotta go." Grant ran out of the building like a man being chased by a pack of hungry wolves, or worse yet, one pretty little woman.

Hannah wanted to send him on his way with a swift kick.

And she might have if she could get her knees to stop wobbling.

Suddenly her spine stiffened, if not her knees. What if he'd kissed her knowing a kiss would make her stay away from him? And by staying away from him, she'd naturally stay away from the Rocking C, which meant she'd never know for sure what went on out there.

She thought of the few times she'd seen Parrish in action. The man had a masterful front he'd put on for others who questioned whether he should be allowed to adopt children with no mother in the home. Her skin still crawled when she thought of the times Parrish had rested a loving hand on her shoulder while he spoke of his devotion and wanting to help those less fortunate. She'd known full well that the same so-called loving hand would punish her brutally if she didn't smile and call him daddy for the onlookers.

Grant wasn't like that. Her heart knew he wasn't. But what if her heart was reacting to a handsome man who made a public display of his affection for his children? He'd said he never let them go to school. He made it sound like he was protecting them. But what it amounted to was the children were cut off almost all the time. Had Hannah's intervention stopped him from doing exactly what he wanted to do? Getting his children back home and putting them back to work?

Hannah couldn't trust her instincts about Grant. And she couldn't face him.

Hannah closed her eyes and prayed for wisdom. Her prayers kept being interrupted by the memory of Grant's strong arms and how wonderful it felt to be held.

Stirring restlessly, she knew she couldn't go out to the Rocking C to inspect again. She didn't trust herself. Chewing one stubby thumbnail, Hannah decided that as long as he left the children in school she'd know they were released from any hard labor for a few hours every day. So she'd stay away from the Rocking C as long as the children were here. But if Grant pulled them out, she'd have to go back.

She thought of Grant's head lowering toward her, pulling her close, and something very sweet and rather desperate turned over in her chest. She'd shared lots of hugs with her sisters in her life. But she'd never been held by a man.

She'd seen moths fluttering toward a burning lantern. They'd fly straight into the flame and be burned, sometimes to death. The moths never learned, or maybe as they burned to death they finally did. Until it hurt that badly, the pull of the warmth and light was too powerful. Even if Grant had done it to keep her from finding out his secrets, mesmerized by the heat of his arms and his kiss, she still felt the pull.

How humiliating!

Even more humiliating, what if he tried to kiss her again? She knew deep in her heart that she might well kiss him back.

While the children settled in their desks, she headed for the outdoors, hoping the sharp cold would ease the burning in her cheeks and cool her crazy thoughts about Grant and how badly he needed a mother in that house of his.

She wanted to—had to—avoid Grant, and to do that she had to keep his children in this school.

NINETEEN

He had to get his children out of that school!

He practically fell down the steps of the schoolhouse in his hurry to escape whatever had happened in there.

He slammed into something soft. His attention abandoned the disaster that was Hannah, and he saw that he held Shirt Lady in his arms. She leaned toward him; her lips seemed to be pursed. She might be going to kiss him.

A door opened behind Grant and he turned, knowing it had to be the schoolhouse door. Grant looked straight into Hannah's eyes. She was just a couple of yards away at the top of the three steps. She was flushed, her lips still shiny and swollen, looking as bothered as a woman could be. He knew it was about that kiss. He was mighty bothered himself.

Hannah saw him and her expression turned to horror. He read every bit of what she was thinking. Grant, holding someone else, another woman, seconds after he'd been kissing the daylights out of Hannah.

Lips came at him, and he saw them just in time to dodge. Shirt Lady missed his lips and grazed his neck ever so slightly. He shuddered. Her lips were soggy and flabby and...

Hannah made a sound that distracted him from his revulsion. A wounded wildcat growl, part pain, part fury, all dangerous. She was in a good position up there to pounce, too.

Grant braced himself to be buried under two women.

Hannah's expression of horror and fury changed to utter contempt. She whirled around, her tattered skirt flying, and stormed back into the schoolhouse, slamming the door so hard the whole building shook.

Sick to imagine what Hannah thought about what she'd witnessed, Grant turned back and saw Shirt Lady zeroing in on him again with those disgusting lips. He'd rather kiss one of his longhorns, one who'd just sucked up a river full of brackish water. He ducked before he could commit his third act of stupidity concerning a woman's lips in less than a minute.

Shirt Lady almost fell, for the second time, because of his clumsiness. Then she staggered and cried out with pain. Her hands tightened around his neck.

He reached up to free himself.

"No, please, be careful. My ankle. I think I sprained it. If I let go, I'll fall."

Grant stopped in his headlong effort to free himself from these poison ivy arms. He shook his head to clear it, knowing he was still reacting to Hannah—to what had happened inside the school and out. There was no sense knocking Shirt Lady over just because he was upset with the schoolmarm.

"Sorry. Here, let me get my arm around your waist."

Hannah wanted to get her hands around Grant's neck.

She should have gone all the way inside, but that window, right by the door, was too handy, and she looked out at that lowdown, stinking polecat as he slipped his arm around his girlfriend, seconds after the skunk kissed Hannah!

She should have moved on, but it was like she wanted the pain. Hannah watched Grant practically sweeping the horrible seamstress off her feet. Standing, staring, Hannah knew it was a good thing to see. Let it burn her eyeballs to cinders so she'd remember.

She'd always been afraid of men. Her father had taught her well. But for some awful, ridiculous reason her common sense had deserted her with Grant. Even when he was scowling and snarling like a smelly old ogre, she'd never been scared. That just proved that not only was she right to be afraid of men, her instincts were also never to be trusted.

Boiled down to its simplest form. . .she was an idiot.

Prudence smiled and leaned close. Grant slid his hands up her arms. Hannah couldn't see his face, shadowed by his hat, but she could see that nasty Prudence, batting her eyes like a Texas dust devil just blew straight in her face.

Hannah finally had all she could take. She forced herself to turn from the window.

School!

She was a teacher. She had students and responsibilities and a life that had nothing in the world to do with that awful, lowdown Grant or his appalling mistreatment of both Hannah and that dreadful Prudence.

Hannah smoothed her hair and forced her breath to come more evenly. She wished her heart would stop thudding. More than thudding, it seemed to be breaking, but she couldn't imagine why. She'd barely had one kind thought about Grant in all their brief, unpleasant acquaintance.

Well, there'd been a few kind thoughts. More than a few in all honesty. And a few pleasant moments. Extremely pleasant.

Then she decided, despite her firm belief that God wished her to be honest in all things at all times, this once she'd go ahead and lie to herself about those kind thoughts and pleasant moments and dwell on the bad ones. She'd pick them apart, see that even worse things lay beneath Grant's disgusting behavior.

She squared her shoulders as she imagined shoving him off that train platform the first day. She'd have saved herself a lot of time and trouble if only she'd known.

Feeling marginally cheered by the image, or at least capable of not bursting into tears in front of her class, she marched into her true calling. Working with children. . .only children. . .no man ever!

Grant firmly unfastened Shirt Lady's clinging hands. He controlled the urge to gag as he peeled her loose. "Should I help you to the doctor's office?" Doc Morgan was nearby. That'd get rid of her right away.

"No, I don't think that's necessary."

Grant stifled a groan.

Prudence smiled. "I don't think it's broken. I just need some help getting home." She looked up at him, and she must have had something in her eye. Her lashes flapped as if she was trying to dislodge a dirt clod.

"I'll help you then." What choice did he have? His natural inclination, which was to shake her off him like a slimy leech, would leave the woman lying in the dust. He didn't know much about women, unless they were his children, but he was sure dropping Shirt Lady in the dirt wasn't right.

He slid his arm around her back. His head cleared enough that he realized the woman was almost letting him carry her. Her ankle must really hurt. Grant walked the length of the meager Sour Springs Main Street with Shirt Lady clinging to him.

Mabel came to the door of the general store, wiping her hands on her apron. "Howdy, Grant, Prudence."

Grant controlled a flinch. Prudence. He thought of her as Shirt Lady, and he wasn't going to stop now. He was determined to never know this woman well enough to learn her name.

"Good morning, Mabel."

Expecting Shirt Lady to say something about her injury, Grant hesitated. Then it seemed like it was too late somehow. Oh well. Surely Mabel could see the woman limping.

"Tell Harold thanks again for coming out to help yesterday." Grant reached up and tipped his hat.

Harold appeared in the door behind Mabel with a big grin on his face. "Mornin', you two."

You two? Like they were a couple or something? Grant had to fix that misconception.

"Can we hurry along, Grant, honey? I'm anxious to get home."

Honey? Grant was suddenly almost pulled along. Prudence didn't seem to be favoring her ankle as much. That was a good sign.

"So, when are you going to keep our next date?" Prudence's voice had a piercing quality that carried up and down the street. Grant was sure Mabel and Harold could hear. He saw Doc Morgan grinning at him as the man unlocked his office.

"What date?" Heart sinking, Grant knew these fine citizens of Sour Springs were drawing the wrong conclusion. And he hadn't cleared a bit of it up by the time they'd reached the shirt shop.

"You said you were too busy to come for supper the other night, remember? Come on in now and have a bite of my seed cake and some coffee."

Prudence kept dragging him, but Grant drew the line at actually going into her store. He didn't want to be alone with the little ivy plant for even a second. He dug his heels into the wooden sidewalk. "Gotta go. No time for cake." Wasn't that pretty much what he'd said last time, and look how much trouble that had gotten him into.

"Then when, Grant?"

It came to Grant in a flash that instead of fighting he should go along with her. Better the town folks knew there was nothing going on between him and Hannah. Of course nothing could ever come of a date with Shirt Lady. His skin crawled when he thought of that almost-kiss he'd dodged.

The woman had definitely set her cap for him, and he couldn't let her go along believing they might be suited. But one date would solve a lot of problems between him and Hannah. He made a promise to himself not to be alone with Prudence for a second. He'd just come to her door, take her for a nice public ride so Hannah and everyone would see them but nothing improper could be even whispered, then he'd drop her off and run like a scared rabbit.

"Um, how about we go for a ride some evening?"

"I'd be proud to make dinner for you. I'm an excellent cook." Prudence must have that dirt back in her eyes again. With her ankle hurting and her eyes all stinging from the dirt, it was a wonder the woman didn't want to go on inside and get some rest.

"It wouldn't be proper for us to be alone in your room, Prudence. But we can take a quick ride. Just this once. You know"—Grant felt he had to be honest. The woman needed the truth—"I'm not planning on taking a wife. I've got a house too small for a gnat to find a place to settle in. I'm running all day every day to keep up with the children, and I'm planning on taking in more when the need arises. There's no room for a wife in that."

Shirt Lady's eyelids stopped flailing and her smile went kind of hard around the edges, but Grant was impressed that she held onto it at all. The mention of the children bothered her. And hearing that they couldn't do more than just take a single ride had to pinch her feelings.

Half expecting the door to slam in his face, instead she said, "I'd enjoy your company, Grant. Even if it's not a wife you're looking for, we could be good friends."

Somehow, Grant sincerely doubted he could ever be friends with a woman who didn't like children. He decided he'd said enough for now though. "I'll come for you on. . ." He hated to do it of an evening; he was too tired. He didn't want to give up Saturday; he got a lot done on Saturday with the children home. It didn't seem proper to do something he was dreading as much as this on the Lord's Day, so Sunday was out.

"Come Friday night, please. Not too late, so the dark doesn't catch us out riding."

Well, the woman had beaten him to the asking again. It didn't suit him a bit, but at least he'd be getting it over with soon, except. . . "Uh. . .can we wait a little longer?" He had to be sure Josh was well. Like maybe a year or two?

"How about a week from Friday then?"

Grant couldn't think of a single excuse. He wasn't prepared. If he'd known this was coming, he'd have practiced excuses. But who could predict a thing like this? His shoulders slumped. "A week from Friday sounds fine. I'll be here. . .before the supper hour. We'll take a short ride, but I want to get home to my young'uns for the evening meal. Don't want them alone at night."

Her smile hardened again. It was a purely frightening expression. But most things about women frightened Grant, so he didn't know if he could trust his reaction.

"Fine. I'll see you next Friday then." She closed the door with a sharp click that didn't sound near as friendly as her words.

Grant turned and almost ran to his wagon. Women were a mystery to him, and he'd had two mysteries fetched down on him in a single morning. Then he saw Mabel, still wiping hands that had to be bone dry by now, and she gave him a smug smile that he had no idea what it meant.

Three mysteries.

He leapt to the wagon seat. Tossing the brake free with a thump of wood and iron, he yelled.

The horses cooperated nicely and took off as if Shirt Lady chased them, flying on her broomstick.

Finally, Grant found someone who understood him—his horses.

"Why couldn't you get him in here?" Horace emerged from the back room.

"All you'd have needed to do was get the door closed then rip your dress and start screaming loud enough to draw a crowd. He'd have been forced to marry you and the land would be ours."

Prudence scowled at the filthy man. "He's coming by next Friday night. We'll finish this then. I think you should be here to knock him in the head. Then after he's been in here a good long time and comes around, I can act out the whole scene. As soon as he's conscious, I'll get the preacher in here breathing fire and brimstone, and he'll force the marriage."

Prudence went and made sure the window curtains were drawn shut. "I know just how to do it, too. I was hiding behind the school, waiting for my chance to get Grant in here, and I watched in the window at that crowd who came to toss Grant's kids out of school. Those folks will believe the worst of him because he's an orphan."

"People are always suspicious of orphans." Horace headed for the back room. "I remember how we got treated, like we was dirt. Trash under their feet. We deserve some payback for growin' up that way."

Purdence's temper flared, and there was only one person handy to take it out on. "Why'd you sleep so late? Now you can't get out to the dig all day because someone might see you." Prudence noticed Horace's steps falter. "What? You're hiding something."

Horace turned slowly, his eyes narrow and shifting.

Prudence braced for him to solve this with fists.

"I went to LaMont and didn't get back until late last night. I overslept."

"I know and spent half of what we should have made in the saloon." Prudence jammed her fists on her hips and felt the thrill of daring him to shut her mouth.

He stalked toward her. "There's more. Monday morning early, one of those riffraff kids from the Rocking C came on me. I had to shut his mouth for good."

"You killed him?" Prudence's mouth watered. She loved a man

strong enough to take what he wanted. Horace was the strongest man Prudence had ever known.

"Yep. I'm surprised you didn't hear about it in town."

"There was a fuss yesterday. I heard Grant's son fell. I reckon that's what it was about. It must not have bothered anyone too bad. Things were normal with Grant and his get this morning." Prudence walked back to the window and peeked through the burlap curtains to stare at the school building.

"No one's gonna make much ruckus about one dead orphan." Horace came up and shouldered her aside. "And he was one'a them black-skinned ones, too. No loss all the way around."

"Stay back from the window!" Prudence shoved his hand away from the curtain.

Horace wheeled and grabbed the front of her dress in one fist and shoved her against the wall so hard the shop shook.

Her head slammed against wood. She saw stars.

"I'll go where I want to go."

Her knees buckled, but he held her up.

"Do what I want to do." Horace clamped one massive stinking hand around her throat. "And you'll keep your mouth shut about it." With a vicious laugh, his yellow teeth broken and bared, he tightened his stranglehold. "You hear me, Prudence?"

"Yes." She could barely whisper.

"Good girl." He kissed her.

When she kissed him back, he let her breathe.

TWENTY

Grant forked fresh clean straw into the last horse stall, tossing around ideas and horse bedding with equal abandon.

He'd always taken the kids out of school for their own good. Only now, when there was no reason to take them out, Grant realized how much he liked having them around. Joshua was here, but right now the boy was sleeping, and he was a quick healer. He'd be in school in a couple of days. Grant hadn't been alone like this since those painful few months after his pa and ma died.

He hated it!

He worked hard just like always, but now, all day long, he heard no childish chatter from Benny, no thoughtful questions from Joshua. Marilyn never called out that the noon meal was ready. Sadie never giggled and whispered secrets to her sisters. He even missed Charlie, and the boy had yet to speak a kind word.

With the children here, Grant was always needed for something.

Had he taken his kids out of school on the least excuse all these years because he missed them? That meant Grant had sacrificed his children's education so he wouldn't have to be home alone.

Stabbing his pitchfork into the last of the straw, Grant refused to admit it was all his fault. The Brewsters had made it impossible. Breathing a sigh of relief, Grant remembered Festus Brewster. That thug had driven them away. If he'd have been in that posse this morning, there'd have been no going home without his children.

Looking around his tidy barn, Grant saw a few spots that could use attention and attacked them. The hours of the day crept by.

"Pa, what are you doing?"

Grant yelped, so lost in thought he almost jumped out of his skin. He jerked away from his bucket of water and looked at Joshua. Up and around. Grant smiled, so relieved he was speechless. "You look better."

"Is something wrong?" Joshua moved carefully, but he came on into the barn.

Grant realized what the boy had said the first time. "I'm...uh...just..." *acting like a madman.* Grant couldn't say that because Joshua would ask why and Grant wasn't about to admit that, if he *was* a madman, it was Hannah who had driven him crazy.

"I'm cleaning the barn floor is all."

"Are you planning to sleep out here?"

Good idea. No, bad idea. Grant didn't want to sleep in the barn. The barn was cold. But good excuse. "Maybe. Thought I'd see how it cleaned up." So that meant he wasn't a lunatic for scrubbing the barn floor on his hands and knees. Or at least Josh wouldn't realize he *was* one.

"We probably ought to all move out here and move the animals inside." Joshua grinned. "They have a better house than we do."

More cheerful now that his son was here, Grant got up from the ridiculous scrubbing. "Dumb idea anyway. I just had some spare time." Then Grant realized that it wasn't just Hannah-induced insanity. It was also boredom. That he could admit.

"It's so quiet around here with the young'uns all in school. I hate it. How can the father of six be so lonely?"

"I was bored, too. That's what made me come out here."

"You're looking good, Josh. Real good. Give yourself time to heal though." In other words, please don't go back to school and leave me.

"I think I can go back to school tomorrow."

Grant kept his smile in place by pure force of will. He didn't want the boy to stay sick after all. "How about your memory? Do you remember any more about what happened?"

Josh rubbed his head with his good arm, avoiding the spot with the stitches. He favored the arm that'd been knocked out of its socket. But he didn't have the sling on today, and his eyes seemed clear.

"I can't remember anything after I set out hunting that cow." Worry cut creases into Josh's forehead.

Grant was sorry he'd brought it up.

"I don't know what happened at all. I can't believe I fell off that cliff. I've been playing on that slope since I first moved here."

"The doc said it's normal to lose your memory around an accident. It may never come back." Grant didn't want to say the next words, but he felt like he had to warn the boy. "I scouted up that hill. It looks to me. . ."

Josh's eyes narrowed when Grant hesitated. He came farther into the barn. "What?"

"I think. . ." Grant hated saying the words, but the boy had to be warned. "I think you were hit on the head by someone." It looked to Grant like Josh's knees wobbled. He stood and rushed toward his son. "Let's sit down a minute."

Sheaves of straw, bound tight and set ready to bed the horses, were stacked close at hand. Grant helped Josh ease down on one and took the next one over. A person with black skin wouldn't go pale, but Grant had a feeling that all of the blood had flowed out of Josh's head.

"I'm sorry. Maybe I shouldn't have said anything." Grant clenched his hands between his knees and stared sideways at his son. "But you and all the young'uns need to be on your guard."

Josh steadied after he sat down and gave Grant a man-to-man look. "I'd rather know, Pa. We're all raised rough, except maybe Benny. We can handle bad news and we don't scare easy. I know I'd rather hear what I'm up against than have trouble sneak up on my flank. Do you have any idea who it was?"

Grant shook his head. "Tracks were wiped clear if there ever were any on that stony ground. The back side of that hill is that stinking spring. We never go anywhere near there and the cattle avoid it. They want no part of that foul, oily water or that black tar seeping out of the ground. I've got no idea who it was, but that's a good overlook for this property." Grant looked around his ridiculously clean barn. "What have I got anyone would want?"

Josh stared into the distance, thinking. "I've heard there's a way to get lamp oil out of a seep like that. I suppose someone might be sneaking in there to fill a lamp."

"You can't fill a lamp with that kind of sulfuric sludge. I know men who have tried it."

"No, you have to refine it. I read of such a thing in a newspaper once. But I don't know if I've ever heard of a refinery around these parts."

"Besides, if someone does think they can do it, all they'd need to do is to ask permission, I'd just say they could have it. There's nothing there to try and kill a man over."

"If I could just remember what happened!" Josh's fists clenched together between his splayed knees.

"Don't fret on it. It'll only give you a headache. Doc says your memory will either come back or it won't. Nothing we can do to force it."

"I know, but it's frustrating." Josh shrugged then winced at the shoulder movement.

"You should stay home a good week, Josh." Grant's spirits lifted at the thought. But he didn't want the boy to stay hurting. That was pure evil. Nothing wrong with a little coddling though. Of course the boy was as tall as Grant and took care of himself with adult confidence. But still, a father could fuss over his son.

Grant sighed and said a quick prayer for the boy's aches and pains to heal. He threw in a plea for forgiveness for the selfish wish to have his family back. And while he was at it, he asked God to take his loneliness away.

Hannah flashed into his thoughts, and Grant quit praying and focused on his son.

"I'll take things a day at a time. If I'm up to the ride to town tomorrow, I'll go. Any time I get to hurting, I'll stop and laze around awhile." Josh grinned, his smile broad and white against his black skin. "You're in need of a few more children, I'd say, Pa."

Grant smiled back even though he saw no humor in it. He *did* need more children.

Joshua stood slowly, protecting his shoulder, aching head, and tightly wrapped ribs from any sudden moves. "I was lonely in the house, but coming out here was more effort than I expected. I'd better go on back in and rest."

The instant Josh wasn't there to witness it, Grant's smile faded away. Just imagining Josh leaving made Grant's ears echo with the silence of his barn and his house and his life.

Hannah crept back into his thoughts. Thinking of her made the loneliness a thousand times worse.

Grant tried to think of something more constructive to do, but the barn was pure clean to the bone. The horses were brushed. The stock cattle were fat and healthy. The chickens had given up their day's supply of eggs and been fed.

Grant sighed and went back to his bucket. A madman scrubbing the barn floor.

Joshua went back to school, and Grant had a new problem.

As much as he missed his kids, he started dreading them coming home, because then, instead of thinking about Hannah to fill the silence, he had to hear about her. They came home full of excitement about their lessons, news about the Easter pageant, and endless tales about how much they adored Miss Cartwright.

Something else to drive him crazy!

To prove he was crazy, he noticed all the cobwebs on the barn ceiling. He started knocking them down—as if spiders didn't have a right to live outside. But he needed something to do!

Once the spiderwebs were gone, Grant hunted for any spot he couldn't eat off. He'd already cut a winter's supply of firewood, splitting it down to toothpick size.

He enjoyed the weekend with his children more than he ever had. They went to church together. Grant noticed Hannah never even looked his way. He'd have liked a chance to apologize for kissing her. But he saw Prudence bearing down on him after services and ran for home.

He worked and played side-by-side with his family all weekend. And then they left again.

He spent the next week working himself to death, moving his longhorns from the high pasture of his rugged ranch to the valley. A five-man job that could have been handled in a half day if he'd waited until Saturday with the children helping. He'd done it by himself.

The meaner and more feisty those half-wild cattle had been, the more Grant liked it, because only when he straddled the line between life and death did he forget about how much he'd enjoyed kissing Hannah.

By midday Wednesday, the winter term of school was near two weeks old, and he could count the hours since he'd put his hands on Hannah. His rough, work-reddened hands wrapped around her slender waist.

He kept thinking about that ride he'd promised Prudence, too—his stupid plan to make Hannah mad enough to never get close to him again. But to make the plan work, he had to survive an evening with that child-hating battleaxe. Shuddering with dread, Grant tried to figure out why he'd thought that was a good idea.

Looking around frantically for something to occupy his mind, there was nothing left outside so he started on the inside. He scrubbed the kitchen floor and baked bread and a couple of pumpkin pies. When the kids got home, the young'uns ran outside to play and do their chores as they always did. No reason for them to spend time in this dinky house if they didn't have to.

Sadie and Marilyn stayed behind to start supper and saw the baking Grant had done.

"Don't you like how we've been cooking, Pa?" Marilyn asked, her blue eyes downcast.

"You've been doing fine, honey." A lot better than him.

He looked at the blackened pies. "I just. . .uh. . .had some spare time today. I used to cook a lot, but since I've started having grown-up daughters, I haven't kept my hand in. The bread didn't rise like it should've, and I burnt one of the pies and forgot to add eggs to the other one. I guess that's why it's kinda flat-like."

"Then why'd you do it?" Sadie frowned at him. "I mean, if you have extra time, a lot of parents are coming in to work on the pageant. Easter is early this year, and it's already the end of January. Maybe Miss Cartwright could find something for you to do."

Grant flinched at that woman's name. She seemed to be all the children talked about.

"Almost every other parent has helped, especially the mothers. And since we don't have a ma, maybe we aren't doing our share." Marilyn looked at Sadie. "Shouldn't he come in and work with Miss Cartwright? Don't you think that'd make her happy?"

"Does she seem unhappy?" Grant bit his tongue too late to stop the words.

Sadie turned away from the mess he'd made of supper and studied him like he was some kind of bug she'd caught crawling out of the cornmeal. "Does it matter to you if Miss Cartwright is unhappy, Pa? Are you worried about her?"

Marilyn caught the overly interested tone in Sadie's voice, and the two of them exchanged a quick glance. His daughters, full-grown women and as stubborn as the rest of the female breed, snagged his arms and pulled him onto a bench. They sat down beside him.

"What's going on, Pa?" Sadie asked, her eyes shining. "Are you sweet on Miss Cartwright?"

Grant surged to his feet. His daughters held on tight and plunked him right back on the bench between them. Marilyn got up and stood so close he couldn't escape without knocking her over—which he hated to do, but still he seriously considered it and saved the idea in case it came to that.

"What kind of question is that to ask your pa?" Grant tried out his best I'm-the-Head-of-This-House voice. He'd never used that voice much, mostly because it didn't work worth a lick. "You girls behave yourselves now. I'm sorry I messed up supper, but you can see clear as day I needed the practice."

"We've been trying something fierce to get Miss Cartwright to come out again." Marilyn leaned down, her eyes narrowed as she studied him. "She seemed to want to learn how to sew a riding skirt, and she asked a lot of questions about cooking. I was sure she'd be back, worrying about orphans the way she does."

Grant had never been one to turn a child over his knee. He'd just never found it necessary. Most of his children were so happy to live with him—sometimes after a rocky start of course—that he'd never had to resort to such as giving a whoopin'. He reckoned Marilyn and Sadie were a little old now for him to start in. But still—

"Now she won't come." Sadie leaned in from the side. "Pa, did you do something to hurt her feelings? Did you try and steal a kiss or—"

Grant erupted off the bench. "Now, you girls just stop that."

Marilyn didn't get knocked clear over, but that was only because Grant caught her and set her aside on his way past.

"We're not havin' that kind of talk around here." Grant grabbed his hat as he ran out the door.

The girls were giggling. One glance over his shoulder, just before he hid in his immaculate barn, showed the two of them standing in the doorway of his crooked little house with their heads together, chattering like a couple of pea-brained magpies.

"All right, children. You're dismissed for morning recess."

As the classroom emptied amid shouts of joy, Hannah held two slates together on her desk, studying Charlie's handwriting. Charlie's was so beautiful, full of loops and swirls, it made Hannah think of an ancient Bible handwritten by monks.

Benny's wasn't so good. He'd have been all right except he'd taken to copying Charlie's style. All he'd done is end up with words Hannah couldn't read. She mulled over how to redirect Benny's attempt at beauty without hurting his feelings.

Maybe she should talk to Charlie, get him to tone it down. But it was a shame to stifle such creativity.

"Miss Cartwright?" Marilyn's voice broke her concentration.

Hannah glanced up, surprised to see Marilyn and Sadie still in the room. The children usually all stormed out for recess. "What is it?"

Sadie held up a small bundle, wrapped in brown paper. "This is some extra fabric we had at home. People give us things like this all the time, and we can't begin to use it all. We've been wanting you to come out and learn to sew. But since you haven't, Marilyn and I thought maybe we could work on it here."

Hannah thought of her worn dress. Heavily patched, faded until it was colorless, nearly torn to shreds when she'd fallen off Rufus that day at Grant's, only wearable because of Sadie and Marilyn's talented needles.

Looking down at her frayed cuffs and the drab gray color that had once been blue gingham, she remembered stealing it off a clothesline when she was still in Chicago, over four years ago. The way she'd gotten it was a disgrace even more so than the way it looked. She'd never had the money to spare for a new one, but it didn't matter because she wore it now as penance. A reminder of the depths to which she'd sunk to survive. The rags of a street urchin because a thief didn't deserve better.

"Girls, I can't take that fabric." Hannah shook her head. "You might need it for yourselves. No, absolutely not. Thank you, though. I should get paid soon. Then I'll buy some cloth. I would be very grateful for your help then." Getting paid would be wonderful. Right now she was eating each day solely because of the generosity of Grant's children. A situation that had to end.

Marilyn kept coming. "Now Miss Cartwright, I'm afraid we can't let you wear this dress anymore. It's indecent and. . .and. . ."

Sadie pushed past her sister. "You're shaming us, miss. Why, anyone who sees you thinks you aren't paid enough and this town doesn't care about you, and it's just plain hurting the honor of the good town of Sour Springs, Texas."

One corner of Hannah's mouth turned up. *Oh yes, the highly developed skill of all orphans—the ability to manipulate.*

Marilyn stepped past Sadie, and the gleam in Marilyn's eyes sent a little thrill of fear through Hannah. "The plain facts are, Miss Cartwright, people in this town are generous to Pa with things like fabric. You saw the pile of it in our kitchen when we were digging around for a patch for your dress, now didn't you?"

Hannah remembered the little mountain. It was a fact that the family had more cloth than they'd ever use. "I saw it."

"Well, this is how it's gonna be." Marilyn arched her eyebrows at Hannah, and Hannah remembered that the girl was a big help with the teaching. She was old enough and strict enough to do it better than Hannah ever could.

"Marilyn, don't take that tone—"

"We're going to make you a new dress," Marilyn cut her off. "You can help us and learn something or you can stay out of our way."

"You can make it, Marilyn, but you can't make me wear it." Hannah didn't like the direction of this conversation. It put her on an equal footing with these girls when she was supposed to be in charge.

"We will make it and you will wear it, even if we have to 'accidentally' rip a big hole in that dress, which would take about two seconds and next to no effort."

Hannah gasped. "Marilyn, you wouldn't!"

Sadie's eyes got wide with what could only be admiration. She stepped up beside her sister. "The honest truth is that even if we don't do it, it's going to happen someday. You'll snag it on a nail or a rough corner of a wooden chair or have another run-in like you did with Rufus, and your dress is thin as paper."

"And when that happens," Marilyn went on, "you won't have anything to put on. You'll be standing here with your dress hanging in tatters with nothing to change into because you don't have another dress. You need this dress now, made of good sturdy cloth so something *disgraceful* doesn't happen. Or at least you need to have it so, when something disgraceful *does* happen, you're ready."

Sadie jerked her chin in a way that seemed to say everything was settled. "So we are going to make this dress, with or without your help. And if you don't want to wear it, we'll just stuff it in a corner of the classroom to be used in the event of a disaster. Then you'll be happy enough to have it."

Hannah glared at the girls. Then she glanced down at the patches Grant's girls had sewn on the sleeve of her dress. There was another big one on the back and the cloth didn't come close to matching. When the girls had sewn her dress back together, they'd commented on the tissue-thin cloth. She knew she needed to replace it soon for the sake of decency. But her pay hadn't come yet, and Hannah didn't know how to sew when she could afford fabric. And she'd die before she let that dreadful Prudence sew for her. . .as if Hannah could afford to pay someone for a job Hannah was ashamed she couldn't do for herself. And now, here stood these generous, blackmailing children offering her fabric.

She knew Grant hadn't been consulted, although in fairness to him, she admitted he'd have probably let her have the cloth. But the girls hadn't asked. And that probably made her a thief yet again. At the very least she was a beggar. The only food she had was a share of the children's lunch every day, something they'd also manipulated her into without Grant's knowledge, since their excuse for each one sneaking her bits of their food was that they didn't want to hurt their pa's feelings by not eating every bite of the mountain of food he sent.

Between Grant unknowingly feeding her, his daughters offering her fabric to dress herself, and the knowledge that what she wore was stolen, she could hardly look the girls in the eye. She couldn't have looked them in the eye anyway. They walked past her.

Turning, she watched them clear her desk, spread dark green wool out, and begin talking about what to do next. With a huff of disgust, she went up to stand beside them. "Oh, all right, you little monsters. Tell me what you're doing and go slow."

The girls started giggling, and before long Hannah took up the giggling and was in the middle of her first sewing lesson.

Sadie pulled a tape measure out of her pocket. "Stand up straight, Miss Cartwright. You're so slender I'm afraid we'll make it too big."

As they worked, the girls chattered pleasantly. Hannah learned far more than she wanted to about Marilyn's affection for Wilbur Svendsen.

"We need to find a man for Miss Cartwright before she's too old to have children," Sadie announced.

Marilyn gave Hannah a quick glance then started giggling. She covered her mouth as she laughed louder. Through gasps for air, she said, "Miss Cartwright could use a beau for sure."

Sadie ran the tape from Hannah's shoulder to the tips of her fingers. "That is unless you already have someone sparking you, Miss Cartwright."

"I most certainly do *not* have anyone sparking me. It's not proper for you to ask me such a question, Sadie."

Sadie and Marilyn exchanged a strange, satisfied look.

"And anyway, I can't cook or sew." Doing her best to sound falsely forlorn, Hannah said, "Why, any poor husband of mine would most likely not survive. I think I'll just keep teaching if you don't mind. I believe God has given me a gift for teaching, and I plan to devote my life to it."

Sadie said, "Well, husband or not, it won't hurt you any to learn to sew."

Grant's girls told her what each measurement was for and how to lay out the fabric to cut. In the end they made her do most of it herself, just like any good teachers.

When the time came, they wanted her to cut, but she refused. Sadie took over, and Hannah flinched every time the scissors snipped for fear the precious piece of cloth would be ruined. But Sadie cut and chatted as if she did it every day.

TWENTY-ONE

G rant went through the whole mending basket.

He even darned some socks, although he was afraid his uneven stitches might cause a blister or two. But it wasn't a bad job all in all. He hadn't had grown daughters to do for him at the first, and he'd learned some things. He ran like a scared rabbit when the children came home so there was no way Sadie and Marilyn could ask about it.

But when he came in to supper, Marilyn next-thing-to-attacked him with a bolt of cloth. "Pa, I've been thinking. Since Wilbur's been sparking me, I need to get some experience making clothes for a man. It's all your fault I don't know how to do that."

Grant backed away from her, looking between her and that length of brown cloth in her hands. "Why's it my fault?"

Sadie came up behind him and blocked the door so he couldn't escape. "Because you never let us make you any clothes."

"I don't need any new clothes."

"Yes, you do, Pa." Joshua sat leaning against the wall, reading a schoolbook, with his long legs drawn up to his chest so he wouldn't stretch across the whole floor and trip everyone who came by. "Sadie already made a whole new outfit for me just this year, but that was before Marilyn came. I don't need anything. Marilyn is sure enough right that she doesn't have much practice."

"You don't want me to be a failure as a wife, do you, Pa?" Marilyn wheedled.

"I don't need clothes." Grant grabbed the fabric out of Marilyn's hands with too much force, feeling an almost desperate need to stop her.

The gleam of mischief faded out of Marilyn's eyes. Grant hadn't noticed it was there until it was gone.

Grant held her stare for as long as he could stand it. "What?"

"When's the last time you let us make you something?"

Grant folded the fabric clumsily as he went and set it on a teetering pile of cloth that he'd been given by kind ladies over the years. There was quite a heap of it, enough to keep his children in clothes for a long while.

"We're not wasting cloth on me."

The touch on his shoulder turned him around. Sadie smiled at him. "Now calm down."

Grant fought the pull of her sweet charm. Sadie, his youngest daughter in that first group of children he'd adopted, had always held a special place in his heart—of course *all* his children held special places in his heart. Still, he knew how he responded to Sadie. He had a hard time denying her anything. His stomach twisted for fear he'd calm down. He didn't *dare* calm down. He'd end up doing something he didn't want to do.

"You're trying to store up everything for us, aren't you?" Marilyn's voice pulled him back to look at her.

Grant frowned. "You kids are growing. There's no call to waste good fabric and time on me when you boys will tear the knees out of your pants by tomorrow night and need new. There isn't always fabric to be had."

"You've got quite a few dollars in the bank these days, don't you, Pa?" Joshua waited in silence. The kind of silence that made a man talk, even when he didn't want to say a word, just to end that silence. And how did Joshua know what he had in the bank? That wasn't anything proper to speak of with children. Grant had certainly never told him.

"Even if I do, there are hard times in ranching. We've got some cash money built up for now, but a hard winter might cost us a crop of calves and we could be in trouble. You kids need things. Your shoes wear out and your arms and legs sprout. I spend what needs spending and save the rest for a rainy day."

Grant noticed Charlie looking down at his outfit. Everything the boy had on was new. Grant remembered the shame of having clothes come to him secondhand. Not that his children didn't wear hand-me-downs; they did. But when they first came to the family, they got one set new, right down to socks and boots, made just for them.

Charlie, settled on the floor on the far side of the fireplace, raised his eyes. Those hostile eyes, so suspicious, carrying a world of anger around on his thin shoulders. Grant saw the war in the boy. He wanted to get mad about the clothes because he reacted to everything with anger. But what was there to get riled up about with clean, freshly made, nicely fitting shirts and pants?

Grant also noticed something sticking out of Charlie's pocket. The little corner he could see had the look and shape of a pocketknife. Charlie didn't own a pocketknife. Grant knew that for a fact. And how could the boy have any money? With a sinking stomach, Grant knew it had most likely gotten into Charlie's pocket in a dishonest way. Charlie wouldn't be the first orphan to have a knack for thieving. Just because a boy had enough food and a warm bed didn't always stop things from sticking to his fingers. Sighing, Grant knew he had something else to deal with. He said a silent prayer for his troubled son.

Looking at his children, Grant's eyes landed on Libby with her new dress. After Grant had fixed her worn little shoes, he got her new ones at the mercantile and fixed the soles on those. Now she had a pair for good and another for home.

The little angel was settling in well, but Grant had to clear up this fuss about clothes and go for a walk with Charlie.

"I think we've got enough cloth to spare to make you a pair of pants and a shirt." Sadie stepped to Grant's side as Charlie rose to his feet. The two of them exchanged a glance then turned to face Grant. Grant noticed Charlie tuck that knife deeper in his pocket.

"And you need new boots, Pa." Sadie crossed her arms. "Yours are worn clear through on the bottom. They have to be cold."

Grant studied his boots. They were the ones his ma and pa had gotten for him when he was sixteen, just a couple of months before they died. They'd seen to it he had a new pair the two years he lived with them. But that was when his feet were growing as fast as summer grass. His feet hadn't grown since then. Why buy new? Two leather thongs held the soles on, and his toes peeked out in half a dozen places. He'd slipped new pieces of leather on the inside because the bottoms were worn thin as paper, and he'd sewn buckskin on over the heels a couple of times. "I'm fine."

Sadie reached past him and snagged the piece of fabric off the pile. "Please, Pa. It makes me feel selfish to have nice things and see you go without."

Marilyn stepped up behind Sadie, her blond head nodding. "We're not going to make one more new thing for anyone in this house until we get you out of these rags."

Benny dodged in front of Sadie with his wide, loving eyes. "Are we selfish, Pa? Do you think we are?"

"No, son. Not a one of you kids has a selfish bone in your body."

"You must think we are, or you'd have something nice for yourself once in a while," Sadie said. "You gave up your room, and now you sleep on the floor without complaining."

"I didn't even think of that when I was so mad at Benny. You don't even have a room." Charlie's hand slid deep in his pocket to hold the knife. The boy looked up and Grant caught his eye. A faint flush of red that screamed guilt rose on Charlie's fair cheeks.

"Now, you guys stop it. The kitchen is a room. No one's using it at night. It's a waste not to have someone sleeping in it. I'm closest to the fire. Why, I'm the selfish one. If you kids'd just think about it, you'd be fighting me for the kitchen floor."

He scanned all those worried young faces. None of them was buying it for a second.

"You never have anything nice for yourself." Sadie held up the yards of brown cloth. "And we never even noticed till now. We really *are* greedy and selfish."

This had started out differently. Grant had seen the teasing light in Marilyn's and Sadie's eyes. He'd known they were up to something that had only a little to do with clothes. But they weren't teasing anymore. Somehow he'd made them feel bad. The last thing he ever wanted to do was hurt a child.

"You young'uns are the most generous people I've ever known. There's nothing greedy about any of you. It's not that. It's just. . ." Grant looked at all of them. "You're such fine young people."

Charlie dropped his chin to rest on his chest and studied the floor as if it held the meaning of life.

"I'm pure lucky to have gotten you. We've all lived through hard times. What if there's not enough? What if we run short of something? Yes, we may have fabric we'll never use, but if times got hard, we could maybe sell it. There's always a day coming when there might be a need for us."

"It makes no sense for you to dress in rags," Marilyn said. "Using up three or four yards of fabric that came to us as a free gift will not change a thing if hard times come. I want you to let Sadie and me make you some new clothes. If you love us at all, you'll let us share with you one tiny bit as much as you share with us."

Grant tightened his jaw. An almost desperate fear twisted around inside him when he thought of wasting anything on himself.

A tug on his hand pulled his attention away from Marilyn's stubborn eyes. Libby held his hand. She looked at him then lowered her eyes to study a patch in his flannel shirt torn away from the nearly rotten fabric. She reached one tiny finger into the hole in his shirt, stuck her finger on in through the hole behind that in his union suit, and poked him in the belly.

She wiggled her finger back and forth and tickled him. With a little laugh he jerked away, surprised to find out he was ticklish. She smiled up at him and reached her twitching finger toward him again.

Grant jumped back and glanced up to see all of his kids with their eyes focused straight at him.

"You're ticklish," Benny said.

"Pa's ticklish." Sadie's dark eyes almost caught fire as she came toward him, her fingers raised in front of her, wriggling around like ten worms.

"You're gonna get some new clothes, Pa." Sadie gave him a diabolical smile. "We're not going to leave you alone until you say yes."

With a scream, Benny jumped on him, tickling his belly. Libby latched onto one of Grant's legs, and that tripped him as he tried to get away from Benny while laughing. Marilyn, Sadie, and Charlie stepped back to watch him go down under them, but Grant saw a gleam in Charlie's eyes like he wished he could be part of the wrestling match. Sadie looked like she'd be willing to attack if need be. Joshua laughed from his spot on the floor.

"Okay, okay, okay!" Grant laughed as he tried to escape his tormenting children. They quit attacking as quickly as they'd begun. Grant dumped them off him, pretending to be rough but very careful not to hurt either of them. Through laughter, he said, "Make the blasted clothes. Just don't tickle me anymore."

"New boots, too?" Sadie said with an arch of her eyebrows and a twitch of her fingers.

Grant collapsed flat on the floor. Gasping for breath, he said, "Yes, fine, new boots, too, you little monsters."

Sadie and Marilyn exchanged satisfied nods that made Grant

759

wonder what they were up to. But he'd never known how ticklish he was, and he didn't want to go through it again. He stood patiently while the girls measured him.

He tried Joshua's boots on and when they were too tight, the young'uns wouldn't be satisfied to let Joshua guess at a fit. Under threat of another attack, he promised he'd go to town the next day and let Zeb at the livery measure him for new boots. With that, his cantankerous household settled down to do their studies.

As he sat with Benny, going over his lessons, Grant wondered what he'd ever do with fancy clothes. Then he wondered if Hannah would like the way he looked in them, and if it weren't for the tickling, he might have gone back to refusing. It didn't matter anyway. It was too late to stop 'em. Once the girls had gotten him to go along, they'd been cutting quick as lightning, most likely afraid he'd weasel out of his bargain somehow.

"Pa, you remember when you first brought me and Sadie home?" Joshua drew Grant's attention, and Grant realized Joshua had been watching the sewing just as he had. "You sewed all six of us a new outfit of clothes."

Grant laughed. "Yeah, I really made a mess of 'em, didn't I?"

Joshua shook his head. "We should have saved 'em just as a bad example. Even then Sadie was better at it than you. And she was only five."

Sadie nodded over her needle and thread. "And you made me a dress."

Sadie and Marilyn looked up from their fine, neat stitches.

"Pa sewed you a dress?" Marilyn looked at Sadie as if she'd grown another head.

"I'd seen my ma do some sewing. Even threaded a needle for her. I didn't really know anything. But Pa's hands were so clumsy." Sadie started giggling until she had to set her needle aside. "He made Joshua a pair of pants so big, Joshua and Will could've both fit inside them."

All the children snickered. Even silent little Libby giggled behind her fingers.

"They weren't that bad," Grant said between his own chuckles. "It beat what you were wearing."

"We were all in rags, even worse'n what you've got on now." Joshua nodded. "When you made Sadie try on her new dress, it dragged on the floor in back and her knees showed in front. Plus there was no hole for her head, so you just hacked an opening with your knife."

"And then you cut the back off so it wouldn't drag, and then it was too short so you cut the front off." Sadie quit talking so she could laugh full time.

"Good thing it was about four times too big around for Sadie," Joshua said, leaning his head back against the wall, his shoulders shaking with laughter. "Will ended up wearing it as a shirt as I recall."

"Sadie got better at it quicker'n I did." Grant shook his head.

"Sadie taught me most of what I know." Marilyn grinned at her little sister.

"You picked it up fast enough." Sadie picked up her needle.

"And Cassie was ten," Joshua added. "And she knew a few things that helped us along. And you boys pitched right in to help on the ranch."

Grant remembered that little gang of orphans. Joshua, Sadie, Will, Cassie, Eli, and Sidney. They'd all been starving. It was a cold morning, and they didn't have a single coat between 'em. Will had tried to pick his pocket. Grant had caught him and known right away he was dealing with a street urchin just like he'd been near all his life.

He'd convinced Will to trust him, and before long he'd been carrying out food from a diner. . .a diner that wouldn't'a allowed black children inside. He fed six little kids breakfast while he fretted over how to take care of them forever.

Grant could see people in a huge city like New York ignoring hordes of children. The problem was just too huge for a lot of people to deal with. But it made him furious to think of the citizens of a good

Texas town like Houston letting those children scurry around in alleys without taking them in.

He'd been riding his horse, planning to sign up for the Confederacy if he could ever hunt up the War. He'd seen those children, banded together, Will acting as the father, ten-year-old Cassie mothering the littler ones, Joshua and Sadie, black, but accepted as members of the family without a question. Grant had been planning to fight for the Confederacy, just because that's what a good Texan did, but after seeing Joshua and Sadie, and knowing what danger they were in running around loose in the South, he couldn't have taken part in any fighting that supported slavery.

With no paperwork and no permission, he'd claimed them as his adopted children and taken them home. He'd found his calling in life.

Soon after the War, the first orphan train came through Sour Springs.

"Cassie and I both learned a sight quicker than you, Pa." Sadie basted a sleeve onto the shirt she was making for him.

"A fractious longhorn would'a learned quicker'n me."

The family laughed again.

Sadie looked up from her work. "Now Cassie's sewing for her little ones, just like Megan and all your other grown-up daughters. You would have made everything easier if you'd have rounded yourself up a wife before you started collecting children. That's the proper way of things."

"I was too young to get married." Grant flinched when Sadie and Marilyn exchanged a quick glance. "I'm still too young to get married."

Marilyn said quietly, "But not too young to have children, right?"

That set the whole bunch of them off in a fit of laughing again, and Grant felt his cheeks warm up even as he laughed along. He'd never explained to his children about the vow he'd made to care for young'uns. He'd told some of them when they'd grown up, after they'd left his home, but the ones who lived with him would never know. He didn't want them to think he was sacrificing anything for them, because he wasn't. He got so much more than he ever gave. But talk of marriage led to thoughts of Hannah, and kissing her, and how she'd stood shoulder-to-shoulder with him and offered to sacrifice her job for his children.

And that made him desperate to think of something else. He couldn't think of a way to talk to Charlie about that knife without embarrassing him in front of the family, so Grant left that for later and settled in beside Benny to help him wrestle with the words in his reading book.

Maybe it was time he polished up his skills for working inside the house. It'd keep him busy and keep his mind off Hannah if he'd do the sewing. He could stab himself a few times with a needle anytime she bloomed inside his head.

The girls could teach him fine stitchery and dressmaking. As Benny droned out the words of a psalm, Grant stared down at his callused hands and wondered if it was hard to crochet lace.

"Pa." Marilyn came up behind him while he leaned over Benny's book. "The fabric's cut now and the basting done, so while Sadie is busy sewing, I think I oughta cut your hair."

"Cut my hair?" Grant whirled around to face his daughter. The gleam in her eyes near to set him running out of the house.

"I need to practice on a man, since I'm getting married soon and all. Just turn around and sit still." She opened and closed the scissors with an ominous snip.

Grant glared at the little troublemaker.

She glared right back.

Finally, rolling his eyes, he turned around and ignored her to the best of his ability. . .while she scalped him.

763

TWENTY-TWO

Grant had put up with the new clothes and a haircut, but now it was eating him alive.

He ran his hands through his stumpy hair, wishing he could sleep. Lying on the kitchen floor, listening to the sound of his children breathing, living, fed and warm and safe, there was no way to explain to them the desperate burden he felt for unwanted children. He'd had Parson Babbitt tell him once that he needed to trust God to care for His sheep. That Grant, try as he might, couldn't care for them all.

Grant wrestled with the worry. He could feel those children, cold and hungry, out there, begging for a coin, just enough to keep the front of their stomachs from rubbing against the backs. The hard wood of his floor was a reminder of the hard life of a child who had no one to care if he or she lived or died.

He could still remember little Sadie when he first laid eyes on her. Her body shivered so hard in the cold, the skirt of her thin little dress waved back and forth. It haunted him to think of all Sadie had suffered before she'd come to him.

As he lay there, the clothes the girls were making started to bother him more and more. That cloth was wasted being cut and sewn into something for him. Anger burned low in his belly until he was furious thinking of it. But the children were right. It was a kind of foolishness to wear rags, thinking it would feed one hungry child.

"Trust," the parson had said. "God is in control."

If God was in control, then why had He given Grant a tiny glimpse of family? If God was in control, why had Grant's parents died? If God was worthy of trust, then Grant had to accept that He wanted children like Libby to be frightened beyond their ability to speak.

Sadie, cold and shivering. Grant opened his eyes and ruffled his short hair. He stared at the dark ceiling, the nightmarish image of his freezing daughter. Her skinny little bare knees shaking beneath a skirt that she'd grown out of years before. Rolling onto his stomach, he wondered how many nights in his life he'd been left sleepless with this torment.

God, why would You make a world where children lived, hungry and cold, in an alley? How can I believe You're in control when the innocent suffer like this?

It was a sin to spend money on himself for new clothes. And new boots were a foolish waste while children froze.

He listened to the wind whip around his ramshackle cabin and knew it was so much better in here than out there. There were more children out in the cold. He couldn't go to New York and get them without abandoning his family, but what if some were close to hand? He'd found Joshua and Sadie in Houston. It was a long trip, but Grant should be looking for them, bringing them home. He had six, but there was room beside him on the floor. He could squeeze in six more if he tried.

He rolled back to stare at the ceiling, and his heart cried out to God for sleep and peace and for a chance to take care of all the cold, hungry children who needed a home.

A creak on the ladder to the loft pulled him out of his worry. He saw Charlie backing down the steps, as silently as possible. "What are you doing?"

Charlie froze and looked down. Even in the barely existent light from the fire, Grant saw Charlie's guilt. What was going on? Grant was afraid he knew.

Charlie's rigid muscles relaxed and he climbed on down. "Just. . .
uh. . .couldn't sleep."

He was running away. Grant had seen the guilt in Charlie's eyes
when he'd realized Grant didn't have a room. Between the anger the
little boy carried around and the desire to leave before he got left, the
boy would use this as an excuse to move on. Probably planning to steal
a sack of food on his way out the door.

"Pa?"

Grant sat up and leaned forward. He turned so his back leaned
against the table leg. "Yeah, what is it?"

"I'm just restless is all. The wind is keeping me up, I suppose. A cold
wind makes me think of bad times I had before I came here."

Pa pushed his bedroll aside. He rolled to his knees and grabbed a
couple of logs and threw them onto the fire. Charlie dropped down in
front of the licking flames, and the two of them watched as a friendly,
reassuring crackle lit up the room.

"Did I wake you?" Charlie asked.

"I wasn't asleep."

"Are you sure?

Grant shrugged. "I don't think so. Maybe I dozed off. The night can
trick a man."

Grant rested his palm on Charlie's shoulder, and Charlie flinched
like a child might who'd been treated harshly by a man's hand.

"It sure enough can." The boy sat frozen under the touch.

"It can trick a man into thinking only dark thoughts. It can trick
a man into making some small thing into something large without
the light of day to shine on his worries." Grant felt Charlie's fear and
tension and let go of him. Turning around, Grant rested his back on the
stones that framed the fire. Charlie visibly relaxed and leaned closer to
the warmth of the crackling fire.

Grant decided the boy wasn't going to say anything more. "I was
awake because. . .I don't. . .need new clothes. I want to be ready in

case there are children who come along. I shouldn't have let Sadie talk me into those duds. I should leave Joshua in charge and go see if there have been any children abandoned nearby."

"And leave the family alone?"

"No, I can't do that."

A silence stretched between them as the smell and warmth of the fire soothed and eased the knots tying up Grant's thoughts.

"Pa, it's not the new clothes that are bothering you. It's not even thinking about children who might need you."

"Yes, it is."

"It's the devil."

"What?" Grant sat forward. He hadn't expected to hear that from the boy.

Charlie, crossing his ankles, propped his elbows on his knees and rested his chin in both hands. "The devil is who torments good folks in the night. He whispers doubt in your ear. He stirs up anger. He picks at any little mistake you've made, or thinks you've made, and blows it up big. That's Satan, stirring and stirring trouble, like a pot he's trying to boil over, hoping he can spill sin through your soul and slop it all over the people around you."

Grant's eyes narrowed as he considered that. "I reckon you're right, son. When I'm up and about, busy with you kids and life, I know I'm doing God's work. But if you could have seen Sadie when I found her..." Grant couldn't go on for a minute. He scrubbed his hands over his face and combed his fingers through his short hair.

When he was sure his voice wouldn't break, Grant continued. "I remember other little children when I ran the streets of New York. I saw them die, run down by carriages. I saw older children beating on them. I saw them dead from the cold. They beat on me, too." Grant paused. "I saw the younger ones grow up and turn mean and get in trouble. I was right along with them. I'd spend time in an orphanage, then I'd run off, then the police would catch me doing something and send me back. I felt my own innocence die, replaced with anger and cruelty. As I got older, I saw new little ones show up. I knew what was ahead of them. I couldn't do anything for them then when I was young. But now I can."

Grant leaned toward his troubled son. "I want you here, Charlie. If I found others in need, I'd bring in ten more. I'd find the room for 'em. Maybe I should build a great big house and, who knows, maybe find room for a hundred. They could stay here until they're grown and. . ."

"You can't be a real father to a hundred children at once, Pa. You couldn't even feed them. And you could never give them a father's love, not enough to change their lives."

"Maybe I could. I'm glad I've had each one of you kids."

"Even if we've done bad?"

Charlie was talking about the knife. And maybe some other things Grant hadn't caught the boy at. "The funny thing is I seem to love the one who's going through the hardest time the most."

Charlie sat up straight. He and Grant studied each other. Grant didn't want to force a confession out of the boy. Instead, to make it easier, Grant said, "I saw the knife. If you give it to me and tell me where you got it, I'll slip it back. No one needs to know it was stolen."

Charlie sat silently for a long time. Grant gave him as long as he needed.

Finally the boy fished into his pocket and handed the knife to Grant, then reached in again and brought out a handful of coins. "I took it from the Stroben's Mercantile. Some money, too."

Grant nodded. "Things stuck to my fingers when I was young. It's not right. But when you live like we lived, sin starts to look like the only way to survive."

Grant patted the boy on the back, careful to be gentle. "I look back now at the food I took and the clothes and other things and I know it was wrong, but I know I'd do it again to live."

This time Charlie allowed the touch.

"But you don't need to do that anymore, Charlie. I don't have a lot of money for a knife and to give you young'uns spending money. But you'll never go hungry. You'll never be cold. And I think, if you asked, they sometimes hire help at the mercantile, delivering supplies in town. You could earn the money for this knife if you really want it."

Charlie slouched again. "No one's gonna give me a job. I've tried that before."

"You might be surprised. Harold's a good man. He'd make you work hard, but he'd pay you fair."

Charlie's eyes lit up in the flickering fire. "You think so?"

"I could ask him for you. Or, if you felt brave enough, you could take this knife back to him, tell him what you did, and ask permission to work off the cost. I think Harold would respect that. I know God would."

"Why do you suppose God lets children live on the streets? Cold, hungry, hurt?"

Grant sighed. The exact question he had been wrestling with for years. He knew the truth. It just wasn't easy to accept. "I think, Charlie, that God doesn't really care that much about our bodies."

"What?" Charlie seemed upset.

Grant tried to explain himself. "Oh, He does care. He loves every one of us so much. He knows the numbers of hairs on our heads. But I think God sees inside us, and what's in there is more important than food or clothes or good health. God cares about souls. He cares about us, one soul at a time. If a child dies, cold on the street, but he knows the Lord, then there is rejoicing in heaven. And a lot of street kids do have a beautiful, childlike faith in God."

"A lot don't."

"A lot of warm, well-fed people don't, either. God loves people one soul at a time. And His truth is written in all their hearts so every child has a chance to believe." Then Grant added, as much to himself as to Charlie, "I can only help the children God puts in my path, and I've done that. If God wants me to have more children, He'll send them.

All those years ago, Will didn't try to pick my pocket by accident. He and his friends were sent into my path by God. It wasn't an accident that little Benny got put on an orphan train at such a young age. He was mine and God got him here. Marilyn didn't just happen to show herself at the exact instant I took a shortcut through an alley. It's not a coincidence Mrs. Norris broke all the rules for Libby by letting her join the other orphans. I know each of you children was meant to be mine. That includes you."

"And any other children that are meant to be yours will be sent here." Charlie was clearly visible by the now-roaring firelight. The crackling wood, the comforting smell, and the soft whoosh of heat coming from the hearth seemed to mute the howling wind outside, or maybe the wind had died. Or, Grant thought, maybe Satan had been vanquished, at least for tonight.

Charlie yawned.

"You'd better get yourself to bed, boy. Morning comes almighty early around this house."

Charlie nodded. "It's long past time for rest, and that's a fact. Uh. . .Pa?"

"Yes?"

"I think God wants you to let the girls dress you up. I think this is something you should do for them and not fight it. Your reasons not to spend money on yourself. . .I understand them, but now and then it's okay to have a new pair of boots if your feet are really cold."

Grant nodded. "I reckon that's a fact."

"If you'll give me back the knife and money, I'll go have a talk with Mr. Stroben tomorrow after school."

"I'll come with you if you want."

Charlie was silent for a long time. Grant though he saw the boy's shoulders trembling. At last he said, "Yeah, I guess you'd better, in case he calls the sheriff."

Grant gave Charlie a gentle squeeze on the back of his neck. "He won't. I'll come by the school and walk over with you."

"Thanks." Charlie climbed back up the ladder.

Grant lay awake until he heard soft snoring coming from overhead.

Sadie braced him about the boots first thing in the morning.

Grant promised he'd go in and order a pair from Zeb. He meant to ride in along with his family when they were heading to school, but a cow had delivered her baby out of season and needed to be driven into the barn before the calf ended up as food for the coyotes.

Grant told the children to go on ahead.

"Pa, you're just trying to get out of buying new boots." Marilyn crossed her arms and refused to get in the buckboard.

"No, I'll order 'em. I promise."

"Today?" Sadie asked, standing shoulder-to-shoulder with Marilyn.

"Yes, today."

His older daughters, suddenly a bossy pair of mother hens, climbed into the wagon. After she was perched on the wagon seat next to Joshua, Sadie hollered, "Make sure and wear your new clothes to town. You're shamin' the whole family wearing those rags."

Grant would have felt worse about shaming them if Sadie had been able to keep the smile off her face. "Scat, all of you. Get down the road to school, or I'm turning you all over my knee."

He could hear them laughing until they were out of sight. Handing out punishment had never been his strong suit.

Grant rode out to round up the cow and her calf. The cow seemed bent on killing Grant for messing with her baby. And the calf, wobbly and shivering, needed tending. Grant's shorn neck froze him the whole time. With one thing and another, he didn't get back to the cabin until well past noon.

When he came in, he saw his new shirt and pants all folded neat as a pin on the kitchen table. Resting on top was Joshua's new Stetson. Grant wondered if this was a hint for him to buy a new one, or if Joshua was offering Grant the hat.

Too tired to worry about it, Grant shed his only pair of pants and noticed his old clothes were not only rags, they were filthy rags. Oh, the girls kept other things washed up nice and tidy, but Grant only had one pair of clothes. How was he supposed to have his clothes washed if he was wearing them? Once in a great while, he'd shed his things and get along in an even older pair he'd kept, but those had holes that were next-thing-to-indecent, so he usually just hung on to his pants and shirt and shooed the girls away to clean someone else up. After a morning dodging slashing horns and flailing hooves, he was coated in dirt and sweat. He'd also ripped a couple of new holes in his rags.

Maybe God had stepped in last night, knowing what a fierce mama cow could do to fabric so rotten sharp words could shred it. Grant thought about his talk with Charlie last night. The talk had brought a considerable new peace in Grant's heart. He accepted that God had sent children who needed him into his path. How had that orphan train picked the little town of Sour Springs as the last stop?

For that matter, how had he happened to be in Houston all those years ago? He was hunting for the War. Why had he thought he'd find it in Houston? It'd made sense to him at the time. And if Grant was honest with himself, he knew Houston wasn't a huge impersonal city like New York. The good folks there wouldn't leave six children on the street. People would have stepped in and found them homes—well, maybe not Sadie and Joshua. There could have been trouble there. Grant's heart rebelled at the thought that Sadie and Joshua would have been turned over to some slaver for the remaining years of the War. It didn't sit well to trust God to bring children to him, but Grant knew it was right.

Grant turned his attention to the wreckage of his old clothes. Imagining how the girls would fuss if he dirtied up his new clothes the first time he wore 'em, he took a quick bath, even washing what was left of his hair—a blamed nuisance in the middle of the day.

He found a nasty bruise on his stomach where the cow had landed a hoof. A scrape ran from his hip to his knee where she'd hooked him with her spread of horns. He'd worn his chaps or that cranky old cow would've poked a hole right into his leg. Shaking his head at his battered body, he dried off and dressed. Then he noticed his old clothes, piled beside the tub. They really were rags. Not even fit to save for scrubbing the floor. He knew Sadie was teasing him some, but he probably *was* shaming his young'uns by wearing them.

With a resigned sigh, he did what he had to do. He tossed his old rags onto the fire and grinned to think of telling the girls he wanted another set of clothes right away so he'd have one for good and one for work.

It was midafternoon before he headed for town. He brought along an extra horse so Charlie could stay in town with him.

Stopping first at Zeb's, he found out it'd take a week to get his boots. With some grumbling about highway robbery, Grant paid for them. Then he went to the mercantile and warned Harold and Mabel about the coming talk with Charlie, just to give them a little time to decide how they wanted things handled. Grant bought himself a new hat while he was there and went to pick up his light-fingered son. His children came flooding out the schoolhouse door and embarrassed him half to death with their fussing over his clothes and hat.

They went together to Ian's blacksmith shop, and Grant visited with his grown-up son while the two of them hitched up Grant's team that boarded at Ian's during the school day. Before he was done, Joshua, even with his tender ribs and gimpy arm, was beside them helping out.

"Pa, most of the other parents have been in to school helping with little things." Joshua glanced uncertainly at Ian, one of Joshua's many older brothers.

"True enough," Ian said. "Megan did some sewing for costumes. I like her staying close to home, with the baby on the way, but if I bring her the material she's able to sew."

"Yeah," Josh went on. "And Ella Johnson and Agnes Mackey, along with a lot of other mothers, are bringing cookies and cider for a party afterward. Mr. Mackey fashioned a cross. He and Mr. Harrison brought it in and we're using it for the play. Almost everyone has come by and offered to help."

"Well, it sounds like she's got everything handled already. Don't reckon she needs me underfoot." Grant buckled the leathers across the broad backs of his horses.

"Ian donated some lumber so she can knock together a little set of steps for us to stand on." Joshua passed a strap under one of the horses, and Grant caught it and fastened it. "But I don't think she's got anyone to help her build 'em."

"I'll go do it for her." Ian started leading the team outside to hook it up to the buckboard. A horse shifted and snorted in a back stall of Ian's shop. It drew all their attention. "No, I've got to finish shoeing a horse. I told Zeb I'd have it ready tomorrow morning. Well, I'll shoe the horse now, and maybe I can get Miss Cartwright's carpentering done tonight."

"You shouldn't leave Megan alone, not with the baby so close." Grant fell silent, knowing what he needed to do.

Joshua looked Grant straight on. "I can do it, Pa. I still ache some but I'm up to it. But since you haven't done anything, and you've got the most kids of anyone in the school, and the main reason she has to build the steps—she calls 'em risers—is because there are so many of us, I think it's the right thing for you to offer."

Grant's temper started heating up to hear his son reminding him of his responsibilities. Grant was a fair enough man to know he wasn't really mad at Joshua. He was embarrassed not to have helped. But that didn't stop him from doing a slow burn. And mixed up with his mad was a sharp ache to see Hannah. She could hurt herself trying to build things. For heaven's sake, she'd near burned herself to death trying to pour coffee. Anything could happen if she was turned loose with a hammer. Grant knew for sure the little woman didn't have the skills a body needed to build risers, whatever they were.

Grabbing the crown of his hat to clamp it as firm as iron on his head, he said, "I'll do it. First, Charlie and I need to go to Stroben's Mercantile. Then I'll send him on home. He won't be long, Josh, so travel slow so he can catch you. I don't like any of you on the trail alone these days. You leave the evening chores for me. I don't want you reinjuring yourself."

Harold arranged for Charlie to work for him after school for the next month to earn the knife. Grant sent Charlie home and headed for the schoolhouse like it was his own doom.

When he got inside, he found the priggish little teacher eyeball-deep in a mess. . .as usual. She knelt at the front of the classroom, wrestling with a long piece of board. Several nails were clamped tight between her lips, and she had a hammer tucked under her arm.

Joshua's polite scolding burned in his ears as he strode to the front of the room. She turned, a pleasant smile on her nail-holding lips as she heard him approach. And then she saw him, and that smile shrank off her face like wool washed in boiling hot water.

"Let me do that." Grant pulled the board out of her hand.

She stared at him, acting as mute as Libby.

He held out his hand. "And get those nails out'a your mouth before you stab yourself to death with 'em."

She removed the nails and laid them in his hand.

Now that her mouth wasn't occupied, Grant moved to stop her before she could start yapping at him. "Joshua said you needed help. What do you want me to do in here?"

TWENTY-THREE

W hat was he doing in here?

Feeling a little like she'd swallowed the nails, she tore her gaze from Grant and looked at the pile of wood in front of her.

"Hannah?" Grant's sharp voice jerked her out of her daze.

She looked at him. His face was red as a beet, his jaw clenched until he bared his teeth when he talked. He looked furious.

"What did I do now?"

Grant blinked. Startled into relaxing his jaw a bit, he said, "You didn't do anything."

"Then why are you so mad at me?"

"I'm not mad. I'm here to help build this riser Joshua said you needed for your pageant. What is it, anyway?"

"Well, you look mad clear to the bone, Grant Cooper. And if you're going to come in here and be unpleasant, I'd just as soon do it myself."

Grant's eyes narrowed. She felt like she stared straight at a gunslinger at high noon. "My name isn't Grant Cooper."

Hannah stood and walked straight up to his cranky face. "Your name *is* Grant Cooper, and I've listed all your children, except for Sadie, with the last name of Cooper, and listed Grant Cooper, you"—she jabbed him in his chest with her index finger—"as their father. Since you're too stubborn to name yourself, I did it for you."

The red in Grant's face turned an alarming shade of purple.

"*Fine*." He could have dissolved the nails with the acid in his voice.

Hannah was glad he didn't have them in his mouth because she needed them.

With a choppy slash of his hand, he said, "Call 'em whatever you want."

"I will." Hannah gave her chin a little jerk.

"But just remember, I came in here offering to help and you started right in calling me names."

"What names?"

"Stubborn and unpleasant."

"I wasn't insulting you."

"Yes, you were."

"I was asking you why you were being so stubborn and unpleasant."

"I'm *not* stubborn and unpleasant."

"Well, that's my point exactly. If you *were* stubborn and unpleasant, and you came in here acting like this, I'd just think, 'There goes Grant being himself.' But since you *aren't* those things, I had to wonder what set you off."

Grant dragged his hat off his head as if he had to keep his hands busy so he wouldn't strangle her.

Hannah was distracted from his temper by his haircut. The man looked purely civilized.

"So, the thanks I get for offering to help is to be braced with more of your insults?"

Hannah clapped her mouth shut from defending herself. She'd give him this one point to end the quarrel he'd started. Besides, just because something was true didn't mean it wasn't insulting to point it out. And anyway, she did need help with the risers.

Inhaling long and slow to get her pounding heart to settle into a normal rhythm, she said, "You're right. I just thought after last time you were here, you might. . ." She stopped. What crazy impulse had made her bring up his last visit? Maybe the same impulse that kept her remembering, day and night, how much she'd enjoyed kissing him. And how badly she'd wanted to do him violence when she'd seen him holding Prudence in his arms. She'd heard the gossip, too. Grant was definitely sparking the seamstress. They'd walked arm-in-arm down the street. Behaving that way in public was nearly an engagement announcement.

Trying to move on, she said, "I'd be grateful for your help. Here's what I planned to do." She described her idea for risers. She'd seen such a thing at a church in Omaha one time and heard them called such, but she couldn't figure out how they'd made them.

From her description, he began hammering, knocking together sturdy risers so quickly she could barely follow his flashing hands. He made two sets without speaking to her beyond grunting.

Hannah stood off to the side the whole time, doing little more than giving directions, and precious few of those.

After setting them in place, he turned to go.

"Grant?" When she said his name she looked down to avoid making eye contact and noticed she'd twisted the frill around the middle of her new green dress into a knot. She released her death grip on the fabric and tried to smooth away the wrinkles.

She glanced up to see Grant freeze. Then his shoulders slumped, and he turned around to face her. Hannah saw a look of pain on his face. She forgot what in the world she wanted to say to him as she closed the distance between them.

He looked at her, long and quiet. "New dress?"

Hannah kept swiping at the mess of wrinkles she'd made. This fabric had come from Grant. She'd thank him if she wasn't afraid he knew nothing about it.

"Sadie and Marilyn helped me make it." Distracted by the knowledge that she could get the girls in trouble by telling the truth, Hannah forgot about how awkward things were with Grant. True, the dress she was wearing now had come from him, but she'd been paid since then and gotten enough cloth for a riding skirt. She and the girls were already done with it.

"I got my first pay. I earned ten dollars for the first two weeks of school. I wasn't supposed to get paid until I'd worked a month, but Sadie encouraged me to tell the school board I needed the money. She said they would understand, and they did. I bought fabric for. . .uh. . . for myself." Hannah went back to twisting her skirt. "And my students turned the tables on me and became teachers. With your girls working together, I had this dress done in no time."

"Money," Grant said with the first relaxed smile Hannah had seen on his face today. "I remember the first time I earned an honest dollar. It's about the sweetest feeling on this earth."

Hannah smiled and set aside the story about the girls bringing her fabric. There was always time to tell him later. "I've never spent much on myself. Before I came here, even if I did find some work, there was. . ."

Hannah almost said Libby's name, thinking of how her injured little foot had taken up every spare penny. Catching herself in time, Hannah wondered what Grant would say about all the lies. Libby was doing well from what Hannah could see. She still never spoke, but her limp was barely noticeable these days, thanks to the shoes Grant had fashioned for her. Libby smiled easily and ran around with the other children in school. Emory Harrison, Gladys's youngest son, enjoyed quieter play than the roughhousing big boys, and he and Benny had become Libby's champions around the playground. There was no reason to bring up her relationship with Libby to Grant. Silent Libby certainly wasn't going to spill the beans

"There was what?" Grant asked.

Hannah drew a blank for a few seconds. "There was. . .uh. . .oh, just always something more pressing to spend it on."

"The girls forced me to get some new clothes." Grant looked at himself. "They sewed them up for me, the whole outfit just last night."

Hannah had noticed how tidy he looked. "And you got a haircut?"

"Marilyn sheared me like a sheep. My girls set on me like a pack of wolves. Told me I was shaming them with my old clothes. When they were done, I looked like this." Grant held his arms out and looked down at himself, shaking his head. "Kids."

"You look really nice." Hannah almost choked when those words slipped out.

"So do you." Grant closed his mouth so quick Hannah heard his teeth click together.

They stared at each other. Hannah knew what he had on his mind—the same thing she had on hers. Hannah felt as if a team of Clydesdales had just galloped into the schoolroom between them and they were pretending not to notice.

Forcing herself to do the right thing, she said, "We never should have. . ."

"Hannah, I owe you. . ."

Speaking on top of each other, they both fell silent.

Into the silence, Grant said, "I want to apologize for the other morning. I took. . .uh. . .that is. . .improper familiarities passed between us. I. . .I don't. . .it won't. . .we can't let that happen again."

Hannah thought of Prudence. He was getting ready to confess that he had betrayed his intended with that kiss. She had to stop him before he cut her heart completely out. "You're right. We can't. I was as wrong as you. I'm here to teach school and nothing else. And you've got someone else, I know. Thank you for your help with—"

Grant kissed her again, quick as a striking rattlesnake, only way, way nicer.

He practically jumped away from her. Shaking his head, he turned and rushed out of the building, muttering something Hannah couldn't hear.

It was a good thing the risers he'd made were well-built because Hannah barely managed to stumble over to them before her knees gave out. She sank onto them hard enough that if they'd been rickety, she'd have squashed them flat to the floor.

TWENTY-FOUR

Grant did the chores the next morning so fast he was finished before the wagon rattled down the lane, taking his family to school.

Charlie rode his own horse so he could stay in town to work. Grant planned to ride out to meet the boy when he returned.

Jamming the pitchfork into the haystack, he headed to the immense pile of split wood, wondering if he should make each piece a little smaller. He had to find something, anything, to keep his mind off Hannah.

Worse yet, he was facing a ride with that child-hating Shirt Lady. He shuddered every time he thought of that awkward hour he'd have to spend with the fool woman.

He stared at his tiny, ramshackle house. He looked at the looming mountain that rose up behind it, covered with trees that clung to the sheer slope.

Most of the woodlands surrounding the Rocking C were either scrub or older trees that wouldn't work for a log cabin. Three small stands held trees the right size. He'd considered chopping down these trees a hundred times and rejected the idea because it was so dangerous. Even in the summer he'd avoided them. Now, in the bitter winter with its short, dreary days, it was a nightmare.

Perfect!

It beat his other plan—holding his head under a bucket of ice water until his thoughts cleared of confounded women making his life a living nightmare.

He jogged to the woodpile, snatched up his axe, and headed for the stand of young trees. Sure it might kill him, but if he died, Joshua, Marilyn, and Sadie could manage. And until it did kill him, he'd be clinging to the side of a mountain for dear life, which would keep him from saddling up his horse and riding to town to see for himself if Hannah's hair was as thick and soft as he remembered. It had come to mind around a thousand times that, as long as he kissed her anyway yesterday, he might as well have touched her hair just once, to check and see if—

With a near howl to stop his wayward thoughts, he charged the mountain. Gripping the axe handle as if holding onto his last shred of sanity, he headed up that slope.

He fell halfway off the mountain a dozen times that morning. He tossed the axe away and grabbed a tree as he slid past and always scrambled right back up to work. The pile of trees at the base of the mountain grew fast, and Grant thought he was getting the knack of being a mountain goat. It's not like he was falling off a cliff or anything. He'd just slide along, sometimes get to rolling a little, and catch himself as soon as possible. He slammed into a couple of trees and that hurt. But thanks to the peril, it definitely took his mind off Hannah.

Mostly.

With no notion of time passing, he sidled along the treacherous bluff, chopping even while he knew he was acting like a maniac. The hillside was slippery with half-melted snow and so steep that, when he cut a tree, if it didn't snag, it fell most of the way to the house.

He came close to forgetting how much he wanted to see Hannah again toward the middle of the afternoon when he was so exhausted he couldn't see straight. Cutting down a whole forest was a stroke of genius.

Joshua came home driving the wagon.

The young'uns saw the load of lumber that had tumbled to within a hundred feet of the cabin.

"What are you up to, Pa?" Josh yelled from below.

"We're building on. You go ahead and start chores. I'm almost done here." It wasn't exactly true, because Grant intended to keep chopping down trees for the rest of his life if it helped keep his unruly thoughts in order. But it was true enough, because he had nearly enough for the two extra rooms he had in mind. For now, he was almost done.

With cries of excitement, the children ignored his wish to be left completely alone and immediately jumped in to help.

Grant thought of Charlie riding home alone from Harold's and the lowdown polecat who had attacked Joshua still running loose. Grant had to quit and go ride his son home, then go back to face Shirt Lady. He was out of time.

The children were so excited, begging to help, Grant almost quit going crazy with his wayward thoughts. "You young'uns can't go up that hill. It's too steep. And I don't want any of you working the axe. Josh, you could be chopping, but you're too beat-up and you girls haven't had enough practice."

"We could hitch up the horse and drag the logs into place. Just tell us where you want them." Marilyn's eyes flashed with excitement.

Sadie looked like she wanted to jump up and down just from thinking of the new rooms.

Grant didn't want them to do a thing. This was his project. Meant to keep him busy working himself near to death for the rest of his life. "Leave it. There's plenty to do with chores."

"But you'll be back with him in just a few minutes, Pa." Benny started climbing around on the teetering mound of tree trunks, risking his life.

Grant's stomach clenched when he realized his children might be in danger and he shouldn't leave them. Then his heart lifted. He'd tell Shirt Lady the ride was off and blame it on his children.

She'd hate it.

She'd hate him.

She'd never come near him again.

Grant smiled for the first time all day.

But he had to ride in and do it. That'd still take awhile because she'd no doubt nag him near to death. He'd better make sure the young'uns didn't worry.

"Uh. . .after I get back with Charlie, I have to ride back to town for. . .for. . ."

"For what, Pa?" Sadie asked.

"I'm supposed to go out riding with. . .with. . ."

Sadie and Marilyn whirled to face him, their eyes blazing with excitement.

His throat dried up and ached as if he'd swallowed a cactus thorn.

"With. . .who?" Marilyn clutched her hands under her neck.

Sadie took a step closer. Grant noticed Josh grinning and wondered what the boy had in his head.

"With that. . ." The thorn grew into a whole prickly pear, and Grant cleared his throat and wished for a drink of water. "That. . .seamstress woman. . .Prudence." Confound it, he'd gone and learned her name. He'd have his hands full forgetting it now that he'd actually said it out loud.

Marilyn's hands dropped to her side in fists. Sadie gasped. Josh's grin shrank away. Benny straightened from his wild scramble and rolled off the pile of lumber.

Grant snagged him in midair, glad for the distraction. "Now, you quit your climbing. While I'm gone, I want you to—"

"Prudence?" Sadie screeched like to break a man's eardrums. "You're going out riding with *that* nasty woman? Why, she won't so much as look at any of us. Last week at church. . ."

"How did you get mixed up with her?" Marilyn talked over the top of Sadie. Both of them tore into him in a way no child should ever speak to a father. As a matter of fact, the way no person should ever speak to another.

"I can't stand her, Pa." Benny squirmed to get loose of Grant's hold. "I ran into her once in the store. I mean ran hard into her. But it weren't on purpose. It was an accident. And she got so mad I thought she was going to take a swing at me. She doesn't like. . ."

Josh started in, too. "One time we just passed on the street and she made a face like I smelled bad. She held her skirt off to the side like she was afraid my skin would stain her. . . ."

Grant took a moment to thank God for Libby's muteness and Charlie's absence. Sure Grant hated being alone. But when his children were here, it didn't mean it was okay for them to yell at him.

The noise went on until Grant was afraid Charlie would be home on his own. "Okay! Enough!" Grant took a long route around the mob his children had become. "I told the woman I'd take her for a ride and a promise is a promise." One he intended to weasel out of, but he'd do it face to face, like a man. A weaselly man, but still. . .

"I'm going!" Grant was madder at himself than his children were, so their yelling barely vexed him. They tagged him to the barn, yapping and nagging to beat all, which at least got Benny away from that log pile.

Grant's ears were ringing by the time he hitched up the wagon and rode out of the yard. Spending time with that nasty, child-hating Shirt Lady wasn't going to be that much different than home. He planned to talk fast while he told her there'd be no ride then run for home.

He sat up straighter. He'd ask Charlie to wait at work rather than ride the boy home and go back. With that as an excuse, Grant wouldn't even be much delayed. He remembered that determined look she'd had while cornering him into the ride. If he couldn't head her off, he'd pick up Charlie and take the boy along for the ride. Make sure Charlie sat between them on the buckboard. Better yet, maybe he and Charlie could sit on the seat and they'd stick Shirt Lady in the back by herself. Bringing a surly child along on their date ought to put the perfect finishing touch on any ideas Shirt Lady might be hatching in her brain.

For the first time, Grant worried that Charlie might be settling in and cheering up. A good-natured child wouldn't get under Shirt Lady's skin nearly as much as a sullen, sly child. Sorely hoping Charlie hadn't turned happy on him, Grant hurried the horse toward Sour Springs.

"Tonight's the night." Prudence looked at Horace. This was it. Tonight they'd get it done.

She'd be married to Grant by sundown and his property would be hers within days. The man would then take an unfortunate fall off his horse. She'd inherit, sell to someone who recognized the value of that seeping oil, then head for California with Horace. A man who was too dumb to know he had an oil field in his backyard deserved to have it taken away.

"I know what to do." Horace slurped the last of his coffee and slapped the tin cup on the table. "Get this table cleaned up. He'll be here soon enough. You don't want him seeing there's two people living here."

"I'll get him inside somehow. The sprained ankle worked last time, except he left me at the door. This time I'll force him to bring me in. Collapse if I have to."

"All we need is to get him one step inside. I'll be behind the door and knock him cold. By the time he comes around, the whole town will know he's been in here too long. Won't matter what he says, they'll believe you." Horace rubbed his hands together. Prudence could see he was already counting the money.

Prudence tried her best not to let the greed shine in her own eyes. "Stop talking about it. I'm afraid he'll see it in my face how much I'm looking forward to our marriage." Prudence laughed.

Horace put his hands on her. Money always brought out the animal in him. He pulled her hard against him.

"Stop it. It's almost time for him to get here. Don't mess me up."

Their eyes locked. "This is the big score, Prudy. The one we've been waiting for."

The light in Horace's eyes made Prudence's heart bound with excitement. He lowered his head to mess her up good just as they heard the clatter of wagon wheels pull to a stop by the shop door.

"He's early. Maybe he's lookin' forward to his big date." Horace let her go with a crude laugh.

Prudence's living quarters were in the back of her shop. She hurried ahead of Horace to let Grant in. Horace followed, and as Prudence brushed the wrinkles out of her prettiest gingham dress and straightened her hair, Horace slipped behind the door, his eyes hot and excited.

Prudence knew he wanted to finish this now. So did she. If she could just get Grant to take a single step inside. . . She inhaled slowly, concentrating on replacing the hungry look of greed with one of adoration for the stupid fool now knocking on her door.

She reached for the knob.

Grant pulled his hat off his head as Shirt Lady swung the door open. "I don't have much—"

"Grant, you're here at last." Prudence threw her arms around his neck and came at his lips again.

Grant ducked and he accidentally kinda butted her in the lips with his head.

"Oww." She pressed one hand to her mouth and clung to him with the other.

He pulled loose quick while she was distracted. "Uh, sorry about that. I'm a clumsy one, for a fact. Listen Shirt. . .uh. . .I mean. . .uh. . ." Grant had to think for a second, but he remembered—much to his dismay. "Prudence. I've got a. . .uh. . .the thing is. . ."

Her eyes met his, something sharp and knowing in them. She glanced down at his feet as he backed away. She could tell he was canceling their ride most likely.

"I left this dangerous pile of logs. . . ."

"My fault entirely, Grant, honey. Don't worry a speck about that little bump." She slipped past him and practically ran to the wagon.

"Now, Prudence, the thing is. . ."

She climbed up that wagon quick as a squirrel scaling a tree trunk. Grant sighed. Now he was going to have to get her down. He'd told Harold he had to run an errand and to keep Charlie working for another few minutes. But Harold wanted to close up shop, so there just wasn't going to be time for a ride. He slumped as he followed after.

"Let's go, Grant. You promised." She shined those wide eyes on him, and he thought he saw tears getting set to fall. Well, he'd been a father to girls for a long, long time. A few tears didn't matter a bit to him. Women went with waterworks just like a beaver and buckteeth.

"I can't take you riding." Grant choked on her name. The woman made him feel as awkward as an ox trying to sled down a hill on a toboggan, and there was no denying it.

He thought of Hannah at that moment. Of course he thought of Hannah most moments, so that came as no surprise. No ox on a toboggan with Hannah. He hadn't put a foot wrong there when he'd kissed her. Except he shouldn't have done it at all. But he'd never come within a mile of knocking her in the head. Probably a shame. A good head butt might have ended all of Grant's troubles. But no, everything had gone just right. In fact, it was so right he'd. . .

"Hi, Harold." Shirt Lady's overly loud voice drew him back to the present. "Grant and I are going for a little ride."

"No, I'm not!" Grant decided. Since the woman was determined to have her way, he'd have to be doubly determined to get rid of her. "If you'd have let me finish, I was trying to tell you I've got a problem out at the ranch and I can't take time for a ride. Plus, I've got to get Charlie home. With Joshua hurt and. . ."

"Joshua hurt?" She stopped her babbling to Harold and turned on him.

Grant got the impression that he'd said something important, but he couldn't think what.

"Yes, with him hurt, I don't like leaving the children alone."

"I heard he died." The little witch's eyes narrowed into something that made a shiver run down Grant's backbone.

"Where'd you hear that?"

A long silence stretched between them. Then, talking too fast, she said, "I heard he fell off. . .off. . .I mean I heard he fell. I heard it was a long fall, and I guess I assumed he'd died."

Grant suddenly didn't give two hoots and a holler whether he hurt Shirt Lady's feelings. "You thought I'd have a son die and just go on as if it were nothing? I talked to you in town the day after it happened. You think I'd send the rest of the children to school the next day? You thought I'd agree to go riding with you a day after my son died?"

The longer he talked the more furious he got. It was all true. The woman really did believe all of that. "You didn't notice in this little town that there wasn't a funeral? Or what'd you think I'd do? Just toss him in a dirt hole and pay it no mind?"

The nasty hag's face turned stony, and she didn't answer his questions. Well, what she'd said before was all the answer he'd ever need. "Get down from the wagon. Now! I've got to get home. There'll be no ride now. . .nor ever."

Prudence held the spot and Grant crossed his arms. At last she moved, swinging down, slipping and tumbling toward the ground.

Instinctively, Grant moved to catch her.

She cried out in fear and pain. And instead of guilt or regret, all her caterwauling made Grant's stomach turn to be this close to the battleaxe.

His children had been right. Of course, he'd already known it. He wanted to kick himself for thinking this was a good idea, all because he wanted to make sure Hannah didn't have any crazy ideas about him just because. . .just because he. . .he had. . . crazy ideas about her.

Shirt Lady said in a tearful voice, her arms clinging around his neck, "Just help me inside. The ankle you hurt storming out of the school and colliding with me is acting up again."

Grant practically lifted her off her feet in his hurry to get shed of the woman. "Fine."

"I didn't mean to offend you with my comment about Joshua. I just heard he had a terrible fall. I thought terrible meant that he'd died. I didn't think about funerals and such. Please don't be angry with me, Grant. Please!" Her voice rose to a screech and tears now flowed freely from her eyes.

"Okay, I misunderstood." Grant didn't think so, but he'd do about anything to get her to quit squalling. Anything but go on a ride with her. He hustled her the few steps to her door while she seemed determined to drag along like a freight wagon with the brake on. "But I've got children. And you don't like children. That's as clear as the Texas sky. That makes us a bad match, and there's no point in wasting time denying it. We won't be going on any rides, ever." He swung her door inward and stepped back, letting loose of her waist.

She gasped in pain and caught at him. "Just please, get me to the chair."

He let her grab his arm but kept it extended, holding his body well away from her. For some reason the woman had a knack for ending up hanging from his neck. Her clinging arms gave him chills. Like ice cold chains were wrapping around him.

Grant saw a straight-backed chair only a few feet into the murky store. How could the woman see to do any sewing? "Okay, but the door stays wide open." He took a step in.

"Pa, you need any help?"

Grant turned and saw Charlie just a step behind him.

"Yeah, reckon I could use some help. She fell off the wagon and hurt her ankle and now she needs me to help her inside."

"Miss Cartwright, could you help, too, please?" Charlie said, turning to look back.

Lifting his eyes, Grant looked over Charlie's shoulder.

And there stood Hannah, her lips pursed, her arms crossed. Ready to start in nagging him, too, most likely.

Grant wished mightily for a chance to climb back up that mountain and tangle with cliffs and trees and a razor-sharp axe. His life made sense when he was doing things like that.

"I'll be glad to help, Charlie." Her eyes were as bright and burning hot as the blue at the heart of a flame. "What exactly is the problem, Prudence?"

"Uh...I...my ankle is..." Shirt Lady straightened and took her arm off Grant's neck, favoring her leg but standing well enough.

"I thought you were limping on your right leg when you first fell. Now it's your left. Did you injure both of them then?" Hannah's chin lifted, defiant and strong, but Grant saw the hurt in her eyes.

And why wouldn't she be hurt? He'd kissed her twice now. The woman had a right to believe, if Grant was an honorable man, that he wouldn't do such a thing unless he had feelings for her.

Grant let the child-hating Shirt Lady go to stand or fall on her own and had his hands full not reaching for Hannah and that pert chin and sassy...

"Good night, then, Grant." Shirt Lady stepped back and closed the door with a hard snap.

"Pa, what were you doing with that mean old hag?" Charlie said it plenty loud for Shirt Lady to hear. Grant didn't even consider shushing the boy. "Why, she told me after church the other day that I smelled like a—"

"I'll see you tomorrow at school, Charlie." Hannah spared Grant one last look, contempt laced with pain. Then she whirled away and headed for the diner straight across the street. Her ankles were working just fine. Why couldn't Hannah ever collapse in his arms?

Unable to stop himself, Grant rushed after her. "Hannah, wait." He caught her arm just as she stepped into the alley, where she'd go around to the back to climb the stairs.

She jerked free and turned on him. "Wait for what, Grant? For you to start yelling at me? Or maybe parade your girl around in front of me and the whole town? And would that be before or after you try and steal another kiss?"

"She's not my girl. I just. . .I just wanted. . .you to know there wasn't going to be anything between us. The woman's been pestering me for a carriage ride and I thought. . ." Grant's voice faded away.

"You thought you'd make it clear that you were just dallying with me when you. . .when you. . ." Her eyes brimmed with tears

Grant would have done anything to make it up to her. He could feel his control slipping. "Hannah?" He suddenly loomed over her. He hadn't meant to get this close or be this angry or feel so out of control.

"What?" Those fire-blue eyes faded to warm instead of burning. Instead of hurt there was longing. He suspected she could see that longing reflected back at her in his speckled eyes.

"Get upstairs right now."

"But I. . ."

"Right now, Hannah, before I give you one more reason to hate me." The eyes held. The moment stretched.

Grant took rigid control of himself and waited and hoped she'd go away and stay away. He clenched his hands to keep from reaching for her. He clamped his teeth to keep from asking her to come see what he had planned for his house. He locked his neck to keep from lowering his mouth to hers. He prayed to God for the self-control not to break all of his promises.

Neither of them moved. It was as if a cord bound them and stretched taut between them. Suddenly the cord snapped. Hannah whirled and ran down the alley and around the corner.

Grant held himself still as he heard her door open then slam shut. "Good for you, Hannah."

Then he turned to see Charlie sitting on the wagon seat with a weird, satisfied look on his face. He'd ridden a horse to school, and now it stood tethered to the back of the buckboard. Even the horse looked smug.

Feeling beset, Grant practically leapt into the wagon and headed his horses toward home.

Being a father was the only thing Grant had one bit of talent for. Although he was discovering he had a gift for making women cry. With a stifled groan, he knew the addition he had planned for his house wasn't going to be enough.

He pulled his Stetson low on his brow. "How'd you like your own room, son?"

"You wrecked it! I remember the day all you had to do was smile at a man, but you're getting old and tired and ugly." Horace had followed her into the back part of the store.

Prudence kept her eyes on Horace's fists and moved to the far side of the table in her back room. She was leery of him, but she was also thinking. "We're not beat yet."

"How'd'ya figure that?" Horace's eyes, cold and watchful as a rattlesnake, could have cut her flesh.

"So he won't come in here by himself. Not willingly. Well, we'll just bring him here unwillingly. You're out and about his place working."

"Digging in that stinking black tar, filling buckets, breakin' my back!" Horace picked up a chair in front of him and heaved it across the room, snapping its legs.

Prudence swallowed and talked fast. "You sneak out there next time, wait until all those brats leave for school, and you knock him senseless. Tie him up and hide him away, then keep him until dark and sneak him in here. We'll keep him overnight. Maybe we can even force some liquor down his throat while he's out. The next morning he'll have to come out, and I'll make sure there's a lot of ruckus. I'll stage a scene right in front of the whole town, crying and saying he promised to marry me, that he spent the night. He'll be forced to marry me on the spot."

Prudence went to close the door that separated the living quarters from the store. The heavily curtained front window had a slim opening, and through it she saw that snippy schoolteacher stalking away from Grant. Prudence knew human nature enough to recognize the light in Grant's eyes as he watched her go. If Prudence didn't move fast, she'd lose Grant to Hannah. She didn't have much time to stake her claim.

Grant followed the schoolmarm into the alley, and they disappeared from sight.

Seeing the teacher reminded her of all the fuss Sour Springs was making over this stupid passion play at the school. Her mind, always sharp, focused on that now.

"Wait, I've got another idea, an idea that'll catch him good, right in front of the whole town. We'll try that before you dry gulch him and drag him in here. He's a tough one. I can see it in his eyes. Catching him won't be that easy. But he's soft in the head on collecting children." She leaned forward and outlined her plan.

Horace's fists relaxed.

A floorboard creaked in the front of the building, and Prudence's eyes went to the closed door. She swung a hand at Horace. "Someone's out there. Get behind that curtain."

Horace concealed himself quickly. The fat old coot could move fast enough when he was swinging a fist or hiding out. Too bad he was so slow with his digging. She wouldn't have to put up with the nuisance of people wanting sewing done. She was sick of working for pennies.

She smoothed her skirt, plastered a smile on her face, and went out to the front. No one was there. She looked around the room then strode to the door. She pulled it open and noticed it squeaked. If someone had come in, she'd have heard for sure.

Shutting the door again, she scanned the room then shook her head as she studied every shadowy corner of her dumpy little business. Her eyes caught a crack of light coming from beneath the window that opened onto the alley between her store and the mercantile. She went to it and raised it a bit. She didn't remember ever opening it, so why hadn't it been closed?

Maybe Horace had wanted a breath of fresh air? And maybe if she asked him, he'd use those fists of his this time.

She slid the window open and closed and noticed it moved silently.

A rattle of a wagon drew her attention and she saw Grant drive away with that blond boy that had ruined her plans. She'd delight in seeing that child be sent down the road.

After they drove away, she stayed in the front, piddling with her fabric and a shirt she was overdue to deliver, giving Horace plenty of time to calm down.

TWENTY-FIVE

Grant got home to a warm supper and cold shoulders. The girls slapped food on like they were trying to give the table a good beating. Even Joshua, Charlie, and Benny were mad at him. Libby seemed a little huffy in her silent way, too.

Well fine! He'd managed to head-butt Shirt Lady. Hannah hated him. His children were furious. And he might as well admit he was good and sick of himself. He ought to form a club for people who hated him and charge membership. He'd be a wealthy man.

The only sound besides pottery on wood and the clink of silverware was chewing.

Grant wolfed down his food as fast as he could swallow to keep them from burning him to a cinder with their glaring eyes. He got done eating long before they did and practically ran out of the house toward the barn. Once there, he found the chores were done perfectly, and when he came out, he saw the young'uns had managed to get two rooms' worth of logs stacked and ready for building while Grant had been in town making enemies. He grumbled over all the help. He'd intended for this job to take him years.

He stepped into the kitchen to overhear his children settled down to their dinners, speaking at last. "Miss Cartwright has the pageant planned for the Saturday night before Easter. We'll have to drive into town at night." Benny spoke around a mouthful of roast beef.

Grant resisted the urge to hammer his head good and hard on the door. If he could only get through one night without hearing Miss Cartwright this and Miss Cartwright that. He saw a look pass between Charlie and Sadie and decided Charlie had told what went on in town, and since his dealings with Shirt Lady had turned into a disaster, they seemed ready to talk to him again.

Sadie wiped Libby's mouth with gentle hands and tucked the napkin more firmly under Libby's dimpled chin. "I've been asking and asking for Miss Cartwright to come out after school or on a Saturday or Sunday to work on her sewing. She needs a lot more practice. But she is really busy with the pageant."

Grant gripped the doorknob until it seemed likely to snap off.

"You're doing a wonderful job as Mary," Marilyn told Sadie as she served Benny more mashed potatoes. "There's a little nativity scene included as part of the Easter story. Miss Cartwright calls it a passion play."

"We've all been given really good parts, Pa." Charlie sat next to Benny. Charlie's shoulders were straighter, and he barely resembled the hostile, defiant boy who had moved in here such a short time ago.

"I get to sing a solo," Sadie added.

"Thanks for going in to help Miss Cartwright the other day." Joshua reached his long arms halfway down the length of the table and snagged the meat away from in front of Benny. "The risers are going to be great for the singing. All of us can get in rows and nobody's head is lost behind the person in front."

Grant sighed as the children chattered happily. Libby still remained silent, but she smiled and had a good appetite. He heard Gladys Harrison's name several times. It seemed that Hannah's chief critic had become her right hand. Everything was going fine at school. More than fine. Fantastic.

Grant wanted to scream!

He had no excuse to take his family out, and that meant he had to listen to All-Hannah, All-the-Time. And that meant he could never forget about her or how much he wanted to spend more time with her. If he did, sure as shooting he'd end up kissing her. He'd already proved he wasn't equal to the task of behaving himself in that area. And someone would catch them, and he'd end up married to her, which meant, in a world full of children, they'd add a few more.

Stirring restlessly, Grant forced his thoughts away from the stunning temptation of having children with Hannah and thought of all the unwanted children who needed him. He'd promised himself and God long ago that he'd devote his life to helping these lost little ones. He was *not* bringing more children into the world.

So that left marriage out. That left Hannah out. That left Grant with a lot of unruly thoughts and feelings that he had no idea what to do with. And that left him with some rooms to build.

"I know it's late, but I think I can level the ground and lay the first few logs for the foundation of the new rooms while you young'uns are doing your studies."

A mighty cold night, he'd rather be out building than listening to his children talk about Hannah.

"I don't have any homework, Pa." Joshua had always been an exceptional student. Right now, Grant wished the boy was dumb as a fencepost because he didn't need this house addition to go up any faster.

"I don't have any either." Charlie stood from the table.

"Maybe you two should stay in and help Benny and Libby with whatever homework they have." Grant pulled on his coat and listened to a rising wind whip around the cabin. Good, this oughta about kill him—which should keep his mind occupied.

"No need, Pa," Sadie said as she cleared the table off. "I'll wash up, and Marilyn can watch over the studies. As soon as we're done, we'll be out, too."

Marilyn began settling the little ones at the end of the kitchen table

Sadie had already cleared. "Miss Cartwright and Mrs. Harrison both say I'm old enough right now to be a schoolteacher. If it wasn't for Wilbur, I might consider it. I could probably take a term somewhere while Wilbur is making up his mind about building a cabin. Mrs. Harrison is going to ask around and see if there are any openings in the county. I could even teach a spring term."

Grant flinched to hear of one of his children growing up so soon. "I think this spring is too early, Marilyn. You're just sixteen."

"I'll be seventeen in a month, Pa. We've had teachers younger than that at school and there's a real need."

Grant looked at his daughter and thought of how well she did running his house and caring for her little brothers and sisters. He knew she could handle a school. "I don't want you out on your own just yet."

"I could help a lot of children who might not get an education otherwise. Besides, I'm almost through all the books. Miss Cartwright says I'll graduate this spring. And the schools are real careful to find a good place for the teacher to live."

"All except Sour Springs," Charlie said. "Working at the mercantile is kinda fun. I run all over town, carrying packages. I'm getting to know a lot of people. When I made some deliveries to the diner, I peeked in Miss Cartwright's room to see where she lives."

"Charlie, you shouldn't be sneaking around." Grant spoke sternly then ruined it by adding, "What's it like?"

"It's hardly bigger than our loft."

Grant looked up at the tiny triangle of space over his head. "That small?"

"Well, she can stand up straight in the middle, but it's not much bigger. Her room is cold, too. There's no heat except what comes up from the diner, and they shut that all down at night. I saw half a loaf of bread and no other food. I don't think she had enough money to feed herself at all until her first pay came in. Now, it's barely enough to make do. Most schools let a teacher live with a family, and then they can have their meals and a warm house. It's no wonder this town can't hang on to a teacher."

"Hannah's cold and hungry?" Grant's heart started beating too hard. He hadn't known. She'd never said a word. Of course, when had they exchanged normal words? They were either fighting or. . .

"I'm sure she'll be okay. Warmer weather is coming. She'll only have to be cold a little while longer." Sadie smiled at him, but it wasn't a friendly kind of smile. "And after all, she's an orphan. I'm sure she's *used* to being cold and hungry. I'll bet she doesn't even mind suffering anymore."

Grant's eyes narrowed. Sadie and Marilyn exchanged another one of those confounded female glances.

Joshua pulled on his coat. "Miss Cartwright said I'm going to graduate this spring, too, Pa. Ian offered me a job at his blacksmith shop."

Grant thought of his son Ian, who'd gone out on his own black-smithing after living with Grant for only a year. As soon as he was set up in business, he'd come back and scooped up Megan, one of Grant's daughters, to marry. That had been a first. Ian and Megan had two children and one on the way. The blacksmith shop was a success, and Ian hustled to keep up with all the work. It was a fact Ian could use the help.

Joshua's dark eyes flashed with excitement. "I'm thinking I can work for him and file on a homestead. I've already got my eye on a good spot out near Will's ranch."

"You have to be twenty-one to do that." If Joshua and Marilyn left, he'd be down to four kids. He wouldn't even need to add on to the house.

"Who's to say how old I am, Pa?" Joshua buttoned his coat up to the neck. "You always make us pick a birthday for ourselves so we can have birthday cake, and all I know about my age is what I guessed at. I don't have any record of being born. If I say I'm a full-grown man and do the work of a full-grown man, then I don't see why the people filing homestead claims should disagree."

Grant saw Joshua slip a quick look at Sadie and Sadie looked back. Grant was shocked. Sadie did know her birthday. She'd be sixteen in a few months, the same age as Megan when Ian married her. Sadie'd been with Joshua since before Grant found them in Houston. She'd have her birthday about the time Joshua graduated from high school, got a job, and had his house built. If Sadie hauled off and married Joshua, Grant would be down to three kids.

"When we're done here we can start building a cabin for Josh." Charlie went out the door following Joshua.

The boys disappeared, closing Grant inside with the girls and Benny. If he wasn't careful, they'd build on to the blasted house without any help from him at all!

Sadie, Joshua, and Marilyn all growing up right in front of his eyes. Grant pulled his old Stetson on tight against the cold wind, saving his new one for going to town, and went outside to add on a room before his whole confounded family moved out on him.

There wasn't another orphan train due for two years.

Jogging to catch up with his boys, he thought desperately that he was getting plumb short of children!

TWENTY-SIX

The day Gladys Harrison dropped in unexpectedly at school and caught Hannah handing out the award for champion speller to Emory, Hannah knew her position as teacher was secure for life

Gladys seemed to have completely forgotten which children were orphans and which weren't. Emory, Libby, and Benny were best friends, and Gladys was as kind to them as if they were her own. Blessed with a beautiful singing voice, Gladys worked tirelessly helping the children learn songs for the pageant.

The day three new students showed up at the school, along with their burly father and browbeaten mother, Hannah doubted she'd last until the end of the week.

Mrs. Brewster stood slightly behind her husband and studied her clutched hands. Mr. Brewster spoke rudely to Hannah, scowled at Joshua and Sadie, and left after making a few veiled threats.

The three students, two boys and a girl, managed to disrupt the whole school.

Hannah would never have made it to morning recess if it hadn't been for Joshua, Marilyn, and Sadie.

Joshua kept interfering when Wally, the older boy, would get too disruptive. He stepped in when the boy, nearly as big as Joshua but in Charlie's grade, tried to pick a fight with Charlie.

Sadie spent all morning diverting the little girl, Celia, who was about Sadie's age and pulled hair and tattled with every breath.

Hannah had her hands full with Cubby, a first-grader who was as big as two of Libby, his classmate, and didn't seem able to sit still for a minute.

Marilyn taught the rest of the school by herself.

At one point, Joshua came to the front of the room to ask a question. Since Joshua had yet to need a moment's help with his lessons, Hannah wasn't surprised when he whispered, "This is the family that made Pa pull us out'a school every year. They joined a wagon train to head west, but something must have happened to bring 'em back. No way will we get through the first recess, let alone the whole day, without Wally knocking someone down."

Hannah shared a worried look with Joshua. "We have to keep that from happening."

Hannah saw Cubby get up from his desk and go to the window.

Marilyn came up to the two of them. "No matter what we do, these boys will still hit someone, and Celia will run crying to her father to tell lies. She's always hated Sadie especially."

Hannah couldn't stay and plot strategy for another second. When the window wouldn't open, Cubby had pulled a length of firewood out of the woodbin and approached the glass.

Just before it was time for recess, Charlie stood from his desk and said loud enough for everyone to hear, "I'd like to stay in from recess today and practice the pageant. I want to know my part a little better."

Charlie knew his part, letter perfect.

Hannah caught on instantly. "Let's all stay in from recess. It's a really cold day anyway."

The howl from the Brewsters was deafening.

Hannah did her best to act surprised. "You children don't have a part in the pageant, do you? Would you like a part? We've got plenty of time to work you in. Or, if you'd like, you can go on out and play while we keep working."

803

Hannah saw smiles break out on every face in the room but three. The Brewsters didn't confine their cruel mischief to orphans.

"I was thinking Ma should be here for practice," Emory suggested.

Gladys lived over a mile from town, but maybe tomorrow. Her heart lifted as she thought how much help Gladys would be, even if only as a witness.

"Ma was going to stop for coffee at Mabel's," Emory said. "She always lingers when she does that. I'll bet she's still there, just across the street. She'd be glad to come over."

"Emory, why don't you run over right now and see if she can come."

"And if she's gone, maybe Mabel will come back with me." Emory nodded and dashed out of the room.

Wally Brewster reached out his leg to trip the little boy as he ran past, but somehow Joshua was there, not saying or doing anything except being in the way. Emory had to slow down and make a wide detour around Joshua, and that kept him away from Wally. Emory escaped unscathed.

"Why does he get to go out and we don't?" Cubby started banging his fist on the desk.

"Why, you can go out, Cubby," Hannah said brightly then kept talking to slow them down so Emory could make a clean getaway. "It's time for recess all right. I'll work on a part in the play for all three of you tonight. Tomorrow you can stay in at recess and practice with us." Hannah looked out the window and saw Emory disappear into the mercantile. "But for now you might as well go play."

Wally got up, shoving his desk out of line with the others. Celia pinched Sadie so hard Sadie jumped out of her desk with a squeal of pain. Cubby kicked Libby as he passed her. Hannah caught Libby because the little girl looked inclined toward revenge. The three Brewsters stormed out of the schoolhouse door.

"Joshua, watch to make sure Emory gets back inside without trouble," Hannah ordered.

Joshua headed for the window.

The minute the Brewsters were gone silence reigned. Hannah breathed a huge sigh of relief until she remembered that the recess couldn't go on forever. And it wasn't fair for the rest of the school to go without a recess so they could hide from the Brewsters. This was no time for relief.

Hannah didn't feel it was appropriate to discuss the naughty children with her students. Instead she began working on the pageant just as Charlie had suggested.

Gladys and Emory showed up almost immediately, and Hannah could tell from Gladys's disheveled appearance that she had hurried over. Hannah wondered how bleak a picture Emory had painted. Gladys gave Hannah a commiserating look then dove into working on the play.

Gladys stayed for the rest of the day. Hannah even allowed a short outside recess after the children ate their dinner. She and Gladys stayed on the playground the whole time. Despite the Brewsters' best efforts, the school day passed and some learning even went on, mostly thanks to Marilyn.

Hannah excused the children after school, but none of them left. They usually exploded out of the building. Instead they sat quietly until the Brewsters were long gone. A few, whose parents arrived in wagons to drive them home, left.

"Cubby'll be waiting for me after school cuz I made him look bad in reading," redheaded Gordy O'Reilly said. "Can I just sleep here, Miss Cartwright?"

Gladys ended up escorting the children who lived in town, including taking Charlie to work. She got Zeb at the livery to hitch up his team and take the children home who lived close enough to town that they were expected to walk.

In the end, only Grant's family, who brought their own team, was left. Just when Hannah had decided she'd have to rent a horse and ride along with them to see they got home all right, Charlie came into the schoolhouse with a wild, nervous look on his face about a half hour after school had let out. Wally Brewster had slowly begun to focus most of his considerable angry mischief on Charlie, who wasn't inclined to be pushed around.

"They were hanging around awhile, but their pa called them home." Charlie started handing out his family's coats. "I explained things to Mr. Stroben, and he let me off work early. If we head out now, we'll be fine."

They all loaded into the wagon and hustled away.

Hannah went to her room and collapsed. She ached in every muscle of her body from the hard work and tension of the day. She was never going to survive teaching school with the Brewsters in residence.

Grace couldn't survive one more minute in this canyon! She waited until no one was watching.

Daniel had been eagle-eyed ever since she'd made her first break for the high trail out of the canyon. She'd only made it out three more times. Each time he'd caught up to her, let her have her visit with Tillie, then, contented, she let him drag her home.

But now, he'd been lulled into a false sense of security with the coming warm weather. He didn't realize she could almost hear the snow melting, one flake at a time. Spring had long come to the valley of their canyon, but winter would not let up its hold on the gap.

Matthew had given up his nap at fourteen months of age. Grace sighed when she thought of how lively her little boy was. Nowadays, Matthew went out to work with Daniel for long stretches and never came back with more than bumps and bruises—he was a sturdy little thing. So, when Daniel climbed the hill behind the house to start chopping down trees to add onto the house so the baby could have a room right next to her and Daniel's, and all of the boys followed him, Grace saw her chance.

This time it wasn't about seeing Tillie or Sophie. She had much more in mind.

Grace put on sturdy hiking boots, sneaked out the front door, slipped past the barn, and headed up the canyon wall. She thought as she climbed that she might possibly have a fever. Or maybe she just felt a feverish need to escape. Whatever it was, she couldn't help making a break for it from time to time. And this time she was going all the way. She was going to see Hannah.

She was nearly to the steepest part of the trail when Mark caught up to her. "Runnin' off again, Ma?"

Grace scowled down at the little imp. Only not so little anymore. He was nine now, and as wily as ever. "Did you tell Pa?"

"Nope, I decided just to trail along in case you needed help. I don't mind a visit outside every once in a while."

"Well, why don't you convince Pa to go along with me then? It's a plumb nuisance having to escape when he's not looking."

"Maybe he'll come around. I heard him say he's going to turn his attention to the high pass trail as soon as the new room is done."

"Well, good. That'd make this a lot easier."

"So, you think you're gonna die havin' this baby, Ma?"

"Ma's not gonna die, Mark. You take that back!"

Grace stopped and turned.

John was just a few yards behind him. Luke tagged along a few yards farther back.

"What are you boys doing?"

"We're coming, too." Luke grinned. "Busting out of the canyon is fun."

"Pa says Ma's gonna most likely die havin' this baby." Mark started up the trail toward the canyon wall. "I just don't think it's a good idea to get our hearts all set on her surviving. I think it'll be better if we plan for the worst."

"Mark!" Grace turned and walked faster toward Sophie's.

"Could we have two or three this time, Ma?" Ike appeared on the trail just a few paces behind Luke.

Grace stopped to see her fourth son. She threw her hands wide in exasperation. "Your pa cannot have helped but notice you're all gone."

"You're not gettin' the hang of sneakin' like you had oughta, Ma." Mark came back to her side and took her hand.

Grace held on as she plodded toward the most treacherous part of the trail. She'd have to let go of Mark and use her hands and feet and cling like a scared cat to the little handholds. But it was only a hundred feet of sheer rock face, with the occasional perfectly good handholds. Then she'd go over the peak. There were some touchy spots on the other side, and then things eased off some. "Well, I'm still practicing. I haven't been at it as long as you have."

Grace came to the base of what she thought of as The Spike. The trees quit growing and the canyon wall turned to pure rock. It reached upward at an almost vertical angle, came to a point, and dropped on the other side just the same way, with only a few outcroppings of rock on the other side that were big enough for a person to sit and rest. Daniel had cut handholds and footholds in it, because he worried about getting out in case of an accident. It used to be a life and death matter to scale this cliff. But now it was just hard work. He'd been complaining about her abusing all his efforts for something as frivolous as having tea with Tillie or Sophie. The man had no idea where she really wanted to go. She touched her pocket and wondered if she'd brought enough money for train fare for eight.

She gritted her teeth and took a step toward the first grip, but Mark beat her to it. He raced up the sheer wall like a scampering mountain goat. John headed up right behind him and Luke was next.

Ike paused as he drew alongside her. "Go ahead. I can catch you if you fall."

"No, that's fine. I'll slow you down. When you boys get to Adam and Tillie's, have them send a horse back for me."

Ike nodded and went straight up. She envied him his youth and strength then remembered she wasn't that much older than he was.

As she reached for the first handhold, she heard footsteps. She knew they'd come. She turned around just as Abe emerged from the treeline with Matthew on his back. She tapped her toe as she waited. Honestly, if they were all going out, she was tempted to stay in.

Abe nodded to her and began his climb. She noticed Matthew wasn't just clinging for a piggy back ride. He'd been strapped like a papoose on Abe's back. He faced backward.

"Hi, Ma!" Matt waved as Abe ascended. Grace waited until they'd gone a ways. She wasn't in any mood to have Matt's drool dripping down on her head.

The only reason she didn't go home now was because they'd figure it out and come on back. Then she thought she felt the baby kick, which was impossible. She couldn't be more than two or three months along. But it reminded her of this claustrophobic canyon. That kick was like a kick up the mountain.

She reached for the handhold again, knowing the only one left was Daniel, but the boys were good at sneaking. If she'd gotten away with only them noticing, he might be awhile coming. He'd come along soon enough though. He knew she liked having him along on the way home.

She was a dozen feet up the cliff when a handhold crumbled and she began sliding backward. She didn't even scream. She'd learned to flatten herself against the rock and slide to the bottom. A few scrapes were all she'd get.

She'd only gone a few feet when Daniel caught her by the back of her dress. "I didn't hear you coming." She turned, smiling, her feet back on solid ground. "Thanks." She held her breath, afraid he'd haul her home.

He pinned her between himself and the cliff and scowled. "Grace, you are determined to die one way or another, aren't you."

"I just want to have a little visit." Let him assume it was with Sophie. "I don't mind a few scrapes on my hands."

"A few scrapes?" Daniel loomed over her, looking down, disgusted. "How am I supposed to go gallivanting all the time and still get my chores done?"

"You're going to get cranky wrinkles if you don't stop looking at me like that."

"Well, good. If my face is set in permanent wrinkles, it'll save me using my frown muscles."

Grace ran one finger down the corner of his mouth, tracing the deep furrow. "I'm sorry I make you frown. But Daniel, I just have to go for a visit once in a while."

"You've never had to before."

"That is the honest truth. I don't know what's changed, but this year I just have to." Her finger rose, and she ran it down the lines that were working themselves in between Daniel's blond eyebrows.

Daniel shook his head to escape her finger, but his scowl eased some. "Can this be the last time, please? The gap has to thaw pretty soon. I'll take you and we'll have a visit, but then we come home and stay home. I've got to get that room built, and I've got cow and chicken chores. Having to run to the neighbors so often is a strange quirk that I don't like to see you developing, Grace. You're strange enough as it is."

Grace nodded. She didn't bother to tell him that she was going to see Hannah. She'd only be gone a week. . .or two. By then, surely she could hold herself to home until the thaw. "I can't seem to stop being strange though, Daniel. You know, I've wondered before if maybe I'm not all that strange. Maybe women and men are just different."

Daniel shook his head. "You're not going to get away with this by blaming it on being a woman."

"Why not?" Her finger lowered to his frown again.

His eyes dropped to her lips. "Quit distracting me."

"I'm not." Grace smiled, hoping to distract the dickens out of him so he'd be a good sport about it when she headed for town.

"Oh yes, you are. And you know it."

"Is it working?"

"I'll say it's working." Daniel kissed her right there on the mountainside.

The boys had been pestering the McClellens for a long, long time before Grace and Daniel caught up.

Hannah trudged home after surviving another day.

Grant still hadn't taken his children out of school, and that surprised her. Was it possible they weren't telling him about the Brewsters? Once Grant found out about the Brewsters' return and how awful they treated his children, he was bound to take his young ones out.

Hannah, slumped exhausted in her single chair, wished Grant was here so she could tell him it wasn't just orphans. The Brewsters were nasty to everyone. Gladys and the other townspeople had learned to trust Grant's children.

She stood up, her spirit renewed. If Grant took his children home, he'd be quitting on the school, quitting on the town, and worst of all, quitting on his children. He'd be making them feel like they were being picked on when they weren't—well, they were, but no more so than anyone else.

"I'm not going to put up with it." Hannah paced in her tiny, sloped-ceiling room as she focused her anger on Grant—the quitter! "You're going to keep your children right here in my school, and when things get tough, you're just going to have to get tougher."

She declared to the empty room, "I'm not going to let him run away!"

TWENTY-SEVEN

Hannah wanted to run away.

The school became a daily struggle. Hannah knew that only sheer stubbornness, combined with the need to feed herself, plus endless prayer kept her going back.

She wrote parts for the Brewsters. One minute she'd try and teach them their parts, and they'd refuse to join in the pageant. The next minute Hannah would excuse them from being in the play and let them quit practicing, and they'd complained about being left out.

The Brewsters were allowed to go outside for every recess, and the rest of the students mostly stayed in. Hannah let them all out for a few minutes, but the second the Brewsters started trouble, Hannah would announce play practice, and the students, except for the Brewsters, would run for the schoolhouse like they were running for their lives. Even though it was well into March, a cold spell had settled in and shortened recesses weren't a great hardship, except her students needed to run off steam. The whole school fairly buzzed with pent-up energy, and Hannah began to have discipline problems in addition to the Brewsters.

Marilyn was good at teaching the school. Charlie was always right at Wally's side, diverting the big boy's flair for cruel mischief onto himself. Hannah watched Charlie like a hawk in case she needed to step in, but Charlie always seemed to be one jump ahead of Wally. In fact, Charlie seemed to enjoy the chance to taunt Wally and attract the boy's wrath.

All of the parents had taken to meeting their children and seeing them home from school. Ian now rode out with Grant's family until he was sure they were in the clear.

Hannah found herself spending all her time protecting Sadie from Celia and Benny and Emory and Sally from Cubby. Through it all she never gave up trying to force a little learning into the Brewsters' stubborn heads.

Hannah collapsed after another stressful day, grateful to have survived. It was two days before the pageant. All of the children had already headed home. She sat in her desk chair and prayed fervently to live through tomorrow. It was too much energy to pray for more than strength sufficient for the day.

The pageant was getting closer.

The Brewsters were getting more unruly.

The winter was dragging on.

And Hannah was considering applying for a job at the diner.

Before she was anywhere near done catching her breath, a red-haired woman, very pregnant, carrying a toddler, came in the classroom. "Miss Cartwright, I've wanted to come in and introduce myself any number of times."

Hannah couldn't resist returning the warm smile. "You have to be Gordy's mother." Hannah thought of the vivid curls and the abundance of freckles on one of Benny's classmates.

The young mother laughed, as the toddler squirmed in her arms. "Yes, I'm Megan O'Reilly. You wouldn't say Gordy looks like me if you could see his pa."

Hannah heard a soft Irish lilt in Megan's voice. "Your husband's a redhead, too?"

Megan smiled, running her hand over the red curls on the little girl bouncing and patting her mama's mouth with pudgy hands. "We're a matched pair and that's a fact. Ian is Sour Springs's only blacksmith."

"I'm glad you found time to come in." Hannah stood and waved Megan into the only adult chair in the classroom. It was a cinch the young woman wouldn't fit behind a student's desk. "Sit down. Please, you look like you've got your hands full."

Megan lowered herself gratefully into the chair with a soft groan.

Hannah perched on her clean desktop. "I wanted to get around and visit all of the children in their homes, but I've been slow getting it done. I had no idea teaching and putting on the pageant would be so demanding."

The little cherub in Megan's arms blew spit bubbles and squealed as she tried to get down. Megan wrestled with her like she'd done it a thousand times before. "I wanted to help you, but Ian hasn't been letting me get far from his sight these last few weeks, not even for church. My time is close, and our babies come fast. He's afraid I'll get caught out and have the little one along the trail."

Hannah was tempted to get the woman out of the school right now for fear she'd give birth on the spot. She didn't say that of course. "I understand. I appreciate that you wanted to help."

"The main reason I came in wasn't because of the children but because I wanted to talk to you about Grant."

Hannah's heart sank. Had word finally gotten out about what went on between her and Grant in the school, not once but twice? Maybe one of the other children saw the two of them through a window. Hannah opened her mouth to ask for forgiveness.

"Grant is my father."

Hannah's mouth dropped closed. "Your. . .your. . ."

"I know." Megan laughed. "I'm only about five years younger than he is. He's only two years older than Ian, and he's Ian's father, too. It makes me laugh to think of him as our pa, but I called him that for the years I lived with him. I wasn't the first child he adopted, but I was mostly grown so I had a bunch of little brothers and sisters from the minute he plucked me off the train."

Suddenly Hannah was intensely curious. She'd heard about the twenty children, and it made sense that some of them were still around, but she'd never wanted to ask who was an orphan and who wasn't, partly because the question could be hurtful but mainly because she'd been avoiding the whole subject of Grant like he was a full-blown plague.

"Do many of Grant's children live around Sour Springs?"

"There are six of us still around, plus the six still living with him. My husband lived with Grant for a year before he was out on his own. Ian never should have been put on an orphan train. He was near seventeen and no one wanted to adopt a boy that old, which meant he was a leftover."

"A leftover?" Hannah asked, masking her horror at a person being called such a thing. Megan had said it almost affectionately.

"Yes, we had no more scheduled stops before we turned around and headed back to New York. So Sour Springs is the end of the line. Any children who get this far aren't going to be adopted. Grant found that out and started showing up at the train station when an orphan train pulled in. He takes any children that are leftover."

Hannah saw it now. Crystal clear. Leftovers. "I heard Grant talking with the lady who rode with the children."

Megan's face lit up in a smile. "Martha. She's a saint. She and her husband took in more than a dozen leftover children themselves when they were younger."

Hannah knew her instincts that Grant couldn't be trusted had been born from her own awful experience. She still resisted believing in him fully, but she knew her lack of trust was her own problem, not his.

"The real reason I wanted to talk to you about Grant is that I wanted to thank you for whatever you've done to keep my family in this school. We've been afraid, Ian and I, that whatever resentment people in this town feel toward orphans might spill over onto our children. We were half expecting to end up teaching Gordy at home, too. But he loves coming to school, and he's found good friends and is welcome in people's homes."

Hannah stood, her jaw tense, her fists jammed against her slender waist. "Well, for heaven's sake, why wouldn't a sweet little boy like Gordy be welcome in anyone's home? What is wrong with this town that you'd even worry about such a thing?"

With a quiet smile, Megan said, "We heard that you are an orphan, too."

Hannah said rigidly, "That's right."

"And that you didn't have a very nice time of it with your adoptive father."

Hannah didn't respond.

"So you know what's wrong with people. You know what it can be like. You know how much an orphan longs for a family. I reckon that's why I've had so many little ones so quick, having a family just means so much to me. It's the same reason Grant has promised God to give his life to orphans. He's vowed to have no babies of his own when there's a world full of children who need a home. And to Pa, that promise includes never getting married because married folks"—Megan patted her substantial belly—"tend to have children."

"Never have children of his own?" Hannah felt a little lightheaded. "He promised God?"

"He just can't bear the thought of bringing more children into the world when there are so many now who need love. He told me that, once I was grown and gone, when I was pestering him about finding a wife. He never tells his children about it. He doesn't want them to think he's giving up anything. He's committed his life to children. He's a wonderful man." Megan heaved a sigh then hoisted herself and two babies—one inside, one out—to her feet. "I didn't mean to go on so long. Ian will be hunting me if I don't get on. But I wanted to meet you and thank you for your kindness to my son and my little brothers and sisters."

Hannah didn't want to let her go. She had more questions that needed answers. But she didn't dare ask any of them since the basis of all of them was, "What is a man who never wants to get married doing kissing me?" and, "How can I get him to do it again?" And maybe she'd ask, "Is wishing a man would break his promise to God an unforgivable sin?"

TWENTY-EIGHT

On the night of the pageant, Prudence waited with the patience of a stalking cougar for Grant's wagon to pull up to the schoolhouse.

She'd watched him at church long enough to know he'd be late. Always last in, first out. Those worthless orphans were the cause of his living like that. Her mouth watered when she thought of how she'd rid this town of that trash. The fact that she'd been an orphan didn't matter. She'd made a life for herself. She'd left the horror of her childhood behind when she teamed up with Horace. The fists of one man were easier to take than the hands of many that she'd had to endure to earn coins on the streets of Boston.

The milling around of the crowd settled down as everyone got inside.

Horace came up behind her and slid his arm around her waist. "Tonight's the night."

Prudence nodded. "If this doesn't work, tomorrow we take what's ours by force. But we won't need to. I've got it all planned."

Horace kissed her neck and laughed. She hated the stench of him. It never went away since he'd been working Sour Spring. But they'd get their land, they'd get their money, and they'd leave this stench behind. She hugged his hand tight and leaned back against him, laughing as she counted the money and saw their lives stretched out ahead of them. No more cold weather. No more working that sharp needle. No more hard times. Grant was their way up, for good this time.

She saw his wagon pull into town and straightened. "This is it."

Horace turned her around and kissed her soundly. "Do it without messing up."

Prudence nodded and slipped away from him, then pulled on her cloak. She peered through the window in the front door. She had to time it just right.

Guilt alone got Grant to his children's pageant.

To avoid the sin of skipping the Easter program, he had to break his promise—given only to himself but a promise just the same—to avoid Hannah. His avoidance plan was all he could come up with to keep from kissing her again.

His children's excitement defeated self-preservation. Here he stood unloading the children from his wagon when he should have been home adding more rooms onto his house. He was up to six new bedrooms, and he had one more stand of trees he could attack.

As he jumped down, he noticed that Joshua looked him square in the eye. Charlie had picked a birthday and declared himself thirteen. The boy was probably closer to eleven, but Grant didn't care, unless the boy decided to haul off and build a house and get married, too.

Grant sighed, shoved his hands in his pockets, and let the children go ahead as he secured the team to a hitching post. He trailed glumly behind the others to the brightly lit school as he considered the grand nest he was building that might well be empty soon. He'd deliberately come late, hoping to have only a few minutes to get the kids inside and pick out a spot for himself in the back.

The children ran ahead and he was alone as he stepped into the small entry area. The last in, he stood gathering his courage, holding the door open like an escape route he didn't dare take. He pulled on the knob to close himself in with Hannah. Sure the whole rest of the town was here, but Hannah was the only one who was haunting him.

Prudence slipped in. His arm stretched out holding the doorknob in such a way that she stepped into what was nearly a hug. She had that look in her eye that she'd used a few times, right before she attacked him with her lips.

He abandoned the door and backed away. He got just far enough that she could get some real speed up when she swung at him. So unexpected was it, Grant stood and took the full force of the slap without even ducking. The sound echoed in the hallway. She hit him so hard he staggered back into the wall, dazed and barely registering Shirt Lady's words.

"You promised," she yelled so loud a little dust sifted down from the rafters. "You lied to me."

Trying to make sense of her words, Grant shook his head as she launched herself into his arms. A thundering sound that Grant thought at first was from the blow he'd taken was a room full of people rushing into the little entry all at once.

"You said you loved me."

Grant looked down, trying to figure out what was going on. She caught him in a near stranglehold, and this time he wasn't quick enough. She landed her fishy lips right square on his. He tried to lift his head, but her grip was like iron. He did look up though. Straight into Hannah's horrified eyes.

Grant pulled at Shirt Lady's arms and tore her loose. Freeing her lying lips only gave her back the ability to speak her awful words. "You said we'd be married, or I'd have never let you be with me as only a married couple should be. I might even now be carrying your child."

The crowd gasped. Hannah's face went pure white.

Grant saw Marilyn and Sadie cover their mouths, but their expressions were of shock, aimed at Shirt Lady. They didn't have a single spark of doubt in their eyes.

Joshua pushed into the room and shook his head, scowling. "Pa wouldn't do that."

Shirt Lady broke into desperate sobs.

Grant saw the trust of his children solid in their expressions. He knew they believed him. But the rest of the town—the folks who barely tolerated him and his family to begin with—looked shocked.

He tugged on the little leech still clinging to him but without being rough with her, not wanting to be seen abusing a woman on top of everything else. He couldn't get her loose.

Gladys Harrison's eyes grew stone cold as she crossed her arms. "What's the meaning of this?" Gladys said. "If you made this poor girl promises, then you'll stand by them."

Quincy shook his head, thinly veiled contempt on his face.

Then Grant saw Hannah. The color had faded from her face until Grant thought she might faint. And it wasn't contempt or shock or anger he saw there. It was pain. He'd hurt her. Again.

"This isn't true." Grant nearly choked on the words. The humiliation made his face heat up until his ears burned. "I don't know what she's talking about."

The crowd kept filling up the little entry.

People he respected, people he thought respected him, glared at him. Harold, Mabel, Doc Morgan, the parson. Mixed in were others who looked at Shirt Lady with disgust. Will, Ian, and Megan. His own younger children looked confused. It couldn't get any worse.

Then Festus Brewster shouldered his way into the entry. "Startin' a whole new generation of orphans, huh?" Brewster's pockmarked face, wrinkled from years of grim anger, settled into creases of derision.

"No, I've never told her I was interested in marriage."

"Just playing around?" Brewster shoved Grant's shoulder, pushing him hard against the outside door. Shirt Lady held tight and staggered back with Grant. "Foolin' with a woman just like the trash you came from and all the rest of this riffraff."

"Don't deny our love, Grant." The crying rose to a wail. "Anything but that."

Parson Babbitt stepped just behind Brewster. He didn't shout, but that only gave his words more power. "This can't be allowed, Grant. You know you've got to do right by this woman."

"But I didn't do this."

The parson shook his head, his eyes burning.

Grant felt guilty even though he'd done nothing. Nothing except possibly lead her on by agreeing to that ride. He'd known she was interested in him. Would she disgrace herself in front of the whole town like this because she was so desperate to marry him? What woman would behave like this? Could she really love him this much?

His guilt must have shown on his face, and everyone interpreted it as an admission that the liar's words were true because he saw the doubt on many faces shift to anger.

"You'll do right by that girl, or I'll see you run out of this whole county," Gladys said.

"You and your young'uns should *never* have been allowed in this school." Festus's hand came down hard on Grant's shoulder until Grant had to lock his knees to keep from being pushed to the ground. "You're like a disease this whole town'll catch if we let you get close."

Gladys and Quincy Harrison nodded; Agnes and others joined in. Muttering voices rose to a low roar.

The parson looked tired, but his voice was firm. "You will do the right thing by this girl, Grant."

"No, I . . ."

"I love you, Grant. Don't leave me in shame. I'm ruined if you don't marry me. Ruined!" She looked up, her eyes swollen nearly shut with tears. Her nose ran. Her skin was mottled red and white. Grant couldn't remember ever seeing a more repulsive sight.

"You'll ruin every good woman in this town, you and the rubbish you've taken in." Festus was three inches shorter but twice as wide, and he outweighed Grant by fifty pounds. Festus had been harassing him ever since Grant was a teenage boy, taken off an orphan train here in Sour Springs by the Coopers. Festus, sixteen at the time, had made school a nightmare for Grant. And Festus's children had tormented Grant's children from the beginning. He knew the Brewsters'd come back to town and he'd been expecting trouble. The trouble had never come.

Until now.

"My young'uns come home from this school every day wearing a stench from sittin' next to the dung heap of your family. I've been busy gettin' settled'r I'd'a been in here afore now to clear out this rat's nest."

Shirt Lady wept and pleaded.

The parson frowned.

Brewster pushed and goaded.

Grant's fists clenched.

He saw Hannah and knew he'd ruined this play that had meant so much to her. He'd somehow allowed this scene and shamed his children, undone all the hard work that had allowed them to be accepted in the school.

"You will do right by this girl, Grant." The parson had always been a supporter of Grant's. Now he looked so disappointed. Grant felt his will being crushed. The guilt and the trapped-rat feeling choked off any more self-defense."

"Many of us in town saw you courting her." Harold looked between the crying woman and Grant. "You can't walk away from this responsibility."

Mabel nodded.

Charlie slipped up to Grant's right side. "He's not going to marry you," Charlie shouted in his childlike voice, high enough to carry over the madness.

"You stay out of this, boy." Festus Brewster put his hands on Charlie, and Grant saw red.

Charlie was tough, a fighter, but he had taken on too big a target with the likes of Festus Brewster.

Festus was diverted from hassling Grant. He looked down at Charlie with a sneer on his whiskered face. "You're another one'a them orphans. Stay out'a this. I don't need to hear nothin' from the trash they sweep up off'a the alleys in the city and dump on us."

"You get away from Pa, and you. . ." Charlie jabbed this woman who had turned herself into Grant's noose.

Grant noticed the little cry-baby, frowning in anger, in contrast to the tears that kept falling. He had the first inkling that, whatever her motives for crying and shouting lies, Shirt Lady wasn't all *that* upset. Just determined.

His humiliation faded, and his head worked for about two seconds before Festus grabbed Charlie by the front of his shirt and lifted him off the ground to eye level. With a vicious shake, Festus said, "I told you to stay out'a this."

"Get your hands off him." Grant caught Festus by the wrist. The night, so hopeful, so full of the Lord and the joy of the season of resurrection, was ruined and Grant was in the center of the whole mess. Everything was ruined for his children, for all of the other pupils and parents, and for Hannah. It was supposed to be a night of joy; instead it was going to be a brawl. The match was lit by Shirt Lady's accusations, the crisis deepened by Festus, but the situation was pushed into a free-for-all by Grant-the-orphan, the one who brought all of these unwanted children into their midst. Because Grant wasn't going to stand by and watch Charlie take a beating at Brewster's hands.

Just as Festus appeared ready to toss Charlie to the floor and turn on Grant, Charlie reached into his pocket and pulled out a sheet of paper. "This is a marriage license. The lady who threw herself at Pa is married. Her husband has been hiding out in her house all this time."

The whole crowd froze. Eyes blinking, the parson reached between Charlie and Brewster's burly stomach and took the paper.

Shirt Lady grabbed at the document.

The parson evaded her and stepped out of her reach. Then he looked at her, fire and brimstone in his eyes. "What is the meaning of this?"

She let go of Grant's neck to wrestle the parson for the paper, but the parson blocked her. "I don't know where the boy got that."

Grant saw the cold, calculating look harden her features. He saw something close to pure evil as she dove for that paper.

Grant stopped her.

Charlie spoke into the stunned silence. "I deliver parcels all over town. The day Pa came to tell Prudence he couldn't go riding with her, after she tricked him into asking her, I looked in her window after Pa told her he wasn't interested in seeing her ever. I saw her with a man. A man standing with his gun drawn, held backward like he was going to hit someone with it.

"You, Pa, if you'd have gone inside. While you were talking to Miss Cartwright, I sneaked inside and hunted around. It didn't take long to find that paper. I knew she was up to something, with all her lies and the way she chased after you. So I kept it."

The parson held up the document for all to see. "That's what this says. She's married. It's dated ten years ago."

Hannah spoke up. "I saw a man in her room the first night I was here. The night of the blizzard. Then again one other time. I didn't know her well enough to wonder who was there, and then I forgot all about it."

Grant looked up to see Hannah pushing her way through the crowd, closer to him.

"And then, when I was delivering to the sheriff's office, I found this." Charlie held up a wanted poster with Prudence's picture and a man's, wanted for pulling cons up and down the Mississippi River.

Prudence slid quickly sideways and reached for the doorknob.

Grant slammed a flat hand against the door to keep it closed. The sheriff fought his way from the back of the crowd and grabbed Shirt Lady's arm. "Let's go across to the jail and talk about this." He looked down at Charlie and studied the wanted poster. "There's a good reward for these two. It looks like that's yours if we can round her husband up."

Charlie said, "Give it to Pa."

"No," Prudence screamed. "It wasn't me. It was my husband, Horace. He's hiding in my shop right now. I'll help you catch him." Prudence's voice rose until it was a wonder she didn't shatter the schoolhouse windows. "He forced me to do this. He beats me. I didn't want to hurt anybody."

Joshua looked more closely at the wanted poster, and his eyes sharpened as he rubbed his head. The stitches were gone, but he'd carry the mark all his days. "That's him. I remember now. That's the man who hit me with his gun butt and knocked me off that cliff."

"We'll want your testimony if it comes to a trial, Josh." The sheriff tucked the poster in his shirt pocket.

"If?" Grant asked. "Why do you say if?"

"These two are wanted for a whole slew of crimes, and they've hurt some powerful people with their cons. That's why the reward is so high. They'll probably want to take them to trial in Mississippi. Here we can charge them with assault and attempted murder, but the charges back East would lock them up for the rest of their lives. I'd as soon see them found guilty back there and be done with them."

The sheriff pulled a clean handkerchief from his pocket and stuffed it in Prudence's mouth. "We want to keep her quiet so we can snag her husband."

"I'll help you bring him in, Ned." Harold went out. Several other men followed.

The door closed.

Parson Babbitt came to Grant's side. "I'm sorry I doubted you, Grant. I know you well enough that I should have taken your side from the first second. It's just"—the parson shook his head—"I've never seen a woman do something like that before. I can't fathom that kind of public humiliation, and to force a marriage."

"But why?" Gladys asked. "Why would she want Grant so bad?"

"Oil." Charlie held up one more piece of paper. Grant really should scold the boy for all his sneaking around.

"What about oil?" the parson asked.

"I found this paper right by the marriage license. Her husband's been digging at the spring. Buckets of oil are worth money if you ship it out of LaMont. He wanted to own Pa's land. She'd have married Pa. Then she'd be part owner."

"B–but how would her being part owner do her husband any good?" Grant was still too befuddled to make sense out of any of this.

"She wouldn't be *part* owner if you were dead, Pa." Charlie scooted closer to Grant. It chilled Grant to realize the vicious plans Prudence and her husband had in store for him. But that chill was swept away as Grant realized his most recent problem child had finally truly joined the family.

Grant rested his hand on the young shoulders. All of the boy's wiliness had paid off for Grant. All the sneaking and lying and stealing had saved the day. Grant knew he had to have a serious talk with the boy.

But maybe not tonight.

Brewster grabbed Charlie by the front of his shirt and lifted him off his feet. "I want you and all of yours out of this school."

Grant's stomach sank, and his eyes flickered to Hannah's face. He was still going to ruin this night she and his children had worked so hard on. But he couldn't let Brewster hurt Charlie. He reached for Brewster.

"You let Charlie go!" The tiny voice brought dead silence to the room.

Grant, along with everyone else, turned toward that voice.

Hannah gasped. "Libby!"

Everyone in town knew about the little girl who never spoke. She charged straight up to Brewster and stood side-by-side with Charlie, her little fists clenched, her jaw tight and angry. Her tiny anger even stopped Brewster in mid-rant.

Grant couldn't hold back a smile as he reached down and picked Libby up. "You spoke. Libby, honey—" Grant wanted to laugh and dance and spin the little girl around, but he didn't want to scare her back into her shell of silence.

Charlie looked up at the little sister he'd ridden into town with. "Hey, Lib. You've got a pretty voice."

"Thanks, Charlie." Libby's sweet smile bloomed.

Hannah came to Grant's side and grabbed Libby out of his arms. "Oh, Libby, honey, honey, you talked!" She looked to be planning on the dance Grant had thought better of. He smiled as Hannah gave Libby a kiss on the cheek.

Grant saw the love and joy shining in Hannah's eyes.

When Hannah glanced at him, her cheeks flushed a bit and she whispered, "Libby is my little sister."

"Your sister?" Grant tried to add and subtract all that Hannah was telling him. "That's why you tried to mess things up at the train station? You wanted her to come with you?"

"Not really. I mean, we had a plan that she'd just duck away from the train and get herself left behind. Then the two of us would hide. We knew no one would let me keep her if we asked permission, but we pulled the same trick in Omaha and it worked. Of course we were supposed to be in a big anonymous city. Not tiny Sour Springs."

Hannah caught Grant's arm, her touch gentle, her eyes warm. "We never dreamed anyone would adopt a little girl with a limp. When you took her, I could only think of Parrish, my adoptive father, and how cruel he was, how he made us work in the carpet mill then took all our money and barely fed us. I didn't know a man could ever be so kind."

Hannah's hand settled on Libby's back. "And now she finally feels safe. Safe enough to speak. Safe enough to fight a bully to protect her big brother."

Grant took Libby back and was honored that Hannah let him have his daughter.

Libby twisted in Grant's arms, glared at Brewster, and jabbed a finger right at his nose. "I'm not going to let you hurt my brother."

"We're not going to let it happen either, little gal."

Grant looked past Libby and saw the parson, determined and focused right on Brewster.

The parson, a man of peace, took hold of the town bully. All of a sudden ten sets of hands were laid firmly on the bully's arms and shoulders.

Will, Ian, Joshua, Doc Morgan, Zeb, Quincy, more and more people throwing into this fight on Grant's side. He'd learned to expect the worst from this town, but now they were standing with him.

Festus's hands were wrenched loose from Charlie's shirt without any blows being landed. Charlie slipped away and the crowd closed around Festus.

The parson spoke for all of them. "God says to turn the other cheek, but tonight I think He's on our side. He doesn't expect good people to quietly stand by while a bully abuses a child. We won't let you hurt one of God's precious children."

Festus wrenched against the hands restraining him.

"And they're all his children, Festus," Quincy Harrison added. "Wherever they were born and however they came to be in our lives."

"Harrison, you've always been on my side." Festus raised his glowering eyebrows at Quincy.

"And I've always been wrong," Quincy replied. "I've seen the error of my ways, and I'll not side with you while you harm these youngsters. I'll not stand by while you hurt this fine young boy or Grant or anyone else in this town."

When Festus looked around and saw everyone in the town siding against him he quit struggling.

"Caring for children is a sacred trust." The parson took his hands off Brewster and pushed Grant aside so he faced the man. Grant, holding Libby tight, gave way.

"God's given that trust to you, Mr. Brewster. He's given you children who can grow up hating like you do or loving as God wants them to." The parson quoted: " 'But whoso shall offend one of these little ones which believe in me, it were better for him that a millstone were hanged about his neck, and that he were drowned in the depth of the sea.' "

They were familiar words. The parson's voice was as clear as a night sky. As pure as God's Son and His sacrifice of love.

"You will behave decently tonight or you will be thrown out. Your choice, Brewster."

Festus didn't answer.

"And from this day on," the parson added, "if you harm Grant or one of his children or anyone else, you will answer to the whole town."

The parson's voice lost its edge and became softer, kinder. "Festus, please, if you only knew how much God loved you, all the turmoil would be gone from your life. God wants to fill you with His peace."

"Peace?" A look of longing shone on Festus's face so intense and personal that Grant felt he should look away.

"Yes. Do you stay in peace or leave this building?"

Grant saw the war inside Brewster and prayed. It was the first time in Grant's life that he'd ever been able to pray for Festus.

Finally, into the endless quiet, speaking barely above a whisper, Festus said, "I. . .I'd like to stay."

The parson laid his hand on Festus's head like a baptism. "Good. I'm glad. And later I'll walk home with you and your family. You've got some decisions to make about your life."

"Can we have the pageant now?" Libby spoke into the silence, and the exasperation in her voice broke everyone into laughter.

Into the chaos Hannah spoke, "Let's get on with it."

Everyone filed into the schoolroom and settled into chairs. Grant felt the presence of the Holy Ghost in that room on that warm spring night.

The children lined up. All of them recited the old familiar story of Jesus' crucifixion and resurrection. It sounded fresh coming from childish lips.

The highlight of the night came near the end.

It was impossible that Hannah had planned for Libby to have a speaking role. But now, from the place she'd stood in the front row, singing along, Libby stepped forward. Reading from a slate, Hannah must have quickly written up for her, Libby's voice rang out. " 'Go ye therefore, and teach all nations, baptizing them in the name of the Father, and of the Son, and of the Holy Ghost. Teaching them to observe all things whatsoever I have commanded you: and, lo, I am with you always, even unto the end of the world. Amen.' "

Grant prayed that he lived up to the Great Commission. He prayed that, in his own small corner of the world, he did teach. He did baptize. He did spread the word, at least to his own children, that God was with them.

The whole building finished the program with a quiet verse of "Just as I Am." As the song faded, the parson said a quiet closing prayer.

When Grant saw Festus Brewster bow his head, Grant realized he couldn't hold on to the foolish promise he'd made to himself to avoid Hannah. She deserved to be thanked for all her work and the new sense of closeness and community she'd brought to Sour Springs.

Grant went over and took her hand. "The pageant went perfectly."

TWENTY·NINE

"The pageant was a disaster." Hannah smiled despite the fact that she was dead serious. "What are you talking about?"

"No, it wasn't," Grant objected.

"We had six little singers who kept running down to sit with their parents. I could barely hear the students saying their parts over the din. Gordy tripped over his robe, landed on Emory, and the two rolled down the risers punching each other. Benny and Libby got into a tug-of-war over the cross and ended up in a slap fight, and—"

Marilyn rushed up, interrupting Hannah. Grant's daughter's face blazed so pink Hannah could see the blush in the part of her white-blond hair. "I can't believe I pushed that big paper stone, and it started rolling and knocked into Megan holding her baby. If Ian hadn't moved so fast, I could have hurt them both."

Hannah patted her shoulder. "It's a good lesson to learn."

"Why's that?" Grant asked.

Hannah grimaced. "I have plans for a Christmas program next winter, and I considered asking Megan if we could use her baby."

Marilyn gasped in horror and covered her face with her hands. "No, the poor little thing will never survive!"

"I'm sure Benny wouldn't stage a tug-of-war over a real baby like he did with the cross." Hannah had a brief vision of Benny and Libby doing just that and shuddered. "We'll think of something."

832

"Those were all little things," Grant said. "The pageant was perfect."

Hannah shook her head.

"I'm never going to convince Wilbur to marry me now," Marilyn said. "He'll be scared to death of what might happen to our children."

A young man Hannah thought had better be Wilbur came up behind Marilyn and hooked his arm around her slender waist. "You're not getting out of marrying me," he said, talking into the back of her neck. "I think you're gonna be about the finest mother who ever lived." He dragged a giggling Marilyn away.

"I'd better get Marilyn through her books quick." Hannah turned and smiled at Grant. "I've heard Wilbur's clearing land for his house."

Grant stepped just a bit closer to Hannah. "I want you to know—"

Megan came up beside them. "Thanks so much, Miss Cartwright." She put her arm around Grant. "Didn't know if I'd make it here or not, Pa. Ian kicked up a fuss, but I wouldn't hear of missing it. You know how Ian is."

"I know." Grant nodded. "It won't be long now."

"Till you're a grandpa again." Megan started laughing and several others around her joined in. Even Hannah had to laugh at Grant, so young, being a grandpa.

Grant crossed his arms and furrowed his brow. "This'n'll be my tenth grandchild. I'm used to it."

The whole crowd laughed again.

Gladys had helped arrange for cookies and cider, and the parson said a heartfelt prayer.

The party began winding down and the crowd headed for home.

As they stepped outside, Will held his lantern up to light the way to the hitching post.

Hannah watched them all leave then closed up the schoolhouse, her heart singing with the success of the Easter pageant, despite the fiasco with that horrible Prudence. Her heart still glowed with the kind words and the many thanks.

With a smile, she walked through the quiet night. Her pleasure faded as she let herself into her lonely room. Tomorrow was Easter, a day that was the foundation of her faith. But it would just be another lonely day for Hannah.

Of course Parrish had never made the day memorable. Once she'd escaped Parrish and lived in one hideaway or another with her collection of brothers and sisters, she'd spent Easter focusing on the holiness of the day, but she'd rarely gone to church or had the means to prepare a special meal. At least tomorrow she'd attend services.

She realized as she prepared for bed that she didn't even have any food in her room. The diner and mercantile were closed tomorrow because of the holiday, so she couldn't buy any. The pageant and the Brewsters had claimed all her attention for so long that she'd neglected almost everything else. With a sigh, Hannah realized she'd have to go without food on Easter. Well, she'd done without food before. It wouldn't kill her.

The night had cooled and the diner's heat had burned away and faded. So she'd be cold as well as hungry. After all she'd survived in her life, she didn't mind her little room and an occasional day of cold and hunger. She did mind the loneliness though. She'd never been alone on Easter before.

Self-pity grew and she indulged herself in it as the loneliness overwhelmed her. She wept into her pillow even as she knew she was being selfish.

Libby was safe at the Rocking C.

She prayed for her big sister, Grace, and wondered if she'd ever know what happened to her. After the foolish tears were spent, she settled into her cold little bed.

As Hannah walked out of church the next morning, Charlie rushed up beside her. "Miss Cartwright, have you made plans for today?"

Hannah smiled down at him. "No, I haven't."

"We'd like you to come out and celebrate Easter with us at the Rocking C. Joshua bagged himself a huge turkey, and the girls have been baking since dawn. A lot of Pa's grown children are coming and bringing food along. We're going to have more food than even all of us can eat. We'd like it very much if you could come."

"Well, I don't know." Of course the answer was no, but Charlie looked so hopeful. Hannah decided she'd find Grant to turn down the invitation rather than disappoint Charlie.

The crowd was thinning fast, everyone hurrying home to their Easter dinners. Grant was nowhere in sight. She didn't see his wagon either, or any other of his children.

"Do you know the way through the pass?"

"I know the way."

"Then I'll head back. Put your riding skirt on, and I'll tell Zeb to have any horse but Rufus saddled up for you and waiting out front of the diner."

Hannah nodded but didn't answer his question. There was no possible way she could spend the day with Grant.

Charlie headed toward the livery that would, Hannah realized, be closed today. Charlie would figure that out soon enough.

Hannah hurried around the church, searching for Grant to tell him she couldn't come. His wagon was nowhere to be found. She hurried toward the livery, but Charlie had vanished and the building was locked up tight.

Not sure what to do, she walked home to find a quiet, gentle-looking mare standing, bridled and saddled, right outside her door. "Charlie!" Hannah's voice seemed to echo down the deserted Sour Springs street. Charlie didn't answer. With a shake of her head, she admitted she was thrilled to not spend the day alone and rushed inside and ran upstairs to change into her riding skirt.

The horse behaved perfectly and the high trail was clear and dry.

When she rode up to the Rocking C, she pulled the reins so abruptly the horse backed up a few paces. Where had Grant's little cabin gone?

A sprawling log ranch house stood where the humble home had been. So completely had it been transformed, Hannah could barely remember the other house. The center jutted out nearly twenty feet farther than it had. There were impressive additions on each side and the roof was higher. It wasn't just bigger, someone had taken the time to make it beautiful. A neat porch with dozens of slender support spindles graced the front. There were shutters on each window, and the land around the house had been leveled with well-rocked paths leading to the barn. It looked like someone had worked himself near to death to make it so lovely.

And the children were all outside. Hannah remembered that Grant had said the children spent all their time outside, and from the looks of things, it was the absolute truth. Libby ran along, keeping up with Benny, her limp a distant memory. They chased after Charlie, whose sullen scowl was long gone. Joshua rode his horse toward the corral. The two older girls sat on the porch steps visiting.

Benny yelled, "Miss Cartwright's here."

Joshua tipped his hat at Hannah. "Happy Easter, Miss Cartwright!"

Hannah noticed that Joshua carried himself with the same assurance as Grant.

Charlie came over and held her horse. "Glad you could make it, Miss Cartwright."

"Hannah!" Libby came running toward her, and Hannah swept her little sister up in her arms and had to swallow back tears at the sound of her voice.

Marilyn and Sadie got up and walked toward her with all the poise of women. The air fairly rang with "Miss Cartwright" and "Happy Easter," shouted by six happy children.

Hannah remembered last Easter, Libby and her alone in a cold, dilapidated shed with only stale bread to eat. The change from last year to this was nothing short of miraculous. She couldn't remember another time in her life when she'd been welcomed into a family like this.

Regaining her composure, she thanked Charlie for his help with the horse and headed for the house carrying Libby.

"Are you going to help us cook, Miss Cartwright?" There was no missing the fear in Sadie's voice.

Hannah couldn't help but laugh. "No, your meal is safe."

Hannah would have said for sure that a black person couldn't blush, but Sadie proved her wrong. Then all the children started laughing and the awkward moment passed.

The children thronged around her. Even Joshua hurried out of the barn to join them. Hannah and the children headed for the greatly enlarged house, not a cabin at all anymore. "Do all of you have your own rooms now?"

"Some of us still have to share." Joshua fell into step beside Sadie. "Pa turned the back room into an entryway like it was supposed to be, although he made it way bigger and stuck two more bedrooms on the back. He tore out the wall to the old bedrooms to make the kitchen bigger and pushed the front wall out a whole bunch. Then he added two bedrooms on one side, plus the loft is three times as wide as it was and twice as high. So we have five bedrooms counting the loft."

Hannah noticed Sadie steal a glance at Joshua. Had Grant noticed the attachment between these two?

"I have my own room," Benny bragged. "I have the loft to myself, and it's huge cuz Pa made the kitchen huger'n ever."

Hannah's eyebrows arched. "It sounds like he's been busy." He'd never come again after he'd built the risers, until last night. She'd noticed because she'd been wondering if he might steal another kiss. Not that she wanted one, but a girl could wonder. . .couldn't she?

"We all helped." Benny rammed his shoulder into Charlie, and Charlie smiled and slung his arm around his little brother's neck. The two looked like they'd become best friends in the months since Hannah had found Benny bleeding from Charlie's assault.

"Marilyn and I have been sharing a room so we decided to stay together," Sadie said.

"Especially since I'm getting married soon," Marilyn added with a shy smile.

"You're planning to finish school first, aren't you?" Hannah asked with a stern frown.

Marilyn nodded. "With spring work, Wilbur might be awhile finishing the cabin. I'll be through all my books by the end of this term."

Hannah studied the girl. Marilyn was telling the truth, but Hannah had seen a determined light in Wilbur's eyes last night. Hannah decided to push Marilyn through her books fast.

"And I've already filed a homestead claim." Joshua shook his head at the new house. "We've got this great big house after all these years. Pa'll rattle around in it with the two of us gone." He glanced at Sadie again and the two smiled at each other.

Hannah subtracted another child from the house very soon because Sadie wanted to be with Joshua, and though she was young, she was a mature young woman who knew her own mind. That left Grant with three children in this sprawling home.

"I've got the biggest room." Benny puffed out his chest.

Sadie sniffed and gave her little brother a gentle shove. "You might have the biggest room, but ours is the warmest cuz it's closer to the fireplace. And it's the prettiest. It doesn't matter how crowded it is when we sleep. We never go inside 'cept for bedtime and meals anyway. I think Pa's gonna need more kids. It's gonna be lonely with only four of us, plus Pa."

"Only four children. . .what a tiny family." Joshua shook his head and smiled down at Sadie. "I want lots more kids than that."

Sadie shoved him sideways, and he pretended to stagger and nearly fall.

The whole group started laughing.

"It's a good thing he made the kitchen huge because Will's family is coming today and a bunch of our other brothers and sisters," Benny added. "We have the biggest and bestest family get-togethers of anyone."

"Ian and Megan can't come," Sadie reminded them. "Ian's too nervous."

They all laughed over that. High holiday spirits nearly burst out of them as they dragged Hannah toward their new home.

Then Grant rode into the yard.

Hannah only had to look at him for a second to see he had no idea she was coming for dinner.

She turned a dismayed look on Charlie.

He smiled at her and held the door open to the ranch house. He leaned close enough to her to whisper, "Trust me."

Although it made absolutely no sense, Hannah did.

THIRTY

G rant turned away from the celebration in front of him the minute Hannah went in the house surrounded by his children. Riding his horse into the barn, he got down, his movements uncoordinated. He pulled the leather off his horse with unsteady hands and gave it an extra bit of grain to avoid going inside for a little longer.

"What is she doing here?" He asked the question directly to God.

With no excuse not to go in, Grant turned toward the house and came to a dead stop, afraid of what he'd say if he had so much as a second alone with her. And he knew what he'd promised God and the desperate need of all the orphaned children in the world.

"God, why did You let her come here?" Grant heard no thunderous voice. No finger of fire carved answers like commandments on stone. No burning bush spoke to him. No still, small voice whispered to his heart.

He was so alone in his barn, with his family all surrounding Hannah in his house, that his ears almost echoed with the aloneness. Grant knew that somehow the answer to all his aloneness was in that house and in that woman.

Grant, alone in the empty barn, asked, "What about my promise, God? What about all the children who need me?" Grant ran his hands over his face, trying to wash away the temptation to be selfish away. "I had a good reason for that promise. There are still orphans suffering.

"I can't give as much to a child if I have a wife to consider and children of my own." Something bloomed in Grant's heart as he thought about having children of his own, maybe a son with speckled eyes. Maybe a daughter with Hannah's brown curls.

He needed to trust God with his loneliness. He needed to trust Hannah with his love. A weight lifted, and Grant looked up to heaven to thank God.

When he lowered his eyes, he saw Hannah coming into the barn. Looking a bit fearful, she said, "Dinner is almost ready. Will's here and several other families are coming down the trail." Hannah's lips trembled. "You know it will be the first Easter dinner of my life?"

Her expression turned so vulnerable Grant couldn't stay away. Walking toward Hannah, he walked toward his future. She kept moving in his direction just as steady and solid as the mountain behind his home.

They met, and Grant reached out to grasp her hands. "You can be with me for every holiday from now on, Hannah. You can be a mother to all these children. They've already claimed you anyway."

Grant lifted her left hand and kissed it. "I love you. I think I fell in love with you when you crawled under my kitchen table chasing potatoes."

Hannah smiled warm enough to bring summer to Texas. "And I've loved you ever since you spent an afternoon fixing up Libby's shoe so she could walk without a limp. Even when it went against every hard-learned lesson of my life, I still loved you."

"Will you marry me, Hannah? Will you join our family and make our house a home?"

Hannah hesitated, and Grant's heart dived hard enough it'd break if it hit bottom.

"I have a lot to learn about how to be a woman. My upbringing didn't teach me a lot of what I need to know."

Grant's heart didn't crash after all. He smiled and then he laughed. "You'll learn." He wrapped his arms around her waist and lifted her off the floor. He swung her around joyfully, and she squeaked a little and laughed with him.

"Between Sadie and Marilyn and me, we'll teach you all you need to know." Grant lowered her to her feet and kissed her. Not the stolen kiss of those brief times at the schoolhouse, but the honorable kiss of the only man who would ever be given leave to kiss her.

He lifted his head, his heart thundering. "Shall we go in and tell the children?"

"Yes, I can't wait."

They turned to leave the barn. She'd never change her mind if it meant disappointing them. He slipped his arm around her waist and urged her along.

Hannah started moving, such a perfect fit in his arms that Grant decided he was never going to let her go, not even for one more day.

Hannah moved closer to him as if she was cold. She leaned against his shoulder. He thought his shoulder was the perfect size and plenty strong. She could lean on him for the rest of her life.

"You know, you're younger than quite a few of my children."

Hannah's brow furrowed. Then she shrugged and smiled. "Considering Ian's age, you're almost younger than a few of your children. That's a tricky thing to explain."

The wonder of her, alive and loving in his arms, was nearly too sweet for him to bear. They opened the ranch house door, and Grant saw a couple dozen sets of shining eyes staring straight at them, Will and his family, and several others.

"I asked Hannah to marry me. She said yes."

The children exploded with noise and hugs.

In the midst of the chaos, Hannah pulled Libby into her arms in a way that let Grant know how much she'd missed her little sister. His heart overflowed just watching them be truly reunited.

He looked past his present brood of children and saw wagons and horses hitched here and there. The rest of his family had arrived. His family finally had a ma. The dinner was forgotten for a long time as they celebrated this special day.

After they ate, the whole family hitched up the wagon and went to town for a wedding. Grant pulled his wagon up beside the church, Hannah at his side, the wagon box full of children.

He looked behind him and saw what amounted to a parade, following him down Sour Springs Main Street. Doors started opening as curious townsfolk noticed the commotion.

Putting on the brake, Grant scrambled to beat his sons to Hannah's side and help her down. Joshua slapped him on the back. Ian came out of his house behind the blacksmith shop with his hand resting on Megan's back and his daughter hanging from his hand. Gordy saw Benny and Libby and dashed toward the crowd.

Will laughed and shouted, "Everybody's invited to a wedding!"

Grant lowered Hannah to the ground, her face shining with excitement. Something caught in Grant's throat to think this beautiful, smart, feisty, loving woman was excited. Excited to marry *him* of all people.

Suddenly he knew everything in his life had been preparing him to love this woman the way she needed to be loved, and her life had been a preparation to be his perfect match. He could thank God for the things he'd been through, even thank Him for the things many hurting children were going through. Ian being sent out here when he was so old. . .because Megan was here. Josh and Sadie. . .the streets had prepared them for each other. And Marilyn and Wilbur. Somehow Wilbur, from a strong family with two great parents, had grown up to have that perfect place in his heart for Marilyn with her broken past.

He could breathe more deeply, thank God more fully. His eyes open, his head unbowed, Grant could still pray his thanks with every step.

A hard slap on his back made him realize he'd been holding Hannah, her toes still dangling off the ground, smiling like a maniac as he watched her and prayed.

"Put her down." Will came up beside him. "And if you'd like to have a little talk about the facts of married life, I'll be right here to help you. . .Pa."

The whole crowd erupted into laughter. Grant gave Will a sheepish grin and didn't admit he had a few questions. He reluctantly put Hannah on the ground and slid his arm around her while he gave his irreverent son a shove.

The parson came out of his home, which was next door to the church, and quickly caught on to the celebration. His wife was a few steps behind him.

Walking arm-in-arm with Hannah, Grant approached him. "Can we tear you away from your Easter dinner to perform a wedding ceremony?"

The parson smiled. "I'd be proud to, Grant."

As they headed in, Sheriff Ned came up beside Charlie. Grant noticed and stopped to listen.

"We picked up Horace with no trouble. And by the time those two got done accusing each other of being the real bad guy, we had confessions for a lifetime of criminal activity. You've earned that reward, boy. The U.S. Marshal will be bringing five hundred dollars for each of them two crooks within a week."

"A–a thousand dollars?" Charlie's face went pale, and then he turned to Grant. "It's for the family, Pa."

"No, boy, that money's yours. You earned it." Grant still needed to scold Charlie about his sneaking ways. Thinking of a life tied to Shirt Lady made it real hard for Grant to get too upset. But God wouldn't approve of such underhanded means, no matter that it had turned out for good.

Charlie shook his head. "I don't need that kinda money. You'll put it in the bank for us, won't you, Sheriff? In Pa's account?"

The sheriff nodded.

"We'll settle this later," Grant said, mussing Charlie's hair. He needed to pray about whether it was right to give a young boy so much money. . . especially as a reward for being a sneak thief.

There wasn't much ceremony to the wedding. Grant refused to turn loose of Hannah long enough to let her walk down the aisle. The only delay was in having the guests troop in, which took awhile considering the whole town was idle and available due to it being Easter Sunday.

Grant held both her hands, and she held on just as tight, while the parson had them swear vows before God. Never in history, at least Grant couldn't imagine it, had vows been given with such sincerity.

Grant barely had time to kiss the bride before his whole family surrounded them to offer congratulations.

The townsfolk all brought out their leftovers from Easter dinner and turned the wedding into a party that lasted until the sun set. Grant's grown-up children were the last to leave the reception.

Grant turned to his new wife. "Let's stop at your room and get your things, Hannah."

Hannah smiled. "I'll be glad to see the last of that place."

Grant followed her upstairs with all of the children coming behind to help carry things.

Except there were no things, or almost none.

"Charlie said this was small." Grant was appalled at the size of the room. His head came to the peak of the roof, which slanted sharply. "And where are your things?"

Hannah blushed and pointed to a small pile of clothes that tucked easily into her satchel. She also produced proudly two dollars and fifteen cents.

"I've been saving my wages."

Grant turned to the children who were pushing their way inside. "Go on back down kids. There isn't room for all of us in here." The understatement of a lifetime.

They all seemed to need peeks. Then they grabbed the few bits of Hannah's possessions, ran into each other coming and going, but finally were all gone.

"You've been living here for three months?" Grant ran his hand up and down Hannah's arm.

With a reluctant nod, Hannah said, "It's awful, isn't it? Let's get out of here and go live in the mansion you built."

Grant kissed the pretty smile right off Hannah's face, caught her hand, and they left behind the teacher's quarters for good. He headed home with his wife. Newlyweds who already had six kids.

After a festive evening meal, Grant wanted to suggest the children all head for bed. It was a little early, but he had a powerful yen for some quiet time with Hannah. A pang of guilt hit him for wanting his children to go away. Truth to tell, he wasn't sure just what the point was of quiet time with Hannah.

From the looks of Megan, Ian had figured out what to do with a wife. Grant would die before he'd ask his son's advice.

Of course he lived on a ranch. He had a fair notion.

Marilyn left for a ride with Wilbur.

Hannah took the last coffee cups into the kitchen to wash. Grant looked after her, confused and fascinated.

He rose from his chair and opened his mouth to shoo the children off to bed just as his front door slammed open and a wild-eyed woman rushed in.

Grant backed away. The woman looked unhinged and that was a fact.

"Hannah?" She shouted so loud Grant was tempted to cover his ears. "I heard Hannah was here."

Before anyone could answer, an explosion of noise and shoving came through the open door. Five boys arguing at the top of their lungs clogged in the door, battling to get through first.

"Climbing out of that canyon is stupid an' if you do stupid things, you're stupid, an' that's that."

The boys came in two sizes. Medium and large. One of the medium ones ripped his hat off his head and whacked one of the larger ones in the face. They had to be brothers—no brood could look this much alike and not be.

"Hannah, where are you?" The blond-haired madwoman ran into a side bedroom.

Grant hoped this wasn't another one like Shirt Lady. He stayed well away from her.

"Don't you be calling Ma stupid." Blinded, the bigger boy fell over the younger, and both landed on the floor so hard the lantern sitting in the center of the table rattled.

The wrestling boys shouted. The larger one roared through his fingers as he rubbed his stinging face. "That ain't right to insult her like that, Mark."

"But it *is* stupid." The smaller boy jumped out of the fight, threw his coat toward a pair of antlers on the wall, missed, and hit another boy in the face with the garment.

"Hannah! Hannah, are you here?" The crazed woman dashed back into the room shouting, ignoring the chaos in her wake.

"Don't call me stupid, stupid." Mark was knocked sideways by a smaller child yet. Grant hadn't noticed him at first. Three sizes. Small, medium, and large. The toddler jumped on Mark's back, screaming until Grant thought his ears might bleed.

The toddler grabbed Mark around the neck and pretended his feet had spurs and Mark was a stubborn horse. The little boy screamed for Mark to "Giddyup."

"Hannah!" The female voice cut through the chorus of shouting boys.

A giant replica of all of them came into the house last. "Man oh man, was it ever stupid to come all this way, Grace."

"Grace?" Hannah came dashing in from the kitchen then froze for just a second until Grace, ignoring the riot that came in the door after her, and the terrible insults being hurled right and left, turned and looked at her.

"Hannah?" With a little scream, Grace threw her arms wide. "Oh, Hannah." Grace ran toward Hannah, and Hannah ran toward Grace.

They caught each other and swung each other around in a circle, laughing and crying at the same time. Grant had heard enough about

Hannah's childhood now to know who Grace was. But he'd never expected her to come with a crowd attached.

Joshua quickly snatched the lantern off the table and left the room with it and another breakable lamp. Sadie backed Benny and Libby into a corner to guard them, and Joshua came back and stood beside her. Benny looked between them, thrilled to see the newcomers.

Charlie scaled the ladder to the loft with a third lantern so it was out of reach but the room didn't fall into complete darkness. He left it well back from the side of the attic, swung his legs over the edge, and began climbing down into the fray.

Grant was tempted to yell for Charlie to stay up there where it was safe and send the rest of the family up, too.

Mark began bucking and hurled his younger brother on a flying trip toward the ceiling.

Their father snagged Matthew in midair. Settling his son on his hip, the adult man turned to Grant and offered his hand. "We found someone in town to direct us out here. We just came in on the train. My wife was bound to visit her sister. I'm Daniel Reeves and these are my boys." Daniel seemed to yell every word, far too loud to be explained away by the riot. He swept his arm at the chaos and didn't bother trying to point out who was who.

Grant appreciated that. "I'm Grant Cooper." They shook hands.

"Grace has kinda made a habit of escaping from me this winter. Every time I relax and quit watching her like a hawk, I'll be switched if she doesn't disappear."

Grant did his best to listen to Daniel over the crying women and the screaming boys.

"My contrary wife made me bring her here." Daniel smiled and blushed just a little. "Women are the almightiest hardest critters to figure out, Grant. I can't get mine to be submissive worth a lick. I've got it underlined in the Bible and everything. But she's just plain stubborn."

Grant had been raising girls for nine years. He could probably give

Daniel a little advice. It would start with, "Don't call her stupid. . .or stubborn. . .or a critter."

Then he looked at the six children Daniel had managed to father and wondered if Daniel had some advice that could make the coming night go more smoothly for Grant. Grant had no idea how to ask. "Uh. . . Daniel, did you hear Hannah and I got married today?"

The crying women had turned on Sadie and Libby and were chattering like a flock of chickens.

Hannah pulled Sadie close and introduced her as "my daughter."

Grace began crying as if her heart was breaking.

"What is that infernal woman crying about now?" Daniel pretended to drop Matthew and the boy screamed and laughed. Daniel flipped him upside down, dangling him by one ankle for a couple of seconds while the boy shrieked and swung his fists at his pa's knee. Then Daniel swooshed his son around by the leg, flipped him right side up, and tossed him head first over Daniel's shoulder. The little boy clung like a burr and swung himself around and ended up riding piggyback on his pa.

"Too many menfolk." Grant had seen it all before and accepted it. "Women like to talk to other women from time to time."

Daniel nodded earnestly, soaking in every word Grant said, even though his son was strangling him and yelling for a horsie ride. "She's expecting another young'un, too. Probably die from this one." He looked over at Grace. "I am surely gonna miss that woman."

"Ma's gonna die!" Matthew shouted right into Daniel's ear.

Grace whirled around and fairly screamed. "*I am not going to die*, Daniel Reeves. You quit saying that. If I hear you say that one more time, I swear this is going to be the first baby ever born where we lose a father."

Hannah looked wide-eyed at Daniel. With a glance at Grant, Hannah pulled Grace back into the little circle of women.

Two of the medium-sized boys—they had to be triplets because there were three that were a matched set—rolled under the table wrestling and tipped it over.

Daniel shouted, "You boys get outside!"

Shouting with joy, his boys vanished, along with Benny, leaving the door wide open. Grant, his ears ringing, prayed for his son to survive this visit.

After a moment's hesitation while he looked between the women and the open door, Charlie grabbed his coat and went out after the others. Grant hoped living most of his life on the mean streets made him tough enough to survive the Reeves boys.

The Reeves stayed the night. Grant had no choice but to spend his wedding night with the menfolk in the barn, and Grace slept with Hannah. Grant's children skipped school the next day, and by nightfall, the Reeves family still showed no signs of leaving. Of course the train wouldn't come through for a week, so there was no escaping the Reeves until then.

Grant was ready to start building on to his house, maybe a big playroom with no breakables. Something with a lock on it, so Grant could shoo them in there and pen them up.

By midweek, Grant worked up the nerve to ask Daniel, in carefully discreet terms, about being married. Near as Grant could tell, Daniel thought women were a dangerous temptation from the devil, died at the drop of a hat, and a man with any sense at all would move himself permanently into the barn.

Terrified by Daniel's dire predictions, Grant didn't ask questions after that.

Grant barely kept from tearing his hair out while he waited for the visit to end. The only thing that saved him from a bald head was the joy he saw on Hannah's face—on the few occasions he saw her face since he was living full-time in the bachelor quarters in the barn now—as she talked nonstop with Grace.

Grant did his best not to shout for joy when Daniel declared it to be time to go home. Grace, relaxed and happy, went along with her family without protest.

After the Reeves tornado spun itself back toward west Texas, and Grant repaired the furniture, their home went back to normal.

THIRTY-ONE

"Peace and quiet at last." Grant sank into his rocking chair, enjoying the relative silence of his household with only eight people in it.

"It just seems quiet without the Reeves." Hannah glanced away from the room and smiled at Grant. "We've still got six children making noise."

Libby looked up from where she sat at the table listening to Marilyn read.

"I think you and Ma had better only have babies one at a time, Pa." Josh pulled his harmonica out of his pocket.

Laughing, Hannah shook her head. "Are you really going to call me Ma, Josh? I'm pretty sure you're older than I am."

Grant settled more firmly in his rocking chair. "I like the sound of Ma. I think you kids had oughta all call her that."

"But she's my sister, Pa." Libby screwed up her face and pouted. "Do I have to call her Ma, too? That's kind of confusing."

Sadie and Joshua started to laugh.

"Well, you could call her Hannah for your sister"—Marilyn pushed the book aside—"Miss Cartwright for your teacher, Ma because she's married to your pa. . . She's right. It is confusing."

"Well, we'll keep it simple and you can call me Ma." Hannah sat struggling over the knitting lesson Sadie and Marilyn had assigned her.

Grant did his best not to laugh at the mass of knots.

"But I declare if Will and Ian start calling me Ma, I don't know if I'll put up with it."

"They can call you Grandma instead." Libby nodded innocently. The whole room erupted into laughter.

Grant jumped to his feet and scooped his little daughter into his arms. Once she'd started talking, the little girl seemed to be catching up for years of silence. "I never get tired of hearing you talk." He danced her around the room, whirling and hoisting her toward the ceiling.

"Say something else, honey," Grant cajoled as he tossed her in the air. "C'mon, let me hear that pretty voice."

Libby giggled. "I love you, Pa."

Grant stopped in midstep. He pulled Libby into a bear hug. "Thank you, sweetheart. The day God brought you and Charlie and your meddling big sister into my life is one of the very best days of my life. And you did that without saying a word."

"I'm not a meddler, Grant Cooper. You take that back." Hannah came and stood in front of him, her hands on her hips, doing her very best to look fierce when the sparkle in her eye told him she was fighting not to laugh.

"I know a way to make Pa behave, Ma." Libby giggled as if saying the word *Ma* was hilarious.

"How's that?"

"Pa's ticklish."

Hannah's eyes zeroed in on him. Benny roared like a Comanche warrior, a six-year-old Comanche warrior. They ended up in a pile on the floor, tickling and laughing and being the biggest, happiest family ever sheltered by a Texas mountain.

And later, when the house was quiet and Grant finally had her alone, he found out Hannah was ticklish, too.

DISCUSSION QUESTIONS

1. Hannah has a passion for children to the point she's willing to sacrifice anything to save them. When she rode out after Grant in the blizzard at the beginning of the book, did you root for her or think she was so unwise that it annoyed you?

2. As Grant finds himself falling for Hannah, he goes to increasing silly lengths to keep her out of his head. He had an almost desperate calling to protect all the unwanted children in the world. Discuss the conflict in his heart between romantic love and a father's love and why he couldn't resolve the two.

3. Why do you think God put people in the world who go hungry, who are cold and unwanted and abused?

4. Could a seventeen year old boy emotionally "father" children? Is Grant's feeling that he was better than nothing good enough? Discuss whether Grant is being a father out of an honorable calling or just plain loneliness.

5. Hannah has no womanly skills. When Grant's daughters start matchmaking, they start by teaching her to sew. Are their motives because she needs a prettier dress to attract Grant or to really teach her a skill?

6. The part of the story about oil was a good look at how something once considered a nuisance became a source of power and wealth. Discuss the inventions and discoveries that have changed the world.

7. The Orphan Trains ran from 1854 to 1929 relocating an estimated 200,000 orphaned, abandoned, and homeless children. Have you ever met someone who came west on an orphan train. Some are still living. Do you live in an area where Orphan Trains stopped to find adoptive families? Discuss whether Orphan Trains are a great idea or a terrible one.

8. If you read *Calico Canyon*, you'll know that Hannah was unable to turn her back on a child in need. She'd find homes for the orphans she protected then turn around and find herself with more children. Grant similarly had a special heart for children. Do you think children have been devalued in our modern society? Do parents today think, "What can a child give to me?" rather than, "What can I give to a child?" Are many children now viewed more as a goal fulfillment for parents with a ticking biological clock than a treasured gift entrusted to us by God for shaping and molding into godly adults? Explain your thoughts.

9. Are Grace's antics in *Gingham Mountain* a fair depiction for a pregnant woman with "cabin fever"? Have you ever been "trapped" or a tiny bit crazy while you were pregnant—or just housebound—especially with a house full of children?

ABOUT THE AUTHOR

Mary Connealy is a Christie Award finalist. You can find out more about Mary's upcoming books at www.maryconnealy.com and www.mconnealy.blogspot.com. Mary lives on a Nebraska ranch with her husband, Ivan, and has four grown daughters: Joslyn (married to Matt), Wendy, Shelly (married to Aaron), and Katy. And she is the grandmother of one beautiful granddaughter, Elle.

Mary loves to hear from her readers. You may visit her at these sites: www.mconnealy.blogspot.com, www.seekerville. blogspot.com, and www.petticoatsandpistols. Write to her at mary@maryconnealy.com.

Other books by Mary Connealy

MONTANA MARRIAGES SERIES
Montana Rose
The Husband Tree
Wildflower Bride

SOPHIE'S DAUGHTERS SERIES
Doctor in Petticoats
Wrangler in Petticoats
Sharpshooter in Petticoats

Nosy in Nebraska
Black Hills Blessing